Lloyd C. Douglas, best novels

In this book:

Magnificent Obsession

Forgive Us Our Trespasses

Doctor Hudson's Secret Journal

Lloyd Cassel Douglas (1877 –1951) born Doya C. Douglas, was an American minister and author. He was born in Columbia City, Indiana, spent part of his boyhood in Monroeville, Indiana, Wilmot, Indiana and Florence, Kentucky, where his father, Alexander Jackson Douglas, was pastor of the Hopeful Lutheran Church. According to the 1910 Census Douglas was listed as a Lutheran Clergyman. He was married to Bessie I. Porch. They had two children: Bessie J. Douglas, 4 at the time and Virginia V Douglas, 2 at the time. They employed a cook, Ms. Josephine Somach. He died in Los Angeles, California. Douglas was one of the most popular American authors of his time, although he did not write his first novel until he was 50. His written works were of a moral, didactic, and distinctly religious tone. His first novel, Magnificent Obsession, published in 1929, was an immediate and sensational success. Critics held that his type of fiction was in the tradition of the great religious writings of an earlier generation, such as Ben-Hur and Quo Vadis.

In this book:

Magnificent Obsession…………..…….Pag. 3

Forgive Us Our Trespasses…….……Pag. 129

Doctor Hudson's Secret Journal…….Pag. 293

Magnificent Obsession

CHAPTER I

IT had lately become common chatter at Brightwood Hospital—better known for three hundred miles around Detroit as Hudson's Clinic—that the chief was all but dead on his feet. The whole place buzzed with it.

All the way from the inquisitive solarium on the top floor to the garrulous kitchen in the basement, little groups—convalescents in wheeled chairs, nurses with tardy trays, lean internes on rubber soles, grizzled orderlies trailing damp mops—met to whisper and separated to disseminate the bad news. Doctor Hudson was on the verge of a collapse.
On the verge?...Indeed! One lengthening story had it that on Tuesday he had fainted during an operation—mighty ticklish piece of business, too—which young Watson, assisting him, was obliged to complete alone. And the worst of it was that he was back at it again, next morning, carrying on as usual.
An idle tale like that, no matter with what solicitude of loyalty it might be discussed at Brightwood, would deal the institution a staggering wallop once it seeped through the big wrought-iron gates. And the rumour was peculiarly difficult to throttle because, unfortunately, it was true.
Obviously the hour had arrived for desperate measures.
Dr. Malcolm Pyle, shaggy and beetle-browed, next to the chief in seniority, a specialist in abdominal surgery and admiringly spoken of by his colleagues as the best belly man west of the Alleghenies, growled briefly into the ear of blood-and-skin Jennings, a cynical, middle-aged bachelor, who but for his skill as a bacteriologist would have been dropped from the staff, many a time, for his rasping banter and infuriating impudences.
Jennings quickly passed the word to internal-medicine Carter, who presently met eye-ear-nose-and-throat McDermott in the hall and relayed the message.
"Oh, yes, I'll come," said McDermott uneasily, "but I don't relish the idea of a staff meeting without the chief. Looks like treason."
"It's for his own good," explained Carter.
"Doubtless; but...he has always been such a straight shooter, himself."
"You tell Aldrich and Watson. I'll see Gram and Harper. I hate it as much as you do, Mac, but we can't let the chief ruin himself."

* * * * *

Seeing that to-morrow was Christmas, and this was Saturday well past the luncheon hour, by the time Pyle had tardily joined them in the superintendent's office each of the eight, having abandoned whatever manifestation of dignified omniscience constituted his bedside manner, was snappishly impatient to have done with this unpleasant business and be off.

When at length he breezed in, not very convincingly attempting the conciliatory smirk of the belated, Pyle found them glum and fidgety—Carter savagely reducing to shavings what remained of a pencil, Aldrich rattling the pages of his engagement book, McDermott meticulously pecking at diminutive bits of lint on his coat sleeve, Watson ostentatiously shaking his watch at his ear, Gram drumming an exasperating tattoo on Nancy Ashford's desk, and the others pacing about like hungry panthers.
"Well," said Pyle, seating them with a sweeping gesture, "you all know what we're here for."
"Ab-so-lute-ly," drawled Jennings. "The old boy must be warned."
"At once!" snapped Gram.
"I'll say!" muttered McDermott.
"And you, Pyle, are the proper person to do it!" Anticipating a tempestuous rejoinder, Jennings hastened to defend himself against the impending din by noisily pounding out his

pipe on the rim of Mrs. Ashford's steel waste basket, a performance she watched with sour interest.

"Where do you get that 'old boy' stuff, Jennings?" demanded Pyle, projecting a fierce, myopic glare at his pestiferous crony. "He's not much older than you are."

Watson tilted his chair back on its hind legs, cautiously turned his red head in the direction of Carter, seated next him, and slowly closed one eye. This was going to be good.

"Doctor Hudson was forty-six last May," quietly volunteered the superintendent, without looking up.

"You ought to know," conceded Jennings drily.

She met his rough insinuation with level, unacknowledging eyes.

"May twenty-fifth," she added.

"Thanks so much. That point's settled, then. But, all the same, he wasn't a day under a hundred and forty-six when he slumped out of his operating room, this morning, haggard and shaky."

"It's getting spread about too," complained Carter.

"Take it up with him, Doctor Pyle," wheedled McDermott. "Tell him we all think he needs a vacation—a long one!"

Pyle snorted contemptuously and aimed a bushy eye-brow at him.

"Humph! That's good! 'Tell him we all think,' eh? It's a mighty careless, offhand damn that Hudson would give for what we all think! Did you ever..." He pointed a bony finger at the perspiring McDermott, "...did you ever feel moved to offer a few comradely suggestions to Dr. Wayne Hudson, relative to the better management of his personal affairs?"

McDermott rosily hadn't, and Pyle's dry voice crackled again.

"As I thought! That explains how, with so little display of emotion, you can advise somebody else to do it. You see, my son,"—he dropped his tone of raillery and became sincere—"we're dealing here with an odd number. Nobody quite like him in the whole world...full of funny crotchets. In a psychiatric clinic—which this hospital is going to be, shortly, with the entire staff in strait-jackets—some of Hudson's charming little idiosyncrasies would be brutally referred to as clean-cut psychoses!"

The silence in Mrs. Ashford's office was tense. Pyle's regard for the chief was known to be but little short of idolatry. What, indeed, was he preparing to say? Did he actually believe that Hudson was off the rails?

"Now, don't misunderstand!" he went on quickly, sensing their amazement. "Hudson's entitled to all his whimsies. So far as I'm concerned, he has earned the right to his flock of phantoms. He is a genius, and whosoever loveth a genius is out of luck with his devotion except he beareth all things, endureth all things, suffereth long and is kind."

"Not like sounding brass," interpolated Jennings piously.

"Apropos of brass," growled Pyle, "but—no matter...We all know that the chief is the most important figure in the field of brain surgery on this continent. But he did not come to that distinction by accident. He has toiled like a slave in a mill. His specialty is guaranteed to make a man moody; counts himself lucky if he can hold down his mortality to fifty per cent. What kind of a mentality would *you* have"—shifting his attention to Jennings, who grinned, amiably—"if you lost half your cases? They'd soon have you trussed in a big tub of hot water, feeding you through the nose with a syringe!"

"You spoke of the chief's psychoses," interrupted McDermott, approaching the dangerous word hesitatingly. "Do you mean that—literally?"

Pyle pursed his lips and nodded slowly.

"Yes—literally! One of his notions—by far the most alarming of his legion, in so far as the present dilemma is affected—has to do with his curious attitude toward fear. He mustn't be afraid of anything. He must live above fear—that is his phrase. You would think, to hear his prattle, that he was a wealthy and neurotic old lady trying to graduate from Theosophy into Bahaism..."

"What's Bahaism?" inquired Jennings, with pretended naïveté.

"Hudson believes," continued Pyle, disdainful of the annoyance, "that if a man harbours any sort of fear, no matter how benign and apparently harmless, it percolates through all his thinking, damages his personality, makes him landlord to a ghost. For years, he has been so consistently living above fear—fear of slumping, fear of the natural penalties of overwork, fear of the neural drain of insomnia...Haven't you heard him discoursing on the delights of reading in bed to three o'clock?...fear of that little aneurism he knows he's got—that he has driven himself at full gallop with spurs on his boots and burrs under his saddle, caroling about his freedom, until he's ready to drop. But whoever cautions him will be warmly damned for his impertinence."

Pyle had temporarily run down, and discussion became general. Carter risked suggesting that if the necessary interview with the chief required a gift for impertinence, why not deputize Jennings? Aldrich said it was no time for kidding. McDermott again nominated Pyle. Gram shouted, "Of course!" They pushed back their chairs. Pyle brought both big hands down on his knees with a resounding slap, rose with a groan, and sourly promised he'd have a go at it.

"Attaboy!" commended Jennings paternally. "Watson will do your stitches, afterwards. He has been getting some uncommonly nice cosmetic values, lately, with his scars; eh, Watty?"

The disorder incident to adjournment spared Watson the chagrin of listening to the threatened report of Jennings' eavesdropping, an hour earlier, on the dulcet cooing of a recently discharged patient, back to tender her gratitude. Emboldened by his rescue, he dispassionately told Jennings to go to hell, much to the latter's faunlike satisfaction, and the staff evaporated.

"Let's go and eat," said Pyle.

As they turned the corner in the corridor, Jennings slipped his hand under Pyle's elbow and muttered, "You know damned well what ails the chief, and so do I. It's the girl!"

"Joyce, you mean?"

"Who else?" Jennings buttoned his overcoat collar high about his throat and thrust his shoulder against the big front door and an eighty-mile gale. "Certainly, I mean Joyce. She's running wild, and he's worrying his heart out and his head off!"

"Maybe so," Pyle picked his footing carefully on the snowy steps. "But I don't believe it's very good cricket for us to analyze his family affairs."

"Nonsense! We're quite past the time for indulging in any knightly restraints. Hudson's in danger of shooting his reputation to bits. Incidentally, it will give the whole clinic a black eye when the news spreads. If the chief is off his feed because he's fretting about his girl, then it's high time we talked candidly about her. She's a silly little ass, if you ask my opinion!"

"Well, you won't be asked for your opinion. And it's no good coming at it in that mood. She may be, as you say, a silly little ass; but she's Hudson's deity!"

Jennings motioned him to climb into the coupé and fumbled in his pockets for his keys.

"She wasn't behaving much like a deity—unless Bacchus, perhaps—the last time I saw her."

"Where was that?"

"At the Tuileries, about a month ago, with a party of eight or ten noisy roisterers, in the general custody of that good-for-nothing young Merrick—you know, old Nick Merrick's carousing grandson. Believe me, they were well oiled."

"Did you—did she recognize you?"

"Oh, quite so! Came fluttering over to our table to speak to me!"

"Humph! She *must* have been pickled! I thought she was getting on, all right, at a girls' school in Washington...Didn't know she was home."

Jennings warmed his engine noisily, and threw in the clutch.

"Maybe she was sacked."

Pyle made some hopeless noises deep in his throat.

"Too bad about old Merrick...Salt of the earth; finest of the fine. He's had more than his share of trouble. Did you ever know Clif?"

"No. He was dead. But I've heard of him. A bum, wasn't he?"

"That describes him; and this orphan of his seems to be headed in the same direction."

"Orphan? I thought this boy's mother was living—Paris or somewhere."

"Oh yes, she's living; but the boy's an orphan, for all that. Born an orphan!" Pyle briefly reviewed the Merrick saga.

"Perhaps," suggested Jennings, as they rolled into the club garage, "you might have a chat with old Merrick, if he's such a good sort, and tell him his whelp is a contaminating influence to our girl."

"Pfff!" Pyle led the way to the elevator.

"Well, if that proposal's no good, why don't you go manfully to the young lady herself and inform her that she's driving her eminent parent crazy? Put it up to her as a matter of good sportsmanship."

5

"No," objected Pyle, hooking his glasses athwart his nose to inspect the menu, "she would only air her indignation to her father. And he likes people to mind their own business—as you've discovered on two or three occasions. He keeps his own counsel like a clam, and doesn't thank anybody for crashing into his affairs, no matter how benevolent may be the motive...It would be quite useless, anyway. Joyce can't help the way she's made. She is a biological throwback to her maternal grandfather. You never knew him. He was just putting the finishing touches to his career as a periodical sot when I arrived in this town, fresh from school. Cummings was the best all 'round surgeon and the hardest all 'round drinker in the state of Michigan for twenty years; one of these three-days-soused and three-weeks-sober drunkards. This girl evidently carries an over-plus of the old chap's chromosomes."

"You mean she is a dipsomaniac?"

"Well—that's a nasty word. Let's just say she's erratic. Ever since she was a little tot, she has been a storm centre. Sweetest thing in the world when she wants to be. And then all hell breaks loose and Hudson has to plead with the teachers to take her back. Oh, she's given him an exciting life; no doubt of that! And lately it's booze!"

"Hudson knows about that part of it, of course!"

"I presume so. How could he help it? She makes no secret of it. At all events, she's no hypocrite."

Jennings sighed.

"Rather unfortunate she has this one embarrassing virtue; isn't it? But, that being the case, I dare say she'll have to go to the devil at her own speed. We must persuade Hudson, however, to clear out and take a long leave of absence. He can take her along. Lay it on with a heavy hand, Pyle. Be utterly ruthless! Tell him it affects us all. That ought to fetch him. I never knew anybody quite so sensitive to the welfare of other people. Save that card for the last trick: tell him if he doesn't clear out, for a while, he will do up the rest of us!"

* * * * *

For the first half hour of their conference, which was held in the chief's office the following Tuesday, Pyle stubbornly held out for a trip around the world, Joyce to accompany her father. Indeed, the idea had seemed so good that he had armed himself with a portfolio of attractive cruise literature. He had even made out an intriguing itinerary—Hawaii, Tahiti, ukeleles—Pyle was a confirmed land-lubber with a dangerously suppressed desire to lie on his back, pleasantly jingled, under a trans-equatorial palm, listening to the soft vowels of grown-up children unspoiled by civilization—the Mediterranean countries, six months of hobnobbing with brain specialists in Germany. The latter item had been included as a particularly tempting bait. Hudson had often declared he meant to do that some day.

The chief listened preoccupiedly; tried to seem grateful; tried to seem interested; but as Pyle rumbled on with his sales-talk the big man grew restless, refilled his fountain-pen, rearranged his papers in neater piles, had much difficulty hunting a match-box. Then he shook his head, smiling.

No, much as he appreciated Pyle's friendly concern, he wasn't going around the world; not just now. Of course he had been sticking at it too steadily. Lately he had had it on his mind to build a little shack in some out of the way place, not too far off, and put in there from Friday afternoon to Tuesday morning, at least in decent weather, tramp, fish, botanize, read light novels, sleep, live the simple life. He would begin plans on such a place at once. Spring would be along soon.

"And—meantime?" persisted Pyle, gnawing at the tip of his uptilted little goatee.

Hudson rose, slammed a drawer shut with a bang, swung a leg over the corner of his desk, folded his arms tightly, and faced his counsellor with a mysterious grin.

"Meantime?...Pyle, I hope this won't knock you cold. I'm going down to Philadelphia, week after next, to marry my daughter's school friend, Miss Helen Brent."

Pyle's eyes and mouth comically registered such stunned amazement that the Hudson grin widened.

"And then the three of us will be spending a couple of months in Europe. I've arranged with Leighton to come over from the university and take care of such head cases as Watson can't handle. Watson's a good man; bright future. Oddly enough, I was on the point of asking you in to talk this over when you said you wished to see me."

Pyle bit off the end of a fresh cigar and mumbled felicitations, not yet sufficiently recovered to pretend enthusiasm.

"Doubtless you think me a fool, Pyle."

Hudson took a turn up and down the room, giving his colleague an opportunity to deny it if he wished. Pyle puffed meditatively.

"Seventeen years a widower," mused Hudson, half to himself. He paused at the far corner to straighten a disordered shelf of books.

"A man accumulates a lot of habits in seventeen years." He returned to his desk-chair. "Sounds like the wedding of January and June, eh?"

Had Jennings been in Pyle's place, his eyes would have twinkled as he replied, *"January!* What! You? January? Nonsense, Chief! Not a day over October, at the farthest!"

Pyle smiled wanly, and shifted his cigar to the other corner of his mouth.

"I came by this valuable new friendship early last year when Miss Brent was made Junior advisor to my Joyce."

Something of sympathetic comradeship in Pyle's reviving interest, now that he was partially coming to, encouraged Hudson to toss aside what remained of his reticence and tell it all.

To begin with—Miss Brent was an orphan; parents reputable Virginians; most interesting French background on her mother's side; same kind of blood that the guillotine spilt in 1789..." Quite pronouncedly Gallic, she is—at least in appearance."

Jennings, had he been there, would have been audacious enough to suggest, slyly chuckling, "Oh—in that case we should amend June to *July!*" Then he would have watched the chief's face intently.

But Pyle, who had no traffic with psychoanalysis, attached no significance whatever to the fact that the young lady's probable temperament was somewhat on the chief's mind.

"About Thanksgiving," Hudson was saying, "Miss Brent, after a brief encounter with influenza, left the school and spent a few days at home. No sooner was she gone than Joyce slipped out, one night; attended a party, down in the city; defied some house rules as to hours; flicked all her classes next day; stormed until the shingles rattled when they rebuked her; and, in short, contrived to get herself suspended, notwithstanding that her record—thanks to Miss Brent's influence—had been quite above reproach ever since she matriculated, a year ago last September."

The story went forward rather jerkily. Hudson was not given to confiding his perplexities to anybody. Pyle discreetly remained silent.

"Well—she came home and plunged immediately into a series of hectic affairs; out every night; in bed most of the day; nervous, testy, unreasonable. I can't tell you, Pyle, how thoroughly it did me in...She's all I have you know.

"At my wit's end, I suggested that she invite Miss Brent up to visit us through the holidays. Twice before had she been our guest for a few days, and I had seen something of her on my occasional visits to Washington. Believe me when I tell you that this charming girl was no more than across our threshold last week, than Joyce was another creature, poised, gracious, lovable—a lady!"

He paused to take his bearings before going further; impelled to explain how the swift movement of events, that first evening at dinner, amply accounted for his decision to ask Helen to marry him; reluctant, even in the interest of plausibility and self-defence, to give words to the memory of that occasion. It had all been so natural; so unimpeachably right; so precisely as it ought to be! He had remarked—perhaps a bit more ardently than he intended, for his heart was full—how happy it had made him—and Joyce—that she had come. "I don't see how we can ever let you go!" he had said; to which Joyce had added impetuously, "Why need she ever go? She's happier here than anywhere else; aren't you, darling?"

Pyle recrossed his legs and cleared his throat to remind the chief that he was still present.

"As a matter of fact, Miss Brent is certain to be happier with us than she was at home. Since childhood, she has lived with an uncle, her father's elder brother, an irascible, penurious, not very successful old lawyer. There are no women in the family. And I have reason to suspect that her cousin, Montgomery Brent, is a bit of a rake, though she has idealized him out of all proportion; calls him 'Brother Monty,' thinks him vastly misunderstood by his father and everybody else...that kind of a girl, Pyle...espouses the cause of homeless cats, under dogs, misunderstood cousins, my flighty, wilful Joyce...and now—thank God—she has promised to join forces with *me*! I think she's making something of a mission of it, Pyle. I was quite willing to wait until she had finished school in June; had some serious misgivings, indeed, about that; but she dismissed the thought lightly. If I needed her, I needed her *now*, she said...I hope to God it works out!"

Pyle said he believed it would; moved to the edge of his chair; looked at his watch; asked if this was a secret.

Hudson stroked his jaw, his eyes averted.

"I don't object to their knowing...Let's consider it sufficient, for the present, that I'm going to Europe with my daughter." He mopped his broad forehead vigorously. "The rest of it they can learn in due time. Report to Aldrich and Carter and the others that I'm off on a vacation."

"Any special word for Mrs. Ashford, Chief?" Pyle paused with his hand on the door-knob.

Hudson thrust his hands deeply into his trouser pockets and walked to the window, staring out. "I'll tell her myself, Pyle," he answered, without turning.

* * * * *

Doctor Hudson named his isolated retreat Flintridge. It was quite remote from the beaten trail of travel. A mere acre had been tamed to serve the cottage for which his hasty sketches, before leaving, were elaborated and executed in his absence by his loyal friend, Fred Ferguson, the best architect in town.

It was an inhospitable bit of country, thereabouts. Sheer cliffs, descending abruptly to the black water (a long flight of wooden steps led to the little boat-house and adjacent wharf) had discouraged such colonization as had long since developed the western shore, two miles distant. Deformed pines clawed the rocks, sighing of their thirst in summer, shrieking of nakedness in winter.

Almost from the first, Flintridge never knew certainly, for there was no telephone, when its master would appear for a week-end. It anticipated, made forecasts, baked ineffable angel food cakes, caught vast quantities of minnows for bait, and held itself in instant readiness to welcome the big man with the ruddy face (just a shade too ruddy, any heart diagnostician could have told him), silver-white hair, grey eyes with deep crows-feet, and expressive hands eloquent of highly developed dexterity.

When and if he came, it would be on Saturday, late afternoon. Once only had he brought Joyce and Helen—strangers, passing them, presumed they were both his daughters—but that was merely temporizing with his promise to seek a retreat. And he now needed days off, if ever; for his young wife's gregarious disposition and charming hospitality had multiplied his social obligations in the city.

How easily she had adjusted herself to his moods! How proud he was of her, not quite so much for her exotic beauty, as because of her exquisiteness of personal taste and the tact with which she met the rather exacting problems of fitting neatly and quickly into his circle of mature acquaintances. It delighted him that she chose the right word, wore the right costume, intuitively knew how to manage a dinner-party without seeming concerned as to what misadventures might have occurred in the kitchen. Yes; the affair was "working out"—how often he used that phrase!—immeasurably better than he had dared hope.

Even the women liked her! They had accepted her on approval at first; but when it became evident that she had no intention of taking on airs because their grizzled spouses fluttered about her with the broad compliments privileged to fifty addressing twenty-five, they admitted she was a dear.

But, however pleasant it was for Hudson to note his wife's growing popularity, certified to by the increasing volume of their social activities, his new duties contributed little to the reinvigoration of that fatigued aorta which had worried Pyle.

"The chief's in better fettle—think?" said Jennings.

"Temporarily," conceded Pyle. "But you don't mend an aneurism with late dinners, three a week. I'm afraid he'll crash, one of these days."

Not infrequently some visiting colleague—for Brightwood now not only attracted patients from afar but had become a mecca for the ambitious in the field of brain surgery—would be driven out into the country to rusticate for a day or two. They seemed singularly alike, these brain-tinkers from otherwhere; moody, abstracted men, in their late forties and early fifties, most of them; seldom smiling, ungifted with small talk, not unusually inclined to be somewhat gruff. Hudson preferred to hold conferences with them at the lake, for their conversation would be tiresomely technical. And anyhow, men who trafficked daily with Death could not be expected to enliven a house party.

A devoted pair of middle-aged twins served as caretakers at Flintridge. What time Perry Ruggles, of the stiff knee, hairy throat, and Airedale disposition, was not tinkering the boat engine with greasy wrenches or trolling in and out of season for bass, he was teaching little patches of apathetic soil to take a maternal interest in iris and petunias. On Saturdays about five o'clock, he would put on his other coat and limp down to the gate that admitted from the narrow ridge road; and, having opened it, would flick little stones off the driveway with his good foot.

Martha, his buxom sister, wrought ingenious quilts, concealed from the taciturn Perry the vandalisms of an impertinent, bottle-fed fawn; was silly over a pair of tame pheasants whose capacity for requiting her affection was as feeble as her need was great; scratched her plump arms gathering early berries in anticipation of some high moment when her pie would be approved with a slow wink, of which the learned guest, profoundly discoursing of surgical mysteries to his celebrated host, would be entirely unaware.

On Saturdays, about four-thirty, having again made sure she had laid out the doctor's pyjamas on the bed, and turning the vase of roses on his chiffonier a little more to the advantage of the tallest, Martha would take her stand before the window in the sun-parlour, her knuckles pressed hard against her pretty teeth, devoutly praying for a swirl of yellow dust and a flash of glittering nickel at the bend of the ridge road, visible through an open lane of dwarf spruce.

At the sound of gravel crunching under heavy tires, she would dash to the door and fling it open, always hoping—and hating herself for it—that the doctor had come alone or, if not alone, accompanied by another man. She had been uneasy, abashed, and awkward in the presence of young Mrs. Hudson, whose beauty had stirred remembrance of a certain pre-Christmas shopping excursion when she was nine...There had been a French doll, so beautiful it had made Martha's little throat ache with longing. Her wistful eyes had gushed sudden tears, and she had put out a hand, tentatively.

"No, dear," her mother had cautioned. "You may look at her, but you mustn't touch."

* * * * *

On the broad mantel in the "gun room" (there had been a bit of chaffing about the "gun room," seeing there was only one gun in it among all the miscellaneous instruments of sport—golf clubs, fishing tackle, and the like) an impressive row of silver cups testified that Wayne Hudson was no less expert at play than with the more important implements of surgery.

It was a frequent remark of his intimates that Hudson possessed an almost uncanny capacity for projecting the sensitiveness of his cognitive fingers to the very tips of whatever tools he chose to manipulate. There were nerves in his niblick, in his casting-rod, in his scalpel.

"A lucky devil!" bystanders used to remark when he had successfully made a long putt up-grade on a sporty green.

"An uncommonly good guesser!" his confrères agreed occasionally, when some quite daring prognosis—probably defining the exact location of a brain tumour on such cryptic evidence as the arc of an eyebrow, the twitch of a lip, the posture of a hand in repose, or the interjection of an unbecoming phrase into casual conversation—was verified.

Among the trophies on the mantel—whose inscriptions always amazed a visiting colleague, marvelling at his distinguished host's diversity of proficiencies—there was a tarnished triple-handled aquatic prize won by Doctor Hudson when, in the early days of his internship, he had taken a First in a mile swim.

"Still swim?"
"Regularly."
"Enjoy it?"
"Well—it's good for me."
"Keeps your weight down?"
"Perhaps. But, in any event, it's good for me."

Some time in the course of his visit, the visitor would rag his athletic host upon the excess of his prudence; for the most conspicuous article of furniture in the "gun room" was an elaborate but not very decorative inhalator of the super-type used by life-savers at busy wharves and crowded beaches, equipped with nickelled oxygen tanks and a complication of mechanical mysteries.

"What's that thing?"

Hudson would tell him, briefly, brusquely.

"What do *you* want with it?"

"Oh, somebody might fall in. The water's deep out here."

It was clear enough to the guest, if he ventured to press his queries, that Doctor Hudson did not enjoy any talk about aquatics. The guest found himself wondering why. Perry Ruggles could have explained, had he been disposed. There had once been a very anxious hour at Flintridge, down on the narrow pier. Not even Martha knew. The next time he had come out, Doctor Hudson had brought the inhalator, and had explained its use to the terrified Perry who thereafter stood in dread of the thing. It became a grim spectre that haunted his life. Some day, he suspected, he would be obliged to experiment with it. The responsibility constituted a steady, remorseless threat that tortured him and kept him awake nights. Some sharp, man-to-man candour had been handed to the surgeon, that afternoon, by his uncouth caretaker. It had been a long time since anybody had called Wayne Hudson a fool to his face. He accepted the degree with dignity.

"Perhaps I am, Perry," he replied soberly. "You probably wouldn't know. But, however that may be, the thing you're to keep in mind is that this top valve controls the oxygen; and if you have occasion to use it, don't get excited and forget."

* * * * *

Not a few men of importance to the surgical world resident in widely-spaced cities, recalled having had brief and somewhat disquieting conversations about swimming, while guests at Flintridge, when, one Sunday morning in early August, they read the front-page dispatch which reported that Doctor Wayne Hudson, widely known brain surgeon of Detroit, had drowned, the late afternoon before, near his summer place on Lake Saginack.

At their breakfast table in Seattle, Doctor Herman Bliss read the shocking headlines to his wife, and when she had commented sympathetically, he added:

"Not only very sad, my dear, but very strange!"

Pressed for explanation, he reviewed for her the incidents of a visit he had paid to his friend at the lake cottage, and the heavy constraint which had fallen upon their conversation when he had made some inquiries about his host's enjoyment of the water.

"Do you suppose," conjectured Mrs. Bliss, "that there could have lurked in his mind some vague mirage of the fate that waited for him?"

Her husband pursed his lips and shook his head. "I don't take much stock in such theories," he declared, almost too vehemently to be convincing.

"But you told me once that Doctor Hudson was 'prescient'!"

"Only a form of speech, Grace. Nobody is prescient. However, Hudson was extraordinarily sentient; psychic to an uncommon degree."

"But why did he persist in swimming," inquired Mrs. Bliss, "if he was afraid of it?"

"For that very reason, unquestionably. I never knew a man so impatient of normal people's timidities, or more passionately eager to make himself independent of fear. Doubtless this was the one thing that gave him anxiety, and he was resolved to master it."

"But—by the same logic," objected Mrs. Bliss, "he might have jumped off a precipice, if he found himself afraid of that."

"Not quite the same thing! Here was something he had been able to do with ease, skill and safety. Now, for some reason, he had suddenly become afraid of it. An experience of cramp, perhaps...Might happen again. The fear filtered through his thinking...Had prided himself on living in complete mental liberty...Knew now that he was housing a dread! So long as he gave that phobia the hospitality of his mind, he would be, by that much, no longer his own man; so he decided to go to the mat with his antagonist. I fancy that explains."

The newspaper account further detailed that by a singular coincidence the inhalator which Doctor Hudson owned, and kept at his cottage, was in use on the other side of the little lake at the exact moment of his own tragic need of it.

A few hundred yards off shore, near his grandfather's estate, "Windymere," young Robert Merrick, alone in his sailboat, had been knocked unconscious by a jibbing boom and pushed into the water.

"Must have been drunk," indignantly commented Doctor Bliss. "Things like that don't often happen to sober people."

Excited bathers, informed that there was an inhalator at the Hudson cottage, had rushed a speed-boat across for it, and after an hour's heroic exertion, were successful in restoring the young man to partial consciousness. It was said that he would undoubtedly recover.

"Unquestionably! He would!" growled Bliss.

It was believed, said the dispatch, that had the inhalator been immediately available and promptly applied, Doctor Hudson's life might have been saved. The caretaker, Perry Ruggles, observing the evident distress of his employer, had rowed quickly to the spot, dived for him, dragged his limp body into the boat. Desperately, Ruggles had set forth with his unconscious passenger towards the Windymere beach, and had rowed until his strength failed. Small craft, attracted by his signals, hurried to him; found him huddled over the lifeless body of Doctor Hudson, weeping hysterically, while the little boat drifted in the middle of the lake.

"Never saw such dog-like devotion as old Perry's. I suppose he went in after him, clothes and all; bad leg too."

Robert Merrick, the paper continued to explain, was the only son of the late Clifford Merrick and Mrs. Maxine Merrick, now resident in Paris. He had only that day returned from an extended visit with his mother, having gone abroad immediately after finishing at the State University in the mid-year senior class. He was further identified as the grandson of Nicholas J. Merrick, retired founder and large stockholder of the Axion Motor Corporation, with whom he made his home at Windymere.

"Hope this youngster will be able to realize how valuable a person he is," said Doctor Bliss, putting down the paper, "now that he has had his life handed back to him at such a price!"

There was still another coincidence connected with this event. The village physician, suspecting that Merrick's head injury might be in need of more skilful examination than he could give it, had sent him in a swift ambulance to Brightwood Hospital. At that moment he did not know that the man who had made Brightwood famous for its brain surgery would be unable to see his young patient.

"What do you suppose the boy said," speculated Mrs. Bliss, "when he learned what it had cost to save his life?"

"Well," reflected the doctor glumly, "from my own observation of the type of young cub whose father is dead, whose mother lives in Paris, whose doting grandfather is a retired millionaire, and who gets himself bumped off his boat by a boom in broad daylight, I should suppose he just scratched a match on the head of his bed and mumbled, 'Whadda yuh know about that!'"

CHAPTER II

SLOWLY and carefully—for he was still limp from his battle with pneumonia, resultant from the prolonged use of a lung-motor in the inexperienced hands of excited people—two nurses had trundled young Merrick up to the well-appointed solarium.

"It won't hurt him a bit," Doctor Watson had said, "and there is at least the suspicion of a breeze upstairs."

Parking his chair in an alcove somewhat sequestered from the general assembly of convalescents, most of them white-turbaned like himself, his uncommunicative attendants had pattered quickly away as if relieved to be off to more pleasant undertakings.

Their scamper added to his perplexity. Yesterday he had tried to explain the prevailing taciturnity of the people who waited on him: it was the weather. The muggy, mid-August humidity accounted for it. If doctors were brief and brusque, nurses crisp and remote, it was because the patients were fretful...everybody out of sorts...naturally.

But, even so, something more serious than a low barometer ailed this hospital. Its moodiness was too thick to be interpreted by a murky yellow sky, the abominable rasp of cicadas in the dusty maples, or the enervating heat. Brightwood was in trouble; nor could Bobby shake off the feeling that he, himself, was somehow at the bottom of it; else why this conspiracy of mute glumness in their attitude toward him? My God!...He might as well have been some penniless bum, fished out of the gutter, and patched up for sheer humanity's sake...Didn't they know who he was?...Why, his grandfather could buy up the whole works and never miss it!

It wasn't that they'd neglected him, he was bound to admit. Somebody had been always hovering over him...God!...What a ghastly experience he had been through!...That fog...drifting in greyish-white, balloon-like billows across the road—impenetrable, acrid, suffocating—a damp, chilling, clinging cloud that pressed painfully against his chest, swathed his arms, clogged his feet...That trip back from Elsewhere!...Would he ever live long enough to forget? It made him shudder to remember it!...That unutterable fatigue!

Sometimes it had been more than he could bear. After he had plodded, staggering, groping his way for a few shaky steps, the Thing would rush him, with a roar like heavy surf, and hurl him incredible distances back toward oblivion. Then the violence of the storm would subside, followed by an ominous silence...Was he really dead, this time?...Suddenly, the Thing would swoop him up again and pitch him deeper into the stifling fog...

After years and years of that—he had grown old and stiff and sore with his hopeless struggle—the situation had begun to clear. Now and again there were ragged rents in the fabric of the fog through which certain landmarks might be fleetingly recognized, as steeples and spires come up, faintly, on an acid-touched plate. These hazy perceptions were, at first, exclusively olfactory. He had read, somewhere, that the nose was more integrally a part of the brain than the other sense organs. Perhaps the smelling faculty (he had taken more than a casual interest in physiology) was the oldest of all the perceptive organs; earliest to evolve. But no; that would be feeling...feeling first, then smelling...It had amazed and amused him that part of his mind seemed to be trudging alongside, analyzing the predicament of the rest of his mind, wading through the fog.

Now there had come a much wider gap in the drifting cloud, and through it breezed a combination of identifiable odours; strong scents crushed hard against his face; smell of good wool, and, buried in the wool, iodoform, cigarette smoke, chlorides of this-that-and-the-other, anæsthetics, antiseptics, laboratory smells, hospital smells.

A weight shifted about on his chest. It was warm. It throbbed. It pressed firmly, rested briefly, moved a little space, paused again, listened; went back to spots it had visited before; listened, more intently.

Then the weight had lifted and the medley of smells vanished. Through the next rift in the fog, voices were speaking from a vast distance; one of them calm, assured; the other bitter, unfriendly...That had been the beginning of his perplexity...

"I believe he's going to pull through!"

"Doubtless—and it's a damned shame!"

After that, there had been a complicated jumble of voices—one of them a woman's—before the fog closed in on him again. Occasionally, the cloud would tear apart, and he would take up his load...he seemed to be carrying some enormous weight...and plod on woodenly. He would have yawned, but deep breathing had gone out. They weren't doing it any more...quite too painful. One breathed in short, dry, hot gasps...glad to have them at the price...Tom Masterson had confirmed that fact...Tom—doubtless this was part of his delirium—Tom had sat by the bed; and, queried about the new style of breathing, remarked, "That's the way we're all doing it...Not nearly so good as the old way, of course, but better than none."

Another smothering billow of fog had engulfed him; but the Thing wasn't in it. He didn't mind now, so long as the Thing was gone.

He opened his eyes and glimpsed a square of blue sky through a real window. The curtain fluttered. A motor churned in a court somewhere below; gears rasped, gravel scrunched. Ice tinkled in a glass, near at hand. A starched nurse, eyes intent on her watch, fumbled for his forearm. The sharp tip of a thermometer dug cruelly into the roots of his tongue. That was what ailed it, then—all this awkward gouging while he had been unconscious.

He had become aware of the steady drone of an electric fan, the metallic whir of a lawn-mower in parched grass; had dully explored his cracked lips with a clumsy tongue; had regarded with apathy the nurse who bent over him; and, after a few hoarse croaks, had contrived to ask where he was. She told him. Sluggishly, he surmised that his presence at Brightwood indicated there was something wrong with his head. There was; it ached abominably, and was bandaged. He felt of it gingerly, and inquired.

"A hard bump. But you are doing very nicely. Drink this, please!"

And then he had slept some more. A dim light was burning when he awoke. Everything was very quiet; so he decided to go to sleep again. Another day came...two or three of them, maybe...he couldn't remember.

A young, red-headed doctor, in a white coat, had appeared and asked some questions of the nurse. He seemed a friendly person...but young. Doctor Hudson was the big man at this place. If there was something the matter with his head, he wanted Hudson.

"I say," he had called, stiffly turning his eyes toward the doctor, "why doesn't Doctor Hudson look in? He knows me. I've been at his house. Does he know I'm here?"

"I'm Doctor Watson, Mr. Merrick. I'm looking after you. Doctor Hudson is not in the city..."

After Doctor Watson had left the room, he had beckoned the nurse to the bedside. Had Miss Hudson called?...No; but that was because he wasn't seeing visitors yet...that is, not many...Yes, his grandfather had been in...and a Mr. Masterson...The accident?...Oh yes, they would tell him all about that, a little later...What he needed now was sleep; lots and lots of it; no worry or excitement...What we wanted now to make us well was sleep...Then we could have visitors, and the visitors would tell us everything we wanted to know...That kind of silly baby-talk!...Hell's bells!

This morning however he had grown impatient. These people were carrying their stupid silence strike too far! Obviously he had been in some sort of a scrape. Very well...It was not the first time. There would be some way to settle it. There always had been. Was he not accustomed to paying for smashed fenders, broken china, splintered furniture, outraged feelings, and interrupted business? If anybody had a grievance, let him make a bill of it, and he would draw a cheque! It wasn't any of this hospital's business, anyway! Or...was it?...What could he have done to their damned hospital?...Run into it?

"Tell me this much, won't you, Miss...?"

"Bates."

"...Miss Bates; just how did I get this whack on my head?...And I won't ask you any more questions."

"There was a mast or something flew around and knocked you off a boat."

"Thanks."

A mast had knocked him off a boat! He grinned; tried to remember. Well—that was that; but how did the hospital get in it?

* * * * *

At noon, his nurse had been relieved for an hour by a no less important factotum that Mrs. Ashford herself, superintendent of the hospital.

She sat by the window with a trifle of needlework in her hands, apparently intent upon it; but quite aware of her patient's mood and expectant of an outburst.

Bobby studied her face and decided in its favour. It was a conclusion to which patients at Brightwood customarily arrived with even more promptness, but he was in no state of mind to lose his heart impetuously to anyone in this establishment where he was being treated with such contemptuous indifference.

He found himself guessing her age. Everybody indulged in such speculations on first sight of Nancy Ashford. Her maternal attitude toward the staff, the nurses, the patients, was premised solely upon her white hair. The fact that she had come by it in her early twenties, at the time of her husband's fatal illness, in no way discounted the matronly authority it gave her as the general counsellor at Brightwood. Notwithstanding her quite youthful face and slim, athletic figure, many people who outranked her in years called her mother—a perfect specimen of the type that instantly invites confidences. She had become a repository for a wider diversity of confessions than come to the ear of the average priest.

Doctor Hudson's tragic death had been a deeper sorrow to her than anybody connected with Brightwood was ever going to know certainly—whatever might be guessed; and the business of bearing it with precisely the right outward expression of regret was the most serious problem she had ever faced.

For fifteen years Mrs. Ashford had grown more and more indispensable to Doctor Hudson. Entering his experimental hospital as an operating nurse, shortly after the death of her husband—a promising young surgeon and a protégé of the brain specialist—she had quickly and quietly transferred many an administrative responsibility from her chief's shoulders to her own, almost without his realizing how deftly she had eased him of an increasing volume of wearisome details. The time came when her decisions represented the opinions of Doctor Hudson, and went unquestioned. Nobody was jealous of her influence over him, or of her calm authority over the institution. Improvident young internes sought her counsel in their troublesome business affairs. Nurses told her their love stories. Patients laid their hearts bare to her; confided everything from minor domestic perplexities to major crimes; wrote to her after they had gone home; not infrequently proposed marriage to her; deluged her with Christmas gifts.

"Isn't she sweet?" the women patients would say. She was not. The word was silly, applied to her. She was understanding, tactful, and, above all, strong; with the face of a young woman, the mind of a man, and the white hair of a matron.

There were some other things about Mrs. Ashford which, had young Merrick known, might have changed his attitude toward her that morning, as she sat jabbing her needle into the bit of tapestry and waiting for him to blow up.

Doctor Hudson had taken her for granted. He had grown accustomed to confiding every difficulty to her, and only rarely was he disposed to debate any of her opinions. There was no phase of his professional life to which she was a stranger. Even some of the strictly private enterprises to which he gave himself with stealthy concern—thinking them effectively concealed—she had discovered, either by chance or shrewd guess; and from that knowledge she had long since deduced at least a vague and troublesome idea of the motive back of them. He would have been amazed—perhaps somewhat annoyed—had he known that Nancy Ashford almost knew the one important secret of his life.

How deeply she cared for him, and the nature of that affection, the surgeon suspected, but resolutely refused to recognize. Anything like a mutual admission of their actual dependence upon and attraction for each other would, he felt, lead to unhappy complications. He could not marry her. Joyce would have disapproved.

"A nurse?...Why, Daddy!...You wouldn't!...You mustn't!"

On the morning that he told Nancy he was to be married the next Tuesday to Joyce's college friend, she had said quickly, "A very sensible thing to do. She will make you happy. I am so glad for you."

"I had hoped you might think that," he replied, obviously relieved.

Luckily for both, they were not facing each other. He was tugging on his rubber gloves, in the little laboratory adjacent to his operating-room, and she was buttoning his long white coat down the back. He pretended not to notice how long it was taking her.

"All right, back there?" he sang out, with attempted casualness, glancing over his shoulder.

"Quite all right now," she had answered, in a tone that matched his for lightness; but—it was not quite all right...Nothing would ever be quite all right again.

Bobby had felt his heart warming toward the lady of indeterminate age who busied herself with the needle, evidently unaware of the tumult of his mind. He decided to disturb her peace. He would ask a few questions which he had been at some pains to compose. They sounded a bit bookish, as if memorized...It was clear enough, he said, that he had been in some kind of a mess. He was forever getting into messes. That appeared to be his occupation. It was customary with him, he recited, with what sounded more like silly bravado than he had intended, to be in a bad scrape and not know the full particulars until the next morning. What was this one about? Had anybody else been hurt? He could not recall. If there were damages, he would gladly pay.

It had turned out to be a surly speech, as it progressed; mostly because Mrs. Ashford did not look up from her work, or seem properly attentive to the petulant complaint. Mistaking her effort at self-control for but another exhibition of the indifference under which he had fretted, Bobby grew irascible. In the very middle of a spluttery sentence however he broke off suddenly and regarded her with perplexity. As she raised her eyes to meet his, he saw that they were brimming with tears. Her lips trembled.

"What have I done?" he demanded huskily. "It's something very terrible. I can see that in your face. You've simply got to tell me. I can't stand this anxiety any longer!"

Mrs. Ashford put down her work on the table, came to the bedside, and taking one of Bobby's hands in both of her own said, "My friend, something has occurred here that makes us all very, very unhappy. It happened about the time that you came here. We are not recovered from it. But it was not your fault, and the damages cannot be settled. You need give yourself no further concern about it."

Not a bit satisfied, but assured by Mrs. Ashford's tone that their discussion was at least temporarily a closed incident, Bobby made no further effort to press his inquiries. He murmured his regrets that there had been any trouble and sank into his pillows, disquieted, but—whatever was the matter it was no concern of his. That was good. That was ever so much better than he had feared.

It had been a very welcome diversion, an hour later, when Doctor Watson had suggested the solarium. In the rumbling elevator, Bobby had made a feeble effort to be jocular. It was impossible that the grief which had seemed to distress the matronly Mrs. Ashford would be equally experienced by so young and pretty a girl as the slender blonde who stood at his elbow, silently awaiting their arrival at the top floor.

"I'll bet you a box of candy against a pleasant smile," he said, grimly, "that we do less talking in our hospital than any place else on earth."

Instantly he realized it was the wrong thing to have said to her. She did not challenge his statement. It was not that she was offended. It was rather as if she had not heard him. She was in trouble. She was in the same kind of trouble that affected everybody else in this hospital. It plunged him again into the gloom from which he had partly extricated himself through the not very reassuring statements of Mrs. Ashford.

Squelched to a shamed silence by the girl's rebuff, he gazed steadily ahead, conscious of flushed cheeks, as they wheeled him into the alcove, adjusted his pillows, half-lowered the blind, moved the screen closer to isolate him from the others and, without a word or a smile, hurried away.

He must have been there an hour or more before he learned what he thought he had wanted to know.

In the course of that hour, failing of scraping together enough remembered facts to be of any service in the solution of his problem, he had gone wool-gathering in all directions.

Perhaps it was his sense of utter desolation and loneliness that had set him going over the path of his singularly bitter childhood.

* * * * *

Bobby Merrick had grown up about as independent of the normal restraints imposed upon children as could have been possible in civilized society.

When he was a little lad, his father, Clif Merrick, had been too much occupied with business—what time he was not yacht racing, deer hunting, or on other journeys not quite so clearly explained—to pay any attention to the sensitive child beyond an occasional pat on the head as he passed him on the stairs in tow of a governess; or a brief and clumsy tussle in imitation of paternal playfulness. The big man was always half drunk when he made these rough overtures of comradeship. The boy dreaded seeing his father approach, of a late afternoon, with a flushed face, suggesting a good romp together.

On such occasions, if she was present, Bobby's neurotic mother usually intervened.

"You're much too rough with him, Clif," she would expostulate. "He's only a little boy. You hurt him! Stop it, I tell you!"

"Nonsense!" his father would reply, glancing toward the governess for approval, "you don't know anything about boys. Does she, Bobby?"

In all truth, she didn't; but the lad would be distressed over the episode, hardly knowing what answer was expected of him.

Once—how vividly he remembered this!—his mother, upon being sarcastically scorned in his presence for the way she was "bringing up a soft little mollycoddle, with his hands full of dolls and dishes" (true enough), had shocked him by screaming, in a shrill falsetto, "Leave him alone; damn you! I won't have you bullying him any more when you're drunk! You touch him again and I'll call the police!"

The police! For his father! Bobby remembered that it had made him ill—nauseated. The governess had had to carry him upstairs, where he was awfully sick. He even remembered what it was he had eaten—currant pudding. He had never cared much for currants thereafter.

Clif Merrick so steadily ragged the child, after that, about his girlish toys and trinkets, that Bobby himself revolted against the soft programme the women had made for him and gratefully approved when his father suggested boxing lessons. Strangely enough, he found himself happy with the new sport. Eager to test the value of the instruction he was receiving, he occasionally slipped away from the big house about time for school to be out in the afternoon, attired in an immaculate black velvet suit with white lace cuffs, and waited at the corner for somebody to yell "Sissy!" When he returned home he would be very dirty and greatly in need of repair, but grinning from ear to ear.

When he was twelve, Bobby's father had died suddenly of pneumonia brought on by exposure while duck hunting in nasty weather. Young as he was, the boy realized that his mother's bereavement was accepted by her with a calm fortitude out of all proportion to her weakness for indulging in self-pity.

One of her remarks, upon their return from the cemetery that bleak afternoon, was chiselled indelibly upon her son's mind. None of the epitaphs he had regarded with childish curiosity, as they drove slowly along the narrow, winding roads, was carved deeper. Sometimes, when he thought of it, he winced; sometimes he grinned.

"Well," she said, handing Colleen her furs, "that's *that*!"

"Yes, ma'am," dutifully replied Colleen, accustomed to occasional outbursts of caste-forgetful confidences vouchsafed by her mistress, "it certainly is!"

And then, apparently dissatisfied with her rejoinder, which had taken an almost too casual view of the matter for one who entertained so wholesome a respect for death, Colleen added, sepulchrally, "It must have been very hard, ma'am, to leave him out there."

Upon which followed the memorable elegy spoken by his mother.

"Well; *I'll know now where he is*!"

Sometimes, when, as a collegian, Bobby was at that exact state of intoxication where the tragic in a man's experience becomes distorted into broad, screaming farce, and even sacred memories make wry faces and put out their tongues in scorn of everything decent, he would recall his mother's elegiac comment, laugh uproariously, and pound his knee. "What a corking epitaph!" he had shouted once, and had instantly cursed himself for a drunken fool.

* * * * *

Bobby could not remember precisely when he had become conscious that his father and mother despised each other. It must have been while he was still a mere baby. By the time he was eight, they had stopped quarrelling, their mutual contempt too ponderous for so frail a vehicle as speech. Unquestionably she had suffered much; but it was no use trying to champion her cause. She was entitled to her son's pity, and had it. He would have been glad enough to have respected her, too, had that been possible.

Petulant, selfish, suspicious—Maxine Merrick was no end difficult. Her only proficiency was her skill as a pianist; and aware that it was the sole endowment she was in a position to transmit, she had begun to teach the child piano technique almost before he knew the letters on his building-blocks.

A restless soul, she was; temperamentally cursed with "floating anxiety"; pretty, after a fashion...a transparent blonde...always attracting attention at the opera where she quite took one's breath away with her beauty at thirty yards; given to fits of melancholy, for which there was plenty of excuse, God knew; dissatisfied with her own personality which she constantly endeavoured to improve, either by tinkering with her face and figure, or by taking her dishevelled mind to quack psychiatrists and will doctors for adjustments. She was on the sucker list of all the advertising mountebanks in town; talked seriously about palmistry; had paid a considerable sum for a horoscope which related her affairs somehow with the movements of Arcturus; frequently had her fortune told.

She vibrated between institutions for the care of the body and the cure of the soul. Having spent a busy season of assiduous devotion to the business of being plucked, picked, dyed, frescoed, and massaged; sitting long and painful hours in the studios of beauty experts, Maxine would suddenly experience an unaccountable surge of disgust, and make off hurriedly to some sanitarium de luxe where, in seclusion almost conventional, she lived on unsalted insipidities, and listened of evenings in the lounge to mellifluous harangues on personality expression...nerves in order...the will to live...life at its utmost; followed by less sidereal comments by the chief of staff concerning the importance of internal purity—not of the conscience, which was out of his field, as the piracy of his bills attested—but of the colon, to which he referred with a bland candour somewhat disconcerting to the newer arrivals, still serving their novitiate in the by no means unexacting vocation of hypochondria.

During these spells of improving her health and personality, Maxine would lose many pounds and add as many new words to her pathological vocabulary. It suited her mood, during such retreats, to become as disdainful of her appearance as a Thibetan lama.

One day, for no apparent reason other than caprice, there would be a flurry of trunks and boxes, tickets and taxis, and a swift return home, to the utter consternation of yogis who had been fattening on her patronage, and the indignant amazement of pallid charlatans whose income would be alarmingly depleted by the sudden demobilization of her crusade for the Perpetual Light. It would be generally rumoured among the patients that Mrs. Merrick was a brilliant social leader..."simply required, my dear, to stop and rest for a few weeks, now and then, if you know what I mean"...which was nonsense; for Clif Merrick never took her anywhere, and she could have numbered her friends on her fingers.

On these excursions in quest of youth, beauty, sweetness and light, his mother never took Bobby along. He remained at home in the custody of grafting servants and an endless procession of young governesses, none of whom ever stayed longer than a few weeks. The prettier ones were the quickest to go...sometimes on an hour's notice. He had put on quite a scene when Miss Newman had left without so much as saying good-bye to him, and had been slapped by his father for the racket he was making.

Shortly after Maxine had been assured that henceforth she would know exactly where Clif was, the big house on Piedmont Square was sold, and Bobby was taken to Europe where his mother rapidly improved in health and spirits. He was placed in a school for rich waifs at Versailles, where he fraternized with youngsters who had become an embarrassing liability to divorced parents. On brief vacations he joined "Maxine"—as he obediently called her—in Paris, scowling his distaste when, in the presence of her new friends, she chattered baby talk to him, to which he made sour replies in a voice that frequently skidded off the treble clef. She had filled her spacious apartment with wigged and bangled old harridans, who swapped dull prattle about their aristocratic relatives for caviare and champagne and was inordinately vain of her *ménage,* which Bobby impudently insisted would better be called her *menagerie.*

There were lonely summers at Brighton and Deauville, lonely Christmases at Cannes; private schools and sycophantic tutors; trains and hotels; brief, dry, hard friendships with over-sophisticated, unwanted boys like himself, envious of their mothers' Pekingeses, and not infrequently dizzy with pilferings from the decanter on the sideboard.

At seventeen, he had been sent back, alone, to enter a high-toned prep school in Connecticut where, for previous lack of a balanced intellectual ration and experience of steady discipline, he survived only until Thanksgiving. Headmaster Bowers saw him off on the train and returned to lead the chapel exercises. Ineffable calm sat on his brow, and his voice was vibrant with unfeigned gratitude as he announced, "We will stand and sing the Doxology."

Through the influence of old Nicholas, Bobby was then accepted, provisionally, in another preparatory school, a Military Academy not quite so close to salt water..."It's just a ritzy reform school," he wrote on his first day, to his perplexed grandparent, who replied, in substance, that, if that were so, it was quite the place for him. To his instructors there, he gave more bother than any other six, but contrived to stay on. Through these days, he renewed his abandoned taste for boxing, under a preceptor who cuffed him about, shamefully, until he discovered that the boy was game and thereafter took an interest in him. It was Mr. Bowman's boast, when Bobby finished with them, that albeit he was a bit frail in algebra, he could lick his weight in wildcats.

* * * * *

It was at the State University, however, that Bobby had struck his stride. Neither a loafer nor a dunce, he easily ran circles around the average student in such classes as stirred his curiosity. Zoology?...He ate it up! Physiology...psychology...chemistry...he was constantly amazing his friends by his ardent boning, especially in chemistry, in the face of his utter indifference to scholastic credit in the courses he disliked.

His David-and-Jonathan friendship with Tom Masterson had been good for him; better for him than for Tom, a likeable youngster with an insatiable ambition to be a short-story writer.

They had found each other as rushees at a luncheon for freshmen in the Delta Omega house, and decided on the spot to room together. Young Masterson, however eager to emancipate himself from the restraints of a rather severely disciplined household, was something of an idealist, and opened up a new world to Bobby who, listening at first because he liked Tom, and later because he liked what Tom said, learned from his youthful tutor a love for the classics which, in the original, he had despised.

But Masterson, not having been brought up on cocktails, was not much advantaged by the tardy instruction he received in exchange for his Greek and Roman mythology. Once he started—no matter what the hour, place, or circumstance—Tom could be depended upon to continue drinking until he was unconscious. Bobby, approximately sober, would get him home, somehow, and put him to bed with all the solicitude of a mother. Apparently it never occurred to him that he was jeopardizing his chum's future.

"Poor old Tommy!" he would say, unlacing his shoes. "I'm afraid you'll just never learn to drink like a gentleman!"

Nor was the Merrick influence much of a blessing upon the Delta Omega house into which he and Tom moved as sophomores. Had he been less lovable, he might have been less dangerous. His charming irresistibility was fatal to the good resolutions of many a chap who honestly wanted to stay sober and do his work. Even the seniors—by custom disdainful of juvenile society—once they were in debt to him for lavish hospitality which was at first reluctantly accepted, found themselves careening over the road in Bobby's big touring-car, late Friday afternoons, en route to his grandfather's home on Lake Saginack.

And the indulgent old man, believing they would all have a better time if they had the house to themselves—and eager to be out of the racket—would be driven in to the city to find sanctuary at the Columbia Club. The neighbourhood used to protest, but old Nicholas always reminded them—when they complained of drunken demons, for whose conduct he was presumably responsible, driving recklessly with open mufflers and raucous sirens, at all hours of the night—that boys would be boys. When they smashed something, he paid for it.

Not infrequently Bobby's week-end guests went back to Ann Arbor on Monday morning without a nickel; wearing their very socks by permission of their host, who owned them after an all-day poker game on Sunday. How often them promised themselves, "Never again!" but it was hard to stand out against Bobby's insidious smile. Moreover, the food and service at old Nicholas' country palace was a tempting diversion from the near-starvation of fraternity fare and the discomforts of a crowded house where nothing ever received anxious thought and respect but the impending payments on the mortgage.

* * * * *

For some time, Bobby had been conscious of a dull rumble of conversation, just beyond the screen. It began to annoy him. Some stupid ass was airing his home-brewed philosophy.

"All this here talk about Providence...Providence; bah—I say!...Take this very case, for instance!...Here is a noted man who has made himself so useful that people came to him for thousands of miles for help that nobody could give them but him!...Look at me, for instance!..."

Bobby scowled, and muttered, "Yeah!...Look at you!...It's bad enough to have to listen to you!"

"Look at *me*! I came here clear from Ioway; and lucky enough I got here when I did...Last operation he ever performed, they tell me!...And they might have saved his life too if that pulmotor thing, or whatever it was, hadn't been in use on that drunken young What's-his-name with the rich granddaddy! What right had he to be alive, anyhow...now I ask you?"

It may have been Bobby's sudden pallor that attracted the attention of the nurse who sat at the little desk by the door. She quickly crossed the room and asked if there was anything he wanted. Bobby swallowed with a dry throat, attempted a grateful smile, and replied weakly, "Perhaps I should go back...feel better in bed...not very strong yet. Tell them, will you?"

His exit from the solarium was effected with such promptness that the patients observed it. Who was this youngster? Questions were asked and answered. The man who had discoursed of the unseemly ways of Providence was deeply contrite...Wished he'd known, he said.

Bobby's nurse stepped out into the corridor, after putting him to bed, and an interne passing by remarked, "So he knows all about it."

"Well, he had to find out sometime, didn't he?"

18

"Yes—but he's a pretty good scout...And it was a rotten way to dish it up to him!"
"You should worry," snapped Miss Bates.

* * * * *

For hours, Bobby Merrick lay with his eyes closed, motionless, but not asleep. At first, he was hotly indignant. What right had these saps from Ioway, or wherever, to pass judgment on what kind of people had a right to live? How could anybody be so small-minded as to hold it against him that his life had been saved, even if it could be shown that Doctor Hudson might have been rescued if the oxygen machine had been available? It wasn't his fault. He hadn't borrowed the damned thing! He hadn't asked to have his life saved at that price, or at all!

And then his resentment over this monstrous injustice gave way to steady thinking. Perhaps, after all, he was under a certain obligation to this dead man. Very good; he would show his appreciation of what it had cost to save his life. He fell to wondering whether Doctor Hudson had left his young wife and Joyce properly provided for. Joyce was extravagant. He knew what it must require to keep her going. He had had her in tow, occasionally, himself.

"See if Mrs. Ashford is free to come here for a moment," commanded Bobby. The nurse nodded stiffly, left the room, and, in a few minutes, Mrs. Ashford stood by the bedside.

Assuming what he believed to be a mature, conventional, business tone—the tone of large capital about to indulge itself in a brief seizure of magnanimity—he inquired, without preamble, "What sort of an estate did Doctor Hudson leave?"

"I do not know," she replied; and after a pause added crisply, "Why?"

The dry crackle of that "why?" irritated him. She had given him reason to believe that she was sympathetic. Surely she might know he was not asking this question out of sheer curiosity.

"You seem to infer that it is none of my business," he retorted.

Nancy Ashford coloured slightly.

"Well," she snapped, "is it?"

Bobby's face felt hot. He was at a serious disadvantage, and she was not helping him; not making the slightest attempt to understand him.

"You might at least credit me with an honest wish to do something about all this, if I can," he expostulated angrily.

"I am sorry if I offended you,"—with forced composure—"You were thinking of giving some money to the family?"

"If they need it—yes."

"Whose money?"

Bobby raised up on one elbow and scowled.

"Whose money? Why, my own, of course!"

"Some you earned, maybe?"

For a moment, he was speechless with exasperation over the studied insolence of her query. Sinking back upon the pillow, he motioned to her to leave him. Instead, she took her stand at the foot of his bed, and, hands on hips, militantly began an address distinguished for its lack of polite ambiguity.

"You invited this," she said thickly. "You called me in here to get some information about the Hudsons, and I'm going to tell you! And then you can pay them off...with your grandfather's money! Do you know what killed Doctor Hudson?...Worry! They said it was overwork that weakened his heart. I know better! The only thing that counted in his life, besides his profession, was Joyce. He saw her going to the dogs. Part of that was your fault! You've had a reputation for ruining all your friends!"

Bobby Merrick lay stunned under the attack, his eyes wide with amazement at the woman's audacity.

"The poor chap tried to pull himself together." Her voice wavered a little, but she went on with resolution. "Built that little house at the lake, went swimming when he wasn't able; knew he wasn't able; had provided a lung-motor for emergencies; and then, at the moment when he has to have it—*you're* using it! *You*—of all people! And now you casually suggest settling the bill with money!"

Something in his look—it was the look of a hurt animal—checked Nancy's passionate diatribe.

"Please forgive me," she muttered agitatedly. "But, as I say, you invited it. You wanted to know, I have told you."

Bobby swallowed awkwardly, and rubbed his brow with the rough sleeve of his cotton smock.

"Well," he muttered hoarsely, "you've told me. If you've said everything you have to say, I won't keep you."

She started toward the door, paused, turned about, walked slowly to the window and stood looking out, her left elbow cupped in her right hand, the slim fingers of the other tapping her shoulder, agitatedly, at first; then meditatively. Bobby watched the slowing tempo of her fingers, cleared his throat nervously, and decided to meet her half way.

"That was really all I had to offer; wasn't it?...just money?"

She returned slowly to the bedside, drew up a chair, sat down, and rested her plump arms upon the white counterpane close to his pillow.

"You have something very valuable besides money; but you'll never use it." Her tone was judicial, prophetic. "It's in you, all right, but it will never come out. Nobody will ever know that you had it. The money will always be blocking the way...You were much disturbed to-day, because you overheard an impolite insinuation that your life wasn't worth saving at the price of Doctor Hudson's. Naturally, you resented that. Your indignation does you credit...However—crude as that man was, what he said was true, wasn't it?...You admitted it was true when you decided to put up a cash difference. But you can't justify yourself that way. It might make things more comfortable for the Hudson family; but it wouldn't help you to live with yourself again."

She had taken his hand in hers, maternally. Disengaging his eyes, she stared upward absorbedly, and murmured, as if quite alone, "He'd never do it, of course...Couldn't!...Wouldn't!...Too much money...It would be too hard...take too long...but God!... *What a chance*!"

Bobby stirred uneasily.

"I'm afraid I don't get you...if—if you're talking about me."

"Oh, yes, you do!" She nodded her head, slowly, emphatically. "You know what I mean...and you wish you were up to it...but—" pulling herself together resolutely, "you're not; so we won't talk about it any more...Is there something I can get for you before I go?"

Bobby raised a detaining hand, and their fingers interlaced.

"I think I know now what you're hinting. But it's quite impossible, as you say. It's worse than impossible. It's ridiculous! Doctor Hudson was famous! Nobody can ever replace him!...Oh, I say, Mrs. Ashford; that's quite too bad! I didn't mean to say the wrong thing, you know!"

For Nancy's eyes had suddenly tightened as if wincing under sharp pain, and her white head bent lower and lower in a dejection strangely out of keeping with her aggressive personality. He ventured to touch her hair in a clumsy, boyish caress, murmuring again that he was sorry.

"That's all right, boy," she said thickly, regarding him with weary eyes, suddenly grown old. "You needn't worry about *me*!...*I'll* carry on!...My little problem is quite simple compared to yours."

She straightened up, patted his hand, and smiled.

Bobby raised on one elbow.

"You're a good sport, Mrs. Ashford!"

"Thanks!...You like people to be good sports; don't you?...So do I. I'd rather be a good sport than worth millions!...I expect you're a pretty good sport too; aren't you, Bobby?"

He relaxed on his pillow and studied the ceiling.

"Your—what you were talking about—would be a sort of sporting proposition; wouldn't it?"

"Quite!"

"Years and years!"

"For life!...There would be no discharge in that war!" She extended her hand, as one man to another.

"I'm going now...Sure you're not angry with me any more?"

He shook his head, with tightly closed eyes, and gripped her hand. The emotional tension of the past half hour was taking advantage of his physical weakness. Hot tears seeped through his lashes, and trickled down his temples.

Nancy withdrew her hand, stood for a moment silently regarding him, her knuckles pressed hard against her lips; then turned away and quietly closed the door behind her.

CHAPTER III

"YOU say he's different," pursued Joyce interestedly. "How do you mean—different? Sober, perhaps?"

Masterson chuckled.

"Don't be a fool!" she growled. "You know very well what I meant."

He returned his empty glass to the silver tray on the table, settled himself comfortably into the cushions of the garden swing, and so frankly considered the slender shapeliness of the girl in the wicker chair that she shifted her position uneasily.

"Yes," he replied, reverting tardily to her question, "he's all of sober, and then some. He's owlish...morose...prowls the night like Hamlet...has an idea that people resent his having been saved from drowning."

"How absurd! Did he tell you that?"

"As much as."

She thumbed the pages of the novel that lay in her lap and frowned.

"Well—and what is he proposing to do about it?...Sulk?"

Young Masterson indicated by a slow shake of the head, eyes half closed, that the problem was too vast for him, and meditatively tapped the end of a fresh cigarette on the arm of the swing.

"You'll discover for yourself that Bobby is greatly altered since his accident. I can't quite make him out. Yesterday, when I saw him at Windymere, I expected to find him in better spirits. He is almost well now; has been walking about on the grounds for days. But he seems thoroughly preoccupied. I suggested it might improve his disposition if we threw together a little cocktail, and he said, 'You know where the makings are: help yourself.' I shook up enough for both of us, but he wouldn't join me; and when I ragged him about it, he replied, from about ten miles off, that he'd 'another plan in mind.'

"'Something that doesn't include gin, evidently,' I suggested; and he nodded cryptically.

"'Something like that,' he replied. You know about how little he discloses through that poker face of his, when he decides to be *incomunicado*."

"So—you dared him to tell you, I suppose."

"No; I just kidded him a little, but he didn't take it very nicely. Just sat—and posed for 'The Thinker.' 'What's the big idea?' I said. 'Gone over to Andy Volstead?'"

"What did he say?" demanded Joyce, as the pause lengthened.

"He said, 'Hell, no!' and then mumbled, down in his throat, that he'd gone over to Nancy Ashford."

"And who's Nancy Ashford?" she inquired, sharply, flushing with annoyance over her disclosure.

"You ought to know," smugly enjoying her vexation. "She is the superintendent of Brightwood Hospital."

"Oh—you mean *Mrs.* Ashford. I hadn't thought of her as Nancy. They must have become quite well acquainted. Why, she's an old lady."

"Well—so much the better; wouldn't you say?"

She met his banter with a grimace.

"You spend too much of your time thinking up story plots, Tommy. It's affecting your mind."

"Maybe so," agreed Masterson dryly. He stretched his long arms over the back of the swing and regarded her with an inquisitive smile. "Your own story grows more exciting every minute. What else do you want to know about Bobby?"

Joyce offered him the concession of a crooked smile.

"Did he say whether he was coming in soon?"

"Nary a word on that. However, he may not feel himself quite up to it yet...Rather awkward situation, you'll admit."

She nodded, and there was a moment's silence.

"You have Bobby and me all wrong, Tom. We were together pretty steadily...in December...before Helen came..."

Masterson broke in with an unpleasant chuckle.

"I'm surprised that you remember anything about December," he teased. "My own recollection of it is very pale."

"Yes; I'll admit it was rather dreadful. Especially the evening we celebrated your birthday. That must have been a mighty rough night on the sea. Incidentally, I have not seen Bobby since. When he finished at the university in February, he sailed for France to visit his mother, without a line to me that he was going. I had two short letters from him later. Then he turns up at home; next day this dreadful thing happens to us."

She hesitated before going on.

"So—now you know exactly how thick we are. Does it sound—romantic like?"

"Of course, you're bound to keep it in mind," observed Masterson soberly, "that Bobby feels quite terribly about the—the thing that occurred out there at the lake. Never having met Helen, he is a bit shy about meeting her now. He may fear she would be slightly prejudiced against him, under the circumstances."

"I'm afraid she is," agreed Joyce reluctantly. "Entirely natural that she would be."

"How is Helen, by the way?"

"Oh, she's steady—the darling! Want to see her? I'll tell her you're here."

She rose, handing Masterson her book.

"Helen has been entertaining a queer little lady for the past hour or more, but I think she is free now. The caller was one of father's patients, I presume. So many people have been here lately...all sorts...people we had never heard of who come with tearful gratitude to tell us what father had been to them. Really, it has kept us quite stirred up. I wish they wouldn't...And letters?...To-day there was a long one from a man in Maine hinting that father had saved his life, somehow, years ago. He didn't state the particulars...Seemed rather secretive, as if there were some big mystery behind it; as if there were something he wanted to tell, but couldn't. Very queer...I'll go and call Helen."

* * * * *

She turned toward the big white house with the green shutters, and Masterson's eyes appraisingly followed her graceful movements as she crossed the lawn...Some girl!...He set the swing gently in motion and inhaled deeply from his cigarette...A thoroughbred! So, she was Bobby's, then? What the devil did Bobby mean—trying to keep this a secret from him? Well, if she considered herself Bobby's property—and obviously she did—Bobby's pal must be loyal. However, a man could look at her, couldn't he?...And wish she belonged to him?...A compliment, in a way...perhaps...debatable question, probably...But seriously, why shouldn't an artist in creative writing have as much licence to admire beauty for its own lovely sake as a painter—no matter whose girl she thought she was? What a type! Not many blondes like that left in this dyed and painted world...Original colours, these...Pale gold and milk white; with the slinky-footed gait of some wild woods thing...Some girl! But what made her think Bobby was interested in her? Or—was he? If so, he had kept his sentiments carefully concealed...

Joyce's reappearance through the shrubbery, accompanied by her step-mother, interrupted Masterson's day-dreaming. The two offered a striking contrast. Mrs. Hudson was Latin in every feature and curve, in the glossy blackness of her shingled hair, the arch of her brows, the utter lack of self-consciousness in her posture and carriage. Joyce was perfect Saxon; slightly the taller. Leading the way, she seemed the older.

He strolled to meet them. Helen waved her hand, upon sight of him. She had adopted the rôle of being years his senior, much to his amusement. They had often made a little game of it—he, cast for the part of a spoiled nine-year-old, which he carried off with amazing skill; she, the exasperated but polite mother, endeavouring to keep her whelp in hand without making too much of a scene. They had done it, quite spontaneously, at the Byrnes, one evening. Laura Byrne, upon her own testimony, "had about passed out," Senator Byrne had said the skit was worth a fortune in vaudeville "big time". They had thought it not half bad, themselves.

The conventional uniform of the bereft had only accentuated her youth. It called attention to her girlish vitality, deepened her dimples, whitened her throat; as a severe frame on a bright etching will heighten its colours; emphasize its values.

She extended a small hand and smiled. Her recent experience had left traces. She was pale and a bit remote, her appearance suggesting convalescence from a serious illness.

The smile fluttered momentarily and was gone; but it was essentially the same smile that one waited for, plotted for, tried to recapture in memory, analyzed without success. Once Masterson had attempted to persuade one of his women in a story to smile like that; but she couldn't learn it. He had written, of "Gloria"—

"It was more than a smile. It was a little sonata, in three movements. It arrived first in her eyes, which gradually grew wider and bluer. Almost imperceptibly, but very disturbingly, the patrician brows lifted, ever so little, as if they asked permission. That was the *adagio* movement.

"Then, suddenly, the sonata played upon her lips, as when an organist seeks with one hand a lower bank of keys for the melody. They parted to disclose the smallest, straightest, whitest of teeth. That was the *scherzo* movement.

"Instantly, however, as if the lips had become alarmed at their own audacity, they closed, demurely. But the smile lingered in her eyes—in the outer corners of her eyes—long after her pretty mouth had done with it; and that was the *largo* movement. *Largo dolcemente.*

"And the beholder? What of him? Ah—but his pulse ran on into throbbing, pounding *strotto!*"

Masterson knew the description was silly. He had added, rather helplessly:

"—a vastly disquieting smile; a smile to be smiled with discretion, preferably among strong-minded, elderly men—relatives, if at all convenient to have relatives at hand."

Helen Hudson smiled. To-day it was a sonatina. The movements were *adagio, andante, lento;* but it was no less stirring for its chastened mood.

* * * * *

"It seems a long time since we saw you, Tom," she said, in her husky contralto, motioning him to a place beside her in the swing.

Joyce had remained standing.

"Tommy," said she, "I had promised Ned Brownlow I would go for a ride with him. He's out front now, waiting for me...Mind if I go?"

"Depart in Peace!" Masterson held up two fingers, pontifically. "I am in excellent hands."

Joyce's slim fingers trailed caressingly across her stepmother's shoulders as she moved away. "I'll not be long, dear," she said.

"Have you been getting out, at all?" inquired Masterson, with comradely solicitude.

Helen shook her head.

"Too busy! Callers come here at all hours; people one can't very well refuse to see; patients of Doctor Hudson's and others he appears to have befriended in one way or another. I presume you recall the quite unusual number of floral remembrances..."

"I never saw so many!"

"Well, Tom, those flowers came at the direction of people from many places; from persons whose relation to us was very difficult to establish. Fully a score were unidentifiable by anyone at Brightwood. And these callers I am receiving daily are mostly unknown to us. They come to inquire if there is anything they can do for Joyce and me. Yesterday a queer old Italian turned up and tried to present me with a thousand dollars. That's just a sample. Their stories are quite different, what there is of them—for they are strangely reticent—but one fact is common to all...sometime, somewhere, Doctor Hudson had helped them meet a crisis—usually involving money loaned; though not always money; sometimes just advice, and the aid of his influence."

"He surely had a big heart!" said Masterson.

"Yes, certainly; but there's more to it than that. Lots of men have big hearts, and are generous with their money. This is a different matter. His dealings with these people were something other. They all act as if they belonged with him to some eccentric secret society. They come here eager to do something, anything, for me, because they want to express their gratitude; but when you pin them down and invite them to tell you by what process they got into our family's debt, they stammer and dodge. It's very strange.

"Since two o'clock, I've been listening to a story that perplexes me more than any of the others; probably because I prodded a little deeper into the mystery. An old lady I didn't know existed came to tell me what a wonderful man Doctor Hudson was, and could she be of any aid to me?...I'd like to talk it over with someone. Would it bore you?"

"Tell me—please!"

"Well—it all began, said Mrs. Wickes, with an operation on her husband. Doctor Hudson had warned them it was hopeless. The family was left destitute. She says there was no bill sent from the hospital; that Doctor Hudson found a good position for the older boy and sent the girl, who had some talent for drawing, to an art school...She pointed to that lovely marine over the mantel in our living-room, and said, 'That's hers. She gave it to him. It was exhibited by the Architectural League in New York.'...Doctor Hudson had stood between them and disaster, she said, until they were able to look out for themselves; and when, a couple years later, she went to his office with a small payment on the debt they owed him, he refused to accept it; said, at first, that he had had enough joy out of it, and didn't want to be repaid any farther. She quite insisted; and he said, 'Did you ever tell anybody about our little transaction?' 'No,' she replied. 'You told me not to—and I didn't.' 'Then,' he declared stoutly, 'I *can't* take it back!'

"Of course, she was dissatisfied to leave it that way—she has all the instincts of a lady—but when she pressed him to take the money he explained, 'Had I considered this a loan, I could accept its repayment. I did not so regard it, when I invested it in your family. You have all been much more successful and prosperous than I thought you were going to be. So—since I believed I was giving it to you outright, I *can't* take it back now because, in the meantime, *I have used it all up, myself*!'"

"Pardon me," said Masterson, "I don't believe I quite understand. What was that last thing he said to her?"

Helen nodded, mysteriously, and repeated the inexplicable phrase.

"You may well inquire," she went on. "I asked Mrs. Wickes what that meant, and she grew restless. 'I can't say that I rightly know,' she stammered.

"'But you have a suspicion!' I said.

"At that she hurriedly changed the subject by taking a bulky purse from her handbag. She pressed me to take the money. It had been invested, she said, and now she wished to restore it to us.

"I said to her, 'If Doctor Hudson refused to accept it, so shall I. You had best reinvest it. Put it back where it was, if it yielded a good rate.'

"'Oh, I can't do that,' she replied. 'They're quite done with it, you know.'

"Well, after that, I gave it up! She was over my head!"

"Perhaps she's a bit cracked," hazarded Masterson.

Helen was thoughtful.

"Yes; she would be cracked, and we could let it go at that, and smile over it, if she was the only one of her species."

"You mean that you've entertained some more like her?"

She nodded.

"Yesterday, a quite well-known merchant called on me. You would recognize his name. His affair with Doctor Hudson dated ten years back. He wanted to pay me a pretty large sum of money which he said was interest on a loan. I thought it odd that he was coming forward with it after so long a time, and he confessed that Doctor Hudson had refused it. So did I, of course.

"My curiosity had the better of me, and I pressed him to tell me about it. He said that about ten years ago he was on the rim of failure. He had started in business for himself; had over-reached; and, as if he was not having enough anxiety, his wife passed through a lengthy and expensive illness. He had built a beautiful home. It was more than half paid for. He decided to let it go at a cruel sacrifice to get cash to put into his tottering business. He listed the house with a real estate concern. It was worth thirty-five thousand dollars. He was offering it for twenty thousand. There was a temporary depression of real estate values. Well—next day, he said, Doctor Hudson came to see him.

"'I understand you're selling your home for twenty thousand dollars. Why are you doing that? It's worth twice that much.'

"The young merchant explained that he must have money immediately, or his business would fail.

"'I'll lend you twenty thousand,' said Doctor Hudson. 'I haven't it, but I can get it. Pay me the principal of this loan when you are prospering again. I shall not expect any interest, because I have use for it, myself; and you are not to tell anyone, while I live, that we have transacted this business.'"

"What an odd deal," commented Masterson.

"Wait until you hear the rest of it," said Helen quietly. "Within three years, my caller said, he had returned the money, and was insistent upon paying interest on the loan. Doctor Hudson refused to take it. And what do you think he said when he declined to accept the money?"

"Give up!"

"He said, 'I can't take it, you see; for *I've used it all up myself*! 'Now—that's five distinct times I've heard that phrase, in the past week! What do you make of it?"

"Queer!" said Masterson. "Couldn't have had something to do with his income tax, could it? You know...so much allowed for gifts, charity, and the like."

"Tommy, don't be foolish!"

"Well—have you a theory?"

"Not the faintest glimmer of one." Then, animatedly, "Did you ever hear the story of Doctor Hudson's early life?"

"No; does it offer a clue to these queer performances of his?"

"Not at all...at least, it offers no clue to me. Perhaps...to a psychologist, which I am not...But, I think I'd like to tell you...It's no secret.

"You see, Wayne's parents were very poor. They lived on a farm upstate somewhere. He had to look out for himself, early. As a boy he had wanted to be a surgeon. He came to Detroit, at fifteen, to enter high school, and worked in the home of a Doctor Cummings..."

"And married his daughter! I knew that much."

"You're going too fast...In the Cummings home, Wayne Hudson was errand boy, hostler, accountant, and, on occasion, nurse, cook, private secretary, and rescue squad."

"Rescue? How's that?"

Helen hesitated.

"This Doctor Cummings was a very capable man, with a large practice; but unfortunately he drank too much...periodically. At intervals of anywhere from three weeks to two months, he would disappear for days. It was Wayne's duty to track him down, clean him up, bring him home, and meantime invent excuses for his absence and serve as a shock-absorber between the doctor and all his interests—the hospitals, the patients, the family."

"Not a very pleasant occupation for a high school boy."

"No," agreed Helen, "but calculated to mature him early. And it was not by any means a thankless task. Doctor Cummings was of course deeply appreciative and in his repentant moments assured him of his lasting gratitude. He sent Wayne to college later, and guaranteed his medical training with a life insurance policy, which, strangely enough, became accessible exactly when he had most need of it, for Doctor Cummings died when Wayne was a senior in college."

"Perhaps that helps to explain Doctor Hudson's marriage while he was still a medic," commented Masterson. "Doubtless the girl was fond of him. He felt under heavy obligations to the family. That...and the propinquity...so he married her."

"Not quite that," corrected Helen. "He was very fond of her; had given up everything to be in Arizona with her until she died. For more than four years, she was his chief concern. Naturally, he couldn't give proper attention to his work. He told me he had days of depression, while in the medical school, fearing he had mistaken his vocation, after all. His studies were hard, and he had much difficulty keeping up with them."

"One would hardly think that Doctor Hudson had ever found his studies difficult."

"He continued to find them so, for fully a year after his wife's death. Then, something happened! No; I do not know what it was. He did not tell me, and I did not insist; but something happened! One day he became conscious of a new attitude towards his books, his profession. He worked whole nights in the hospital laboratory, without fatigue. Then, soon after, through an odd circumstance, he was obliged to do a difficult operation at three o'clock one morning on an emergency case—a head injury. It attracted much attention. From then on he specialized in brain surgery. You know how well he succeeded."

Masterson closed one eye, and considered her thoughtfully.

"I can see," he said, measuring his words, "that it's somehow in the back of your head that this rather remarkable change in him...this quite sudden step-up from depression...sense of failure...halfway notion to quit medicine and sell bonds or something...into prompt recognition and success...I think you suspect that it's all tied around this—this funny business of his charities? Am I right?"

She nodded.

"Mostly however because here are two mysteries about him. I suppose I have tried to relate them...unconsciously, perhaps. They may have no association, at all...Maybe he would have told me all about it, had he lived...But—we've talked enough about mysteries, Tommy. Let's go and look at the asters."

Masterson followed her through the garden, admiring her childish enthusiasm over the autumn flowers. It was as if she caressed them. He knew she expected him to go now, and toyed with his keys.

"Don't stay in too closely," he admonished. "These people will wear you out."

"I'm taking a few days off...going up into the country to-morrow, to see Martha, our caretaker's sister. She's not very well...dreadfully broken up, you know; and I haven't seen her since it all happened."

"Might I drive you up? I should like to!"

"Thanks; but I shall want my car while I am there."

"We might tow it!"

"Oh—do you really want to go up there so badly as that? I'll tell you what you may do; drive Joyce up to Flintridge, Sunday afternoon. Probably I'll be lonesome by that time."

They strolled together to the gate.

"How fine it is that you and Joyce still have each other!"

"Yes; isn't it?"

He stepped into his car, waved a hand, and disappeared around the corner. Slowly Helen retraced her steps to the garden, sauntered along the narrow path, stooped to cup her pink palms around a garish dahlia. How fine it was that she and Joyce still had each other...Or had they?

CHAPTER IV

AS old Nicholas arose from the table that Saturday night, he said, no more to his tall grandson than to himself, "I am glad I could live until now!"

The past eight years had been dreadfully unhappy for him. It was not that there had been fresh reasons for unhappiness, but leisure to realize how much of life's solider satisfactions he had missed.

From his 'teens until his retirement from the business he had organized, Merrick's consuming passion had been concerned with the development of a great industry; an enterprise singularly difficult in that it lacked the natural guidance of established precedents. There were rules to be made for it, but none to be followed. It was a business without an ancestry.

Men who dealt with any product in the field of ceramics had thousands of years of good tradition back of them. Weavers, tanners, jewellers, masons; builders of houses, ships, cathedrals; growers of grain, fruit, cattle—these people could plot their economic curve and determine future policies by past experience. It was not so of motors.

The rise of that industry had been meteoric, dramatic! A prosperous young bicycle factory turned its attention to the experimental manufacture of a horseless carriage, as a tentative sideline. Young Merrick's stockholders were frankly sceptical of the venture in the face of public hilarity over the noisy, undependable, cumbersome, dangerous gasoline buggy.

And then—one day—the power-driven vehicle was suddenly an accepted fact. But the distance between the fox-statured *eohippus* and the draft horse was no wider than that of the evil-smelling little rattle-trap of an automobile, when Nicholas Merrick first made its acquaintance, and the strong, swift, silent, streamline motor-car which eventually developed.

Its evolution involved hazards as foolhardy as investments at Monte Carlo. A bewildering succession of revolutionizing inventions made the business over, again and again, while investors wrung their hands and shrieked discordant counsel into the ears of apprehensive directors. Costly machinery, installed yesterday, would be scrapped to-day to be replaced by costlier to-morrow. Those were days when the man who bore the final responsibility for such a chaotic enterprise found that twenty-four hours' devotion to business was demanded by this unprecedented industry, plunging impetuously over an uncharted course, narrowly skirting ruin every few weeks, and turning sharp corners every day.

Responsive to general clamour, prophetic of great fortunes to be made, innumerable companies hastily entered the motor-mart where competition became merciless, unscrupulous. Disaster was inevitable for all but a few of the keenest, the bravest, the luckiest. Merrick experienced all the anxiety of a pioneer leading a long wagon-train of scared emigrants across a trackless desert without a compass. For fully thirty years, but little of his time or thought had been deflected from his exacting responsibility.

When, therefore, at seventy-two, he wearily dismounted from the tiger he had ridden—an event which called for a brilliant complimentary banquet at the Chamber of Commerce in the suburban town of Axion—he was a very tired old man with a fortune estimated at twenty millions, a high blood pressure, and a large stock of disquieting memories.

Clif...God!—what a tragedy!...Clif's mother—a timid, brown thrush of a woman—had died when the boy was twelve. Nicholas had scarcely missed her. They had built the big shops, that year. He saw little of the boy. Occasionally there would be a brief and stormy session—Nicholas violently hortatory, Clifford calmly insolent—but nothing ever came of it beyond estrangement.

Nobody could say he had not done his utmost to surround his son with opportunities. Surely if money could have done it, Clif had a chance. Nicholas had always silenced his own misgivings with that reply.

"God knows I've spent enough on him!...I can't nurse him, myself!"

But now that enforced idleness had brought opportunity for serious reflection, Nicholas milled it all over, elbows on knees, empty hands dangling. The old alibi was no good. Nor was there any reasonable expectation of better things to be expressed by the new generation. Bobby was a lovable youngster, to be sure. Nicholas rejoiced in his steady wit, his winning smile, his unfailing consideration of his grandfather's moods, but he gave no promise of success. Beyond the fact that he played the piano like a professional artist, possessed an unusual capacity for making and retaining friendships, and had contrived to finish his college course, Bobby held out no encouragement that he would ever do anything worth a thought. He would drive and drink, gamble and golf, hunt and fish, marry some dizzy, dissipated, scarlet-lipped little flapper and tire of her; he would summer in Canada, winter in Cannes, clip his coupons, confer with his tailor, subsidize the symphony orchestra, appear on the stationery of a few charities and on the platform when the Republican candidate for President came to town; and, ultimately, be pushed into a crypt in the big, echoing, gothic mausoleum alongside Clifford, the waster.

Oh, there had been an occasional ray of hope; a mere phosphorescence, just enough to make the darkness a little more dense when the flash was over.

On the last day of his grandson's senior year...it was a mid-year class, with ceremonies deferred until commencement...Nicholas had driven over to the little city of the State University, lunching with his old-time friend the head of the Department of Chemistry. He had straightened and beamed when Professor Garland said, "I don't know whether you're aware of it, Merrick, but that wild young cub of yours has the making of a chemist."

"Honest? Speak to him about it; won't you, Garland? It would mean more—coming from you!"

Garland had made a lengthy rite of mixing his tea and hot water before replying, "Chemistry's hard work, old chap! Your boy knows he doesn't have to work!"

And when Nicholas' face fell, Garland added, consolingly, "You can't blame him. Why should he put on a rubber apron and puddle in nasty stews and noxious stinks when he can get some joy out of life."

* * * * *

To-night a great weight had been lifted from old Nicholas. He had not been prepared for the news of his good fortune, and though his spirit sang, his sagging shoulders testified to the gravity of the load he had now thrown off. He laid a brown, parchment-coloured hand affectionately on Bobby's arm, and together they sauntered from the dining-room into the spacious library. This was the old man's sanctuary. The walls were covered, literally from walnut-beamed ceiling to Chinese rug, with cases filled with unexcelled and unexplored classic literature. The mental pabulum on which Nicholas fed, these days, consisted for the most part of mystery stories strangely alike in plot and technique. It was not that Nicholas had no mind for better reading. It was only that he was tired of thinking.

They strolled into the library, and the weary old fellow sank with a sigh into the depths of his favourite chair. A gaudy-jacketed detective story lay, face downward, on the table. Bobby took it up, read its title aloud, and grinned.

"Light, Grandpère?"

He offered a flame at the tip of the old man's cigar.

"Exciting yarn?"

Nicholas puffed energetically for a moment, like a leaky bellows, and replied, "The inspector is just questioning the cook, Bobby, and she says she knows the shot was fired at exactly eleven-ten, because that is the time she always puts out the cat."

"You should be pretty well acquainted with the kitchen habits of that cook, by this time, Grandpère. It's the same one, isn't it, in all these stories?"

"By no means, sir," protested Nicholas. "The last cook was a man!"

Bobby was restless to be by himself and eager to divert his grandfather to his novel so that he might escape. The emotional strain of the past hour had been decidedly wearing. The confidence he had extended to the old man represented many days of serious thought; and nights too when he had paced his room for hours considering his tentative decision from every possible angle of objection. Now that he had resolved upon his course, it was only fair that he should inform his grandfather. He had done so. He had made a conscious effort to avoid a dramatic moment. He hated scenes; he had been brought up on them. But old Nicholas had passed through quite too much despair and anxiety not to be raised to an exalted mood by the young fellow's calm announcement of a programme committing him to a task at once expensively sacrificial and, as to duration, interminable.

For a moment, after Bobby had flung out the words, the old man had sat stupified and incredulous. He had put down his fork. His jaw sagged and his chin chopped up and down as in a shaking palsy. The deep wrinkles about his mouth had joined the wrinkles about his eyes, in a series of half-circles, as he peered across the table. He dug his gnarled old fingers into the snowy cloth, rested his weight on his elbows and demanded, in a rasping treble, "How's that, Robert? I don't believe I caught what you just said! Say that again!"

Bobby had said it again, slowly, calmly, convincingly. Old Nicholas' seamed face twitched, and he rubbed the corners of his cavernous eyes with the back of his mottled hand.

"You are a brave boy!" he said, his voice breaking.

Then, ashamed of his weakness, he violently cleared his throat, straightened his back, and declared with dignity, "I congratulate you, sir! I cannot remember when any member of my tribe has made a decision of greater moment than yours! May God—bless you!" The benediction was spoken with a quaver...It was almost too much for both of them.

For an hour thereafter, Bobby had outlined his future plans with a breadth of scope and clarity of detail certifying to the vast amount of time and thought he had spent on them, the old man following every word with eager nods of his leonine head, and occasional hard bangings of his fist upon the table to emphasize his approval. "Yes, sir," he would shout, tumultuously, "you can do it! You will do it! You have it in you! I always thought you had!" His mood was reminiscent of the good old days when it required a deal of table-pounding to convince the directors that a radical and immediate change of policy was necessary to meet new conditions, no matter what it cost.

Now that the first tidal wave of enthusiasm had broken and surfed, Bobby wanted the subject temporarily dismissed. He had lived with his problem—eaten it, dreamed it, walked the floor with it, gone to the mat with it, cajoled it, cursed it, for a month; and, having now brought it to something like a climax, he was ready to see it tabled.

Sensing his grandson's restlessness as he stood toying with a paper-weight, Nicholas deliberately located his place in the book, meticulously polished his glasses, and smiled a very obvious adieu.

"Think I'll step out for a little stroll, if you are to be reading, Grandpère," said Bobby.

Nicholas nodded several times; puffed noisily, contentedly, buried himself in his story.

Immediately Bobby's back was turned, however, he put down the book and stared after the receding figure, his old eyes wide with a new interest to which he had not yet become accustomed. Bobby looked back, as he passed through the doorway, and grinned. Nicholas caught up his book, frowned heavily over some abstruse passage he had just come upon, and puffed mightily on his long cigar.

* * * * *

Changing his pumps for tennis shoes and his dinner coat for a light sweater, Bobby let himself out through the carriage door, upon the driveway. There was a half moon in an unclouded sky and a few fireflies. He trudged aimlessly on the drive, left it for the grass, wandered along the narrow path by the rose arbor, found himself near the huge twin pillars of the gate, strolled out upon the highway. It was not a busy thoroughfare, but a narrow, gravelled motor-road serving chiefly the widely-spaced country estates fronting on the western shore of the lake. It was very quiet to-night. Hands in pockets, head tilted forward in moody meditation, he strode along indifferent to his random journey, his eyes becoming accommodated to the gloom.

He was glad he had told his grandfather. To-morrow he would drive down to Brightwood and tell Nancy Ashford. It was like having strong anchors to windward that these two people should share his secret. He hoped Nancy Ashford would be content to say, "Very proper! Much as I expected!" and let it go at that. He wasn't much of a success in moments crammed with sentimentality. It was all right in the case of Grandpère, of course. He was an old man, and a bit mellow. But he hoped Nancy would be sensible.

Bobby had walked a mile. A hundred yards ahead of him, at a sharp bend of the road, a pair of glaring headlights tilted at a precarious angle indicated that a car had listed heavily to starboard...In the ditch, he surmised. He heard the sudden churning of the motor, as power was violently applied to impotent wheels. "Green driver," he reflected. Again the roar of the straining motor proclaimed that somebody was making a bad matter no better. "Fool!" he muttered; and quickened his steps.

Evidently the driver had sighted him, and, unsure of his intentions, was making a final effort at extrication before he reached the car; for, as he came within a few feet of it, the engine fairly bellowed with exasperation and the big coupé shuddered. There was a young woman at the wheel.

"My God, sister," shouted Bobby, when the racket had subsided, "don't do that any more!"

Sister accepted the admonition with wide eyes into which Bobby now gazed interestedly at close range. She smiled, and he reconsidered his earlier opinion of her. She was probably unaccustomed to driving in soft gravel; unacquainted with its treacheries; might be a most excellent driver almost anywhere else.

"Is it really down very deep?" she inquired, with anxiety.

There was a curious huskiness in her voice that gave it an intimate, just-between-us, confidential timbre.

Bobby walked to the rear and looked.

"Very!" he declared. "To the hub. Your differential is flat on the ground."

Her face was perplexed. "I don't know what that is," she admitted, "but I'm sure it shouldn't be."

"No," said Bobby paternally, "they do better when they're up off the road."

She sighed, and dabbed at a warm neck with a trifle of lace.

"It's my fault, I suppose," ruefully, "I was driving rather fast; and at that sharp turn a car came whopping toward me with the sort of lights they use on aviation fields. I turned out, slipped off..."

"And here you are!" finished Bobby. "Lucky you didn't upset. You might have been badly hurt."

She searched his shadowed face, slightly stirred by the note of concern for her safety...might be safer without it. What she saw caused her no anxiety.

"Well, at least we have no broken bones to worry about. All I have to do now is to get this car back on the road. Anything to suggest? I'm awfully helpless about such things. Not meaning," she added quickly, "that I'm in the habit of ditching my car."

"I'm sure you're not," said Bobby encouragingly. "This gravel is very slippery."

"What do you think I'd better do?" she asked, in a tone that quite relinquished all further responsibility into his hands.

It was as if she had leaned her slight weight against him. For the past half hour, he had been thinking himself the loneliest, most utterly detached person on earth. His important resolution had quite cut him off from his habitual round of interests, but had not yet keyed him on to any new ones. Nobody had ever been so desperately in need of friendship.

He rested an elbow on the ledge of the open window and became whimsically didactic.

"In cases like this, when the local power-plant has proved insufficient, it is customary to seek aid. One calls in the neighbours. They, having suspected all along that their services might be required, have gone early to bed, and must be pounded out with loud noises and the offer of a king's ransom. Having bathed, shaved, dressed and breakfasted, they come, growling, with a snorting tractor..."

"And when they are all ready to pull, the tow-line breaks, and they must drive the tractor to town for another."

"Something like that," agreed Bobby.

"Your advice seems clear," she said, matching his mood. "First, one goes for the neighbours." She tallied the item on her fingers. "But which one?"

"Which one of the neighbours?" Bobby countered with a chuckle. "Or which one of us?...I'll go, of course, gladly. But," he added commandingly, "you're coming along! I won't have you out here alone in a stalled car!"

It was spoken spontaneously. Doubtless it meant nothing more than an unintentionally peremptory way of saying he considered it unsafe for her to be left by herself on this unfrequented road. But the fervent phrasing of it, the implied possessorship he had put into his "I won't have you out here alone" brought her a queer sensation. Nobody had ever used precisely that tone with her before. She felt...well...as if she were being absorbed...ever so little...just the tiniest mite of her; like the first almost invisible trickle of fine sand pouring through the needle-slim neck of an hourglass; nothing to be alarmed about, surely. She could easily enough reverse the glass, whenever she wished. For the moment, it was not unpleasant to let it run; just for the novelty of it. It wouldn't be much. She would see to that. In a half hour, she and this delightful chap, with a clean-cut profile that might have graced a Grecian coin, would go their ways. If it pleased him to issue orders, she would humour him by coming to attention and clicking her heels.

Bobby opened the door and offered his hand. She took it without hesitation and stepped out upon the road.

"Should I have locked the gears?" she asked,

"No," drawled Bobby, "it'll be here when we come back." They both laughed.

Leaving the highway, they entered a thickly-hedged narrow lane, cut through a dense tract of tall firs.

"I hope you know where we're going," she said, as Bobby strode forward.

"Can't say that I do," he confessed. "I never was in here before; but I think it must be the private road to the Foster estate. Doubtless we will find one of the farmers' cottages presently."

The girl trudged along beside him, taking two steps to his one on high heels not meant for hiking in country lanes. A sheep scuttled out of the left hedge and dashed frantically across the road, a few feet ahead of them. Instinctively she caught at Bobby's sleeve.

"Oh—but that startled me!"

"Here! Take my hand!"

It was a small hand that she gave him, and he held it as if he were leading a little child. Absurd as he was bound to admit it, his attitude toward her was proprietary; and, incautious as she knew it to be, her response to it was spontaneous. She had a sensation that just the smallest imaginable emanation of herself was being quietly assimilated by the strong fingers of this dominating boy.

Mentally, Bobby tightened his grip; physically, he led her as one would a younger sister.

"We might encounter all sorts of adventures," she suggested. "Suppose we ran into a nest of—of counterfeiters!"

"There aren't any counterfeiters, any more," scoffed Bobby. "They're all bootlegging...More profits and less risk."

"Oh—how I hate it!" she cried, passionately. "What a vulgar, beastly thing it's come to be! It never concerned me, one way or the other, until lately. But now...it's destroying my best friend!"

Bobby was annoyed at his sudden stab of jealousy. But what right had he to be jealous?

"I have good reason to hate it too," he rejoined bitterly; adding, with a growl, "but I believe I've got it licked!"

"Oh, I hope so!" she exclaimed, with a quick intake of breath. "It would be such a pity..."

Her sentence hung suspended, and for some time neither spoke.

"That's the first time anybody ever said to me that it would be—a pity."

So—the time had come now to reverse the glass. She would do it at once...presently...but not abruptly...How did one up-end an hour-glass gradually, imperceptibly, she wondered. Perhaps the proper technique would occur to her...Meantime...the silence was lengthening; and silence, at this juncture, was disturbing.

"You knew it—without being told, didn't you?"

"I'm not sure that I did. It wouldn't have mattered much to anybody."

"How silly!...No one concerned whether you fling yourself away?"

"That did sound melodramatic, didn't it?...as if I wanted to play Orphan Annie."

"You've been rather—down, haven't you?" Careful!...careful!...The glass couldn't be up-ended by any such process as this!

"Horribly!...But—I'm not now!"

"That's good!...Fresh grip?"

Neither of them knew just why there was a momentary tightening of their hand-clasp. Naturally, the word suggested it. The sudden pressure of his fingers about her hand was but an affirmative; perhaps an acknowledgment of her encouragement. And her quick response was a mere friendly note of confidence to a fellow human, who had been down and was now on the way up. But each was aware—and intuitively conscious that the other was aware—of a compact; a curiously indefinable sense of belonging...She released her hand, a moment later, and instantly realized it was the wrong thing to have done...The withdrawal only seemed to be a retreat after an avowal...More than that, it hadn't come about nearly so casually as it should. Her fingers had slipped slowly out of his hand, detained ever so slightly by his lingering pressure...So, she had turned the glass, had she?...

"Oh, I see a light!" she cried. "In a window!"

With droll predictions of the manner of welcome they might receive, they quickened their steps, and presently knocked at the door. A farmer opened it and stood framed in the glow of an acetylene lamp suspended from the ceiling. Two small children hugged a leg apiece, registering curiosity.

After a brief parley, the man retreated for his cap, joined the pair outside, told them he would be along soon, and went for his tractor.

Bobby made no attempt to resume the conversation interrupted by the sighting of the cottage. He took his new friend's small hand, however, as they turned to retrace their steps, and tucked it under his arm. She gave it without shyness.

"You'll be going back to college, I expect," he hazarded.

"No, not this year...And you?"

"Oh, I'm through," said Bobby, maturely. "Beginning my professional course in a few days."

"Law—maybe?"

"Is that what you would pick for me?"

She laughed.

"I think I should know a bit more about you before I selected your profession."

"Well...if you were a man..."

"I should go in for surgery."

"Any special kind?"

"Yes," she replied, with quick decision, "I would be a brain surgeon."

"That's odd!"

"Why?"

Her question went unanswered. The noisy tractor was overtaking them. They were near the highway, and conversation gave way to the business at hand.

After much manœuvring into position, the farmer was ready. Bobby took the wheel of the coupé, its owner waiting at a discreet distance until the car should be tugged back upon the road. It was simply done, but the emergency driver of the coupé stammered something about the possibility that the steering apparatus might be in need of inspection. Sometimes a strain like this affected the steering gear, he said. He was not pressed for specific explanations. Perhaps, he suggested, it would be best to run down to the village and make sure everything was safe. He would gladly go with her if she wished...It was quite agreeable to her, if he would be so good, and would he mind driving?...Under the circumstances, perhaps that would be better.

She asked the farmer for his charges and paid him more than he asked. He thanked her, awkwardly, feigning reluctance to accept so much. As she entered the car where Bobby sat at the wheel in proprietorial pose, his heart beating rapidly, the farmer, eager to be friendly, said, "That sure is one peach of a car! It looks just like the Packard that Doctor Hudson used to drive around up here."

"It is," said the girl quietly. "Good night; and thank you again."

Mechanically, Bobby Merrick put the late Doctor Hudson's big coupé in gear, and they were off toward the village.

"It seems all right, doesn't it?" happily remarked the young woman in black who owned the big coupé that Doctor Hudson used to drive around up here.

Apparently, her new friend was not yet quite sure enough to reply. His eyes were intent upon the road ahead, and he grasped the wheel so tightly his knuckles were white.

Bobby was stirringly conscious of her on the seat beside him, more conscious of her than he had ever been of any woman he had known. There was no actual, physical contact; but she was most overpoweringly *there*.

"It's all right," he muttered thickly.

"I was on my way to the village, anyhow," she continued. "I do hope the little drug store will still be open."

Apparently her driver was not posted on the nocturnal habits of the druggist, for he did not venture an opinion.

The accelerator received an extra pressure at that moment, and the powerful car suddenly bounded forward.

"I can't tell you how grateful I am," said the girl, a bit perplexed by his silence. "I'm sure I shouldn't have known what to do, if you hadn't happened along."

Bobby was occupied with the adjustment of the ignition lever.

"But I'm afraid I'm putting you to a great deal of inconvenience," she added anxiously.

He spoke at length, as from a considerable distance.

"The car is in perfect condition," he said. "I'll get out here. You need not go to the garage." The brakes were applied with determination, and the car came to an abrupt stop. Bobby opened the door on the left and stepped out.

"Oh, but you're miles from where you found me!" she exclaimed. "Do let me put you down where you'd rather be. Please!"

He could not meet her eyes. "I was just sauntering," he said absently. "It's no matter."

She slipped over behind the wheel and held out her hand. It trembled a little as he wrapped his fingers around it. She was bewildered. Whatever had she said to hurt him?

"Good night, then; and thank you so much!" Her voice was unsteady.

He retained her hand for an instant, said "Good night" in a tone that might mean weariness, dejection, or disappointment, turned, and stepped away into the darkness. She engaged the gears. The car moved slowly, tentatively, hesitatingly forward. Bobby watched the little red tail-light until it vanished at the next turn.

A half hour later, he sat down at his piano in the tomby drawing-room at Windymere, and, vastly occupied with his reflections, toyed with an experimental ending to Schubert's "Unfinished Symphony."

CHAPTER V

IT was late afternoon of the last Sunday in September. Nancy Ashford's snug retreat, immediately adjacent to the general administrative offices in Brightwood Hospital, had proved too small to house the radiant spirits of herself and her guest. She had gratefully accepted Bobby's suggestion that they take a drive. Sitting close to him in the big, gaudy, rakish roadster, her elbow touching his, it pleased Nancy to indulge the fancy that passers-by might think him her son. Her life had been filled and emptied twice. It was brimming again.

Nothing could have been more clear to the white-haired hospital superintendent, as she greeted her expected visitor, at the door of her little office, that afternoon, than that he was hopeful of stating his errand in a manner to insure against its reception with surprise or emotion. He had a very business-like air, and she determined to match it.

He had blurted out his story immediately upon arrival. Tossing his hat upon her desk, and seating himself by her on the little divan, he had said brusquely, "Well, I'm resolved to do it. It will be no surprise to you; for it was really your idea in the first place, even if you didn't specify the details. It's all arranged now. I am entering the Medical School at the University, a week from Thursday...Are you glad?"

Nancy had reached out a hand for his, winked back the sudden tears and bit her lip in an effort at control. Her eyes shone. But she did not speak.

"Of course," continued Bobby hurriedly, as if reciting lines, "I have no illusions in this matter. It means a long, hard grind of drudgery, and I am not naturally industrious. It will be five years, at least, before I can even guess whether I am likely to succeed, or have only been making myself ridiculous. I take chances of becoming an obscure second-rater. In that case, I shall have become merely absurd at the cost of a very great deal of time and trouble. People would grin. They would say—I can hear them—'Yeah; he's the fellow that thought he'd be another Doctor Hudson.' But maybe the threat of that will put a little more fight into me. It's foolish, I suppose, to hope that I might sometime be even a halfway substitute for him; but—I can move in that direction, anyway."

"I felt confident you would come to some such decision as this, Bobby," commented Nancy quietly, "and I feel even more sure—now you have decided—that you will succeed."

"Your hope will help—a lot!"

"Now you will be wanting to learn all you can find out about Doctor Hudson, won't you?"

* * * * *

At this juncture, the tiny office had seemed stifling. They would ride Bobby would drive and listen; Nancy would do the talking. For fully twenty miles they had been weaving swiftly in and out of the Sunday traffic on crowded boulevards; and, now, with speed reduced, were traversing a more quiet suburban street. Nancy had been recalling some of the more singular facts in the life of her hero, especially relating to his wide diversity of philanthropic interests and his odd whim of keeping them a secret.

"Did his family know?"

"I doubt it. Joyce was a mere baby when he began doing these queer things for people, and it is unlikely that he ever told her. And Mrs. Hudson, during a call she made at the hospital only last Thursday, asked some questions indicating he had not confided that feature of his life to her. Many of his wards and beneficiaries have been coming to see her with expressions of sympathy, and some with proffers of assistance if she needed it. She was naturally curious."

"Yes; I know just a little about that. Learned it only to-day. Tom Masterson dropped in, as I was preparing to leave Windymere, at noon. He had driven Joyce up to the Hudson cottage, where Mrs. Hudson is spending a few days. He came over to inquire if I would join them there for the afternoon. I told him of my engagement in town."

"Perhaps you should have gone. You could have telephoned to me. Have you seen Joyce at all?"

"Not since I'm back from France."

"And I presume you never met Mrs. Hudson."

Bobby wished that question had not been raised. Perhaps it would be near enough the truth to reply in the negative. On second thought, absolute sincerity with Nancy Ashford was but her rightful due. He decided to be honest.

"Yes," he answered reluctantly, "I spent a whole hour with her last night, on a country road"—adding after a considerable pause, "But she doesn't know it."

"Meaning what?" demanded Nancy, in amazement.

Briefly he narrated the whole circumstance of their meeting. Nancy Ashford's blue eyes widened. Underneath the boyish recital ran a strong current of unmistakable personal interest which Bobby's attempted tone of casualness failed to conceal.

"I think you liked her, Bobby. Didn't you?"

He essayed a smile of indifference. He might even have been able to delude himself into the belief that Nancy accepted the smile as a sufficient answer to her query, had he not been so audacious with his little deceit as to look her full in the face. What he saw there of incredulity and disappointment instantly sobered him. There was no use trying to keep anything from this woman.

"My dear," he confessed, with an unsteady voice, "I like her so much I'd rather we didn't talk about it."

His big car had idled to a full stop alongside the kerb flanking a little park. They were both silent for a while. At length, Nancy said mechanically, "Well, of all things!"

"Yes," agreed Bobby abstractedly, "something like that." There was another protracted pause.

"And she did not know who you were?"

"I couldn't tell her."

"How long do you think you can maintain your—incognito?"

"Oh, that should be simple enough," Bobby declared, in a tone of self-deprecation. "I took pains to invent an alibi for the evening, when I talked to Masterson, in case some inquiries might be made. But Mrs. Hudson has probably forgotten all about the little episode by this time."

Nancy laughed.

"Bobby Merrick, do you really believe that a young woman of Helen Hudson's temperament could produce the impression she made on you without being fully aware of it? You confessed how acutely conscious you were of her—that was your phrase, wasn't it?—as you sat together in her car. Do you think you would have had that sensation had she not shared it?"

"Of course; why not? See here—you're taking altogether too much for granted in this case. Mrs. Hudson was no more than courteous, friendly, appreciative of a little favour. She had no reason to think me interested in her. In fact, I was almost rude to her when we parted." He did not feel it necessary to add that her car had crept along, in low gear, for fully two hundred yards, apparently reluctant to leave.

"Yes," said Nancy significantly, "she would notice that!"

"And she would know—by my abruptness—wouldn't she?..."

"Know what?" persisted Nancy ruthlessly.

"Why—that I was not interested."

"Dear boy, how very little you know about her!"

"Meaning that she has unusual gifts for interpreting other people's private thoughts?"

"No—Foolish! Meaning only that she is a woman!"

They strolled under the elms, stopping to watch some small boys sailing toy boats on the little lagoon, dappled with lily-pads. A bench was found unoccupied. By common consent, their discussion was resumed of Doctor Hudson's queer penchant for concerning himself with the private perplexities of nobody knew how many people, and the thick wall of secrecy with which these strange negotiations were surrounded.

* * * * *

"You may as well put it down as a fact," Nancy was saying, with strong conviction, "that the curious manner of Wayne Hudson's costly investments in these cases, from, which he never expected or accepted any reimbursement, was occasioned by no mere whim. He was not given to whims. He was not an eccentric. I never knew him to do anything without an adequate motive. Nobody could have said that he was reckless with his money or incompetent in business. He could drive a shrewd bargain. He knew when to buy and when to sell. Plenty of business men, with more commercial experience, asked his advice on probable trends in the real estate market and took his judgment about industrial stocks. I am convinced he did these strange things for certain people, in this furtive way, with a definite motive. In some fashion, which I don't pretend to understand, his professional success was involved in it. When you find out what that motive was, you'll know why Wayne Hudson was a great surgeon!"

"Do you know any more about it than you have told me?" regarding her searchingly.

"There is a little book—a sort of journal—I think you have a right to know about it. He kept it in the office safe, along with valuable records; some relating to professional matters, some to private business affairs. The book was there when I took over the management of Brightwood. Once—we were looking for some insurance papers—I asked Doctor Hudson whether the little book concerned hospital business..."

"Couldn't you tell?" interrupted Bobby.

"It was not written in English, nor in any other language I ever saw."

"What did it look like—Spanish, German, Greek?"

She shook her head, and resumed her story.

"I asked him what the little book was. I vividly remember how earnestly thoughtful he grew, and how he stood, for many minutes, rubbing his temple with the tips of his fingers—a trick of his when trying to arrive at an important decision—saying, after a long wait, 'It's just a personal record.' And then he added, smiling, 'You are at liberty to read it, if you can.'"

"Did you ever try?"

Rae Losdrom Jin u stren
Leyny red w Adom N Y u
preek u N C Medor Gevrns
w Hvnah E Ets bltt u Aig eird
Haii yo w Ratibo yua eloh u
edhso Hohva str w R G Iossi
Mr Aos u iht PS est yron w
Front I icpew lb. u Odig hanihr
ile w M D Panarp oed u Ailiay
wres w

"*Did* I?" she echoed. "Hours and hours—lately."

"Get anything out of it?"

"Headache!"

"I wish I could see it!"

"I'll show it to you! Nobody has a better right to it. I told Mrs. Hudson there were many valuable documents of the doctor's in the hospital safe, and she insisted that we keep them until she was up to looking them over with me; so the book is still there."

"Let's go back," he said impetuously.

Darkness had fallen before they arrived at Brightwood. Nancy brought the book from the safe, and laid it on the desk before him. He sat down, and took it in his hands—a plain, black, leather-bound journal, eight inches by five, and more than an inch thick. On the flyleaf was written, in Doctor Hudson's quite distinctive hand, the single sentence.

TO WHOM THIS MAY CONCERN

"Nobody could be any more concerned than I am!" He glanced up at Nancy for approval. She nodded.

"Now turn over to the next page, and see what you make of that!"

Bobby stared long and hard.

"It's in code!"

Facsimile of first page of the Hudson journal.

"You will find it difficult," said Nancy. "The way I have it figured is this: Doctor Hudson purposed not to have the matters which he kept secret divulged during his lifetime. The fact that so many of these odd wards of his are bobbing up now, ready to tell their stories of his strange dealings with them, convinces me that they were all virtually sworn to secrecy while he lived. Now that he is gone, they tell. I think the mystery is all contained in this book. Whoever reads it, knows the real story. Perhaps the doctor was willing it should be known after he was done with it, but made it inaccessible to anyone who might chance upon it while he lived."

"He's made it inaccessible enough—I'll say!" Bobby growled. "Did you ever see the like?"

"This first page," explained Nancy, "is unquestionably a sort of preface. You notice that all the other pages are completely filled. This one has only ten lines. It must be a foreword; an explanation; dedication, perhaps...You take it along with you...Know any Greek?"

Bobby shook his head.

"Oh, I know the alphabet," he qualified, smiling.

"That's enough...What's the last letter?"

"Omega," recited Bobby glibly.

"And Omega is a sort of stop-signal, isn't it? A sign for the end of something?"

He nodded.

"How many letters are there in the Greek alphabet?"

Bobby closed his eyes and counted on his fingers.

"Twenty-four."

"Omega being the twenty-fourth—and signifying the end!"

"Right!"

"Now, what is the twelfth letter?"

"Mu," answered Bobby, after another calculation.

"Well, if Omega means 'finished,' what do you suppose Mu means?"

"'Half finished'—I suppose."

Bobby soberly returned to the preface of the little book and found, at almost regular intervals, the letters μ (mu) and ω (omega).

"Is that a clue?"

"I think so," said Nancy, "but it did me no good. I just offer it to you for what it seems to be worth."

* * * * *

Not at any given moment of his long drive home did Bobby Merrick realize exactly where he was, as he swiftly covered the familiar road to Windymere. At midnight, he put up his car; went to his room; sat down before his desk, with Doctor Hudson's private journal, a pencil, and a thick pad of paper; and at dawn was still experimenting without a glimmer of encouragement.

Meggs, opening the door to call him to breakfast, found him sitting fully dressed, with his head on his arms, asleep, and tiptoed downstairs, his eyes shining.

A few minutes later he whispered to the cook, in a tone of victory, "You lost your bet!"

"Drunk again?"

"Quite!"

CHAPTER VI

THE glowing ellipse cast by the heavily shaded lamp at the head of her bed shone upon the weapons with which young Mrs. Hudson had armed herself against drowsiness when, at midnight, she had retired with a novel, two magazines, and a leather writing case embarrassingly stuffed with unanswered letters, resolved to stay awake until Joyce returned.

Shortly before two, she had lost the battle and now slept with the light shining into her troubled face. Not that the trifling incident of dropping off could have worried her; but it was all of a piece with the general failure.

Had the late Doctor Hudson been subpœnaed to the witness-box on the day of his death to report on the success of the marriage he had contracted on behalf of his daughter, he, being unusually fastidious about truth-telling, might have found it an awkward question.

The three of them had stood up, that crisp January morning at St. Andrew's, in the presence of Uncle Percival and Monty—and the Senator Byrnes, who had run over from Washington—not so much as a bride and groom, attended by a grown daughter, cordially consenting; rather as a pair of strikingly lovely young women, attended by an elderly, distinguished guardian, invoking Church and State to legalize and bless their comradeship and give them a deed to it.

That it was candidly a *mariage de convenance* (the French for it was more euphonious than the English equivalent) caused Doctor Hudson no serious misgivings. He nursed no illusions on that subject, aware that if all the world's weddings were limited to romantic attachments in which no material advantages were at issue on either side, the human race would long since have been exterminated; and that if it were unethical for a young woman to marry with the knowledge that she could not immediately give herself with unqualified devotion to her husband, the Holy Virgin herself was at fault.

Immediately upon the consummation of his wedding, however, Doctor Hudson had found himself falling sincerely in love with his girl-bride, and the comradeship he had sought to insure between Helen and Joyce was put in jeopardy.

Joyce was a poor sailor, and the first three days were rough.

"No, darling; not a thing...Please run along. I'd much rather you did."

So when, on Sunday noon, she had been persuaded to come down to the blanketed chair they had prepared for her on B-Deck, she realized that she was being solicitously attended, on either side, not by an indulgent father and a devoted college chum, but by a man and his wife—good friends of hers, unquestionably, but, well—there you were!

All three of them tried to twist the contemplated relationship back into focus, but it wouldn't go. Perhaps their very efforts to do so made it impossible. Hudson, in Paris, had enthusiastically encouraged Joyce in her shopping extravagances; and Helen, eager to join in her husband's approval, may have overdone it.

"What an exquisite coat! So glad you found it, Joyce! How very becoming!"

It was the right attitude without a doubt, but it hadn't the right inflection. It wasn't as one girl to another, but as an ingratiating stepmother over anxious to be generous, affectionate.

There were no disagreements. Perhaps it might have cleared the air if there had been. Nor was there any constraint on the surface. It was too deep to come to the surface. That was the difficulty. Everything they said to each other was amplified—as through a loud speaker—intensifying their mutual assurances of devotion until it took on a tone of unreality. Each knew the other was trying hard to be natural. Each knew the other was playing a difficult part. Almost desperately, they scrambled for the old position; but they had lost the way to it.

Shortly after the death of Doctor Hudson, the distance between them increased markedly. For the first few days, they had clung to each other with a re-dedicated bond that promised to be, if not a restoration of their earlier comradeship, at least an earnest of future indispensability...possibly to become a more valuable relation than any they had heretofore sustained. But it was not for long.

Joyce's grief, inconsolable for a week, quickly exhausted itself. It was only common honesty in her when she declared one day that she wasn't going to sit moping any longer, for, volatile as she was, any protracted mourning would have been mere affectation, even if she were capable of it, which was doubtful.

Presently there came a disquieting furtiveness in her explanation of late hours. Helen's gently tactful queries, implying an uneasiness about her social programme, were either dismissed lightly with a chaffing reply, or met with a brief—albeit friendly—hint that one was quite old enough now to know where one wanted to go, and with whom, and until when. She was not to trouble her pretty head about her flighty Joyce. She was to live her own life and stop worrying about trifles.

"Don't sit up, darling!" Joyce would protest, at nine.

"I'm going out with Ned." (Or Tom, or Pat, or Phil.) "We may be late, you know. Where? Oh—I'm not sure...to dance, some place, I suppose...and a bite of supper, later...Crystal Palace, maybe...Gordon's, perhaps."

"I don't like your going out to Gordon's, Joyce. Really—that's not a nice place. Tell me you won't...please!"

"Oh, very well! Only one can't do all the deciding. One's escort has something to say about that too."

* * * * *

On the rose counterpane lay several letters; one of them from Montgomery Brent, brief, brotherly, suggesting that his counsel would be at his "little sister's" disposal should she be troubled about business matters, now that her responsibilities were increased.

"Only too glad, you know, to straighten out the kinks for you when it comes to income tax, investments, and the safeguarding of your estate. That sort of thing is my daily work."

"The dear boy!" she murmured half aloud, as she re-read it, "How decent of him; and not a bit bad idea, either. I wonder does he really know anything about business. He ought to by this time."

Montgomery, whom it pleased her to think of as her brother Monty (never more affectionately than now that she felt so desolated), was five years her senior. College not agreeing with him after his sophomore year, Monty had brought his saxophone to the jazz-market. Not quite satisfied to make a permanent profession of bouncing and writhing and puffing himself purple every night from eight until two in the front row of a dance orchestra, he had made some friends among the chalky-fingered youngsters who posted the board at a down town brokerage office. In a few months he had a desk and a small salaried position in the organization.

"I'm a broker!" he would reply maturely, when some young thing coyly inquired, while they danced, what college he attended.

Doubtless he was doing well enough now. He had not borrowed from Helen for more than a year; had given her an expensive silver vase for a wedding present, appearing on that occasion in a morning coat, striped trousers, and spats, the only man present who had given no quarter to the request for informal dress...It wasn't a half-bad idea. There was one friend left, anyhow—good old Monty!

Another letter was a brief note, written to Joyce, by the young Merrick person, dated from Ann Arbor; evidently composed with much care. It left many things unsaid which its author assumed would be read into it. He had entered the Medical School, hopeful of becoming of some use, eventually, to the profession which her father had so conspicuously adorned.

"I never would have picked him for the part," Joyce had interpolated, as she read that much of the letter to Helen. "Rather quixotic, don't you think?"

"Did it on impulse, likely," Helen had remarked.

"Rather fine of him, though—at that! Wouldn't you say?" championed Joyce.

"I'll tell you a year from now," Helen had replied, half-audibly.

Joyce had continued reading to herself. With a gesture of impatience, upon finishing the letter, she tossed it across the table, and savagely dug into her grapefruit.

"I think you had better answer it, Helen. The only human, personal line in it is for you. Write and tell him you hope he gets on well with his teachers, and makes A in everything," she snapped, with frank asperity.

The only human, personal line read, "Please convey my sympathy and regards to Mrs. Hudson, whom I hope I may soon have a chance to know."

Helen had made no further comment. Her opinion of the Merrick person was based solely upon Joyce's disquieting references to him—a spoiled youngster with loose habits and too much money. It was clear enough that the girl entertained an infatuation for him which he had made no effort to capitalize. Helen was glad of it. She had no wish to meet him—had dreaded the day when he might turn up. It was enough that he had been the cause of her husband's tragedy...Not his fault, of course; but she hoped he would not make it necessary for her to try to be nice to him. It was a closed incident. She was relieved.

The letter had remained in her pile of morning mail, beside her plate. Later, it had been tucked into her portfolio. She had read it again, in bed. Well, it was no concern of hers, whether he made good or not. At least, he was out of Joyce's calculations...One questionable friend less to worry about.

* * * * *

Helen was awakened with a start, as the door of her room was cautiously opened far enough to admit the flushed face of Joyce.

"You Joyce?"

The door was closing, slowly, cautiously.

"Sorry, darling...Good night!" came in muffled tones from beyond the door.

"Come in, dear!" called Helen.

There was a considerable delay before the door opened again. Joyce came in, jerkily, all but asleep on her feet, dazedly rubbing her forehead with the back of the hand in which she clutched her crumpled hat; the other groping, uncertainly, for something to support her. She leaned heavily against the foot of the bed, swaying dizzily.

"Oh!—but, my dear!" cried Helen, in consternation, propping herself up suddenly on her elbows. "What in the world—! Where have you been?"

"Gordon's!"

Joyce ground out the guttural between tensely locked jaws, and smiled fatuously.

Helen sat up and peered incredulously, silently, at her dishevelled step-daughter, who grew restive under the inspection.

"Been—been writin' letters?" Joyce surveyed the litter on the bed with a pitiable attempt at casualness.

Helen nodded briefly, and pressed both hands tightly against her forehead in a gesture of despair, which Joyce decided to ignore.

"And if there isn't ickle Bobby?" She leaned far forward over the foot of the bed and with elaborate precision flicked the letter contemptuously with her finger. "That!—for you!—Doctor Merrick!"

"Why—Joyce Hudson!—you're drunk!"

Helen stepped out into her slippers, caught up a kimono, and put her arm about the girl's sagging shoulders.

"Who? Me?" giggled Joyce amiably. "Me—drunk? You should shee Tommy!"

"Let me help you to bed," pleaded Helen brokenly. "No—here! You may sleep in my room."

Joyce fumbled helplessly at her buttons with one hand, the other clumsily mopping her dripping brow with her little hat. Presently she crumpled on the bed, and Helen tugged off her dress and laid a cold towel across her eyes.

"Thanks, darling!" mumbled Joyce, between heavy sighs. "Much bother...too bad...all my fault...Don't blame Tommy. Tommy nice boy! Goin'—goin' to marry Tommy...Well—can't you congrat—can't you felic—I'm afraid I can't say it very distinc'ly—but aren't you glad—about Tommy and me?"

"Let's wait and talk it over in the morning, dear," soothed Helen, turning the towel and patting it about the flushed temples.

"No—sir!" babbled Joyce, with an expansive gesture, "We're goin' talk about it—" she brought a slim, lovely hand down with a clumsy slap on the pillow—"ri now!" The towel was brushed aside, and she gazed up militantly with swollen eyes. "Tha's just like you! You cry! I come home—all happy—to announce my engagesh to Tommy—and you cry! What's the big idea? Do you want him?"

Bridling her impatience, Helen urged the drunken girl to leave off and go to sleep. Maudlin tears of self-pity bathed Joyce's face.

"Nobody loves me!" she wailed. "Nobody but good old Tommy!...But I won't marry him!...I won't!"

Presently she relaxed, licked her stiff lips, sighed deeply, and slept. Helen knelt by the bed, her face buried in the covers to escape the heavy fumes, and wept piteously. Wayne

Hudson had left her with a responsibility quite too serious to be met. Only one thing had he expected of her. She had failed him.

* * * * *

At length, rousing stiffly from the cramped position in which she had fallen asleep through sheer fatigue, and nervous exhaustion, she mechanically collected the scattered letters from the floor, turned out the light, and went dejectedly to Joyce's bedroom. She put down the letters on the little vanity table and bathed her face with cologne.

Bobby Merrick's rather stilted note lay open before her as if inviting attention. Between the lines it announced that he considered himself under a moral obligation to Doctor Hudson...She had been disposed to waive that implication aside as a mere pose...a bit of ephemeral martyrdom to be toyed with until he tired of it...a pretence of gallantry. She averted her eyes from the letter, perplexed, accused by it. Was she too under a certain moral obligation to Doctor Hudson? Young Merrick was trying to discharge his! How about hers?

She carefully folded the letter, and stood for a long time preoccupiedly deepening its creases with nervous fingers. It occurred to her that she would like to have a long, confidential talk with Bobby Merrick. Perhaps he might have something to suggest...She stared at her haggard reflection in the mirror and shook her head. No—the way out did not lie in that direction. She tucked the letter into her writing-case, and tumbled wearily into bed.

CHAPTER VII

AT one o'clock on the morning of Thanksgiving Day, young Merrick solved the riddle to which he had devoted much of his spare time for nearly two months.

After only a week's sporadic work on it, he had written to Nancy Ashford:
"When the light breaks on this it will not come like a valley dawn. The book is going to be pitch dark up to a certain moment, and after that it will be clear and bright as a June morning. There's no half-way business about a job like this. Either you can read it all, with ease and understanding; or you can't read a syllable!"

The Thanksgiving recess having begun at noon on Wednesday, Bobby determined to spend the brief vacation on the cryptic journal. It would be a good time. Distractions and interruptions would be reduced to a minimum, for no sooner had the noon whistles blown than the student quarter was as deserted as if warned of an impending epidemic of the Black Plague. He had made a tentative promise to have evening dinner on Thanksgiving Day with old Nicholas "provided I finish a problem it is important to complete at once."

All Wednesday afternoon, he turned from one futile experiment to another, most of them being variants of schemes already tried. It annoyed him that he seemed unable to bring his attention to a sharp focus. Now he would sit at his desk for an hour, sharpening pencils and gazing glassily at the mocking script. Now he would fling himself across his bed and, supporting himself on an aching elbow, set down columns of letters in every manner of eccentric sequence. Oblivious of the passing time, his own discomfort, his need of exercise, he continued to lay out diagrams and tear up paper. Night came down and he turned on the lights. Midnight found him very weary, his brain operating mechanically, sluggishly. He tapped his teeth with his pencil, and went wool-gathering in spite of himself. He even made a brief mental excursion on foot along the highway to the north of Windymere and assisted a motorist in distress. Recovering himself, impatiently, he pursued his endless diagrams.

Then a fresh idea occurred to him. Here was something he had not yet tried. He wrote the first few words of the unintelligible script in a running line, utterly disregarding the spaces between them. (It had long been his practice to reproduce the letters in capitals, thinking this might help to simplify the words.)

Now he broke in two what was obviously the first sentence, at the point where the Greek letter "μ" indicated a half-stop, and set down the remainder of that obvious division immediately below it:

R A E I O S D R O M F I N
E D R C N I E Y U Y R E D

Moved by sheer caprice, he wrote the lines again, the second division lacking one space of meeting the left margin:

R A E I O S D R O M F I N
 E D R C N I E Y U Y R E D

For full five minutes he stared at this combination until the lines blurred and blended. Of a sudden, his heart speeded up. His pencil shook as he rapidly re-wrote the letters, mortising the lines:

READERICONSIDERYOUMYFRIEND

"*I have it*!"

He shouted, aloud; laughed, ecstatically, half hysterically. How ridiculously simple it was—now that he had cracked it open. Within five minutes of feverish copying and mortising, he had decoded the brief message of the first page:

READER I CONSIDER YOU MY FRIEND AND COMMEND YOUR PERSEVERANCE HAVING ACHIEVED THE ABILITY TO READ THIS BOOK YOU HAVE ALSO THE RIGHT TO POSSESS IT MY REASONS FOR DOING THIS IN CIPHER WILL BE MADE PLAIN AS YOU PROCEED.

* * * * *

With the long strain relaxed, Bobby awoke to the fact that he was wolfishly hungry. He dressed for the street, a broad grin of self-satisfaction on his face. It was good to have conquered something! As he stood before the glass, knotting his scarf, he glanced at the little black book on the table as a gladiator might have regarded a recumbent antagonist.

Stepping out into a stinging sleet-storm, invigorated by its tonic thrust, he squared his shoulders, lengthened his stride, took deep inhalations, laughed joyously, sang the Marseillaise, and marched to it, swinging his long arms with a triumphant swagger.

There was a little chop-house only a block south of the Michigan Central station where one Tony held forth all night. Tony was typical of the occasional small shopkeeper, erudite barber, philosophical cobbler, or picturesque restaurateur to be found in every college town, by whose eccentricities, combined with a sincere interest in varsity athletics and the institution at large, they contrive to achieve local fame.

Many a full professor at the State University would have been happy and lucky had he been able to call as many undergraduates by their names as Tony. The turnover in population in a college town being bewilderingly rapid, Tony's eleven years' residence in Ann Arbor had made him a fixture, an institution. It was as if he had been there since the sixth day of creation.

He was reputed to be quite well to do, in spite of the fact that he extended credit and made unsecured loans to students with a naïve faith that would have closed a bank in forty-eight hours.

On the cigar-case lay open a cheap day-book. Attached to it, by a cotton string, was a pencil. If a student came into Tony's place without funds, he ordered what he liked and upon leaving wrote his name and the amount of his indebtedness in the book. It was not necessary to establish one's credit. One wrote in the book. When one got around to it, one paid off the score, leafed back through the book, located and personally deleted the item. Tony unemotionally accepted the payment. His failure to smile his thanks over the liquidation of the debt was in itself a pretty compliment. Having known it would be paid, there was no occasion for breaking out into rapture.

Tony himself came on duty at six in the evening and stayed the night. Nobody ever saw him at his place of business in the daytime, capable assistants being in charge through the breakfast and luncheon hours.

"Tony, how come you work only at night?" he was frequently asked by his clients, as he plunked platters of ham and eggs on a bare wooden table.

"You rather I not be here at night—eh?" Tony would inquire, grinning, quite aware that in the noisy protest which this rejoinder would evoke, their original inquiry would be forgotten.

Periodically young reporters on *The Michigan Daily,* hopeful of developing what they suspected was an unusual flair for feature writing, would engage Tony in conversation about his business; how much did he lose annually through bad loans and loose credit; why did he work only at night when business was unimportant; and sundry queries phrased in the best conventional manner of journalistic impertinence. But no story had ever appeared on this subject, Tony invariably taking refuge, when hard pressed, behind his inadequate knowledge of English.

"I couldn't get anything out of him. He's too damned dumb."

"Yeah?" the sophisticated Sunday editor would reply. "My boy, you have made the customary blunder of mistaking Tony's depth for thickness!"

* * * * *

Bobby Merrick knew from experience that Tony would be on hand to-night, to attend to his pressing wants. He would be served with amazing rapidity a steak well able to hold its own alongside many a more snobbish cut of select beef with a Parisian name, all buttoned up the back with mushrooms and presented with stiff salaams on a silver-mounted plank at a cost ten times the tariff Tony levied. There would be freshly-made coffee and a salad worthy of an exacting palate.

Tony knew exactly when to stop rubbing the bowl with garlic.

Bursting into the little café, Bobby found himself the sole patron. Tony, drowsy but amiable, made haste to draw out a chair for him. With the grace of a courtier, he took his guest's heavy fur coat and deftly shook the snow from its shoulders.

His client enumerated his desires with the eloquent conviction of one who knows exactly what he wants, and Tony made off with his instructions.

"Needn't bother about the potatoes, Tony," called Bobby, as his host began to rattle his pans.

"Out dam' late, doc!" shouted Tony, above the hiss of the hot grill. He had an unerring instinct for identifying medics; probably because they were older than the rah-rahs, and had a pungent smell. Medics were always highly aromatic of their future trade.

"Baby case, mebbe?"

He liked to make the young medics think they looked old and wise enough to be internes, at least, or out on call, understrapping for their snug-in-bed betters. Eventually the more industrious and persistent would be "doctored" officially, some fine June morning at Hill Auditorium, in the sonorous tones of the President; but every one of them had long since received his degree from Tony. They chaffed one another about it; but never chided him, or suggested that he discontinue the practice.

"No, Tony," drawled Bobby, "nothing like that. Not for a long time yet. And no babies—ever!"

Tony plopped the thick stone dishes down with a comforting clatter on the bare table, adorned only by deep-carved initials—some of them to be pointed to with pride; many of

42

them reminiscent of excellent stories without which the university traditions would have been seriously impoverished.

The steak was a masterpiece. The potatoes had arrived, magnanimously unmindful of the guest's feeling of indifference toward them. There was a head of chilled lettuce, half the size of a small cabbage, dripping with a creamy Roquefort dressing not to be had in that exact degree of all-rightness in more than six other places in the North Temperate zone.

"Coffee, doc?"

"You bet, Tony! Strong as brandy and hot as hell! I'm in great need of nourishment!"

Tony put down the steaming mug, thrust his big thumbs under his apron-string, in the vicinity of his waistcoat pockets, and considered his voracious customer with deep satisfaction. The next best thing to broiling a choice steak was watching a healthy client making proper use of it.

"No babies—eh?"

Bobby shrugged a shoulder and shook his head.

"Eye-ear-nose—mebbe? Lots of dem fellers."

"Heads!" declared Bobby, stoutly abjuring ophthalmology, otology, and all their works.

"Ah—so?" Tony grew excited. "I show you a head! You like for to see heads? Look, doc!" He bent down and offered for minute inspection a four-inch strip of bare white scalp. Straightening, he lightly tapped the scar and nodded several times very solemnly, "I dam' near die...Very bad!"

"Accident?" inquired Bobby.

"Railroad!"

"Wreck, maybe?"

Tony chuckled.

"Nah! Work on da railroad. Jus'—what you, call—wop! Not ride."

"So after you were hurt, you thought you had enough of working on the railroad, eh?"

"I'll say da world!" concurred Tony, whose amazing use of the prevailing slang was by no means the least of his conversational charms. "Doc Hudson—he set me up here."

"You don't tell me!" Bobby put down his fork and gave attention.

Tony nodded vigorously.

"Doc Hudson—Detroit—he fix me. Patch da head. Put me in da business. Great feller! Too bad he die!"

When it was evident that his patron wanted to know all about it, Tony was eager to furnish information. The sanguinary account of his accident was recited dramatically with much stress upon the grisly details, not omitting a quite voluminous report of the minor incidents leading up to the event, many of which were less essential to the pathology of the case than to the histrionic technique of the narrator.

All but dead, he had been; yes. The company surgeon had called in Doctor Hudson. Hudson had done "da eempossible!" But never again must Tony be working under the hot sun—never!

"'But what I do?' I cry. 'I starve; mebbe?'...'Can you cook, Tony?' he say."

It developed into a long story. Doctor Hudson had spent a whole day helping Tony locate a suitable place for his little restaurant; had guaranteed the rent of the building; had been present at the purchase of the range; had deposited to Tony's account in the leading bank a sum sufficient to carry him until his income was assured.

"I never heard about this before, Tony," said Bobby.

"No! Nobody know! Doc say, 'Tony! Tell nobody. Not while I leeve.' He dead now. I can tell!"

Bobby's glassy look of abstraction was mistaken for waning interest in the story, and Tony had no wish to bore his guest. He would return to the medic's pet interest. It was reasonably sure he would be attentive to an inquiry about his own aspirations.

"So!—You do heads, too, mebbe—like Doc Hudson?"

"I hope to, Tony. Some day," said Bobby, rising.

"Great feller—Doc Hudson!...Nobody know!"

* * * * *

Young Merrick paid his bill, donned his coat, said good night, lingered with his hand on the latch. Tony had begun clearing the table.

43

"I say—Tony!"

Tony put down a double handful of dishes.

"Did Doctor Hudson ever tell you why he wanted you to keep it a secret about his setting you up here?"

Tony inserted his thumbs under his apron-string and strolled forward, meditatively shaking his head.

"Dam' funny feller! He say, jus' like I tell you, 'Tony, I fix you so you no more work in da hot sun. While I leeve, you tell nobody.' I say, 'Doc, you one dam' fine feller. I pay you back some day.' He say, 'Nah—but, Tony,' he say, 'some dam' cold night, eef a feller come een, hongry and broke—'"

"Yeah?" prodded Bobby; for Tony had apparently changed his mind about the advisability of this confidence and had dismissed the rest of the sentence with a gesture. His red face crinkled with perplexity, and he rubbed the side of his bulbous nose with a corner of his apron. Nodding, jerkily, after the manner of an old man, he turned away, and was resuming his interest in the dishes.

"What then?" pursued Bobby—at his elbow.

"Doc say never tell nobody while I leeve."

"You mean—you never tell about these fellows who come in here hungry and broke?...Listen! I'll bet you a new fur-lined overcoat against a package of fags that that little account book, over there, on the case—and all these fellows who come in here hungry and broke—"

Tony interrupted. His face was very serious. He picked up his tray, and, as he straightened dignifiedly, he replied, in a thickening dialect significant that he was about to submerge and become incommunicable, "Ees eet dat you would make old Tony onhappy? Da leetle book! Eet ees for me to know! Doc Hudson—he say, 'Tony—you tell nobody!' For why he say that, I do not know; but—I tell nobody!"

"I'm sorry, Tony!" said Bobby contritely. "I had no right to intrude in your personal affairs. I beg your pardon."

Tony smiled absently.

"Oh—eet ees all right," he said reassuringly. "Gooda night, doc. Come again!"

CHAPTER VIII

HAGGARD from a sleepless night and the experience of more mental agony than he had suspected himself capable of, young Merrick sank dejectedly into a club chair on an early train for Detroit.

In response to the long and excited telegram he had sent her from the railroad station while en route to Tony's, the night before (he heartily wished, two hours afterward, he had not sent it), Nancy Ashford had wired she would be waiting for him at the Michigan Central depot.

It was the picture of her, radiant with anticipation and bubbling with questions, that he dreaded most. Nancy must not be hurt.

As for himself, he would get over it. Somehow he would be able to accommodate himself to the utter abandonment of his cherished illusions about Doctor Hudson, and the hero-worship that had held him up in his dull, monotonous grind at the Medical School; though, now that the bottom had fallen out of everything, he wondered how he could go back and tread the mill again.

But, however difficult that might be, it was simple enough compared to the pending job of sitting down beside Nancy Ashford and hunting for pleasant words with which to tell her that her sainted Wayne Hudson, to whom she had unrequitedly given her full devotion, was crazy.

He was not even an interesting lunatic. A lunatic, often as not, was a brilliant mind that had blown up under compression—blown up splendidly, with a loud report, the neighbours hurrying with straps and stretchers to collect the débris and lug it off to the mad-house.

No, this man Hudson had not been good enough to himself to explode so that everybody could hear it and know what the big bang meant. He was just a plain nut!...Can you feature it?...Grown-up man...of good standing professionally, respected and admired...toiling interminably over the detailed report of what some wild-eyed crank had told him of impossible experiences, and then going to the enormous bother of concealing that hodgepodge of delusions in a code—a performance worthy the mind of a seventh grade schoolboy playing sleuth with a toy pistol.

Returned from Tony's, wide awake and exultant, he had resolved, late as it was, to decode a few pages of the journal. He had read patiently at first, with a broad smile of anticipation. Presently he found himself wishing the eccentric author would soon have done with his commonplace preliminaries and settle to business in the disclosure of his big secret—for it would have to be a big one to justify all this elaborate hocus-pocus of the code.

Surely nothing was discoverable, so far as he had gone, that required any thick wall of secrecy. It might be difficult to induce the general public to read it, were it printed in English for free circulation; but to pretend it was a deep mystery was idiotic.

After awhile he had come upon a paragraph that drew down the corners of his mouth and dragged a bitter "What t'ell!" from an oversmoked throat. He pushed the little book aside contemptuously; rose, paced the floor, lighted his pipe, tossed it clatteringly upon the table; undressed and went to bed—but not to sleep.

His disappointment was the most serious jolt of his life.

Never until three months ago had he ever taken any stock in "big moments," "crucial decisions," "great renunciations," "consecrations," and the like. If people suddenly left off doing one thing and went galloping away in another direction, it was because they had sighted something more to their advantage. As for the legends of Saul and Saint Francis and Joan—well, if there was any substratum of truth in them, the psychiatrists could explain it.

Nor had he ever had any patience with that sticky confectionery of sentimentalism, that daintily perfumed moonshine, which effeminate visionaries referred to as "ideals." He had always been willing that all such blather should be left to the exploitation of preachers, poets, and the sob sisters.

Lately he had changed his mind about that. The coincidence of his having been saved from the lake at the same hour a valuable life had been lost in it, and at the price of that life, had stampeded him into a grand orgy of sentiment. He could understand Saul and Joan...Hudson had become his ideal, his star, his sun, his totem-pole!...Now it was all over!...

There had been an old story about an idol that had fallen down because it had clay feet. His had tumbled over with vertigo...sick in the head! To have grown to manhood without an "ideal" of any kind; to have espoused one, belatedly, with crusading zeal; to have discovered, after burning all his bridges behind him, that his hero was a sap!...It was a nasty wallop!

He had gouged his hot face into his pillow and decanted his wrath to its bitter lees...It wasn't that he had any fault to find with Hudson's penchant for poking a prehensile snout into other people's affairs with a passionate urge to do his one good deed per day, like the Boy Scout his silly little journal proclaimed him...but...My God!...Hudson wasn't the first man in all human history who had titillated his ego and busted the buttons off his weskit by doing alms!...What a pother about nothing!

At long last he had drifted off into an uneasy sleep, growling that he had a damned good notion to go on to New York in the morning and hop the first boat for Cherbourg...His passport was still alive...Grandpère would gladly send it to him...Then he wouldn't have to stop and face Nancy...What a rotten trick that would be!...And Grandpère?...The dear old boy had taken a lot of pride in him lately...

He would be in Detroit now in five minutes. He must be careful not to offend Nancy. Why not hand her the journal and the code-key and make off hurriedly to keep some urgent engagement? He could say his grandfather needed him badly. It would be true enough if he said he himself was sick.

She was waiting for him at the gates, wide-eyed and smiling when he first sighted her from the tunnel; a bit perplexed as he drew nearer...So it was plastered all over his mug, then!...He tried to pull a smile—a sickly smirk he knew it was; slipped an arm through hers; inquired, without meeting her eyes, if she'd had anything to eat, which she hadn't; told the porter to check his bags; and propelled Nancy to a quiet corner of the station restaurant where he made much ado about helping her with her coat—nervous as a caged fox.

"But I thought you had succeeded, dear." She followed him with inquiring eyes as he multiplied his little attentions and made no end of trouble for himself trying to find a place for her umbrella. "You don't resemble a conquering hero. You look more like the man who had set out after a beautiful butterfly, under the impression it was some kind of a bird; and found, after battering its wings to bits, that he had captured a worm."

Bobby put down the menu, which he had begun to pore over assiduously, and emphasized his rejoinder by planting a long index finger close to her plate.

"Now you've said it! I went after a butterfly and came back with a worm!"

"And whose fault was that—the butterfly's?"

"Take your base, Nancy," he conceded with a chuckle.

"Take my base—indeed!...What about?...Your wild pitching?...I tell you it was a safe hit and a home run!...But—no matter about the butterfly. Wake up, stupid; and let me into the secret!"

At that he attempted to rally, cleared his throat, made pretence of rolling up his sleeves. He wasn't going to let Nancy down. Maybe he himself could carry on without the guidance of the Hudson spectre; but Nancy couldn't. He would save the honour of her precious ghost if he had to profess faith in voodooism, necromancy, and witchcraft!

"I'm tired; that's all...Up nearly all night. Let's talk to the waiter first."

She was not reassured, but willing to be patient.

"It's simple as addition!" he declared, when the waiter had trotted off. "That is—" pleating the tablecloth with restless fingers, "the mere mechanics of converting the script into readable sentences is easy enough. But—to understand what it's about, once you've done that..."

He broke off suddenly and smiled...By the Lord Harry—he'd been handed his cue—at last! Now he could make his speech! He'd tell her the stuff was too deep for him! That would be infinitely better than to say it was childish piffle!

"Why—how very exciting!" exclaimed Nancy. "Out of one mystery into another!"

Bobby took the book from his pocket and opened it on the table before her, their heads close together. He was smiling now, quite pleased with his decision to let her explain it to him.

"Look! I'll read you the first page...Easy enough, isn't it?"

Nancy was ecstatic. She spread her hand over Bobby's and gripped it hard. Almost too good to be true, wasn't it? He nodded, adding mentally, "or even entertaining."

"How far have you gone?" she inquired, leafing the unintelligible pages. "Aren't you just thrilled to death?"

Bobby had no enthusiasm to match hers, try as he would.

"Over to here...about twenty pages. Thrilled? Well—no; not that, exactly...Just stupified...It's over my head, you see...I suppose I'm like your clumsy naturalist chasing a butterfly. I've been expecting so deuced much, and have worked so long to pry the lid off this thing that, now it's off, maybe I've damaged it somehow, or perhaps I haven't the mentality to—"

Nancy clutched his hand again—savagely.

"Look me straight in the eyes, Bobby Merrick! You've not been yourself for one instant since you arrived. You can't put anything over on me! I've been all through you with a lantern! You're trying to keep something back! I won't have it! Come clean, now— and tell me all about it! What's the trouble, boy?"

Bobby flushed and hung his head like a naughty child caught in the jam-pot.

"Aw—the stuff's no good!...Bunk—if you ask me...If anybody else but Doctor Hudson had—I say, Nancy, are you quite sure he really did write this? It isn't signed, you know."

"Don't talk nonsense!...What's it about?"

"Well—it isn't exactly religion, I guess; but it reads like those goofy tracts that shabby chaps with dirty whiskers toss into the open window of your car...slush you can have by the ton for a whole lot less than the asking! And why he should have gone to the pains of jiggling the words all out of shape, as if they spelled some precious secret, the good God only knows! If anybody else had written it, I'd say he was all unhooked!"

Nancy had been tapping the table with her finger-tips, thoughtfully, impatiently, indignantly, and now explosively.

"How old are you, Bobby?" she snapped.

"Twenty-five-goin'-on-twenty-six," he recited, in the tone of one six-goin'-on-seven— a pleasantry she failed to acknowledge.

"Well—when Doctor Hudson was just coming into national renown for having performed the first head operation of its kind in the history of surgery, you still had some of your milk teeth to cut and were galloping about the nursery on a stick-horse! When he wrote this 'bunk,' you hadn't learned to wash your own ears! I don't mean to be too rough with you, sonny; but you need a drubbing, and you're jolly well going to get it from your Nancy Ashford this day!"

"Go ahead!...I'd rather you were sore at me than—than—"

"Hadn't nerve enough to finish it, had you? You were trying to say you hoped I wouldn't discover that Doctor Hudson was a fool...Don't give yourself any concern about that. I won't!...I presume you never had your attention called," she went on, biting her words into bits, "to the psychology of the genius. Why should you, indeed? Freshman medics aren't troubled much, I presume, with excursions into the rarer altitudes of psychiatry which deal with obsessions. They're kept too busy peeling the pelts off cadavers; trying to remember which is incas and which is stapes; trying to distinguish carpal from tarsus!...Oh, *I* know! You needn't hoity-toity *me* with your wisdom!"

She suddenly sighted the open-mouthed waiter.

"Here!...If you're looking for something to amuse you, take this cold coffee away and bring a fresh pot...some that was made this morning—preferably."

Bobby burst out with a peal of laughter as the fellow paddled away.

"Nancy—you're a scream!...Do go on!"

"I mean to!...I'm going to give you your first information about the genius-type...The genius won't pigeon-hole! He won't card-index! He won't file...And because he won't, the dull-eyed dolts who hadn't needed any trimming to fit whatever pack they properly belonged to, think him crazy. They can't understand him, so—he's unhooked! He romps away where they can't follow, so—he's gone wild!...He bestrides an idea and rides it furiously across country, over ditches and fences, through people's houses, trampling down fields and gardens, knocking even his best friends down, and never knowing it...never looking back...or caring a tinker's damn...so long as he can retain his seat on that one tremendous idea!

"Now—our Doctor Hudson was that sort of a person, and he became obsessed with an idea. He conceived a notion...I'm sure I don't know how he came by it; maybe this book tells; I have hoped it would...that his professional success depended upon certain eccentric philanthropies which had to be kept secret to be effective. That much I managed to guess, long ago...Then the thought occurred to him, apparently, that he would put his theory into such shape that his heirs or successors or admirers might have a go at it. But he wanted to be insured against the ridicule of some pinhead who, pouncing upon it by accident—"

Bobby raised a hand.

"You're getting rather excited, aren't you?"

"You find it ridiculous that he employed this silly cipher," she continued, lowering her voice. "Well—suppose he'd written it in Latin, which he easily could have done without a lexicon; would that have caused you any less bother?...Or Greek! He could have done it in Greek! How much Greek do you know—beyond the letters on your fraternity badge?...He wanted to make somebody dig for it—I tell you—and that was all of a piece with his obsession! It was part of it!"

"You win, Nancy," admitted Bobby quietly. "You and I think the same thing about Doctor Hudson. We just say it differently; that is all...I said he must be mentally unhooked, and you say he was a genius and that all geniuses are unhooked...Very good...Now we can read the little book together and understand each other—even if we can't understand the book."

* * * * *

"I'll give you a brief digest of what I've read so far...Nancy—it isn't that I begrudge him the time I've spent untangling this involved cipher. It's only that there's really nothing in it that calls for such mysterious handling. You'll see!"

"I won't be sure about that until we've read the book—all through."

Bobby fingered his notes.

"The story begins about a year after the death of Joyce, his first wife. Her long illness had slowed him up; absorbed all the neural energy that should have gone into his professional training. On the edge of failure and in deep depression, he was half-minded to give up surgery and go into business...It occurred to him, one day, that Joyce's grave should be marked..."

"Ah—there you are!" ejaculated Nancy, with suppressed excitement.

Bobby glanced up, inquiringly.

"That tombstone was a milestone!" she explained, with emotion. "How often, when he wanted to date some event in his experience, it would be 'shortly after I had erected the little marker for Joyce.'...Do go on!"

"He went to a concern dealing in memorial stones and selected an inexpensive monument. On the blank form he wrote his wife's name and the vital dates. The manager asked if he wished a brief epitaph. It seems to have been customary, at that time. Unable, on the spur of the moment, to think of an appropriate sentiment, and eager to close the business at once, he was advised to stroll out into the production department and look about. Perhaps he might see something there that appealed to him.

"So—he went through the factory, where monuments were under construction, and there he accidentally came upon this man Randolph."

"You speak of this man Randolph as if he figured somewhat in the tale. I never heard of him."

"Yes, Randolph is by way of being the hero of the piece, as far as I have gone. I leave it to you to say, after you've made his acquaintance, whether Randolph is an apostle of light or as mad as the Hatter. Personally, I haven't any use for him. He makes his début in the story as an exceptionally gifted hypnotist...Turns out to be a sort of—miracle-man."

"Are you trying to tell me," demanded Nancy, "that Wayne Hudson took an interest in a person of that sort?"

"Well—you shall see...This Randolph fellow was in a studio partitioned off from the main production room. He was not a mere stone-cutter, but a sculptor—an uncommonly good one...Artist type. The piece he was doing, according to the journal, was a triumphant angelic figure, heroic size, gracefully poised on a marble pedestal, altar-shaped; an exquisitely modelled hand shading the eyes which gazed toward the far horizon, entranced by some distant radiance...It had all the combined delicacy and strength of a Canova—"

"Are you quoting?"

"Yes; it's in the book—just that way."

"But Doctor Hudson knew practically nothing about art!"

"He may have known more about it than you thought. He was heavily influenced by this crazy Randolph, as you shall see; and Randolph was a consummate artist."

"Oh, I wonder—do you suppose it could have been Clive Randolph? You know—the sculptor who did that group of children in the Metropolitan. He has been dead for years. Why, Bobby, I do believe he used to live here in Detroit!"

"Likely as not." He put his pencilled notes down on the table and sat for some time with half-closed eyes, absorbed. "Another genius," he mumbled. "Nancy, geniuses do have a right to be batty, don't they?"

"Certainly!" Nancy glowed. Bobby was seeing the light.

He took up his memorandum.

"Well, on the face of this altar-shaped pedestal was engraved, in high relief, in ecclesiastical letters, these words: 'Thanks Be to God Who Giveth Us the Victory.'"

Nancy murmured that she thought it odd.

"How do you mean 'odd'? It's in the Bible somewhere, isn't it?"

"Doubtless," she conceded, with a nervous laugh. "It could be in the Bible, almost anywhere, and still be odd, couldn't it? But what I mean is that it seems queer to find Doctor Hudson reciting a quotation from the Bible. He wasn't the tiniest mite religious!"

"Don't you be too sure about that!" he warned.

"Why, Bobby, he was not only unconcerned; he was almost contemptuous of religious organizations; hadn't been inside a church, except at weddings, for twenty years. He was soured on churches as a small boy; told me once—it was when some quite dreadful evangelist was here and the papers were full of his cheap vulgarities—that the churches in his village were forever haranguing people to 'come apart from the world,' when they had nothing to offer in exchange for such renunciation but the vestigial remains of medieval superstitions!"

"But, couldn't he have been interested in—in the supernatural without being a church adherent?"

"Well, would he?...It isn't customary."

"Oh, well! if you propose to analyze this thing in the light of what's customary, let's go to the football game and quit torturing ourselves...I ask you!...Is it customary for a man to conduct his ordinary charities by stealth; scampering, squirrel-fashion, into his hole and pulling the hole in after him, at the approach of anyone who might discover he had done somebody a good turn? Is it customary for a man to write the story of his madness in a kiddish cipher? I'll tell you what he was!...one of these old-time mystics!...believed in fairies...had visions...played with the angels!"

"Bobby Merrick—you're c-r-a-z-y!"

"No—not yet; but I've a queer feeling I'm going to be."

Nancy pushed back her plate and impatiently waved the waiter away when he asked if everything wasn't all right.

"No—" Bobby slowly shook his head, judicially. "It wasn't really religion that he had; not what I think of as religion, anyway. I don't pretend to know much about it, but isn't religion just a more or less perfunctory acceptance of a lot of old myths abstracted from the folk-lore of the Jews; tries to make people say they believe this and that about God; imagines it knows what God wants humanity to do—sometimes waiting sadly for mankind to do it, and at other times pushing people about so that they've got to do it, willy-nilly; takes up subscriptions to send barkers to the so-called heathen, warning them they'll seethe in hell if they don't leave off calling their God whatever-it-is and call Him something else?"

Nancy laughed.

"It isn't that bad, Bobby. It couldn't possibly be that silly. People do get a lot of comfort out of their religion, or they wouldn't stick to it."

"Comfort!" he echoed. "I'm glad you used that word. I believe I can tell you now what I think was the difference between this stuff that Doctor Hudson had—and the conventional sort of religion. Ordinary religion is intended to bring comfort. Believe such-and-such, and have comfort, peace, assurance that all is well and a Great Somebody is looking after things. Well—this religion that Hudson had certainly brought him no comfort!...Rode him like the Old Man o' the Sea...lashed him on...hounded him by day and haunted him by night...worked him like a slave...obsessed him!"

"He could have given it up, couldn't he, if it annoyed him?"

"Ah—there you are! Now you've touched the vital spot! No! He couldn't give it up because it furnished his motive power! It was what kept him going!...Says it made him—professionally!"

"I'm afraid you've let this book get horribly on your nerves, Bobby." Nancy drew on her gloves. "Let us go out to Brightwood, where we'll not be interrupted, and see what it's all about."

Bobby was slow to rise.

"Nancy, my whole attitude towards this matter is changing, since talking it over with you. I don't mind telling you I was never so disgusted or disappointed in my life as last night when I tried to read this stuff. But that was because I expected it to be a normal account of a normal man's experiences. And when I found it wasn't normal, well—I committed the usual blunder of pronouncing it silly!"

Nancy was radiant.

"Exactly!...So long as he was saying the customary thing, the normal thing, the thing you understood, he was sane! When he got to the unusual, the thing you did not understand, he was crazy!...That's the way the average mind operates; but you daren't make snap judgment like that, for you're to be dealing with queer heads all your life!"

* * * * *

Throughout the long taxi drive to the hospital, their conversation studiously avoided the mystery they had confronted. They talked of his medical course. What did he like best? She shuddered when he spoke of his delight in anatomy.

"One gets used to that," he assured her. "And old Huber's a prince! He handles those poor cadavers as if they were our relatives. I'll bet if some of them had been given as much tender consideration while alive as Huber gives them in the lab, they might have lived longer...Buries their ashes, Huber does, at the end of the semester...conventional interment—bell, book and clergy...Contends that these paupers and idiots and criminals, however much they may have burdened their communities while they lived, have so completely discharged their obligation to society by their service in the lab, that they deserve honourable burial...A fine old boy is Huber, believe me!"

The talk shifted to Nancy's affairs. She admitted she was worried. Rumour had it that Joyce Hudson was quite out of bounds; that Mrs. Hudson, apparently, could do nothing with her any more. She was being seen at the wrong places, with the wrong people.

"Do you suppose there is anything you could do about it, Bobby? Joyce is still your friend, isn't she?"

"I presume." His tone lacked interest. "I haven't seen her for nearly a year, you know."

"It may be just a notion of mine, but I always thought Joyce was a little in love with you, Bobby."

His gesture denied it.

"She isn't; but—suppose she was!...Would that be a good reason for my mixing in, over there? I'm not in love with her. No—I don't believe my obligation to Doctor Hudson involves my serving *in loco parentis* to his daughter."

"I'm not so sure it doesn't," reflected Nancy. "You've had an ambition to finish out his life for him, and part of his job was Joyce. There were times when all of his job was Joyce! You've no idea how much he gave up for her! Why, he even married—to keep her straight!"

"That shouldn't have been much of a sacrifice." Bobby grinned.

"Have you ever seen her—since?"

"Never tried to."

"Still think about her sometimes?"

"Why do you want to know?" His tone hinted that he would like to close the door between them—not rudely, but—to close it, nevertheless; and, prompt to feel it, Nancy disclaimed her right to inquire.

"Forgive me, won't you? I haven't anything to do, you know, but amuse myself wondering about things like that."

"Then I mustn't do you out of your occupation."

* * * * *

Nancy hung their coats in her closet, drew up a chair beside him, and together they faced the book again, agreeing that she should read the script, letter by letter, while Bobby arranged it into words.

"First, let me finish telling you the part I have already deciphered," he said, putting down his pencil. "Randolph pointed to the epitaph and inquired, 'How do you like this one?'

"'Means nothing to me!' replied Doctor Hudson. 'If there is a God, He probably has no more interest in any man's so-called victory, which can always be circumstantially explained, than in the victory of a cabbage that does well in a favourable soil.'

"'Then you're related to God same as a cabbage!' chuckled Randolph. 'That's good!'

"He resumed his work, deftly tapping his chisel. 'I used to think that,' he went on, talking half to himself. 'Made a little experiment, and changed my mind about it.' He put down his mallet, leaned far forward, and, cupping his mouth with both hands, confided, in a mysterious tone, '*I've been on the line*!'"

"He must have been crazy!" Nancy muttered.

"Tut, tut!...What's come of your genius theory? You're willing Doctor Hudson should be one—why not Randolph?"

"Quite right! Go on!...But he does sound a little off, doesn't he?"

"Decidedly!...And dangerously, I should say!...The most cold-blooded, calculating, sacrilegious lunatic you ever met!...I'll show you. Here is the exact copy of my translation! Listen to this:

He did not have the tone or stance of a fanatic; spoke quietly; had none of the usual tricks by which aberrations are readily identified; talked well, with absolute self-containment. "Victory? Well—rather! I now have everything I want and can do anything I wish!...So can you!...So can anybody! All you have to do is follow the rules! There's a formula, you know! I came upon it by accident!" He took up his chisel again.

He was a queer one. I felt shy and embarrassed. Clearly, he was cracked, but his manner denied it. I tried to remember he was an artist, with permission to be eccentric; but this was more than an eccentricity. He made me shivery. I wanted to get away. So—I was backing through his doorway when he called, "Doctor—do you have victory?"

"Victory over what?" I demanded, impatiently...I had not told him I was discouraged; hadn't mentioned I was a doctor...I never did find out how he guessed that—the question being eclipsed by more important mysteries.

"Oh—over anything—everything! Listen!" He climbed swiftly down from his scaffolding, and gliding stealthily toward me as if he had some great secret to impart he whispered into my ear—his hand firmly gripping my coat-lapel, somewhat to my own anxiety—"Would you like to be the best doctor in this town?"

So—then I knew he was crazy, and I began tugging myself loose.

"Come to my house, to-night, about nine o'clock," he said, handing me his card, "and I'll tell you what you want to know!"

I must have looked dazed, for he laughed hilariously, as he climbed up again. I laughed too as I reached the street—the epitaph matter having completely left my mind for the time. I had never heard so much nonsense in my life. "Like hell," I growled, as I started my car, "will I waste an evening with that fool!"

"This writing is authentic, Bobby."

At nine o'clock, I was at Randolph's door...When these words are read I shall be unable to answer any queries as to my motive in going there that night. And that will be fortunate; for I have no explanation further than to say (and this will unquestionably be regarded with distrust and disappointment) that I was propelled there against my wishes. I had no thought of going; went in response to some urge over which I had no control. ...I was down town to dinner, that evening; returned home at eight; went immediately to bed—quite contrary to my custom, for I never retired before midnight—and began reading a book, unable to concentrate on a line of it. I could not keep my eyes off the clock. It ticked louder and louder and my heart beat faster and faster until the two of them seemed synchronized. At length, becoming so nervous I could no longer contain myself, I rose, dressed hastily, dashed out for my car, and drove to Randolph's address without regard to boulevard stops or angry traffic officers. My mouth was dry, my heart thumping.

"How do you like it—far as we've gone?" he asked.

Nancy's elbows rested heavily on the desk, her clenched fists digging deeply into her cheeks.

"Why, Bobby—isn't this just *awful?*" she whispered. "*It's tragic!*"

"You'll think so—presently. It hasn't begun to get awful yet!"

His eyes travelled back to his copy.

"You had not intended to come, had you?" inquired Randolph, taking my hat.

"No!" I replied, sourly.

"That's what I feared," he said, gently, "but I felt so sure you needed to have a talk with me that I—"

"That is what I want to know!" I demanded. "*What did you do?*"

He grinned slyly, rubbed his hands together softly, satisfiedly, and said, "Well—I earnestly wanted you here; and, as I told you, this morning, whatever I earnestly want—*it comes*! *I wanted you here*! *You came!*"

He motioned me to a seat—I was glad enough to accept it for my knees were wobbly—in a living-room furnished in exquisite taste. His daughter, whom he had gracefully presented, promptly excused herself, and left us alone. Offering mea cigar, he leisurely filled a long-stemmed churchwarden pipe for himself, and drew his chair closer. In his velvet jacket, at his ease, he was all artist; quite grizzled, wore a short Van Dyke beard; had a clear, clean, grey eye that came at you a bit shyly and tentatively, but left you no way of escape.

He lost no time in preliminary manœuvres. Reaching to a small book-table, at his elbow, he took up a limp-leather Bible. I knew then that I was in for it. Impetuously, I resolved upon an immediate, if inglorious, exit. Savagely, I put up a protesting hand and said firmly, "Now—if it's that, I don't care to hear about it!"

"See?" shouted Nancy. "What did I tell you?"

To my surprise, he put the book back on the table, and calmly puffed at his pipe, thoughtfully, for a while; then replied, "Well—neither am I—except as it's really an important history of a great religious system. Quite useful, I presume; but I'm not specially interested in it—except one page—" he blew a few smoke rings, his head tilted far back against his tall chair "—and I have cut that page out...I just wanted you to see this particular copy of the Bible. I was about to say—when you plunged in with your impatient remark—that this copy of the Bible lacks the secret formula for power. I keep that one page elsewhere!"

"What's on it?" I inquired, annoyed at my own confession of interest.

"Oh—" he replied casually, "it's just the rules for getting whatever you want, and doing whatever you wish to do, and being whatever you would like to be. But—you're not interested in that; so we'll talk about something else."

"What is on that page?" I demanded—my voice sounding rather shrill.

"Do you really want to know?" he challenged, leaning forward and fixing me intently with his gaze.

"Yes!" I barked.

His next words came slowly, incisively, single-file.

"*More-than-you-have-ever-wanted-to-know-anything- before*?"

"Yes!" I admitted—and meant it.

"Say it!" he commanded.

I repeated it: "*More-than-I-have-ever-wanted-to-know-anything-before*!"

His manner changed instantly.

"Good! Now we can talk!"

He went down into an inside pocket and produced a morocco wallet. From the wallet, he extracted a folded page. I read it, and he carefully interpreted its meaning.

Nancy's eyes were a study, when Bobby stopped reading to search her face.

"Are you prepared now for a complete knock-out?" he inquired. "If so—I'll give you the next paragraph."

I did not leave Randolph's house until four o'clock, and when I finally went out into the dark, considerably shaken, I was aware that my life would never be the same again. Whatever of success has come to me in my profession dates from that hour and can be explained in terms of the mysterious potentiality which Randolph communicated to me that night.

There was a long silence between them.

"That's almost as far as I've gone," said Bobby.

"Far enough—I should say!" Nancy's deep sigh was ominous of dejection.

"Then let's call it a day." He rose, and glanced at his watch. "You and I can't help knowing that this is something Doctor Hudson must have written when he was under very heavy pressure of work; half dead on his feet; seeing things; hearing voices. Perhaps we shouldn't be reading it at all. Maybe it isn't fair to his memory. How about giving it up—and forgetting we ever went this far into it?"

Nancy tapped the table, thoughtfully, with her fingertips.

"I wonder what was on that page!"

He laughed.

"That sounds like Doctor Hudson! That was what he wanted to know. Now it's your question! I'm bound to confess I'd like to know too." He gripped her arm in strong fingers. "And—no matter how stiffly we revolt against this thing, we're sure to be sneaking back to it, one at a time, to investigate; so—perhaps we should be honest with each other, and look into it *now*! Are you willing?"

She nodded, without looking up.

"Take warning! It's likely to make us as nutty as he was!"

Lighting a cigarette, Bobby strolled to the window, hands in pockets. He turned, and leaning on the window-sill, faced her studiously.

"Not me! I'm not going to do it. I can't afford to dabble in such stuff. It isn't good for me. I had no idea I could be so impressionable toward this sort of thing. You can go into it, if you want to...I'm out!" He dismissed it peremptorily, with widespread fingers.

Nancy's voice was husky.

"You'll not be able to get away from it! You're too far in!...And you know it!...It's got you!...I know it's got *me*! I understand now why he went to the Randolph house, that night! There's something—something sort of inevitable about it!...A form of insanity, maybe; but—once it beckons to you, it's got you! You may as well come along—first as last!...It has curious, invisible tentacles that reach out and wrap their feelers about you...and draw you up...and into...and drag you along..."

"Stop it, Nancy!...That's ridiculous!"

* * * * *

Young Watson could hardly have chosen a less opportune moment to put his head in. Mrs. Ashford had a caller, and it was clear that both hostess and guest were labouring under an unusual mental tension...having something of a storm, indeed! Realizing he was *de trop,* he was for making a hasty retreat, when Nancy recalled him.

"Come on in! You remember Mr. Merrick."

"Quite!" extending his hand. "I shall always remember you as putting up the gamest fight with pneumonia that I ever watched! And now, I hear, you're having a battle with old man Gray."

Turning to Mrs. Ashford, he stated his errand:

"Your Mr. Folsom is rapidly slipping out. In an hour or two he will be quite unconscious. He inquired for you a few minutes ago. Perhaps you will want to run in and see him. There seems to be none of his people in town."

Murmuring regret, Nancy rose to go.

"Will you wait for me?"

Merrick nodded.

"I'll go on with this. Take your time. You'll find me here when you come back."

The door closed softly behind them.

* * * * *

I reached out my hand greedily for the page Randolph had unfolded, but he shook his head.

"Not just yet," he said, smiling at my eagerness. "I mean to let you see it; but I must tell you something about it, first. This page contains the rules for generating that mysterious power I mentioned. By following these instructions to the letter, you can have anything you want, do anything you wish to do, be whatever you would like to be. I have tried it. It works. It worked for me. It will work for you!"

Combined impatience and incredulity brought a chuckle from me which he did not resent.

"You saw that piece I was working on when you came in, this morning?"

"Beautiful!" I exclaimed—sincerely.

"You liked it that much?" He was pleased with my enthusiasm.

"Nothing short of a masterpiece!"

"Perhaps I should be more grateful for that compliment, doctor; but I really have had very little to do with it...You may be interested to learn that I was an ordinary stone-cutter until about three years ago, hacking out stamped letters with a compression chisel. From my youth, I had cherished an ambition to do something important in stone. But there was never any money for training; never any time for experiment. Such crude and hasty attempts as I had made, from time to time, had netted nothing but discouragement.

"One day, I went to the church my little girl attended, and heard a preacher read what is on this page. It evidently meant nothing to him, for he read it in a dull, monotonous chant. And the congregation sat glassy-eyed, the words apparently making no impression. As for me, I was profoundly stirred. The remainder of the hour was torture, for I wanted to get out where I could think.

"Hurrying home to our bare little house, I found—with considerable difficulty, for I was not familiar with the Bible—that page from which the minister had read. There it was—in black and white—the exact process for achieving power to do, be, and have what you want! I experimented."

* * * * *

Nancy's face, sober and troubled, appeared at the door.

"Bobby," she said softly, "I don't like to leave you alone so long, but my patient seems to want a hand to hold. I'm afraid I must stay with him a little while."

"Quite proper," he agreed, with more than a glance at her. "Stay with him and don't worry about me. I may have something very important to tell you when you come back. It looks as if the big mystery may be cleared up now at any minute."

She hesitated, and was about to ask a question; but, seeing how complete was his absorption, withdrew and quietly closed the door.

With that, Randolph handed me the magic page. Some twenty lines of it were heavily underscored in red ink. In silence he puffed his pipe while my eye traversed the cryptic paragraphs, and when I looked up, inquiringly, he said:

"Of course, you will not realize the full importance of all this, instantly. It seems simple because it was spoken dispassionately, with no oratorical bombast or prefatory warning that the formula he was about to state was the key to power!"

Edging his chair closer to mine, he laid a long hand on my knee and looked me squarely in the eyes.

"Doctor Hudson—if you had a small, inadequate brick house, and decided to give yourself more room, what would you need for your building?...More brick...If you had a small, inadequate steam-engine, you would want more steel to construct larger cylinders—not a different kind of steel to house a different kind of steam, but merely more room for expansion...Now—if you had a small, inadequate personality, and wanted to give it a chance to be something more important, where would you find the building materials?"

He seemed waiting for a reply, so I humoured him.

"Well—according to the drift of your argument, I presume I would have to build it out of other personalities. Is that what you're driving at?"

"Pre—cisely!" he shouted. "But—not 'out of!'...*Into*!...Glad you said that, though; for it gives me a chance to show you the exact difference between the right and wrong methods of making use of other people's personalities in improving one's own...Everybody is aware, instinctively, that his personality is modified by others. Most people go about imitating various scraps and phases of the personalities that have attracted them—copying one man's walk, another's accent, another's laugh, another's trick of gesture—making mere monkeys of themselves...This theory I am talking about doesn't ask you to build your personality *out of* other personalities, but *into* them!"

"I'm afraid all that's too deep for me," I admitted befuddledly.

He rose and stamped back and forth in front of the grate, shaking his shaggy mop of grizzled hair, and waving his long-stemmed pipe as if trying to conjure a better explanation.

"See here! You know all about blood transfusion. That's in your line. Superb!...One man puts his life into another man...Doctor—how do you accomplish a blood transfusion? Tell me in detail!"

* * * * *

Merrick glanced up as the door opened.

"Is he gone?"

Nancy nodded, soberly.

"What has been happening since I left?" she asked, drawing up a chair beside him.

He pushed his notes toward her and watched her face as she read.

"Just what *is* the best process of blood transfusion? Let's see how much you know!"

"Well—it's simple enough, except for one obstacle. The blood must be kept from coagulation as it passes from the donor to the recipient. Even when the artery and the vein are attached by a little cannula, the blood soon clogs the glass; so, to avoid that stoppage, the vein of the recipient is passed through the cannula and cuffed back over the end of it. Then the cannula, carrying the vein, is inserted into the artery of the donor. The point is, you see, to insure against any outside contact."

"Bobby—what was on that page?"

"I haven't learned yet."

"Do you think he is ever going to tell us?"

"He's got to, sooner or later. Let's read on. I imagine we're close to it now."

Nancy took the pencil and began to copy from his rapid dictation.

I explained the principles of transfusion, briefly, and Randolph seemed mightily pleased, especially with that feature of it which concerned the problem of coagulation.

"Bright boy—Bobby!" cried Nancy. "You did know, didn't you?"

He acknowledged her sally with a grimace and continued dictating.

"You will notice there," pointing to the page in my hand, "that this first step toward the achievement of power is an expansion—a projection of one's self into other personalities. You will see that it has to be done with such absolute secrecy that if, by any chance, the contact is not immediate and direct—if, by any chance, there is a leak along the line of transfer—the whole effect of it is wasted! You have to do it so stealthily that even your own left hand—"

Nancy tossed her pencil down on the desk, and relaxed in her chair.
"Bobby! I've got it! *I can find the page!*"
"Is there a Bible handy?"
"I'm afraid I haven't one, dear."
"Well—that can come later, then. Continue!"

Randolph returned to his chair, and went on, in a lowered voice:
"Hudson—the first time I tried it—I can tell you the incident freely because nothing ever came of it, although it had cost me more than I could afford, at the time, to do it—the chap was so grateful he told a neighbour of mine, in spite of my swearing him in. He had been out of work and there had been a long run of sickness in the family, and he was too shabby and down at heel to make a presentable appearance in asking for a job. I outfitted him. He told it. A neighbour felicitated me, next day. So there was more than sixty dollars of my hard-earned cash squandered!"
"Squandered!" I shouted, in amazement. "How squandered? Didn't he get the job?"
Randolph sighed.
"Oh, yes," he said. "He found a job. I was glad enough for that, of course. But—that didn't do *me* any good! You'd better believe—the next time I made an outlay I informed the fellow that if I ever heard of his telling anybody, I would break his neck."

"Did you ever hear of anything more diabolical?" broke in Nancy, indignantly. "Can you imagine such fiendish selfishness?...Just doing it to benefit himself! Not even willing the other fellow should be grateful!...And yet he thought he was getting himself connected with God, that way!...It gives you the creeps!"
"Well—keep it in mind he's obsessed with a delusion."
"Possessed of a devil—I'd rather believe!"
"Maybe Doctor Hudson will explain it...Let's proceed."

He laughed merrily at the remembrance of the incident.
"The man thought I was crazy!" he added, wiping his eyes.
"And you weren't?" I inquired in a tone that sobered him.
"Really—it does sound foolish, doesn't it? I mean—when you first hear of it. I don't wonder you're perplexed."
"I am worse than perplexed," I admitted, bluntly. "I'm disgusted!"

"You and me—both!" interpolated Bobby, under his breath.

"You might well be," admitted Randolph, "if I were trying to get power, that way, to stack up a lot of money for my own pleasure. All I wanted was the effective release of my latent ability to do something fine!...And, as for being disgusted because I requested the man not to tell anybody what I had done for him, if that offends you, you wouldn't like the Lord himself!...For he often said that to people he had helped."

"I'm sure I don't know," I said..."Not very well acquainted with what he said...Go ahead with your story."

"Thanks...But, first let me lead you just a little farther into the general philosophy of this...On the night of the day I made my first successful projection of my personality—I cannot tell you what that was—I dare not—I went literally into a closet in my house, and shut the door. That's the next step in the programme, as you have read there on that page. You see—I was very much in earnest about this matter; and, having already bungled one attempt, I was resolved to obey the rules to the letter...Later, I discovered that the principle will work elsewhere than in a closet. Just so you're insulated."

"Oh—Randolph—for God's sake!" I exploded. "What manner of wild talk is this?"

"Good!" interrupted Nancy. "It was high time he called him!"

"I confess I can't understand," said Randolph, impatiently, "why you find this so hard to accept! Why—it's in line with our experience of every other energy we use! Either we meet its terms, or we don't get the power. What did Volta's battery or Faraday's dynamo amount to, practically, until Du Fay discovered an insulation that would protect the current from being dissipated through contacts with other things than the object to be energized?...Most personalities are just grounded! That's all that ails them!

"So, I went into a closet; shut the door; closed my eyes; quietly put myself into a spiritually receptive mood; and said, confidently, addressing the Major Personality,—*I have fulfilled all the conditions required of me for receiving power! I am ready to have it! I want it! I want the capacity to do just one creditable work of statuary!*

"Now—you may be inclined to believe that I experienced only a queer delusion, at that moment. As a scientific man, you may think that my mental state can easily be accounted for by principles well-known to psychology. If you think that, I have no objection. The fact that a process of achieving power by the expansion of the human personality admits of an explanation, in scientific terms, does not damage its value at all, in my opinion. I dare say the time will come when this matter is made a subject of scientific inquiry.

"But—whether it is explicable or not, I can truthfully assure you that upon finishing my experiment in that closet, I received—as definitely as one receives a shock from an electrode, or a sudden glare of light by opening a tightly-shuttered room—a strange inner illumination!

"It was late in the night. I came out of that dark, stifling little closet with a curious sense of mastery. It put me erect, flexed the muscles of my jaw, made my step resilient. I wanted to laugh! I tried to sleep; and, failing of it, walked the streets until dawn. At eight-thirty, I approached the manager of the factory and asked for six months' leave. When he inquired my reason, I told him I had it in mind to attempt a piece of statuary.

"Something we might use, perhaps?" he asked.

"I am confident of it," I said, surprised at my own audacity. It was enough that I had determined to survive somehow, without wages, for six months; but now I had made an extravagant promise to the manager. He was thoughtful for a while and then said:

"'I'll give you a chance to try it. For the present, you are to have your usual pay, and a studio to yourself. If you produce something we can place, you will share in the sale. Your hours will be your own business. I should be glad if you succeeded.'

"I began work at once in a flutter of excitement. The clay seemed alive in my hands! That first day was a revelation. It was as if I had never really lived before! All colours were more vivid. I want you to remember that, Hudson. See if you have the same reaction. Grass is greener; the sky is bluer; you hear the birds more distinctly. It sharpens the senses—like cocaine.

"That night, I went into my closet again, and was immediately conscious of a peculiar intimacy between myself and That Other; but it was not so dynamic as on the previous night. I decided that if I was to get any more power that way, I would have to make some further adjustments of my own spiritual equipment.

"That was on a Friday, the tenth of June. On the first day of September, I invited the manager in to see the cast I had made. He looked at it for a long time without any remark. Then he said, quietly, 'I have some people who may be interested in this.'

"It was the figure of a child, a chubby little fellow about four years old. The boy was posed on one knee. He had just raised up from his play with a little dog that stood tensely alert, in front of him, with a ball in his mouth, waiting for the child to notice him. The boy's shirt was open at the throat. His tight little knickers were buttoned to broad suspenders. The legs were bare to the knee. He was looking straight aloft, his little face all squinted up with baffled amazement, wonderment, curiosity. His small square hand shaded his eyes against a light almost too bright for him, the head tilted at an angle indicating that he had heard something he could not quite understand and was listening for it to be repeated.

"The next afternoon, the manager's clients came in—a man and his wife. She was in black. They had recently lost their little boy. She cried at first, heart-breakingly. But, after a while, she smiled. It made me very happy when she smiled. I knew then that I had been able to express my thought.

"I was told to go on with my project and put it into white marble...Quite incidentally, the people adopted the boy I had used for a model."

* * * * *

It was about four o'clock when I left Randolph's house that night. I was in a grand state of mystification. I went home resolved that I would make an experiment similar to his. Before I went to bed, I tried to project my thoughts to some remote spiritual source, but was conscious of no reaction whatsoever. In the morning I decided that I had been most outrageously imposed upon by an eccentric and scowled at my own reflection in my shaving-mirror. Nobody but a visionary could do these things with any hope of success, and I was, by training and temperament, a materialist and a very cold-blooded one, at that. All that day, however, I was aware of being on a quiet, unrelenting search for some suitable clinical material to be used for an experiment in the dynamics of personality-projection...The strangest feature of my mood, however, was the fact that the power I had begun, rather vaguely, to grope for—under Randolph's urging—was not the mere satisfaction of an ambition to make myself important or minister to my own vanity...For the first time, my profession seemed to me not as a weapon of self-defence but a means of releasing myself!

The last thing Randolph said to me, at the door, was this caution: "Be careful how you go into this, my friend! I do not know the penalties this energy exacts when misused...I've no notion what dreadful thing might have happened to the Galilean if he had turned those stones into bread!...But, I warn you!...If you're thinking of going into this to feather your own nest, you'd better never give it another thought...I'm not sure—but I think it's terribly dangerous stuff to fool with!"

My own experiences are hereinafter set forth as possible aids to whomever has had the curiosity to translate this journal. I trust I have made it quite clear why I have chosen this peculiar method of passing it along. Had I ventured to report my experiments, it would have been at the expense of my reputation for sanity. I do not know of a single friend to whom I could have told these things without putting an unpleasant constraint between us. It has been a hard secret to keep. It is equally hard, I am discovering, to confide—even with the realization that these words are unlikely to be read during my lifetime. I dislike the idea of being thought a fool—dead or alive.

You—whoever you are—may be inclined to read on—perhaps personally interested in making an experiment; perhaps just curious. I wonder—would it be asking an unreasonable favour—if you would not consent to stop, at this point, if you are smiling?...You see, some of these experiences of mine have meant a great deal to me, emotionally. I don't believe I should want them laughed at...If the thing hasn't gripped you a little by now, put it down, please, and think no more about it...If, however, you seriously wish to proceed, let me counsel you, as Randolph counselled me, that you are taking hold of high tension! Once you have touched it, you will never be able to let go...If you are of the temperament that demands self-indulgence to keep you happy and confident enough to do your work—and many inestimably valuable people are so built and cannot help it any more than tall men can help being tall—leave all this alone, and go your way!...For if you make an excursion into this, you're bound! It will plaster a mortgage on everything you think you own, and commandeer your time when you might prefer to be using it for yourself...It is very expensive...It took the man who discovered it to a cross at the age of thirty-three!

* * * * *

Young Merrick pushed back the papers and turned slowly to face Nancy but their eyes did not meet. They felt strangely embarrassed in each other's presence, and sat for many minutes in silence...Bobby spoke.

"'Bound,' he said. 'Once you go into it, you're bound.' Hudson has had me bound ever since he died!...He should have been content with that."
Nancy rose and rested her capable hands on his shoulders.
"It's a good place to stop, wouldn't you say?"
He agreed. Perhaps they might have an hour or two together to-morrow. He had half promised his grandfather he would be out for dinner. Tom Masterson had talked of going, too.
"Are you meaning to take the book along?"
"I'll match you for it!"
"Heads!"
He slapped a coin on his wrist.
"Sorry, Nancy...I'll bring it back to-morrow."

CHAPTER IX

"GRANDPÈRE," said Bobby, slowly twirling the stem of his glass, "I wish you would tell Tom about the time you and Mr. Anderson butchered the pigs at the Country Club."

The talk had been growing too serious. Masterson had an annoying tendency, when exhilarated, to become didactic. It was all clever enough, informative, interesting—but more dogmatic than suited the temper of a Thanksgiving dinner.
By a circuitous route they had arrived at the problem of caste in America, Masterson conducting the excursion and pointing out the essential facts of interest to be noted along the way. Bobby was for a change of topic. Old Nicholas had some convictions on this subject. He would probably not express them to the same degree with which he believed them; but Masterson must not be encouraged to deliver himself of too many sentiments unshared by his genial host.
"Why shouldn't there be a leisured class? Loafers—if you like that word better? This was about the only sign America had exhibited that she was maturing, ever so little, in a few restricted zones. Wasn't our brand of democracy dangerous? Referendum—huh! What did the average voter know? Every nation that had become great had achieved its distinction through the leadership of small social and intellectual minorities!"
Masterson was still talking—Hyde Parking, almost—a bit flushed about the temples. Bobby determined upon a change of subject.
Old Nicholas was not in accord with many of young Masterson's views, but he liked his views better than the manner in which he delivered them, and liked both the views and the delivery better than the way he drank his wine.
Meggs had been told to bring up a long-neglected bottle of choice Burgundy. In the opinion of the elder Merrick, wine like this deserved to be caressed, its colour admired, its fragrance inhaled, its story reconstructed. It was to be sipped, drop by drop. It pleased him that Bobby seemed to know how. Liquid sunshine, it was; sunshine that had warmed the pleasant banks of the Rhone, in tranquil days before the war. One did not toss it off at a draught. Masterson gulped it. It was good to see Bobby close his eyes as his lips touched the rim of the glass, as if he saw merry groups of bare-legged little girls tramping it out in

the shade at the corner of some Provençal vineyard. The boy was maturing rapidly, reflected old Nicholas. He had the posture and gesture of a man.

"Bobby occasionally insists upon this story," said Nicholas obediently, "I have repeated it, at his request, many times."

"And each time it is better," commented Bobby, appreciatively.

"Let's have it then, by all means!" shouted Masterson, much more boisterously than he had intended, an error he instantly endeavoured to correct by bowing very formally and dignifiedly in an affirmative to Meggs' unspoken query as the bottle was again tilted, tentatively, inquiringly, over his glass. Meggs had tried to put into the gesture just the right degree of reserve, but the finesse was a bit too subtle for his customer.

* * * * *

"Well," said Nicholas, clearing his throat, "it was this way. You see, where Axion now stands, there used to be nothing but pasture fields. Joe Anderson and I, when we were kids, had a contract with most of the village folks to drive their cows out to pasture, every morning, in the summer, and bring them home in the evening to be milked. Each cow was worth a dollar a month to us.

"Out there, in those fields, where we freckled-faced youngsters, with stone bruises on our calloused feet, sat all day, whittling kite sticks, playing mumble-peg, and bragging about the teams we captained at school—three-old-cat; you never played it, either of you—Joe and I later built a couple of big factories which quite changed the look of the landscape.

"These factories also brought changes in most people's mode of living. Many men, who might have spent all their lives in ordinary financial circumstances, came to have quite a little money. They built big houses, and their children took on airs. It was hard to recognize the place, after a while, and even harder to recognize some of the people.

"Well, no matter how much absorbed we became in our business, Joe and I remained, through the years, just kids—to each other. I suppose it was a subject for many little jokes with other people. We kept up our boyish relations—always bragging about our speed, strength, and endurance, whenever we met, and invariably in the language we had used in the old days. Like 'Gemunee Crickets!' and 'Gosh darn ut!' and 'Fer the love o' Mike!' It was rather silly, I'll admit; but we enjoyed it.

"Joe and I used to help our fathers with the hog butchering in November. Every family, in those days, had a few hogs in a pen. The time came, when we were in our late 'teens, that the annual slaughter was left pretty much to our management, and we usually combined forces—pulling it off at the Anderson place, where they had better facilities for such work. We became quite expert butchers, and were very proud of our accomplishment. I dare say our fathers flattered us in the hope of making us too vain to see how glad they were to dodge the job.

"Well, one day, after Joe and I had retired from our business concerns, we were having lunch together at the Country Club. It was brand splinter new; had been open only a week. The only natural hazard, on the golf course, was a little stream where Joe and I used to fish for crawdads and minneys. Nobody ever said 'minnows.' On the knoll, where the new club house stood, there had been quite a nice little grove. Joe and I used to sit among those trees, on a log, slapping mosquitoes, and watching for grey squirrels. He owned an old muzzle-loading shotgun. Mighty dangerous toy, too. Wonder we weren't killed a dozen times.

"We were having a good time reminiscing. It seemed queer to be sitting there, on that spot, lunching at a solid mahogany table sprinkled with Venetian doyleys that slid about under crested silver. Everybody belonging to that club had plenty of money, and the club house had been built and equipped without regard for expense. There was a lot of swank too. The servants seemed to have been let into the secret that this was one of our better clubs. The institution was by way of becoming a bit snobbish, we feared. Practically all the natives who belonged to it had been derived from quite humble origins, like Joe's and mine; and we worried a bit about the decline of the old democracy. It struck us that the mere fact of our having accidentally made a little money didn't require us to pretend we were of the British peerage.

"At adjoining tables sat some of the second-growth crop of Axionites—male and female—talking about polo and Derbies and regattas and Biarritz and grouse in Scotland;

and we thought the general tone of the place should be improved. So we fell to discussing some of the good old times the Axion boys and girls used to have before the automobiles came along and scared the horses off the roads, and drove the cows out of the pastures to make room for the golfers. Then, one of us remembered about the butchering.

"Joe recalled that one time we put on a contest to see which of us could dress a hog in the shortest time. I recalled the incident perfectly, but was sure I had won the small stake we had put up. Joe disputed me so strongly that the neighbouring tables became interested and, presently, alarmed. When we observed that we had collected quite a sizable audience, we obligingly continued our debate chiefly for their benefit. The upshot of the argument was that Joe and I bet a thousand dollars aside that each of us could dress a hog in less time than the other. The old chaps, when they heard of it, insisted that the contest be held in the grillroom, and a book was made which, I learned afterwards, involved bets running into scandalous sums.

"The engagement was put on the club calendar. I'm not sure it was pointed to with much pride by the younger set; but the old fellows seemed to want it there, and, seeing their wishes really had to be consulted, more or less, the polo crowd waived their objections. On the next Tuesday, after luncheon, no man went back to his office—if he had one. Two live pigs—pretty good sized ones, too—were fetched in crated. A tarpaulin was spread on the grill-room floor, and Joe and I stripped to the skin and put on butchers' togs. We went through it, from squeal to sausage. I was told, afterwards, that the club house had to be gone over, from crypt to spire. They had grease on the stairsteps and bristles in the soup and cracklings in the rugs for days thereafter."

"Did it improve the democratic tone of the club?" asked Masterson, laughing.

Old Nicholas shook his head and smiled.

"No. I don't think so. Once you outgrow the simplicities, you can't recover them or even remember them with any satisfaction. It's not far, you know, from corn pone to plum pudding, but it's a long way back!"

"What do you make of our new second generation, Mr. Merrick?" inquired Masterson.

"You mean—yours and Bobby's, perhaps? Yours is the third, you know—counting from where I am. Well—I presume there's more to be hoped for from yours than from the one that immediately preceded you."

Nicholas' eyes strayed in Bobby's direction, and he continued, "There's a youngster, for example, preparing to be a doctor. His father, at his age, was an amateur deer-slayer. When Clif heard about this hog-dressing episode, he was considerably excited. I said, 'But, Clif, I heard you bragging about skinning and curing a buck.' 'Oh, well,' he said, 'that was quite a different matter.'...And—I 'spect it was," he added generously, after a pause.

"Our family"—there was a trace of cynicism in Masterson's tone—"has been curiously undisturbed by the problems incident to the accumulation of large fortune. My father is the editor of a small town paper in Indiana. His father was a country doctor, his grandfather a Methodist circuit rider. All the trouble that money has ever given us has been how to get enough of it to pay our bills...But, so far as Bobby is concerned, he isn't running true to type, at all...He's a biological—or, should one say—a fiscal sport?"

Nicholas was meditative.

"Well, yes—Bobby's case is, as you say, somewhat unusual."

Masterson's corrugated brow signed that he was tuning his kettledrums to this key and would presently be holding forth again unless promptly checked.

"Let's not bother to diagnose my case," protested Bobby, with an amicable growl. "Besides, I haven't done anything yet. And this is no time for serious talk...Grandpère— how about telling Tommy the story of the time you and Mr. Anderson bet on which one of you could mow the most hay in an hour."

Masterson furtively glanced at his watch and was caught at it by old Nicholas who immediately pushed back his chair, ignoring Bobby's suggestion, and led the way toward the big drawing-room where he paused to toy with the music on the piano desk.

"What's this 'Unfinished Symphony,' Bobby?...Mind playing it for us?"

"Not much in a mood for that one, Grandpère...Too stuffed. We need something a bit livelier."

"How about this one—'Neapolitan Nights'?"

"Pretty good; but it's rather soft and sticky too for a holiday celebration."

"Something with a lot of bang in it, then," said Nicholas, sinking with a satisfied sigh into a deep chair.

Masterson edged up to Bobby and muttered, under his breath, "I say, do you think your grandfather would take it nicely if I ran along? I've promised to look in, later, at

Gordon's. There's a special little party on there to-night...a Revue...Wouldn't care to come along, would you?"

"Who will be there?"

"Oh—everybody! The old gang...that you've snooted so damnably for months!"

Bobby was thoughtful for a moment; then, quite on impulse and greatly to Masterson's surprise, he said, "I believe I will, Tommy. I'd rather like to see the bright lights again, myself. It's been a good while."

Masterson drummed nervously on the top of the piano. Recalling himself suddenly, he said with enthusiasm, "Attaboy, old mole! Let's tell Grandpère and hop...Just make the eight-twenty-five...In at midnight. Right time to be there."

"You weren't taking anybody, were you?"

"Well—yes," Tom admitted hesitantly. "That is, I had a tentative arrangement to pick up Joyce Hudson, around midnight, and drive her out—provided it was quite agreeable I should return from here. But there's no reason why you can't come with us, is there?'

"Not so good!...Don't care to horn in...But—I'll run down with you and spend the night at Grandpère's club...Have to be there in the morning, anyway...Perhaps I'll drop in for a look at Gordon's...We'll see."

Old Nicholas was glad enough to have done with both of them. So long as they stayed, he must be mindful of his sacred obligation as host. Late that afternoon he had arrived at a most perplexing situation in *The Tragedy in Stateroom 33*, and was feverish to discover whether the pilot, whom the count had tied up in the closet, would contrive to release himself and warn the American girl before the motor-launch returned with the conspirators.

"Willing you should go?" rumbled Nicholas, as they scampered upstairs, "Great Snakes!"

CHAPTER X

GORDON'S!...Gordon's—the colourful!...Gordon's—the exotic!...Gordon's at two-thirty in the morning!...Brilliantly lighted, packed to suffocation, strangling in the smoke, sticky with sweat; shrill with gin, begotten of dirty messes in mouldy cellars and proudly carried in monogrammed silver flasks; clamorous with the new music but lately imported, duty free, from the head waters of the Congo and brought to triumphant perfection by the highest paid orchestra in the States—fresh from New York where its engagement had been abruptly terminated by a padlock...Gordon's Gardens!

Fiddles squeaked, saxophones squealed, oboes giggled, clarionets wailed, tubas yawped, triangles clanged..."Lament of the Damned," perhaps?...Not at all!..."I'm Lonesome and Blue for You."

Bobby Merrick, waiting in the rococo lobby for his coat check, listened with the ear of a man from Mars and drew a crooked smile.

His coming had been quite on impulse. Long before the train had reached Detroit, he had made up his mind not to go out to Gordon's. The announcement of his decision had, he observed, eased the constraint that had fallen upon their talk. Tom had brightened, visibly, though making gallant pretence of disappointment.

"I've a book that interests me," explained Bobby. "I'd rather go to the club and read it than mill around with a lot of high school sheiks."

"And then there's your rheumatism, Uncle Dudley!" sniffed Masterson. "You ought to be careful at your age...Aw—why don't you snap out of it?"

"No—I've graduated from all that stuff. It's the bunk! It's too depressing, Tommy...Everybody pretending!...Little chap at the next table poking his fork occasionally into a cold dinner that costs him seventeen dollars for the two of them—half his week's wages...Hopping up with his mouth full to push Mazie around again through the wriggling pack, wishing he had the courage to ask her to marry him, and wondering where he'd dig up three hundred for a sparkler...Mazie wouldn't wear one that cost a nickel less...And that sad wail they dance to; though—God knows—one can't blame Clarence for liking sad music. He's a sad young man. His credit's bad with his papa, and he's been drinking too much Dago mash."

"Have you ever thought of joining the W.C.T.U.?"

"Don't get peevish, Tommy. You run out to Gordon's and give 'em what you got for your last story, and I'll go read my book."

"That must be a damned fine book. What's its name?"

"Oh—it's a treatise by a medical man. You couldn't read it."

"Taking yourself rather seriously, aren't you?"

"Aesculapius is as jealous as Jehovah, my son."

By consent, they had stopped ragging each other, and Bobby was asking interestedly about various members of the set from which his attention had lately been deflected.

On mention of Joyce's name, he inquired casually, "Seeing much of her, these days, Tommy?"

Masterson nodded.

"Serious?"

"I wish it might be thought so."

"Upstage with you, is she?"

"Quite!...And you damned well know why!"

"Nonsense! I haven't seen her for a whole year!"

"Well, it isn't nonsense...not with her. You're very much on her mind, doc."

Bobby repudiated the idea with a gesture.

"Fine girl!...Wish you luck, Tommy!"

"Thanks! Go bump yourself off, and maybe I'll have it."

"By the way, Tommy, do you see something of the young Mrs. Hudson occasionally?"

"Of course...Gorgeous...Irreproachable and unapproachable!...Goes nowhere...In mourning, you know...Southern old school notions about weeds—and all that...She'll come out of it one of these days and stir up a sensation!...Lovely?...Gad!...Don't know her, do you? Well, then you've never been anywhere and hain't seen nothin'!"

"Bad as that? I'll call sometime and give myself a treat."

"You'd better not...You've hard work to do, and shouldn't be distracted."

The train groaned and ground into the ugliest station between Bombay and the Aurora Borealis, and they parted to hail taxis, promising each other an early meeting.

* * * * *

Cordially welcomed and comfortably established at the Columbia Club, Bobby slipped out of his clothes and into a dressing-gown to resume his work on the Hudson Journal. It was the beginning of a new chapter which took the reader into the author's confidence more intimately than before, as if, having met the latter half-way by the very act of proceeding with the translation, the legatee of the book was now on new terms of comradeship.

< br>

It is important that you should know how serious are the conditions to be met by any man who hopes to increase his own power by way of the technique I pursued under instructions from Randolph.

I must mention them, at this juncture, because it is quite possible these words may be read by some impulsive enthusiast who, eager to avail himself of the large rewards promised, may attempt experiments from which he will receive neither pleasure nor benefit; and, dismayed by failure, find himself worse off in mind than he was before.

Indeed, this was my own experience at first, Randolph having neglected to warn me that certain conditions were imperative to success. I learned them by trial and error.

It must be borne in mind, at the outset, that no amount of altruistic endeavour—no matter how costly—can possibly benefit the donor, if he has in any manner neglected the natural and normal obligations to which he is expected to be sensitive. Not only must he be just before attempting to be generous; he must figure this particular investment of himself as a *higher altruism,* quite other than mere generosity.

Every conceivable responsibility must have had full attention before one goes in search of opportunity to perform secret services to be used for the express purpose of expanding one's personality that it may become receptive of that inexplicable energy which guarantees personal power.

My own life had been set in narrow ways. I had had but small chance to injure or defraud, even had I been of a scheming disposition. There had been a minimum of buying and selling in my programme. I had lived mostly under strict supervision—in school, in college and as an interne—with no chance to make many grave or irretrievable blunders.

Once I began to discharge my obligations, however, it was startling to note how considerably I was in the red. For example: I found that there were a good many men, scattered here and there, who had been scratched off my books. Either actually, or to all practical intents, they had been told to go to hell. In some cases, there had been enough provocation to justify my pitching them out of my life, I thought. But, more often than otherwise, they were to be remembered as persons with whom I had sustained some manner of close contact—close enough to make a disruption possible. I discovered that almost without exception the people I had pushed away from me—consigned to hell, if you like—were once intimately associated with me...So far as I was concerned they had gone to hell taking along with them a very considerable part of me!

To lose a friend in whom one had invested something of one's personality was, I discovered, to have lost a certain amount of one's self.

The successful pursuit of the philosophy now before you demands that you restore whatever of your personality has been dissipated, carted off by other people. If any of its essential energy has been scattered, it must be recovered.

The original proposer of this theory, aware of the importance of insuring against such losses, advised that all misunderstandings should be settled on the spot. When an estrangement takes a friend out of your normal contacts with him, he leaves with part of you in his hand. You must gather up these fragments of yourself, by some hook or crook, so that you have at least all of the personality that rightfully belongs to you, before you attempt its larger projection.

In the next place: you may make the mistake of seeking far and wide for opportunities to build yourself into other personalities through their rehabilitation. A happy circumstance kept me from doing that. Strangely enough, the first really important service I was permitted to do, prefatory to experimenting with this mysterious dynamic, was for the daughter of the man who had shown me the way to it...I risked what small repute I had, and put a mortgage on whatever I might hope to acquire by the performance of an operation that saved her life, and, quite incidentally, brought me three pages of comment in the next edition of the *Medical Encyclopædia*.

Bobby left his papers as they were, dressed carefully, called a taxi, and proceeded to Gordon's. He had no one definite answer to give to himself for his sudden decision. If queried, he would have had to say that there came a moment when he felt he was needed at Gordon's. Certainly he was not going in quest of pleasure.

* * * * *

His arrival at the famous cabaret could not have been better timed. An hour earlier he would have found a noisy, chaffing welcome at a table of silly and excited friends hopeful of seeing him as drunk as themselves; half resentful of his appearance sober.

Because it was a festival night, the cabaret's bill of amusements was more elaborate than usual.

The girl chorus, obviously much the worse for the holiday hospitality—during intermissions they were accorded many courtesies at the tables of diners—were softly caterwauling the refrain of a popular opera song, while a huge fellow, open-shirted, velvet-trousered, and bandanna-ed in a bandit rôle, held the spotlight with a solo dance.

Aleppo was the headliner on the bill. Primarily an acrobat and strong man, with fancy dancing and a bit of florid song to supplement his feats of agility and strength, Aleppo's versatility was acknowledged with tumultuous applause. Smug satisfaction and self-assurance were spelled in every line of his swarthy face as he executed his intricate dance steps.

Bobby waited, just inside the entrance, until the number should be finished. He was too far from the stage to hear Aleppo's announcement. Some time afterwards, he learned that the cad had called for a volunteer dancing partner from the audience. A tall blonde, in blue chiffon, was unsteadily mounting the steps to the stage. She lurched into the big dancer's arms, and he swung her into rhythm with him in a fast and furious fox-trot. The girl was Joyce Hudson.

The crowd cheered them lustily. The orchestra took fresh interest. The chorus receded to give them room.

Eager to offer a final thrill to his audience, the huge Aleppo lifted his amateur teammate to his shoulder. No one but an experienced acrobat could have met the situation gracefully. Aleppo continued to spin about the stage with light steps. His burden meant nothing to him. Dizzily drunk, Joyce swayed, clutched at Aleppo's shaggy head for support, and sank back limply over his shoulder, while he, with big, muscled arms encircling her knees, revolved like a top, quite as if the act had been rehearsed, and he need have no concern about his partner's safety. Joyce's hair stood straight from her head and her arms wildly groped as the rapid revolutions of the dancer whirled her through the air.

Bobby could not remember later how he arrived at the stage. There was some ruthless elbowing through the crowd, chairs upset, tables pushed aside, as he made his way. He ran up the steps and confronting the dancer with an outstretched arm commanded him to stop. His face was grim and pale. With an ironical smile, Aleppo eluded the intruder, and Bobby rushed. Pandemonium broke loose among the tables, and the diners jostled about the foot of the stage.

Tom Masterson forced his way through the crowd, climbed the steps, and clutched at Bobby's sleeve.

"What the hell's the matter with you?" he screamed. "If Joyce wants to have a bit of fun with this fellow, what business is it of yours?"

The orchestra had stopped now. Aleppo put Joyce down, and she crumpled on the floor. Several girls from the chorus bent over her, and one ran for water.

With a pugilistic swagger, Aleppo strode forward. His beady little eyes flashed dangerously. His pugnacious jaw seemed coming along somewhat in advance of him. His big fists were clenched. Baring his teeth in a crooked grin, he snarled: "Now!—You're so damned anxious to get into trouble—"

"Look out!" shouted Masterson, "Don't do that!"

"Sock him!" yelled some youngster from the crowd.

Aleppo advanced belligerently until he was within reach of a surprise.

There were three quick, crunching blows in his face, a right to his left eye, a left to his right eye, and a right to the point of his chin. The big fellow's knees buckled under him, and he collapsed without a sigh.

It was very quiet at Gordon's for a moment. Everybody was stunned by the sudden turn of events.

Roughly pushing Masterson aside, Bobby turned to Joyce, stooped and gathered her up in his arms, and started down the steps of the stage, the crowd falling back to make way for him.

"Just a minute!" shouted Masterson, pursuing him. "I'll take care of her. You needn't be so officious!"

Bobby turned toward him, and said in a low voice, "You should have taken care of her a little sooner!"

Masterson was in a drunken rage over his humiliation.

"Well—if you think you can get away with that—"

He clutched Bobby's throat, ripping off his collar; clawed at his hair; his cuff-link dug deeply into his friend's cheek, and the blood flowed freely, dripping from his jaw to his shirt bosom.

Supporting his limp charge with his left arm, Bobby let loose a short-arm jab at the pit of Masterson's none too able stomach, which demoted him to the ranks of the noncombatants, and, taking Joyce again in his arms, marched forward, pushing chairs and tables out of his way with their bodies.

At the door, the burly head waiter barred his progress.

"Did you bring this young lady here?"

"No! But I am taking her away!"

"Well—not so fast! Let's look into this!"

Again Bobby lowered Joyce's feet to the floor, steadied her with his left arm, and growled, "Open that door! I have no intention of mixing it with anybody else here to-night, but if you try to stop me I'll put you to sleep alongside your little friend up there."

The bruiser hesitated. Someone shouted, "Let him go, before the joint gets pinched! He'll see her home! Here—take her coat!"

* * * * *

The crisp blast of cold air swept Joyce back to partial consciousness.

A waiting taxi drove up under the *porte-cochère*. Bobby lifted her in, told the grinning driver to head east on the boulevard and he'd let him know presently where they wanted to go, and seated himself beside her.

Confusedly she recognized him, looked up dully into his face and mumbled thickly, "Oh, Bobby, you came at last, didn't you? I've waited so long! I've wanted you so?"

She nestled her head against his shoulder, and he put his arm around her, spared the necessity of replying, for her revival was brief. In a moment she slumped and slept.

Now he'd got her, what should he do with her? It occurred to him he might take her some place and sober her up before presenting her at home, an idea he instantly rejected. She wouldn't be even approximately normal for hours. Joyce was drunk, and no mistake!...Had he really done her a good turn with his swashbuckling excursion into her affairs? Perhaps it would result in more damaging notoriety for her than had she been left to go her own gait...Could he and Tom Masterson ever be friends again?...Doubtful.

The driver turned his head for definite instructions, and Bobby gave Joyce's address. He'd have to take her home. Maybe he could put her into the house without stirring it up. He shook her awake as they neared the corner.

"Joyce! Where is your house-key?"

She began to fumble with her coat, and, acting on the clue, he discovered it in an inside pocket. The taxi drew up at the kerb and the driver obeyed his fare's order to shut off the engine and wait.

Rousing, as the cold air rushed in through the opened door, Joyce twined her arms about Bobby's neck and kissed him on the cheek. He was bleeding, but she was too far gone to notice.

It was easier to carry than drag her. The front door was quickly reached, opened and closed quietly. He remembered the appointments of the house. Depositing her on the davenport in the living-room, he drew off her slippers and covered her with a heavy steamer rug. Her face was bloody. That would undoubtedly call for explanations which would drag out the whole story, adding even more discredit to her plight and more chagrin to someone else whose dignity better deserved protection.

Presuming there must be a lavatory on the main floor, he looked about for it, and having made experimental forays into two coat closets, finally discovered the little wash room off the library; dampened a towel, and was on his way back with it when he heard a throaty voice that had never quite left his consciousness. It so completely bridged the weeks that it seemed to take on exactly where it had left off, "Good night, then—and thank you so much!"—"Joyce, you've been hurt!"

There was no reply...and a moment's silence. Doubtless she was noticing the light in the library. Perhaps she had observed his coat, tossed across a chair. He decided not to be caught in ambush...They met at the door.

She seemed not quite so tall as he had remembered her, possibly because the little red and black slippers had lower heels. The disarray of her bobbed head, her tousled bangs, made her look like a child suddenly roused from sleep, to which juvenile effect her suit of Japanese pyjamas contributed—black with red poppies, buttoned high about her throat. Bobby was aware of the exquisiteness of her ensemble, but all that he saw distinctly was her bewildered blue eyes searching his with mystification.

On sight of him she gasped with surprise; put the back of her hand to her lips as if warding off a blow; stared inquiringly at his blood-smeared cheek.

"Why—it's *you*!" she whispered. "Whatever are you doing here?"

"I brought Joyce home...I'm sorry I startled you...I'd rather hoped we might not have to disturb you."

"But I thought she was going away with Mr. Masterson. Was he hurt? You've been, I see! Was there an accident?"

"Something like that...Nothing serious at all...And Joyce isn't hurt. She's just—just pretty tired and sleepy."

"Her face is bloody...You were going to do something about it, I notice."

He handed her the towel.

"You'll find she's not hurt. That blood she rubbed off me when I brought her in. I thought I would wash it off so you wouldn't be alarmed when you saw her."

For a long moment they stood gazing, appraisingly, into each other's eyes—hers wide with curiosity, hurt with disappointment, but half-sympathetic; his, eloquent with appeal for suspended judgment; both of them at a loss for words to meet their predicament; unable to release themselves from this speechless recognition of their brief comradeship's claims.

"So—you knew you were coming to my house, then...Perhaps you'll tell me who you are...You didn't say—that other time."

Into Helen's eyes, and, an instant afterwards, upon her lips, there came the suggestion of a smile. Bobby hesitated: then blurted out, "Merrick."

"So you're Bobby Merrick!" Her eyes narrowed. She dug her little fists into her ribs with a defiance that would have seemed deliciously absurd had the occasion been less serious; for she had not been naturally cast for tragic rôles and her costume was everything but militant. "You hadn't brought us enough trouble, had you? What we'd been through wasn't quite sufficient! You must add a little humiliation to it! You've brought Joyce home to me drunk! You look as if you had been drinking, too!...Fighting, weren't you?...If you could only see yourself!...Oh!"

"Yes—I know. I'm not very pretty to look at—and the evidence isn't good. Joyce will tell you all about in the morning...Meant it all right...Sorry."

"You'd better go now."

He caught up his top-coat.

"It's too bad!" he muttered, half to himself, as he passed her.

As if he were already out of the house, Helen sank down on the davenport at Joyce's feet, put both her hands over her face and cried like a little child threatened with punishment. It was a devastating scheme. She seemed so pitiably alone, so desperately in need of a friendly word.

With arrested step, Bobby regarded her with a deeper compassion than he had ever experienced, swept again with that strange sense of their belonging. He turned and took a hesitating step toward her. Suddenly aware of him and divining his thought, she slowly shook her head.

"No...There's nothing you can do for us...but go!"

His voice was torn with pity.

"I can't leave you this way...Am I to remember you—always—sitting in a crumpled little heap—crying because I had hurt you?" He bent over her with extended hand. "Say good night to me, won't you?"

Her eyes travelled up to his face.

"You're still bleeding," she said dully. "Better do something...Go in there and wash it off."

Tossing aside his coat, Bobby returned to the little lavatory, disinterestedly mopped at his stains and flung down the towel, bitterly...She was waiting in the open doorway when he turned; leaning limply back against the door-post, face upturned, eyes closed, with a roll of surgical bandage, adhesive tape, and scissors in her hands.

"You're mighty thoughtful." He reached for the dressings.

"Not at all," she said evenly, ignoring his gesture. "I'd do as much for a hurt dog...I was too upset to notice that you really needed attention...Come over here to the light. I'll try to fix you."

He followed her to the table. With deft fingers she shaped a gauze pad, sheared off some strips of tape, and gave her attention to his torn cheek with all the impersonal interest of a veteran nurse in a charity clinic...The sleeves of her jacket slipped back as she reached up...The touch of her hands on his face, the warm nearness of her, the little tremulous catch in her throat when she breathed, set his heart racing furiously.

"There!" she said at length, lifting the longest lashes he had ever seen, and looking inquiringly into his eyes, "Does that feel better?"

* * * * *

Hours afterward, when her tempest of indignation had subsided through sheer fatigue, her self-reproaches began to eclipse the scorn she felt for him.

Exquisitely tortured, she had lived it over and over again, each second of it—for it had all happened swiftly—as one who follows the minutia of motion on a slow film.

Perhaps, had she turned away at once, he might have stammered his appreciation and left...How indiscreet of her to have looked up, at close range, to inquire, with honest solicitude, "Does that feel better?"

It felt so much better, apparently, that he must express his thanks by taking her hand, as it was withdrawn from his face, lifting it quickly to his lips. She jerked it away from him angrily...Later, as she thought it over in her chaos of angry shame, she reflected it would have been better had she submitted dignifiedly to his impulsive gesture of gratitude...and signed him to be off.

He stood humiliated, abased, as if she had struck him a blow. Then, huskily, measuring his words, he said, "I wonder if you would have done *that* to a hurt dog, grateful for a little unexpected kindness."

What a slyly mean advantage to have taken of her sympathy—of her instinctive courtesy!

"That was awfully rude of me...I've been through a lot, to-night...I'm not quite myself...Please go—now."

She should have commanded; not entreated.

"I know you have been cruelly troubled...and it nearly breaks my heart!" he had said.

As she milled it over, with her flushed face buried deep in her pillow, she tried to explain how it all happened. For an instant, when he had put his arms gently about her, she forgot that he was Bobby Merrick. Bobby Merrick was just some mythical person she didn't want to know. She remembered only that this was the quiet, pensive, lovable chap who had led her like a little child along a dark country lane...And she was so desolately lonely and in need of tenderness.

He softly touched her wet eyes with his handkerchief...How could she have stood there, calmly submitting to his impudent attentions?...What had she been thinking of to allow herself to be placed in such an impossible predicament? What a beast he had been to make capital of her yearning for a bit of human kindness...at a moment when, he knew, her whole world was breaking up under her feet!...Well, he surely was made aware, before he left, what she thought of his despicable treatment of her!...Hadn't she told him, so bitterly, so scathingly, that he had cringed under it?...But—that was small balm for her injured pride...She had actually stood with her forehead pressed against his arm, while his slim fingers caressed her hair, utterly unable to exert her will...dreamily visioning a thin trickle of fine sand pouring into a small red-brown heap at the bottom of an hour-glass...and wondering how to shut it off...Why—she must have been hypnotized!

"Won't you forgive me—now?" he whispered.

Why couldn't she have freed herself, smiled; agreed—in a matter-of-fact tone, "I'll not hold anything against you. Good night."...She repeated into her pillow several variants of that commonplace, devoutly wishing she could remember having said it; trying to persuade herself she really had.

But he had pleaded so wistfully!...She had lifted her eyes, and her lips were parted to speak a single word of friendly assurance when—it happened...And she had offered no resistance!...Oh—how cheap he must think her! How little respect he had had for her—widowed because of him—and, worst of all, he would probably be cad enough to imagine that she had responded to his kiss...It was the haunting fear he might think she had shared it that tortured her most.

Of course—she had done what she could, quickly, savagely, to reinstate herself in his regard. Breaking free, she had pushed him from her; forbade him ever to speak to her again; left the room in a grand state of emotional tumult without so much as pausing to glance at the stupefied Joyce, heavily sleeping through a scene that could not have failed to interest her, had she been aware of it.

Seated before her mirror at nine, gazing remorsefully at her haggard reflection, she straightened, stiffly, and said aloud, "Well, whatever he may care to think, I'm certain I didn't."

* * * * *

Sleepy servants at the Columbia Club grinned and exchanged winks when Bobby arrived at a quarter to four, sullen and dishevelled.

"Teddy," he growled to the elevator boy, "bring me a bottle of Scotch and a syphon of soda."

He disrobed, mixed a stiff drink, and another, and a third, in swift succession, scowled hatefully at himself in the bathroom mirror and muttered "Piker!"...He had forfeited the thing he most wanted—the only thing he wanted in this world!...Now she would never consent to see him again...She had said it, and she meant it. He had imposed upon her kindness; had stampeded her into an impetuous response to his sympathy which she would regret with self-loathing...What was the good of anything—now?

The Hudson journal lay on the desk where he had left it; a sheaf of club stationery beside it, scrawled with rows of letters.

He gave the book a contemptuous push with the back of his hand and it fell into the waste-basket.

"Damned silly nonsense!" he muttered. "To hell with all that kind of blah!"

CHAPTER XI

"PLEASE be seated, Mr. Merrick," the secretary had said, stiffly, twenty minutes ago. "Dean Whitley is busy now."

A qualitative analysis of Mr. Merrick's scowl as he sat fidgeting would have resolved it into two parts curiosity, three parts anxiety and the remainder annoyance. .Of chagrin—a trace.

The note had said eleven, and he had entered while the clock was striking. It had not specified what the dean wished to see him about. That would have been too much to expect. Courtesy and consideration were against the rules governing the official action of deans.

Big universities, like monopolistic public utilities and internal revenue offices, enjoyed high-hatting their constituencies; liked to make an impressive swank with their authority; liked to keep people waiting, guessing, worrying; liked to put 'em to all the bother possible.

Mr. Merrick glowered. He glowered first at the large photograph of an autopsy suspended above the secretary's desk in the corner...Seven doctors owling it over a corpse. All of the doctors were paunchy, their pendulous chins giving them the appearance of a covey of white pelicans. They were baggy under the eyes...a lot of fat ghosts swathed in shrouds. The corpse too was fat. Why conduct a post over this bird? Any layman could see at a glance what had ailed him—he was a glutton. Let these wiseacres take warning in the presence of this plump cadaver, and go on a diet of curds and spinach before some committee put them on a stone slab and rummaged in their cold capacious bellies to enhance the glory of *materia medica*...They were the bunk—the whole greasy lot of them!

Having temporarily finished with the autopsy, Dean Whitley's impatient customer glowered over the titles of the big books in the case hard by...Simpson's *Nervous Diseases*...the old sap. You had to read his blather in front of a dictionary; weren't ten words in the whole fourteen pounds of wood-pulp with less than seven syllables...Mount's *Obsessions*... Why was it that these bozos thought it unscholarly to be intelligible and undignified to be interesting? And as for obsessions, old Mount was a nut himself—one of these cuckoos that tapped every third telegraph pole with his cane and spat on fireplugs...If he missed one, he had to go back, it was said...About the same mentality as Fido's. Well, Mount ought to be an authority on obsessions!

A tall, rangy medic came out of the dean's sanctum, very red but with a jaunty stride, crossed the room in four steps and banged the door...Bet it was no new experience for that door!

Distracted from his invoice of the book shelf, Mr. Merrick glowered at the bony maiden who rattled the typewriter. Smug and surly she was; mouth all screwed up into an ugly little rosette, lashless eyes snapping, sharp nose sniffing...Easy to see what she was doing—writing a letter to some poor boob inviting him to come in at nine and see the dean...She ought to add a postscript that he would be expected to spend half of a fine June morning in this dismal hole waiting for his nibs to finish the *Free Press* and his nails, take his legs off the table, and push a buzzer to let the beggar in.

"Dean Whitley will see you now, Mr. Merrick."

* * * * *

"Mr. Merrick," said Dean Whitley, after Bobby had taken the chair recommended to him, "I must have a friendly chat with you. During the first few weeks of last semester, you gave promise, I am informed, of an exceptionally interesting career in the medical profession. Shortly after the mid-semester examinations, which I see you passed with the highest marks of your class, you began to slip. You quickly used up all your cuts. You became disinterested and disgruntled. What's the trouble?"

"I think you'll find I've been doing average work, sir."
Dean Whitley shook a long, bony finger.
"Exactly! Average work! Do you hanker to be an average doctor?"
"Well—when you put it that way—of course not."
The dean tilted back in his swivel-chair and clasped his hands behind his head.
"Your case is somewhat unusual, Merrick. You are the heir apparent to a large fortune. You did not have to seek a vocation. It was a surprise to all your friends that you came here. Your line of least resistance was polo. But you plunged into your work with an enthusiasm that put the whole first-year class on its toes and challenged the instructional corps to offer the best it had. Now—precisely what has happened to your spirit? Is there anything we can do to put you in the running again?"
Bobby twisted the links of a platinum watch-chain, head hanging.
"You're quite right, Dean Whitley. I suppose it was the novelty kept me alive at first."
"Yes—but see here!" The dean reversed a sheaf of tabulations and pushed it across the table. "Just follow that line from opening day to the Thanksgiving recess, and there isn't a cut! You didn't flick a class!...Pursue it the rest of the way and see what you did to your scholastic credit!...What happened to you on or about Thanksgiving?...Perhaps you should be treated for it—whatever it was. You're too promising to lose if we can save you!"
"I just got tired of it. Too much drudgery."
"It wasn't drudgery before!"
"Well—I think I began to notice that it was, about that time."
"Ever think of giving it up?"
"Oh—no, sir! I can't do that!"
"Why not? You don't aspire to be a mere second-rater, do you?"
"I suppose I'll have to content myself with that. I'll have plenty of company, won't I?"
The dean fiddled with a paper-knife and looked down his nose glumly.
"This is very disappointing!...Sure you don't want to give me your full confidence and let me try to help you?"
Bobby moved to the edge of his chair, and took up his hat.
"There's nothing you can do, sir. Thank you for your interest. I'll try to do better."

* * * * *

On the front steps he met Dawson, a first-year medic with whom he had a mere nodding acquaintance. Dawson was a lean-faced, hollow-eyed, shabby chap, who had a desperate time of it trying to keep up. Slightly older than the average, more was expected of him than he was able to deliver. Not infrequently he was scornfully panned by his instructors who seemed to enjoy watching him wince under their satirical jabs.

A question, having been muffed by three or four, would be tossed at him in some such fashion as, "And of course *you* wouldn't know, would you, Mr. Dawson?" Seven times out of nine, he wouldn't. Bobby's sympathy had been excited, occasionally...What were they trying to do to the poor devil?...Drive him into the river?
"Hello, Merrick!...Been deaning?"
"Oh yes," said Bobby brightly. "But not in the way you probably suspect. You see, the dean and I meet frequently for a game of cribbage. He's good too. I presume you're having tea with him presently?"
Dawson was grim.
"Naw—I'm going in to tell him I'm through and that they can all go to hell!"
"That would be a great blunder, Dawson." Bobby became owlishly didactic. "They might go—and where would that leave you? You see, my son, every time you send a man

to hell, with whom you have had close personal contacts, he takes part of you along with him. And then, some fine day, when things are ever so much better with you, and you need to collect all there is of your scattered personality for some noble purpose, a considerable chunk of you is missing—and—and you have to go to hell after it."

"What's the big idea? Trying to kid me? If so, don't! I'm in no mood for it...Up to the last ditch—if you don't mind my weepin' on your neck!"

"How about a bite of lunch together?" suggested Bobby, amazed at his own proposal of hospitality to this morose, threadbare fellow. "All you're seeing him for is to tell him to go to hell. Put it off till to-morrow. He won't object to the delay."

Yielding with a crooked smile to Bobby's persuasion, Dawson fell into step.

"Anything you'd like to get off your chest?" inquired his host, after their order had been given. "Perhaps you'd enjoy singing a few verses of your hymn of hate. If so, go to it—and I'll join you in the chorus where the fancy damning comes in."

"Thanks, Merrick. You're a good sort. Perhaps it wouldn't be bad for me to let off steam. I'll tell you a little about it...I always wanted to be a surgeon...prattled about it as a child...never thought of anything else...thought of it as a novitiate in holy orders thinks of his vocation!...After college, I was out for three years trying to scrape up enough to bring me back...Got discouraged: gave it up; fell in love; married. The girl revived the old hope in me...Worked like dogs—both of us; she in an office, I selling bonds...So we came, last September...She found a job...Then the baby came...lot of expenses. Living was higher than we figured...I began to work down town nights in a bowling-alley...setting pins for freshmen to knock down one at a time...How's that for your inferiority complex?"

"Well, it certainly wouldn't drive a man into a state of hallucinatory omnipotence; that's sure!"

"A woolly caterpillar!...That's what it made of me!...No wonder I was a dunce!...And now—as if I hadn't already enough to...But—hell—what's the good of talking about it?"

"Drive on!" commanded Bobby. "It's no farther through to the other side than to back out. Let's have the rest of it. You were a caterpillar and a dunce—and now you're something else again?...What's happened lately?"

"My wife is sick. No—nothing acute. Just fagged and undernourished and neurotic; says she's a dead weight on me and wishes she were dead. She's brooding over it. I'm half afraid to go home for fear I'll find that she has destroyed herself!"

"She should be out in the country for the summer," advised Bobby. "Fresh air, good milk, sunshine."

"Might as well suggest a trip to Europe," muttered Dawson. "We've nothing."

"Hasn't she people she could go to for the summer?"

"Nobody...There's a tight old step-father who threw her out when she married me. He'd picked a yokel for her who lived in the neighbourhood...My mother is a widow, living with my sister, up state. They're poor too and crowded."

"How about a little loan? You're not always going to be on your uppers. Almost anybody would consider that a safe investment, I should think."

"I don't know any one I could approach with a proposition like that."

Bobby's guest ate hungrily. His hand trembled when he cut his meat.

"I have a little money that isn't in use just now."

Dawson shook his head.

"No!—By God, I didn't tell you my story with the hope of panhandling some money out of you. You're probably like all the rest of the medics—just scraping along...Thanks all the same, old man...It's mighty generous of you...No—I'm going to give it up and get a job!"

"You didn't understand me, Dawson. I didn't mean to propose handing you the price of next week's groceries. I'd like to lend you, say, five thousand dollars."

Here was one chap that had accepted him as a pal in poverty...Natural enough, though. Dawson had had his nose to the grindstone; kept aloof from the others. He needn't have heard that there was a wealthy student in the class...And this interview had not been of his seeking.

"You mean that?"

"Of course!...You didn't think I'd joke with you about a business matter involving five thousand dollars, did you?"

Bobby would never have suspected the fellow of so much sparkle and spontaneous wit. He expanded as if some miracle had been performed on him.

"Merrick," he said solemnly, as they reached the street. "You've come near saving a couple of lives to-day!...Mind if I run home now?...I've got to tell her!...I say—wouldn't you like to come along?"

* * * * *

They were a shabby pair of rooms on the third floor of a third-rate apartment house over north of the big hospital, disorderly with the clutter incident to an attempt to make a bedroom, dining-room, nursery and kitchen of such cramped quarters.

Marion Dawson had no apologies to offer for the appearance of her house. Bobby liked her for that. He was instantly delighted with this pale, tawny-haired, hazel-eyed young woman who gave him a man's hand-grip and unloaded a chair for him without a flurry of embarrassment. The baby was dug up for inspection and greeted the visitor with big, blinking eyes, amusingly like his father's. Having had no experience with babies, Bobby regarded this one with something of the same solemn interest it bestowed on him. Marion laughed.

"You can't get acquainted with him that way," she exclaimed. "You've got to boo at him, or something! He expects it, you know. He wouldn't think of making a little ass of himself by booing at you; but he'll be dreadfully disappointed if you don't make some idiotic noises at him."

Bobby knew he was going to like this girl.

"Marion," said Dawson, with an unsteady voice, "Mr. Merrick is going to lend us some money. He says we're a good risk. I'm not sure about me; but I know you are."

She dropped her air of banter and stared at their guest for a long moment, trying to realize the significance of her husband's announcement; then said, with deep feeling, "So—after all we've been through—Jack is to have his chance, at last!" She put a hand on his shoulder. "Dear boy!...It has been so long—so hard for you!"

She reached out her left hand to Bobby and clasped his with grateful fingers. "What a lovely thing for you to do!" she said.

"Oh—everybody has his troubles," stammered Bobby, hoping the situation would be spared a debauch of sentimentality. "The least trouble in the world is a shortage of money."

"Unless one hasn't any," chuckled Dawson.

* * * * *

Bobby arrived late in the little amphitheatre of the surgical clinic, that afternoon. The operation proved of exceptional interest. He found himself leaning far forward. That night, he almost enjoyed his Brill. Before he went to bed at one, he wrote to Nancy Ashford, to whom he had owed a letter for weeks.

"I had a very interesting visit to-day with a young medic and his wife—the Dawsons—" his second page began; but, after looking at the words critically for a moment, he crumpled the page and started a fresh one with no mention of the Dawsons.

"Have you ever deciphered the rest of the journal?"

He had sent it back to her with the brief statement that he didn't care to bother any farther with it...He wasn't the right type to pursue any such philosophy with hope of pleasure or profit, he said, and it really wasn't sporting to read it for curiosity's sake—especially after Doctor Hudson's request that one stop when one's personal interest had flagged.

"Perhaps you will tell me, at least in a general way, how it all came out if you completed it...I learn, in reading about unusual obsessions, that a marked mystical tendency occasionally shows up in the minds of very materialistic people who deal practically, otherwise, with all their interests. I dare say Doctor Hudson was a typical case."

Two days later he had her reply.

"Mrs. Hudson has the journal now, along with all the other things we kept for her in the office safe. I doubt if she has made any effort to discover what it's about. Perhaps she hasn't opened the box in which she received them. At all events, she has not queried me, as she might have done if she had been mystified by the code...I feel confident she would let you have the book, now that your interest in it is revived.

"Yes, I deciphered the rest of it...An amazing record!...If it were done into a book, it would sell a hundred thousand! People would pronounce it utterly incredible, of course; but they would read it—and heartily wish it were true. And I have a notion they would be sneaking off to make experiments, no matter how they might have giggled when discussing the theory with their friends.

"I wish I dared tell you...you know why I cannot...about the quite startling experiences I myself have had lately...It's all true, Bobby. You do get what you want that way, if what you want contributes to the larger expression of yourself in constructive service...You even get letters that had been so long delayed you wondered if you'd been forgotten...Does that sound foolish?"

It sounded foolish.

"I'm sorry," mused Bobby, folding the letter. "Nancy had such an interesting mind. Now she'll be goofy for the rest of her life...Glad I stopped the bally nonsense before it got me."

He smiled bitterly over Nancy's suggestion that he ask Mrs. Hudson for the journal...His contrite note of apology, dated December first, had not been answered. For the first two weeks, he had shadowed the postman.

* * * * *

On the Sunday morning that young Mrs. Dawson and the baby were taken to the country, Bobby, on pressing invitation, joined the party.

The place they had chosen was a quiet cottage owned by a middle-aged widow, a few hundred yards from the shady shore of Pleasant Lake—an hour's railroad trip to the north.

Relieved of his long anxiety, Jack Dawson had lost his pallor. His step was elastic; his shoulders were squared. As for Marion, she was radiant.

They made a picnic of it, and ate their lunch on the lake shore—Jack, junior, left in the custody of Mrs. Plimpton who immediately on being alone with him, decided he would be all the better for a bit of old-fashioned rocking and a few Gospel songs.

"Now—none o' that!" declared Marion, setting out the contents of their basket. "You two old doctors have plenty of chances to talk wisely about disabled gizzards, all through the week. It makes me sick to eat my meals off the operating table, anyway."

Apparently they had known nothing of Bobby's wealth before he had interested himself in them. Doubtless they knew now. But the Dawsons' attitude toward him was unchanged. There was not a trace of shyness or sycophancy. Thoroughbreds—they were. He wished he had a sister exactly like Marion Dawson.

The men took a later afternoon train back to town, separating at the station.

"So long, Bobby," said Dawson. "Thanks much for coming along. See you soon. Glad the stuff's going better for you. You've certainly given me a shot in the arm!"

"It's been good for both of us," said Bobby.

* * * * *

That night he carried out a decision he had resolved upon the day before. Randolph had seemed able to get all the information he wanted from a certain important page of the Galilean report on the one man who apparently knew the principles imperative to an expanded personality. Bobby considered himself entirely capable of pursuing such research as Randolph had made.

He had never owned a copy of the Bible. Yesterday he had bought a testament. The salesman had laid out quite an assortment. Bobby had chosen a copy that looked more like an ordinary secular book than the black ones with limp leather covers. His choice was based upon his expectation of treating it as he would any other book.

He leafed in it, back and forth, for a long time before he came upon the particular thesis which the sculptor had considered important to a man's quest of a dynamic personality. He read it with as much intensity of concentration as he might have studied the map of a strange country through which he expected to travel.

There was a certain quaintness of phrase that intrigued him and commanded his interest. On and on he read, far into the night, without weariness. The little book amazed him. When and if he had thought about it at all, he had considered this ancient document a jumble of soporific platitudes, floating about in a solution of Jewish superstitions, and accepted by simple-minded people as a general cure-all for their petty anxieties and a numbing narcotic to dull their sense of wanting what they couldn't have.

It was rapidly becoming apparent to him that here was one of the most fascinatingly interesting things he had ever read. Not only was it free of the dullness he had ascribed to it; it kept hinting of secrets—secrets of a tremendous energy to be tapped by any man with sense enough to accept the fact of it as he would any other scientific hypothesis, and accord it the same dignity, the same practical tests he might pursue in a chemical or physical laboratory.

It was astounding to feel that he had in his hand the actual textbook of a science relating to the expansion and development of the human personality. How queer that people seemed bent upon setting it to music, and drawing long faces while they piously intoned it! How ridiculous! And how unfortunate! This wasn't the libretto for grand opera, or epic stuff to metre into maudlin little hymns! This was a profound, scientific thesis! The very act of chanting it would be proof you didn't know what it was about!

* * * * *

One of Merrick's most important discoveries, that night, was the fact that unlike the usual scientific dissertation, which would be accessible only to the trained mind, there was enough of simple counsel in the book to be of high advantage to the least sophisticated. It was not a treatise intended for highbrows. But it was plain to see that the potential constituency of the book was sharply classified into groups. With the utmost candour, the Galilean had postulated three types of general capacity related to one another as 5:2:1. He had been entirely frank about saying to his intimates, in an intensive seminar session, that there were certain mysteries he could and would confide to them which he had no intention of discussing before the general public for the reason that the majority of people would be unable to understand.

He noted, also with keen interest, the numerous occasions when the Galilean, having performed a service for someone, would ask him, as a special favour, not to tell anybody about it.

"Practising his own theories, all right!"

It was clear, from the record, that men became interested in this strange, uncanny power by various processes of introduction to it. One man would see the remarkable power and beauty of it in the hands of another, and would resolve to have it for himself if it cost him his last dime. The matter was stated pictorially in a fable concerning a man who saw a pearl in another man's hands and sold everything he had to buy it. It was further stated that occasionally a man came upon this almost incredible thing by sheer accident. There was a story of a traveller who, while taking a short cut across a field, stumbled upon a treasure chest. The book did not say what was in the chest. It just reported that the traveller gave up his journey, went home, converted everything he had into funds, came back, and bought that field.

But nothing struck Bobby more forcibly than the constantly reiterated advice to approach life audaciously. Anything a man really wanted, he could have if he hammered long enough at the doors behind which it was guarded. If he didn't get it, it was because he hadn't wanted it badly enough! No matter how patently futile it was to continue battering the door, any man who wanted anything earnestly enough could open any kind of a door!

"Got to have bloody knuckles," reflected Bobby, "before you can say you tried it and it wouldn't work!"

The fable accompanying this proposition told of a poor widow, with no influence at all, who wanted justice from a rich man. The judge was an utter rascal. The woman had no attorney, no friends, and no case; but she kept coming until she wore the judge out.

He found himself entering more and more confidently into the mood of the man who had proposed these principles of what he called a more abundant life, particularly struck by the poise and audacity.

* * * * *

At length, he closed the book and closed his eyes. He was not conscious of formulating a definite request. Had anybody told him he was praying, he would have been greatly surprised. He was endeavouring to construct a mental image of the kind of a man who might be likely to have proposed such a philosophy.

The thing that happened to him came quite without further invitation than that.

As he attempted to analyse it, later, the sensation he experienced—the most vivid and vital experience he had ever had—was as if a pair of great double-doors, somewhere at that far end of a dark corridor in his mind—in his heart—in his soul—somewhere inside of him—had quietly parted, shedding a soft, shimmering radiance upon the roof, walls and pavement of the long hall. The walls were covered with maps, charts, diagrams, weapons, and glittering instruments and apparatus in glass cases.

It was only a fleeting glimpse. The doors parted but a very little way. They quickly closed, and left the corridor so dark he could no longer tell where it was.

Rousing, bewilderedly, he became conscious of a curious sense of exultation. Had he been asleep? He did not think so.

He rose and walked unsteadily about the room, trying to recover as much as possible of his momentary illusion.

"Doors!...Light behind doors!...Light shining through!...I wonder if the corridor was always there waiting my discovery!...Perhaps I can do something to open those doors wider...I must!...Well, one thing is sure: I've seen it! It's there! It's real!...Maybe I'll never get very far with it—but—it can be done!...Randolph wasn't as crazy as I thought!"

* * * * *

Next morning, as he was starting to the dean's office to arrange for his summer course in the face of old Nicholas' urgent request that he knock off until September and return to Windymere, he received a note from Nancy Ashford.

"Perhaps you've read it in the papers, but I'll make sure, for I know you will be interested. Friday night, Joyce Hudson and Tom Masterson slipped over to Toledo and were married. Mrs. Hudson expects to sail, on Saturday the tenth, for Europe. She just called up to inform me of her plans...Leviathan...I thought you'd want to know."

At intervals, all day, he debated the advisability of sending flowers to the ship, and decided against it. She would probably consider it an impertinence. No—he had irretrievably cut himself off...All that he had left now was his mounting interest in his work, into which he plunged with renewed enthusiasm.

CHAPTER XII

IT was nine o'clock in the morning—early September.

The last of the summer trippers had gone, reluctant to leave all this beauty behind them and pledged to a prompt return...With their hands filled with bulky bouquets of garden flowers, graciously bestowed by long-time servants who seemed sincerely regretful over their departure, they had edged along the slippery seats of the station bus to make room for the tardy, scurrying back from one last look at the blue bay from the terrace wall. They would go down the hill to Bellagio, cross the bay to Menaggio, and take a funny little funicular over the mountain en route west—and home.

The Villa Serbelloni was very quiet, this morning...Not that it was at any time a rackety place, even when filled to its small capacity. There was something about the ineffable tranquillity of the old mansion that slowed one down to its leisurely tempo; that mellowed the voice and blurred the vision.

Its atmosphere seemed strangely sedative, giving a curious unreality to the whole region. One felt one's self walking about through a Corot. The changing cloud-shadows on the mountains and the bay, synchronized with warming wisps of autumn breeze, played unaccountable tricks with one's estimates of distances and hours. One never knew certainly whether it was Tuesday or Thursday—or cared.

Somebody had declared it was as if the picture were blurry...out of focus. There were no sharp, angular outlines either to the purple hills or the turquoise lake below. The very pebbles on the carriage drive were unreal, each wrapped with a tiny, shimmering aureole of pale opal...Each grape, in the shapely clusters dependent from the trellis sheltering the breakfast nook, was encircled by an amber nimbus as if glowing with some inner radiance...An excellent place for day-dreaming.

To appreciate it properly, however, the guest must bring to the little arbour a quiet, unworried mind, else the timeless calm of the place would only accentuate the internal tumult...Unless one were at peace with himself, here, he could be more desperately lonely and depressed than in a desert.

The arbour was all but deserted. Except for the elderly English couple at the last table in the row against the low terraced wall, absorbed in their letters, groping occasionally for the handles of their coffee cups, Helen Hudson had the place to herself. She was so lonesome she watched with comradely concern the antics of an ambitious bee that disputed her right to the little jar of honey.

It might never be determined where was the next to the loveliest spot in the world...La Jolla?...Lake Louise?...The Columbia River Highway?...Royal Gorge?...Grand Canyon?

During her three years abroad, Helen had successively shifted her allegiance from the Grand Canal under a full moon to the Upper Corniche Road, the Amalfi Drive, the Neckar glimpsed through the tree-tops from the crumbling balconies of Heidelberg Castle.

But there never could be any doubt about the *loveliest* scene in the world. She faced it—Lake Como—from the little arbour flanking on the east the Villa Serbelloni, on the hillcrest overlooking Bellagio...looked at it without seeing it to-day; for her eyes were preoccupied.

* * * * *

Her morning mail had practically confirmed certain harassing suspicions. It was reasonably sure now that Monty had been manipulating her estate to her serious disadvantage. How to protect herself against grave misfortune—if indeed that misfortune had not been already guaranteed—without plunging her family into disgraceful publicity, was too intricate a problem to be solved.

Not at any time since her commitment of all her affairs to Monty, upon his renewed persuasion, a year ago, had his remittances been in full of her expectations.

When, in January, he had written that North-western Copper was in the midst of a "reorganization" which was temporarily depressing its value and reducing its dividends, she had been disposed—albeit puzzled—to accept his statement as correct. She made no pretence of understanding the explanation he offered with an infinitude of befuddling detail phrased in a jargon utterly incomprehensible. The situation troubled and inconvenienced her, but she had tried to believe what Monty said. There was nobody at hand to query; no one she cared or dared to consult by correspondence. She had made Monty her business agent with full power of attorney. She was in his hands to do with as he pleased. It was most disturbing.

In mid-July, he had written lengthily his deep regret and disappointment that North-western Copper was making so slow a recovery; still in a tangle over "reorganization" difficulties, "refinancing" problems, and "the tiresome delays of senseless litigation"—Monty was gifted with an extraordinary capacity for redundant ambiguities. In short, North-western Copper had passed its semi-annual period of accounting to its stockholders without declaring any dividend at all...He was sorrier than he could say—but, of course, it wasn't his fault.

Stunned to the realization that she was alone in a foreign country without income or any assurance that it might be restored, she had spent whole days fretting about her next move in this awkward predicament.

It had occurred to her that something might be liquidated of her holdings at Brightwood. She was aware that her inherited stock in the hospital had no market value. It was not at all like ordinary commercial or industrial securities. The income was small and uncertain; the stock itself being worth just what some philanthropic purchaser might be willing to pay for it.

Moreover, there was a sentimental value attached to it in her mind. Under no circumstances, short of actual pressing need, would she have consented to part with it. But, sentiment or no sentiment, she would have to live. Her funds were very low.

After a month of worry, she had written to Nancy Ashford. Rejecting, after some debate, the thought of confiding the exact state of her affairs, she limited her inquiry to the possibility of converting her Brightwood stock into cash at the earliest moment a purchaser could be found. Mrs. Ashford would be surprised and disappointed, doubtless, but she would have to think what she liked about it. The real reason could not be divulged.

* * * * *

"Now—I wonder exactly why she wants to do that?" Nancy had said to Doctor Merrick, upon receipt of it. "Surely she has enough to live on...The income on her North- western Copper can't be a penny less than six thousand a year...Preferred stock...sound as Gibraltar...Do you suppose somebody has been defrauding her? She knows so little about business."

"Who's handling her affairs while she is gone?"
"Nobody—so far as I know...There's nothing very complicated about her business...I think she said her brother—her cousin, rather—would assist her in making out her income tax report."
"D'you know anything about him?"
"Not a thing...Might he be handling her money?"
"Unlikely...Why should he?...Unless she gave him carte blanche to buy and sell; and she wouldn't do that."
"What shall I say to her, Bobby?"
"How much is her Brightwood stock worth?"
"Conservatively?" Nancy grinned.
"No—optimistically!—a Micawber appraisal!"
"About twenty thousand, I should think...Want it?"
"Yes...You tell her you have contracted to dispose of her Brightwood stuff for—for twenty-five thousand dollars...Tell her the man wishes to pay for it in twenty-five monthly instalments...That will insure her against being broke, over there; and meantime..."
"Yes?...Meantime?"
Doctor Merrick moved toward the door.
"Oh—I don't know—I'm sure...It's her affair."

* * * * *

Again Helen took up the long letter she had just received from Mrs. Ashford with its life-saving enclosure and the definite promise of more to come. The possession of it filled her with misgivings. She had snapped an important tie connecting her with Doctor Hudson's most cherished interest. It was like closing a door on something he had lived for.

There was no reproach in the letter, either direct or implied...Easy to detect a note of anxiety, however.

"I hope this disposal of your Brightwood stock does not mean that your income from other sources is in any way depleted...Is there anything you would like to have us look after for you?"

Following the briefly clear statement of the deal she had made, and the terms of the sale, Nancy Ashford had served up a potpourri of local news...You wouldn't know Detroit!...New clubs, new theatres, swagger hotels, metropolitan shops!...Even the hospital was adding a new unit. Plans already drawn.

"Young Doctor Merrick is with us now. Or perhaps you knew that. Of course it is a delight to me to see the rapid progress he is making, for I've always been interested in him...Naturally he has a great advantage over the typical interne because, having known from the first day of his medical course that he was going in for brain surgery, he comes here with more specialized knowledge and experience that any other young doctor who ever joined our organization...Already Doctor Pyle is treating him with a deference that amuses me. (Doctor Pyle is *so* short with the cubs.)...Bobby got permission to fit up a little laboratory of his own. There was a small alcove—perhaps you recall—just off the main solarium on the top floor. We had it partitioned. You should see the apparatus he has installed. It's more of a physical than a chemical laboratory, I think...Glass-blowing!...A forge!...A blast-furnace!...All manner of electrical things!...You can't get any information out of him...I was in there yesterday, and asked him if he was making a new radio set, and he said, 'Something like that.'...But that doesn't mean much when he says it, except that he wishes you wouldn't bother him.

"Oh—I never had a bigger thrill in my life than at his graduation! I had hoped so much for him, all along...And when it came to the big day...with his name starred on the Commencement programme (he hadn't said a word to me about his taking second honours!) well, I just sat there and wept silly tears...His mother couldn't come, so I pretended I was his mother...And you should have seen his grandfather! Proud? When the class marched across the platform for their diplomas, dear old Mr. Merrick stood in his seat, trying to wave his handkerchief and blow with it at the same time, until somebody pulled him down by the coat-tails."

The sheets trembled in Helen's hands as she read.

The last line on that page—it was numbered eight—had been scratched out, but was still legible:

"The young doctor who received—"

The next page had been originally numbered twelve. That had also been ineffectually deleted in favour of nine.

On second thought, Nancy Ashford had omitted a considerable part of her letter.

* * * * *

"Here's that draft for a thousand," Bobby Merrick had said, as he stood by Nancy's desk.

"Thanks. I've just finished writing to her. I'll get it off to-day."
"That's good!...By the way—you said nothing about the Dawsons, did you?"
"Why—yes...Rather I'd not?"
"Leave it out...I don't think she'd be interested much...and—well, I have a reason."
"As you like," said Nancy, hastily extracting the pages on which she had written:
"—first honours is Doctor Merrick's closest friend...Damon and Pythias...the kind of a friendship you read about! They worked together throughout their medical course—same speciality. First honours now carry a prize offered by Mr. Owen Simmons (Simmons Turbine Co.)—a year in Vienna, all expenses, scholarship, liberal allowance, etc...The Dawsons were here last Thursday—the day your letter came. She was going to New York to see her husband off.

"Actually, the three of them were like brothers and sister. I couldn't help being jealous. They were closeted here in my office for a whole hour, and when they came out, and I met them in the hall, Mrs. Dawson was all excited. She seemed so happy that I said, 'You look like Christmas morning!' 'Why shouldn't I?' she replied, laughing. 'I'm going along!'...'To Europe?'...'Absolutely!'

"They have a dear little boy—going on four. I never saw a child so beautifully trained. Doctor Merrick went along with them to New York and brought little Jack back with him to stay at Windymere until Mrs. Dawson returns. I dare say old Mr. Merrick can be found, at this minute, leading the pony he has bought for him."...

* * * * *

There was a letter from Joyce:

"No, darling, I'm sure you will take no pleasure in thinking or saying 'I told you so.' For that wouldn't be you...Never a day passes that I do not scourge myself for the abominable way I used you that winter when you were trying so hard to step in between me and myself.

"I wasn't fair to anybody through those days. Not even to poor Bobby. I never told you the straight of that. I meant to; but, you see, I telephoned to him the next morning and asked him to come and see me. I'd a hazy notion that he was—well—kind to me the night before, and I thought he might renew our friendship. He made some excuse. I was hurt and humiliated. I knew something had happened to cause an estrangement between you and Bobby, for—can you forgive me, darling?—I noticed a letter you had from him shortly afterward, and peeked into it. He wanted to be forgiven for causing you a lot of suffering. I knew that meant he hadn't told you all the truth. You thought he was in that souse party at Gordon's, and I just let you think so—after he refused to see me again. The honest fact was that he went there sober and fought everybody in the place to get me out when I was so blind drunk I didn't really learn what it was all about for three days. I know Bobby means nothing to you and that you despise him, but it's only fair to him that you should know how he happened to bring me home, that Thanksgiving night.

"No, darling, it's not any better. It's never going to be any better. I know that now. Tommy can't help it. One night he comes home drunk, surly and obstinate; the next night drunk, silly and sentimental; the next night drunk, argumentative and critical; the next night drunk, savage and abusive—but always drunk. I can definitely count on that! I never know what mood he will be in—whether I am to be upbraided for imagined indifference to him and his work (little enough he does of it!) or pestered with pretences of an affection neither of us feels—but I can always be sure of one thing: he will be drunk!

"At first, he claimed he wrote better when stimulated, and I believed him; drank with him—all times of the day, in all sorts of places, with all kinds of people. He said it helped him to the local colour necessary to his story writing. I took his word for it. Then I saw that it was rapidly doing him up. He was losing his magazine market. His things began to come back with curt little notes. I hated to nag him, but the time came when I had to rebel against being dragged about with his greasy crowd of drunken pretenders to some sort of literary or artistic talent—would-be's and has-beens!

"Now he is out on his own, doing little or nothing. Thank God, we don't have to worry about the rent or where the next meal is coming from. Dear old dad saw to that. So long as they continue to mine copper in the Upper Peninsula, Tommy and I can go through the motions of living, but it's a dull business and life has gone flat. I would leave him to-morrow if it were not that I feel under a sort of obligation. I'm as much responsible for his habits as anyone. What would you do in my place?"

* * * * *

So—nothing whatever ailed North-western Copper or Joyce would be having trouble with her dividends. She would write to Monty and press some serious questions. Had Monty volunteered to look after her business with the purpose of appropriating her income? Why had she not sought counsel before putting herself at his mercy? There were plenty of reliable trust companies...Perhaps there was an explanation...Well, he should have his chance to offer it...very soon, too! She would write to-day!...No—to-morrow. She wasn't up to it to-day...So he was taking Brightwood by storm, was he?...Glass-blowing!...Whatever for?...What had surgery to do with glass-blowing?.. Why hadn't he told the truth about that episode at Gordon's!...She was glad his letter of apology had been too vague for Joyce to understand...Poor Joyce!

Gathering up her mail, she arose from the table, smiled at old Martino as he drew back her chair, and strolled slowly down the winding carriage-drive. The gay little parasol refused to share her trouble, and brightened her face. She descended the narrow flight of steps to the next level of the mountain road that spiralled up from the village; followed a graceful arc of it to the second long flight which widened to a street flanked by picturesque little shops.

Yesterday she had promised herself that this morning she would make an excursion to the Villa Carlotta. Diagonally across the bay, on a heavily wooded shore of indescribable beauty, the famous home of an absentee prince was open to tourists...Some important Canovas, some rare orchids, a wide variety of exotics...She must see them. Everyone did.

There was no lack of attentive service as she stepped down into the red-and-blue canopied motor-boat...It required many assistants at the little wharf in front of the Villa Carlotta to attend to her disembarkation. The diminutive parasol was handed up to the nearest member of the reception committee, the Baedeker in its leather cover was passed to another, the field-glasses on a strap were unslung from her shoulder; and, regretting with a gesture of dismay that there was nothing further to take off, she reached up both hands and permitted the envied pair who remained uncommissioned to help her over the gunwale.

Smilingly collecting her possessions, she ascended to the huge iron gates and into the coolness of the great hall—ceiled, walled, floored with white marble.

A young American woman, about her own age—possibly a little older—was seated on a graceful marble bench—the only place in the room where one might sit—intent upon the famous Cupid and Psyche. She was modish in a grey tailored suit with a close fitting grey hat fringed with tawny curls.

With a brief glance they took each other's measure, nodded, smiled. Helen sat down beside her.

"It's the best thing he did, don't you think?" ventured the girl in grey.

"Exquisite!"

Well—she ought to know what things were exquisite, reflected Marion. The word described herself...Somewhere in this vicinity she expected to meet a young woman with blue eyes, long lashes, blue-black hair probably coiffed in what was known as a wind-blown bob, a smile as tantalizing as Mona Lisa's, and a voice that made you think of a 'cello. ("Bobby—for Heaven's sake!" she had protested. "Are you sure it isn't like a heavenly harp?"..."Well—something like that," he had agreed.)

"What else is there to see?" she inquired, after a long silence.

"I never was here before," Helen replied. "The gardens, I think, and some foreign trees and ferns. Shall we look? You're alone, aren't you?"

"Quite—alone and lonesome."

The patter of their heels echoed through the spacious corridor as they sought the autumn sunshine. On the terrace they hesitated, inquired of an attendant, and took the broad path northward through the artfully landscaped gardens.

"You came over from Bellagio?"

She had. Last night she had arrived from Lugano, and was stopping at a little hotel in the village...Thought she'd stay a week, perhaps.

"Oh—then you must move up to the Villa Serbelloni. I'd be so happy if you did!"

Immediately they had disclosed their identities, the budding friendship developed with all the rapidity natural to a meeting of two lonely fellow-countrymen in a foreign land. Young Mrs. Dawson's story was quickly told.

"He'll be all the better for not having me to bother with until he settles into his routine," she explained. "And, anyway, it's my first experience of Europe. I want to ramble about and see things."

"Queer you should have come to Bellagio direct from Paris. I'm glad you did, of course; but there's nothing here but an amazingly fine view...People don't, you know. They go to—oh, down into the château country, or along the Riviera; Rome, Naples, Florence...How did you happen to come here?"

"I read about it in a book...long time ago...Always wanted to come here!"

It was fun to search for mutual interests. Doctor Dawson had just finished the Medical School in June. His first honours had taken him to Vienna. Brain surgery—that was his speciality...Helen had had a letter, just this morning, from a friend in Detroit who knew intimately the young doctor taking second honours in that class. Without doubt, Doctor Dawson knew him well.

"Merrick?" Marion's brows wrinkled in an attempt at remembrance. "Oh, yes—tall, serious chap, wasn't he? But, you never met him—"

"I've seen him...I think that describes him—pretty well."

"What a duck of a grotto!...Let's go down!"

They descended into the mossy, fern-fringed enclosure and rested on the circular stone seat, facing a stucco Pan on a graceful pedestal.

"What did he have to be so serious about?" queried Helen. "Surely things should have come easy enough for him!"

"Do you think he looks serious?...Why—he's the most roguish thing I ever saw!...Serious?...With that impish grin?"

"Oh—you mean Pan!...He's a little devil!"

"And you were still thinking about young Doctor Merrick." Marion pinioned her lower lip in an understanding smile and mysteriously half closed one eye. "Maybe he wasn't serious, at all. He wouldn't need to be. Awfully rich, isn't he?"

They wandered on, occasionally coming upon delicious surprises—a short flight of worn steps by a wall mantled with Banksian roses descending to a shady water-gate—a little classic pavilion, the flagging strewn with fugitive yellow leaves. Marion loosed her imagination, prattling of romances and intrigues sheltered by these sequestered nooks, through the years.

"He's at Brightwood now," observed Helen, at the first full stop in her new friend's rhapsody. "That was Doctor Hudson's hospital; so—naturally—I'm interested."

"Yes—you would be." Marion smiled, cryptically.

It was far past noon now. The little boat that had brought Helen over was moored at the wharf. They were helped into it. Neither spoke for full five minutes—Helen regarding their silver trail on the placid water, Marion's eyes held by the lovely terraces and gates of the Villa.

"I think," said Marion dreamily, "that is the most wonderfully beautiful place I ever saw!"

"What I can't understand"—Helen's face was a study in perplexity—"is how they could have helped knowing each other—intimately...Taking the honours together...and specializing in the same thing...a very restricted field, too!"

Marion turned and regarded her with a slow smile.

"If I'd known I was ever to find somebody who was so interested in him, I'd have made it my business to get acquainted...Let's poke about in some of those funny little shops before we go up...Want to?"

* * * * *

Marion Dawson went to her room that night—she had moved up to the Villa—with many troublesome misgivings. So far as the success of her mission was concerned, it was assured. Bobby had sent her to find out the whole truth about Helen's financial misfortunes and to put him on the track of their possible remedy. He had confided that his interest was in the main philanthropic. Had Doctor Hudson lived, she would not have met this disaster; and Doctor Hudson's death was more or less chargeable to him. At least, he admitted a heavy responsibility. Her welfare was his concern.

"Sure there isn't any more to it than that, Bobby?" she had teased.

"I wish there was more to it," he had confessed, "but there can't be...I've quite put that idea out of my mind...Frankly—she hates the sight of me!"

It hadn't required much feminine intuition to discover that Bobby's estimate of Helen Hudson's attitude toward him was exactly wrong...How she could delight him, if she wished, with an impressionistic report of to-day's conversation...But that wouldn't be fair...Precisely where was her allegiance in this matter?...It was traitorous enough to extract Helen's confidence about her money difficulties—but that would be ultimately to her advantage. When she learned—if she ever did—how her financial anxieties were relieved, she would not question the method...But she would never forgive a breach of confidence about her interest in Bobby...Really, it was most unpleasant—being a spy.

All afternoon they had been together, rambling in and out of the crooked little streets; at four, grinding laboriously up the hill in the ancient fiacre with the high, steel-tired wheels; at seven, tarrying over their dinner in the arbour—each conscious of a friendship destined, they felt, to become very valuable. Helen had insisted upon her having a room next her own, on the south side where the big balconied windows looked out upon the bay...To-morrow they were having an early breakfast so they could catch the little steamer on its first trip of the day to Como.

"I'd flick this job to-night," wrote Marion, "and come straight home, if it wasn't that I knew my detective work would benefit her. She's been terribly lonely, awfully troubled; and she's going to tell me all about it in the next few days. I won't have to ask her a single question. She's going to tell me of her own accord. But I do feel so mean, Bobby, with this deception. What an adorable creature she is! I never met anybody to whom I was so quickly drawn. Please don't ever let her find out about my part in this. I don't believe I could bear it if she learned I had cultivated her for a purpose!"

* * * * *

The shopkeepers in little Bellagio became quite accustomed to the sight of two remarkably attractive young American women on their streets, and the skippers of the pleasure craft, plying Lake Como, were proud to have them for frequent passengers. Every morning they breakfasted together in the arbour, every evening they strolled, arm in arm, through the lovingly tended gardens of the hotel.

There was very little about each other's story that they did not know now. Their confidences had been tender, girlish, unreserved. It was no ordinary friendship. From the first moment, they had been irresistibly attracted, and made no effort to sustain the reticence each would have felt, naturally, toward a stranger.

All forenoon of that tragic Tuesday, which they were to remember with agony, they had hiked along a tortuous mountain road above Menaggio. Helen had laid bare her whole dilemma in the case of her business dealings with Monty, and was strongly counselled to wait a while and do nothing until her return to the States, seeing that her income was assured for the present...With the bars all down, she talked freely about Bobby too, confessing by her tone all that she hesitated to put into words.

It began to rain after luncheon. They agreed upon a siesta, and went to their rooms...An hour later, Helen, having wakened, decided to write some letters. She remembered she had left her guide-book in Marion's room. Quietly turning the knob and finding the door unlocked, she tiptoed across the room, smiling at the sleeping face on the pillow, and took up her Baedeker from the writing-desk. Beside it, stamped and ready for mailing, was a bulky letter addressed to *Dr. Robert Merrick, Brightwood Hospital, Detroit, Michigan, U.S.A.*

She was stunned...as if someone had dealt her a blow over the heart. Scarcely able to breathe, she groped her way blindly out of the room, so fearful of rousing Marion that she left the door ajar rather than risk rattling the latch. For a long time she sat on the edge of her bed, shoulders bowed, hands listless on her knees. The world had caved in. With hot cheeks, she recalled some of the things she had whispered to Marion Dawson—confidences no Inquisition machinery could have twisted out of her...Doubtless all these impulsive confessions had been spread on paper to satisfy the curiosity of Bobby Merrick. It was clear enough now!...What an odd coincidence they had thought it—she and Marion—that they had been brought together in this accidental way, and found the dearest friendship either of them had ever known!...Coincidence—indeed!

* * * * *

Marion slept heavily until five and roused with the uneasy sensation that something unpleasant had occurred. It was raining torrents. The room was dark. A strong draught was blowing through. The door was open. She distinctly remembered having closed it.

Suddenly she gasped and clutched at her throat with both hands. She walked with short, reluctant steps to the desk. Helen's Baedeker was gone! It would have been impossible for her to recover it without noticing the letter. She flung herself across the bed, swept with remorse.

A half hour later, frantically drumming on her temples with her fingers, she resolved to take the letter to Helen and beg her to read it. She would tell the whole story, and try to explain how she came to be involved in this benevolent treachery.

Heart pounding, face flushed, she tapped gently at Helen's door and received no response; tried the latch and found it locked.

Returning to her room, she nervously dressed for dinner, and went slowly down the winding staircase; searched the lounge, glanced into the dining-room; finally summoned her courage to approach the desk of the concierge.

"Has Mrs. Hudson come down?" she asked, with a dry throat.

"She is gone, madame...You did not know?"

"Gone?...You mean she has left the hotel?"

"About four o'clock, madame."

"But—where?"

"She left no address, madame...She said she would send for her trunks, later."

Marion turned slowly away and retraced her steps spiritlessly to the foot of the stairs; then, after some hesitation, came again to the desk.

"Will you see if there is a message for me?"

Obediently he went through the motions of inspecting several pigeon-holes on the wall behind him and thumbed a pack of letters, looking for something neither of them expected he would find.

It poured hard all night, and the Villa Serbelloni—if not the loneliest place in the world—was a close runner-up to the Continental Hotel in Milan, for that distinction.

CHAPTER XIII

THE girl with the pink hair, languorous lashes gummy with an overdose of mascara, and ugly black muffins over her ears, was informing Mr. Brent that a Doctor Merrick was in the lobby and wished to see him...No, he hadn't said.

"Mr. Brent is dressing for dinner and can't come down," she said coyly, with one hand over the mouthpiece. "He says can you tell him on the phone what you want. Just step into booth number two, please."

"Tell him I'll be right up."

She relayed the message, while the tall young man with the shoulders of a discus-thrower and the tapering waist of a fencer tapped the high counter in front of the switchboard with slender, impatient fingers.

"He says it won't be convenient," she reported, visibly reluctant to transmit the blunt discourtesy.

"What's his room number?" inquired Doctor Merrick, unruffled.

"Three hundred and seventy-eight; but—he said he couldn't see you, you know."

"Here, boy," to the bell-hop at his elbow, "put those bags in check, and then show me up to three hundred and seventy-eight."

Mr. Brent was not dressing for dinner. He was packing a trunk; and chairs, bed and table were littered with clothing, papers, books, toilet articles and mussy linen. The room was in great disorder. It was with a very surly scowl that he opened the door to inspect his visitor.

"Merrick—you say? Never heard of you. What's wanted?" He planted his short, stocky bulk defiantly in the doorway, hands on hips.

"Ask me in and I'll tell you," said Merrick quietly.

Brent reluctantly stepped back.

"Oh, very well," he snapped, peevishly. "But make it peppy. I'm busy—as you see...Thought I'd sent word down that I didn't care to be bothered."

The loud-checked coat that matched the trousers he had on was lifted from the back of a chair and tossed on the bed.

"Sit down—if you want to."

Young Merrick ignored the sour invitation and proceeded to state his errand.

"I live in Detroit where I am associated with Brightwood Hospital."

Brent's face, pallid, and bristly with two days' beard, went a shade paler.

"Yeah?"

"You may recall that Brightwood Hospital was brought into prominence by your cousin's late husband—Doctor Hudson."

"Well—and then what?" growled Brent, insolently.

"It came to our attention, about thirty days ago, that Mrs. Hudson—now in Italy, as you know—was obliged to dispose of her interest in the hospital."

"And how's that any of your damn business?" demanded Brent, stepping toward Merrick belligerently. "You're just a doctor, aren't you? Couldn't she sell her hospital stock, if she wanted to, without consulting you?"

"Quite true," replied Merrick, determined not to lose his temper. "She had no occasion to confide in me, and didn't. But if we are interested in her welfare, I should think that might meet with your approval. You've been managing her affairs, haven't you?"

"Yeah! And I don't need any help!"

"I happen to know that you do. That's what I came here to talk about."

"And what makes you so powerfully interested in my cousin?" Brent sneered. "Trying to get your fingers on her money?"

The fingers were restless.

"I advise you not to presume too far on my patience, Brent."

"When you get too impatient, you can leave!...You want to marry my cousin, I suppose—but have to make sure, first, that she has plenty to keep you!"

"Just for the moment," cautioned Merrick, "we'll not be talking about Mrs. Hudson. We're going to talk about you!...And that North-western Copper stock!"

"What do you mean, you low-down, sneaking spy?"

"I mean that in the last twelve months you've lost upwards of one hundred thousand dollars on the ticker and the ponies...That last big flyer in oil—along in May, wasn't it?—wiped out the North-western Copper completely!...I'm here, as Mrs. Hudson's friend, to find out exactly what you propose to do about it."

Brent's face was livid. He stamped to the door and threw it open.

"Now—out you go, damn you!—or I'll call the house detective!"

Merrick turned to the untidy desk and took up the telephone.

"I'll save you the trouble," he said quietly, lifting the receiver.

"Put that down!" screamed Brent, slamming the door.

Merrick smiled and obeyed.

"You're not anxious to talk to a detective, Brent. But you're going to talk to me! Do you want to come clean on all this, now, and tell me about it—or do I have to break you in two over that table? I can do it, you know; and I'd like to!"

Blind with fury, Brent lunged savagely with his fist. Stepping aside to let it go by, Merrick caught the shaking wrist in a vice-like grip of his left hand. With the other, he gathered up a large handful of Brent's throat, pushed him to the table, and bent him over it—back—back farther, until the purple neck was corded with distended veins, and his laboured breathing signed it was a good time to ease up.

"Like to talk business now?"

Brent raised heavily to one elbow, and his hand fumbled in the desk drawer.

"Drop that gun!" Merrick closed down on the wrist until Brent's fingers released their hold on the automatic. It fell to the floor. "That shooting project costs you extra." Once more Brent's Adam's apple and environs were compressed until his breath came in agonizing little whistles.

Merrick stooped and picked up the gun, emptied it, pocketed the cartridges, and waited for his host to recover.

After some minutes he sat up, rubbed his bloodshot eyes clumsily with his fists, and felt gingerly of his neck.

"Well," he croaked, "now you've proved you're bigger than I am, what do you want?"

"I'm no bigger than you are, Brent. Your trouble was that you rushed me with your eyes shut. Just took a long chance that maybe, somehow, your blow would land. That's probably what ails you, all along the line. You close your eyes and whang away, hoping you'll strike something by accident...That afterthought of yours about the gun...you'd be in a nice mess by now if I had let you shoot me...Some little gambler, you are!"

"I'd rather take a chance on the chair than the pen!"

"That proves what I'm saying...And—speaking of chairs and pens, crawl over there to your desk and sit down. I'm going to have you write something for me."

"If you think you're going to extort a confession from me, Merrick, you've another think coming."

"Confession? Nonsense! I've enough evidence in my pocket to send you up for twenty years...I want you to write a letter to your cousin. I'll dictate it. Don't make any mistakes in it, for I'm going to mail it myself."

Brent slumped off the table and sweeping the desk clear of its litter took up a pen.

"Begin with her address and your customary salutation. Continue as follows: In view of the uncertainty of your income from your North-western Copper stock, I have disposed of it—"

Flinging the pen down, Brent shouted, "Do you realize you're forcing me to write this letter?"

"Oh, rather! That's why you're writing it! Proceed, please."

"Do you know what that is?...compelling me to write this?"

"What is it?"

"Why—it's—it's—"

"You think up the name for it after I'm gone...Pick up that pen!...You've got that about your disposal of her North-western Copper? Now—go on...I have taken its equivalent for you in Axion Motor Corporation, preferred—"

Brent hesitated and glanced up mystifiedly.

"I don't understand!"

"That's unimportant," said Merrick crisply. "It's none of your business, in fact. You're just acting as my clerk for the moment. You have nothing further to do in your cousin's business affairs after writing this note:—'Axion Motor Corporation, preferred; five hundred shares listed to-day at two hundred and twenty-six. This stock is held by the Trust Department of the Fourth National Bank of Detroit from where your dividends will hereafter be remitted to you regularly'."

"How do I know that's true?" growled Brent.

"You don't; but—as I said—it's no affair of yours. Have you written it? Now—one more paragraph:—I find that an important business errand requires me to go immediately to Buenos Aires—"

"But—I'm not going to Buenos Aires!"

"Oh, yes, you are!...Sailing on Saturday...You're just packing up, now, to leave for Washington to get the passport I've arranged for you. From there you go to New York where you sail on the *Vigo*... Get on now with your correspondence:—'I do not know how long I shall be away; so I am transferring my entire responsibility for your business to the Trust Department of the Fourth National Bank of Detroit. Mr. T. P. Randall will verify this and give you a clear statement of your affairs in a short time...' Now add whatever pleasant amenities you may have the crust to write to a woman you have robbed, and sign your name to it...and address an envelope."

While he wrote, Merrick took out his wallet, extracted a steamship ticket, and counted two thousand dollars in bills of large denomination.

"There." He pointed to it, as Brent finished. "That is for you. Take it—and be off! And if you're in the market for any advice, I'd suggest that you quit trying to be a sport, which you most certainly aren't; make some new connections; find a few honest friends; get yourself a respectable job; buck up—and be a man!"

His face distorted, Brent fumbled with the money, and blindly groped out with his hand. Merrick ignored the gesture. He was not fond of the movies.

"You can get out of the country, can't you?...I've fixed things for you so you'll have no trouble about the passport, unless you're wanted for some other crime...Sure you'll not be stopped?...Haven't been robbing anybody else besides your little cousin, have you?"

"No! No!...God—but I've been a rotter!" Collapsing in his chair, Monty buried his tousled head in his arms.

"You don't have to remain a rotter, Brent...Start fresh!...Go straight!...You can do it!...I'm going now. If you have any trouble getting off, wire me. There's my card. And I presume I needn't tell you that Mrs. Hudson is never to know anything about this little transaction of ours."

"You mean," said Brent, looking up perplexed, "that she's not going to know you've given her all this money? What do you expect to get out of it?"

"That's my business!...No—I think I'll tell you...just to clear your mind of any nasty suspicion that my obligation to her may be somehow to her discredit...Do you recall the story of her husband's death?"

Brent nodded.

"Do you remember that a young man was resuscitated, while Doctor Hudson was drowning?"

"Yeah—I remember...some rich guy...By God—it was *you*?"

"Yes! My life was saved, that day, by a machine which might have brought Doctor Hudson around, if he'd had a chance at it...Had Hudson lived, you would not have squandered Mrs. Hudson's money...Do you understand now?"

"Was that why you became a doctor too?" inquired Brent, wide-eyed.

"That would be a good enough reason...but—no matter about that...I just wanted you to know the nature of my interest in your cousin...I don't give a damn what you think about me, but I'd prefer you'd think straight about her!"

"So—you figured he had handed your life back to you—sort of—and you had to make good with it; is that it?"

"Something like that."

For a long time Brent sat staring up glassily, and when he spoke his voice came from a distance.

"God!—I never heard of such a thing!...And here you've just handed my life back to me!...If I were the kind of a person you are, I suppose I'd have to do something about it, wouldn't I?"

"Oh—not necessarily...I was a good while debating whether to do anything about my affair...I was a pretty rummy lot, Brent...I'd have ducked it if I could."

"How do you mean—rummy?...Hadn't stolen anything, had you?"

"Never needed to steal anything...Had everything...Had too much!...Corrupted a lot of people with it!...You've had too little. I suppose that's the main difference between us."

"D'you think there's anything I could do—to square up for what you've done for me?"

"Perhaps—if that sort of thing interests you?"

"What—for instance?"

Merrick rose and took up his coat.

"You'll have to figure that out for yourself."

"I'd like to, you know," said Brent earnestly.

"You mean that?" challenged Merrick, putting both hands on Monty's shoulders and looking him squarely in the eyes.

"Yes—more than I ever meant anything in my life!"

It seemed to Monty that his athletic young benefactor would never emerge from the brown study into which his words had driven him. He stood, leaning against the table, hands deep in his pockets, oblivious to his surroundings.

"In that case," he said slowly, "I presume I'll have to help you. I don't want to! But—there's just a slim chance that...See here! You shave and dress for dinner. I'll be in the lobby when you come down. We'll eat—and I'll tell you all I know about it. After that—it will be up to you!...Better put some iodine on those scratches...Sorry I hurt you."

* * * * *

They went in a taxi to a down town restaurant. It was somewhat after the dinner hour and their table in the corner permitted them to talk undisturbed. Counselled to forget the experience of the past two hours, Monty had regained his self-confidence and listened with rapt attention to his host. If it was not good soil for the reception of a new idea, it was for no lack of sufficient plowing and harrowing.

"I am going to tell you a strange story, Brent, about a sculptor named Randolph. If it seems incredible to you, I shall not be surprised. It was to me when I first heard it."

It was a long story. Dinner courses came and went. In the hour, Monty had spoken but once.

"He'd quite lost his mind, hadn't he?"

Dessert glasses had now been pushed aside and cigars lighted.

"Of course," Merrick was saying, "if you should decide to experiment with this projection of yourself through investments in other people, you must be prepared for all manner of failures, disillusionments, disgusts. You will frequently go to no end of trouble and expense for somebody who turns out to be a pest and a piker. You will be imposed upon, lied to, lied about! You will run into cases of ingratitude so rank that it will sicken you! But—now and again, you will manage to put the thing over...and when you do you will discover it has squared for all the failures you've had!"

He paused, and his mood seemed reminiscent.

"I expect you're wondering," risked Monty, "whether you've been wasting your time and money on me."

"So far as the money's concerned, I'm afraid that wasn't an investment in you. I just wanted to be rid of you. But—you're quite right about my wondering whether it's really been worth while to confide to you this theory of personality projection."

"Do you mind if I inquire whether you think it would give you additional personal power in your undertakings, if I managed to make good?"

"Oh, unquestionably!"

"And—if it ever got out—that you had started me on the way up—then this whole investment of yours in my behalf would be a total loss to you?"

Merrick smiled and toyed preoccupiedly with his ashtray.

"Well—no!...Randolph was a bit obsessed, you know. He was for breaking people's necks if they told of his investments in them. That was going it rather stronger than necessary...Hudson was careful to caution his beneficiaries against telling, and threw every possible safeguard around his investments to protect them from discovery; but I don't believe he felt they hadn't been worth doing if the facts leaked out...The really important feature of it is here: if you succeed in expanding your personality, I shall come in on the reward by just as much as I've been responsible for it...In the process of expanding yourself, you are almost sure to help somebody else make himself bigger. He, in turn, energizes other people...If you know anything about chemistry, you will be helped by considering this as a process of catalysis...Personality projection is like any other investment. The thing goes on! It earns compound interest. If you were the agent that set it going, the credit's yours...Some of it will be going at full blast long after you have been declared dead. In actual fact, the real *you* may be more alive, as to personality energy, fifty years after you're gone, than when you seem to be at the top of your power!"

"But—if your beneficiary does not succeed in making good on your investment?..."

Merrick shrugged.

"In that case, you can see for yourself that nothing comes of it."

"But—you tried! Isn't there any satisfaction to be had of that?"

"Oh, it's good practice, I suppose...But—if you had spent twenty thousand dollars and six months' time sinking an oil-shaft, and got nothing but a dry hole, would you have much satisfaction in reflecting that—at all events—you'd tried?"

When they parted at the kerb, Brent said, "May I write to you, sometimes, and report?"

"Glad to have you...But you needn't try to tell me what you're doing for anybody else. That's your affair. Write and tell me if it works—but not what you did to make it work. Do you get me?...Good luck!...Good-bye!"

* * * * *

Bobby went to the Ritz-Carlton for the night, stood for a long time at the counter of the Western Union office in the lobby trying to compose a cable to Vienna, gave it up, bought a few magazines and took the elevator.

Having made himself comfortable in a dressing-gown, he drew up to his desk and wrote:

"Dear Marion: I've been racking my brain for a solution to your problem, but nothing comes. You have lost a friend and I see no way for you to regain her at present. I learned to-night that she is in Nice. But I don't want you to go there seeking a reconciliation, for you wouldn't do it without making things bad all around. You would be obliged to say that you went to Bellagio as my agent to discover what had happened to her money. I've arranged—guided by your report—for the complete untangling of her affairs. She has recovered in full. But the machinery devised to effect this restoration of her property without offence to her is frail enough. I believe and hope it will go, but it won't stand any wrenches being tossed into it.

"The postscript to your letter broke me all up. She left Bellagio about four, you said...drenching rain...heartsick and betrayed...by you and me—who would have laid down and died for her!...Stuffy little steamer to Como...Probably spent the night there—or maybe caught a train over to Milan...wondering where to go...what to do next! My dear—was there ever a more pitiful state of things?...Consult Jack about this. Ask him if he sees any other way out. If neither you nor he can think of a plan by which you can communicate with her without jeopardizing everything we have tried to do for her, better keep away! I'm devastated over the situation, but—there you are!"

Then he wrote a letter to Helen which he had no intention of mailing, tore it into small bits, undressed, went to bed, tried to read, turned out the light, relaxed.

For a long time it had been his custom, just before dropping off, to attempt an inward look. His corridor—as he called it—was, of course, a mere hallucination developed and encouraged by his own quest of it. He had long since decided that the corridor was but an eccentric property of his own imagination, located somewhere in that No-Man's-Land between fading consciousness and sleep.

It amused him to search for it, and, by practice, he had been able to arrest the clouding of his consciousness at the exact phase where his curious phantom resided.

The clearness of it depended upon his mood; and his mood—in respect to the corridor—was determined by the projects he happened to be working on in the field of personality projection.

Usually a very thin, faint pencil of promising yellow light streaked down the middle of the corridor's rough flagging—the flagging was always rough as if paved with cobblestones. There would be but an instant of it. The big doors would part, and the light would shine through...just enough to nourish a great hope.

To-night—perhaps because of the investment he had made, his intense concentration upon the subject he had endeavoured to make clear to Brent, and the emotional strain incident to both—his mood, he found, was unusually conducive to a materialization of the corridor.

As he neared that grey twilight of consciousness, it came sharply into focus. The doors, instead of parting a little, slowly, tentatively, were opening! The corridor was flooded with a shimmering radiance.

After that, events moved with bewildering swiftness. The corridor suddenly seemed objectified—a thing apart from himself—and he walked into it! A terrific roar deafened him...Finding the blinding glare at the big doors too painful to face, he turned his attention to the objects against the wall, blinking in his effort to accommodate his eyes to the dazzling light.

All endeavours to recall, afterwards, exactly what he saw there were futile. They belonged to a narrowly restricted phase of half-consciousness, and were not to be reconstructed elsewhere. He was left only with a very hazy impression that he had seen his own laboratory—the oven, the black switchboard, the little vice screwed to the table. His diminutive blast-furnace was at top heat. White flames jutted out about the hinges. Doubtless that accounted for the roar. There was also a nebulous recollection left that the door of the five-foot cabinet, containing all the apparatus he had been at such pains to manufacture over a period of many months, stood wide open...He had almost decided, a few days earlier, to dismantle it and have it carted off before some inquisitive colleague in the hospital discovered what an audacious thing he had had in mind, and chaffed him about...

Well—be he waking or sleeping, sane or crazy—there it was!

In the lowest compartment there was a box containing the vacuum tubes; *but they were not arranged in the order of the tubes in his cabinet*!

He had summoned all his efforts to concentrate on that illusory tube-box, and the exertion aroused him to full consciousness.

Tossing aside the bedclothes, he leaped out drenched with perspiration and trembling so he could barely stand. For an hour he sat at his desk, drawing diagrams of another experimental hook-up of his tubes. He was unable to shake off the impression that he was on the edge of discovery. A strange sensation of exultancy possessed him.

Mechanically putting on his street clothes, he went down into the deserted lobby and sought the outer air. For miles and miles he walked, neither knowing nor caring where he went; walked with long strides, seeing nothing; utterly absorbed by the curious experience that still clung to him like a garment...When dawn broke, he found himself down at the ferry-docks.

Returning to the hotel, he bathed, breakfasted, and drove to the station. Securing a compartment, he went to bed and slept dreamlessly all day. When he awoke it was dark, and for a moment he was unable to recall where he was. Then remembrance came, and he smiled broadly. A strange sense of mastery exalted him. He laughed, and recalled Randolph. Randolph had laughed. Randolph had found the grass greener; everything tuned up to a higher key; every sensation more intense. He laughed as Randolph had laughed!

"And once I thought him crazy!"

He sat on the edge of his berth and stared hard at the shiny mahogany walls of his compartment, his eyes wide with the interest of his pleasurable self-analysis. He laughed.

"And once I thought Hudson was crazy!"

The jolting of the trucks over the rail-ends, the clank of chains, and the wail of flanges tortured by a sharp curve, stirred him out of his rhapsody. The sound of his own laughter still echoed in his brain. He rubbed his forehead roughly with the back of his wrist, and swallowed with a dry throat.

"My God!" he groaned. "I wonder if I'm going mad!"

CHAPTER XIV

YOUNG Merrick discovered, within a week, that when a man begins to suspect he is slipping mentally his disorder fattens on itself.

He became morbidly introspective, exaggerated the significance of his little tricks of manner, caught himself doing things automatically and wondered what else he might have been doing of which he had no recollection.

Then, in the course of two hours, one Friday morning, Pyle had said, "You're not quite par these days. Something bothering you?..." Watson had said, "I'll look after that Weber case, Merrick. She had a notion you're too young. Silly nonsense, but we'll have to humour her..." Nancy Ashford had said, "What is it, Bobby? Tired?"

That settled it. At noon he told Pyle he was going out to the country for a couple of weeks. He spent the afternoon gutting his little laboratory, assisted by an orderly who packed the apparatus into boxes. His first intention was to store the stuff in his suite of rooms near the hospital. On second thought, he shipped the whole of it out to Windymere. Perhaps he might amuse himself if time dragged.

Farmers along the roads near Lake Saginack grew accustomed to the sight of a tall, slender chap, in knickers and white sweater, walking rapidly on the highway; learned who he was; vainly speculated about the cause of his leisure. One tale had it that he was discharged from the hospital for drunkenness, another that he had decided to give up medicine and loaf. Meggs' curiosity, reaching that state of compression which demanded that he either blow off or blow up, ventured to inquire of Bobby why he had come home, and was informed that his young master was recovering from "a slight touch of leprosy."

Old Nicholas aged markedly during the first week, but made a gallant effort to disguise his worry, a well-intended deceit which added to his grandson's anxieties. The old man's excessive solicitude annoyed him. He reproached himself for making wild remarks for the sole purpose of seeing to what ridiculous lengths he might lead his grandpère in assenting solemnly to his nonsense.

"Believe I could persuade him a cloud resembled a camel," thought Bobby, "and then talk him into the notion that it looked like a hawk."

More than two weeks had passed before he had any inclination to rig his laboratory. Somehow it seemed related to his mental dishevelment, and the thought of it had been repugnant. One morning at breakfast, he announced impulsively that he wanted the use of an attic room for a workshop.

Nicholas was delighted. Carpenters, plumbers, and electricians were in the house before noon, taking orders from a young scientist who obviously knew exactly what he wanted, surprising them with the breadth of his practical information about their trades.

That night at dinner, Bobby was more like himself than he had been at any time since his home-coming.

The farmers who lived near the highway missed him; presumed he had finished his vacation, or he had been reinstated at the hospital, or had gone "gallavanting to furrin parts."

Old Nicholas worried more about him now than before; feared his close confinement in the attic would do him harm.

Bobby rarely came down to the first floor. Most of his meals were sent up to him, and as often as not the tray was returned almost untouched.

* * * * *

It was on Thursday about nine. The lights in the laboratory had burned all Wednesday night. Bobby was haggard and stubbly with three days' beard. Meggs had tried the door, found it locked; had knocked and been told to go away.

Taking in his left hand the tiny knife, attached to the end of a long green cord, Bobby reached up and slowly moved the lever along the dial of the rheostat.

The little scalpel came alive!

For a long time he sat there on his laboratory stool with the dynamic thing in his hands, too deeply stirred to make a sound, trembling with ecstatic happiness.

Then he switched off the current, put down the scalpel on the bench, rose, stretched his long arms until every fibre was at top torsion, and laughed boyishly.

* * * * *

Old Nicholas was quite swept off his moorings when Bobby strode into the library, shaggy as a tramp, hollow-eyed, pasty from lack of sleep, and said he wanted to use the telephone.

"Is anything the matter, Robert?" he quavered, rising hurriedly, and taking him by the arm.

Bobby shook his head and smiled. The operator was in the process of giving him his connection.

"I want to talk to Doctor Pyle, Nancy...No! Everything's quite all right!...Yes...That you, Doctor Pyle?...I wish you would come out here!...Yes—very urgent!...That's fine! Thanks! Bring your bag along and we'll put you up!"

"What's it all about, son? Feel all right?" Nicholas had dropped into a chair and his face was twitching.

"Very much all right!" shouted Bobby, patting him on the shoulder. "I'll tell you about it after a little! I want to run up and shave first. Then I want my breakfast...Meggs!...I'll be down again in a half-hour for a thick slice of ham, two eggs turned, a pair of flapjacks, and a pot of strong coffee."

* * * * *

Doctor Pyle was consumed with curiosity when he arrived. Nicholas could not tell him exactly what was wanted. He was to go up to the attic when he came. Robert wished to see him there.

"You can come along, Grandpère!" called Bobby from the head of the stairs.

Nicholas trudged wheezily after Pyle, and they entered the laboratory.

"Hello, Doctor Pyle," greeted Bobby radiantly. "Got something to show you! Wanted you to be the first to see it!"

He held up the gleaming little scalpel, dependent from yards of green-clad wiring, leading to a tall cabinet.

"Take it in your hand!...Now look!" He stepped to the switchboard and drew a lever.

"Look out!" he warned, as Pyle lifted the knife for closer inspection. "Don't let it burn you!...Know what it is, don't you?"

Pyle slowly nodded his head, eyes still intent upon the glowing blade.

"Humph!...Cuts and cauterizes instantly, eh?...Hummm!...Takes care of the hæmorrhage as it goes, eh?...Hummm!...Well—that means we're to have some new brain surgery, doesn't it?"

He reached out a hairy hand.

"I needn't tell you what you've done, Merrick!...Thank you for letting me be the first to congratulate you!"

Then, turning to old Nicholas, who had been standing by, his face puckered with baffled curiosity, he also extended his hand to him.

"Mr. Merrick, your grandson has invented a device that will completely revolutionize brain surgery, and make a new science of it! Operations which have never yet been successfully performed will now be comparatively safe. Within the next thirty days, his name will be as familiar in the clinics of Europe as yours is among manufacturers of motor cars!"

Old Nicholas' chin vibrated spasmodically. All he could say was "Indeed!...Indeed!"

He threw an arm around his grandson's broad shoulders, and mumbled,

"Why, Bobby!...Indeed!"

* * * * *

Pyle could not stay the night, but consented to remain for dinner which was called earlier than usual for his convenience. When he had gone, old Nicholas and Bobby, deep in their chairs in the library, talked of the invention.

To the latter's pleased surprise, the old man asked questions which showed with what tenacity he had retained his interest in physics; for there had been a time when Nicholas Merrick had had to know a great deal about electricity.

Bobby was so delighted with the lucidity of his grandfather's queries and the comments, that he drew the small coffee-table between their chairs and proceeded to make a detailed diagram of his coagulation cautery, Nicholas following with keen attention.

"It was the vacuum tubes that had you stumped, eh?...And the success of that came, you say, as a sort of bolt out of the blue...How do you mean?"

"Did you ever go to bed, Grandpère, with a problem on your mind, and find in the morning that you'd worked it, somehow, in your sleep?"

Nicholas rubbed his jaw.

"I've heard of such things. Can't say I ever had that experience myself...Was that what happened to you?"

Bobby pushed the table away, and shifted his chair until their knees touched.

"Grandpère," he said, soberly, "I'm going to tell you something that you may have trouble believing. It's a long story, and I'll have to begin at the beginning."

Nicholas' contribution to the conversation, during the next hour and a half, was limited to an occasional "Indeed!...Incredible!...You don't tell me!"

When finally Bobby had made an end of it, the old fellow sat for a long time in deep meditation.

"I had never suspected, Bobby, that you were interested in religion."

"Not sure that I am, Grandpère."

"But that's what this is! You've been talking about this 'Major Personality' that supplies our personalities with added energy, as we ask for it and obey the rules for getting it...Well—that's God, isn't it?"

"Doubtless...Just another way of saying it, maybe."

"I've always shied off from the subject, Bobby. But, of late, it has been much on my mind. I'm quite disturbed, these days. I'm in a mental revolt against death. It's sneaking up on me, and there's nothing I can do about it. Death holds all the trump cards...It takes me a little longer to get out of bed in the morning than a month ago. It is just a bit harder to climb the stairs than it was last week. The old machine is running down. I don't want to die. I understand that when a man actually faces up to it, nature compounds some sort of an anæsthesia which numbs his dread and makes it seem right enough; but that thought brings me small comfort. I have been accustomed to meeting all my emergencies with my eyes open, and I don't get much consolation out of the thought that I'm to be doped into a dull apathy—like a convict on the way to execution—as I face this last one...I wouldn't mind so much if there was anything—after that...Bobby, do you believe in immortality?"

"I wish I was as sure of a few other things that bother me," replied Bobby, instantly, "as I am of the survival of personality. Once you've experienced a vital contact with the Major Personality, Grandpère, you become aware that the power of it is quite independent of material things...To my mind, that's clear. Personality is all that matters! The roses in that vase have no meaning for each other; no meaning for themselves. A tiger doesn't know he is a tiger. Nothing in the world has any reality except as it is declared real by our personalities. Count personality out of the scheme, and there's no significance left to anything! Include personality in the scheme, and the whole business is automatically explained!

"I've thought a good deal about the soul lately, Grandpère. It strikes me that the things one reads about souls are frightfully misleading. They inquire, 'What are you doing to, for, and with your soul?' as they might ask 'When are you going to turn in your old car?'...I can't say 'my soul,' as I would say 'my hat,' or 'my canoe,' or 'my liver.'...I *am* a soul! I *have* a body! My body is wearing out, and when I can't tinker it back into service any more, I'll drive it out to the junk-pile; but I don't have to be junked with it! I'm tied up to the Major Personality!...like a beam of sunshine in the sun!...I'll not lose my power unless He loses His!...If that's religion, Grandpère, I'm religious! But I'd rather think of it as science!"

"Bobby—are you a Christian?"

"That's what I'd like to know myself, Grandpère...For some time I have been very much absorbed by the personality of Christ. Here was the case of a man who made an absolutely ideal adjustment to his Major Personality. He professed to have no experience of fear. He believed he could have anything he wanted by asking for it...The story interests me at the point of his bland assurance that anybody else could do the same thing if he cared to. I'm amazed that more people aren't interested in that part of it...Now—if that's being a Christian, I'm a Christian."

"Is that what the churches teach, Bobby?"

"I'm sure I don't know; for I never go to them. From what I gather, they approach this whole subject sentimentally. They regard the soul as a sort of congenital disease that ought to be cured. The soul has been passed along, from one common carrier to another, like a trunk with a bent lock and a broken hinge, labelled 'Received in Bad Order.'...And as for the things you read in the papers about the churches, either they're campaigning for money to build something, or helping to elect a new prosecuting attorney, or stopping a prize-fight, or panning some other sect's belief, or raising hell with one another inside their own bailiwick...Maybe you and I had better start a church; eh, Grandpère?"

"Very good," approved Nicholas, grinning. "I'll build it and you be the parson."

"It would be just like all the rest of 'em...Nobody would want to go to the bother and expense of making his own connections with his Major Personality...He'd decide to sing about power...Fancy!—singing about power! Watt didn't sing for his! And Faraday didn't produce the dynamo by reciting 'I believe in Volta, Maker of the dry battery and Father of the Leyden jar, and in his successor Ampere, who codified the formulæ for electrodynamics, and in Ben Franklin who went at it with a kite.'...No, sir! By the Great Horn Spoon—No!...Faraday did his in an attic, alone, on an empty stomach!" He rose with a prodigious yawn and sauntered toward the door.

"I'm off to Brightwood early in the morning...Think I'd better turn in!"

Old Nicholas struggled heavily to his feet.

"Bobby, I'm not physically able to go around trying to nose out some opportunity to experiment with your theory. Keep your eyes open and let me know if there's anything I can do. You arrange for it: I'll furnish the money."

"That wouldn't get you anywhere...You can't do this with a cheque book!...By the way—did you know that old Jed Turner, up the road here, had to kill seventeen of his Holstein cows, last week? The State Vet condemned them as tuberculous...Jed's all broken up about it."

"I wonder if he has a telephone."

"Oh, you can easily send for him to come over."

Nicholas' eyes brightened. He rubbed his hands.

"Thanks for telling me, Bobby. I'll let you know how it comes out!"

"That you won't! I never want to hear about it again!"

"Maybe you were thinking of doing it yourself," said Nicholas. "If so, I'll not get into it."

"No, Holsteins are not in my line. That's your job...And Grandpère—while you're over in that neighbourhood—I noticed, the other day, that Jim Abbot's ten-year-old boy is dragging a leg in a brace that didn't look right to me...Why don't you hop into your car to-morrow, and have Stephen drive you about through the district? You'll be amazed what it does to you to make connections with people who need you!...Oh, I know you've done a lot. It was big stuff when you contributed a hundred thousand to the hospital in Axion; but you couldn't do it without getting your name on a bronze tablet in the main hall. You drop in at Jim Abbot's and inquire all about the boy. If they ask you to stay for noon dinner—corned beef and cabbage—you stay! I know you can't eat boiled cabbage at home, because it isn't good for you; but you'll be able to eat it at Abbot's, and it won't hurt you a bit. I'll guarantee that on my honour as a medic!"

"Run along to bed!" Nicholas slapped him vigorously on the back. "Glad we had this talk! Glad your worries are all over! Now you can be happy again!"

"I'm not looking for happiness, Grandpère...She's out of my reach!"

"Since when was happiness a she?"

"Mine is!"

"Going to tell me about that, too?

"Sometime, maybe...Good night, Grandpère."

CHAPTER XV

THE *Aquitania* had crept up the river that morning with exasperating caution. It was the day before Christmas. The more impatient compared tedious experiences in customs; hoped goodwill toward men might have percolated through to the baggage inspectors; wondered if they could get Pullman space on the two-forty-five in case they missed the one-twenty.

Her furs muffled high about her throat, Helen Hudson ventured to the frosty rail of B-deck as they passed the Battery, and found the stinging breeze a bit strenuous. She had avoided three consecutive winters, and the fast trip from Nice to New York had not been free of discomfort.

A spluttery scrawl from Joyce accounted for her sudden decision to return. She had read the letter on a stone bench by the sea wall, a stone's throw from the Casino pier, one week ago this morning...It had been that kind of a journey.

"All packed and waiting for the taxi," Joyce had begun. "Going back to Detroit. Why Detroit, I don't know, unless because it seems to offer something like anchorage. I'll try to find some employment there—anything to occupy my mind...The past month has been a nightmare! Quite unendurable! Last night, Tom struck me a savage blow on the breast with his fist...deeply penitent afterwards...wailed his remorse like a little child...But I told him I'd had enough!...I'm through!...He left, early this morning, ashamed and glum. He thinks I'll be here when he comes home to-night, though I made it plain enough I was leaving...I wonder, darling, would it be asking too much of you to come back and be with me for a few weeks. I do need some good counsel, and I'm bitterly lonely...It's a shame to drag you back to Detroit in mid-winter—but could you? I've nobody but you! I need you desperately!...Cable me at the Statler...I'll be wild with joy if you say you'll come!"

It had taken only an hour to decide. Creasing the letter with puzzled fingers, she had risen and walked mechanically along the Promenade des Anglais for fully half a mile; had slowly retraced her steps, past the Negresso and the Ruhl, so deep in her problem she barely noticed the strollers recruited from a dozen nations. By the time she had reached the little park fronting the Jettee, Helen was ready to concede that Joyce had won her case.

She had called the roll of all the alternatives to a return trip. Why not cable Joyce to come over? But no—Joyce had set her heart on finding some employment. She would find none along the Riviera. Joyce wanted to begin life again. She couldn't do it lounging in Nice. Joyce was bitterly lonely. Well—Nice wouldn't help that very much...After all—she did owe Joyce some attention. She must go!...It was almost as busy an afternoon as the one on which the had impulsively migrated from Bellagio.

Slowly the big ship warped into her slip; sleety, salty hawsers were wound upon huge rumbling spools somewhere deep in her vitals; the covered gangways were hauled up from the dock and opened to the swarm of restless home-comers. Almost everybody had located wide expectant eyes in the steam-breathing crowd that huddled at the openings of the wharf-shed.

Helen felt very much alone. She exchanged tentative good-byes with the few friends she had made on board; doubtless she would be bumping into them again in the Customs.

Already a nervous little caucus had convened under the big H, half-way down the draughty warehouse where a pile of luggage was rapidly accumulating. Some sat on their trunks with the resigned despair of the shipwrecked on a desert island; some—less experienced—squatted before their gaping bags contemplating last minute amendments to their declaration slips.

Young Mrs. Hudson had done a minimum of collecting in Europe, but it was amazing how many things one unwittingly came into possession of in the course of a mere three years of foreign travel. As she neared her letter, she met a pair of officials headed also in that direction and told them that she was hopeful of spending at least part of Christmas Day with relatives in Detroit. She led them to her belongings and indicated which pieces they were to put the stickers on. She could have brought in the Crown jewels, that morning.

To her delight, the three o'clock train was not crowded; but why should it be? It was Christmas Eve! Normal people were at home. The thought depressed her. For a little while, as the train roared through the tunnel, she missed a home as she had never before.

There was a pleasurable excitement, however, in this return to Detroit. She and Joyce had been very close. Whatever of constraint had come upon their comradeship, in that last

93

trying winter when she had attempted so unsuccessfully to keep the girl from utterly ruining herself, Joyce's urgent need of her drove all that into oblivion.

And there were many other friends in Detroit she would be happy to see again...The Byrnes...Should she go out to see Mrs. Ashford? Why not—indeed? Mrs. Ashford had been good to her...It might be thought strange if Doctor Hudson's widow returned to Detroit and failed to call at Brightwood...Perhaps it would serve the purpose if she invited Mrs. Ashford down town for luncheon and a matinée...It wouldn't be necessary to go out to the hospital...Doctor Pyle would be glad to see her, of course; but she would call on the Pyles at their home...Besides—it would be awkward meeting people one scarcely knew any more, and being expected to remember their names...And as for that glass-blower, who meddled in people's affairs and sent spies about to report on their movements, one would be almost sure to encounter him!...Why should he want to blow glass, anyway?...Imagine!—a brain surgeon spending his time in such silly business!

The sky was the colour of wood-ashes. Big snowflakes flattened against the pane, crumbled, edged toward the lower corner of the sash. No matter where they struck and spattered, or how slowly they made their way, sooner or later, quickly or slowly, they eventually arrived in the corner and packed themselves down hard against the others...Her thoughts were like that. Let them strike where they would—they all contrived to bring up at one spot. She was impatient about it, tugged herself free of her reveries, returned to the magazine story and re-read with utter disinterest the page that had failed to register...Would it pay to take the coupé out of the storage garage? She had not driven on icy streets for so long. Had she lost her nerve? Skidding was dangerous...She watched a snowflake creep across the pane...Her eyes grew reminiscent, tender. She bit her lip. Her cheeks were flushed...Then, vexed with herself, she shifted her position and took up the magazine with resolution.

Had Joyce been effectually cured of her drinking? Would she drift into her old habits, once she had renewed connections with her Detroit set?...And be brought in, at all hours, maudlin and stupid?...An unusually big snowflake went scudding across the glass, clawing for a hold, but unable to stand out against the rule for all snowflakes on this pane...For a brief instant, she was in his arms, and she felt his lips pressed hard against her own...She threw down the magazine and rang the bell for a table. A game of solitaire might divert her.

* * * * *

It was pleasant to be back in an American dining-car...And, all things considered, it would be better to invite Mrs. Ashford to take an afternoon off and come down town...Our diners were so much nicer than the European ones where the passengers were organized into platoons and given so many minutes to devour each course...What a pity she had felt she had to sell her Brightwood stock. Would it make any difference in her relations with Mrs. Ashford?

It was bitterly cold that night as the long train clanked and creaked and screamed along the east bank of the Hudson, and, crossing the bridge at Albany, thrust its black muzzle into the face of a blinding blizzard; but the scurrying landscape, blurry with snow, did not seem so bleakly inhospitable as she had feared. In her berth, she raised on one elbow, drew aside the blind, and watched the sleet-trimmed trees and fences skimming by, half glad she was returning. She snuggled down with her furs against her cheek, and drifted off into an extended debate with somebody, whether she wasn't under a sort of obligation to call at Brightwood, if only for a moment.

* * * * *

Joyce was at the gates, dancing gleefully, arms outstretched, as she sighted her beloved emerging from the concourse tunnel, pursued by two porters staggering under bags plastered with foreign labels. There were some murmured tendernesses, and a moment later they were careening around the circle, tire-chains rattling merrily. Bubbling with excitement, Joyce tried to tell half a dozen stories at once.

"First thing I did, darling, when I arrived—week ago—I went out to see Nancy Ashford. Isn't she the dearest thing? But you hardly knew her. Well—she's regular!...I went out to Brightwood and told Nancy all about it; how I couldn't stick it another minute and had had to leave him; and could I possibly find anything to do, just to keep from going crazy...And, what do you think? They had just lost a file-clerk, and would I like to do that for a week or two, to find out how I would react to the discipline of office hours; and, meanwhile, we could all be thinking and inquiring for something permanent...But, I don't mind if nothing turns up for a while. Really—it isn't dull work, at all; and I quite like it!"

"Oh, you've begun it already?"

"Umm-humm!...That same afternoon!...Just took off my hat and went to it. Honestly—it's a lark. Of course, I knew several of the people—Doctor Pyle and Doctor Carter, and the red-headed Watson boy, who's grown a moustache and glasses since I saw him last; and fully a dozen of the older nurses...And—my dear—you should see the Merrick person!...Don't frown that way!...I know you never liked him."

"You mean I never knew him."

"Of course! That was the whole trouble! You never met him but once, on that awful night! Ugh!...that night!"

Helen patted her hand.

"Forget it! We'll never mention it again!"

Joyce brightened and resumed her monologue.

"Well, as I was saying, all you ever knew about him was that he had a sentimental notion he must study surgery and try to take dear dad's place...And you thought it a piece of impudence, didn't you?...Listen! He's going to come near doing it! Do you know what Bobby Merrick's up and done? He's invented a thing—"

The taxi scraped against the kerb, and the door-man was reaching for the baggage.

"Look! Isn't this foxy?" prattled Joyce, as they entered the lobby. "All done over!...Let's go straight through to luncheon. I'm starving!...There's a place—by the window...Umm! Duck! That's Christmassy!"

"What were you saying about your work at the hospital, when I interrupted you?" asked Helen, as the waiter moved away, scribbling on his card.

"What was I saying?...Oh, yes—about Bobby! He's made an electrical thing that's bringing head surgeons here from all over. I don't know exactly what it is—some sort of a charged knife...awfully complicated...They're doing operations with it at Brightwood that have never been done anywhere before...Something that prevents hæmorrhages, or something. Nancy Ashford told me about it; but she couldn't explain it very well. I saw it—a big, tall, wooden case full of the most intricate machinery you ever saw..."

"Glass things?"

"Umm-humm!...How did you know?"

"Well—they always do have a lot of—of things made of glass whenever they use electricity, don't they?"

"Naturally...Have some of that wonderful celery, darling...Only celery in the world, you know...And handsome? My word! Honestly—I wouldn't have known him! And he always was good-looking!...But the change in him is simply marvellous! I'm half afraid of him...Oh—very professional! Crisp! No nonsense—no—sir-ee! And the nurses are all wild and crazy about him—and he doesn't know they're existing...He's doing some of their most important cases out there, now...Calls me 'Mrs. Masterson!' Isn't that idiotic! Nancy says it's because I'm employed there...Funny—don't you think?"

Helen thought it was funny; thought the whole speech funny.

"Really—" Joyce leaned forward and dropped her voice. "If I had the teeniest right to, I'd lose my heart—utterly! You know I always was a little bit soft about him!"

"I hope you'll not be indiscreet, Joyce."

"Oh, I'll take pains not to let him know I think he's nice," she reassured. "But—I don't want you feeling unkindly toward him. You really can't avoid meeting him, you know."

"Why not?"

"Well—you'll be out at Brightwood, more or less, now I'm there..."

"I don't see how your work at Brightwood would require my presence."

"But—you're going out, aren't you?...Honestly, darling, you'll just have to be pleasant toward him—for my sake!"

"For *your* sake?"

Helen experienced a momentary wave of disappointment...In her long absence from Joyce, she had idealized her somewhat; but—she was the same Joyce, whom no blunders could chasten; the same unchanged Joyce who couldn't forget anything, or learn anything; hopping gaily out of the frying-pan into the fire.

"Yes," repeated Joyce dramatically, "for my sake!"

"Then," said Helen slowly, "I'm sorry I came back."

They ate their duck; but it wasn't very good.

* * * * *

That night they saw "The Hypotenuse." It was a rollicking comedy employing a small cast and simple materials. A young widow and her contemporary stepdaughter furtively concealed from each other, throughout the first act, that the late Judge Haskins' junior partner was of larger interest than was demanded by his professional service as their attorney and business counsellor. Act Two developed some delicious situations, adroitly handled. The audience was delighted.

When the curtain had finally settled, after several trips in response to warm applause which brought them all back together, and then reconsidered them in relays, finishing with mamma and Polly, hand in hand, Joyce turned animatedly to offer comment and surprised an abstracted look on Helen's face. She, apparently, had not been quite prepared for the sudden onrush of lights.

"You're tired, aren't you?" inquired Joyce solicitously.

"It always takes a day or two, I think, to recover from a long journey."

"Awfully jolly show, don't you think? Fancy such a mess! You and I—for instance! We'd be honest with each other, at least! I suppose we'd just cut the deck to see which one was to get him."

"Stuffy in here, isn't it?" said Helen. "Let's go out and prowl in the foyer. Want to?"

* * * * *

Joyce's incapacity for understanding the operations of her own mind was spectacularly displayed, early next morning, as she dressed to go to Brightwood, babbling about herself as a "woiking goil."

Breakfast had been served in their rooms. Helen, exquisite in a dainty lounging robe, was lingering over her coffee and the morning papers.

"I think it's simply marvellous," enthused Joyce, into the mirror, "that I've been able to adjust so quickly to office routine, don't you?...After all these years of indulging myself, sleeping late, pottering, lazing about! I'm happier than I ever thought I could be again. I know now I'll never be contented, any more, without a regular job."

"Glad you like it," said Helen, deep in the theatre advertisements. "What do people say about this new musical comedy, 'Jasmine'?"

"Very tuneful, I hear...Like this hat?"

"Cute!...Suppose Mrs. Ashford might like to come down town, to-morrow, and have dinner with us and see 'Jasmine'?"

"Oh, I'm sure she would love it! I'll ask her. And, darling—she and Bobby Merrick are such pals. Wouldn't it be nice to ask him, too?"

"Not a bit nice! I don't know him! I don't want to know him!" Helen's tone was frankly impatient.

"Well, you could get acquainted with him. *I* know him! Couldn't you consider my wishes a little?" Joyce savagely flicked probable dust from her coat.

"Hand me my pocketbook...there...on the mantel. Thanks!"

Helen opened it and unfolded a letter.

"Oh—it's the one I wrote you!...Well, what about it?"

"Read it...You will see that you asked me to travel five thousand miles to give you some good advice. Now that I've gone to the bother of humouring you, I hope you'll not resent it if I say that your present state of mind in regard to Doctor Merrick is absurd!...If you want to be silly about him, don't annoy me with it! I won't have him thrust down my throat!"

"Well—what's come over you? I hadn't heard that residence in France and Italy made people so squeamish!...And it seems to me that a person with your admiration for people who do really valorous things—at a lot of cost to themselves—would take a little human interest in Bobby Merrick, slaving himself almost to death, when, if he wanted to, he might be lounging on a yacht somewhere in the Mediterranean!...I heard one of the nurses say he had come into a million dollars' worth of Axion Motors when he was twenty-five, and is due for another million when he is thirty! I tell you he deserves some credit!...Good-bye...Don't be peeved!...See you about five-thirty."

Helen rose, after the door had slammed, and stood looking down upon the street...Axion Motors!...A million dollars' worth of Axion Motors!...*Axion!*

CHAPTER XVI

MR. T.P. RANDALL was extremely solicitous in his attitude toward his charming client. She had telephoned him at ten, and they had agreed on a business conference at one-thirty.

He was tall, fifty-five, well-fed; grizzled at the temples. The tailor who had made his waistcoat might have succeeded as a sculptor. He rose, as she entered his padded leather and dark mahogany sanctum, dignifiedly offered his hand, bowed to the top of her close-fitting grey hat from his considerable altitude, helped off the grey fur coat from the grey gown, drew out the throne-like chair for her, seated her, walked around the table majestically, sat down in his swivel-chair, folded his big, pink, newly manicured hands on the bare desk, and said again that he was glad to see her. He mentally doubted his assertion, however, and looked more than a little troubled.

Considering it highly important that he should lead the conversation into safe channels, he talked of Paris, where he had once spent a fortnight, and of Venice, where, he declared, he would like to live; but it was obvious, from the restlessness with which she chafed the backs of her grey gloves, that she hadn't come to hear his impressions of Europe.

At the first semicolon, she leaned forward in her big chair.

"You had a long talk with Mr. Brent about my affairs."

T. P.—he was known as T. P. throughout the Fourth National organization—drew an anxious smile. Now, why the devil hadn't he been told that he was supposed to have talked with this rapscallion Brent? He had been under the impression that Brent was to be presumed as having had all his business with him by correspondence.

"Umm!" murmured T. P., deep in his throat. He gave it just that quality of indeterminateness which might make it pass either for an affirmative, or a mere receipt of information already in hand, or a promise that presently he would discourse at more length about the matter when she had quite finished her remarks.

But she was not going to be contented with his "Umm." He saw that at a glance.

Mrs. Hudson smiled—a bit roguishly.

"There was one man you had to look up to; is it not so?"

Her syntax was unfortunately under continental influence. It made the query difficult to evade...My eye!—was this innocent child with the wide blue eyes leading Detroit's most resourceful side-stepper into a trap?...Well, he'd follow along, and see what came of it. Of a sudden he remembered; he brightened; he tossed up an outspread hand.

"Rather!...Uncommonly tall!...Your cousin, I think."

"Yes," agreed Mrs. Hudson.

T. P. took a long breath, exhaled it luxuriously, and felt relieved.

"Must be six feet three, isn't he?"

"About my height," said Mrs. Hudson. "But—he is my cousin."

"Oh—of course!" T. P. laughed, boisterously. "Of course! You knew I was jesting, of course!"

She did not join in his merriment.

"Odd that you should have forgotten!" she said meaningly.

When in doubt about what next to do, T. P. always fell back on the didactic style. He could stun and bewilder with his voluminous vocabulary of technical terms relating to the upper ether of large finance. He settled sternly to it, ignoring their brief exchange of exploratory thrusts, and discoursed of stocks. Most industrials were good now; motors especially; Axion most assuredly. She could be confident that her money was prudently placed. Moreover, she could sleep soundly o' nights while the Fourth National looked out for her interests...And—by the way—he wanted to show her about through this fine new building before she left, if there was time...Not quite satisfied with her expression, he launched upon an oration of some length, rumbling wisely of economic trends, cycles, the periodicity of financial mutations now happily stabilized by the Federal Reserve. At the first full stop, she said:

"I would like to see my stock certificates."

"To be sure, Mrs. Hudson! Of course!"

T. P.'s tone was paternal. Inwardly he chuckled. If this amazingly good looking young widow had hopes of learning how she had become possessed of her Axion Motors by inspecting her stock certificates, she was about to be disappointed. She had caught him napping in respect to his relations with her ne'er-do-well cousin, and it was up to him to take the next trick in this little game. Well—she would discover nothing new, bearing on the question, from these certificates. Hadn't he told Riley to hustle those shares of Doctor Merrick's back to the Axion office to be re-issued in the name of Mrs. Hudson? Of course!

However—just to make doubly sure. He quite distinctly remembered having written to Blair, the transfer agent of the Axion Motor Corporation, notifying him that, beginning at once, all future dividends on that block of stock were to be forwarded to the address of Mrs. Hudson, who now owned them, and that the certificates would be brought over to him for re-issuance. Surely he had remembered to tell Riley about that. To be on the safe side, he'd inquire.

"I'll send for them," continued T. P., beaming amiably. "Excuse me, please."

He was detained in the adjoining office for fully five minutes, and when he returned he was mopping his expansive brow with a large, monogrammed handkerchief. Resuming his chair, he smiled, not very happily, and said:

"It may take quite a little time. Had we known you would want to see them, they would have been ready for you. We have such things pretty carefully stowed away, you know."

"Yes," said Helen, comprehendingly, "you would have, of course."

"It's rather a pity to keep you waiting so long," regretted T. P. Why the devil couldn't the woman say, "Oh—never mind about them, then."

"I can wait," she replied, settling comfortably in her big chair.

T. P. drummed on the desk with anxious fingers.

"You know we have them, of course, or you wouldn't be getting your dividends."

"Oh—certainly."

"They're just like any other...You've seen stock certificates, haven't you?" He was still amiable, but he was growing desperate.

"Yes...and I would like to see these!" She glanced at her watch.

There was nothing more that T. P. could do about it. He pushed a button, gave an order, tried to be cheerful, tried to be nonchalant; but the conversation was unsatisfactory. Neither of them had the slightest interest in it.

At length the certificates arrived, and he pushed them across the desk.

She slipped the top one from under the broad rubber band, spread it out, turned it over, and noted the endorsement whereby it had been transferred from Robert Merrick to Helen Hudson.

"Thank you!" she said, rising. "That will be all, I think. I shall be in again to-morrow to talk further with you."

T. P. did not waste time, immediately his client had left. He took up the telephone, and in his best bank manner told the switchboard to get him Doctor Merrick at Brightwood Hospital. The contact was no sooner made than T. P. went off the deep end, without ceremony, and reported what had happened. The answer he received consisted of a few words not properly used over the telephone, which really has to draw the line somewhere.

"Now—Doc—you've got to keep your shirt on! I tell you it absolutely couldn't be avoided! It was either that—or tell her we didn't have the stuff at all! Would that have improved the situation any?...Hell!...She's suspected all along. You might 'a' known she would! That woman's no ninny!...What say?...Why—damned if I know, Doc. She left here—pronto—shot out of a gun—a bit flustered, maybe...No—I don't know, I tell you. Perhaps she was. If so, I suppose you'll soon find it out!...Well, I'm sorry as you are, Doc; but you might 'a'..."

There was a metallic click that made T. P. wince. He laid the instrument back on its rack, opened the left lower drawer of the desk, took out a bottle and a glass; poured, swallowed, sizzled and shuddered; replaced the bottle, shut the drawer, lighted a cigar, pushed a button.

"Riley—put those certificates back where you got 'em...and if anybody wants me importantly, call me at the Athletic Club. I've a headache."

* * * * *

Not often was Helen Hudson a victim of emotional stampede. Her poise was not a pose; neither was it arrived at by effort. It was native to her.

This afternoon she simply tossed the reins of discretion upon the neck of her indignation and abandoned herself to the tempestuous rush of it. Mentally at full gallop, she hurled herself at Brightwood.

It was as if a huge, ugly cauldron of anxieties, perplexities, forebodings, misgivings and suspicions, which had been simmering and bubbling for all the dragging months, had suddenly reached that stage of the brewing when it was time to pour.

A taxi waited at the door of the bank as she emerged, half-blind with humiliation. She walked swiftly to it, gave the driver an order, and sat tense throughout the journey.

This abominable Merrick had placed her in an impossible position...No matter about the intent...He had doubtless enjoyed his Galahading...But he had made her his pensioner; treated her like an irresponsible child; helplessly loaded her with an obligation she would probably be unable to discharge...Well, she could disavow her willingness to accept anything further at his hands! She could return the capital of it, at once; and set to work toward a replacement of what she had spent.

Exactly what she was going to say to Bobby Merrick when she saw him, Helen had not yet determined clearly. Of one thing she was sure: she would denounce his officious meddling with her affairs, and let him know exactly where he stood in her regard...He should have it all back!...Oh!...She pressed her shaking fingers against her eyes and tried to cool her cheeks with the back of her gloves.

Barely conscious of the journey, the unhappy girl stepped out of the cab as it stopped in front of the hospital, ordered the driver to wait—she would not be long—and quickly pattered up the broad concrete walk between masses of formal shrubbery coated with glistening ice.

* * * * *

At the desk in the snug little lobby, she inquired for Mrs. Ashford, and was shown into her office, where she quite took that pretty lady's breath away with her exotic beauty.

"Why—what a joy!" cried Nancy, putting forward both hands in greeting. "I knew you were in town, and have been so anxious to see you!"

"Yes," said Helen breathlessly, and with an effort to steady her voice, "I do want to have a good visit with you—and I shall—soon. But not—just now...I find I have a rather sudden errand with Doctor Merrick. Could I see him?...Is he here?"

He was here, and she could see him. Nancy believed he had just now finished an operation, and would probably be at liberty. She would send him in, and they could talk in her office.

Nancy went out, her own heart beating rapidly, and closed the door behind her. For a while, Helen fidgeted on the little divan, fumbled with her pocket-book, latching and unlatching and latching, tapping her little grey-shod toes impatiently on the rug; then, unable to sit still another instant, she rose, walked to the window, and stood gazing preoccupiedly at the street, her fingers busy with her coral beads.

At length, the door was quietly opened and as quietly closed, and she was aware of his presence in the room. She knew he was standing there, just inside the door, expectant, waiting for her to turn and face him...Why in the world didn't she?...Would he cross the little room, and approach her—speak to her?...Perhaps not...But why didn't she turn quickly and confront him?...She had asked for this interview, hadn't she?...She had sent for him to come to her, hadn't she?...What ever ailed her, anyway?...The difficult thing about it was that she had delayed turning about to face him!...Every second that passed made the situation more trying...

After a young eternity, he spoke—rather unsteadily.

"You wanted to see me?"

His quiet query broke the spell for her. She turned quickly, and, leaning against the window, put her outspread hands upon the sill, in a pose that Bobby sorrowfully interpreted as a sort of back-to-the-wall defence; but not defiance. Her head was bowed; her eyes to the floor. It was so thoroughly against his wish and hope that whatever he had done for her should put her into this attitude.

Helen was dismayed at her own sensations. Ten minutes ago, she had been ready to do violence. When she had stepped to that window, she had been aflame with a passionate anxiety to call him hard names; to hurt him, somehow; to let him taste a little of the humiliation he had put upon her...What had happened to her?...She felt deserted even by her own rage...Well—she could not stand there silently any longer.

She lifted heavy eyes to meet Bobby's.

"I must have a talk with you," she said, in that throaty contralto he so keenly remembered; a timbre that seemed to set up all manner of curious vibrations in him.

"Won't you shake hands?" he begged.

"No need!" she said, with a little gesture of futility.

"Then—will you sit down?"

"Thank you—no. I think I can say it—quickly!"

Bobby leaned against a corner of Nancy Ashford's desk, folded his arms and listened.

"I have just discovered that everything I have in the world is—is yours. I have been living, for some time, as your dependent...I didn't know. I'm sure you will believe I didn't know..."

"Of course you didn't know! You have nothing to blame yourself with—in this matter."

She went on as if she had not heard.

"The very clothes I have on me..."

She lowered her head and covered her eyes with her outspread fingers.

Bobby could stand no more. With his heart furiously pounding, he stepped quickly to her, and took her hands in his. For the tiniest instant, she permitted his impulsive gesture of sympathy, and then withdrew from him, shaking her head.

"No! No! I didn't come here to be pitied!" Her voice was firmer now, and there was a note of rising impatience in it. "I've been pitied—quite long enough! All I came to tell you is that all your money at the bank I am going to turn back to you; and, as fast as I can possibly earn it, I shall pay you every dollar I have spent."

Bobby drew a deep sigh of regret, stepped back, and leaned his weight against the desk, his eyes brooding.

"I'm so sorry," he said slowly. "You see—the circumstances were very strange. I wanted to spare you, if I could, a misfortune that would bring you some unhappiness. I guess I went about it the wrong way—but I meant it all right. Won't you believe that?"

* * * * *

For a second, their eyes met in a look that each remembered later, when, that night, the episode was reviewed, inch by inch, and word by word, on sleepless pillows—Bobby solemnly wondering whether, had he taken her in his arms at that moment, their difficulties might have been solved—Helen remorsefully chiding herself for what she feared was a serious disclosure of a feeling she had tried to batter into submission.

"Perhaps you did," she admitted, tugging herself loose from his eyes. "But it doesn't make my position any more endurable. I don't propose to be pensioned by you! I'm going to give all your money back—the capital, to-morrow—the amount I have used, at the earliest moment I can earn it!"

"You mustn't do that!"

Bobby's voice was stern, commanding. He stood erect and faced her determinedly.

"There's more to this than you are aware of...more than I dare tell you! The lives of many people would unquestionably be affected! Whatever you may decide to do with that money, you can't give it back to me! I won't take it! I can't take it...because you see, *I've used it all up!*"

Helen glanced up quickly, her eyes wide with amazement. She swallowed convulsively.

"W-h-a-t?" she whispered. "What is that you say?"

"*I've used it all up*!...Do you know what that means?"

"No! Tell me! What *does* it mean?"

"Sit down," he said gently. "I'll try to explain...It's not easy, though."

She walked with some reluctance to the little divan and sat.

"Perhaps you never had it called to your attention,"—Bobby was feeling his way with caution—"that there is sometimes a strange relation between the voluntary, secret bestowal of a gift, without expectation of any return or reward, and certain significant results that accrue from it in the experience of the giver...Now I am not sure that this money I was so happy to put at your disposal is not that kind of an investment. Shortly after I arranged for it, something of quite tremendous importance occurred—something that dared not be trifled with by either of us...It's almost hopeless to try to make it convincing to you, I know...Can't you just take my word for it—and trust me—dear?"

Helen flushed deeply, and rose—her eyes flashing.

"No—you're not dealing squarely with me!" she retorted hotly. "And I'm not—your—dear! You have humiliated me! There are many things I have wanted to know, and you seem to be able to clear up some mysteries; but you are plainly not disposed to do so. I'm going now. I shall arrange at the bank about the money. And—the rest of it—the part I've spent—I shall pay that back! You can depend on it!" She was at the door, her hand on the knob.

Bobby stepped swiftly to her side and covered her hand with his own.

"Listen!" he demanded soberly. "It is quite important, both for your sake and mine, that we do not set every tongue in this place wagging with the gossip that we met here to have a row. You're ready to go stamping out through the office, rosy with rage. Much curiosity will be aroused and explanations will be in order."

"Then you can make them! I do not feel that I owe anybody an explanation. If you think you do, that is your affair! Let me go, please."

Bobby did not remove his detaining hand.

"My dear," he said, scarcely above a whisper, "I appeal to your good sportsmanship! Granted—that you have cause to be indignant. Granted—that I have blunderingly placed you in an awkward predicament. Let us at least keep our misunderstanding to ourselves. Please! Compose yourself—and we'll go out to face these people as if there were no trouble between us. Wouldn't that be ever so much better?"

She hesitated for a long moment; looked up searchingly into his eyes, like a bewildered little child, and finally replied:

"Agreed."

He released her hand and she walked to the window, took out a tiny vanity case and consulted her reflection, Bobby regarding her with repentant eyes. How wretchedly he had bungled everything—everything!

Presently she turned and faced him calmly, like a stranger.

"I'm quite ready, if you are."

Bobby hesitated.

"But—really—don't you think—" he stammered shyly, "that a wee bit of a smile might help to—to..."

"I'll attend to that when we need it!"

* * * * *

He opened the door and signed for her to precede him. At that instant, she became another person, gracious, smiling.

Nancy Ashford, who had been hovering about, with curiosity and some anxiety, met them. She drew a quick breath, apparently of relief.

"I'm so glad you two have found some occasion to become acquainted at last," she exclaimed, searching their faces eagerly.

"Yes—isn't it?" responded Helen, slightly confused over her cue. "Doctor Merrick and I have been talking of so many interesting things—some of them quite mystifying, I'm afraid."

Ah!...Good!...So that was it!...Mystifying things!...Mrs. Hudson had been asking questions...Somehow she had learned—by a chance word, perhaps—that Bobby Merrick was in a position to clear up some of the strange riddles bequeathed to her by her husband...So—that was what had brought them together...Good!...Nancy was radiant.

"I hope I may soon have a little visit with you, Mrs. Ashford," continued Helen rather breathlessly. "To-day—I'm in something of a rush...Important errands."

At the sound of the familiar voice, just outside the door of her little filing-room, Joyce came bounding into the circle with a shrill exclamation of surprise and delight and a torrent of questions.

"Why, whatever brought you here, darling? Why didn't you tell me you were coming so soon? And you and Doctor Merrick have actually met! How jolly? Oh—now we can have that dinner we talked about! Let's do it to-night! We four! My party! And I'll get tickets for 'Jasmine!' What do you all say? Can you come, Mrs. Ashford?"

Nancy swiftly sought Helen's eyes, and thought she detected a faint expression of annoyance. Should she encourage the dinner project? It was an awkward moment.

Suddenly sensing her own obligation to take a cordial interest in Joyce's proffer of hospitality, Helen smiled inquiringly, and Nancy replied, "I should be very happy, Joyce. Thank you."

"And you can come, too, can't you, Bobby?" persisted Joyce.

He studied Helen's face for a brief second, and found his heart pounding when she glanced up unmistakably interested to hear his reply.

"I'll be very glad to come, Joyce."

Helen glanced at her watch.

"I must be going," she said determinedly. "I'll see you all this evening, then."

The three of them accompanied her to the big, glass-panelled doors—Bobby at her elbow, obviously proposing to see her to the waiting taxi. The pair descended the snowy steps, his hand on her arm, both conscious that Nancy and Joyce were still standing just inside the door, observant.

*****

"We must talk," said Bobby cheerfully. "This game isn't over yet."

"True," agreed Helen, turning toward him with a smile that fairly dizzied him. "And from all indications, you've let us in for a whole evening of this delightful recreation! Whatever made you say you would come to that wretched dinner Joyce contrived to plan? Some more of your good sportsmanship, I suppose!"

Bobby was contrite. His face was overspread with it.

"Don't look like that!" she commanded, her tone oddly out of step with her smile. "They'll think we are quarrelling!"

"Well—" glumly, "aren't we?"

She laughed.

"As a dramatist, you seem to be better as a producer than an actor!"

"But, really, I was going to refuse the invitation. And then, when I happened to glance at you, you seemed so—so friendly about it..."

"What had you thought I might do? Scowl at you? It was your own suggestion that we appear to be on good terms. And now—well, you have taken advantage of me—as usual." She was still smiling. They had reached the kerb. The taxi-driver was churning his engine.

"I'll contrive some excuse," decided Bobby, weakly. "I'm sorry."

"No! You can't do that. We're in for it, and we'll see it through; and I can promise you that my own feelings will not be apparent to anybody." She hesitated for a moment, and added, "Not even to you! I'll guarantee not to spoil your dinner."

Bobby opened the door and helped her in. The warm grasp of his hand on her arm vexed her—thrilled her. Safe in her seat, she no longer felt under compulsion to make further show of amiability. The smile had vanished. He held out his hand, and she, annoyed, was obliged to accept it. He held it tightly.

"Good-bye, dear," he said tenderly. "Please don't think too badly of me. I have blundered, terribly, but—my dear—I do love you so!"

CHAPTER XVII

WHEN Merrick arrived at his apartment shortly after midnight, he slipped out of his dinner clothes and into a dressing-gown, and told Matsu to toss another chunk of pine on the fire and go to bed.

The evening's entertainment had been a gusty symphony set to every key and tempo; brief passages of ineffable tenderness, momentary measures of hope, drably padded intervals of manœuvring and modulation, spiced, with occasional breath-taking crescendos that went ripping shrilly up the chromatic scale precariously freighted with anxiety. The finale, unfortunately, had brought up on a most disquieting diminished chord...Considering the evening, in total, its moods were as fitful and erratic as Sibelius' *Valse Triste.*

He had hoped to bring to it the sportsmanly spirit of an athlete entering upon a vigorous contest. His dear antagonist had promised that nobody—not even he—should be aware of her irritation and resentment, and he knew she would keep her word. If hers would be a difficult part to play, his would be more so. All she had to do was to register cordiality. Whoever, with any social experience at all, had not learned how to dissemble in pretence of amiability when thrown with persons whom one disliked? As for him, the part he had drawn called for a cool casualness; not the stiff restraint of renunciation, or a show of ascetic indifference, but the calm courtesy of a man toward a woman he had barely met. It would be his task to carry this off convincingly—this with a heart aflame.

As he gave himself a brief inspection in the cheval glass before starting down town, he seriously pledged his own reflection that he would maintain an attitude of dignified chivalry toward the woman whose promised pretence of friendship, for an evening, would probably be little short of torture. And he had seen through, almost valorously—all but to the end.

And yet, remorseful as he was over that one brief but utter breakdown of self-discipline, which now made their relations more difficult than ever, he tingled to his nerves' ends with memories of those few enchanted moments when, even fully aware that she but kept her contract, her comradeship had seemed sincere.

In the mood of a miser, eager to be alone to finger his gold, he impatiently dismissed the solicitously lingering Matsu, lighted his pipe, and eased himself into a deep chair before the crackling fire, determined to live the evening over, item by item, and recover its most stirring sensations.

* * * * *

Pursuant to instructions from Joyce, he had called for Nancy Ashford. Regally stunning in crimson, with her youthful face, glistening white hair, superb figure and resilient step, Nancy was worth all the pride he had in her. He told her so, and she thanked him—for that, and the flowers.

Nothing ever escaped her eye. She remarked, as he helped her into the limousine, that Richard had a new cap and puttees.

"You haven't had him in uniform before, have you?" she inquired. "I thought you had some democratic convictions on the subject."

"So I had," he admitted, "but I've changed my mind. He's part of an institution, with his uniform on, and it helps him keep out of mischief. At least, that's the theory. Besides, he likes it."

There had been a lot of rambling chatter like that, to which he had contributed with unusual animation; but Nancy dodged from under the fusillade of inconsequential talk presently, eager to be enlightened.

"Bobby," she said, as his beautiful new car had swung into the current of boulevard traffic, and lengthened its stride, "something tells me this is to be a rather difficult event."

"You always were a keen observer, Nancy," he conceded.

"One didn't have to be gifted with occult powers to see that the atmosphere at Brightwood, this afternoon, was heavily charged."

"Pardon the interruption, but—I like you tremendously in that colour. You are very beautiful to-night, dear."

"Meaning that you don't want to tell me about it?"

103

"Well—perhaps...Something like that."

"Very good, then. I shall shut my eyes, ears, and mouth. I am the three wise monkeys. I'll pretend I don't know that you two have had a quarrel."

"That's a dear!"

"And I shall also pretend I don't know that you silly things are so deeply in love you're afraid to exchange glances for fear your secret may be discovered."

"I still think you are beautiful, Nancy."

"But dumb!"

"No, no! Not that!...Quite exasperatingly to the contrary!"

At this she had forgiven him, squeezed his hand, called him her dear boy; and, for the rest of the trip, discussed hospital affairs in a most business-like manner.

* * * * *

They stepped out, at the Book-Cadillac, into a big-flaked snowstorm, and hurried to cover through the revolving doors. Joyce and Helen were awaiting them, by appointment, on the mezzanine, Joyce almost boisterously gay, swishy and sinuous in some green taffeta confection, wearing the corsage he had sent her; and, unless he was much mistaken, she had tucked a cocktail or two under his orchids, for there was a taut nervousness in her canary gestures and a strident overtone in her voice hardly to be had for less bother than the embarkation of about three jiggers of gin...If Helen observed it, she was apparently resolved to ignore it. Seeing it was an occasion for the wholesale ignoring of unpleasant facts, there was probably no reason why she should cavil at this one...What an adorable creature she was...in the black velvet...and the pearls...and his orchids. So she had actually consented to wear them!...Score one against the beloved enemy!

* * * * *

Curiously enough, Joyce, from the first moment, had seemed bent upon hurling them at each other, almost violently...Maybe it was the gin...Perhaps her instinct told her there was some unspoken bond between them which it was her duty to make articulate...Of course, it was always difficult to guess what, how, or whether Joyce was thinking...But, whatever her motive, if she had one, she was at no pains to disguise her intention to make this little party the occasion for a rapid development of their budding acquaintance...as if it were some fungus that must mature now or never.

Indeed, she had been utterly ruthless. Over the salad, she had chinked a momentary gap in the conversation by murmuring to herself, in an exaggeratedly stilted style, "Mis-ses Hudson!...Doc-tor Merrick!...Dear me!"—with a shrug and a sigh—"I had hoped they might be Bobby and Helen by this time!" To which Helen had replied, leaning toward her, in an apologetic, maternal undertone, "Drink your milk, little one. There's a good child!"...They had laughed, their merriment in the nature of applause.

* * * * *

The hotel was suffocatingly crowded. Some big trade convention was on, and the public lounges and foyers were swarming with fussy fat men, wearing long blue and gold badges on their lapels, beads of perspiration on their foreheads. Dozens of them were milling about, bound in as many directions, teetering themselves crabwise athwart the current, begging pardons, right and left, in the tone of "Gangway!" Their corrugated brows certified that unless they managed to squeeze through, the whole enterprise, after all this trouble and expense, would be futile.

Their weary wives sagged in every available chair, conscious of their redundant knees, pecking at fresh marcels with nervous fingers. A few of the more intrepid attempted a languorous indifference toward their unaccustomed cigarettes which, however, they regarded gingerly and at arm's length, as foolhardy urchins hold sputtering firecrackers—nonchalantly, but with secret concern at the tail of the eye.

Joyce had impetuously taken Nancy's arm and led the way.

"Keep close, you two," she shrilled, over her shoulder, "and don't get lost. We must hurry, so we will not be late for the theatre!"—and had swept Nancy along into the squirming pack.

Bobby had offered his arm to Helen and she had taken it; not perfunctorily, but as if she wished to do so...She really needn't have done it...Neither Joyce nor Nancy could observe them...She might have ignored his gesture...It was not necessary she should play a part at that moment.

They were jostled in the crowd. He had drawn her closer to him, and she had responded...No—it was not merely that she had been pressed against him from without...She had responded...There was a difference. He had drawn her closer to him, and she had responded!...

He relighted his pipe, mechanically, and absently held the match until it nipped his fingers.

She had responded so generously that he could feel the warm, soft contours of her against his arm...She needn't have done that...It was not in the book of her play...Yet, it was what she would have done if there had been no estrangement between them; or would she?...Probably not...It was hard to think straight about this affair.

Until now, no words had passed between them except their brief salutation at meeting, and Joyce's patter had sent even that into eclipse. He felt he should be saying something to her. He despised dull commonplaces, but the silence must not be permitted to grow any longer.

Of a sudden, he had become audacious.

"I led you this way, once, through a very dark lane," he heard himself saying.

"Oh—was it?" she laughed. "I thought we went hand in hand. I felt like a little girl being led to her first day in the kindergarten."

"So—you do remember!"

"Rather! I don't know what I should have done that night without you." And she had looked up into his face and smiled. He wondered if she could feel the pounding of his heart...They were entering the dining-room...Joyce waved a hand from a table halfway the length of the room.

"Tell me something, while we're thinking about that," continued Helen, confidentially. "Why didn't you let me drive you home, that night, or at least put you down as we passed your gate?"

"Because I preferred you shouldn't know me. I thought that if you knew, you might—" He had broken off, lamely, groping for a word.

"That was a very appropriate way to begin a friendship like ours," she said crisply, "seeing it was destined to be full of little deceits and riddles."

"I am sorry," he said. He must have appeared appallingly so.

"Well—don't be, then!" she commanded hotly, with a savage little tug at his arm. "You look like Hamlet! Grin, I tell you! Your Nancy Ashford knows well enough we have been quarrelling! I saw it in her face this afternoon. I'm not going to do this farce all by myself!"

He had looked down into her big blue eyes, amazed at this outburst so startlingly out of keeping with her serene expression, and laughed aloud. As he reviewed it, now, he laughed again. It had been absurd...beyond belief!

* * * * *

"What's the joke?" demanded Joyce, as the waiters drew their chairs.

"Long story," said Helen briefly, "and the good man laughed at it once. I can't have him hearing it over again."

Nancy looked puzzled. He was secretly pleased over her bewilderment, and amused to see that the little episode had put a crimp in her omniscience.

"Your curriculum is all prescribed," Joyce was saying, as the waiters hurried away, "all but the dessert. That's an elective. Otherwise, you take what the institution thinks will be good for you. No, darling," she added, turning to Helen, "it isn't veal. I remembered that you had already worked off your credits, majoring in veal."

"Do tell us some of your other experiences abroad!" Nancy had begged. "I'm hoping to go over, for a summer, presently, and I'm awfully keen on travel tales."

How graciously she had complied! And how charmingly she talked of her impressions. Most of the larger cities he knew almost as he knew his own, but she had seen things that

105

he had missed—intimate glimpses up narrow streets and into quaint shops where, it seems, she had frequently made the acquaintance of a whole family...How tenderly she talked about little children!...

* * * * *

"In Assisi, I once made some wonderful friends that way, in a little shop," she was saying. "I'm afraid I began visiting the Bordinis, at first, to improve my colloquial Italian. Of course, I always bought some trifle to pay for my tuition, or brought along something for the children; but after a while, I found myself going there because I liked them and really needed their friendship. And, one day, little Maria, about three, took dreadfully ill. For three weeks, she just hung on to the mere edge of life. They were all so terribly worried. And, not having anything very important to do, I was in and out, frequently, through those days—"

She interrupted her story to unfasten from within the neck of her gown a little silver cross.

"Maria's mother insisted on giving me this when I left Assisi."

The trinket was passed around the table. When it came to him, he had inspected it, with a feeling of reverence. It was holy—for many excellent reasons.

"I did not want to take it," pursued Helen, "for I am sure it was the most treasured thing she owned. It had been blessed by the Holy Father himself, when, as a young girl, in nineteen hundred, she had accompanied a pilgrimage to Rome."

"So that's why you're wearing that cheap little cross!" exclaimed Joyce. "Does it bring you good luck?"

Helen smiled.

"Perhaps," she answered. "At least, I like it better than any other jewellery I have."

"Very naturally," commented Nancy understandingly.

Joyce was quite attentive.

"You must have been the family's main prop, during their trouble, to earn their enchanted cross. Let's have the rest of the story. What all did you do for them while Maria was sick? Help keep store? Were you the nurse? Go on, darling! Tell us all about it!"

At that point, he had been unable to restrain himself. Quite to his own amazement, he had held up a protecting hand.

"No, no, Joyce! We really daren't ask Mrs. Hudson to tell us that!" Instantly he had felt embarrassed by his own remark.

"How funny! Why shouldn't she tell us?"

He had turned to Helen, at that, and asked soberly, "Did you ever tell anybody that story?"

"No! Now that you ask—I don't believe I ever did."

"Then I wouldn't, if I were you. This is a very valuable little keepsake, and its chief charm is in the fact that nobody knows but you what you did to earn it."

"How perfectly ridiculous, Bobby!" shouted Joyce. "Did you know he was so superstitious, Nancy?"

"I had suspected it—a time or two."

Helen was regarding him with perplexed, wide eyes as he put the little fetish into her palm with a gesture that had been perilously close to a caress, for his finger-tips had lingered there.

"Sometimes I have thought of sending it back to her. You seem to have ideas on this subject, Doctor Merrick. Perhaps you will tell me; should I?"

"By no means. It wouldn't be valuable to her any more if she accepted it. She really can't take it back now, you see, because—because..."

Helen's lips were parted, and she was a bit breathless as she urged, insistently, "Yes?—because—because what?"

"Well—because—by this time she has possibly—probably—used it all up, herself."

She stared at him steadily for a moment, as if she had seen a ghost. Then, half-articulately, and for his ears only, she murmured, "So—that's—what—that—means!"

"Yes—exactly! That's what it means!"

Her eyes were misty and her fingers trembled as she refastened the little cross inside the neck of her gown.

"I'm glad you told me," she said, under her breath. "I have so often wondered."

* * * * *

Joyce put down both hands with a sudden gesture of impatience.

"What on earth are you people talking about!...Do you know, Nancy?"

"Oh—vaguely, I think," she replied..."You liked the little towns best, didn't you, Helen? Let's hear some more about them. There was Bellagio. Tell us about that."

"Oh, do!" echoed Joyce. "You wrote such wonderful letters from there. What was the name of that little hotel—on the top of the hill?"

"The Villa Serbelloni?" Helen grew moody. "Yes—I quite liked it, at first; but I grew very lonely there. I became so unhappy I left, one afternoon, on a moment's impulse—in a drenching rain."

"Why—what was the matter, darling?" inquired Joyce solicitously.

"Just sheer loneliness! The season was over, really, and almost everybody had gone away. There was a young woman I had found congenial, but she turned out to be a writing person, and seeing that was what she was there for I couldn't impose myself on her when she needed all her time for writing; so, one dreadfully lonely, stormy day, I left."

"Ever see any of her work?" Nancy wanted to know.

Helen shook her head.

"Perhaps you should make some inquiries," suggested Joyce. "Maybe you figured in some of her tales, yourself. Wouldn't it be odd to pick up a story and find oneself cavorting about in it?"

During all this Bellagio talk, Helen had addressed herself chiefly to the others. As she replied to Joyce's comment, however, she turned her eyes slowly in his direction.

"It's quite possible I may have qualified for some minor part in a story; for I had been as garrulous as a high school girl before I discovered her occupation."

"I am sure you were the heroine of the piece," he had declared stoutly. "I would swear to that!"

"You seem as certain as if you really knew." She had leaned slightly toward him. Her nearness gave him a chance to mutter, in an undertone, "I do!"

* * * * *

The talk had drifted, then, to ships. Nancy was anxious to know all about voyages; what to wear, how much and whom to tip, how long in advance one should book passage to insure good space.

"Helen had hers on a day's notice, coming back," remembered Joyce.

"But it's not always that way," Nancy argued. "I recall a quite hectic experience we had in getting accommodations for some friend of Bobby's who was suddenly required to go to Buenos Aires."

He had glanced apprehensively at Helen, and found her staring into his eyes, her brows knitted in perplexity. Quickly collecting herself, she said:

"Perhaps the season had something to do with the congestion. When was it?"

"When was it, Bobby?" queried Nancy. "You ought to remember. You were no end excited over getting him off by that boat. It must have been about a year ago; possibly a little earlier than this."

"Something like that," he had agreed disinterestedly.

The waiters had handed them menu cards. Joyce and Nancy had their heads together in consultation over parfait flavours. Helen had raised her card until it screened her face from them.

"That was very good of you," she said softly. "I never guessed—until now."

"I didn't intend you should. I hope you will never give it another thought. I'm sorry the matter inadvertently came up."

Her face was studious for a moment; then brightened, suddenly, with illumination.

"Oh—I see!" she murmured.

"I wonder if you do."

She nodded her head vigorously.

"It is something like—like my Bordinis—and my little cross, isn't it?"

"Yes—exactly like that!"

Joyce had put an end to their cryptic by-play with a demand for light on the dessert problem...It had been a very tender moment. As he mulled it over now, analytically, it occurred to him that had he been called away, on some emergency duty, at that juncture, he might at this moment be exulting in the hope that their misunderstanding had been definitely cleared...

* * * * *

He rose and paced the room, digging his finger-tips into his temples, paused at the little table, re-filled his pipe, replenished the grate, and sank again into his chair. A small cathedral clock on the mantel wearily tolled the first quarter.

Those four strokes, when, on occasion, they caught his attention, invariably sent a momentary cloud drifting across his mood. It was not so at the half. The clock seemed to have cheered up, noticeably, by that time. It was almost reassuring when it came to the third quarter. But, always, that jaded, resigned, mocking, Amarish da—de—di—dum at the first quarter impressed him with the solemn asininity of whatever he happened to be doing and the futility of everything he was planning to do. It was exactly as if Eternal Destiny stretched its long arms and yawned. He could never be sure precisely what it said. Sometimes the strokes were but four gradations of an articulate sigh of inexpressible fatigue.

The vibrations still lingered. He glanced up. It was fifteen minutes past two...He resumed his reflections, moodily, realizing that his memories, from this point, would be disturbing.

* * * * *

The short trip to the near-by theatre had been uneventful, made in his own car. As it drew up at the kerb, he had heard Helen exclaim to Nancy, "What a beautiful car! What is it?"...He had not caught Nancy's reply; but she knew.

They were very late, having lingered long at dinner...Gropingly following the usher's little electric torch, they had dodged guiltily into their seats which fortunately were on the aisle.

A nimble chorus marched mincingly across the stage, single file, in close formation, like a garish caterpillar; coquetted, shrieked a piercing blast, broke ranks, and were joined by the male contingent which sauntered in from the wings. There was a stormy repetition of the theme song, a final deafening screech, with arms aloft, and the lights burst on as the curtain fell.

Joyce, who had insisted on leading the way, leaned to the left, across Nancy and Helen, to hand him the seat checks...How vividly every trivial incident stood out now, chiselled in high relief...He had reached for the ticket-stubs, his movement pressing him close against Helen's bare shoulder. His hand had lightly brushed her arm. Every chance contact swept him with a suffocating surge of emotion. It was only by the sternest resolution that he resisted the urge to touch her.

He could not remember what the chatter was about at this first *entr'acte*. Joyce seemed to have provided most of it—some amusing incident of "Jasmine's" opening night in New York. Nancy was her best listener; Helen smilingly half-attentive, half-preoccupied.

The orchestra trailed in, twitched its E-string; the director raised both hands, swept his crew fore and aft with a final inspection; and they were off at full gallop in the descending darkness.

He had wished he was not quite so acutely conscious of her beside him, fearing she might sense the physical out-groping of himself toward her. Nancy's experienced observation recurred to him. He had told her how keenly aware he had been of the girl in the car beside him, that night in the country. Nancy had pooh-poohed his naïve notion that Helen was, of course, ignorant of his sensations.

"Nonsense!" Nancy had scoffed. "Do you imagine she could have that effect on you without sharing it?...How little you know about women!"

It was near the close of the second act that the catastrophe occurred.

He had not been following the silly, threadbare plot with enough attention to realize what, if anything, it was aiming at. His mind had been concentrated on the magnetic presence beside him, what time he was not day-dreaming of the happiness he would find in surrounding her with the things she ought to have. It was not until he had irretrievably blundered that he came awake to the fact that he had unwittingly insulted her.

The dashing ingénue had returned—it was a colourful scene of a country house party—in a luxurious limousine. The fact that she was penniless; that the car was the property of the brazen broker who had been pursuing her throughout the play with gifts and attentions obviously to be credited on account; that the imported gown she wore was his by purchase—all this was of no significance to him...At that moment, the only fact of any interest to him was the quite good-looking limousine.

Impetuously, he had turned to Helen—their heads had touched, lightly, for an instant—and whispered, "I heard you say you liked my new car. I'm not using it much. I'd like to lend it to you for the time you're here."

Perhaps, even then, the most serious blunder of all might have been avoided had she been quick with an emphatic refusal...Unsuspecting that her silence meant nothing more encouraging than that she had been stunned by his raw audacity, and heartened by that misinterpreted silence, he had groped shyly, his heart pounding, for the hand that he knew lay, palm up, very white against the black velvet.

Perhaps she had intuitively divined his intention...Perhaps the slight movement of his arm gave her warning...Or, did she choose that exact second to toy with her strand of pearls?...He would probably never know how it had happened...The warm velvet stirred uneasily under his brief caress.

The curtain was falling. The house was flooded with light. He glanced apprehensively toward her. Her cheeks were flushed, and her little fist, tightly clutching her handkerchief, was pressed hard against her lips.

* * * * *

On Joyce's suggestion, they strolled in the lobby. On the way up the aisle, Helen had taken Nancy's arm, and Joyce, observant, had tarried until he fell into step with her. Animatedly, she had carried the full responsibility for their desultory talk. He was glad, for his mind was in chaos.

When the signal summoned to the last act, they returned in the order in which they had made their exit, and when their seats were reached, Helen led the way in, leaving Joyce beside him.

What a beastly cad she must think him!...But—surely her own good sense would tell her he had not meant it!...Not that way!

He hadn't the faintest idea what the last act was about; sat through it suffering every imaginable torture. After a few eternities, the wretched thing was done.

Their parting was brief, conventional, without one single understanding look into each other's eyes.

In the morning, he would find her and attempt an explanation...The clock tolled the four quarters and struck three...He had an operation to do at nine.

Wearily he flung off his clothes and went to bed. As he relaxed on his pillow, sick at heart, the chimes offered a cynical comment on his adroit handling of the evening's complicated problem.

* * * * *

Upon his arrival at the hospital, in the morning, the desk notified him he was requested to call Mr. Randall at the Fourth National Bank, to which he paid no attention.

Having finished his operation, he called the Statler and asked for Mrs. Hudson. She had checked out.

CHAPTER XVIII

THE Bruce McLarens were entertaining Dr. Robert Merrick at luncheon in their cosily furnished apartment. It was Sunday, and the three of them were just back from Grace Church where the appearance of the distinguished young surgeon in the minister's pew, in company with Mrs. McLaren, had excited a genial buzz of pride and satisfaction.

Bobby Merrick's recent spectacular contribution to the cause of brain surgery had been made much of by the press, somewhat to his own dismay; for he had the honest scientific worker's shyness of publicity. It had been quite embarrassing to see his invention described in the argot of journalistic ballyhoo, and he was not nearly so grateful as he would have liked to be for the well-intended eulogies on the editorial pages of the dailies, and the sentimental twaddle which embellished his biography in the digests and reviews.

Of course, it really had been a corking story, well worth its two-column head on page one. The scribes had left nothing out. Young Doctor Merrick's utter abandonment of the leisure to which he had access by virtue of his large fortune, to give himself tirelessly to the most difficult and discouraging speciality known to surgery, was played up for all that the traffic would bear. Had he not promptly barricaded himself against the fleet of feature writers who bore down upon him, the matter would unquestionably have been worse.

"You really owe something to your public!" one of them had twittered, as if she were talking to some movie-struck flapper who had won *The Times'* beauty contest.

It was even recalled that Doctor Merrick's life had been saved, some years ago, at the same hour when another eminent brain surgeon, the late Dr. Wayne Hudson, had drowned in Lake Saginack. One paper (pink) had broadly wondered if the wealthy young Merrick's immediate decision to enter a medical school where he trained to espouse brain surgery might have been influenced, if not indeed directly caused, by that tragedy; but, lacking the details, and unable to twist them out of the unhappy hero or his associates, it had been content to toss out the hint and let the public draw its own conclusions.

Within eighteen hours after the news broke, Bobby had decided that if the liabilities of front page publicity were pitted against the assets accruing therefrom, his account with Fame was already in the red. It was obvious that a new star was better off for a low visibility. His mail was crammed with importunities from every known species of beggar; appeals from alleged philanthropies ranging all the way from foundations guaranteeing international understanding to wildcat altruistics for the relief of hectored blue-jays. He was the recipient of home-brewed poetry extolling his merits, slobbering songs hymning his praise and hopeful of publication at his expense, saccharine love letters, many of them enclosing photographs. He was besieged for luncheon talks. He became a fugitive, darting from cover to cover.

Even out at Windymere, where he sought seclusion for a week-end, shortly after the persecution set in, he was exasperated to find his grandfather proudly and—for him—garrulously accommodating a severely tailored young woman who required some intimate knowledge of Bobby's boyhood to adorn a magazine story.

"Ah—Robert—surprised to see you!" exclaimed old Nicholas. "We were just speaking of you. This young lady..."

"Yes, I see," Bobby had responded icily. "I dare say she will pardon us if we change the subject."

"That I will not!" giggled the visitor.

Nicholas had looked very foolish and helpless over the situation until Bobby came to his relief by summoning Meggs.

"Tell Stephen to drive this lady down to the station, Meggs. She is anxious to make the 4.16."

* * * * *

As for his colleagues in the profession, their gratitude and generous felicitations had been a source of much pleasure. Every day brought dignified encomiums from well-known men of his own speciality, thanking him for the unselfish manner in which he had promptly made his find available to his fellows. He had had letters from every civilized country of the world.

Now that sufficient time had elapsed for his sudden fame to jellify, Bobby had shyly crept out into the open to resume his normal schedule of activities and recreations. He had not yet become accustomed to the stares, whispers, and nudges, which singled him out in public places; but, seeing he couldn't sneak about forever like a hunted thing, he masked his self-consciousness the best he could and took his punishment with an assumption of nonchalance. To-day he had even risked going to church.

* * * * *

Doctor McLaren had preached a scholarly sermon to a large audience of good-looking people—fully half of whom were under forty—on a topic he hoped would be of special interest to his important guest.

Indeed, what Dr. Robert Merrick was going to think of that sermon had loomed so large in the popular young preacher's mind, while preparing his discourse, that it was with much difficulty he had restrained himself from the use of a scientific phraseology quite beyond the ken of his customers—albeit, as church audiences went, they intellectually registered A-plus; and freely admitted it. Grace Church was quite conscious of its modernity.
"Really, the most forward-looking—indeed the only forward-looking church in town!"—Mrs. Sealback was remembered to have said in prefacing her suggestion of Doctor McLaren as the proper person to invoke the divine blessing on that session of the Social Congress which had programmed a discussion of Birth Control.
"As to what?" President-of-the-Social-Congress Mrs. Cordelia Kunz of Grand Rapids had inquired drily, tapping her notes with a cunning little lorgnette. "Forward-looking on economic questions, social problems, political issues—or merely posing as the last outpost of orthodoxy?"
Mrs. Sealback, slightly dizzied and not a little nettled, had replied that she was sure she didn't know exactly how far or in what direction Grace Church led the way to freedom—and snapped her purse several times, quite noisily, to emphasize her disclaimer of further interest in the matter—unaware that the brusque gavel-swinger from up state had indeed touched a mighty live wire.

* * * * *

Obedient to the necessary precautions, however, Doctor McLaren had made a few last-minute substitutions for certain erudite terms he feared might overshoot his congregation; but, even with these begrudged alterations in the cause of clarity, the address was as one scientist to another, and the people who heard it were at once flattered and befuddled by its charming inexplicability. They, too, wondered what Dr. Robert Merrick thought of it, and were glowingly proud of their wise young pastor.

And they had every right to be proud. The Rev. Bruce McLaren, Ph.D., was by no means an intellectual coxcomb or a solemn blatherskite with a fondness for big words and an itch to achieve the reputation of a savant. His scholarship was sound, and the sermon that morning was a credit to it.
Deacon Chester, warmly gripping his pastor's hand, shouted above the shrill confusion of the metal-piped postlude that he guessed it was the most profound sermon ever delivered in Grace Church! The statement was entirely correct; nor was the word "guess" used in this connection a mere colloquialism. Had Mr. Chester been a painstaking stylist—he was a prosperous baker of cookies by the carload lot, and not averse to admitting that he had left school at thirteen—he could not have chosen a word more meticulously adequate than "guess" to connote his own capacity to appraise the scholarship disclosed by that homily. Had a photographic plate been exposed to Mr. Chester's knowledge of the subject which Doctor McLaren had treated, it could have been used again, quite unimpaired, for other purposes.

* * * * *

The warm friendship which had arisen between Doctor McLaren and Doctor Merrick dated from a raw March evening when the rangy, bronze-haired preacher had been brought into Brightwood, unconscious and breathing stertorously, with an ugly and dangerous smash in the right squamous temporal. He was muddy, bloody, and limp. It had looked black for him, that night; and the only recess Doctor Merrick had permitted himself, from the time he finished the necessary repairs at nine until the next morning at seven, were brief pacings up and down the corridor in front of his important patient's door, tugging nervously at cigarettes, and disinterestedly accepting the sandwiches and milk brought up by a nurse at three.

Bobby Merrick had liked McLaren from the first moment; liked the length and strength of him as he lay on the operating table, subconsciously making his good fight for life; liked the shape of his broad forehead, the cut of his ears, the cleft of his chin, the hardness of his well-tennised right forearm, the texture of his hide, the elliptical curve of his thumb. All these things were significant. Had Doctor Merrick been required, he could have written a two thousand word paper on the character of Doctor McLaren before ever he had heard him speak.

He had liked his patient, next day, for the inherent poise he exhibited when, rousing for the first time to a vague consciousness of his surroundings, he had taken in the situation at a glance, and, apparently considering it as all in the day's work, had dropped off to sleep, at the nurse's suggestion, without bothering to ask questions. Bobby had liked him even more, a few days later, for his quite superior capacity to take his punishment—and there was a lot of it—without flinching or grousing. And, finally, he had liked Doctor McLaren's state of mind when, a week after the accident, he had spoken calmly and without rancour of the drunken insolvent who had run him down in a safety zone.

"He probably feels bad enough about it," remarked McLaren, in his deep bass, mellowed by an ancestral Scotch burr. Anyway, I'm not going to press the matter, or make myself wretched by mulling it over."

"That's amazingly good sense!" Merrick had commented, privately resolving to see more of this man when he was up and had his boots on. He had never known a preacher before. His rather nebulous opinion of the clergy had been collected from cartoons, the quips and jibes of paragraphers, and satirical sideswipes at the profession roughly projected from the stage and screen. He had lately thumbed, scowlingly, a nasty novel vilifying men of this vocation. He was not conscious of an active dislike for them, but shared what seemed to be the unchurched public's general belief that preachers were—to put the matter laconically—a bunch of saps.

Every day, the young surgeon found himself more and more pleasantly attracted by his patient, enjoyed his droll comments, offered in moments when drollery came high, admired the adroitness with which he parried the friendly railery of doctors and nurses—chaff invited by his own whimsical humour. Almost everybody in the organization at Brightwood was in to see him, at one time or another, during his convalescence; and it was quite unanimously held that he was a good sport.

And no less cordially interested had been the Brightwood household in the brown-eyed, deep-dimpled Mrs. McLaren who had appeared, anguished but admirably controlled, a half hour after her husband's arrival. They had telephoned her that Doctor McLaren was seriously injured, suggesting that she come at once. When she came, there was no hysteria...Would Doctor McLaren recover? They couldn't say. It was too soon to tell. He was very, very badly hurt...She took the blow standing, and they rejoiced in her pluck. She was invited to stay the night, and they were at pains to give her every scrap of available information about her husband—both good and bad.

From the first, Mrs. McLaren was adopted at Brightwood on unusual terms. When Doctor Merrick told her, at noon, that her husband was putting up a very encouraging resistance, and had at least an even break in the decision, she did not stage a scene. There was a momentary tight closing of her eyes, a quick breath of relief, and a misty smile; but no theatricals. She had herself well in hand. Bobby liked her for that. He was glad to have her about. Sometimes, when her husband was asleep, she would read to other convalescents. On several occasions she offered first aid to hysterical next-of-kins, who waited while operations of interest to them were in progress. One day, upon invitation of Doctor Pyle, she went into the operating-room to see "some interesting surgery"—from which entertainment she hastily excused herself, however, when a diminutive saw began making noises that played the deuce with her digestion.

The McLarens were, by popular suffrage at Brightwood, "all to the good."

* * * * *

One afternoon, the Reverend Bruce said to Doctor Merrick, as the latter sat by his invalid chair, visiting—not very professionally, but with a hope of hearing a few more Scotch stories: "Beloved, I'll soon be out of here, and I'm just a bit anxious about my bill. My income is small, and my present balance at the bank, if there is one, would amuse you. Of course, I know what the hospital charges are, and I can manage to pay them. But I have been afraid to ask about your fee, thinking perhaps the shock wouldn't be good for me. Speaking of the Scotch—what are you going to charge me?"

"Well—I'll make you a proposition, dominie. You have given me a chance to patch your head. I'll give you a chance to do something for my soul. And we'll call it square. I'll take it out in trade. How's that?"

"It's mighty generous," rumbled McLaren, in a tone at least three added lines below the bass clef. "I'll expect you to come in and attend my church, soon as I am in the running again."

"Oh—do I have to go to your church for this treatment?"

"Well—I came to your hospital, didn't I, for mine?"

"You win!" said Bobby submissively. "I'll be there!"

* * * * *

Pursuant to his promise, he had gone to Grace Church on that fine May morning, after having telephoned the McLarens he was coming, and having accepted their invitation to return with them to their apartment, afterwards, for luncheon. Betty McLaren had quite enjoyed the sensation of presenting him to many of their friends. She had been very proud of Bruce's performance in the pulpit. She was having a good day...Would Doctor Merrick have two lumps or three; cream or lemon; and wasn't he surprised to see so many young people in the congregation?...Doctor Merrick would have one lump; neither cream nor lemon; and was it anything to be surprised at that young people went to church?

"Oh—quite!" replied Doctor McLaren, helping his guest to a portion of a delicious omelette. "That's our one great satisfaction! You see—the students and the young business and professional people have outgrown the old traditions and are eager for an—shall I say an intellectual approach to religion. We have been trying to give it to them."

"I noticed that," said Bobby. "Your sermon was very scholarly; and they liked it, I am sure."

"Well, doctor—if you don't mind being helpfully candid with me, exactly how did it strike you—as a scientist?"

"Oh, I'm not much of a scientist. A surgeon doesn't have to be a scientist—just a good mechanic."

Betty McLaren protested with a laugh.

"Come now, Doctor Merrick! The very idea! You—not a scientist? We know better than that!"

"At all events, you have the scientific outlook—the scientific approach," insisted Doctor McLaren. "Perhaps you noticed at what pains I was to avoid the old stock phrases of theology."

"I fear I wouldn't recognize them as such," confessed Bobby. "But—what's the matter with the old terminology?"

"Obsolete! Misleading! We'll have to evolve a new vocabulary for religion, to make it rank with other subjects of interest. We've got to phrase it in modern terms; don't you think so?" Doctor McLaren was eager for his guest's approval.

"Perhaps," agreed Bobby tentatively. "I don't know. Whether people could learn any more about religion by changing its names for things of concern to it, I'm not sure. It just occurs to me—casting about at random for a parallel case—that the word 'electricity' means 'amber.' All that the ancients knew about electricity was that a chunk of amber, when rubbed with silk, would pick up a feather. Now that it has been developed until it will pick up a locomotive, electricity still means amber. They never went to the bother to change the name of it. Maybe they thought there was at least a pleasant sentiment in retaining the name. More likely, they never thought about it, at all. Too busy trying to make it work, I suppose."

"Humph! That's a new idea. Then you think it doesn't make much difference about the phraseology of religion?"

"It wouldn't—to me," replied Bobby, hoping he had not too ardently objected to a pet theory of his host.

"Well—there seems to be a demand for a more adequate interpretation of theology. We are trying to be a little less dogmatic in our assertions and a little more honest. For instance—I think it's ever so much better to say frankly that God is an hypothesis than to attempt to offer proofs which fail to stand up under their own ponderosity."

Bobby was tardy with a rejoinder, and both McLarens silently quizzed him out of the tails of their eyes. Surely he ought at least to believe in the Deity as an hypothesis!...He observed that they waited.

"I'm afraid I don't accept that," he said at length, rather shyly.

"Oh—Doctor Merrick!" reproved Betty disappointedly. "You don't mean to say that you do not believe in God, at all!"

"I mean that I do not think of God as an hypothesis."

"But—my dear fellow," exclaimed McLaren, "we really have no hard and fast proofs, you know!"

"Haven't you?" asked Bobby quietly. "I have."

The two forks in use by the McLaren family were simultaneously put down upon their plates.

"Er—how do you mean—proofs?" queried his host.

* * * * *

Bobby wished then that he had smilingly deferred to the minister's theory. He had no relish for controversy. And this was no place for it, had he been no end a debater. Moreover, he knew he was not in a position to explain what he had called his proofs. Lamely he admitted that what he had considered sufficient evidence for the existence of God might satisfy no one but himself. He privately hoped the conversation might soon find safer going.

"You're probably arguing from 'design'," McLaren suggested bookishly.

"Oh—probably," said Bobby, with a gesture of dismissal.

"The whole business of institutionalized religion," resumed McLaren, didactically, "demands reappraisal! It appals me to contemplate what must be the future of the Church when all the people who are now fifty and up are in their graves! This oncoming generation, now in its adolescence, is not in the least way concerned about organized religion. Religious enough, instinctively, I dare say; but out of sorts with the sects; weary of their bad-mannered yammering at one another over matters in which one man's guess is as good as another's, and no outcome promised either in faith or conduct, no matter whose guess is right!"

"Is it that bad?" commented Bobby. "I hadn't known the churches were losing ground. There seems to be such a lot of them."

"Yes—too many!" grumbled McLaren. "Too many—of the wrong kind!...Take so important a matter, now, as the nature and mission of Christianity's author, himself. A Christ who can help us to a clearer perception of God needs to be a personality confronted with problems similar to ours, and solving them with knowledge and power to which we also have access—else he offers us no example, at all.

"But here we have a majority of the churches trying to elicit interest in him because he was supernaturally born, which I wasn't; because he turned water into wine, which I can't; because he paid his taxes with money found in a fish's mouth, which—for all my Scotch ingenuity—I can't do; because he silenced the storm with a word and a gesture, whereas I must bail the boat; because he called back from the grave his friend who had been dead four days, while I must content myself with planting a rosebush and calling it a closed incident! What we want is a Christ whose service to us, in leading us toward God, is not predicated upon our dissimilarities, but upon our likenesses!

"In our church, we're trying to offer a Christ who is not a mere prestidigitator—a magician who feeds an acre of people from a boy's lunch-basket—but a great prophet and an understanding friend! Don't you think a man can accept that, and still be a sound scientist?"

Bobby accepted a light from his hostess's hand, and slowly nodded.

"I know very little about the conflict between the traditional estimate of Christ and the more recent theory. Viewing it superficially, I should say that neither system would appeal very strongly to this age. Isn't the modern school just substituting a new metaphysic for the old one? Our generation is doing all its thinking in terms of power, energy, dynamics—the kind you read about, not in a book, but on a meter! Why not concede the reality of supernormal assistance, to be had under fixed conditions, and encourage people to go after it?"

"That sounds a little as if you believed in prayer, Doctor Merrick," said Betty wistfully.

"You mean—getting down on your knees to wish you had something?"

"Oh, it's more than that!...Asking God to give it to you!"

"Well, that depends on your credit."

"Agreed!" nodded McLaren.

"I'm afraid I don't quite understand," said Betty.

"Why, he means that unless one has been living up to one's best ideals, it's useless to ask for God's approval and assistance. That's obvious."

"No," said Bobby. "That is not what I meant. If you're interested, I'll tell you a story."

* * * * *

For the next two hours—they had moved to the library on Bobby's hint that they had let themselves in for an extended tale—the McLarens sat scarcely daring to trust their own hearing.

Eager to give them all the steps of his spiritual progress, in their exact sequence, he had begun back in Randolph's studio. Carefully picking his way with a care to the avoidance of any act of his own, performed in pursuance of the Galilean theory of availing prayer, he laid the facts before them in a dispassionate recital.

He finished as he had begun. He could hardly expect them to believe it, he said. He hadn't believed it; had been disgusted by it; intellectually offended by it; in violent revolt against it; but—well, there it was!

"How utterly trivial," said McLaren humbly, "my whole programme of preaching seems in the face of such astounding possibilities! Why—we've been trying to teach religion without—without knowing what it's about!"

"Oh, I shouldn't go so far as to think that!" consoled Bobby. "You've inspired people to take stock of themselves. They can't help being better for every serious thought you've given them about life and duty. That's ethics. And ethics is decidedly important. This thing I've been talking about is not in the field of ethics. It belongs rather to science. We have been at great pains to construct devices and machinery to be energized by steam and electricity and sunshine; but haven't realized how human personality can be made just as receptive to the power of our Major Personality."

"I feel, to-day," said McLaren, "as if I'd been doing nothing—exactly nothing!"

"By no means! You have been doing some highly necessary work in clearing away the old superstitions; the old irrelevancies. That's not labour lost, you may be sure! Only—as I listened, this morning, I couldn't help wishing that this new interpretation of religion which you are so splendidly equipped to offer might go further and show how soundly scientific religion is. You counselled us, to-day, to accept the evolutionary hypothesis. You said—if I recall correctly—that we could explain everything we have and are by that theory...Now—I don't agree with you. Perhaps our bodies derive from some pre-human type of life. Perhaps all romantic literature is but an elaboration of the animal's urge to reproduce itself. Perhaps our brains are but refinements of elementary nerve ganglia that used to respond, automatically, to the necessity for food and shelter...It hasn't been proved. You were ever so much more sure of it, in your pulpit, than my biology professor was, in his classroom...But—assuming a physical evolution, biology has no explanation to offer for human personality. You ask old man Harper how he accounts for aspiration, penitence, inquisitiveness about our origin, concern about our future—and he'll say, 'I'm not a theologian, sir! I'm a biologist!'"

"And I suppose you're hinting," smiled McLaren, "that my chief business is to account for aspiration, penitence, and man's passion to be a time-binder—and if anybody inquires what I think about evolution, I'd better reply, 'I'm not a biologist, sir! I'm not a theologian!'"

"Something like that," agreed Bobby.

"I wonder if we modernists," said McLaren, after a considerable pause, "are not somewhat in the predicament of Moses, who had enough audacity to lead the slaves out of their bondage, but lacked the ingenuity to take them on into a country that would support them. We've emancipated them; but—they're still wandering about in the jungle, dissatisfied, hungry, making occasional excursions into paganism and experimenting with all manner of eccentric cults, longing for the spiritual equivalent of their repudiated superstitions—sometimes even wishing they were back in the old harness!"

"It's worth while to have fetched them out of that," said Bobby. "It ought to be equally interesting to lead them on. They mustn't go back! But they will—if they're not pointed to something more attractive than the jungle you say they're in."

* * * * *

As he left the house at four, McLaren followed him out to his big coupé parked at the kerb.

"Merrick," he said rather timidly, "would it be asking too much of you to come to my church again next Sunday? I'm going to have something a little more constructive to offer—and I'd like your reaction."

"I would gladly, but I shall be on the briny deep. Sailing Saturday to France, en route to Vienna to see a colleague. I'll be happy to come when I return."

He stepped on the starter and the powerful engine hummed.

McLaren gripped his hand.

"Merrick—just a minute!...We modernists have been trying to show how religion is not at odds with science. What we've got to do now is to show how religion *is a science*! Isn't that what you mean?"

"Exactly! Nothing less or else than that! You have it! More power to you! See you in September!"

CHAPTER XIX

MAXINE MERRICK, pouring their coffee in the sunny breakfast room of her over-Louised apartment in Boulevard Haussmann near the Etoile, glanced up shyly at her distinguished guest, finding it difficult to identify him as her son.

His mouth was somehow different. Ungifted with any capacity for character analysis, she was unable to define the change, but some dormant instinct told her it was other than merely functional; it was organic, structural.

It was not an austere mouth, neither was it pessimistic; but it had put off its adolescent wistfulness. It no longer entreated or anticipated, or even inquired; it accepted. The mouth had none of the tight-buckled smugness of self-imputed infallibility; none of the haughty protrusion of authority in repose; but it looked as if it were concerned only with facts, and had learned to be very particular about them. If they had really been shown to be facts, the mouth accepted them—let the facts be fair as a May morning or ugly as sin.

And his eyes were somehow different. They seemed deeper set, not as if they had winced but retreated from sights they had found disagreeable—experienced eyes that were used to looking at suffering, but not without great cost to themselves. They were not sad or weary eyes, but one felt they had seen so much they would not again widen readily with surprise. They did not cynically defy you to startle them; but you knew there was nothing you would be likely ever to say or do that would make them blink with amazement.

There was a difference in his hands; same long, slender, artist fingers—but they had left off groping uncertainly for things. They had achieved a sureness, a poise, a confidence not to be had at less expense than the honest, tireless, discriminating experience of dealing with facts—let the facts be no end unpleasant.

In short, they were the mouth, eyes, and hands of a surgeon.

Bobby's decision to go in for a profession had failed to impress her favourably. Beyond a feeling—which she tardily and peevishly expressed—that he was enslaving himself unnecessarily, she had been left unstirred by his resolution. His completion of his medical course evoked only a request that now he was finished with school she dared say he would be able to run over and spend the summer with her. Later, when he had settled to the routine of an occupation demanding a devotion all but cloistral, she confided to her intimates how unfair it was that he should give his life to strangers when his own widowed mother stood in such desperate need of him. Her infrequent notes, in purple ink and big sprawling letters, blubbered with self-pity and petulant accusations of indifference; but her mileage was about as good as ever, and she was rarely alone except when asleep.

When, however, it had been called to her attention—she never read the journals or reviews herself—that a young Doctor Merrick of Detroit—could it possibly, her informant wondered, be her own Bobby?—had been making himself famous by the invention of a remarkable surgical instrument, her pride knew no limits. Suddenly aware that she had sacrificially offered him, years ago, on the altar of humanitarian service, and had been waiting hopefully for the day when her unselfish renunciation of her maternal claims on him might be publicly recognized, Maxine hastened to collect the tribute due her valiant and uncomplaining martyrdom, inviting all and sundry to view the stake whereon she had sizzled through the long-drawn days when her faith and hope were under fire.

For the space of a week she romped about among her acquaintances, accepting with happy tears their high-keyed chirps of felicitation, and cabled a mawkishly sentimental message to her son which fervently thanked the good God for making all her wonderful dreams come true, and cost her four hundred and fifteen francs.

This morning, Maxine lacked but a decade of looking her age, and felt even closer to it than she appeared. At no little cost she had planned the brilliant luncheon she was giving to-day at two when Bobby was to be triumphantly exhibited to a half dozen young old ladies—mostly self-exiled Americans who had either outlived, outgrown or outworn their relatives—and as many modish and musty old gentlemen with grey moustaches and ginny breaths. She had been bland with her statement that they were exceptionally favoured by this invitation to meet her boy prodigy, and privately hoped he had matured sufficiently to justify the story of his wide distinction. It had not occurred to her that he would return to her with that kind of a mouth, those eyes, those hands, which accused her of being not a day under fifty-six.

Accustomed to playing rôles on short notice, suggested by her own volatile caprices, she determined to meet this awkward circumstance on its own ground. She would enjoy being the mother of a lion, even if the fact that the lion was no longer a cub would make it difficult for her to be quite so kittenish as usual. She was giving herself a dress rehearsal, this morning, of the new part, and was almost matronly.

"You'll love them, Bobby!...Such dears!...And—Bobby—" she held up a warning finger and twinkled it mysteriously—"I've asked my adorable Patricia Livingstone to come with her mother. We've been so anxious to see you two together. You'll be enchanted with her!"

Bobby grinned amiably and said he was going to be happy to meet them all, especially someone his mother considered adorable. It was obvious she was preparing for this event as if it were a coronation, and he was resolved to humour her. God knew it was little enough he had ever been able to do for her pleasure. He would to-day atone for all his failures to be what she wanted him to be by going cheerfully into an affair which, he suspected, would establish his utter asshood as a fact beyond controversy in the opinion of any sensible person present.

Considering the will—in this instance—equivalent to the deed, he later scored up the party to his credit; though he was unable to attend it.

* * * * *

Bobby Merrick's decision to request a four months' leave had been based ostensibly upon an extended correspondence with Dr. Emil Arnstadt of Vienna. Arnstadt had been long at work on the coagulation cautery project before the Merrick invention was announced. Immediately he had sought full information about it which was promptly and cheerfully given. Then had sprung up the warmest attachment between them, leading to Arnstadt's ardent hope that Doctor Merrick would come to Vienna for a leisurely conference on their mutual interests.

"We have much to give each other," wrote Arnstadt. "It is well we should meet."

In the scales alongside Arnstadt's intriguing invitation was an importunate letter from Jack Dawson, down on all fours in supplication.

"No small matter, I tell you, to be asked into conference with Arnstadt! You've got to come. It's equivalent to a command! You've got to come for my sake! You must realize I've never felt decent about the way I came here as the winner of a prize you tossed into my lap. You shouldn't have done it. Of course, as it has all turned out, you've more achievement to your credit than had you written that exam in full for old Appleton and taken the persimmons you so jolly well deserved. I never had any illusions, old chap, about my winning the first honours and this prize. You handed them over to me because you thought I needed them more than you. I never felt easy about it. But—now that Arnstadt wants to do you this honour, don't refuse. It will make me a heap more comfortable, I can tell you!"

But these pressing invitations to Vienna were not the actual driving reasons why Bobby Merrick had decided to spend the summer in Europe. The real tug, he was bound to admit, resided in the fact that Helen Hudson was conducting a small party of tourists through Italy and France. He had a hope of meeting her. She was interfering with his work, disturbing him in his sleep, making him restless, absent-minded, distraught. However she might regard him, he must see her again, if to no better purpose than to change the torturing mental picture he carried of her, shamed and hurt by his unintended impudence. Some kind of reconciliation must be attempted. He had accepted his expulsion from his Fool's Paradise, and no longer cherished the notion that he could reinstate himself with Helen; but it would be worth the trip to see her—let her be indignant, indifferent, or contemptuous. He must dispose somehow of this haunting picture of her, hurt and humiliated.

He had kept track of her movements through Joyce, who had quite voluntarily confided the essential facts of Helen's sudden departure from Detroit the next morning after the execrable theatre party. It was apparent that Joyce had not been informed—and equally apparent that she very much wanted to know—what business had drawn her young step-mother impulsively out to Brightwood, that winter afternoon. In Joyce's mind there seemed an inevitable sequence relating that event to Helen's sudden departure for New York, early next day, on some unexplained errand.

Short of actually putting a thumbscrew on him, Joyce's inquisitiveness to learn how much Bobby knew about it was persistent, ingenious, desperate; but she received small pay for the news she offered as bait.

Exactly why Helen Hudson wanted or needed employment badly enough to become a routing agent in the office of the Beamond and Grayson Travel Bureau, Joyce couldn't imagine. It was so unlike her. She hated routine. She wasn't used to taking orders or keeping hours. She was about as practical as a Persian kitten on a satin pillow.

Bobby had had to listen to an inordinate amount of this, astounded at his own patience, though in his honest moments he reflected that had Joyce not prattled so volubly of her own accord he would have been obliged to prime her to it.

He was thankful enough for her gift of garrulity the day she told him Helen was about to leave the New York office for Cherbourg, as the conductor of a small party.

"Does Joyce annoy you, Bobby?" demanded Nancy Ashford one afternoon, with her disconcerting directness.

"Oh—not at all!" he had replied, feeling a bit silly.

"As I thought!...She has just been offered an interesting position as a home visitor with the Juvenile Protective League. I shall press her to take it."

Duly pressed, Joyce accepted the new job. On her last day at Brightwood, she cornered him as he was leaving the hospital at five.

"I won't be seeing you any more, will I?" she said. "I'm leaving, you know."

"Why—that is true," he replied, as if it had not occurred to him before. "You'll be busy, and you know how this ties me up here. I do hope you like your new work. You must let us know how you get on with it, Joyce."

118

"You couldn't come and see me sometimes? I'm going to be horribly lonely." It was evident that the speech cost her something. She forced it with an effort.

"Oh—I don't go anywhere...Unsocial as an oyster...This business is cruelly confining. Some day I hope to have a little more time for—"

She laughed, nervously, mirthlessly.

"Don't say any more, Bobby. It's plain you don't want to...Good-bye! I may not see you for a long time."

He took her cool hand and repeated his good wishes. The episode left him uncomfortable. It had been a decidedly awkward situation. Maybe, if old Tommy could be bucked up, somehow, Joyce might be willing to give him another try. It was worth looking into.

* * * * *

Arriving in New York that Friday morning, the twenty-second of May—he was sailing on the *Majestic* the next day at four—Bobby had hunted his old friend down and was startled at the change in him. Tommy was seedy, shiny, spiritless, and had skipped patches under his jowls in shaving...Not much wonder Joyce wanted some other employment besides looking after Tommy.

They had lunch together and tried heroically to recover their long lost collegiate mood, but it was rough going. Too much water had gone under the bridge...Too little water had gone into Tommy.

"Sometimes—" Masterson furtively pushed a soiled cuff back into his coat-sleeve, and attempted to steady his leaky spoon—"sometimes, I've had a notion to end it. If I wasn't such a damned coward, I'd have done it long ago."

So—there being at last a definite motion before the house, Bobby discussed it. Masterson was of the artist type that required a deal of encouragement and adulation. It couldn't be laid on too heavily. Tommy had always possessed an almost infinite capacity for absorbing glory, laud, and praise. Unquestionably Joyce could have kept her man on the rails had she been a little less frugal with his necessary rations of ambrosia. Well, it was high time he had some. Bobby fed him on the rich confectionery of appreciation all day and left him hilariously drunk with it at midnight—drunk as ever he had been on whisky. He was going to perk up and show 'em, by the Eternal, that he had the stuff! He'd been temporarily depressed, but—as Bobby had said—that was naturally to be expected of any man gifted with so sensitive a creative imagination! And he'd been drinking too much; but he could stop it. He would stop it! And there was his hand on it! The worm had turned!...And a good deal more like that.

Before he turned in, Bobby wired to Nancy.

JOYCE URGENTLY NEEDED IN NEW YORK STOP TOMMY HAS FINISHED WITH J BARLEYCORN STOP IS FULL OF REVIVED AMBITION STOP DEMANDS REGULAR MEALS ENCOURAGEMENT COMPANIONSHIP STOP STRONGLY COUNSEL HER TO HELP HIM MAKE GOOD STOP PUT IT UP TO HER AS IMPORTANT SOCIAL SERVICE STOP SHE WILL STILL BE WORKING IN INTEREST OF JUVENILE PROTECTION STOP YOU NEED NOT TELL HER THAT STOP AFFECTIONATELY MISTER FIXIT P S AND HERE IS HOPING FOR BETTER LUCK THAN USUAL IN MANAGING SOMEBODY ELSES BUSINESS R M

Sunday afternoon he was roused from a nap in his steamer-chair to receipt for a radiogram. He smiled with pleasure.

JOYCE LEFT FOR NEW YORK AT NOON.

* * * * *

"Patricia paints beautifully!" continued Maxine, passing Bobby his cup.

"Does she, indeed?"
"Batiks."
Bobby's eyes wandered disinterestedly over the headlines on the front page of *Le Matin* at his elbow.
"Any news?"
"No...But—what's this?...Seven Americans hurt in a railroad accident near... *Oh, my God*!"
Maxine rushed after him as he dashed from the room and found him telephoning for a taxi. For the next five minutes, while he frantically tossed a few necessities into a bag, she hovered at his elbow, extracting broken phrases from him..."Terrible accident...my best friend...have to go...awfully sorry...No!...No!...Have to go—at once!"
"But—Bobby!...My party!...Surely, you wouldn't do such a thing to me!...Be reasonable!...You can start to-night, just as well!...Oh! I think this is just too cruel—too cruel!"
He wasn't hearing her...Luncheon?...Ridiculous!...He kissed her wet face and rushed out...There was no time for the sluggish automatic lift. He ran down the stairs. Ordinarily, the deafening roar of the propellers exasperated him; gnawed the insulation off his nerves, bit by bit. To-day he was barely conscious of the racket. He had seen nothing on his way to Le Bourget field, and was equally indifferent to the receding landscape as Pierre Laudée tilted up his ship's nose and climbed a steep grade into the clouds for what he boasted, that afternoon, was the record flight from Paris to Rome.
Bobby still clutched the newspaper in his hand; unnecessarily, for he could recite every word...Late last night...Naples-Rome express...wreck near Ciampino...open switch...seven Americans among the injured...Mrs. Helen Hudson, conductor of a touring party...fatally hurt...removed to the English Hospital on Via Nomentana, in Rome.
He remembered the place...little hospital...Ardmore—good man—chief of staff...throat specialist. He knew of him.
The day dragged on. Sometimes he relaxed from his tension, sank back into the cushions, limp, and wondered how much of the quiver of him was due to the ship's tremor. Then his anxiety would sweep over him, drying his throat, nauseating him.
It was an interminable grind. And it seemed almost as long again to creep in, at a thirty-mile snail-pace, from the landing-field to the hospital.
The taxi turned in at the hospital gate and slowed down as it followed a gravelled driveway hedged with masses of shrubbery. It drew up under the porte-cochère. He had not remembered it to be such a gloomy, taciturn forbidding place as it appeared to-day. He wondered if that was the way Brightwood looked to people who came, heart-sick with anxiety, to inquire whether their beloved still breathed.

CHAPTER XX

YES—Doctor Ardmore was in, admitted the desk in the lobby, but it was to be doubted if he could be seen...Yes—so very busy to-day...Mrs. Hudson?...She was still living...Would he sit down?...The desk was sympathetic.

Bobby nervously scribbled a message.
"Take that card to Doctor Ardmore," he commanded, "and make sure he gets it!"
In a few minutes a stocky, greying man of forty-five came quickly down the corridor and reached out his hand.
"Yes—I'm Ardmore. Only to-day we were speaking of you, Doctor Merrick. This is indeed a great pleasure...Now—you have come about your countrywoman, Mrs. Hudson...My friend, I fear we are not to save her...No—nothing has been done yet...Too soon—you will understand...Cerebral concussion...Donelli must wait a little...He thinks to-night it may be safe to try...but he has no hope...Conscious? Oh—fitfully; partially. We have had her quieted, you know...She is aware that she is totally blind—I am sure of that."

"Then the contusion covers the occipital lobes!"

"Exactly! Squarely on the back of the head! Very deep lesion!...Then there are the fractured ribs. That's bad too. Lowers the resistance...Donelli had decided at noon that it was useless to attempt the head operation, but now he's going into it...He does not see too many of these cases...I could wish—but—my God, man! *You're* here! You shall do it! Donelli will be very grateful!"

Bobby's heart was pounding.

"You really think he might want me to?"

"Want you? He'll say you're a godsend! Donelli's an excellent surgeon, but he does not specialize. You'll win his everlasting appreciation!...Come—we will go to your patient...I shall be responsible for Donelli's full approval...Come—please."

"Just a moment, Doctor Ardmore," said Bobby, tugging loose from the arm that was propelling him down the corridor. "I have something to say to you before I see Mrs. Hudson. Let us go some place where we may talk privately."

Ardmore led the way into a small parlour.

"I think you ought to know," said Bobby, "that this young woman's life is more to me than of professional concern; more than might be implied by the fact that we are fellow countrymen and acquaintances...I have had hopes of making her my wife."

"My word!—What a situation!"

"Yes, isn't it? Now, I'll tell you the rest of it. We have had a very serious misunderstanding. That is to say—she is misunderstanding me. That being the case—perhaps it would be much better, in the event she has an interval of consciousness, that she be left unaware that I am her surgeon."

"But," objected Ardmore, "might not that fact put a little more resistance into her?"

"Not the kind we want."

"Well—you ought to know...I shall tell the nurse and endeavour to keep your identity secret."

* * * * *

It was the droop of her mouth that brought the scalding tears to Bobby's eyes. For a moment he thought he couldn't bear it.

Ardmore, observing how deeply he was affected, felt some concern. This was not an affair into which an operating surgeon dared to fetch his emotions. He gripped the visitor's shoulder with five vice-like fingers and muttered, "Steady! You're her doctor; not her lover!"

He motioned the nurse to follow him out into the hall and left Bobby alone with his patient. She roused slightly, drew a short, painfully interrupted sigh that made her wince; the lips tightened momentarily, and relaxed again into the pensive droop.

Booby took the hand that lay on the white counterpane and held it in both of his. There was the very faintest imaginable pressure in her fingers. Dear little chap! She was at least vaguely aware of a friendly handclasp, no matter where it came from. That was that much—anyhow!

The door opened and Ardmore returned with the nurse whose eyes sparkled. She shared an important secret.

"Perhaps you would like to make an examination, doctor," said Ardmore.

Bobby nodded. The nurse led him to a wash room and found him a smock and gloves.

The patient was placed in position and the temporary bandages were removed. Bobby stood stunned at the sight. It was, as Ardmore had said, very, very deep. He gave a quick, almost articulate intake of breath as he touched it...Again the English doctor's strong fingers gathered up a large handful of his young colleague's shoulder and growled, "Remember! She's your *patient*!"

"There's nothing to be gained by waiting," said Bobby. "Send for Doctor Donelli, please. We will go into this as soon as he arrives."

* * * * *

It was six o'clock when Helen was laid upon the operating table, and seven-thirty when she was transferred again to the wheeled bed on which she had come.

During that hour and a half, Bobby Merrick, by a supreme effort of his will, was a brain surgeon, and Helen Hudson was a patient—a case—a precariously difficult occipital contusion.

When they had wheeled her in, he feared for a moment he would be unable to achieve that professional attitude. He hesitated, before making his first incision, as he might have hesitated had the scalpel been aimed at his own heart. Once that deft stroke had been accomplished, he was all surgeon.

Donelli stood by, attentively, gently sponging away the blood; marvelling at the uncanny accuracy with which the veins were clipped with forceps almost before they had a chance to signal their location; regarding with envious admiration the swiftness and sureness of those slim, strong, experienced fingers.

Twice Merrick had glanced up anxiously into the eyes of the anæsthetist—it was no small matter to be conducting ether into those pummelled lungs—but, apparently satisfied with what he read there, applied himself with renewed concentration to his task.

It was a terrific strain, and the little group in the operating room was strangely silent. By common consent it was understood that a moving drama was being enacted here—a tragedy, perhaps. Any breath might be her last. That would depend upon the skill of the surgeon. Life and death here were to be determined by the promptness and accuracy of decisions in the removal of the clots. Too deep meant death; not deep enough meant blindness for life!

When the operation was all but finished, Donelli inquired, with an entreating look and a hand outstretched for the needle, if he might not do the scalp stitches; but Merrick shook his head.

The little procession crowded through the door. Bobby walked shakily into the adjacent dressing room; sat down on a white enamelled stool, his shoulders slumped; and contemplated his hands...Her blood!...Donelli and a nurse helped him off with his rubber gloves and out of his smock. The impulsive Italian himself insisted on mopping his guest's face with a cold towel, eager to show his sympathy. It had been the most stirring event of his experience in a vocation singularly exposed to dramatic situations.

They tried, a little later, to persuade Merrick to eat something, but his dinner consisted of a stiff drink of brandy which he gulped greedily as a toper. It was useless to argue with him. He was determined to go at once to his patient's bedside and wait results.

"But—there's nothing you can do," expostulated Ardmore. "It will be hours before you can determine anything more than you know now, unless—of course..."

"Exactly!" muttered Merrick. "It's the *unless* that concerns me!...That—and the threat of a quick pneumonia."

Donelli and Ardmore went to dinner. As they parted at the hospital gate, the Italian said, "It's too much to hope for. Our young friend will be deeply grieved. But—it was a masterful piece of work!"

* * * * *

Her room was in semi-darkness, but Merrick's eyes, once they were accustomed to the gloom, caressed the loveliness of her face. He had not bandaged her eyes. They were closed; and the long black lashes—incredibly long lashes—made heavy shadows on her darkly flushed cheeks. Her breathing was regular, quiet—almost too quiet, at times, and he would rise from his chair by the window and move anxiously toward the bed, his nerves keyed to the breaking point.

Mostly he sat resting his elbows on his knees with his chin in his hands, staring at her face, occasionally rousing when a longer breath, exhaled shudderingly, would bring him to her side, his stethoscope intent.

About midnight, he took a turn up and down in the corridor, and upon re-entering the room, whispered into Julie Craig's ear:

"Is her clothing in that closet?"

"Yes, doctor...Can I help you?"

He shook his head, stepped to the wardrobe, and after some search brought out a soiled and torn blue gown, fumbled at the neck of it, and, having found what he sought, restored the garment to the closet and closed the door.

Julie Craig watched him interestedly as he sat toying with the bit of jewellery he had abstracted from his patient's clothing. Doubtless it was one of his gifts to her. There was some delicious secret connected with it. She wished she knew.

After a while, he rose, and, bending over her, whispered:

"You may go out and take a bit of exercise. I shall call you if you are needed."

* * * * *

Dawn was breaking. The little clock ticked energetically on the bureau. Birds twittered sleepily, outside the window. Bells tolled matins.

There was a weary sigh from the bed. Julie Craig bent over it, solicitously.

And then, in that dear voice, curiously like a muted 'cello, between hysterical little sobs, Bobby Merrick's patient murmured:

"Oh—Blessed God—*I can see*!"

CHAPTER XXI

JULIE CRAIG was a romantic little thing, and the drama in which she had been assigned a rôle was quite to her liking. It was not a fat part as to voluminosity of lines, but it kept her almost continuously on the stage in the thick of action.

Very thrilling it was to feel herself the chief custodian of so valuable a secret. She had resolved to safeguard it against any hazard until the impressive moment arrived for its sensational release.

As for Doctor Ardmore's attitude toward the matter, he was so hilarious that morning, to learn of the complete success of young Merrick's operation that it mattered little to him when or how his attractive patient should discover the identity of her benefactor. Ardmore was British. It occurred to him that whatever misunderstandings might have estranged these two interesting young Americans, the machinery of reconciliation was now in good running order. If they couldn't execute some kind of a treaty in the face of this theatrical life-saving event, they deserved to go their separate ways without expectation of sympathy.

Donelli, by race and temperament cordial toward the grand opera aspects of the situation, rather hoped the fair patient's identification of Merrick might not be brought about until she was at least sufficiently clear of mind to get a real emotional wallop out of the occasion, and sincerely hoped he might find some good reason to be present when it happened.

Julie was for postponing the great moment as long as possible. To her active imagination it was a situation to be nibbled at appreciatively; toyed with—cat and mouse fashion; savoured, rolled about on the tongue. She could not conceive anything more bitterly disappointing than a prosaic anti-climax, now that the dramatic materials were all in hand for a perfectly whopping curtain! It made her shudder to contemplate the possibility of his popping into the room while his idol was in the throes of nausea, as she was almost sure to be, a dozen times before the day was out. The whole affair, Julie decided, should be insured against a commonplace outcome, and dedicated herself to that movement with almost as much concern as if she were one of the principals.

Pursuant to that determination she had left word at the office that she wished to communicate with Doctor Merrick as soon as he returned from breakfast and the brief nap he had promised himself. When the message came up that the young American surgeon was in the building, Julie went to the stairs to meet him. He greeted her warmly, told her she had been very faithful, suggested she would be better off for a few hours' sleep. He would see to it that she was relieved at once.

She shook her head.

"I am not sleepy. I shall wait until this afternoon. Doctor Ardmore told me my patient was not to know who was treating her. So—I have restored the bandage to her eyes. I told her they should not encounter the strong light for several hours. I hope I haven't done wrong, sir."

"You are very resourceful," said Bobby, endeavouring to keep a straight face. "Is there, by any chance, something else I ought to know before looking in?"

She coloured with conscious pride.

"Yes, sir. If you don't mind, I have told her that since she does not speak Italian fluently, whatever conversation she may have with you is to be interpreted by me...And Doctor Donelli can be asked in, this morning, while you make the examination. Is that agreeable?"

"Miss Craig," said Bobby solemnly, "you're wasting your talents here. You should belong to the diplomatic corps."

"I hope you're not making fun, sir...Doctor Ardmore said she wasn't to know—and I saw no other way of keeping it from her."

"You have done very nicely," commended Bobby. "I'll wash up and change my coat."

* * * * *

Helen had been creeping out of her etherized torpor, at closer intervals of full consciousness, since seven; had even smiled gratefully under Julie's little tendernesses.

"So glad!" she had murmured when Julie assured her she was going to be well and sound as ever.

"And—I can see!"

She raised a white hand and tugged weakly at the edge of the bandage over her eyes. Julie hastened to restore it.

"To-morrow, perhaps," she promised. "He wants them protected to-day."

"Very well," with an obedient sigh, "he ought to know, I suppose."

Julie was a tense little figure when Doctor Merrick came in, arrayed in his borrowed surgical gown, accompanied by the volatile Donelli who greeted her with a bombardment of praise for having contributed so much to this happy eventuality. She returned a volley warning him against an accidental disclosure of their secret. Donelli nodded vigorously and chuckled.

Doctor Merrick stepped at once to the bedside table, consulted the chart, and proceeded to verify the latest pulse-count.

"Please tell the doctor," said Helen slowly, "that the bandage around my chest is so very tight. Could he make it more comfortable?"

Julie dutifully relayed the request in a swift Italian sentence composed of one word of two hundred syllables—mostly vowels.

Seeing that the surgical bandage around her chest had been Donelli's affair, it was only a natural courtesy for Doctor Merrick to permit his colleague to decide whether or not he wished it changed. Stepping back, he silently signed to Doctor Donelli that this matter was up to him. But Donelli vehemently protested, with outspread fingers, that he was only too eager to discover his guest's technique.

The opportunity for a debate not being favourable, Bobby turned down the sheet, examined the broad bandage, unpinned it, unfolded it down to the creamy-white satin skin, carefully inspected the discoloured field of the fractures, and expertly replaced the bandage.

"Oh—that is ever so much better," sighed his patient, gratefully.

Julie shook loose a cascade of musical Italian, and the doctor grunted his receipt of it.

"He has very gentle hands," murmured Helen sleepily.

"Shall I tell him that, madame?" asked Julie, her eyes brightly searching his face.

"No...Tell him I am thankful he has made me see again."

Impulsively Bobby entertained a foolhardy notion. In a clumsy Italian phrase, remembered from boyhood, he mumbled something about the pleasure being all his own—and dismayed by his own audacity, walked to the window to write a prescription.

Julie's eyes were intent upon her patient's half-covered face. She was about to interpret the doctor's remark when she noted that the full lips parted; then, that the lower lip was gently pinioned between an even row of white teeth, while the dimples deepened ever so little and a slow flush crept across her cheeks.

With agitated fingers, Julie re-fastened the smock at the throat, her sentimental little heart beating wildly...She knows!—thought Julie...Bending over her, she said gently:

"But perhaps you understood what the doctor was just saying. Is it not so?"

There was no reply. She had drowsed off again. But the smile lingered on her lips, and the flush lingered on her cheeks.

As they went out, Doctor Merrick beckoned Julie to the door and said, in an undertone:

"You might remove that bandage from her eyes while she sleeps. It will be more comfortable."

* * * * *

Two hours later she roused again. Having soberly regarded Julie for some minutes, she fumbled at the neck of her smock and drew out the little silver cross. Holding it tightly in both hands and pressing it to her heart, she inquired:

"How did you know I wanted it?"
"I did not know, madame; or you should have had it from the first."
There was a long pause.
"When did you put it on me? I just now discovered it."
"I did not put it on you, madame."
There was another long silence.
Observing that her patient was dabbing clumsily at her eyes with the corner of the sheet, Julie hastened to restore her handkerchief; then turned and walked thoughtfully to the window.
"Did you see him do it?"
Julie did not turn from the window as she replied, unsteadily:
"No, madame. He invited me to leave the room."
"The—poor—dear!"

* * * * *

At nine that evening Marion Dawson arrived and Bobby met her at the station.

Immediately upon reading the news of the accident, she had been fortunate in making connections with the best westbound train of the day. Her frantic telegram of inquiry, addressed to the hospital when en route, had been handed to Merrick who had wired reassuringly to her train. She had received the message at ten. It did not greatly surprise her to have a telegram from him, knowing that he would have been likely to see the account of the disaster while in Paris.

"Oh, Bobby—how wonderful!" she exclaimed tearfully, when he told her that everything was favourable to a prompt recovery. "Can I see her?"

"Better not to-night. She will be brighter in the morning."

"And I suppose you two blessed things have found that you're necessary to each other, haven't you?

"Well—not yet," he said, hesitatingly. "You see, I have her at a rather awkward disadvantage. I performed the operation myself. I don't wish to make capital of any obligation she might feel toward me. In fact—she doesn't know I'm here, at all."

Marion was pink with indignation. The taxi-driver stood by the open door of the cab waiting for them to step in; but she ignored the gesture and blazed at her compatriot angrily.

"Bobby Merrick—I think that's simply disgraceful! You've always kept the dear soul in the dark and made her feel irresponsible. And here you are again with some more of your wretched secrets! Well—we'll see if you're going to use her that way, this time! When I see her in the morning, I mean to tell her! You don't need to think I'm a party to any more of these mysteries!"

He rather suspected that she meant it. On the short ride over to the Quirinal where he had reserved a room for her, he told her as much as he could explain of the operation, attempting to divert her attention from her annoyance over his attitude towards Helen.

"I am leaving in the morning for Vienna," he said, after making sure she was receiving proper attention at the hotel desk. "Doctor Donelli can do the dressings as well as I. There is no danger now, and no reason for my staying on; especially since you seem bent on informing her."

"It's the only decent thing to do," retorted Marion obdurately. "She has a right to know...Well—give my love to Jack and tell him I'll be back when Helen doesn't need me any more. I wonder if she'll forgive me!"

"I hope so, my dear; but I wouldn't bet much on it...Good-bye!"

* * * * *

Later in the evening he had a consultation with Donelli and felt confident he was leaving his patient in competent hands. He stepped into Helen's room, found her sleeping, took her hand and held it for a moment, and walked out with only a nod for the nurse who had relieved Julie. At the desk he scribbled a note to her, thanking her for "exceptional faithfulness and originality," and enclosed a substantial tender of gratitude (part of which she used to defray a three months' vacation in Switzerland).

Reconciliation was effected promptly and silently, the next morning, when Marion called. They kissed each other and wept a little. Julie excused herself and left them alone together.

"Helen, dear," whispered Marion, the moment the door had closed, "you could never guess who did your operation?"

"Oh, yes, I could," drawled Helen, smiling.

"Good! He thought he had such a secret! When did you find out?"

She laughed—with a little wince of pain.

"He talked some Italian for me, yesterday."

"And you recognized his voice?"

"Instantly."

"He doesn't know it; I am confident."

"Well, he probably will before the day is over."

Before Marion had a chance to reply, Doctor Donelli came bustling in, trailed by Julie, and smilingly approached the bedside.

Helen looked up inquiringly.

"Isn't Doctor Merrick coming this morning, Miss Craig?"

Julie shook her head.

"He left for Vienna at seven, dear," said Marion. "I told him I intended to tell you he was here, so—off he goes!"

"How like him!" said Helen, smiling.

CHAPTER XXII

DOCTOR MERRICK'S unusual capacity for pin-point concentration upon problems of scientific research was not quite up to par during his collaboration with Doctor Arnstadt. The Viennese surgeon seemed every way satisfied, and rejoiced in his close association with his young American colleague, but Bobby was too restless and distracted to make the most of his opportunity.

Jack Dawson had been quick to understand his friend's mood.

"Bobby," he advised, one early August night, as they were finishing their dinner in the low-ceilinged grill room at Hangel's, "I don't want to meddle, but I believe you really ought to run over to the Imperial City and do your stuff. You're getting to be damned poor company, and I think you have something weighty on your conscience."

Bobby nodded soberly.

"You're right!...I'll go—to-morrow!"

* * * * *

Marion had stayed on in Rome. Jack's daily letter from her constituted the log of Helen's rather tedious trip through convalescence.

It was a great day in Vienna—demanding a bit of celebration that night—when the news came that she had sat up for half an hour.

Now she had been wheeled out into the shady patio...Now she had taken a short walk...Now they were both at the Quirinal, and every afternoon Helen was down in the garden, in the hotel court...Now she was taking drives in the evening...You could hardly find the scar, any more...Helen was so happy.

* * * * *

On the morning of the sixth of August, Jack and Doctor Arnstadt saw Bobby off. After the train had slipped quietly out of the station, Jack went to the telegraph booth and wired to Marion. He did not tell her it was a secret that Bobby was on the way. She would not have kept it, in any event. She was all done with riddles.

"Who do you think's coming?" she cried, romping into Helen's room waving her telegram.

"When does he arrive?"

"To-morrow afternoon—about six!...Isn't it wonderful?"

"I'm going, dear! I don't feel quite up to it."

"Why—the very idea!...You can't!...When you know he's on the way?...He'll be wretchedly disappointed!"

"But—I don't know he's coming—that is, not officially...He probably didn't want me to know, or he would have informed me."

There was no talking her out of it. She was going! That night they paid a farewell call at the hospital. Julie Craig shyly inquired of Mrs. Dawson if Doctor Merrick was still in Europe, and was appalled to learn that he was arriving in Rome to-morrow.

"But—you will have gone, madame!" exclaimed Julie, looking reproachfully at her patient...Surely this affair was being badly managed by somebody.

* * * * *

All that the concierge at the Quirinal seemed to remember at first about the whereabouts of the two young American women was that they had left, that noon, for Paris. Upon further reflection, and in appreciation of the colour of the bank-note which Doctor Merrick was twisting in his fingers, he recalled that Madame Hudson's heavier baggage had been expressed directly to Le Havre. He had himself seen to it. Yes—she was sailing on the *Île de France* on Thursday. At all events, her trunks were.

Bobby spent an hour, pacing up and down the flagging in the garden of the Quirinal, planning his next move. This game of hide and seek couldn't—mustn't go on any longer! He resolved to corner her and take her by force!

He sent a long telegram to Jack Dawson, confiding the full particulars of the enormous audacity he had decided to commit. He had made his reputation with her by various acts of impudence. This would be the crowning deed which would make all his former impertinences seem bland. He was very nervous as he prepared for it.

Events moved very swiftly, once he had come to his decision. He engaged an aeroplane and flew to Paris. Between the racket of the triple engines and the furious pounding of his heart, it was a noisy trip. There was a hasty half-hour with his mother, in which he persuaded her to forgive him on the strength of a promise that he would return and be with her at Christmas.

At the down town office of the French Line, he engaged the most luxurious suite on the *Île de France*. Next morning, he flew to Havre, arriving an hour before the boat-train from Paris.

It was a long and anxious hour. Never had he been so utterly stampeded by his own emotions.

Seeing to it that his light luggage was in his quarters, and having strolled about through the commodious suite to make sure it was ready for occupancy—he had retained enough presence of mind to order the place filled with flowers—he went up to the captain's cabin, renewed acquaintance, and asked a favour.

Then he went down and took up his stand at the foot of the first-class gangway, waiting with an impatience almost too urgent to be borne.

Whatever would she think?

* * * * *

Slowly the train crept into the shed, across the way, and the passengers swarmed in little groups about their hand baggage. Presently the procession began to move stragglingly towards the ship.

Bobby saw her coming, tripping smartly along with two porters attentively close behind her.

Mauve—this time...Snug, saucy, cloche hat—mauve...A tailored suit of mauve that sculptured every curve of her.

She sighted him waiting for her. He knew she had seen him. Now her eyes widened and her lips parted as their gaze met. She advanced steadily towards him with a tread almost martial.

As she neared him, he did not extend his hand, as she had thought he might. He held out both arms; and, to his inexpressible delight, she walked confidently into them, shyly laid her slim fingers on his coat lapels, looked up into his face, and smiled.

"Put madame's baggage in Suite B," said Bobby, in a proprietorial tone to the porters.

"You are travelling with me!" he explained rather unsteadily. "The captain is marrying us, this afternoon!"

"Yes, dear," she said softly. "I know."

Bobby's arms tightened about her.

"How did you know?" he grinned, boyishly.

"Well—let's see. You wired it to Doctor Dawson, and he wired it to Marion, and she wired it to me...Awfully roundabout way to learn one was being married, wasn't it?"

"But—but—you're for it, aren't you?" he pleaded, searching her eyes.

She smiled.

"Perhaps we should go aboard, Bobby. We're blocking the traffic."

THE END

Forgive Us Our Trespasses

CHAPTER I

THE new-laid harvest straw beneath the faded red carpet rustled crisply under Martha's shapeless felt slippers as she padded across the living-room to the cluttered mantel.

With the quizzical grimace of long-neglected astigmatism she adjusted the steel-bowed spectacles that had been her mother's, had of a notion peddler for two dozen eggs and a pound of butter.

The wooden-wheeled clock—a noisy but amazingly accurate and exquisitely ornamented product of old Ferd's, while laid up one winter with a broken leg that had kept him two months sober—clacked irascibly at Martha that another blistering August morning was nearly five hours old. High time, indeed, that the day's work began. Not much wonder the Millers were poor.

Dragging her slipper-heels to the door of the spare bedroom which, in spite of her continued protests, Susan and Greta had insisted on occupying of late, Martha vigorously rattled the latch.

Glumly appeased by assurances from within, she returned to the dingy kitchen and peered into the kettle to see if there was enough water to prime the parching pump under the pear tree.

Then, kettle in hand, she plodded to the foot of the narrow stairs, and petulantly called: "Julia!"

* * * * *

Outstretched on velvet moss so soft and deep it yielded to every curve of her supple young body, Julia knew that if she stirred, the least bit, she would never be able to recapture the complete satisfaction of this luxurious languor.

Doubtless it was too much to expect that an experience so strangely sweet could be quite real. Sooner or later, something or somebody would invade her peace. A tall giraffe would saunter up and thrust his long nose into the top of the banana tree. Giraffes ate bananas, didn't they?... Or a big man with a blue coat and shiny buttons would order her off.... Or there would be a peremptory summons from afar to come at once!

Julia's unbuckled consciousness was already troubled by the persistent echo of a distant call. It had seemed to come from the depths of this tropical forest—a faint but urgent cry for help. The voice had sounded tired, plaintive, persecuted—just like Martha's.

But what would Martha be doing away out here in... in Tasmania? Julia now readily identified her location by recalling a picture in *The Pictorial Atlas,* her omnivorous memory obliging her with phrases from the adjacent descriptive text: "Mountains heavily forested... magnificent scenery... peaks of crystalline rock showing pink and blue... frequent showers... luxuriant vegetation." If this wasn't Tasmania, it was someplace else too far off for Martha to find. Martha never went anywhere, not even to Ligonier on Saturdays. She always saw them off, standing there under the big maple, mopping her tanned forehead with the corner of her brown apron.

"Wish you was a-goin' along, Mat," Hiram would drawl, conscious that he only, by virtue of his clumsy championship of her dour eccentricities, could nickname her without rebuke.

"No," Martha would reply, sacrificially, "somebody's got to stay on th' place—what with them young turkeys and all."

Whoever was calling, Julia had an uneasy sense of guilt over her failure to respond. Whether required to go or not, she at least should have the courtesy to answer. Of course, if it did actually turn out to be Martha—a most improbable event—she would have to obey. One always came when Martha called. Sometimes one came scowling and grumbling, but one always came.

Martha had an uncanny instinct for knowing when one must on no account be disturbed. Had one reached the most exciting episode in a story, Martha needed a few dry chips immediately to revive an expiring fire. Let the sunset be at that phase where vermilion was beginning to be laced with purple, Martha's accusing voice inquired from the kitchen door whether one expected to gather the eggs, or must she go out later and do it herself in the dark and all?... But this couldn't be Martha!

In just a moment, now, Julia would reply to the entreaty. She would draw a deep breath—though deep breaths were rather disconcerting, lately, for they seemed to make her plump round breasts so much more mature than she was, herself—and try to exhale "Coming!" so effortlessly as not to disturb this delightful lethargy. She would wait until the cry sounded a little more distinctly, and then she would answer, "Yes, Martha... Coming!"

Evidently someone else had gone to the rescue, for everything was blissfully quiet again. That was good. So nice not to be bothered. Julia sighed contentedly as a big drop of warm dew dripped from the tip of a sheltering fern-frond and rolled slowly down her cheek.

She opened one eye cautiously—a mere tiny slit—to make sure the tall, slim, slanting date-palm was still there. It was; plainly visible through the vertical bars of her long black lashes.

Was this the one in the *Elementary Geography* or the *Child's Natural History?* No—it couldn't be; for the date-palm in the Geography had a grey monkey in the top, and the one in the Natural History was being climbed by a brown boy with arms as long as his legs, and sharp heels, scampering up out of the tiresome paragraph that read: "The Malay is of pigmy stature, averaging 148-149 cm., with black skin and short woolly hair."... No—this date-palm must be the one in the magic-lantern lecture, last winter, over at Hinebaugh's Schoolhouse.

As for the dripping rubber trees, with the waxy leaves that shaded her like hands folded above her eyes, Julia could locate them certainly. They were from the little conservatory at Fort Wayne... out in Spring Fountain Park... the day she didn't go to the show. And here they were in this immense conservatory—for this really was a conservatory. Julia smiled over her silly mistake. She had fancied herself out in the open... in Tasmania, maybe; and all the time she had been lying here on the moss in this conservatory, exactly like the one in Spring Fountain Park—only twenty times bigger!

But there was no mistaking those moist rubber trees. She had sat under them for a whole hour on a sticky green iron bench, that day last summer, when their family—all but Martha, what with the plums and all—had gone to Barnum and Bailey's circus; only she hadn't seen the show. She had indignantly left them standing there giggling foolishly on the crowded courthouse steps, craning their necks to follow the last of the little elephants at the tail of the pompous parade—the little elephants whose bulbous, bobbing, nodding heads seemed to be saying, "Yes, yes—we're coming."... (Yes, Martha... Coming!)

Hiram and Elmer had been so noisy and silly, and had attracted so much unpleasant comment, that she had suddenly rebelled against the further humiliation of going out to the show-grounds with them.

"Aw—come on!" Elmer had shouted, against the deafening shrieks of the steam calliope. "Don't be a sissy!"

"S'matter with yuh?" growled Hiram. "'Shamed o' yer folks?"

Greta was laughing uproariously over Susan's comment, "Wouldn't it kill yuh, Gret?... Father a-scoldin' the boys fer drinkin' so much, and him just able to stand up."

Julia had been very sorry for her father that day, swaying unsteadily in the broiling sun as he morosely watched the clanking, jingling, garish, pungent parade—his tanned face screwed up into tight little wrinkles, his shaggy grey hair curled in tight little ringlets on his temples, his blue eyes, deep-set, swimming with vertigo. She couldn't bear to see him ridiculed. He belonged to her.

"Please, Greta!"

Greta had grinned, and cracked her chewing-gum.

Julia had been strongly impulsed to slip her arm through her father's, and make off with him; to offer him a hand exactly like his, only smaller and not so brown; to smile into his eyes with eyes exactly like them, only younger and not so weary; to take him along with her—anywhere to be away from these unfeeling people who were not related to either of them except by the mere unfortunate accident that they all happened to belong to the same family. At that very moment, however, he had turned on her reproachfully, stifled a hiccough that hinted at impending nausea, and muttered, "You'd better let yourself go and have some fun once."

"Fun?"

"Yes: their kind o' fun. It won't do you no good to be haughty. You might as well cave in—an' like it! I done it! So kin you! I even larnt to talk like 'em. If you don't want to be lonesome all yer life, you'd better—"

That quite settled it!... Promising to meet them at the Pennsylvania Station at seven-fifteen (they had left old Florrie and the dilapidated surrey at Larwill and had come the rest of the way by rail), Julia had slipped through the sweaty crowd, her cheeks aflame.

Three blocks away she took the street-car—No. 52, a policeman had told her—an almost empty little green street-car that banged its bell furiously at the new demobilizing throng, demanding it to drag its roly-poly, waddling wife and gawky children and their yellow balloons and pink popcorn balls off the rails; had ground dizzily around sharp corners, and lost its few passengers—all but Julia—finally reaching almost open country, where it took the bit between its teeth, tucked its chin against its neck, and galloped over a rusty, hummocky track, the trolley-wheel singing a painfully shrill note, until it brought up with a jerk at the shabby station-shed in Spring Fountain Park.

The grass was seared and badly trampled, and the dahlias were dusty and frowsy in their prim round beds. A black-lettered board pointed an index-finger toward "The Conservatory."

Julia had had the steamy, sweaty, stuffy, little greenhouse all to herself, that afternoon. Everybody else had gone to the circus. She had sat there on the sticky iron bench, hoping it wouldn't come off on her new pink gingham, dreamily transporting herself to the equatorial regions where all this rank, lush, stifled vegetation belonged, finding a strange kinship with it. She sympathized with these cramped, dwarfed, imprisoned rubber trees, and the gigantic ferns with dejected, drooping arms and wings.

And now, to Julia's annoyance, the cry for help was repeated. It came from just outside the conservatory door, this time. Would she, or would she not, come immediately?

The huge dome of the conservatory lifted and disappeared. It was exactly like the glass cover that protected the plate of soggy doughnuts from the flies on the high counter in Ruggles's Restaurant and Pool Hall at Cromwell.... Martha had taken the conservatory by the handle, and lifted it off. One could hear what she was saying now, ever so distinctly. Would she come, this instant, and help get breakfast for Susan and Greta, who, as she very well knew, had promised to be ready at half-past five to go with the other huckleberry-pickers to Wadham's marsh? And wasn't it little enough for her to do, seeing she had begged off from the berryin' to study her algebry, or whatever it was, so she would be prepared for that there County Institute, week after next, which everybody knew she hadn't any right to waste their money on—even if it was her'n, a-teachin' silly paintin' lessons to women as ought to been a-keepin' their children's buttons on—what with them so hard-up and all? And didn't she have any natural feelin's of—"

"Yes, Martha. I'm *coming!*"

Julia sat up, drenched with perspiration, stretched, inhaled an unsatisfactory draught of sultry, humid air, and gazed out through the east window at a chrome yellow sun that already threatened to break an August record. Next Thursday's *Ligonier Weekly Banner* would probably say, in big black headlines, "HOTTEST DAY FOR TEN YEARS!... Highest Temperature Since 1885 Recorded on August the—"

August the whath?... August the tenth? Her birthday! Would anyone else remember?

She reached out a long, slender hand for her stockings, dangling over the back of a chair, and tugged them on. After all, shouldn't she be glad she had a good excuse not to go into Wadham's snake-infested huckleberry marsh and have her arms and legs scratched with briars and nettles while she fought deer-flies with an exasperation close to tears, and shuddered with loathing at the sight of enormous caterpillars, and wiped the slimy cobwebs out of her eyes with sun-blistered, juice-smeared wrists?... Blessings on the pesky algebra!

"J-u-l-i-a!"

"Yes, Martha. I'm coming!"

131

* * * * *

Her entrance into the grim little dining-room was effected with much difficulty. She could have wished that her first appearance before her household, as an adult in good and regular standing, might have been somewhat more impressive.

Circumstances had decreed that Julia must bump her way crabwise through the obstinate swinging-door from the smoky kitchen with a precariously poised platter of bacon in one hand and the big battered coffee-pot in the other, while the family, glancing up from its first round of fried mush and sorghum molasses—with which munitions Martha had preceded her—wondered, not without warrantable anxiety, whether she would make port with all her cargo.

It was not to be expected that her lazy and surly brothers, much less absent-minded old Ferd—whose fork trembled in a long, slim hand that had been obviously intended for more esteemed employment than shingling barns and blowing stumps—would spring to her rescue. That would have been "a-puttin' on style," an affectation held in snarling contempt by Hiram and Elmer. Indeed, their sentiment on this subject was commonly shared by the entire male species, so far as she had been able to observe.

As for Greta, who, at twenty-two, had already well developed an impish talent for the enjoyment of other people's discomfiture; and as for Susan, whose twenty-seven virginal years and one hundred and sixty-seven pounds gave such alarming promise of unarrestable progress in both dimensions that she was frankly envious of her willowy young sister, Julia's predicament was clearly no concern of theirs.

Martha, seated with her angular back to the door, which now capitulated with a savage swish and a sullen bang, cleared a place at her elbow for the brown-stained coffee-pot, and dutifully remarked that this was Julia's eighteenth birthday.

While still in her teens, Martha had accidentally lost an upper canine. Morbidly self-conscious, her misfortune had worried her grievously; but there had been no necessity for replacing the missing tooth. By skilful practice, Martha had been able to conceal this disfigurement with the corner of her lip, a technique which had produced a meticulousness of articulation oddly inconsistent with the slovenly elisions and shockingly bad syntax demanded by her righteous passion to avoid "a-puttin' on airs."

"Yes; your little sister," reiterated Martha, her choice of a pronoun indicating the maternal relationship she sustained to the family, "is came of age."

Brief, bucolic felicitations from the boys were mumbled through the mush, to which old Ferd—so stung with remorse over having no gift for her that he did not even raise his eyes—added solemnly that Martha could always be depended on to remember the days.

Depositing her awkward burdens, Julia stiffened to a martial stance, brought her full red lips to a determined pucker, tossed her curly head airily, and swept the breakfast-table with a look of pretended challenge, as if to say that she was quite grown up now and they must all have a care how they treated her.

A moment later she was repentantly reflecting that previous experiences might have warned her against indulging in this bit of playful pantomime. Julia's sporadic efforts to dramatize some situation for the amusement of her family had been uniformly unsuccessful. It would have been very pleasant, she often thought, to belong to a household quick to interpret and enjoy a little good-natured clowning. It was not that their stodginess and lack of sparkle evoked her contempt: she was too naïve to be contemptuous. Indeed, she had never known—except in *Little Women,* long since read to rags and learned by heart—any such family as the rollicking, bantering, make-believe crew that constituted her ideal home.

On one's birthday, however, it might reasonably be hoped that the family would waive its habitual taciturnity, and humour a whim; so, quite recklessly overplaying her premeditated skit, Julia glared at her brothers and sisters with a mock severity signifying her newly acquired dignity. But they had already returned to their bacon and mush; and, noting that no one of them—not even her father—showed signs of sharing her mood, she doffed her archness, rubbed a damp wisp of blue-black hair from her low forehead with the back of a shapely wrist—astonishingly like old Ferd's, only daintier—and slipped into her accustomed place on the end of the pine bench beside Susan.

"Reckon you'll be too cocky to live with, now yer old enough t' be yer own boss," observed Hiram, who, on second thought, had decided not to leave Julia under the impression that he, at least, was too thick-witted to have taken note of her brief charade.

Equally unwilling to be considered incapable of clever deduction, Greta remarked to her plate that Julia would probably be leaving home, one of these days, to go on the stage.

Old Ferd hitched about in his chair, and for a moment Julia thought he was going to offer a comment.

"Julia's always been a-playin' she was somethin' else besides what she is," said Susan.

"Well—she ain't harmed no one by a-doin' that," growled Ferd. "She come by it honestly enough. When I was her age, or thereabouts—"

"More coffee, paw?" inquired Martha, loudly, as if he were deaf.

"It's sure a-goin' to be a scorcher, Gret," observed Susan,—fanning her goitre with the bib of her apron, and peering through the open doorway toward the road.

"There goes old Len Bausermann with his pick 'n' shovel," reported Elmer, following his plump sister's eyes to the highway.

"He'll be a-diggin' Granny Hartsock's grave today," explained Hiram, without turning to look.

"A saint," murmured Martha, unctuously, "if they ever was one."

"Who—Len?" chaffed Elmer. "That consarned old chicken-thief?"

Susan and Greta laughed immoderately. Martha, easily offended when her piety was ridiculed, drew down the corners of her mouth, and pouted. Elmer explored a defective wisdom-tooth with a pointed quill, and grinned.

Old Ferd knew they didn't care to hear his story—none of them but Julia. He could always be sure of an attentive listener in Julia, though sometimes she asked too many questions.

The family's rude indifference occasioned him no surprise. He had been on the defensive for so long in a home to which he contributed almost nothing, his small earnings claimed by Jake Heffel, that he had no right to be indignant over such discourtesies. He poured the thin coffee into his saucer with a shaky hand, crumbled bread into it, and sprinkled the dish with brown sugar, intent upon his occupation. Julia, toying absently with her food, studied his deep-lined, mobile face, confident that she was following his reminiscences as closely as if he had been given encouragement to recite them.

He was, she knew, skipping hurriedly over the Dresden part of it; the part that most interested her; the part that really mattered. She had never been able to construct a very clear picture of his boyhood home. The blurry impression she had of it was an accumulated synthesis of chance remarks accidentally dropped, and laconic answers to her importunate queries in the rare moments when he seemed willing to talk about his youth.

He would be out in his tiny shop under the big maple, standing at his home-made lathe, turning wooden pins for the mending of Squire Craig's harrow-teeth. The fine hickory shavings would come writhing and screaming from the point of his blue-hot chisel. He would pretend not to notice her, sitting on the old tool-chest, intently watching him.

"Let me treadle it, father. I like to."

The huge oak balance-wheel overhead would lumber to a creaking stop.

"Mind you don't get yer foot caught under it, now!"

Julia would snuggle it between his arms and stand so close, her back to his breast, pumping the broad pedal that made the patched belt go snapping and crackling on the great wooden fly-wheel, threatening to bring it down on their heads; her father's warm, hairy forearm, tense on the chisel, moist with sweat and powdered with fine sawdust, brushing her cheek, almost as if he caressed her.

Panting with exertion, she would look up over her shoulder, and smile, when he signalled her to stop.

"You're more like her every day, Julia!" he would murmur, as the machinery idled to a standstill.

"Because my hair dips down to a point here in the middle?"

"That—and the deep dimple in your chin."

"And she had the same kind of eyes that we have."

"Exactly; that's where we got 'em."

"The others don't have them, father.... Funny—isn't it?"

Thus drawn together in these brief intimacies, there would be some talk about her Grandmother Mueller—Ferd had changed his name to Miller, when coming to Indiana, because the people invariably mispronounced it; or was that the exact reason, Julia often wondered, when she had grown up—Grandmother Mueller who always seemed to be a mere slip of a girl, stooping over the flower-beds in the garden that was so—

"How big was it, father—honestly: big as our potato-patch?"

He would chuckle derisively.

"Our potato-patch! Huh! Six—eight—ten times as big!"

Then there would be some vigorous prodding of memory for more information about the house. It was a great, rambling, stone house with tall, broad chimneys and many gables. Yes—his own room had a gable, and there was a window-seat with a rose-coloured velvet cushion. Wrens nested in a little box under the eaves, and when it stormed, the branch of an elm swept the diamond-shaped panes of the mullioned window.

"And was there honestly a fountain in the middle of a big pool, father?"

"Yes—and lily-pads."

"And really goldfish, like you said?"

"Yes, daughter—but don't you think you'd better go and help Martha now?"

"And you would feed them in the mornings—and they always knew when you were coming, and swam close to the edge to meet you?"

Of late Julia was becoming painfully aware of their lost heritage. Her day-dreams were bounded by the high stone wall, made warm and friendly by the tall hollyhocks his mother loved. On summer afternoons she fancied herself sitting in the rose-arbour, hard-by the large, half-timbered workshop and studio where distinguished guests were so often entertained to tea.

"Tea!—in a shop!" she had exclaimed, the first time he had told her about it.

"But it wasn't a little shop like this here, Julia. Seems to me like it had five or six big rooms. I disremember, exactly. The people came to see the carvings; almost every afternoon, somebody. And there would be exhibitions, couple o' times a year. Lots o' people came then, from long distances, Paris and London."

"Would they talk to you, father?"

"I was just a young feller."

"Going to school?"

"No—I had a tutor.... But I was always a-hangin' around the shop, and I can't remember when I wasn't a-playin' with chisels, and a-makin' things.... Once I heard a Count—I disremember his name—a-tellin' somebody that *Mueller* on a rood screen made it worth more 'n' its weight in gold."

And there was a river.

Julia felt almost certain, as she sat watching her father's slow motions with his spoon, oblivious of the dull prattle of his family's table-talk, that he was dreaming of that river. You went through a thick oaken door set in the garden wall. The door had heavy wrought-iron hinges, and was always locked o' nights with a key that must have weighed all of a pound. You went through the door, and there was the river. The banks were rounded and grassy, and a long row of tall poplars grew on our side, "their leaves always a-flutterin' whether there was any wind or not." He disremembered the name of the river, but "one of the swans was called 'William Tell.'" There were boats, too; a couple o' canoes and a dory and a punt with a red and blue canopy—

"How much did Lafe Shock git fer his gol-danged shoats?" Elmer was inquiring of Hiram.

"Four cents, I heared," rumbled Hiram, puffing at his sputtering pipe. "'Bout enough to pay fer th' corn he'd chucked into 'em."

"Corn—hell!" scoffed Elmer. "Them shoats never seen a grain o' corn. All they ever et was swill!"

"Lot o' good the Shock swill woulda done' em," sneered Greta.

"They was so gol-danged poor," expatiated Elmer, "that I bet Lafe had to soak 'em afore they'd hold slop."

—and a punt with a red and blue canopy; and, sometimes, in the evening, his mother sat in the punt, with her guitar, and sang ballads to him, very sweetly. No—his father never joined them. No—he disremembered what the songs were.

Now Julia was at sea with her father, standing beside him as he stoked his way, with blistered hands, on a slow boat; she was landing with him, bewilderedly, at Castle Garden. Much had happened since the swans and the ballads in the evening; but it was quite impossible to recover intervening events. His father had whipped him savagely when he was sixteen. He wouldn't tell her why; but it had something to do with his mother. She had cried desperately, and that night he ran away. The tutor had helped him get away. The tutor had gone away, too, that same night.

Judging by the confident tightening of his lips, Julia knew he was in New York now, apprenticed to Lamb's Studios. Four years of that passed in a few seconds. Now he was hard at work on the big walnut eagle—his first important assignment—that was to be poised on a lectern for Saint John's in Philadelphia. Lamb's had taken him in on the strength of the Mueller tradition, and had given him every possible encouragement, undisguisedly rejoicing in his budding talent. Every day he was improving his skill; every night he was poring over his new books, determined to perfect his English.

Then came the war. Julia saw the clouds gathering on the seamed old face. It was all over now. He had gone back to Lamb's in a faded uniform topped by the absurd little cap with the stiff visor that he still wore, rather rakishly, on Decoration Day—a day Julia dreaded, for he always marched unsteadily, and joked a good deal, when he should have been silent and dignified.

Now he had returned to the Lamb Studios, stubbly, fuddled, and pungent, after a fortnight's spree. All was forgiven. Soldiers would be soldiers. Lamb's were disappointed, but hopeful. Why, Mr. Joseph Lamb, himself!—(Ferd had been too proud of that recognition to keep it a secret, even if its implications were not to his own credit)—Mr. Joseph Lamb, himself, had pleaded with him to straighten up, and be a man. Surely, nobody could have asked for a better friend, Ferd often remarked, than "Mr. Joseph," who, it was said, had given up his plans to enter the ministry because he thought he could do more for religion by adding something to its beauty. "Mr. Joseph Lamb was a great artist!" Ferd would say. "Yes *sir!*"

No—it wasn't the fault of Lamb's Studios if he had drunk himself practically into the gutter at a time when a returned soldier's dissipation was easily pardoned, but not so easily capitalized in a profession demanding the utmost steadiness of eye and hand. Ferd was so proud of his erstwhile craftsmanship and its stern exactions that he was willing to admit his own inability to meet its requirements, shamelessly confessing the cause of his failure, as if his very drunkenness, at twenty-four, was to be talked about in tones of respect, seeing it had been important enough to collide successfully with an esteemed art.

So—that chapter was finished, then, and her father had ceased being an artist. Julia recognized the exact moment when he "took to the road" en route to Pennsylvania in quest of a distant cousin who owned "a bit of a truck-farm." Oddly enough, no exigency of poverty had ever induced him to part with the books he had bought in the golden days when he was so brilliantly succeeding at Lamb's. He had stored them in New York; had kept himself sober long enough to save the money required for their transportation to his new home; for, now, he had a home. He had married the plump, shy, awkward, yellow-haired daughter of an improvident neighbour who indifferently operated a small sawmill, "mortgaged, by Golly, down to the last cleat in the old pulley-belt."

Julia knew how it always amused him to repeat that phrase. He smiled, now, and glanced up furtively to make sure the family's attention was occupied. She dodged his eyes and took no further risks with them until she was sure he was in "pardnership" with his unthrifty father-in-law, who, hearing rumours of advantages to be had by moving to Northern Indiana, "where everybody was a-makin' big money loggin' and gettin' out railroad ties," had suggested the immediate migration of his populous, penniless tribe.

Ferd grinned again, rather wryly. Julia was not quite sure where we were in the story, now. Perhaps he was thinking about something he had never told her—something not very pleasant, perhaps; something not much to our credit, she feared.

He had taken along to Indiana their simple, mostly homemade, household gear, the precious books—English classics—which were to become a veritable Godsend to Julia!—and his only military trophy, his little brown jug. Occasionally, of a late Saturday night in Heffel's Saloon in Cromwell, when Ferd and his cronies had passed from the bragging stage to the distinctly maudlin, nose-trumpeting phase of bland confessions and remorses over their respective might-have-beens, he would pull himself together long enough to make a pathetic joke of his own disaster.

"Yep"—Ferd would say, grinning drunkenly through his tears—"that was my only military trophy—that there little brown jug."

He glanced up now, out of the tail of his eye, and found Julia regarding him with rapt interest. A bit disconcerted by this intense scrutiny (sometimes Julia's penetrating knowledge of his moods and meditations annoyed him, just a little), he pushed back his chair, and muttered, partly to himself, partly to her:

"Yep—that's the way it goes."

He gnawed off a large bite of Horseshoe chewing-tobacco from the plug he had rummaged from the depth of his overall-pocket, and, without a backward glance, strolled out through the doorway toward his shop.

Perhaps he would continue his reminiscences while he worked on the Snell baby's pine coffin; but he had already covered everything in his story that had any interest for Julia.

135

Except for such minor episodes as the births of his five children, and the death of Minnie, six years ago, his history was an unpunctuated monotony of trivial jobs—building corncribs, replacing timbers in the forebay at Austin's gristmill, planing and hanging Squire Craig's screen-doors every April, and stowing them in the loft of the woodhouse every November—a chronicle as sterile of novelty as the legendary minstrel's redundant report that now another locust came and carried away another grain of corn.

Julia wondered, sometimes, whether her father ever missed her mother. It was obvious that he did not grieve for her. Minnie's biological contribution to Julia's character was no more in evidence than the influence of a hen on a golden pheasant's egg. Julia was all Ferd's.

Minnie had been an ignorant, whining, colourless, unimaginative creature, her quite astounding bulk disproving the adage that stout people are invariably optimistic. Save for the fact that she had been an economical housekeeper (as she had plenty of reason to be), and was thought to put up the best green-tomato pickles in the Oak Grove neighbourhood, nothing important was remembered of her; not even by her own kin.

A litter of empty, overturned, glass fruit-jars on her grave in the Baptist Cemetery which, on the anniversaries of her death, the melancholy Martha stuffed with garden flowers, ironically testified to Minnie's previous relation to other natural objects in a world where she had dully foozled a chance to present society with a rehabilitated wood-carver of exceptional virtuosity, and had contented herself with the excellence of her piccalilli.

* * * * *

A clatter of wheels and harness drew Greta to the door.

"Fer Gosh sakes, Sue, if Bob ain't came with the hay-ladders on! Jolt the very stuffin' out of yuh!" She turned to the abstracted Julia. "You'd better come, too, Miss Stuck-up! Here's that Schrofe boy what's so crazy about yuh.... Hoo-hoo, Bob! We'll be out in a jiffy!"

"Mebby you better go, Julia," advised Martha, maternally.

Julia demurred. It was little enough time she had to review her algebra, even if she studied every minute.

Old Ferd, returning for a tin of water to cool his grindstone, arrived in time to take a hand in the argument.

"Give her a chance, Martha. I'd like to see one of us do somethin' to make our name a little more important than it's been."

Martha picked up a double handful of dishes with a decisiveness of manner that promised an impressive exit, to be followed presently by a great clatter of pots and pans off stage.

"Well—all I got t' say is—"

But the threatened tantrum was played to a thinning house, Ferd had found his tin cup, and was off with it. Susan and Greta were on the way to the wagon. The boys slouched toward the barn. Julia carried her plate to the kitchen, where Martha was sniffing ostentatiously, and vanished with a promise to make the beds, her sister's plaintive whine trailing her all the way upstairs. "'Pears like nobody in this house cares what I think about anything. Just a hired girl... without any pay."

* * * * *

Standing before the severely plain but expertly crafted walnut desk that her father had given her, last Christmas, Julia unlocked a drawer and re-read the precious document it contained.

The desk had become a symbol of the considerable difference between herself and her brothers and sisters. A source of anxiety and embarrassment at first, the desk had come to be a refuge and an inspiration.

On Christmas morning, having presented each member of the family with a fine, large orange, Ferd had made a mysterious trip through the snow to his shop, returning shortly with the desk. Julia's exclamations of delight had intensified the sullen silence. At supper, that evening, Greta's smouldering indignation blazed forth in an irascible comment to which Ferd quietly replied:

"She's the only one in this family that would have any use fer a desk. If any o' the rest o' yuh ever needs one, mebby I'll 'tend to it."

This sarcastic explanation of the gift did little to conciliate them. So much constraint was traceable to the episode that Martha told Julia she had better take her new desk upstairs and keep it out of sight. Susan added that she, for one, would never darken the door of Julia's room while it was there.

But, however painful the situation, at the outset, it developed for Julia a privacy she had never enjoyed before. By common consent, the family left her to herself, implying, a dozen times a day, that she considered the rest of them inferior, twisting her every remark into allusions to their ignorance.

"What shall I do, father?" she inquired one day, in the shop. "They're always trying to act as if they're not as smart as I am."

Ferd grinned, and blew the sawdust off his chisel-handle.

"They don't have t' put on, very much, t' play that."

"But it makes me so miserable!"

"Well—don't cry.... That's what yuh get fer a-bein' smart. Smart people's always miserable. Old man Solomon said that—er somethin' about like it."

"Was he miserable?" asked Julia, with a tearful little smile.

"Gosh, yes! He was the smartest man that ever lived!" Ferd sat down on the tool-chest, laid a dusty hand on her knee, and grinned mysteriously. "Julia, are yuh sure you've found all the drawers in that there little desk? One of 'em ain't got no handle."

Her eyes brightened.

"No," she whispered, excitedly, "I haven't found it. Will you show me?'

He had found it for her the next time the family was out of the house—a narrow drawer set in the centre of a row of six open pigeon-holes and faced by a little pilaster carved to imitate a longitudinal section of a Corinthian column.

"That there's it," pointed Ferd, hugely enjoying Julia's flutter of excitement. "No—it don't come out that way," he said, when she had unsuccessfully grappled with the ornament which defied the best efforts of her finger-tips. "Nobody could ever get it out a-doin' that."

"Do show me, father!"

He had proceeded then in leisurely fashion, immensely relishing her suspense, to demonstrate the strange magic of the secret drawer.

"Now, if you ever want to put anythin' out of sight, Julia," commented Ferd, with a comradely wink, "you'll know how to do it; and it'll take a heap o' tinkerin' with this here desk fer anybody else but you to find out how that drawer opens."

Julia was ecstatic.

Her close inspection of the desk had led to another discovery: Ferd had carved the name "Mueller" on the bevelled edge of the little receptacle for ink-bottles and pens.

"I'm so glad you did that, father. That makes the desk still more valuable, doesn't it?"

Ferd flushed with pride.

"It's the only time, Julia, since I cut the name under the wing of an eagle that holds the Bible in a big church in Philadelphia. It's the way my father cut his name—and his father—and his father's father.... It's a good name, daughter."

Standing now before the desk, Julia withdrew a document—much too long to fit into the secret drawer—bearing the impressive seal of the Great State of Indiana and signed with an affected flourish by the Noble County Superintendent of Public Instruction, authorizing her to teach an ungraded school for the term of One Year. Beside it, in the long envelope, was the covering letter containing a pressing suggestion that the recipient plan to attend a five-day Institute to be held in Albion, the county seat, in late August, chiefly for the benefit of inexperienced teachers.

"Please, God," whispered Julia, wistfully but shyly, for they were not very well acquainted, "let me have a school!"

Nobody in the Miller family exhibited any piety but Martha, who was presumed to have enough for all. Martha's conversation was sprinkled with scriptural allusions, her stock of texts featuring the punitive phrases promising the ultimate rebuke of the proud, the "froward" (whoever they were), and the stiff of neck. Julia, gifted in parody, occasionally employed these solemn exhortations herself, with *ex tempore* improvisations and amendments which amused her, and sometimes frightened her, too; for, she reflected, if there really was a hell, surely the fabricator of any such flippancies was reserving a warm berth.

When Martha, in her thin, flat voice, carolled from the kitchen, "I'm washed in the blood of the Lamb," Julia invariably shuddered, swallowed hard, and muttered, "Ugh!—how nasty!"

"Please let me have the Schrofe School," wheedled Julia, clutching her precious credentials tightly in one hand and with the other pressing her eyes hard to make sure they were closed firmly enough to satisfy the requirements of Deity, who was sure to be suspicious of her sincerity, "so I won't have to come home except on Sundays. But—any school will do. Please, dear God, let me hear from one of them pretty soon. It would be so nice to have word on my birthday. Please!"

Somewhat startled by the inflection of this final word of entreaty, which hinted at an intimacy with the Almighty which, she was aware, impertinently presumed upon a very sketchy relationship, Julia added, humbly "—Unless, of course, it should not be in accordance with Thy Holy Will."

* * * * *

"What have yuh got yer Sunday hat 'n' dress on fer?" inquired Martha, when, a half-hour later, Julia passed through the kitchen, book and slate in hand, pausing to remark that she was going down by the creek where it was cooler.

"I thought I might walk over to Oak Grove, when I am tired studying, and see if there is any mail—about a school, you know."

"Mighty sight o' studyin' you'll get done with that on yer mind. Better to a-gone berryin', like I told yuh. Anyways, all the schools are a-took by now. 'Pears to me like—"

Without waiting for the rest of it, Julia walked out of the kitchen, quickened her steps immediately she was out of sight over the slope behind the barn, tossed her algebra and slate into the grass at the foot of the big willow that overhung the stream, climbed to the highway, and set out at a swinging stride toward the village two miles to the west—two miles by the road, but subject to considerable discount if one cut across Squire Craig's stubble-field, just beyond the Baptist Church, and took the path through the woods along the widening river, pent by the Austin milldam.

There were two high fences and a padlocked gate to climb, and occasionally the Squire's ill-tempered ram contested the audacity of trespassers, but Julia was impatient to peer into the tiny pane of dirty glass—No. 8—in the Post Office which occupied a few square feet in the front end of Baber's General Store.

Halfway across the stubble-field, Julia's steps became shorter and less confident.

Seated, with his back to her, on the top rail of the fence that bounded the woods, was a young stranger, fashionably dressed, his shoulders slumped as if he were lost in serious thought; in trouble, perhaps.

Julia reflected that if he were to straighten himself out to full length he would be very tall.

The stranger's perch must be quite uncomfortable. Julia surmised that he would not remain there long. If she dallied, he might proceed, unconscious of her approach. She stopped, toying with the idea of retracing her steps, but the sun beat pitilessly upon the dazzling yellow field, and the cool maples promised a relief irresistible. Her heart quickened as her pace slowed. She pulled off her dowdy hat, made of cheap lace over a wire frame, and patted the damp curls at her hot temples.

Now the young stranger had turned, and, over his shoulder, was regarding her arrival with frank interest. He stepped down from the fence, on the grove side, consulted his watch, and smiled. It was almost as if he had been waiting for her, thought Julia; as if they had arranged to meet, and she was late. Had he decided to play, she wondered, that they were keeping an engagement? Could it be possible that there was anyone in the world like that? It would be such fun.

Would he not think her a bit stupid if she stared stonily into his friendly eyes, pretending to be offended, pretending to be haughty? Was it not one's duty to be cordial to strangers? Even Martha, prude that she was, believed that one might be "entertaining angels unawares."

Julia had never seen that sort of a smile on a boy's face. It signified nothing but a proffer of friendliness from one young human being to another. It left out of consideration

138

the negligible fact that they were not of the same sex. How different from the awkward, crooked grin of the typical gum-chewing youngster who manœuvred to one's side at a boisterous barn-dance and paid one a clumsy compliment while turning to wink at some equally boorish bystander, as if to say, "I'm a-tryin' to see how fer I c'n git with her!"—as if their relationship implied that she was willing it should be rated an obscenity. She had often been half-ashamed she was a girl.

Julia was within a few yards of the fence, now, making no pretence of indifference to the presence of the tall, athletic chap who awaited her, watch still in hand.

His smile was so disarming that her red lips parted in an honest recognition of the first of its kind she had ever seen worn by a contemporary male. Her ingenuous response to it was quite free of self-consciousness or embarrassment. Toward this handsome, urbane, self-possessed boy—clearly not of her world at all, so far as outward appearances went—she sensed a strange kinship which, she believed, it would have been unworthy of her to deny either to herself or to him.

It was what she had been longing for, all her life, wasn't it? Hadn't she dreamed of an acquaintance with some congenial spirit in whose company she might be... herself? Why dissemble? She owed something to that dream.

"It's much cooler over here," he said, offering her both hands, when, having lightly climbed to the top of the fence, she sat facing him, fanning her flushed cheeks with her crumpled, frumpy hat.

"I know," said Julia.

She took his hands without hesitation or coyness, and joined him.

"But we must keep an eye out for my Uncle Jasper's pet sheep, Otto the Seventh," he said, as they fell into step on the path. "Otto has a vile disposition, and the run of this grove."

"Yes," said Julia, "I know."

He ventured a sidelong glance, as if to inquire whether his new friend had exhausted her conversational possibilities, and met an enigmatic smile.

"Had I kept you waiting long?" she asked, with an earnestness that puzzled him.

He turned about and faced her so soberly that Julia repented her whimsical audacity. Did nobody in the world know how to take a little joke? Was she the only one, after all, who had any instinct for impromptu drama? She took a step forward. He detained her with a light touch on her arm.

"Yes," he said, rather huskily, "I have been waiting a long time... for you."

"Don't spoil it," said Julia, entreatingly. "We were only playing, weren't we?"

CHAPTER II

FOR the first time in the history of the Schrofe School it was being taught without benefit of whips and dunce-caps.

The innovation caused some stir. Discipline had been much less savage in recent years under a succession of female teachers, but the present policy of complete disarmament was viewed with anxiety.

"Fer the girl's own sake," agreed the younger mothers, whose support of her had been swiftly won by the affectionate interest bestowed on their little tots, "them bigger boys oughta be kept in hand. They'll run her out afore Thanksgivin'."

Ham Ditzler, who had put in six exciting winters behind that desk, more than a decade earlier, and now divided his time between odd jobs of plasterin', paper:n', paintin', an' butcherin', in the employ of his erstwhile pupils—("danged degradin' work")—offered to bet (amount of wager unspecified) that the Miller girl would never finish out her term, a prediction which came true, though not for lack of firmness in her schoolroom.

Abner Schrofe, Chairman of the Board of Trustees, when joined in his barn by the four other members, one rainy Sunday forenoon in early October, silently shucked corn during their recital of the public's apprehension based on criticisms offered by the veteran pedagogue.

Upon the conclusion of their remarks, Chairman Schrofe listed heavily to starboard and deftly poured a considerable quantity of tobacco-juice down a convenient rat-hole, thus setting himself at liberty to express the opinion—conciliatorily phrased in terms

139

consonant with the dignity of his office—that Ham Ditzler was nothin' but a damned old sore-head.

Encountering no opposition to this statement, not even from Zeke Trumbull, Ham's son-in-law, with whom he made his home, Abner further deposed that there was more brains in Julia Miller's little finger than Ham Ditzler had in his hull body, adding that he would respectfully entertain a motion a-sayin' it to be th' sense of this here board, duly and properly assembled, that Miss Miller's services was "sadisfactory."

Hez Brumbaugh said he would so move, and suggested that the Chairman inform Miss Miller of their action.

Jake Waters, who since last spring had owed Abner the final Eight Dollars on a Guernsey heifer, 'lowed that Ham Ditzler—after all's said and done, and a-takin' him by and large—was purty much of a gol-darned old blatherskike whose idears wasn't wuth hell-room.

At Zeke's suggestion, this was taken by consent. He modestly demurred, however, when delegated to convey this sentiment to his father-in-law, feeling that it would have "more weight" coming from someone else. The decorum of the board being slightly disturbed by this remark, it grinningly adjourned to the hog-pen to inspect the new "Poland-Chiny" sow that Abner had purchased at the recent Whitley County Fair.

"Please, Mr. Schrofe," pleaded Julia, next morning, after Abner, delightedly to have an official errand at the schoolhouse, had told her he was on his way to settle Mr. Ditzler's hash, "leave him to me. Don't hurt him. I'll think of some way to accomplish the same thing without humiliating him."

Ham, already silenced by a hint from Zeke to the effect that if he knowed which side his bread was buttered on he would let up on the Miller girl, bewilderedly accepted her invitation to make a little talk to the school on the afternoon of Columbus Day, on which occasion he astounded himself and the assembled mothers by confessing the difficulty that an old-timer has in a-keepin' up with th' march o' progress.

An able craftsman of home-made philosophy, Ham spent many meditative hours evolving what he thought was a brand-new theory for the achievement of this here thing they calls success, chattering so volubly about his discovery that it became a community joke.

His convictions on this subject were never better expressed than on the late afternoon of an eventful day in May when, riding home from a service at the Oak Grove Baptist Church in company with Zeke and Lola and their swollen-eyed little daughter Goldie, Ham observed:

"It all goes fer t' show that this here thing they calls success is the fruit of self-confydence.

"If yuh know yer bigger 'n' yer job, and c'n drop the dang thing whenever yuh like and do somethin' better, the people yer a-workin' fer seems t' know it without yer a-tellin' 'em. They take orders as if they was a-spoke by Jehovah, so long as they know yuh know there's sumethin' in prospec' fer yuh a dang sight more important than a-foolin' away yer time with the likes o' them!

"If a teacher, f'rinstance, thinks he's got about all that's a-comin' to him, and has to mind his p's and q's er the Board'll set on him, he just natcherly has t' whale hell outa the brats to make 'em behave.

"If he c'n get along without rules er whips er threatenin's, it's because th' scholars knows that he don't have t' care a tinker's damn whether he keeps his job er not, seein' he c'n leave 'em, if they don't like it, and do somethin' better.... And I bet that's the secret o' success in all th' walks o' life, in ev'ry day an' generation."

Ham leaned far out of the open surrey, where he shared the back seat with Goldie, and improved his impaired articulation by relieving himself of a large quid of tobacco, wiped his stubbly lips with the back of a brown hand, and continued:

"You take this here parson, over in Wayne, what's been a-sayin' lately that th' story about Jonah ain't so, d'yuh reckon they'd let him stay there and be as honest as that if they didn't know the hull town knows as how he's had an invite to a big church in Chicago? Not by a dang sight! They just grin when he goes after the Old Testyment fer a-sayin' that th' Lord God drownded all them heathens fer spite... 'cause they know that if they holler he'll tell 'em t' take their danged ol' church b' th' bell-clapper, 'n' go t' hell!"

"Sh!—Pap!" admonished Lola, without turning. "What kinda talk... right afore little Goldie, too!"

"Well—I wisht I'd a-heared some talk like that when I was about her size," muttered Ham, remorsefully. "Mebby I'd amounted to somethin'."

140

"I wonder," inquired Zeke, "why didn't this here smart preacher in Wayne take that there bigger job in Chi?"

Ham was fidgety with eagerness to explain.

"Now yer a-gettin' to it! That just goes fer t' show how smart this feller is! If he went to Chicago, where mebby he'd be exac'ly the size of his job, er mebby a little smaller, he wouldn't be able t' tell 'em where t' get off at. He likes a-bein' where he c'n tell 'em, if they object t' his preachin', that they c'n take their danged ol' church b' th' bell-clapper, 'n'—"

"Pap—that'll do now!" snapped Lola, adding, growlingly, "Can't we never talk about nothin' else but things as riles Pap and makes him swear, right afore little Goldie?"

"All the same," finished Ham, doggedly reverting to his original proposition, "if Julia Miller hadn't 'lowed, all th' time she was a-teachin', that she was a-goin' away purty soon t' be a rich man's wife, I bet she'd a-had t' larn them sassy young rake-hells all over th' schoolhouse, five times a day!"

Little Goldie wept noisily.

"Shet up, Pap!" commanded Lola. "Hain't yuh got no proper feelin's at all?"

* * * * *

Sometimes, during those early autumn days, Julia's happiness almost suffocated her. As often, it terrified her. Was Martha's grim and hateful philosophy correct? Did people always have to pay the piper? Was this ecstasy the sort of thing you inevitably had to settle for with interest compounded?

Sudden waves of black depression briefly but increasingly inundated her dream-world. Was she living in a fool's paradise? Would the clock presently strike twelve, and send the prancing horses scampering back to rejoin their fellow-mice? Nonsense! She must pull out of this! How silly! Was ever anyone more fortunate than she?

She became very sensitive on the subject of her happiness, eager to keep her radiant spirits within bounds so that Fate would at least give her credit for all the humility and gratitude she would muster. Diligently occupied with the unaccustomed task of disciplining her emotions, sternly warning them to keep their distance from her eyes, her lips, her voice, her hands and feet, Julia was unaware of the outward effect of these suppressions.

"Julia has growed up, almost overnight," muttered old Ferd.

"Who'd a-thought that Julia Miller would age so fast?" remarked Mrs. Abner Schrofe. "She's a *woman!*"

The effect of Julia's self-discipline in the cause of propitiating Nemesis was an unconscious exhibition of that magnetic and covetable type of personal poise not to be had cheaper than at the price of a stoical imprisonment of kinetic energy bruising its fists against the bars and pleading for its right to shout and dance and sing.

Eager to offer any forfeit to fend off the Day of Judgment, Julia had decided to room and board at home, involving a daily tramp of nearly six miles. It was a very real sacrifice, in anticipation; for, in looking forward to her new work, its most alluring promise had been the escape it offered from an irksome home environment.

School had been in progress barely a week, however, before Julia began to doubt the efficacy of her splendid sacrifice. The atmosphere at home had improved. The boys were shaving now, every other day, in honour of the young school-mistress who appeared at their breakfast-table trimly clad for her day's work. Susan and Greta crimped their hair, starched their aprons, and conceded the boarder a right to the exclusive use of her own trinkets. Her father's gratitude for the money she had engaged to pay touched her. Martha's awkward tenderness and solicitude slightly embarrassed her. What a difference a little money made in the general line-up of human relations! Julia smiled, with new understanding, over the story that had gone the rounds about Widow Mercer, who lived near Bippus, ten miles east.

Mr. Mercer, an enthusiastic Maccabee, had left her Two Thousand Dollars in fraternal insurance. There were four sons, all concerned that this large fortune should not be dissipated. They suggested that their mother divide the money among them, and spend her time living in their homes as an honoured guest.

"No," she had replied, quietly. "'Pears to me like an elderly lady with Two Thousand Dollars would be a much more interestin' guest than an old woman with nothin'."

It made all the difference in the world, money did!

One day you were "Julia?... Julia!... *Julia!!* Come here, this instant, like I told yuh, and peel these potatoes!"

One short week later you were "Julia, you just let Susan peel them potatoes, and you go set down till supper's ready."

Nor was this refreshing change at home Julia's chief ground for satisfaction. She was grateful for the opportunity to be alone, two hours daily, with her enchanting memories and high expectations. The vigorous walk quickened her imagination. Fully a third of the trip to school was taken through tall timber on a picturesque wagon-road that negligently waived the right o' way to close-meshed clumps of flaming sumac, and an occasional obdurate oak—a narrow ribbon of a road, carpeted with freshly fallen leaves, frost-sensitized to autumnal rays filtered through the livelier half of the prism, and crisp under her nimble feet.

On the return journey, Julia was always the school-teacher, it being part of her discipline to restrict her thoughts to her professional obligations.

On the early morning trip, however, she was all Zandy's! Her capacity increased for the vivid recovery of her deliriously happy experiences with him. To the very minutia of detail, Julia reconstructed every tone, posture, and gesture associated with those dreamy, unreal afternoons under the shade of the river-willows behind the Baptist Cemetery, not more than a dozen yards from her mother's grave, and the few almost painfully rapturous hours that had transfigured dull and dusty little Albion into the City Delectable!

The first half-mile of the out-bound trip, which brought her to the Baptist Church, where she turned to the left on the busy Larwill Pike, was invariably taken, at that early hour, without encountering any traffic, either on foot or wheel.

Except for the shrill scream of some excited water-bird on the river, and the lonesome clangor of a cow-bell registering the impatience of horns entangled in a wild grapevine down in the glen, there would be no sound but the rhythmic crunch of frosty gravel under her competent heels.

Julia's precious recollections proceeded in orderly sequence. Sometimes—let her do her utmost to concentrate on the opening chapter of the almost incredible story—her memory would insist on turning whole handfuls of pages; but, tugging herself free of the culminating episodes that mattered most, she would pursue events chronologically. She always wanted to be through with the early part of the story before she reached the busier mile of pike, for the full enjoyment of their first encounter demanded a few merry roulades of bantering laughter—her own: Zandy had been so serious. And, besides, she liked to be in the thick of the dark woods when she arrived at the Albion part of it!... Dear, dear Zandy! How tender! How precious!

Julia's reminiscences always began at the fence where they had met on the morning of her birthday. Now they were ambling slowly through the grove. They had left the path, and were wandering toward the river. She was still en route to the Post Office, but they were off the path.

"You have a first name, too?" (I have told him mine.)

"Alexander."

"Quite long and dignified." (I think I must not do that, any more. He doesn't like teasing. He is so serious.)

"So was my grandfather. It was his name. Everyone calls me Zandy. My sister began it when she was a little tot, and I was a baby."

"Do they call you Zandy at Dartmouth, too?"

"Mmm." (Zandy says "Mmm" when he means yes; not "Umm-humm," the way our people do. Martha thinks it queer when I say "Mmm.") "College students are not very formal. Even the profs have nicknames."

"Do they know it?"

"In time. They don't seem to care. We had a big Scot in Math, last year, with an enormous moustache. He discovered that he was 'The Walrus', and pared it down. When that didn't help, he shaved it off."

"And then he wasn't a walrus, any more?"

"Oh, yes, he was still a walrus.... I say, Julia, I'm going to like you, most awfully." (I knew, then, that it was true. Zandy was going to like me. He couldn't have said it, that way, and not mean it.)

"What is your sister's name?" (I think it better we should talk about his sister. I'm afraid my face is red, and my heart is just pounding!)

"Alison.... She's married."

"Does she live in Cincinnati, too?"

"She lives in a Pullman car. Her husband is Roland Forsythe."

"The famous tenor?"

"Mmm... and tanker."

"You mean he drinks?"

"Like a fish."

"Is that why your sister goes along?"

"Exactly—but Alison doesn't mind. She likes excitement. And she thinks Providence has appointed her to keep a great artist sober. She married him for that."

"And she can't?"

"Not much of the time."

"But how can he sing?"

"You don't have to be sober to sing? A good many people never do sing unless they're—"

"It doesn't always work that way. Some people get glum and mean."

"Roland doesn't. He's mean when he's sober. But it'll get him, some day. Leaky heart."

"How I hate it!" (I almost tell him why, for he's sure to find out.)

Now they had reached the gate at the farther side of the woods, and Julia had climbed it, leaving Zandy to wait her return from the Post Office. She had discouraged his going along, reluctant to amuse the loafers who would be sitting in front of Eph Mumaugh's blacksmith shop.... Now she was back.

"Look, Zandy!" (How natural it seemed to call him Zandy.) "I've got a school!—the Schrofe one!—the one I wanted!" (He takes the letter, and our hands touch.)

"Writes like a ten-year-old boy, doesn't he?"

"He probably never went to school much."

"I'll bet he can multiply bushels by dollars." (We are down at the river, again, sitting on the grass.)

"That's where I'm weak... figures. I think algebra's awful!" (I tell him all about having to go to Albion for the Institute.)

"I'll help you. It's easy.... Explain it to you in an hour."

"Will you, honestly?" (Zandy gives my hand a little pat. That was the first time.)

"This afternoon!"

"But I mustn't take your time. You'll be busy!"

"What would I be busy at? It'll save my life." (His father is sore at him because he's decided to be a writer, instead of making nails, and he's changed his course in college, and his father has sent him to the country, all summer, as a punishment, instead of taking him along to Europe, as he had promised.)

* * * * *

Most of the early part of the story would have been covered by the time Julia reached the woods. She had walked rapidly on the pike, and could afford to take the rest of the trip more leisurely.

Now they were sitting on the river-bank behind the Baptist Cemetery. It was Thursday, late afternoon. They had known each other three days. She was reclining against the bole of a maple, using the opened algebra to protect her back from the rough bark. Zandy had just finished reading her the *Rubáiyát*. What a wonderful voice he had! So tender! Her eyes were wet.

"Let me have it a minute. I want to see that verse about—"

She reached for the book.

He took her hand.

"Anybody would know at a glance, Julia, that you were meant for some kind of creative art."

"How would they?"

"Your thumb!"

"What's funny about my thumb?" she had asked, searching his deep-set grey-green eyes.

"Bends back so far.... Open your hand, dear.... Wide.... See?"

"Does yours?... Let me look... Why, the very idea!... Is that what makes you think you can write?... Our hands are very much alike, aren't they?"

A little shiver of excitement always came over Julia when she reached this part of the story.

"We're alike in more ways than that, precious!"

She had made a little effort to retrieve her hands. Zandy had taken both of them in one of his. When he kissed her, she did not resist. How everlastingly right it seemed! She had shared his kiss, a bit clumsily. They were both quite stampeded for a moment. She hoped he would kiss her again: perhaps she could do better. It was rather embarrassing to feel that one had been so awkward. She had done much better, the next time, maybe because it was not so hurried.... Zandy's kisses! They made your heart so big there wasn't room in your chest to breathe!

He had walked back with her, that day, until they could see the chimney of her house. When she stopped, meaning that he mustn't come any farther, he said, "What are you doing, tonight?"

* * * * *

It proved to be an eventful evening. Julia volunteered to accompany Martha to prayer-meeting. At the door of the church, however, she said, "I think I'll run over to the Post Office, first. ... I've a letter that should be mailed to Albion, about my room, you know."

"I thought you had did that," said Martha. "You'll not be back afore meetin' is out!"

But Martha seemed relieved. Julia knew that her sister preferred not to have other members of the family present when she testified to the submissiveness of her burden-bearing. It reflected no credit on her home, where, it was implied, she took all the hard knocks with little to show for them but a chastened spirit.

"You'll not go through them dark woods, will yuh?" Martha cautioned. Julia promised.

Zandy was waiting for her, by the fence where she had first met him. He kissed her lips, her eyes, her hair.... They were made for each other, weren't they?... They would plan to spend their lives together.... Why not?... Didn't she love him?...

Someone was blowing out the malodorous kerosene lamps in the church when Julia returned across the stubble-field with Zandy, the shrill rendition of "God Be With You Till We Meet Again" warning them their tryst was over. They stopped in the darkness for a final embrace.

"It won't be long now, sweetheart."

"Oh, Zandy; I'm so happy!"

The little group on the church porch was separating, Martha's prim voice conspicuous above the others.

They walked home almost in silence, Martha mentally putting into rehearsal the testimony she meant to give, next time; Julia wondering what Martha would be saying if she knew that Zandy Craig was going along with her to Albion where they were to be *married!*

Late in the night, Julia, wide-awake but calm, wondered if she were playing the game squarely with everybody; with her father, with Martha, with Zandy's father, who made nails and was so gruff and domineering; with Zandy's mother, who already had a girl selected for him.... But, as Zandy had said, they had their own lives to live. Her father, her sister, his father, his mother—had they not been given a chance to live their lives, as they liked?... Maybe not.... It was all very confusing. Life was complicated.

"We will do what our hearts tell us is exactly right, darling," Zandy had said. "Nobody in the world has a right to keep us apart. We will keep it a secret, now, but, one of these days, when they see how happy we are, and how right it all was, they will be glad."

* * * * *

Old Ferd remarked at supper, one Saturday evening in early November, that he had met Abner Schrofe, that afternoon.

"Ab says," reported Ferd, proudly, "that Julia is the best teacher they ever had. I'm a-goin' to tell her when she comes down. It's no more 'n' right she should hear it... What's a-keepin' her?"

144

"She's been a-lyin' down most o' th' afternoon, paw," said Martha. "I'm afeard that long walk every day is a-pullin' Julia down, now it's come rainy. She hasn't looked good fer quite a spell."

"She was a-cryin' when I looked in to call her t' supper," said Greta. "Funny fer Julia to be a-cryin'."

"I'll go up," said Martha. "Here, Susan, dish them turnips."

Julia recognized her sister's step on the stairs, raised up on one elbow, dabbed at her eyes with a soggy little handkerchief, tucked a letter under her pillow.

"No—I'm quite all right, Martha. Working pretty hard, you know. Just... sort of unstrung. No—I don't believe I could eat a bite, not now. Maybe, after a while. Run along. It's nothing."

Martha clumped down the stairs, and the letter was unfolded again.

"What a misfortune, darling, if things are as you fear. If it had happened a little later—wouldn't we have been glad? Maybe it isn't that. Try not to worry.

"All one hears about now is the big game with the Chicago Athletic Club on Thanksgiving. Father and mother are coming East for it. How I wish you could be here! Big doings!

"If it's what you think, darling, can you go on, a little while, as if nothing had happened? How long? Maybe I can have a heart-to-heart with my father. But he's pretty hard, you know. Savage old thing, when disappointed. I'm afraid he'd take me out of college. That would set us back. If I can get through this year, the rest will be easy."

* * * * *

Julia had fainted at the Friday afternoon programme with which school closed for the Christmas holidays. The room was packed with visitors and stuffy with festal decorations. When the exercises were all but over, Julia crumpled in a pathetic heap on the floor. Young Jason Schrofe, whose attentions she had regarded so casually that he had quite lost hope, drove her home in his sleigh.

"That settles it," said old Ferd. "She's not a-goin' to tramp through them snowdrifts any more.... You must find a place to board, Julia, closer by th' school."

She smiled wanly and shook her head. She would be all right. No use wasting the money.

She had hoped that the cruel exertion might... somehow... solve the problem. In any event, the long walk daily helped to distract her mind. She might go mad, otherwise.... How long would it be until people noticed?... What would those all-knowing young mothers think of her fainting?... How much torture could she stand in these cruel stays?

"It fairly breaks my heart, darling," Zandy had written. "There you are, worrying your dear little head off; and here I am, starting home for the holidays, unable to bear even a wee bit of your trouble ... and discomfort, too, I suppose. I don't know much about such things."

"The dear boy," thought Julia. "He doesn't know, of course. He probably thinks a woman just knows it's going to happen, on a certain day, and—when the time comes—it happens. And I don't know much more about it, except that I'm afraid I can't keep it a secret much longer ... not even for Zandy's dear sake."

* * * * *

Zandy was in line for the Perkins Medal in oratory. On no account must that event be jeopardized.... Could Julia, he wondered, manage to carry on until the oratorical contest was over? February third, it was. How about it, Julia, darling?

Julia would certainly try. Zandy must not be disqualified for that medal. Perhaps his father would be that much more kind, if he won it. But, dear boy, let's arrange to tell them the very minute the contest is over! It's getting serious! Please!

It so happened that on the very night when Zandy was laboriously composing a letter which began, "My dear Father Miller (for I really want to call you Father Miller, because your Julia is my wife; though I'm afraid you will be annoyed, a little, that we haven't told you earlier about our wedding)"—Greta had whispered to Susan, and Susan, white-faced,

145

had whispered to Martha, and Martha, trembling with fear and indignation, had entered Julia's room without knocking.

Julia was outstretched, her dark-circled eyes were closed, her hands lay supine, palms upward, on the counterpane. Martha looked at her for a long time before she spoke. She swallowed, noisily.

"You might as well make a clean breast of it," said Martha, hoarsely. Julia opened her eyes and smiled.

"In the drawer of my desk, Martha. Here's the key. That long paper. That's it. My marriage licence."

"So you run off and got married, did yuh?"

"Well—not exactly... run off. We were married during the County Institute."

"And you was in Albion, a-livin' with a man, while we thought you was a-goin' to that school that cost all o' Thirty Dollars!"

"He was my husband—and it was my money."

"Humph! He don't seem to set much store by yuh... a-leavin' yuh to face the music. What's his name?" Martha adjusted her steel-bowed spectacles, and stooped under the lamp. "Alexander Craig... who's that? You don't mean t' say it's that rich Craig's boy what was here last summer a-visitin' at the Squire's?"

Julia nodded.

"It's a heap the Craigs would do fer a Miller! You wait till your father hears o' this. He'll make that young rascal sweat! He'll have th' law on him!"

So—at long last, Julia had no further need to punish her desperately ill-treated body. Ungirded—physically, mentally—she felt that her worst troubles were behind her. They could say what they liked, they could do what they would—she had made her last agonizing trip to the schoolhouse. There was some comfort in that, at least.

Old Ferd was torn between grief and anger. He wanted to pour out his rage without delay. He would write to that lousy whelp and tell him, for once, what somebody should have told him long ago—that he was a low-lived coward, a dirty blackguard, and—and—if he ever darkened their door, except to bring the money to pay for Julia's sickness, he would be pitched out!... And he did write that, and more, pounded a stamp on the envelope with a fist that looked amazingly like Julia's, only not so white, and stalked, half-blind with hate, to the Post Office, where he was regarded with fresh interest, the loafers in corduroy coats and felt boots noting his state of mind and winking at one another out of the tails of their eyes. He was aware of it. Everybody knew, damn them!... There was a letter for Julia. She always got the mail, herself.... He would tear it up, and throw it in the river. The sleety gale sobered him, somewhat, on the way home. He did not destroy the letter.

* * * * *

"A couple of years from now, darling," wrote Zandy, a week later, "we will have forgotten all about this. At the moment, things do look pretty dark, don't they? I was all ready to come when I had the letter from your father. He is in a great temper; hardly to be blamed, of course; talked of shooting. Anyone else but your father, I would debate that subject with him. But all I could do for you now would be to stir up a tremendous row and probably make everything more difficult for you.

"I postponed writing to my father until last Saturday; couldn't think up just the right way to approach the matter. He is always so autocratic and hair-triggery. I did the best I could to make him see things. There is a wire from him this afternoon, hundred words, saying he is done with me. That, of course, only means he is very sore. He may come around all right. But not very soon. You have no idea how stubborn he can be.

"So—meantime, I can't stay in school. My mind is too upset, anyway. I shall be out of funds, too. In fact, I'm out of funds now. The month's allowance is just due, and he isn't even going to send that. I've made up my mind to bum my way through to the Coast. This twenty is all the money I have but five dollars. You can depend on me to send you some more as soon as I have it. Don't be discouraged, dear. I intend to succeed. Success is more a gift than an achievement. Some people are born to succeed. I am one of them. You will share. Keep that in mind through these hard days. I shall soon send for you, and we will be happy together forever."

* * * * *

With confidence unshaken, for there was a peculiar contagion associated with Zandy's optimism that gave her courage, Julia watched the last of the snow disappear.

Everything was going to come out all right, as Zandy had predicted. He had started West to find work and make a little home. Then he would send for her... for *them!*

Every few days there came another postal card... from Detroit, Chicago, Davenport, Denver, Spokane. Zandy was on the way.

Presently the lilacs were opening, and the air was vibrant with the hum of all sorts of awakened winged things. Julia could hear the occasional scream of her father's chisel doing a shrill aria to the accompanying rumble of the big wooden fly-wheel.

"Poor old darling," she thought, tenderly. "He's worried about me, and trying to keep his hands busy... dear, shaky, old hands."

"What's father making, Martha?"

"Will yuh let on yer surprised when he gives it t' yuh?"

"Mmm—but maybe you'd better not tell me if it's a secret."

"A little cradle," whispered Martha. "Mind yuh don't let on."

Julia wept a few happy tears. Her father had forgiven her, then. That was ever so much better. It would come out all right, as Zandy had said.

When Doctor Engle came, next day, he was shortly after joined by Doctor Marshall, a specialist from Fort Wayne. Jason Schrofe had driven him up from Larwill.

Doctor Marshall had quiet blue eyes and wore a brown suit that fitted him. He did not talk much, and hardly asked any questions at all. Julia had great confidence in him and felt no shyness in his strong, competent hands.

The charge was twenty-five dollars, and when Julia had counted it out—after Doctor Engle had handed her the pocket-book from her desk—she was pleased to find that there was just enough; a twenty, a two, and three ones. Doctor Marshall looked at the money and the empty pocket-book, and said not to bother about paying it until she was well. He would send her a bill, some day.

"Thank you," said Julia, gratefully. "I'll pay you as soon as I'm up."

"That will be soon enough," said Doctor Marshall. Martha came and sat on the edge of the bed, after the doctors were gone, holding Julia's throbbing fingers. Martha had shown the doctors out, and Julia had heard them talking, downstairs, for a disturbingly long time. Martha's face, always an open book, was troubled. It twitched, as it did when she was worried.

"What is it, Martha? You talked to them. Do they think I'm very sick? They don't think I'm going to—they don't think maybe I'm not going to get well, do they?" Julia's words came slowly, and as from a considerable distance.

Martha pressed her bony knuckles hard against her cheek and swayed slowly back and forth.

"They're a-doin' everythin' they knows how, Julia. We must all put our trust in th' Lord 'n' His precious promises.... Can't yuh let yerself just rest on His Blessed Name?"

Julia turned her face away and stared hard at the white wall, her eyes wide, frightened.

"Would yuh like Brother Miner t' come over from Cromwell 'n' talk t' yuh, Julia? It might be quite comfortin'."

Julia shook her head, and there was a little convulsive shudder of her shoulders. Sighing audibly, Martha drew up the sheet over the quivering shoulders, laid the back of her rough hand against the hot neck, and quietly left the room.

A violent storm was rising in Julia's breast—a devastating tornado of rebellion. Why had Fate played this ghastly trick on her? What had she ever done to earn this dull tragedy? What chance had she had from the beginning? Why had Destiny set her down in this stupid house—her mother a whining fool, her father a shabby old drunkard, her brothers and sisters nothing but clods and dolts?

And that wasn't the worst of it! Fate had opened the door a little way and pointed toward liberty. Love—great love—had come! Why hadn't Fate left her to the tiresome little drudgeries that were the common lot of people badly born? Why this mocking glimpse of freedom?

In her broken-dyked passion, Julia's scorn swept over everything and everybody associated with her disaster. Her father! What right had this drunken old man and his slatternly wife to bring her into the world at all? And this smug, surly, ignorant, superstitious old sister—calmly inviting her, in this hour of break-up, to like it!... to put her trust in the Lord! Mighty little He cared! Nobody cared! Least of all—the Lord! If He saw it, at all, He probably grinned! Another good joke!—saith the Lord.

Martha was back now, seated again on the edge of the bed, wetting her thumb and leafing the thin pages of a book. Julia dully turned her eyes and recognized the cheap little Bible she had earned for faithful attendance at Sunday School when she was nine or ten. Martha was doubtless hunting for some more of those precious promises. What a dull, uninteresting old thing those precious promises had made of her!

Clearing her throat and settling her spectacles more firmly on her thin nose, Martha held up the Bible at an angle that would better the light on the fine print. "No, please, Martha," muttered Julia. "Not now—please!"

"I'll just leave it here, then," said Martha, regretfully. "Mebby it'll be a sort o' comfort just t' have it under yer pillow."

She was gone now, leaving Julia with the precious promises within easy reach. But the storm was by no means spent. With white-knuckled little fists and tightly clenched teeth, rigid lips wide apart, Julia stared up defiantly. In a moment she gave way to the passionate indignation that was all but driving her mad. The precious promises! Bah!... God—and the Bible—and prayer—and the angels—and miracles—and faith that would remove mountains! Bah!... She groped under the pillow, clutched the book, opened it in the middle, utterly blind with hot tears and crazed with desperate anger, and began to claw at the pages with her nails. She buried all her fingers in the book, and tore, and ripped, and crumpled, making snarling little mutterings deep in her throat.

"That!... and that!... for You!" she panted. (Rip!) "And that!... and this!... for Your...(Crunch!)... precious... promises!... Look!... if You can see... You cruel Thing... what I'm doing to your Holy Word!... Now! There!... send me to hell!"

Completely spent by her exertion, Julia lay as one dead under the litter of ragged, crumpled desecration, her shuddering sobs all but subsided; and, fatigued beyond endurance, drifted away from the shameful scene, and slept.

When she woke there was a dim light burning on the table. Her father was sitting on the low rocking-chair by the bed, elbows on knees, his fingers tangled in his shaggy grey hair. Remembering dully, she felt about on the counterpane. Nothing there. So it was only a bad dream, after all. That was good. Her fingers touched a rumpled scrap of paper. It was not a dream. She laid her hand on the torn paper and closed on it.

Roused by her stirring, Ferd glanced up, and their eyes met. Julia's were inquisitive.

Ferd shook his head, and smiled wanly.

"It's all right, Julia. I cleared it up. Nobody seen it. Guess you was a little out o' yer mind fer a spell."

"I'm dreadfully sorry, father," she murmured, penitently. "It was ... an awful thing to do."

Old Ferd caressed the white hand nearest him. With the other, Julia absently rolled the fragment she had found into a tight little ball.

She fell to wondering whether there was anything still legible on the scrap; and, if so, whether it would be some frightful forecast of doom for sinners. Well—she deserved it, didn't she? She recalled her curiosity about the sentimental mottoes that came on thin, narrow, sticky strips of paper wrapped around cheap taffy at the County Fair. ... Funny how people took stock in the silly fortunes told that way.... She remembered a discussion between Martha and Becky Slemmer, one day, over the "messages" they had had by tossing the Bible open at random and reading the first verse at the top of the page.... Martha had come by many a precious promise accidentally... poor Martha.... Becky had laughed over some of hers, and Martha had hush-hushed her, warningly. Becky said you couldn't make much out of it, anyway. One time, after a big quarrel with Zelma in which they had bit, scratched, and pulled hair, she had gone to the Bible for guidance, and the magic verse at the top of the column said, "She is loud and stubborn." Becky was sure, at first, that the Lord referred to her sister, but she wondered afterward. Martha said: "No—Becky. The Lord wouldn't send a message t' Zelma through you. He must 'a' meant somethin' personal."

"Shall I get yuh a cold drink, Julia?" Ferd was inquiring.

"Please, father... and turn up the light a little, won't you, before you go down?"

* * * * *

"You're ever so much better this morning," said Doctor Engle, cheerily.

Julia smiled contentedly, and nodded.
"You're overcoming this toxine, Julia."
"What's toxine, doctor?" she inquired, interestedly.
"Poison."
"Yes," said Julia, thoughtfully, "I have overcome it."
"Well—maybe not all of it yet," he cautioned, stroking his cheek, "but—"
Julia's dry lips puckered determinedly, and she nodded her head with an air of deep conviction.
"All of it," she said, firmly, "all the poison is gone."
That afternoon, to Martha's astonishment and disapproval, Julia demanded pen, ink, paper, and privacy. Protestingly, the weary and worried woman propped her sister up with pillows, and closed the door.
Summoning all her depleted energy, Julia wrote a long letter addressed to her unborn child. The writing was uneven and sprawling, and the lines sagged at the right end, more and more, until the last ones ran nearly off the pages in a pitiful little toboggan toward the corner.
Everything she knew about Dresden was in it; high pride for the things that were Dresden; high hopes for the heir to the Dresden tradition.
Everything she knew about Zandy was in it; poor, bewildered Zandy, so frightfully misunderstood, and showing up so badly when he really had it in his heart to do the right thing.
"I'm going to hide this letter, and hope that you find it, some day, in case anything happens to me. You'll not find it, perhaps, until you're big enough to want to take things to pieces and see how they were put together. I hope you won't find it even then. I hope you won't find it until you're old enough to have had a few harder bumps than just falling out of your cradle.
"I've discovered a secret. It's going to take me through what I have to face. If I live, it's going to make me over into something else than I've been. If I die, I'll die happy. I'm going to tell you what I've found. It's the only thing I have to leave you. If you'll take it, and make use of it, you may need no other fortune."
It was a difficult letter to write. The uncanny experience that had been hers, during the preceding eighteen hours, was not easy to explain. But Julia did the best she could, and with the last physical resource left from the fatigue of writing, she groped her way dizzily to the little walnut desk, with a great effort opened the secret drawer, deposited her letter, and returned to her bed, exhausted.

* * * * *

After her grinding agony was over, Julia slept, and woke, and slept, and dreamed.

In the late afternoon, she became slightly delirious. Martha caught fragments of it, and wept quietly.... Roses overhanging a trellis at the doorway of a little bungalow... Zandy being welcomed with outstretched arms that quickly fell inert from fatigue. ... Then—there was a garden... a high, grey, stone wall... and in the wall there was a door... and beyond the door, a river. ... Martha sobbed chokingly, and turned the iced towel on the hot forehead.... And on the river there was a punt... with a red and blue canopy... and the sound of a tender voice, singing... and a guitar.
When she awoke again, it was almost dark. It was apparent to the watchers that Julia was mildly curious about the presence of the whole family.
Doctor Engle was seated at the bedside with his fingers on her wrist. Her father stood stiffly beside him, his hands clenched. Martha slowly waved a palm-leaf fan, supporting her weary weight on outspread fingers laid against the head of the bed. Susan and Greta stood at the foot, staring wide-eyed. Hiram and Elmer were in the doorway.
Julia's eyes slowly travelled over the group, finally coming to rest on old Ferd whom she inspected with gravity. She attempted a little smile for him—a solicitous little smile

that seemed to say, "What a lot of trouble I'm making you. So sorry." Ferd couldn't face the stiff little smile any longer; closed his eyes, walked to the window, wept.

Julia had kept her secret too long. Through hot, parched lips she asked Martha if she would please take care of the baby. Greta drew a sudden racking sob, and sank to the floor. Susan raised her up and tugged her out into the hall.

"His name," murmured Julia, valiantly battling with the oncoming fog, "is Alexander Ferdinand.... But—Martha—if that's too long a name... for such a little boy... you may call him Zandy."

* * * * *

It was late afternoon. They had just returned from the service at Oak Grove Baptist Church, and its sequel in the Cemetery. The long row of hitching-racks had been quite inadequate. Barely a third of the people had been able to enter the church.

Martha had whispered to the undertaker, and he had laid one of the sprays on their mother's grave, hard-by. Jason Schrofe, observing that his flowers had been chosen for this tribute, tarried, after the others had moved away, and replaced it.

Susan and Greta were busying themselves in the kitchen, sympathetically assisted by neighbours whose voices, restrained but endeavouring to be cheerful, drifted up the stairs where Martha, having laid her borrowed bonnet and veil on Julia's primly made, white-counterpaned bed, was stooping over the cradle.

Old Ferd tiptoed into the room, and Martha glanced up.

"Look at them long fingers," she said. "Like her'n."

Ferd handed her a yellow envelope.

"One o' the Schrofe boys fetched this over from Cromwell."

Martha opened it, read it through, silently, her lips forming the words, and gave it back. Ferd stared hard at the message from Seattle.

COURAGE DARLING IT WILL NOT BE LONG NOW GOOD JOB ZANDY

He tossed the telegram on Julia's bed, and stumbled out of the room, whimpering like a punished child.

* * * * *

That night—as if the Millers had not already furnished enough sensation to satisfy the community—Ferd hanged himself from a rafter in the vacant stall next to Florrie.

Hiram had gone out to throw down some straw, and saw It, from the mow-ladder, slowly revolving. Martha, hearing a hoarse shout, ran from the kitchen and found her brother retching violently. It seemed a long time before they found a box high enough to stand on.

"I was a-feared o' this, all along," groaned Martha.

Greta kept screaming, hysterically, while she tugged at the rope of the dinner-bell that clanged ominously from its perch on the roof of the milkhouse.

The barnyard filled with neighbours carrying lanterns. Milt Mumaugh volunteered to drive to Albion for the coroner, and put his three-year-old roan mare to a gallop.

It was a warm night, but they felt chilly and built a fire to sit by while they waited. About midnight, the wives of the watchers served sandwiches, cake, and coffee.

Abner Schrofe and Doc Engle sat on the doorstep of old Ferd's shop, smoking and slapping mosquitoes.

"Baby a-goin' t' live, Doc?"

"Looks like it.... Poor little devil.... Maybe better off if it died.... Not much of a future for it, I'm afraid."

"Well—as fer that," drawled Abner, "yuh never c'n tell."

CHAPTER III

"AND now, Ferdinand"—Reverend Miles Brumm pursed a public smile—"perhaps you had better mount your new pony, and see how he sits."

"Please, Uncle Miles, I don't want to."

Ferdinand's voice was barely audible, but to the congregation assembled in the parsonage barn-lot there was no mistaking the determined shake of his curly head.

Consternation prevailed in the audience, composed of half the children in Zanesdale, and what Mr. Brumm would have considered on Sunday morning as "a goodly company" of adults.

A medley of encouragement, ridicule, insufferable patronage, and downright contempt volleyed at the embarrassed boy.

"Aw, gwan! Ride him!"... "Don't be scairt of him, Ferdinand; he won't throw yuh!"... "He's yourn, hain't he? Git on 'im!"... "Shucks!—feared of a Shetland pony!"... "Yeah—tame as a kitten!"

Ferdinand hung his head, abstractedly crushed an ant with his bare toes, and was painfully conscious of the rapid beating of a bulging vein in his neck.

"Bet he cost a hundred dollars!" appraised Nathan Himes, who had joined the procession when it passed his drugstore.

"Hundred dollars!" scoffed Bill Trask, the station agent; "that there saddle 'n' bridle cost more 'n' a hundred dollars!"

"My land!" exclaimed Sophie Trask, proudly relaying her husband's versatility to the huddle of women by the big gate, "Mr. Trask says the saddle and bridle alone must 'a' cost more than a hundred dollars! What must the pony be worth?"

Nobody paid any attention to the comment except young Mrs. Himes (her as was one o' them Sheriff Effendorfer girls from over beyond Maples; so stuck up—all of 'em—their noses was out o' joint), who, behind her hand, remarked to Clara Sellars, the lately-from-Wayne peroxide-blonde milliner (less said the better), that the Trasks always knew so much, to which Miss Sellars replied, in a disgusted undertone, "Don't they give yuh a pain?"

Mr. Brumm, aware of the unanimous curiosity about the pony, to which his young nephew had now added spice by his reluctance to exhibit a natural interest in it, felt himself in an awkward situation. He had been unprepared for the episode that had plunged his family into the public eye. No chance had been given him to collect his thoughts or confer with Ferdinand in private.

It was the lad's tenth birthday. At breakfast he had received a large, inexpensive pocket-knife from his uncle, a sticky, acrid-smelling, red-and-green *Child's Illustrated Bible* from his aunt, and three lead-pencils in a slim pasteboard box from Angela. He had put down the apple he was munching, and had gone about, as the custom was, dutifully kissing the donors—Uncle Miles, first; for Uncle Miles was always served first with whatever happened to be in distribution; and then Aunt Martha, who moistened a finger and brushed back the unruly lock that dipped to a point in the centre; and then Angela, whom he tried to kiss on the cheek, for Angela's kisses were wet, and he had a disinclination toward them which he hoped she would realize, one of these days, without too much injury to her feelings.

At that mellow moment—for, however stiffly the family ties were habitually starched, there were festal occasions when something like spontaneous affection had its innings—there was a vigorous rap at the kitchen door. Straightening his frayed cravat, Mr. Brumm had answered the summons. A stranger's business-like voice was heard.

"Mr. Brumm?... How do you do, sir?... Very well, sir.... My name is Thompson. I'm from Chicago; that is, I'm from the Winnetka Stock Farm. Our people has had orders to deliver a pony here for Master Craig—"

Through the open door came the rumble of many voices. Angela wiped her shapely lips on her sleeve and hurried to the window. Ferdinand stared hard at Aunt Martha, listening intently.

"He lives with you, don't he?... It's a birthday gift from his father.... It's Mr. Craig's instructions from Seattle.... I've just got in with it, expressed from our place in Winnetka.... The pony's out here in your lot, delivered in good shape, as you'll see, and if you, or the young gentleman, will sign these papers, I can catch the nine-seventeen back to the city.... Right here you are, sir, on that line; and here, too, if you please. Thanks!... Quite a crowd we gathered up, coming through the village, eh? Guess it's the first time a pony ever came to this town on a passenger train."

Aunt Martha had taken off her brown apron and joined her husband at the back door, nervously smoothing her hair with both hands.

Ferdinand, blinking rapidly, and tapping his front teeth with a restless thumb, squeezed past his aunt, and ventured out upon the back porch, quite overawed by the gathering crowd.

Uncle Miles, with a pumped-up air of heartiness, as if he himself were being presented with a thoroughbred Shetland pony by his admiring fellow-townsmen, breezed forth to the barnyard, delightedly intoning, "Well—well—indeed!... A great surprise, I'm sure!... A pony!... Well—well!"

It was the crowd that remembered the pony was Ferdinand's.

"Heigh! Ferdinand! Come on out! Look what yuh got!"

"Must I, Aunt Martha?" asked Ferdinand, his face twitching.

"Of course, silly!" shouted Angela, clutching his hand and dragging him along.

"Fancy that great big boy having to be tugged out of the house to see a pony!" scoffed Clara Sellars.

"He's only a kid," explained Mrs. Himes. "Awful big for his age; tall as his half-sister, and she must be all of fourteen. I s'pose he's just shy of so many people."

Very much embarrassed, Ferdinand allowed himself to be propelled through the crowd. He drew a stiff, reluctant smile, reached out a slim hand, stroked the pony's velvet muzzle, and was generously rewarded for the tentative caress, the pony sniffing inquisitively at his pockets and licking his hands.

"Aw—look—ain't that cute?" The women cooed appreciatively, and beamed on Aunt Martha, who had joined them, murmuring apologies for her looks and all. They told her she looked quite all right, they were sure.

Miss Sellars, pretending interest in the half-finished sweater that Mrs. Himes was carrying under her arm, whispered, "Did yuh ever see such an old frump?"

"Awful pious, I guess."

"Can't people be pious without—"

"No," said Mrs. Himes, "Sh!—Listen!"

"Well—Ferdinand—" said Uncle Miles.

"No, Uncle Miles." His deep-set, grey-green eyes were perplexed, and his face was contorted as he gnawed his lips. He stepped back, and glanced about as if looking for a way of escape.

Mr. Brumm wiped his brow with a large handkerchief. It would hardly do to send these parishioners of his away with so great a mystery to discuss.

"Don't you like your pony?" he stammered, in a tone that affected to express the general surprise.

"Of course!" Ferdinand's voice was husky under the strain. "But I mustn't have it! I can't have it! You know why!" Hot tears sprang to his eyes, and he scurried through the speechless crowd, disappearing into the house.

"Ferdinand's a little nervous and excited," explained Mrs. Brumm, primly, but obviously shaken by the unfortunate event. "He wasn't expecting a pony, you know, and what with so many good friends coming along, and all—"

"That's it—that's it," said Mr. Brumm, who, upon Ferdinand's retreat, had moved toward his wife to learn what explanation she was offering for this strange conduct. "Ferdinand will be quite himself, presently."

"Yeah—I bet there's a skeleton in the Brumms' closet, all right, all right!" muttered Miss Sellars. "They're badly fussed—both of 'em!"

* * * * *

Ferdinand, face downward on his bed, could hear the children's excited shouts as they took turns riding the pony about the barn-lot. ... It sounded now as if they had taken him out into the road. "Please let me next, Angela!"... "I said first, Angela!"... "These stirrups is too high!"

He heard his uncle's heavy footsteps on the stairs.
"Now, my boy, what's the trouble?" Uncle Miles was serious.
Ferdinand stifled a racking sob.
"You know I can't take anything from *him!*... Sure—I love the pony, and I want it awfully... but I wouldn't take anything from *him—not if he gave me a million trillion dollars!*"
"But you didn't have to show off like that before all our people! What do you suppose they'll think?"
"I don't care what they think," growled Ferdinand into the damp pillow. "It's none of their business, is it?"
"They'll make it their business to find out."
Uncle Miles sat down on the edge of the bed, Ferdinand moving over with a great effort to make him room.
"You are a strange child, Ferdinand, to feel this way about your father." Uncle Miles laid a hand on the twitching shoulder. "I hardly thought it possible for a child of your years to be capable of as much hatred as you—"
"But *you* hate him, don't you, Uncle Miles? Aunt Martha hates him!"
"Hate is an ugly word, Ferdinand. Neither your Aunt Martha nor I hate anybody in the whole wide world—not even your erring father. Whatever mistakes he may have made in letting your young mother suffer and be misunderstood and maligned... and die... it will do you no good to carry a grudge—especially now that he wants to be friendly."
At this, Ferdinand broke down completely, and cried piteously.
"He waited for ten years!... Not one word from him!... Even if you and Aunt Martha did hate him, I kept hoping he would write to me when I got big enough to read.... But I swore, last Christmas morning, I would hate him... forever!"
"On Christmas morning!" Uncle Miles was horrified. "What a day to choose for a pledge to everlasting hate!"
"Good as any," grumbled Ferdinand.
Uncle Miles took a turn or two up and down the room, tugging at his black burnsides.
"Well—if you're sure you don't want the pony"—Uncle Miles's tone was conciliatory—"we'll sell it. Perhaps that would be more prudent, anyway. You've shown pretty good judgment for a small boy. We can't afford a pony, and our people know it. You would only make the other children envious. It's out of keeping with everything else we have.... Suppose we sell the pony, and put the money in bank for your college education: how's that?"
"But—Uncle Miles!"—Ferdinand's voice rose shrilly. "That's all the same, isn't it? I don't want anything he's got! I won't have his ponies, or saddles, or colleges, or anything! He same as killed my mother! Aunt Martha said so! I'm going to write and tell him so! You see if I don't!"
"Now—now!" soothed Uncle Miles. "You wouldn't do that."
He patted Ferdinand on the head and walked slowly out of the room and down the hall to his study, where he slumped into the shabby morris chair by the window and meditatively twisted the burnsides into pencil-points.
Every three months since his marriage to Martha Miller, seven years ago, he had received a draft for two hundred and fifty dollars from his prosperous brother-in-law. It exceeded his salary.
Indeed, his decision to marry Martha Miller—which he tried later to tell himself was based on the fact that she, albeit unsightly and eccentric, was an excellent housekeeper, a paragon of piety, and singularly devoted to his motherless little Angela—had been hastened upon her confiding to him that the baby Ferdinand was something other than a liability.
"It's very sacrificial of you, Miss Miller," he had said, that April afternoon on his return to the Miller home for a brief glimpse of Angela, who, since the revival he had conducted at the Oak Grove Baptist Church in November, had been happily in Martha's

care—"it's very fine of you to have assumed, so cheerfully, the burden of your unfortunate sister's child: very unselfish, indeed!"

Martha had smiled, cryptically.

"I must be honest with yuh, Brother Brumm. Of course, I would 'a' took care o' Julia's baby, like I promised, even if young Craig had disowned it.... But—he remembers."

"Indeed?... Does him credit, I must say.... Does he remember substantially, may I ask, Miss Martha?"

"Two hundred and fifty every quarter." Martha seemed satisfied with the effect of her announcement. "Reg'lar as the clock."

"A thousand dollars a year, Martha, for the keep of a baby?"

Martha nodded, smiled, folded her arms, rocked gently.

"I had a promise from Craig"—she leaned forward and lowered her voice confidentially—"shortly after our poor Julia passed away. He had wrote a-sayin' was there anything he could do, though at the minute he hadn't much to do with, he said, and I reckon that was true.... Give the devil his due, I always say—"

"I'm sure you would, Martha!"

He recalled Martha's prompt reaction to the note of tenderness in his voice. She had smiled appreciatively, puckered her lips self-deprecatingly, touched her hair, rather gingerly; for it was the first time she had done it up over a rat—not one of the larger rats, to be sure, such as the bulky Susan affected; a mere mouse, indeed, compared to Susan's—and was obviously not quite at ease with her greying foretop so heavily shadowing her eyes.

"But—and so—then—Oh, yes; then I wrote him as how poor Julia had gave me th' baby t' bring up, and that I meant t' do so, well as I could. If he ever wanted t' send me anything toward its keep, all well and good, I said, but the baby was mine. I told him as how it was Julia's last words, and it was, almost. I asked him t' promise he would never try t' take little Alexander away from me, or even write to him when he grew big enough t' understand; fer it might make him discontented and all... *and he promised!*"

"Alexander? I thought the child's name was Ferdinand."

"Well, you see Julia had wrote a letter, a couple o' days afore she died, and if the baby was a boy it was to be Alexander. So Craig always calls him Alexander.... We just couldn't; not after what he'd done, 'n' all.... Anyways, that's the baby's other name."

Mr. Brumm had proposed marriage to Martha, that evening, and had been accepted with a coyness he had hardly suspected her capable of in the face of her nun-like, ascetic piety.

On the day of their wedding in December—Mr. Brumm had just returned aglow over the quite brilliant success of his three weeks' revival at Partridge Crossing, Illinois—certain small items of business were under discussion. He and Martha were out walking in the snow on the highway, safe from the hostile curiosity of the family in whose opinion that slick feller Brumm was a-tryin' t' lay his miracle-workin' hands on th' baby's money, an indictment they had hinted at, in his presence, and freely discussed within easy earshot.

Martha had beamed over the prompt victory she had won in gaining his consent to look for a settled pastorate and discontinue his itinerant evangelistic career. Her solicitude over his endurance of cold beds, unwholesome food, and long journeys touched him, even if—as he suspected—there was another reason, quite as good, for her request. As the wife of a minister, Martha hoped to enjoy whatever refracted glory shone upon that office. There would be small comfort sitting at home, unrecognized, with the care of two small children—Angela was seven, Ferdinand three—while her crusading spouse spent blocks of weeks in distant parts.

With this triumph scored, Martha was prepared to be generous when Miles (it was becoming easier to call him Miles) suggested that he would deeply appreciate it if their future negotiations with Alexander Craig might be conducted by himself. It would be much more pleasant, all 'round, if he, as head of the household—and would not little Ferdinand be the same as his own son, now?—were entrusted with this business.

Pursuant to that agreement, Martha had promptly written to Seattle notifying her young brother-in-law of her marriage and stating that hereafter Mr. Brumm was to be considered custodian of the child's funds, adding that the arrangement would undoubtedly make Mr. Brumm even more interested in little Alexander. She hadn't said why.

Shortly before little Ferdinand was eight, Mr. Brumm had received a letter from Craig—they had always referred to him as Craig; not Mr. Craig, which would have denoted an unearned respect for him, or Alexander, which would have seemed more friendly than they felt—inquiring whether it would be considered a violation of his covenant if he wrote to his son on the occasion of his next birthday. The letter was typed on the expensively embossed stationery of *The Puget Sound—Editorial Department.*

Mr. Brumm, who enjoyed letting himself go, a bit, with a pen, had written a reply which, after many revisions, pleased him.

"We live very simply here, as becomes the family of a village clergyman, on small pay, ministering to a by no means well-to-do community composed of persons who for the most part make their own clothes and grow their own food. Your son's wants are few. As you are aware, we have thought it imprudent to inform him of your benefactions. Did he know that we are receiving generous amounts of money on his account, it would unquestionably alter his relation to our household, both in his mind and ours. It would make for constraint, and, perhaps, a breakdown of the discipline which every small boy, however tractable, requires."

There was a great deal more of it, running into all of four pages, redundantly cautioning Mr. Craig that any affectionate gesture toward his son, at this time, would make the child restless in his humble home, and reminding Mr. Craig of his promise to Mrs. Brumm "never to disturb the existing relationship while she lives."

Mr. Brumm had had no reply to that letter which, he felt, deserved adequate recognition, considering the amount of time and labour he had spent on its composition. The quarterly remittances continued to arrive unaccompanied by any personal message. On each occasion, Mr. Brumm receipted with a brief note, reporting on the boy's health and advancement in school, always optimistically. As for young Ferdinand's opinion of his father, they had tried to shape it properly by making the relationship seem as remote as possible. How else, indeed, were they to insure the child's contentment?

Reflecting on it now, in the light of this morning's dismaying episode, Mr. Brumm wondered if they had not slightly overdone their efforts to portray Craig as a selfish, cowardly scapegrace who had fled in terror from the gravest of obligations. He was aware that Martha had spared no ugly words in recounting for Ferdinand the pitiful details of a tragedy which had become an obsession in her cramped mind. Would this hot-headed boy actually write to his father, provoking an open breach, perhaps an investigation? It was a comfort to remember that Ferdinand did not know his father's address beyond the bare fact that he lived in Seattle. But was that a comfort? Mr. Brumm wondered if a letter addressed to Alexander Craig, Seattle, might not be delivered.

* * * * *

Meantime, while Mr. Brumm toyed absently with his beard, there was a dull rumble of conversation drifting in from Ferdinand's room, where Aunt Martha was endeavouring to set everything right. From the boy's protests, it was to be gathered that she was not meeting with much success.

"I was just a-sayin' to Ferdinand"—Aunt Martha rose from the low rocking-chair, and leaned against the foot of the bed as Uncle Miles strolled in—"that we mustn't have any more fuss now about this pony business. It's gone plenty far enough!"

"Well," said Uncle Miles casually, "we'll think it over and decide what's the best thing to do. Ferdinand's going to be reasonable, I feel sure."

His shoes squeaked as he went downstairs. Aunt Martha sighed audibly, and followed him. Ferdinand, fatigued by the emotional storm, yawned, stretched, slept.

After a brief conference in the kitchen, Uncle Miles harnessed the glossy bay mare to the jump-seat buggy, while Aunt Martha, in their downstairs bedroom, changed to her white lawn with the black spray.

"Angela," she called, "your father 'n' me are a-goin' to make a call on Sister Sprecker."

In deference to Ferdinand's distress, Angela had cheerfully consented that the pony should be stabled, and was sitting on one foot in the porch swing deeply absorbed in *The Last Days of Pompeii,* which, after many unsuccessful attempts, she was devouring with interest. The book was lowered to her lap for a moment. Odd—making a visit on Saturday afternoon. Father always reserved Saturday for study.

Aunt Martha did not explain that she herself was to be left with Sister Sprecker, who lived on the pike halfway to Bluffton, while Uncle Miles continued to town for the purpose of sending a telegram, which he could not prudently dispatch from Zanesdale, inquiring of the Winnetka Stock Farm whether they would buy back the pony and equipment. She tiptoed upstairs, and returned to the front screen-door, bonneted and black-mitted for her journey.

"Ferdinand's asleep, Angela. He's been so stirred up 'n' all. Get him a piece when he comes down. We mayn't be back much afore sundown. You peel th' potatoes, 'n' make a good fire about five o'clock."

Briefly disengaging herself from panic-stricken Pompeii, Angela mumbled acquiescence and hoped they would have a good time.

She was a flaxen-haired, large-eyed, precocious youngster whom her father regarded as a valuable asset in his profession. A great deal of attention had been paid to Angela when she was a mere tiny tot by the adoring widows and elderly maidens in whose indulgent care she had been lodged, in at least a score of small towns, while her father was pursuing his evangelistic ministry, previous to his second marriage.

Sometimes she sat beside him in the pulpit, an enraptured and undeniably touching picture of cherubic innocence. Not infrequently she was adverted to, with a tender gesture, when the preacher spoke feelingly of the uninquisitive faith to be found at its best in the heart of a child.

At eight, Angela had sung, "I'll Meet Mother Over There," in a sweet, unaffected, little voice that had utterly devastated with emotion the large crowd on the last night of Mr. Brumm's memorable revival at Unger, shortly after accepting their call.

More than a hundred souls were saved during that revival; and at least a score, already saved, experienced the second blessing. Little Angela herself had publicly professed a receipt of the second blessing, on that final night of the revival, somewhat to her parent's confusion; for this degree, while not explicitly restricted to an adult constituency, had not—at least within his own purview—been undertaken by anyone of Angela's immature years. There was nothing he could do about it, however; certainly not at the moment, seeing with what a spontaneous wave of hysterical exultation the child's bland announcement was accepted. In fact, it was Angela's second blessing that had brought the month's "big meetin'" to an almost painfully triumphant crescendo insuring her father's standing in the community for five successful years.

As was to be expected, Angela, thereafter, was looked to, on occasions when emotion ran high, for a tender song, a fervid testimony, a sugary little prayer—demands which she met so adequately that even she herself could not have failed to realize the value of her talent, had she been infinitely more reticent than she was. Everybody predicted a bright future for Angela. It went without debate that she could expect to be mightily used by the Lord. Aunt Martha occasionally hinted to her husband that it would be a pity if Angela's head should be turned by so much praise; but, observing that his smug smile left something unsaid on the subject of envy, she did not venture to press the matter.

No endeavour had been made to capitalize Ferdinand's piety which was of a much less showy type. He had displayed no prophetic gifts. At Christmas and on Children's Day he spoke short pieces and participated in dialogues, always without enthusiasm or promise of future distinction either as an apostle or platform orator. Privately he despised these exhibitions, and consented to be a party to them only when his loyalty to his uncle was challenged. Especially did he loathe the dialogues. Overtopping by a head all the other boys of his age, he appeared the dolt in a line-up of brighter juniors, albeit some of them might be older than he. It was a sore trial, indeed, when it came his turn to hold up a little white pasteboard card bearing the letter D, and recite, shamefacedly, amid the pardonable titters of the congregation:

"I   am   the   Daisy   that   grows   in   the   spring,
Sweetly adoring the love of our King."

Presently all these letters would spell

and he could stumble awkwardly to his seat beside Aunt Martha, who, smiling benignly, would wet a finger and brush back the lock that had come all the way from Dresden.

Ferdinand accepted Angela's opulent faith at face value. It never occurred to him to be jealous of the marked attentions she received, wherever they went, sometimes in quite glaring contrast to the attitude people manifested toward him. He rejoiced in her well-deserved popularity. He liked Angela. The hazard of childish quarrels between them had been reduced to a minimum by the fact that no question of property rights ever arose. Until recently, Angela had contented herself at play with her dolls and dishes. Ferdinand, when not whittling sticks, amused himself with his small set of smeary rubber-type. They kept out of each other's way.

Of late, however, Angela had been taking more interest in Ferdinand. At first he had been flattered by these friendly attentions; though, on the whole, he rather liked her better when she left him to his own devices. Sometimes she came out to the bench, behind the woodhouse, and sat by him while he whittled toy furniture out of soft pine; sat very close, often hampering him.

Angela confided in him very freely now, as if he were her own age. One of these days she was going to be an evangelist. She could do it now if they would let her. Not only would she do a great deal of good, but she could earn some money. She could have nice clothes. "And I'll get you a really good printing outfit, too, Ferdinand. You want one very much, don't you?"

And when he said he certainly did—very much—she would kiss him, and say: "Never you mind. I'll get you one that you can print a little newspaper on. Wouldn't that be fun?"

* * * * *

Ferdinand was roused by Angela's voice down in the parlour, singing, "That Will Be Glory For Me," to her own accompaniment on the melodeon. He was debating whether he should not go down and ask Aunt Martha for a piece of pie, now that he had slept through dinner-time. It was almost three.

Suddenly the music stopped abruptly. Angela was calling from the foot of the stairs.
"Ferdinand!"
"Ye-es."
"You awake now?"
"Um-humm."
"What are you doing?"
"Nothing."
"Lonesome?"
"No—but I'm hungry."
"Want me to bring you a piece of cake and a banana?"
"Well—if you want to."
She came presently and sat down beside him on the bed, licking sticky fingers.
"Don't you want any?" asked Ferdinand, his mouth full.
"I just had some. Did you know that father and Aunt Martha have gone away for all afternoon?"
"No.... Let's go down and play croquet."
"I'm so sorry you had such an unhappy birthday, Ferdinand." Angela's voice was husky. "I could have cried for you, this morning. Do you feel better now?" She put an arm around him and pushed him back on the pillow.

Ferdinand made a brave show of not being annoyed when Angela bent over him, burying her hot face in his neck, and blinding him with her tousled hair.

"Let me up, Angela. You're smothering me!" shouted Ferdinand. "I don't feel like romping."

"I'm not romping," whispered Angela, trembling.

* * * * *

Ten minutes later, Angela, with very red cheeks, went to the melodeon and continued where she had left off at the third verse of "That Will Be Glory For Me," hoping that Ferdinand's stubbornness meant he was too dumb to understand, or, having understood, would not unintentionally give her away.

The front doorbell rang loudly, and Angela, still scarlet and shaky, answered it. Mr. Trask had brought a telegram for Ferdinand. Whatever was Ferdinand doing with telegrams?

She rushed upstairs with it. He was standing at the window, drumming absently on the pane with his knuckles. He did not turn.

"Look what you got!" Angela hoped the message would be pleasant, at least diverting.

He clumsily opened the envelope and mystifiedly read the telegram several times before its meaning became quite clear. It was signed by the Winnetka Stock Farm.

WE HAVE BRUMMS WIRED PROPOSAL TO RESELL TO US PONY AND EQUIPMENT DELIVERED YOU TODAY STOP IF YOU DO NOT AGREE WIRE IMMEDIATELY COLLECT

"What is it?" Angela was bursting with curiosity.

Ferdinand crumpled the message in his first, and shuffled past her toward the stairway. There he paused, his face working, his eyes brimming with angry tears.

"You're all a lot o' cheaters!" he screamed.

Angela stood in open-mouthed amazement.... So unlike Ferdinand to explode like that!

He clumped down the stairs, savagely shouting: "I hate all of you! Do you hear me? I hate everybody in th' whole damn world!"

Angela brightened.

"He won't tell, then," she reflected.

Ferdinand flung himself out of the house, banged the front gate, pulled his cap far down over his red nose, dug his fists deep into the pockets of his pants (cut down from a pair of his uncle's), and stamped sullenly up the road toward the railroad track, only three hundred yards away. The east-bound Erie Flyer was just due. It always stopped at Zanesdale for water.

Sometimes Ferdinand strolled down to the station and stood close beside the dripping water-tank when, at exactly three-thirty-six, the huge locomotive paused, gasping rhythmically, while the torrent poured into the capacious tender, the fireman on the coal-pile, holding the rope, calmly smoking his pipe, unmindful of his happy privilege.

Most of the fast trains thundered through Zanesdale with a terrifying racket. Ferdinand never failed to experience a surge of hot indignation over this arrogant contempt for his town. He knew it wasn't much of a town; had contempt for it himself; but it was annoying to have the utter insignificance of Zanesdale thrust upon him nine times a day.

He would not have time to run down to the station, now, even if he had been in a mood for running: besides, he didn't care to answer any questions that Mr. Trask might ask, so that he might be able to tell Mrs. Trask the sequel to the pony story which she would promptly explain to the town.

He climbed on top of the gate-post at the corner of Harsh's melon-patch—his favourite vantage when watching the long, black, proud Pullmans flick by, each adding its own little "Psst!" of disdain; and watched Number Nine (he knew all the trains that way) slow to a screeching stop. There was a long hiss of escaping air from the brakes; an acrid smell of greasy, hot metal. The diner was directly in front of him. Little tables with candles on them. A man and a woman, with a black waiter hovering over them. Too late for dinner, too early for supper: this must be "tea." People in stories were always having "tea." Ferdinand drew down the corners of his mouth and hated the man and the woman, though he knew she was a pretty woman. He hated the obsequious waiter, and mumbled, audibly, "Damn nigger!"

The train moved slowly on, so slowly that the locomotive was exasperated by the sluggishness of the heavy Pullmans, and barked a staccato of short, angry demands that it had better get to business, now, or we'd be late again pulling into Washington. Ferdinand climbed down from the post, made a detour around the rear of the melon-patch, and entered the barn through the back door. The pony looked around over its shoulder, stopped munching its mouthful of hay, and blew a long breath that made its soft nostrils flutter.

He advanced slowly and laid a hand on the pony's flank which twitched as if the light touch had tickled; moved forward another step and took a wisp of tawny mane in his fingers; was about to pat the friendly pet on the nose.

On sudden impulse he drew back and muttered, "No—I tell you—*No!*"

Retracing his steps through the back door, half-blinded by tears, he stood for a long time gazing abstractedly into the muddy water of the miasmic, green-scummed little pond that belonged to Flook's Tile Factory; amblingly circled the barn, and moved toward his little workbench behind the woodhouse.

He took the new knife from his pocket, turned it over several times, opened it, closed it with a sharp click; and, deliberately drawing his long arm back to full torsion, he sighted carefully—his lower lip pinioned by a row of uncommonly straight teeth—and threw the knife all of forty yards with such velocity and precision that it landed with a mighty splash exactly when he had intended.

Ferdinand grinned. It was an ugly grin that did something to him on the inside—a brand-new sensation which defied his childish analysis, but seemed to be made up of such ingredients as, "Damn them all!"... "I haven't a friend left in the world!"... "I've got to go it alone!"... "I *can* go it alone!"... "I *will* go it alone!"... *"You see if I don't!... Damn you all!"*

CHAPTER IV

FERDINAND arrived home at five, gaily whistling an improvised tune.

He was in unusually high spirits today; for Miss Carle, who had specialized in Creative English at Wellesley, and was hopeful of teaching it in a college, some day, had detained him again after school to discuss his latest composition as seriously as if they were equals in age and experience.

"But, Ferdinand," she had cautioned, "really, you're quite shockingly cynical, I'm afraid... for fifteen!"

He would have liked to leave the question of his age standing just that way, but when she added, "You're not any older, are you?" he felt obliged to tell the truth.

"I'll be fourteen next May."

"My word!" ejaculated Miss Carle. "Owlish as Omar, when you ought to be out playing marbles."

"I guess I grew pretty fast," Ferdinand admitted, shyly.

"And pretty sour, too," laughed Miss Carle. "But you can write, young fellow! Just be a bit careful how you whirl that battle-axe! You might hurt somebody, and be sorry."

It was evident, at home, that something important was afoot.

Aunt Martha had crimped her hair and was tidying up the house. Apparently all the major feats of putting to rights had been attended to, for she was now at the final stage of patting the sofa pillows and rearranging the trinkets on the mantel—the shepherdess he had carved, a year ago, the china cat that someone had given to Angela when she was five, the oval slab of polished stone that Uncle Miles had picked up on a vagabondish trip long ago in the Petrified Forest. A fire had been neatly laid in the grate, though it was only the second of October and unseasonably warm.

"Mr. and Mrs. Joel Day are coming to call, this evening," explained Aunt Martha, impressively. "Mind yuh don't leave yer things a-lyin' around."

Angela, softly humming while she pressed the skirt of her blue dress on the ironing-board in the kitchen, broke off to say, as Ferdinand thrust a long slim hand into the cooky-jar, "Mustn't scatter crumbs. The Days are to be here, tonight."

Upstairs, Uncle Miles was found straightening books on the shelves in his study. Ferdinand paused in the doorway, half-minded to tell him that Miss Carle had encouraged him about his writing. He was bursting to tell somebody. On second thought, he decided that Uncle Miles might think him boastful.

A neat stack of opened letters lay on the corner of the desk, otherwise bare except for an engagement-pad which occupied a conspicuous position in the middle. The letters were making-believe they were the current mail of a busy man of affairs, the edge of an old telegram protruding slightly from midway of the deceitful pile.

Doubtless Uncle Miles meant to slip up here with Mr. Day for a half-hour's confidential chat about church business while Aunt Martha, in the parlour below, endeavoured to infect Mrs. Day with a more passionate interest in the missionary box, the ultimate unpacking and distribution of which Ferdinand grimly hoped, would put somebody in Paouting-fu [*sic*] to at least half the bother that the recruiting of its miscellaneous contents had already cost him.

He was seldom inquisitive about Uncle Miles's activities, but the engagement-pad caught his eye. He felt the makings of a grin at the corners of his mouth, and dealt with it severely.

A mere glance at tomorrow's crowded programme should be sufficient to inform a sharp-eyed deacon that the new minister was not only industrious and popular, but was a person of orderly mind and much experience.

	October 3
8-9	Correspondence
9-10.45	Study
11	Mercy Hospital (Mrs. Penfield)
12.15	Luncheon YMCA Com. on Evangelism
2-4	Pastoral calls on Brucker, Winona & Swift Sts.
4.30-6	Study
7.30	Midweek Service
8.40	Conference with S.S. Officers

"Don't disturb anything, Ferdinand," remarked Uncle Miles, importantly. "Mr. Day is coming out, after supper... and Mrs. Day ... to make us a little visit."

Ferdinand said he wouldn't, and retreated to his own room at the end of the hall, grinning broadly.

There were a great many things about his transparent Uncle Miles—affectations, pretensions, petty deceptions—which, while they had shocked and distressed him at ten, were only amusing, now. He had quite outgrown his earlier illusions about absolute integrity as an indispensable to anyone engaged in the spread of religion. His observations had led him to suspect that there was as much duplicity practised in Uncle Miles's profession as in any other business, the main difference between sacred and secular callings being that in the latter a man had at least a sporting chance of getting something out of it worth the time and trouble.

Still—Ferdinand was obliged to admit—they had done very well, as ministers' families went. The three years on the rim of Fort Wayne had been good for them. Uncle Miles—what with Angela's undeniably valuable co-operation—had been very successful. The two of them had made themselves known soon after their arrival in the big town. Together they had put on noon meetings in the large railroad-shops, where Uncle Miles had invited soot-smeared mechanics, munching their apple pie, to remember the faith of their mothers—all of whom were presumed to be dead and in glory—and Angela, assured of manner and easy to look at, had sung mellow ballads in keeping with her father's exhortations, accompanying herself on a portable organ which she played so effortlessly that many of the younger workmen wondered if she were actually pumping the thing with her own feet; and, having manœuvred their position to the satisfaction of their curiosity on this point, had remained steadfastly regarding the robust girl's well-turned ankles with an admiration she did not appear to resent.

After that, it had been easy to book engagements at Young People's social affairs in the down-town churches. At first Uncle Miles had imagined that his sentimental little talks, replete with touching anecdotes, were coming into demand; that Angela's contribution merely provided a unique embellishment to his addresses—a delusion he was gradually relieved of, however, as more and more invitations were extended to his gifted daughter alone. But, for all that, Uncle Miles had prospered beyond all reasonable expectations, and the call to the small church in Indianapolis had been no more appreciated than deserved.

They were still poor; not so poor as they had been, back in Zanesdale, but required to practise rigid economies. Aunt Martha, to whom frugality was a virtue, if not indeed an obsession, had succeeded in making poverty a noble estate.

For a long time they had been paying for a "little piece of real estate" in Keokuk, Iowa. It had never occurred to Ferdinand to inquire what the "little piece of real estate" consisted of, whether houses, lands, or business blocks. It had always been a "little piece of real estate," which although involving much correspondence and many receipts of long envelopes from Keokuk, could not amount to very much on their wages, even though they skimped valiantly to make the payments on it.

Ferdinand made almost no demands upon the family purse, considering it no more than his share of the burden to wear the cheapest of clothes—though Aunt Martha didn't try to make them herself any more—and went about, uncomplainingly, with empty pockets. A stated allowance had never been thought of in their family. If Ferdinand wanted a five-cent pencil-tablet, he asked Uncle Miles for a nickel, please, to buy a pencil-tablet; and, to Uncle Miles's credit, the nickel was always forthcoming without argument or reluctance.

Angela had not yet achieved her ambition to appear as the head-liner in a revival. Uncle Miles, finding it quite impossible to leave his local duties for so long a time, and unwilling that Angela should attempt so responsible an undertaking by herself, had put her off; though he kept saying, when she pressed him, that they would surely do it, one of these days; or, if they couldn't, he would see what might be arranged for her "next winter—perhaps."

She had been growing almost rebelliously restless when the call to Indianapolis had eased the tension. She would be making new "contacts"—Uncle Miles's redundant use of this word "contact," especially when he made a verb of it, always annoyed Ferdinand, who was unconsciously becoming something of a stylist—and doubtless "opportunities would develop" if Angela would only bide her time; as indeed they had, for it had been barely a month now since their coming to Indianapolis, and Angela had already been pleasantly spoken of in the newspapers three times (and unpleasantly spoken to in the High School Principal's office twice for her bland nonchalance in respect to Cæsar's Gallic Wars). It had not yet occurred to the Music Committee in Uncle Miles's church that Angela, who had quickly assumed the position of leading soprano in the choir, deserved a cash competence, for no such appropriation had ever been considered; but, on every hand—or at least almost every hand—one heard her appreciatively mentioned as having had much to do with the unprecedented attendance at church services.

Women declared at the Aid Society that they never had any trouble, now, getting their menfolks out of bed on Sunday mornings.

A few of the more conservative were for putting vestments on the choir, something they had never discussed before Angela joined it. One woman, convinced that the congregation, which was almost militantly non-conformist, would not consent to gowns on the choir, wondered—though it took a good deal of courage to say it, even in the privacy of a group of three—whether it might not be tactfully suggested to Mrs. Brumm that

Angela was really a bigger girl than she thought; to which another woman, equally moved to candour, replied, "No—we mustn't do that. It would do no good, anyway. Angela is just one of those people who, no matter how much they have on, always look as if they'd left something off."

As for Ferdinand's attitude toward his uncle's bustling ministry, and the luxuriant Angela's aspirations, it stopped with merely wishing them well. Aunt Martha had long since discontinued her direct appeals to him to prepare himself vocationally to follow in his uncle's footsteps; and Uncle Miles, who had frequently besought the Lord, at family worship, to lead "this lad into the ministry of the gospel"—mostly to please Aunt Martha, Ferdinand always thought—had lately omitted this supplication from his invoice of the family's wants.

Of course, there was no use pretending he had no interest in what went on at their church, for Uncle Miles's profession was singular in that neither he nor his household was ever for a moment free of it. The church was all they lived for. It was at once the hub and the rim, the corona and the periphery of their thoughts and conversation. Such friendships as they had, if not actually originating at the church, eventually brought up there—tentative, temporary, shallow-rooted friendships, for at any minute they might pack up and move elsewhere.

Three years had made structural changes in Ferdinand. They had spread some substantial and nicely distributed flesh on his gangling frame, the additional weight seeming to have given him more self-confidence. He was still rather shy, but had almost outgrown his earlier tendency to a morbid self-dissatisfaction which, at ten, had made him painfully sensitive, touchy, and inclined to mope.

It had been a long time, now, since he had participated in a family scene, contenting himself—when they glanced apprehensively in his direction on occasions brimming with the raw materials of argument—to draw a twisted smile, which, although he had never seen it, he suspected of being somewhat unpleasant. Situations that had once fetched out of him a squeaky and savage indignation, popping off to the ruination of a meal, and hurling him out of the room, and tossing him on to his bed where he would lie for hours hating all visible creation, including himself, were now handled with an indifference so closely akin to contempt that the family sometimes wished he had not tied down the safety-valve.

Aunt Martha, particularly, viewed this change in Ferdinand with prayerful anxiety. Much as she had deplored the lad's occasional releases of volcanic protest—mostly protests against the quite irksome and unquestionably silly inhibitions which she herself laid upon him; for she insisted that at ten he should carry himself like an experienced saint of seventy, while she rigged him in babyish sailor-collars and fussy girlish waists not worn by any child over five, a manner of dress that promoted his misfortune in being oversized to a farce so ludicrous that even he, murderously angry as he was, sometimes laughed himself into wild hysteria over his own appearance in the mirror, a storm usually followed by a fit of rebellious weeping—he often wondered if Aunt Martha did not secretly enjoy such emotional hurricanes.

On several memorable occasions she had knelt, with Ferdinand sourly crouched beside her (venomously despising them both), and prayed aloud—her wailing petitions punctuated with convulsive sobs—that "this wayward orphan, whom Thou in Thine Infinite Wisdom, hast entrusted into our care and keeping, may be just brought under the influence of Thy Blessed Spirit."

All that was over, now. Aunt Martha had herself under much better control. Whether the benign rainbow that arched her had arrived to signal the biologic fact that she had graduated from her rip-roaring middle forties, or whether the promotion from a bucolic atmosphere of country-village piety into the relative sophistication of bigger towns and associated with "city folks" had pushed in a few of the shriller stops in her turbulent spirit, Ferdinand did not know.

Perhaps it was these early experiences of the utter breakdown of emotional discipline that had produced in Ferdinand a mounting contempt for home theatricals. Unquestionably, these unbridled seizures of Aunt Martha's had been bad for him. They had made him despise any sentiment that threatened to invoke tears. He had wept himself out in early childhood.

At thirteen, plus, these deep lesions had healed, but not without leaving some impermeable scars on the lamina of young Ferdinand's soul at the very points of exposure most frequently bombarded in a home where prayer and piety, sentiment and emotion, were all in the day's work.

Adversions and appeals to Deity were, in Ferdinand's opinion, merely an unscrupulous and unsportsmanly method of having your own way in dealing with people who might be so weak-minded as to believe that you and God were at one as to the soundness of your cause. If you couldn't get what you wanted out of the other fellow by wheedle and whimper, purchase or threat, vituperation or violence, you bade him listen while you took it up with the Lord in prayer. You closed your eyes, and, in the lugubrious tone of one making funeral arrangements over the telephone, prosecuted your case while your helpless victim knelt beside you hotly wanting the courage to say, "Either you're a fraud, or your God is a rascal!"

Ferdinand no longer took any stock whatever in prayer—either in the family worship kind of prayer that besought the Almighty to make you sweet-spirited and obedient to His Holy Will, five minutes after you had stubbornly objected, at breakfast on Saturday, to spending the whole afternoon helping old Mullins clean out the church furnace, when you had been looking forward all week to a bit of carving on the fire-screen you meant to give Miss Carle on Christmas; or in the public kind of prayer that asked God to touch the generous hearts of this dear people (Gosh! how he loathed those smug antiques that stood in prim rows in Uncle Miles's prayers!)... and incline them to give sacrificially to some pet scheme they were being badgered into against their wishes.

He had been trying lately not to think about it at all; saying to himself that in any other environment than his the whole matter of religion in general and the activities of the church in particular would be giving him no concern.

Until recently, he had suffered frequent torments, as he watched his feverish disdain burning out to smoking cinders. Could it be that he had "quenched the Spirit"? Uncle Miles was forever warning his flock against the cold apathy that meant one had committed the "unpardonable sin." These past few weeks, he had almost left off torturing himself with these morbid reflections. The "unpardonable sin" was just so much more nonsense—all of a piece with everything else they ranted about and wept over and grudgingly subscribed to.... A lot o' bunk!... Tripe!

* * * * *

Ferdinand tossed his books on the bed and clatteringly rummaged in the disordered lower drawer of his battered, secondhand, taffy-coloured desk for a shoe-brush and the box of blacking. He, too, would be expected to help entertain these precious Days whose threat of a visit had set them all scouring and preening.

Poising one foot on the edge of the untidy drawer, Ferdinand grimacingly recruited a mouthful of lubricant and spat viciously into the noisomely pungent blacking-box. He, too, would be required to come down, with his hair reached high to show he had an intellectual forehead, and smirk for this rich and brittle Mr. Day, who, because his deceased father had organized Uncle Miles's church and paid for most of it, was in a position to make them all jump through the hoop—and like it.

He would have to sit there for an hour and a half, posing for an angel; just as if he gave a damn whether these wonderful Days liked him or not. He smeared the dauber side of the brush into the blacking, and anointed the toe of his shabby shoe.

Angela, of course, would sing for them in her most luscious manner. If the guests didn't ask her promptly, Aunt Martha would direct the conversation into that quarter. "Yes—Angela has been a great help," she would say, in her precise, company voice, "what with her singin' 'n' all."

"Won't you sing something for us now, dear?"—this Mrs. Day would beg, probably hoping she wouldn't. But you could count on Angela... . Well—so much the better. While that was going on, he wouldn't have to do anything.

Ferdinand banged and bumped and smeared the shoe-brush against the desk-drawer as he insured himself against being sent back to "polish the heel as well as the toe"—meanwhile carrying on with his sour prognosis of the evening's entertainment.

Angela, having more than satisfied the customers with her recital, closing it with an extended rendition of "Crossing the Bar," would smile, fold the music, push in the organ-stops, and slowly revolve on the hair-cloth stool to receive the inevitable "My!—ain't that grand?"

And then this Mrs. Day—a feathery, fussy old dame, no doubt—would turn to him.... Ferdinand raised his other foot to the ledge of the drawer and again paid his respects to the vile blacking-box.... Ducking her big-plumed head, coquettishly, and grinning as if she were peering under the hood of a perambulator, she would inquire, "And what do *you* do, Master Ferdinand?"

That's what she would say, and the way she would say it. He had never seen her, but he knew. He had seen Mr. Day. Mr. Day had met them at the train. Uncle Miles had known he would, for he had written promising to do so. And there he was, sure enough, standing on the platform where the day-coach passengers alighted. Mr. Day had known they would be riding in the day-coach, though he himself wouldn't, of course.

Ferdinand had had no difficulty picking him out of the crowd on the platform—a square man, with square shoulders, square hands, square feet, square head, square mouth. He was to be their boss, because he had lots of money. Mr. Day had shaken hands all round and led the way to a shiny new Cadillac. Ferdinand hadn't liked the back of Mr. Day's square head or his square knuckles on the steering-wheel, though he was bound to admit that Mr. Day inspired respect. Mr. Day owned them now, same as he owned his Cadillac. Uncle Miles sitting beside him, with his arm stretched along the top of the seat, as if he were getting ready to hug Mr. Day, was already saying, "Yes, yes; to be sure, Brother Day: ab-so-*lute*-ly!"

Ferdinand transferred his suspenders to his Sunday pants and emptied his pockets on top of the desk.

"Perhaps you sing, too," Mrs. Day would suggest, "like your sister." And then Aunt Martha would heave the long sigh that meant she was going to explain how Angela wasn't his sister, a story that Angela would interrupt presently to reply to Mrs. Day's query.

"Ferdinand whittles," she would say, crossing swiftly to the mantel for the little shepherdess. And Mrs. Day would gurgle, "You don't mean to tell me! Look, Mr. Day, at this perfectly ex*quis*ite, piece of carving!" And Mr. Day, deliberately finishing the long sentence he was on, and steadfastly looking at Uncle Miles from under his square eyebrows—just to show he was the kind of a man who mustn't be interrupted—but reaching out his square hand to signify that he would be pleased to take up Mrs. Day's case as the next order of business, would presently pinch his glasses on to his square nose, owlishly inspect the shepherdess, and say, as he handed it back, "Nicely done, I'm sure."

Ferdinand was tumbling the contents of the top bureau-drawer, looking for a clean collar that had no frayed edges.

"He prints, too," Aunt Martha would add, proudly, though she was forever chiding him for wasting his time with all that type-settin'. Before she and Angela went through with it, he would be sent upstairs for "that meenoo and programme" he had made for the Annual Canvass Dinner at Fort Wayne, last winter. And Mrs. Day would squint at it, and twist in her chair to get a better light on it, and borrow Mr. Day's glasses; and Mr. Day would suggest that Ferdinand might do a lot of the church printing, "just for good practice!"... Gosh!—how he hated these hellish exhibitions!

* * * * *

Ferdinand put his Harvey's Grammar face down on the desk and listened for the doorbell. It would soon ring, now, for he had heard the car-doors slam, opulently. It rang, sharply, as if Mr. Day were saying, "Don't keep us waiting! I paid for most of this house, myself!"... and Uncle Miles was opening the door, his hearty "Well—well!" meaning, "I know you did, Brother Day, and I came running fast as ever I could—ab-so-*lute*-ly!"

They were all talking at once, now, and drifting through the hall into the parlour. Mr. Day was remarking dryly that the floors needed to be gone over, and Mrs. Day—who sounded quite elderly—was asking Aunt Martha, in a high key, how she was finding the house, anyway.

Presently, Angela came to the foot of the stairs and called him. He would have to go. He gave his hair a final scrub with the brush, scowled into the mirror, and started. Hopeful of slipping into the room so quietly they would hardly notice his arrival, Ferdinand made as little noise as possible on the way down.

Slowly negotiating the last few steps, he was able, by the location of their voices, and a panoramic glimpse through the wide doorway, to place their positions—Aunt Martha, first; then Mrs. Day, a white-haired, little old lady, old enough to be Mr. Day's mother (as indeed she was, he soon discovered); then Mr. Day, on the brussels sofa, polishing his glasses with a large silk handkerchief, Uncle Miles sitting close beside him with a hand on Mr. Day's knee.

Another step located Angela, close to the melodeon, of course, talking animatedly, and, for her, rather affectedly, to some unidentified person not yet in the picture.

Ferdinand cautiously moved forward and brought gradually into view a slim, modishly shod foot and a generous glimpse of the first silk stockings he had ever seen, a pair of gracefully crossed, tailored knees, a shapely arm negligently thrown back across the top of the chair—it was a dining-room chair, put there for him, and she had evidently preferred it to the patent rocker which stood vacant—her fur boa tossed back from her shoulder.

Nobody like that had ever been in their house before. Ferdinand hadn't yet seen her face—it would require some courage to do this next step—but he knew she did not belong to their world, at all. Something in her posture told him that.

"Come on in, Ferdinand," called Angela, pleasantly, in the tone of thirty addressing six, which made him know the stylish stranger could not be very old, if Angela was playing grownup.

Summoning all his valour, Ferdinand stepped to the door and found himself staring—open-mouthed, he feared—at the most beautiful woman he had ever seen. She smiled, a slowly widening smile, which seemed to mean they were already friends of long standing, bending her head forward and looking at him from under long black lashes, her lips puckered a little, teasingly, as if to say, "I know you don't want to come in here and be bored; but—let's have it over."

Ferdinand's heart skipped a beat, and then made up for it with a hard bump that put him quite out of breath and made his voice unsteady when, reluctantly detained by Aunt Martha's hand on his arm, he paused to speak to Madam Day and Mr. Day, who obligingly made short work of him to resume their briefly interrupted remarks. All the previously inactive minerals in Ferdinand's blood responded to the first potential magnet he had ever approached, his natural shyness giving way to a new sensation of actually belonging to someone!

She did not rise or offer her hand when Angela said, "This is Ferdinand, Mrs. Day." People, when introduced, always stood up and gravely shook hands. Eighty rose to shake hands with eight. Mrs. Day merely tipped back her pretty head, so he could see the fringe of glossy little black curls under her big picture hat, and smiled, with red lips parted.

He could not speak for an instant. The routine phrase, "Pleased-t'-meetcha," which he had been obliged to mumble so often that it was all one word, would not come. It was inappropriate. He swallowed, rather noisily, and said, "I'm glad—I'm glad to—I'm very glad!"

"By Jove, boy," she drawled, "I really believe you *are!*" She pointed to the vacant chair beside her. "Do you always say such delightfully nice things?"

Angela, hopeful of smoothing over his unsuccessful attempt to manage the usual formula, explained maternally: "Ferdinand is so shy, Mrs. Day. He always hates being introduced.... You can sit in the rocker, Ferdinand. Mrs. Day thought she would like this straight chair better."

"Yes," said Ferdinand, still in a trance, "she would."

He sat down, and while wondering if it would be all right for him to look her straight in the eyes again—wanting to, but afraid he would stare at her—he gazed interestedly at her hands, wishing she did not have gloves on. She leisurely unbuttoned them and began slowly to take them off, tugging at one finger-tip after another. He glanced up, a bit abashed, and they both smiled, understandingly.

"I'm always wondering about hands, too," she said, lazily. "Your sister has been telling me what interesting things you do with yours; but I think I could have guessed—now that I see them."

Ferdinand instinctively spread them out, glad now that he had taken pains with his nails.

"You make things, too," he ventured. "Maybe you paint."

"Rather badly. I've been having better luck, lately, dabbling with wood-cuts. That's great fun!"

"I expect you have lots of carving-tools."

"Too many! I keep experimenting with all these different-shaped chisels, and never use any one of them long enough to—"

"Hard wood?" queried Ferdinand, professionally.

"Oh, dear, no; not yet! I've just begun it, you see."

"I have tinkered with some little designs," confessed Ferdinand, modestly, "but I don't know what they look like."

Angela, recovering from her amazement over the taciturn Ferdinand's easy talk, put in, "He hasn't a press, Mrs. Day—nor hardly anything to work with."

"Pine?" asked Mrs. Day, having briefly turned her head to acknowledge Angela's comment.

"No—oak and walnut."

Mrs. Day's finely modelled eyebrows lifted a little in surprise.

"How would you like to come over, some day, and see what I have been doing? Perhaps I might trade you a reamer or two for some good advice."

"I'd like to!" Ferdinand flushed with pleasure. "But I don't think I could tell you anything that you don't know."

"Saturday—maybe?"

"Yes—after dinner?"

"No—I'm to be out for dinner. Come about two."

She belonged, Ferdinand realized, to a different world from his drab little island where the conversation never rose above the dull tittle-tattle of domestic drudgeries in homes like theirs, and the equally stupid prattle about rummage sales that were to finance a new cement sidewalk around the church and mend the plumbing in the basement. Hers was a world that had dinner at night instead of noon, an unselfconscious world that spoke correctly without stiffness, that moved with dignity but without embarrassment, a world that leisurely went out to the diner for "tea." The difference between her world and his swept over Ferdinand, not to his discontentment, but to his almost painful wistfulness. He felt that she had recognized him as eligible to citizenship in her world, and was glad.

"That's agreed, then. I'll expect you," she said, rising as Aunt Martha—still talking primly to Madam Day, and nervously smoothing her shapeless black skirt—moved toward them, apparently intending to draw Mrs. Day, whom for excellent reasons she was obviously shy of, into the adult section. "Your father can tell you where we live," concluded Mrs. Day, with another smile that sent Ferdinand's damaged heart racing.

Aunt Martha's curiosity spoke in her strained face. Aunt Martha's face was never under good control. Bulletins announcing her every doubt, anxiety, hope, and fear were posted about her restless mouth and myopic eyes immediately upon arrival. At the moment, Ferdinand knew what was going on in her mind as certainly as if she shouted it. She was engaged in a struggle, attempting to be obsequiously courteous to Mrs. Day because it was incumbent on her to be deferential to Brother Day's Mrs. Day, while endeavouring to warn Ferdinand—with one fleeting glare of stern disapproval—that he was on no account to be permitted to come under the influence of this frivolous, worldly creature whom Brother Day—so steady and sensible about everything else—had had the misfortune to marry.

Conversation broke off, in the other corner of the room, in acknowledgment of Mrs. Day's arrival in their midst. Brother Day stiffly stood at attention, tapping his nose-glasses on his thumb-nail. Uncle Miles tardily scrambled to his feet, pulled down his vest, and said, "Well—well!" just as if Mrs. Day had quite taken them by surprise, dropping in unexpectedly.

Madam Day snapped the massive silver latch of her black leather bag several times, and pursed her lips resignedly.

Aunt Martha proffered her chair and drew up another. They were all ready now, it appeared, for Mrs. Day to explain why she had intruded.

"Ferdinand has promised to come and see me," she said, in a tone that hoped she was giving his parents pleasure—"to talk about wood-cuts."

"Very good of you, Sister—er—Mrs. Day," beamed Uncle Miles, in the voice he used when patronizingly commending a shy testimony offered at prayer-meeting.

Mr. Day elevated his chin, stroked the back of his bald head, gazed critically at the ceiling, and tapped his lean knee with his glasses. There was the suggestion of a frown creasing his forehead. Ferdinand wondered if the frown did not mean that Mrs. Day should first have consulted Mr. Day before making her proposal.

"Well"—said he, judicially—"perhaps the lad had better be encouraged to do something more useful than fiddling with wood-cuts."

Aunt Martha, cannily reasoning that, while Brother Day might enjoy handing his wife a surly rebuff, he probably wouldn't thank anybody for being so impertinent as to applaud him, remarked: "Ferdinand comes natural by his taste fer wood-carvin'. His grandpa's folks in th' old country was all wood-carvers. When he come t' this country, he changed the name to Miller because his family name was hard fer folks t' say. Their name was Mueller—M-u-e-l-l-e-r."

"I wonder if they were related to the very famous family of Muellers in Dresden. Do you know, Mrs. Brumm?"

Aunt Martha, hugging her angular elbows and rocking gently, nodded with pride.

"My father was born in Dresden in the house of Frederick Mueller. He was the great-grandson of Hans Mueller."

"Indeed!" exclaimed Mrs. Day. "What a heritage!"

"Ye-es," agreed Mr. Day. "Very interesting."

Angela had slipped over on to the chair recently vacated by the charming Mrs. Day.

"Awfully odd, isn't she?" whispered Angela.

"Hunnh?"

Ferdinand was barely conscious of her comment, so intent was he on the developments in his own case, now under discussion on the other side of the room.

"Odd!" repeated Angela, guardedly, behind her hand.

Ferdinand reluctantly detached his gaze from the object of his adoration, and regarded Angela with an inquisitive stare.

"How do you mean—odd?" he said, absently. "I think she's the most wonderful person I ever saw!"

CHAPTER V

"LOOK, Janet!" Ferdinand laid the limp proof on the imposing-stone, folded his smudged arms, and glanced over his shoulder for her approval. "Rather good, wouldn't you say? How fortunate we could use one of those quaint, diamond-shaped colons on the very first page."

"Perfect!" Janet Day hovered close, snuggling a hand affectionately under his elbow, her cheek pressed lightly against his broad shoulder. "Old Thomas Caxton would be green with envy. Really, Dinny, you're marvellous!"

"It's you that's marvellous, Janet. I would never have known anything about this, but for you."

For a moment she neither responded nor turned away; stood soberly staring at the first page of what was going to be General Bryce's annual Memorial Day greeting to the diminishing survivors of his brigade—a sixteen-page brochure done in two colours on hand-laid Italian vellum, the price no object, for the General was rich. It was the most pretentious thing they had attempted.

Janet had been very quiet and pensive today. Twice, as they had encountered each other, face to face, in the narrow quarters of the little printing-shop that cluttered the whole south bay of her attic studio—screened off to segregate its inevitable untidiness—Ferdinand had been made uneasy by the entreaty in her brown eyes. Janet wanted to ask him something, and didn't dare. Janet wanted to tell him something, but was afraid. Had he done something to grieve her? What could it have been? He had failed her somehow: in what? But no—it was rather as if she, herself, was on the defensive.

Her competent fingers tightened their warm grasp on his arm. Perhaps she was going to talk about it now.

"No," she said, preoccupiedly, "you would have done all this, anyway, sooner or later. However, I'm glad I have had a little part in it.... I want you always to think well of me, Dinny. You've been such a dear, and I'm so proud of you."

Impulsively he lifted her hand to his lips, an act that surprised them both, a little. Ferdinand despised sentiment.

"What is it, Janet?" he asked, gently. "Something bothering you?"

"Now you've ink on your nose, Dinny," she laughed, a bit nervously, he thought. "No—it's nothing. Just moody, because it's raining and dark. I didn't intend it should rain, today."

"Well—if you're sure that's all. I was afraid you were unhappy. I didn't do anything, did I, Janet?"

Shaking off her dolorous mood, and facing him with a twisted little smile, Janet slipped her palms slowly upward on his well-muscled arms, grasped his ear-lobes in her slim fingers, made a gesture of chastising him, and murmured, "Of course not, simpleton."

He had called her "Janet" from the first; ever since that enchanted Saturday, now more than three and a half years ago, when, shy and excited, he had followed the solemn butler over the deep-pile Oriental rugs from the impressive front entrance to the broad, winding stairs, and along a narrower corridor to narrower stairs leading into the huge attic room.

"Master Brumm, ma'am," the man had said, leaving them.

Under a large north skylight, young Mrs. Day—who had not been absent from Ferdinand's thoughts, waking or sleeping, since the night he had met her—sat on a tall three-legged stool before a composing-case, distributing type, her high heels hooked on a rung. Her heavy black hair was braided in one long plait. She wore a short skirt, and a long, green, open-throated jacket with capacious pockets, the costume diminishing her age and urbanity until she was quite another person than the queenly Mrs. Day whose black voile nearly touched the floor, whose white lace yoke had brought up in a tight, ribbed collar that almost reached to her dainty ears, her slim height emphasized by the big black hat with the orange velvet tips, on the night she had made their house, and all the people in it, outmoded and shabby.

Except for the slow, half-teasing, puckery smile with which she turned to welcome him, this girlish Mrs. Day might have been someone else than the mysterious goddess who had been playing the deuce with his imagination and staling his appetite for dinner.

Slipping down from her high stool, she had thrust her hands deep into the pockets of her smock, her head tilted as if in critical judgment of a picture.

"You seem ever so much bigger, taller," she said. "How old are you?"

"It's this collar, I think," Ferdinand had replied, soberly. "Going on fourteen.... Aunt Martha would have me wear it."

"Who's Aunt Martha? Does she live with you?"

"But you met Aunt Martha. Mrs. Brumm is not my mother."

Mrs. Day's shapely arm was thrown up suddenly in a gesture of happy discovery emphasized by a vigorous snap of the fingers, her face alight.

"By Jove!" she shouted. "So—that's the answer to the riddle!"

"My mother died when I was born," explained Ferdinand.

"And your father—what became of him?"

Ferdinand was very sorry that the subject had arisen. He had come, eager and inquisitive, hoping to see Mrs. Day's wood-working equipment; and here we were, wasting precious time.

"He's living... out West... I never saw him.... You're putting the type back in their boxes; aren't you?" Ferdinand drew nearer the case. "May I watch you do it?"

"Oh—we're going to talk about wood-cuts," said Mrs. Day. "But, first, sit down. Tell me some more about yourself."

"There isn't much," he replied, gloomily; but he took the big club chair she pointed to, and began to tell her what little he knew. Seated on a low ottoman at his feet, she listened intently, asking brief questions when he paused. There was, after all, a good deal of the story. It was a whole hour before Mrs. Day seemed satisfied, and they sat silently.

"I think you should have kept the pony," she said, after a long pause. "That must have hurt him, dreadfully.... And you never wrote to him?"

Ferdinand drew a long sigh, with a convulsive catch in the middle of it, and abstractedly twisted Mrs. Day's soggy little handkerchief into a slim rope. Her understanding sympathy and affection had loosed a long-pent flood of suppressed misery. He smiled, feebly.

"That's the first time anybody ever defended my father," said Ferdinand. "Why should I have written to him? He never wrote to me."

Mrs. Day rose, and, walking slowly to the dormer window, stood looking down at the busy street.

"I'm guessing that there's some more of that story... that you never heard," she said, impressively.

Then there had been some hot chocolate and cakes, and Ferdinand became quickly absorbed in Mrs. Day's explanation of the new printing-press which her good friend, Mr. Oscar Zimmerman, had lent her. Mr. Zimmerman had made quite a hobby of art-craft printing; had done some beautiful things; now he had tired of it; had sent her his entire equipment for use while he was abroad.

"He will be so interested in you, Ferdinand. I wrote him you were a Mueller descendant, and that I intended you should have a go at these things—wood-cuts, art printing, etchings."

They became very well acquainted, that day. Ferdinand's name was too bulky and mature, and was abbreviated to "Dinny," which seemed to make him rather light-hearted, as if his name had weighted him.

"You may call me Janet, if you like," she had suggested. "If we're going to play together with these things, you'll probably be teaching me, very soon, and I mustn't be much older than my teacher, you see, or it might discourage me."

"I never knew anyone named Janet, before," said Ferdinand. "I'm glad."

"Dinny, you say the most adorable things... and all unconsciously, too. That's the best part of it. You're developing into a young courtier; I can see that."

* * * * *

Ferdinand was also developing into a young liar, he feared, after he had answered all of Aunt Martha's pressing questions relative to that first visit with the problematical Mrs. Day. Naturally disposed to be suspicious of well-groomed femininity, Aunt Martha was troubled. Ferdinand was required to reproduce the afternoon, item by item. How was Mrs. Day dressed? Was Mr. Day at home? Was Madam Day present? What did she have to say? What all happened?

Ferdinand promoted himself, that evening, from the mere happy estate of apprentice to a beautiful craftswoman. He achieved the dignity of a great story-teller. Baron Munchausen would have been proud of him. Amazing himself by the increasing glibness of his tale, he invented a conversation he had had with Mrs. Day that represented her as most ardently concerned about the welfare of the church, albeit she never attended, due to a slight heart affection which made it dangerous for her to expose herself to strong emotional appeals; garbed her in a sombre dress, laid a grey shawl about her shoulders, had the audacity to put her hair up in curl-papers; located her workroom in the busiest part of the great house; caused servants to stand by her, handing her the things she needed in her work—and wound up with an account of his hostess's admiration for Aunt Martha and Uncle Miles and Angela.... Fearing he had been extravagant in this, Ferdinand decided to risk nothing further and excused himself on the pretence of having to study.

But Aunt Martha was never quite at ease with Ferdinand's two and three afternoons a week—and all day Saturdays—with Mrs. Day.

"I never did like the looks o' that woman," she would say, anxiously, to Mr. Brumm. "You wait!... We'll see!"

And when, at length, having waited, they saw, she muttered, grimly pleased that her forecast had been so prescient, "Didn't I tell yuh? Didn't I warn yuh? Where were yer eyes?"

* * * * *

Dinny carefully unwound the inky string from the type-form and went about the extraction of an upper-case H that seemed a bit defective.

"Rather rubbishy sentiment; wouldn't you say?" he called across to Janet, bent over a wood-cut with a big reading-glass in one hand and a slim reamer in the other, putting stripes in a wind-blown flag.

"Oh—I don't know," she replied, as from a considerable distance. "It's about what one would expect, isn't it, from a mellow old gentleman, trying to be lyrical about war; trying to remember and forget at the same time, like the proud but poor old lady in London who went out to sell papers, mumbling, 'Times, tuppence! Times, tuppence! Lord, I hopes nobuddy 'ears me!'... And no one will actually read this, anyway, you know. They'll be saying, 'What a *lovely* piece of printing! Whoever did it? And especially these bee-ootiful ornamental capitals, and this incomparable tail-piece! Just look at that *flag!*'... That's what they will be saying, Dinny."

"That's rather cynical... for you, Janet," laughed Dinny. "I'm always the one that's scolded for being more concerned over the way things look than what they mean. You must be deteriorating."

He ran the sticky, snapping, black brayer over the face of his corrected galley, and began pounding another proof-page on to it with a plane.

"I think words get their definitions, not from the dictionary, but from the private sentiments of the people who use them," continued Dinny, philosophically. "Take the General's word 'misunderstandings.' That's what caused the war—'misunderstandings.' Fact is, they all understood one another too well. People are forever calling their quarrels 'misunderstandings.' Nonsense! So long as they were misunderstanding, each one could give the other credit for a bit of ignorant honesty. But when they begin to understand each other, they call out the troops and distribute the gunpowder."

"You amuse me, Dinny," drawled Janet, intent on her occupation. "You would never have thought about that, at all, if you hadn't been annoyed because 'misunderstandings' is too long to look well in a line of twelve-point Caslon set to fourteen ems. It's just when they begin to inconvenience us that we find fault with words and have hot debates over them. We think up shorter synonyms that look better on whatever page we're making up, and then imagine we've discovered a new idea, or expressed a pleasanter thought. If 'licentiousness' is too unwieldy, we change it to 'liberty.'"

"'Parsimoniousness' *is* easier to set, if you call it 'thrift,'" agreed Dinny, willing to go on with the game, but a bit bewildered over Janet's choice of an illustration.

"It all depends upon who's talking," she added, absently, "and when. 'Liberty' is a pretty word, isn't it?"

"I should think these old soldiers," pursued Dinny, didactically, "would never want to hear another word about war. It must give them the heebie-jeebies in the night. I saw a team of farm-horses run off with a mowing-machine, when I was a little boy. The man fell off the iron seat, and got tangled in the knives. The scared horses turned short when they came to a fence-corner and had their hind legs nearly chewed off, not having sense enough to stop. I see it yet, sometimes, when I'm slow going to sleep. It's the most reliable of all my pet horrors. Wouldn't you think these old veterans would be just as happy not to be reminded of screaming horses with eyes dangling on a string, dragging their insides after them in long muddy ropes; and neighbour boys with the white splintered ends of bones sticking through their bloody pant-legs, and sticky globs of warm brains—"

"I say! Dinny! Stop it! What a ghastly imagination!"

"I'm going to fetch it to market, one o' these days."

"Going to be a butcher?"

"Going to write a book... called 'Balderdash.' Chapter one—patriotism; two—religion; three—I haven't quite decided on three yet, but it's to be something about the superstition that people with money have a right to play wheel-barrow with everybody who works for them or lives with them. Ever play wheel-barrow, Janet?"

"Yes, I think so. How do you play it?"

"Well—you get down on the floor, on your hands, and I pick you up by the feet and push, and you either have to walk on your hands or bump your nose."

"Oh, yes—I've been playing that, all my life. Nice game!"

For a little while, Dinny rattled on with his sour diatribe against war, Janet remotely keeping track of his excursion.

It hadn't been quite true that she'd always been playing wheel-barrow. Father—God bless him—had been infinitely tender and considerate. How he had humoured her every wish—hers and her mother's. Maybe that was why he could leave so little when he died; almost nothing, indeed, but extravagant tastes. She could have seen it through; but not her mother. Mr. Day had proposed such an easy solution. "You'd be a fool, Janet," her mother had said. "It's a chance in a lifetime." What a pity her mother had died, seeing the sacrifice had been made to please her.

"All this sweet hokum of the General's about 'shot-and-shell,'" Dinny was declaiming. "He's singing hymns about the varnished shot-and-shell piled in pyramids at the foot of the Soldiers' Monument. If he really wants to give the old fellows a thrill, why doesn't he remind them of the slippery shot-and-shell—all ooky and slimy with—"

"I heard you, Dinny, the first time!... Hand me that slide-rule, will you, dear?... But, you see, that's the way to keep patriotism alive."

"Patriotism's tripe!"

"Yes, Dinny.... Come over here and see my flag. Is that any better?"

He bent his five-feet-eleven over her soft shoulder, leaning his weight against the table on an ink-smeared hand.

"Fine, Janet! Much improved!... Now you take my Uncle Elmer; not meaning that he was worth a hoot before he went to Cuba, but just supposing he was. Gets himself all hotted up about his patriotic duty when somebody pounds a drum; sobs into his beer; hep-heps to Havana in boots two sizes too small for his big feet; curries the Colonel's horse; comes home with dysentery from eating spoiled meat that the get-rich-packers unloaded on them; and... Janet—perhaps you might give the eagle's left wing just a bit more spread... and expects to spend the rest of his life lying about in the shade at the Soldiers' Home. Patriotism—rot!... Look out for those stars, Janet! You'll have a deuce of a time putting them back in, you know, once they're out!"

"I know, Dinny. By the way," she laughed, "that's what the General's little book is about; isn't it? He believed that. Once the stars were out, it would be hard to put them back in."

"Rubbish! Sentiment!"

"Then why are we doing this, at all?"

"Because I'm earning money to go to college this autumn." Dinny turned back to his table and carefully peeled off a new proof.

"Speaking of college—has your uncle relented?"

"Him—relent? He's more convinced than ever. Says he has already assured old Dean What's-His-Name that I'd come to Magnolia; says it would do him a terrible lot of damage in the conference, or whatever it is, if I went to a godless State University. Everything's godless that Uncle Miles doesn't happen to know about. Odd jumble of conflicting ideas in Uncle Miles's head. I'd give something for a picture of the inside of it. Long ago, he was out in Arizona and visited the Petrified Forest. Never gets done talking about it. Picked up a piece and brought it home. Fondles it, and says, in a stage whisper, 'That's *a million years old,* my friend!'... But, on Sundays, it's only six thousand years old, so it won't antedate the sun, moon, and stars."

"Don't be too hard on him, Dinny. He can't contradict Genesis, you know. His whole flock would stampede."

"I'll bet Mr. Day wouldn't follow along in that stampede," said Dinny, eager as usual to find something meritorious in Mr. Day, seeing Janet had to live with him—a sore trial, he suspected. Or, was Dinny championing the cause of Mr. Day because he feared that Janet was thinking too much about Mr. Zimmerman, who was at home again, and so frequently visited her?

"No," replied Janet, gravely. "Mr. Day wouldn't follow in that stampede. He never follows. He'd lead it."

"But—you don't mean to tell me Mr. Day believes that old Jewish myth about the universe being created in six days!"

"On Sundays, when he's in church—yes."

"And the yarn about Adam... and Eve made out of Adam's rib?"

"Oh, yes; he believes that, every day and no matter where he is—especially about the rib."

"Meaning... you're a rib, Janet?" queried Dinny, laughing, but half-wishing he had not said it.

"One of the shorter ones, Dinny."

"They're called 'floating' ribs."

"How do you mean—'floating'?... Loose?"

"Oh, no," scoffed Dinny, pretending pride in his superior knowledge of physiology, "they never get loose."

"I should have known that much; shouldn't I?"

"You probably never thought about it, before."

"Don't be too sure about that, my son," she said, in a tone that worried him a little. It wasn't like Janet to be so mysterious. He couldn't quite understand her, today. Even her immediate change of topic was not at all reassuring.

"So—I suppose you'll be going to Magnolia, then."

"I'm in for it, all right. However, I am not particularly interested in science, so it doesn't matter much. The Lit. course at Magnolia is probably no thinner than in many a bigger school. Professors in English Comp. can't tell you how to write. If they knew how to do it, they'd be doing it; wouldn't they? All I want is a chance to do some reading, on my own hook, and plenty of time for scribbling. I can have that at Magnolia. They're much too hard up to enforce any discipline. I can go my own gait."

"I'm going to miss you—terribly." Janet left her work, and stood beside him. Her eyes were troubled.

"That's the only thing about it, Janet. I don't know how I'm to get along without you."

She walked to the window and stood looking out.

"There isn't very much more I could do for you, Dinny; is there?"

"You're the only real friend I ever had, Janet." He put down the brayer and joined her at the window. "Sometimes, I've wondered if I wasn't leaning too heavily; monopolizing you."

"It's been the other way about, dear," said Janet, soberly. "I've monopolized you. You haven't been interested in the girls of your class in school."

"Pooh! They're nothing but silly little gigglers."

"Maybe you wouldn't think so if you made any effort to know them."

"You're all the girl I want, Janet," said Dinny, lightly.

"That's just the trouble. It isn't good for you. I'm not your girl; nor am I your sister, or your mother." She faced about, and abruptly changed the subject. "Oscar—Mr. Zimmerman—wants you to have the stuff he lent us; all the Caxton and Cheltenham and the rest of it, and the seven-by-nine press, and this fancy Caslon, too. He says you're to take it along to college with you. He hopes you will set up a little shop and make it pay your way. Rather nice of him; don't you think?"

"Very!" said Dinny, trying to sound grateful. "But weren't you going to use it, any more?"

"No—not after you leave, Dinny."

He wasn't quite sure whether he wanted to be under such obligation to Mr. Zimmerman. True, it would be of no consequence to the rich bachelor globe-trotter whether Dinny used the printing-equipment or not. Otherwise it would probably be idle in a storage warehouse. But he disliked accepting anything from Mr. Zimmerman. He was candidly jealous of Mr. Zimmerman, of his easy grace, his urbane manners, his charming personality, his casual allusions to the places he had seen—Singapore, Calcutta, Moscow—mentioning them in about the same tone Dinny might have used when speaking of Oak Grove or Zanesdale or Unger. He often wondered if Mr. Day were jealous, too; not that he cared, greatly. Perhaps Mr. Day's private feelings were modified, somewhat, by the fact that Mr. Zimmerman was one of the heaviest stockholders in the Day Wholesale Provision Company. Money made a lot of difference.

"Dinny"—Janet's voice was a bit uncertain—"we're getting awfully crowded and cluttered in this room. Lately, I've been thinking we might move our printing-stuff to larger quarters. I looked at a room yesterday. It's in the Woolford Block on Superior Street—"

Dinny remembered that Mr. Zimmerman owned the Woolford Block, and with difficulty suppressed a scowl.

"—and I can get it for a song. Suppose you run in, next time you're down-town, and see what you think of it."

She took up her purse from the table, and handed him a key.

"Number 306. Go in on Monday, after school, and look it over."

Dinny was in no position to debate the matter. He nodded, and took the key. It was growing dark, though only five-thirty, and the rain was falling in torrents.

"Take my umbrella, dear."

"Thanks, Janet. I'll telephone you, when I've seen the room."

"Good-bye, dear." She reached out her slim hand, and looked up, fleetingly, into his perplexed eyes. It was so unlike her to offer her hand. They never shook hands. Dinny took it, rather confusedly, and was at a loss what to say.

"I'm afraid you're dreadfully worried about something." Dinny swallowed hard, and put his hands lightly on her shoulders.

"'Bye, Dinny!" Impulsively she threw her arms tightly around his neck and kissed him on the lips; then, turning quickly away, walked toward the window, stood with both hands outspread on the broad sill, a mere silhouette in the gathering gloom.

That was the picture he retained of Janet for a dozen years.

With another long, anxious look, he reluctantly went out, and closed the door.

* * * * *

On Monday afternoon, he went to inspect the room in the Woolford Block; went without interest, and weighted by an unaccountable depression.

The room was not empty, as he had expected. All their printing-equipment was there, installed in orderly fashion, ready for work.

On the imposing-stone was a receipted bill for three months' rental. At the bottom of the paper, hurriedly written in pencil, were a few lines in Janet's tall, slim letters:

God keep you always, dear Dinny. Forgive me for going away. I'm not really bad, Dinny. It's just that I'm tired playing wheel-barrow.

He gazed woodenly at the message for a long time, with an aching throat and burning eyes. Then he tore it into small bits, savagely stuffed the scraps into his pocket, went out, locked the door, and clumped slowly down the stairs.... Janet was no better than the rest of them. They were all cheaters! Damn them!

CHAPTER VI

AFTER a wheezing ascent of four steep flights in the wake of his young employer and guide, the gruff expressman had un-shouldered Ferdinand's small, old-fashioned trunk, with a groan of relief and reproach, and had ambled off down the bare, resounding dormitory hall grumblingly fingering the four dimes and seven nickels that totalled his exact charge.

Obedient to some atavism urging him to establish a claim to his new property without delay, Ferdinand laid his coat and collar on the sagging bed, and went through the preliminary gestures of making himself at home. The room was cramped, shabby, and incompletely furnished, but it was his, and the feeling of possession was pleasureable.

The convex lid of the antiquated trunk was thrown back against the dingy wall, and the welcome task of unpacking proceeded; his meagre, outmoded wardrobe, a handful of books, a dozen cheap towels, and the case of carving-tools, over which there had been such a row, Aunt Martha's eloquent disapproval rending the Yuletide peace and reaching an impassioned climax in her unexecuted threat to carry the expensive gift back to that there high-'n'-mighty Mrs. Day with her own hands.

"With love to Dinny from Janet."

It was the engraving on the silver plate inside the velvet-lined lid that had detonated Aunt Martha's tightly corked resentment against a mysterious (and probably questionable) friendship which had ripened without benefit of her sanction, and was increasingly fulfilling her dire prediction that the attachment would wean Ferdinand away from his "humble home 'n' all that it stands fer."

And what right had this Mrs. Day to be "Janet" to a mere half-grown boy, inexperienced, unworldly, and calfishly infatuated? What kind o' "love" was this, we'd like to know, that had the impudence to flaunt itself in the face of his family! And since when had his name been changed to "Dinny"?... "Dinny"—indeed!... *"Dinny!"*—well, we'd see about that!

Ferdinand sat down on the edge of the weak-spined bed with the silver-mounted box in his hands.

Queer—wasn't it?—how an inanimate thing, pieced together of wood and screws and glue, silver and velvet and steel, could take on a personality possessed of so many sensitive, changing moods? One day you couldn't bear to look at it for the worry and chagrin it had caused you. Next day you loved it so tenderly it made your throat thick. Another day you despised it for reminding you of a tragic disenchantment that had all but killed you.

The box of carving-tools and his mother's little walnut desk; living things, they were!

The desk!... One winter Sunday afternoon when he was seven, in a promptly repented unveiling of cankered memories, Aunt Martha had told him the story of the desk; just the bare, ugly, shameful facts about the storm of jealousy it had provoked, a storm which Aunt Martha deplored but partly justified.

"I always said yer grandpa never should 'a' done it. He might 'a' knew it wouldn't set right with th' rest o' th' family; not that I ever cared, myself. I had t' work too hard, goodness knows, ever t' spend any time a-settin' at a desk. But Julia was always his favourite. It broke his heart when she died."

"And grandpa died, too, that same night, Aunt Martha, didn't he?"

Aunt Martha had nodded, shuddered, and laid another stick on the fire.

The desk had come along when Aunt Martha had left "th' old home," her brothers and sisters pressing no claim to a share in it. As a little lad, he saw it only when they moved from one house to another; and not even then, for it had remained thickly wrapped in the dusty burlap in which it had been shipped to Unger.

Shrouded, it had lived in dark corners of attics, damp corners of cellars, a thing neither to be used nor thrown away. It was almost as if they carried his mother's corpse about with them. When they had moved to Indianapolis, Ferdinand had asked for it. Consent was rather grudgingly given. He had one desk, hadn't he? However, Aunt Martha supposed he had a right to it, if he wanted to crowd his room with it. Sometimes he wished he had not insisted. He almost never used it, and when he did he felt depressed.

Perhaps he had better ask Uncle Miles to ship him the desk.... Dinny drew a wry smile. He could put the case of carving-tools in the drawer of the desk, and let them settle their problems between themselves. Now that he was in college, there would be plenty of other things to occupy his attention. New friends and fresh interests would lay his ghosts.

But, what about these new friends; these fresh interests?

The past three hours had been a disappointing surprise. "College" was not quite as he had pictured it, a comradely, democratic, open-hearted aggregation of irresponsible youngsters, bent on getting acquainted with one another by the shortest routes.

At almost every station stop, en route from Indianapolis to Magnolia—so close to Cincinnati as to think of itself as a suburb—young people boarded the train. Doubtless they were going to college; perhaps to Magnolia. A few suitcases were adorned with pink and white stickers, pennant-shaped, cheering for the school. Already he was entertaining a growing sense of loyalty and pride.

For the most part, however, the pilgrims bound for Magnolia, if they greeted each other at all, seemed shy and restrained; a mere nod, "Hello, Buster; back to the mill?"... "How 'r' yuh, Prichard; good summer?"

But this was the day-coach, and these the day-coachers. The distinction gradually dawned on Ferdinand. For some time he had been curious, when the train stopped in the larger towns, over festive sounds on the platform well to the rear. At Richmond, he strolled to the steps, and, leaning out, saw a score or more of well-dressed, high-spirited people, old and young, bidding good-bye to a handful of students, gathered at the entrance to a Pullman, the white-jacketed porter busy with their baggage.

He went back through his own car, and overheard their cryptic banter as they scrambled up the steps, the porter banging the vestibule doors behind them. These, too, were Magnolians—the real, traditional college students of song and story, larkish, noisy, devil-may-care. He wished he had committed the extravagance of riding in the Pullman. It would have made all the difference. Not quite, however, he reflected—not in these clothes.

A month afterward, burning with hot resentment against the discrimination that had bled his pride white, Ferdinand marvelled that nearly four years of intimate association with a person so sophisticated as Janet Day had contributed almost nothing to his knowledge of that other world to whose citizenship he aspired.

Analysing their relations, however, he saw that it was neither his fault nor hers that the friendship had done so little for him in this respect. Such community of interest as they had was based almost exclusively on their shop-work. Ferdinand had never taken a meal with her except the sandwiches, cakes and tea, casually enjoyed during a few minutes of recess from their occupation. Janet was always dressed in an inky, paint-daubed smock, her hair down her back; he was always in his working togs. They rarely talked of anything else than their immediate concerns. Janet had not given him a ticket to the world of smart people.

Alighting from the train, Ferdinand confronted a gay scene. A spirited crowd—modishly dressed, bareheaded, beautiful girls, and white-sweatered, flannel-trousered, handsome fellows—cheered and chaffed the recruits descending from the Pullmans; their classmates, no doubt; old acquaintances: but no—fully half of them were obviously newcomers, like himself. Solicitously in tow of the old-timers, they were now being presented to the welcoming throng. A phalanx of motor-cars was drawn up along the platform, engines noisily churning and clamouring to be off, drivers' seats occupied by debonair greeters, sons and daughters of the other world, the world that rode in Pullmans and came to meet people who rode in Pullmans.

Ferdinand had not been expecting anyone to meet him, and therefore had no occasion to be disappointed; but he was overcome with a feeling of such loneliness as had never afflicted him before. He took up his battered old suitcase, made some inquiries of a policeman whose amused attention was grudgingly distracted from the real people's festivities, boarded a street-car, reached the campus—a gently undulating grove of oaks and elms, zigzagged with winding paths of white, hard-tramped gravel-ribbons that negligently wandered about from one main entrance to another of the dozen or more nondescript buildings of brick, of stone, of cement, of wood, in attempted imitation of every known school of architecture and ranging in age all the way from raw newness to pathetic dilapidation.

He had anticipated, without relish, the quiet chat he would probably have with Dean Sloke. He would be shown into Dean Sloke's office, when his turn came.

"Ah—so you are Ferdinand Brumm, the nephew of my esteemed friend, the Reverend Miles Brumm of Indianapolis, who has been a valuable supporter of Magnolia. We are glad to have you here, Mr. Brumm. Now what can we do for you to make you comfortable?"

Ferdinand was pointed to the Registrar's office. He saw that there was no necessity for seeking an interview with Dean Sloke. There was a long line of bewildered freshmen, leaning an elbow against the long, tall counter. No one of them in any way resembled the urbane youths who had been so hilariously received at the station. Surely they had had time to arrive here, by now. Mailed advice had counselled freshmen to come to the Administration Building immediately upon arrival. Where were these others? But perhaps there was a special room for their accommodation. Maybe the freshmen who came to town in Pullman cars were handled in some distinctive manner, or at some other hour.

He took his place in the line, and, advantaged by his height, surveyed his neighbours. The girl in front of him was a nervous, home-made, little thing; the boy whose broad, square back obstructed her view of the distant goal had the black-tanned neck of a farmer. The criss-cross furrows on the neck announced that their bearer was older than the others by four or five years. He'd been ploughing deep and saving his pennies against the day when he might come to college.

Ferdinand was half-ashamed of himself over this critical invoice of his companions. Come to think of it—this was his own crowd, after all; wasn't it? By what right was he assuming a supercilious attitude, in his mind, toward these yokels?

At length he had reached the impressively business-like, barricaded throne of the Registrar and his self-consciously competent assistants. He answered a few crisp, inquisitorial queries, wrote his name on three or four blanks which were promptly and soundly smacked with a big rubber stamp, counted out forty-two dollars at an adjoining wicket for which he received another emphatic whack on his credentials, moved forward to "Rooms," paid another fee, earned another whack, took his key, picked up the old suitcase he had been pushing along with his foot, and milled through the crowd to the doorway. It moved back, a little, to make room.

Nobody had spoken to him except the perfunctory clerks, nor he to any; though there had been a few shy, bucolic grins accompanying the "Beg your pardon" which went along with sundry unintentional jabs of elbows in the jostling line-up of rookies.

They were a very ordinary lot of people, he thought, on both sides of the counter. Those back of the counter were a bit more seasoned, had learned their tricks, had developed something of the arrogance so appropriately worn by petty officials peering through wickets and sourly handing dipped pens to the public for its signature; but there was no essential difference between the green clodhoppers on this side the barrier and the ripe clodhoppers on the other.

175

As he had stood there waiting, Ferdinand wondered if Magnolia wasn't trying to impress the new arrivals; trying to make-believe she was a big university. Where was this warm, home-y friendliness that bubbled on the comradely pages of the college catalogue? Was all this swanky, big-business-y, card-index-y, cash-register-y atmosphere, this frowning fussiness, this cool official insolence, this elaborate hocus-pocus of labelled wicket-windows and ostentatious thud of rubber stamps a lot o' bunk? His instinct told him the whole affair screamed of insincerity.... "Just a friendly, home-y, little college"—hell!

* * * * *

Ferdinand answered a vigorous rat-a-tat-tat of knuckles and admitted one who, promptly identifying himself as Orville Kling, junior, resident across the hall, candidate for the ministry, leader of the college band in need of new material, and Religious Editor of *The Blossom,* requested pay, in kind, at his first full stop, for his generous tender of a biographical sketch.

With less to tell about himself, Ferdinand made short work of his own story. Pressed for further disclosures, he admitted he had no idea what he would "take up." No—not the ministry; he was sure of that much.... Well—he had no taste for it, no fitness for it, and, to be frank, no interest in it. Kling thought this odd, considering Ferdinand's home environment.

"Hope you'll come down to the Y rooms, second floor, tonight at seven," suggested Kling. "Just an informal little get-together of the fellows to meet the new Frosh; a sing-song, brief devotional service, some short prayers, a few snappy talks; all through by eight."

"Thanks," said Ferdinand, graciously, but without enthusiasm.

"That's the spirit," approved Kling, anxious to exhilarate Ferdinand's wan interest. "It makes all the difference, later, if you begin your college life right."

Ferdinand nodded obligingly, and conceded that this must be true, but his acquiescence lacked fervour. Bent on saving a soul from anæmia, Kling rose to defend his moral precept.

Hands deep in his coat pockets, and rhythmically elevating himself on his toes, he dealt seriously with Ferdinand's limp aspirations to make a right start.

"Yes, sir—it makes all the difference, you'll find. The whole four years depend on the first week's contacts. Down there on Sunnyside Avenue, the upper classmen are teaching the new fraternity pledges to smoke a pipe, scorn the bars, and beat the profs.... Up here, we have different ideas. You'll start right, won't you, Brumm?"

"You mean—at a prayer-meeting?"

"Well—that kind of a beginning would make for safety; wouldn't it?" queried Kling, slightly accelerating the tempo of his adroit bouncing up and down on his toes.

Ferdinand grinned amiably, and walked to the window, leaning against it; long, rangy arms folded.

"I'm pretty well up on prayer-meetings, Mr. Kling. I've been raised on them. And—as for safety, I have all my credits in that, too.... I mean to be friendly, and I'd like to meet the fellows, and I appreciate your asking me, but—"

Kling stopped his bouncing and drew a long face.

"But—you won't be there."

"I don't think so."

Kling smiled bravely, shook his head regretfully, seemed reluctant to leave. His eye wandered about the room.

"Play on anything?" he inquired, brightening.

"No—I'm not musical. Sorry."

"Thought that might be a clarinet. We need another clarinet."

"It's a case of carving-tools."

"Carving-tools.... I never saw any. Mind if I look?"

Ferdinand's consent and the snap of the latch occurred simultaneously. Kling glanced up and smiled.

"They call you 'Dinny,' don't they?"

"Ye-es."

"Rah, rah, rah—Dinny Brumm! That's what we'll be hearing next autumn. You'll be going out for football, of course. They wouldn't let a big fellow like you escape.... Janet your sister?"

"Yes.... Is the athletic field close?"

Kling pointed north with his head, deeply interested in the shining tools.

"'Most everybody's there now, watching the varsity warm up. Want to go over? I'm going."

Ferdinand begged off with an excuse that he had a few errands in town.

"Well—so long, Dinny. See you later."

* * * * *

Supper was at five-thirty, the tenants of the dormitory preferring it early. Ferdinand was not hungry, nor was he keenly disposed to risk further interrogations about his plans for the evening. Waiting until the clangour of the second bell and the last clatter of descending feet had subsided, he put on the rather yellow and battered straw hat that Aunt Martha felt would do quite well enough, though he had entertained some doubts, walked quietly down stairs, down the slope, and turned to the left on Sunnyside Avenue. The broad verandas of the fraternity houses were filled with bareheaded students, some standing, some lounging in the big wicker chairs, some sitting on the railings swinging white-flannelled legs. Ferdinand was conscious of their amused attention, as he passed the Beta House—the last on the row, opposite which one took the streetcar.

A merry voice sang out, accompanied by good-natured chuckles, and followed by a mature growl. "Cut that out, Reddy! What th' hell!"—

"Hey, Reuben! How's the weather up there?"

Ferdinand scowled, flushed, and gave his full attention to the approaching street-car. He wondered if he wasn't going to hate Magnolia.

After supper, at a downtown restaurant, for which he had little relish, he went to the office of *The Morning Star,* and made his way to the Managing Editor's desk. He was a little more sure of himself in this environment, and presented his cause without nervousness.

"What experience have you had?" asked Mr. Brophy, tilting back in his chair, and scrutinizing Ferdinand not unpleasantly from under his green eye-shade.

"I've been doing amateur and semi-professional art-craft printing for some time. Since early June, I was on the display ads with *The Ledger,* Indianapolis."

"How could you work evenings, and go to college?"

"I think I could manage, sir. No classes in the afternoon."

"You'd have to be on from seven to ten-thirty, six nights a week... all but Saturday."

"I could do that."

"Take this out to the composing-room, and set it."

Ferdinand nodded, took the ad-copy, and pushed his way through the metallic racket of linotypes to the row of cases in the corner. It was the first time he had felt at home in Magnolia. The smell of ink revived his spirits, straightened his broad shoulders. Mr. Brophy followed him along, and spoke laconically to the grizzled foreman who nodded without looking up or removing his pipe.

"You may begin to-morrow evening, if you like," said Mr. Brophy, an hour later, glancing over Ferdinand's shoulder. "Ninety cents an hour. Six nights; seven to ten-thirty. Time and a half for overtime. Pay on Mondays. Right?"

"Right!... Thank you, sir."

After a while, the foreman strolled over.

"Pretty fair, for a dub," he growled, fetching his *r*'s rolling up from far back under an Irish pharynx. "Mr. Brophy says you'll be goin' to college, day-times. Sure it won't be too much for ye, me boy?"

Ferdinand lowered his half-filled stick, and warmed to the genial, ruddy-faced Timmy Fagan. No—he could do it, all right. Liked it. Besides—he needed the money. Couldn't stay here without some kind of a job.

"You're luckier 'n most, t' have a trade," said Timmy. "Most uv 'em has to wait table and wash dishes at th' frats."

"I'd see myself doing that!"

"Well—somebody's got t' wait on th' rich boys 'n' girls, 'n' see that they have enough t' eat, when they come in from their tennis, all tired and hungry," drawled Timmy, his eyes wrinkling with delight as he noticed the flexing of Ferdinand's jaw-muscles. "But," he added, "I can see that you'd rather somebody else 'tended to it... . And—now that we're speakin' o' meals, maybe you'd like to come over and have a bite o' honest Irish hospitality on Sunday, say, after the eleven o'clock Mass which you won't be to, bein' a heathen. The missus'll be glad, and th' kids, too. You'll be lonely like, for a while."

Only an ungrateful snob could refuse such an invitation, thought Ferdinand. He accepted gladly, promptly; but, a moment later, and all the way back to the campus, where the dormitory windows gleamed with a welcome he wished he might respond to with more warmth, he was uneasy over his promise to old Timmy. Timmy, God bless him, had him all wrong.... Right, of course, about thinking he would resent the necessity of a job to wait table for these precious young well-to-do's, but quite wrong in thinking that he wanted to hold himself in sour aloofness from them. It was the world they lived in that he most wanted to explore! And how was he ever to invade that world if he approached it via Sunday dinners at the Timmy Fagans'? Perhaps he'd better trump up some excuse.... But Timmy was no fool. Timmy mustn't be hurt.

However—no use worrying about it. Nobody need know. The Fagans probably had no college connections, at all. The "kids" would be freckled little Micks—a half-dozen, maybe, who would show him their toy aeroplane... and that would be the end of it. "Such a nice time, Mrs. Fagan!... Thank you, Mr. Fagan.... Yes, indeed, Mr. Fagan, I'll be glad to!... Good-bye, little Fagans!"

* * * * *

He couldn't help being so tall that his contemporaries presumed him able to get forecasts of the weather, but he could help looking like a Rube. Pursuant to that resolution, he went into town, the next day, strode up to the counter of the best clothing store, and possessed himself of a natty new suit of blue serge.

His immediate college bills had been paid, and there was more than a hundred dollars in his pocket—earned by himself, every cent of it! Why shouldn't he do what he liked with it? His wages were assured. They would amply cover his expenses, with a comfortable margin.

Ferdinand paid for the suit and spent the remaining forty-eight dollars of the hundred he had allotted to this adventure in a neighbouring haberdashery. Uncle Miles, he knew, would have scowled and remarked that even friendly little colleges have a "subversive" (pet word of his) influence on youth; and as for Aunt Martha, she would have had—if aware of his amazing profligacy—a fit.

* * * * *

Up early on Friday, arrayed in all his new finery—the blue, double-breasted suit that squared his shoulders, the soft grey fedora set at a sporty angle on his freshly groomed head, russet shoes, smart fawn shirt, tie a shade darker matching the handkerchief that peeped from his breast pocket—Ferdinand found he still had half an hour to spare before his first encounter with the class in English Composition.

Yesterday there had been mere lesson-assignment sessions in Beginner's Greek with old Appleton, who promised to be a hard taskmaster; Algebra under nervous and self-conscious young Peters who would be lenient (it was devoutly to be hoped); and Latin under the meek and obsequious little Harwood, commonly spoken of as The Bearded Lady.

He would bone in Greek not only because he really wanted to learn it but was afraid of Appleton—a sarcastic old savage. He would toddle along in Cicero, Latin being a cinch for him. And as for Algebra, it could go to the devil along with the inexperienced Peters who was clearly too frightened over his new responsibility to pay much attention to anybody else's dilemmas.

But English Composition was quite another matter. This was going to be a bread-and-butter affair. Ferdinand knew he would be writing, all his life; writing for a career, writing for wages. No fooling, here.

He could have wished that Professor Grover's sketch in the catalogue had hinted at a wider experience. A degree from some well-known university would have added lustre to his biography.

That Professor Grover had not been much of a nomad was obvious. Never had he been taken up, in foreign parts, for vagrancy. He had stayed on home base and kept himself unspotted from the world.

Topping the list of courses offered by the English Department was an impressive and extended survey of the Grover equipment.

WILLIAM ERNST GROVER, A.B., A.M., PH.D., LITT.D.

So far; so good. But the rest of it indicated that Professor Grover's mileage was disturbingly low.

Educated Magnolia Public Schools; Magnolia Academy (grad 1878, with high distinction); Magnolia College (A.B., 1882, *m.c.l.,* Class pres. and hist.; winner Rebecca Winters Dutton medal); Master of Arts (Magnolia College, 1885. Thesis: "Prehistoric Mounds near Magnolia"); Ph.D. (Magnolia College, 1889. Thesis: "Magnolia Under Doctor Swits"); Litt.D. (Magnolia College, 1896). Author: "Magnolians Who Made Their Mark" (Magnolia College Press, 1899), "Fifty Years of Magnolia" (Magnolia College Press, 1902), "Forward, Magnolia!" (Magnolia Ptg. and Engv. Co., 1910).

Three cheers for good old Magnolia; eh, Professor Grover? Ferdinand would have grinned had he been less disturbed over the prospect.

The time came when he did grin; shouted with laughter; slapped his leg and yelled with delight. That was while engaged in composing the article on "Rhododendron College," midway of his junior year. He sold the article to *The Iconoclast,* receiving, two months later, in the same mail, a cheque for one hundred dollars from the editor in New York, and a crisp request for an early interview with President Braithwaite of Magnolia.

"It might have been more discreet," said President Braithwaite, endeavouring to suppress a twinkle, "had you gone to the fauna rather than the flora for a fictitious name. 'Rhododendron' made it a bit obvious, you know.... This about the Pyncheon chickens—facetious enough but cruelly unkind!"

"I had had the chickens in mind for a long time, sir," said Ferdinand, on that occasion. "It simply had to be said."

He did not say how long, but the fact was that this idea had first occurred to him on the morning early in his freshman year when, with a few minutes to spare before going down to his first class in English Composition, he had put aside *The House of the Seven Gables* which he had been reading, and had glanced at the college catalogue's sketch of Professor Grover.

Apropos of "Rhododendron's" policy of recruiting her Faculty exclusively from the ranks of her own alumni, Ferdinand, the junior, wrote:

"Concerned as this institution is over the mental and moral improvement of the outer world, particularly such parts of it as must be reached by water, it occurs to some of us that Rhododendron College might well consider a philanthropy nearer home.

"Year after year, proud of her children, Alma Mater has refused to permit their acceptance of chairs in other schools.

"Yale, Harvard, Princeton, Columbia—does Rhododendron not owe it to these institutions, all of them doing good work and undeniably excellent in their way, to encourage their efforts not only by consenting that a few of our alumni may join their faculties, but by inviting some of their more distinguished sons to accept minor posts on our instructional staff?

"Not a Rhododendron alumnus on the faculty of any other college! Not a single professor at Rhododendron bearing a degree from any other school!

"Should it be said that our policy of intellectual inbreeding insures the integrity of our academic tribe, and guarantees against the debilitating invasion of alien blood, it may be replied that dangers lurk in the way of such aloofness.

"Witness, for example, the tragic plight of Hepzibah Pyncheon's poultry. Generation after generation, they had carried on, gloriously free of any exotic contamination, dourly scornful of the frivolous vulgarians in neighbouring coops. And did not the fateful day arrive at length when these same Pycheon chickens stalked about, spurless, combless, and without plumage; still proud, still grave, still haughty, but lacking the sense of humour necessary to the laying of an egg, to say nothing of the thermal dynamics required to hatch one?

"Featherless, eggless—but not crowless. Even when they were too feeble to scratch, either for provender or reasons of personal hygiene, they still raised their voices in the old pæan of praise that they had been kept free of foreign taints. They had the pip, yes; but, thank God, they were not mongrels!"

* * * * *

Discovering, to his dismay, that the new russet shoes were much too snug, Ferdinand hurriedly divested himself of the entire ensemble, resolved that he would wear none of it until he could wear it all.

Professor Grover was kindly patronizing, playfully paternal. The class would begin by submitting, on Tuesday, a fifteen-hundred-word theme on "Early Impressions of Magnolia."

As the class straggled out, Ferdinand overheard a colloquy in the hall. The Pullmans were talking it over, as they ambled toward the main doorway.

"Freddy says the old boy always asks for that, the first day. He says if you dash off a lot o' rot about the great honour and privilege, and all that sort o' bilge, you're solid with him for keeps; says if you write that when you saw the campus for the first time you just sat down on the grass and cried out loud, you'll be a Phi Beta Kappa when you're a senior."

"Phi Beta Kappa! D'you mean they've got a—?"

"Don't be a silly ass!... Phi Beta Kappa, my eye!"

* * * * *

The elder of the two Fagan kids was a girl with the blackest hair, the bluest eyes, the whitest skin, the evenest teeth, and the most heady smile that Ferdinand had ever seen done into one picture of glowing, high-school-girlish vivacity. Patrick, Kitty's brother, was fifteen.

Timmy Fagan's elder kid was going to resemble her mother, one day, as to amplitude of charms; you could see that. At seventeen, however, this threat, that at forty-two Kitty's physique would probably be redundant, evoked no pity.

The dinner was all that it had promised to be, and more; a gay meal, Ferdinand at his best, glad he had come.

It was over now. Young Pat had left for a ball game. Timmy's eyes began to swim in response to custom's demand for the Sunday afternoon nap. Mrs. Fagan's house-wifely conscience had conveyed her to the kitchen, scorning the volunteered assistance of her attractive child.

They sat in the swing on the little side porch overlooking the trim, tiny garden. Ferdinand was actively in the market for the companionship Kitty was so ready to bestow. He had been quite desperately lonely, almost ill of loneliness.

"You haven't seen our beautiful park yet," said Kitty. "You'll like it, I think. It's very nice, and there's a big lagoon with boats. Lots of people go there, Sundays."

They stood for a long time, at her gate, laughing, bantering, occasionally lowering their voices to brief seriousness, on their return at five-thirty.

Ferdinand regretfully looked at his watch.

"Good-bye, Kitty," he said. "Next Sunday, then."

"Okay, Dinny... 'Bye."

There was a deliciously lilting circumflex accent over the "'Bye" that rang and sang in Dinny's ears, all evening, as he stood at the case and struck large, boastful type certifying that Wembie's would be doing the city of Magnolia a good turn, tomorrow, with some unprecedented values in sheets and pillow-cases.

CHAPTER VII

"NO use," said the nurse, decisively. "He won't see you."

"He's got to," growled Dinny.

"Oh, I don't know as he's got to," countered Miss Lash, suddenly defiant. "The police couldn't make him talk. What makes you think—?"

"Sister"—Dinny drew an ominous frown—"you go back to Mr. Peter Andrews and tell him *The Star* knows all about it, anyway—"

"Thinks it does, maybe," scoffed Miss Lash.

"Which comes to the same thing, so far as tomorrow morning's report of the accident is concerned, he'll find. I'm here to let him correct us on any of the minor details. It's ten o'clock, and we've no time to fritter."

"You certainly have a lot of crust—for a kid."

"You ought to know," grinned Dinny, companionably. "Just a kid yourself." The accusation was ridiculous. Miss Lash was not seriously annoyed, however, and the little nose she made at him developed into a smile.

"I'll try him again," she said, in the manner of a fellow conspirator.

Dinny was covering his first assignment as a reporter. Mr. Brophy had urged him to work full time through the Thanksgiving recess, the display ads being particularly heavy at this season.

"And if you have nothing better to amuse yourself with in the evenings," added the editor, "you may share Anderson's police beat with young Maloney. Anderson's off to see his Alabama relatives. You've been hankering to try your hand at reporting: here's your chance."

Mr. Brophy had been prompt to make his promise good. The Thanksgiving vacation had begun only today at noon, a general hegira leaving the campus all but deserted. Happy to have a congenial companion, Dinny worked on the ads all afternoon and early evening. At nine-thirty, Timmy Fagan called, "Mr. Brophy wants ye."

"You're just leaving for the Protestant Hospital, young feller"—Mr. Brophy tossed him a memorandum scribbled on a card—"to interview an old man, mysteriously shot in the leg; has no police record, good citizen, but won't talk. Make him tell you.... Scatter along, now, and see what you're good for."

"Mr. Andrews says you can come up," announced Miss Lash, amiably. "I told him he'd better get it off his chest; but don't pester him, will you? He's a fine old man, and wouldn't hurt a fly. I won't have him persecuted."

"It seems he's told you," deduced Dinny.

She raised her brows, smiled archly, and led the way, Dinny following with long, confident strides.

"Very sick?" he inquired, as they traversed the third-floor corridor. The pungent reek of antiseptics and spent ether were doing odd tricks with Dinny's unaccustomed nostrils, and the hoarse, unhuman moans of some patient groping out of anæsthesia shortened his steps. Miss Lash grinned.

"No—or you wouldn't be seeing him; superficial wound, no infection, he can go home in a day or two. But"—she paused at the door—"I'll not have him hectored; understand? If he doesn't want to talk freely, that's that, and there's your hat. Promise?"

Mr. Andrews's gaunt old frame was so slight that the bed seemed unoccupied except for the benign face on the pillow. He shyly projected a thin, white hand from beneath the sheet, cleared his throat nervously, and drew a timid, embarrassed smile.

"Nurse thinks I may as well tell you," he murmured, with a weary sigh. "If I don't, you'll probably make it worse than it is, though it's none of the public's business, far as I can see."

"The public," sympathized Dinny, taking the chair Miss Lash had pushed up for him, and sensing with satisfaction the revival of his self-confidence, "is an old hen.... And the newspapers are impudent gossips.... And reporters are a pest.... But—such things being as they are—how *did* you get shot in the leg?"

"My next-door neighbour, out in Lambert Park, is Mr. Charles McCutcheon—" The old man sighed again, deeply, as he watched the name sprawling across the reporter's untidy wad of copy-paper; but, having burned his bridges, there was no retreat. "—A longtime friend of mine. We both work for the Buckeye Implement Company. We have a croquet-ground together, a small garden, and in the winter we play chess."

"He has been to see you, I presume," encouraged Dinny.

"No—er—well, yes; but I had them say I was too sick.... I'll be coming to that, in a minute."

The weary old voice droned on, reminiscently. Charlie was a widower, you know; he, a bachelor; nobody else mattered; went down town in the morning on the same car, lunched together, pretty nearly inseparable.

"'Bout two weeks ago, Charlie's daughter—the one that lives in Pinckney, and doesn't like me very well because I monopolize Charlie—gave him a St. Bernard pup to keep him company, a big-footed, empty-headed, destructive beast that tore up Charlie's house, all day—what time he wasn't tearing up mine—and howled like the devil all night. I could see that Charlie was worried, but he kept saying the dog would settle down and feel at home presently.

"And so, yesterday—wasn't it, nurse?—Charlie had gone down to Tiro to spend the night with William's folks; wedding anniversary, or something. You see, I hadn't slept for more 'n' week. Guess I was kinda out o' my head. Charlie had him out in a kennel at the far end of the lot; but, Gosh! that hadn't helped any.... I had an old revolver that hadn't been fired off for ten years or so. Three o'clock, I was pretty desperate, and put on my pants 'n' went out there. Somehow the hammer got caught in my pocket—"

"You could have made up a story, couldn't you?" inquired Dinny, solicitously.

"I'm not very good at that," replied the old man. "Besides—my leg hurt pretty bad. I managed to get in before it had bled very much, and 'phoned for the doctor. He brought me here—and that's all there is to it. You can print it, if you want to, and all the neighbours will despise me—and Charlie will never speak to me again."

"What did you do with the gun?" asked Dinny.

"Threw the darned thing in the cistern."

"Excellent! Now don't you worry any more," soothed Dinny, patting the emaciated hand. "We'll see you through it."

Dinny caught a car and hurried back to *The Star,* eyes bright with inspiration, so eager to document his scheme for the easement of good old Andrews that it never occurred to him there might also be some inquisitiveness on the part of *The Daily Eagle* concerning this mystery. That night, Dinny recognized for the first time unmistakable signs of his talent as a potential novelist. He warmed to his task. It was an unusual story, and toward the last of it they were snatching unfinished sheets out of his typewriter and rushing them, page at a time, to the lino-typist.

Next morning, December twenty-second, subscribers to both papers were amazed at the difference between the two accounts of this strange affair. According to *The Eagle's* report—a mere stick on page seven—Mr. Andrews had accidentally shot himself while endeavouring to pot his absent neighbour's noisy dog, a minor injury from which he was rapidly recovering.

The Morning Star—(first page, with a carry to three)—offered a long, dramatic story of Mr. Andrews's heroic silence about the shooting. In his delirium, however, the brave old fellow had muttered, "Don't shoot again, lad.... I haven't any money except what's there in my pocket-book.... You can look, if you like.... Take it—and hurry before somebody comes.... I won't tell on you, boy.... It would break her heart."

From these broken fragments, *The Star* had adroitly built up a tale of romance and adventure impressive enough to stand in the museum alongside the mastodon—all lath and plaster and imagination, except the third dorsal vertebra and two molars. Chivalrous old

Andrews! Brave old Andrews! Attacked in his little home by a marauder, he had recognized the wayward son of an old friend.

Nobody knew, nobody was likely ever to know—for Andrews seemed determined to keep his own counsel—what a wealth of romance lay undisclosed in the heart of this kindly old bachelor. Ambitious as she was to print all the news, *The Star* had quietly withdrawn from the bedside of this valiant knight, challenged to match his sportsmanship by declining to press the matter any farther.

That afternoon, industriously distributing big type, Dinny, out of the tail of his apprehensive eye, observed the approach of his boss, paper in hand. He redoubled his zealous interest in his occupation. Mr. Brophy was at his elbow now, but Dinny did not look up. It was a very busy day.

"My son," said Mr. Brophy, reproachfully, "*The Eagle* will probably try for a goal from the field with your Andrews story, tomorrow morning. They'll make us look like a cageful of monkeys."

"I've been thinking a little about that, too, sir," admitted Dinny, confidentially, "but, you see, the tale they tortured out of old Andrews, late last night, was concocted in sheer self-defence. He was resolved not to tell the straight story, so he made one up, on the spot, to satisfy their greedy curiosity. He would have done the same for me, if I had badgered him. Takes all the blame on himself! Risks the good opinion of his neighbours, risks his job at the shop, throws away the lifelong friendship of Mr. McCutcheon.... Shoot McCutcheon's pet? Nonsense! You wait until the people see the picture of saintly old Andrews, in bed at the hospital, near death's door, staring up out of those big, wistful—"

"Hell!—they're going to discharge him this afternoon."

"No, sir. I beg your pardon, sir. They had thought of it, but the nurse and I agreed it wouldn't do. I was out there and told them *The Star* would pay for all it cost to keep him a week, at least."

"He won't stay. Even if he does, he'll talk."

"No, sir. The nurse says his room is rapidly filling up with flowers and baskets of fruit. And Mr. Kellerman was there, making a fuss over him—"

"You mean old man Kellerman?"

"Yes, sir—president of the Buckeye—he was there; and Norton of *The Eagle* tried to see him, but Andrews sent down word to him that they'd practically forced him to tell them the tale he'd made up. The nurse says he likes our version of the affair ever so much better, though he told Mr. Kellerman he didn't think it was very sporting of us to print what he said while he was unconscious."

"Well—I'll be damned!"

"So will Doctor Cummings," drawled Dinny, "for he told me he would. And, as for that—" He hesitated, grinning.

"So will you, I presume," assisted Mr. Brophy.

"*The Cincinnati Democrat* was there, taking pictures, when I left."

"Well," said Mr. Brophy, "it's your affair. Carry on with it. This is going to call for a lot of expert lying, so I'll let you manage the campaign. I've been in the newspaper game for twenty years, my boy, and you're the biggest liar I have ever known."

"Thank you, sir," said Dinny. "D'you think maybe I'd better go out there again?"

"Yes," replied Mr. Brophy. "I think maybe you had; and if old Andrews weakens and tells the truth, you needn't ever come back."

Timmy Fagan had silently joined the party, obviously enjoying himself.

"Timmy," said Mr. Brophy, "I'm going over to headquarters for a chat with Chief O'Brien. I'll be back in half an hour."

"Yes, sir," said Timmy, "but it's all right, Mr. Brophy. I was over there at noon, and he's called 'em off the case. He sent you this long, black cheroot, sir, and said to tell you those greasy Republicans on *The Eagle* could whistle for any more dope on the Andrews shootin'."

"You editing *The Star* now, Timmy?" asked Mr. Brophy, lighting the gift, dubiously.

"Well, sir"—Timmy lowered his voice, confidentially—"we couldn't let th' boy down, sir, seeing it was his first offence. I told the chief he was a fine lad, and I'd seen him at Mass, last Sunday."

"Nonsense, Timmy. Brumm's not a Catholic."

Timmy smiled, omnisciently, and turned toward his stone table. "My Kitty's attendin' t' that, sir."

* * * * *

Dinny Brumm's freshmanhood at Magnolia which, at the outset, had threatened to be drab and uneventful, was not altogether unsatisfactory.

Startled, after five days, by the realization that he was likely to become a lone wolf on a campus where everyone else had entered into budding friendships—his nightly employment, and his boarding at a restaurant in town having made it quite impossible for him to be sociable—Dinny resolved to mend matters by spending an hour, late afternoons, on the athletic field. He could at least relieve himself of the just accusation that he wanted no friends and preferred to go it alone.

At three o'clock on Wednesday, therefore, he had presented himself at the freshman wing of the "training quarters" in the inadequate old gymnasium, where, without asking any questions or announcing his purpose, he was gleefully welcomed by young Assistant Coach Roberts and the awkward assembly of prospective gridiron heroes, the tallest of whom he overtowered.

His whole time having been occupied by other more important matters, Dinny had never taken any active interest in high-school football, but from the first moment of his adventure with the pigskin he seemed to have an instinctive feel for the game.

What came later to be referred to by sports writers as his "reckless courage", was in evidence that first day, possibly attributable to the fact that the savagery of hard tackling, on the open field, appealed to his mood. The utter futility of life had laid so low an estimate on the claims of personal safety that Dinny was indifferent to bruises or the hazard of broken bones.

When, at five, two teams were lined up by Coach Roberts, Dinny observed that the personnel of the combating squads could easily be identified even in their muddy, handed-down toggery. As usual, the real people were on one side, giving battle to the people who didn't matter much. The real people had naturally gravitated, some chemical affinity pulling them together. He found himself playing right tackle on the team that didn't matter much. The Pullman cars were to recognize the Day Coaches to the extent of assisting them for experimental purposes—to try out their own strength, speed, and skill.

There was quite an accumulation of sentiment in Dinny's mind on that subject, and in the ensuing thirty minutes of play he expressed it so convincingly that, toward the end of the game—which attracted a vociferous crowd of spectators who found the battle of the "frosh" more exciting than the experienced manœuvres of the varsity on the adjoining gridiron—there seemed to be a unanimity of consent, on the part of the opposition, when Dinny took the ball, that he might go down the field with it, undetained.

Perspiring, and secretly exultant, Dinny divested himself of the tight-fitting old mole-skins that reeked with the acrid memories of many celebrated engagements, his team-mates and foes respectfully assisting. As he left the gymnasium, he found himself walking alongside Barney Vaughn, against whom he had played in the line. Barney was friendly, inquisitive. Where had Brumm been keeping himself?

"You must drop in and see me," said Barney. "I'm at the Custer Cottage, Sunnyside Avenue. That's where the Sig pledges live, you know."

"No—I didn't know where they lived," said Dinny. "I don't even know what 'Sig pledges' are," he added. "Red-headed ones, maybe?"

Barney ran his fingers through his untidy mop of burnished bronze, and laughed. Then he was serious.

"I'll bet somebody's been getting your goat, Brumm. You played like it. My Uncle! but you were a brute. Look at that elbow o' mine, will you?"

They overtook a couple of seniors, strolling back toward the campus—seniors of the Pullman car variety.

"Yeah," one was drawling, "the barbs were running circles around 'em. Who is this Brumm fellow, anyway? How come we heard nothing about him? Hell of a scouting committee we've got, this year."

"That's what comes of letting the Sophs attend to it," replied the other. "We'd better have Bristol look this bruiser up, and tow him into camp."

Barney winked, companionably, at Dinny, as they passed the self-assured strollers.

"Stock going up, eh?" chaffed Barney out of the side of his mouth. "Couple o' my brethren, those ginks."

"Why didn't you speak to them?"

"Frosh aren't supposed to: you knew that, didn't you?"

"Democratic little school, isn't it?"

At the foot of the slope, their ways separated. Barney urgently renewed his invitation. Dinny evasively mumbled excuses: no time to visit, nose to the grindstone. Thanks, all the same, old man. See you tomorrow.

* * * * *

On Friday morning, as Dinny entered the rapidly filling classroom of Professor Grover, and looked about for a vacant chair, the long arm and beckoning fingers of Barney Vaughn summoned him to a seat in the back row, where he was received with friendly smiles. He realized at a glance that he was in a Pullman car.

Professor Grover, who did not have to eat a whole egg to determine whether it was bad—a quip he often repeated without bothering to enclose it in inverted commas—reported that the papers submitted on Tuesday were, in the main, satisfactory. They would be returned, with notations, to their makers, at the close of the hour. (On the back of the last page of his essay, in red ink, Dinny read, later, "well conceived, meritorious for perspicacity, clarity, and force.")

However, pursued Professor Grover, deliberately, it was not to be supposed that all the papers were of equal value; and, for the benefit of those who hadn't quite caught the idea, he would ask that one of the more excellent themes be read at this time.

Experience had taught him—Professor Grover pulled a benevolent smile—that it was usually embarrassing to the author when called upon to read his own piece aloud to the class. He would therefore request—he adjusted his glasses and glanced down at the unfamiliar roster—he would therefore request Miss—er—Adams to read the paper he had chosen as among the best.

A bit flustered, Miss Adams detached herself from her immediate environment, rather self-consciously approached the sanctum with much nervous jingling of bracelets, bangles, and other light hardware, faced her audience rosily, and began to intore her unknown classmate's anthem of praise to Magnolia in a dulcet tone so cooingly mellifluous that covert grins were exchanged among the more sophisticated.

Barney Vaughn leaned toward Dinny, pressed the back of his hand against the side of his mouth, and whispered, unctuously, "Gawd is love."

Dinny grinned, feebly.

The tender passion of the impromptu score which Miss Adams was fervently attaching to the sticky sweetness of the libretto produced a strange effect upon the class. By the time she had turned the first page, the dullest dolt in the room had his open palm against his mouth, apparently engaged in a battle for air.

Professor Grover smiled, hopefully, as if promising that it would eventually come out all right, and moved slowly back and forth in his chair, his outspread hands rhythmically rubbing his knees. It was easy to see, however, that he was worried. He had only read into this piously grateful tribute to the college far enough to see that it was definitely committed to a loyalty of high degree. He hadn't noticed, at the moment, that it was quite so superlatively silly as it now appeared, set to the sloppily sentimental adagio affected by Miss Adams, whose mark for the semester's work in English Composition he had now determined upon in terms of three flats.

Dinny's flair for satire was not an achievement, but a gift. He had not deliberately planned the early pages of his impressions of Magnolia with a view to disarming the reader in order, later, to smite him with a volley of ridicule.

About midway of page four, it became evident in the mounting flush and occasional hesitations of Miss Adams that even she, herself, infatuated as she was with her elocution, had begun to suspect the increasing digression of the text from the melody, and realized the enormity of the farce to which she was unwittingly contributing the ultimate touch that gave it perfection.

She was reading now the early impressions of the freshman as he watched the masterful manner in which the rubber stamp was affixed to impressive documents, the stony stare of experienced officials which heightened the newcomer's respect for a college of such magnitude that its most insignificant underlings felt the dignity and superiority of their honoured trust, the crispness of their laconic "Next window, please, for that."

Barney inclined toward Dinny, at this juncture, and guardedly whispered, eyes intent upon the reader, "Somebody's been pulling the old man's leg," to which the awe-stricken Dinny added, absently, "The paralysed one."

They were hearing now about the democracy of a friendly little college, the one place in the world where social caste was regarded with the scorn it properly deserved in the opinion of all people to whom the Almighty had vouchsafed even the bare elements of humour.

Dinny sighed, rubbed his red cheek, and reflected that his essay was quite too long. The class must be frightfully tired of it by this time. He glanced at Professor Grover and imagined that the roving eye flashed him a baleful threat of hard times. Pulling himself together and affecting nonchalance, he turned cautiously to Barney and remarked, lips barely moving:

"The old boy should have eaten one more spoonful of this egg before he served it."

Barney thoughtfully dug deep in a trouser pocket and came up with a penny.

"This says you laid it," gambled Barney.

"Vulgar display," whispered Dinny, loftily.

Professor Grover was fussily rummaging through the pile of papers.

"Just a moment, Miss—er—Adams," he broke in, huskily.

Miss—er—Adams lowered the paper and looked up for further orders.

"I think we have heard enough of this essay, now, to gather what must have been in the mind of the writer. It seemed only fair that any slight irritation or disappointment should be recognized. Happily, such sentiments are held by a very small minority. Magnolia does not assume responsibility for the irascibility of newcomers who expect immediate preferments.... We have here another paper written in a better temper, which I shall ask Mr. Bristol to kindly read.... Thank you, Miss—er—Adams."

"'To kindly read,'" observed Barney, "shows the old thing to be human, anyway."

Dinny wiped his brow, and nodded with the pensiveness of a convalescent consenting to a proffered pill; then rallied enough to reply, wanly:

"This must be a rough day on the sea."

* * * * *

During the first two months of Dinny's residence in Magnolia, Kitty Fagan frequently had occasion to come to *The Star,* early evenings, with important messages for her father, the delivery of which would be but the work of a moment.

Not wishing to appear ungracious toward Timmy's lonesome young friend, she would wave a hand, fingers twinkling; and Dinny, resolutely blind to the amused interest of a score distracted from their gainful occupations in the composing-room, would meet her halfway to his case and amblingly accompany her to the door where they would pause and chat amiably for a moment. He always worked half an hour overtime, on his own hook, to make sure he had not visited with Kitty at the expense of the company.

By the middle of November, Kitty's emergency messages for her father had all been delivered, and *The Star,* suddenly bereft of these pleasant interludes scheduled to be played about eight-thirty, twice a week, became mildly curious.

Bert Snyder, on machine No. 1, observing Dinny emerging from the coat-room at ten, sharp, one night, dressed for the street, re-lit his corn-cob pipe, tossed a hot slug bearing the cryptic phrase "etaoin shrdlu" into the bubbling pot, and ventured his guess to Stub Harley, on No. 2, that Timmy had advised her not to come up any more. Stub thought it more likely that Mr. Brophy had set down on it. Pinky Gormer, assistant telegraph, hung a few smeary pages on each of their hooks, and bet there had been a quarrel.... But nobody knew and, after a little while, nobody cared.

On the fourth consecutive Sunday at the Fagans', Dinny realized that he was being gradually, unprotestingly assimilated. Noting that the living-room which gave directly on to the front porch was unoccupied, he did not rap on the screen-door, but opened it and made his way through to the kitchen.

"We heard you coming, Dinny," said Mrs. Fagan, too intent on the beautifully browned chicken she was taking from the oven to give him better attention than a fleeting smile. "I can't think what's come over that gate."

"Where's the oil-can?" inquired Dinny. "I'll touch it up."

"I know," said Kitty, putting down the bowl of whipping cream.

"Let him find it himself.... It's up on the sewing-machine, Dinny, in the back room." Mrs. Fagan vigorously beat the potatoes. "Don't look around in there. It hasn't been picked up."

Timmy met him halfway up the stairs, and said it was too warm for a coat.

Kitty's attitude became proprietary.

"Dinny doesn't want that much sugar in his tea.... Dinny mustn't have another piece of pie, father. It's bad for his wind. If we're going to make the team, we'll have to go easy on the pie.... Dinny, we really must look after those poor fingers: that nasty acid. Can't they use something else on their dirty old type?"

On the fifth Sunday, Dinny met the four of them on the imposing front steps of Saint Vincent at eleven o'clock. It was his first experience in a Catholic church. He knew next to nothing about that institution, and suspected that what little he did know was untrue. Of course, he took no stock in his own family's estimate of it, aware that their passionate prejudice had been slowly percolated through a filter of ignorance and contempt—a musty old filter clogged with nearly four centuries of gritty deposits precipitated from neighbourhood brawls and border wars.

In the questionable judgment of Uncle Miles, whose proud boast it was that his feet had never crossed the threshold of "Rome," the Pope was "the Anti-Christ." Dinny had but a vague idea who "the Anti-Christ" was, beyond his natural deduction that it was a cryptic epithet never employed in eulogy. Aunt Martha maintained that practically all Catholic churches were secret arsenals, their subterranean grottoes stuffed with rifles and ammunition. She wagged her head ominously when she predicted the day of "a great uprisin' that'll make th' rivers run red." This was, on the face of it, mere drivel and nonsense. You could tell, because the rivers were to run red. Aunt Martha was always quite definitely off the rails when she talked in terms of red or any of the collateral hues. She always got excited, hysterical, and incoherent when she discoursed on Sin, which was scarlet, or Salvation, which was crimson.

As they mounted the church steps, pressed close on either side by pilgrims of all sorts, Dinny felt himself a member of the Fagan family. There was something tender and intimate in this new relationship. He would sit in the Fagan pew. He would belong to them, for an hour, in bonds of a common wistfulness. Not that he expected to get much out of it further than the satisfaction of sitting quietly with them. Doubtless he and Kitty would share a hymn-book. There would be a long, tiresome sermon, but they would not have to listen to it. Perhaps he would touch Kitty's fingers, when the clergyman inveighed against some sport or pleasure and they would steal a pious glance at each other, tongue in cheek.

The instant they entered the dim, vasty nave, Dinny found himself quite alone. His Fagans had vanished, their places taken by four strangers who suddenly went about the business of dipping finger-tips in the huge marble shell, touching themselves with an adroitness that could not possibly have been achieved through experience, but must be accounted for by some instinct which Dinny knew he did not possess.

The supple grace of their genuflections set them apart from him and all his kind. The only movement he had ever seen, comparable to it for artless dexterity, was the sweep of a lithe tiger's breast against the bars as it reached the end of its brief journey and turned to pad softly but determinedly to the other corner of the cage.

He followed these people, dressed like the Fagans, halfway down the broad aisle, where, pausing, they dipped again, not by conscious effort, but as if each of them had been gripped by some current flowing from the wood of the pew-end, so that when their fingers touched it, they responded—galvanically.

Kitty glanced sideways and offered him a fragment of a smile—a mere, transparently thin cross-section of a smile—as she slipped swiftly from the seat to her knees beside Pat and her parents. Dinny lumberingly joined her on the bare narrow rail on which they knelt, ashamed of his awkwardness. Adjusting his joints with much difficulty, he distributed his weight so that his elbows on the top of the pew might ease the discomfort of his knees. When all this had been attended to, he glanced down at the profile of the rapt face beside him. The smart little white hat with the blue ribbon looked very much like Kitty's hat. The firm, round, white chin was amazingly like Kitty's lovely chin. The steady fingers, gently moving from one bead to another on her rosary, resembled Kitty's competent fingers. But Kitty had escaped. This girl beside Dinny was a foreigner. Kitty and Pat and good old Timmy and hospitable Mrs. Fagan had left him forlorn, chagrined, and lonely on the beach while they, diving with the skill and precision of graceful seals, had whisked away into their Sea.

Kneeling thus on the hard pebbled beach of that mysterious Sea in which the Fagans were so confidently at home, the sublimity of it all began to lay hold on Dinny Brumm. He realized now that something inside him had been calling, faintly but urgently, all his life, demanding exercise, sustenance, liberty; something aquatic that couldn't walk on the hard ground.

They were back in their seats now, but the mesmeric spell did not lift. They rose, they sat, they bowed, they crossed themselves with sure, deft strokes, Dinny trying to keep pace with them in the rising, and sitting, and kneeling, feeling himself a mere stumbling baby trudging with short, drunken steps in the wake of experienced track-sprinters.

Now the congregation hummed briefly with swiftly flowing, unintelligible fragments of liquid sentences, sentences prodded out of it by stately challenges addressed to the great white and gold and flickering altar by an ornately garbed figure. The celebrant was attended by small boys in vestments, who needed no telling what to do, boys who anticipated each impending phase of the ancient drama, boys whose very backs seemed to disdain such childish fripperies as marbles, tops, and kites, having forsaken all that was secular to pledge their life to all that was sacred.

Presently it occurred to Dinny that these strangers whose pew he shared might be as well pleased with their guest if he made no further ridiculous attempts to imitate them in their worship. The next time they sat, he resolved to remain seated.

He looked about. It was the first occasion on which the Gothic had ever spoken to him directly. The Gothic beckoned him to attempt a spiritual journey.

Dinny's eyes rested on the beautiful window nearest him, a multi-coloured window crowded with brave events upheld and flanked by miniatures of enhaloed saints—enraptured saints bearing massive keys and open books, bearded saints leading submissive lions, beardless saints led by victorious lambs with a fore-foot sustaining a shouldered banner; crowns and crests, shields and swords, cups and censers, purple grapes and yellow wheat-sheaves, and hilltops tipped with spires.

His eyes travelled up until the window narrowed to a pointed arch that led the way to the base of a flying buttress. He gave himself willingly to its graceful curve, and followed along past innumerable sign-posts—all pointing up... Up... *Up!*—each arch, and tip, and spire daring him to leap to another... higher... Higher... *Higher!*—until visibility was lost in the shadows overhead.

Perhaps that was the way Religion really ought to be, thought Dinny. No wonder the Catholics had lasted so long without the necessity of change, reorganization, reappraisals. The old Church invited you to look up. That was all she asked. She made no promises that she could reveal the Ultimate. It was up to you... how far you could see. You looked up—and the Church carried you from one aspiring arch to another until you could go no farther, not because the arches ended, up there, but because your frail sight could no longer follow them into the Mystery whose depths they plumbed.

Meantime, the rhythmic tide of the venerable ritual came rolling, rumbling on in strong, confident waves—music out of a Past that was also a Future; music that took no account of infinitesimal weeks and months, but dealt with a thousand years as if it were only a day; music that never even glanced down to see whether you were following an ox-drawn plough or addressing parliament from a throne, much less noticed whether you rode in a Day Coach or a Pullman; spoken music, drifting from within the chancel, chanted music, drifting from the choir overhead.

For a period there was much made of a small jewelled case, set into the altar; hushed silences bounded by the silvery tinkle of a bell; deep, deep reverence between the silvery tinkle of the bell.

The sweetish-brownish aroma of incense hung in the air, invisible in the nave, though above the heads of the celebrants it drifted like a torn tapestry—a very old, brownish-grey tapestry. To Dinny's unaccustomed nostrils the elusive scent was an indissoluble combination of mingled appeals to the most spiritual of all the senses. He tried without success to analyse its weird effects upon his imagination. At first it seemed to possess a certain medicinal quality—faintly stimulative. No—it was not a stimulant, but an exultant, insisting upon the exultation produced by calm acceptance, confident repose.

There was something primitive about it, too; something woodsy, as if it exuded from the enshadowing trees beneath whose branches valiant men of old had knelt to worship—trees which the Gothic had preserved in stone.... Dinny wondered what strange magic the incense was conjuring in the trained, consecrated nostrils of the transported Fagans.

Aunt Martha had scorned the institution that tried to worship in a heathen language.

"Nothing but gibberish!" declared Aunt Martha, who knew only her mother tongue, and that imperfectly.

Dinny did not find it so. In the mounting radicalism of eighteen plus disillusionment, he was ready to do bumptious battle with any detailed invoice of "I believes," hawked in the language of the clearing-house and the market-place. But there was a sudden tightening of the throat, a burning of the eyelids, when the sonorous phrases came welling forth from the dimly lit chancel:

Et in Jesum Christum... Dominum nostrum... qui conceptus est de Spiritu sancto... natus ex Maria Virgine...

You didn't have to believe it: you just knew it was true.

His eyes groped into the vaulted roof. Up there, out there, beyond there—what? When you had it all explained for you in the patter of the machine-shop, the language of the garage, the department-store, the football field, you waved it away and muttered, "Stuff and nonsense!" It was a different matter when sung to you in an otherwise unused tongue, through an aromatic veil of incense:

carnis resurrectionem... vitam æternam!...

That was the glory, then, of this Catholic religion. It didn't ask to be understood, as Chemistry asks to be understood.

Perhaps that was the whole trouble with Uncle Miles's religion. It explained everything, succeeding only in making itself absurd. Its speculations were hard-and-fast facts to be weighed on the scales, poured into a test-tube, shaken over a flame.

Not much wonder, thought Dinny, this Catholicism had carried on.... Every so often, turbulent little sects had spewed themselves out through the heavy bronze doors of cathedrals to quarrel and dogmatize; obliged, when their fury was spent, to build cheap and ugly little imitations of the eternal thing from which they in their wilfulness had fled.

Every new generation of the self-outcast had revised the imitation. Never were they done tinkering with it, reconditioning it, modernizing it, making it over "to meet the new day." And—meantime—while their most progressive engineers dug deep under the thing to install new heating, climbed high on the thing to equip it with a tighter roof, repainted it, relandscaped it—The Everlasting Church stood fast!... *"sanctum Ecclesiam Catholicam!"*

That was the Sea!

All the time the inquisitive and heady were busily building their little dams, and draining their miasmic ponds, and changing the courses of their impotent, muddy, little creeks, the Sea had steadily throbbed to the tune of the stars without so much as a by-your-leave to any earthly powers. That Sea did not even pause to smile at the snarls and fist-shakings of the engineers. The Sea did not know they existed!... Dinny Brumm devoutly hoped he could learn to navigate that Sea. He went out of Saint Vincent's, into the October sunshine, tentatively committed to the great experiment.

"How did you like it?" asked Kitty, smiling a little, but wide-eyed with genuine concern.

"I really can't talk about it, Kitty," he murmured.

She grasped his arm for a moment, and patted his sleeve lightly.

"*'Dominus vobiscum,'* Dinny!" recited Kitty, gently, gratefully.

"What do I say now—anything?"
"You say, *'Et cum spiritu tuo,'* Dinny."
He repeated the words after her, adding, "dear."

* * * * *

That afternoon—a golden-russet, burnt-sienna afternoon—they climbed the high hill overlooking the city park. The southerly slope of the hill was a cemetery. It was a full quarter-mile to the nearest white stones; a half-mile to the broad granite arch of the old-worldish gateway flanked on either side with clumps of cypress trees.

Dinny was reflective, eyes moody, lips pursed, as he reclined on an elbow, Kitty sitting cross-legged beside him, endeavouring to punctuate the long silences with sprightly talk.
"Wise old owl," she pouted, "come out of your trance."
Their eyes turned toward the cemetery gate, far below. Some secret order in uniform was creeping along, led by a brass band, en route to bury a brother... Chopin's Funeral March... As the band passed under the broad stone arch and through the cypress trees, a whole half-dozen measures were completely obliterated. Kitty supplied the missing passage, keeping time with martial bobs of her bare black head, her pretty cheeks distended as if she blew the notes on the big, shining tuba that presently led the way out into the sun.
"Pumm, pum-te-pumm, pum-te-pum, te-pum, te-pum," pummed Kitty, soberly.
The cortège was marching out into the glow, now, but the dirge was still in the gloom, candidly hopeless of anything to come of this dignified enterprise further than the wretched anti-climax of ropes and shovels and the bouncing of clods on a box.
Dinny lay outstretched on his back, gazing straight up, listening to the wisps of the despairing march which Kitty continued to accompany, softly. Now it was quite stilled again for an instant, while the band rounded the other side of a massive cliff. Presently there swept up the hill a great wave of hope. "Nevertheless!" sang the dirge. *"Nevertheless*—I tell you!"
Kitty scrambled to her knees, facing Dinny, her eyes bright, dancing, her pretty teeth sparkling, keeping time with both hands, fingers outspread, chanting, happily:
"Tra-la—Tra-la—la-la-la- la—la—tra-la" ...
"You actually believe that; don't you?"
"That it's going to come out all right? Sure! Of course! Don't you?"
"I think I do... when... when it's said in Latin."
"I don't quite get you, Dinny."
"Well," he drawled, dreamily, "I think the belief in everlasting life is silly... but *'vitam æternam'* is sound."
"Funny boy!" laughed Kitty. "Old owl!"
Then he told her almost everything he had thought about, that morning in church. On the way down the hill, she promised to ask Father Donovan for some little books he might read, though Dinny was not sure he wanted them.
"I'm contented," he said. "Besides—I would have trouble reading them. Latin's tedious... in large quantities."
"Oh—but this will not be in Latin," explained Kitty.
"Maybe we'd better leave well enough alone," said Dinny, thoughtfully.

* * * * *

Two disquieting books came into Dinny's hands, within three hours of each other, on the next Thursday night.

The first was lent by Father Donovan and delivered into the hands of Dinny, at his case, by Kitty Fagan—a book he opened at one a.m., in his room, and perused for a scant five minutes. Then he closed it with a snap. He had read the English—the modern, workaday English, under the pitiless glare of electric light—the English explanation of The Mysteries.
Here was the "Profession of Faith" for converts:

"I., N. N., having before me the holy gospels, which I touch with my hand and knowing that no one can be saved without that faith which the Holy, Catholic, Apostolic Roman Church holds, believes, and teaches, against which I grieve that I have greatly erred—"

Dinny ran his eye down the page:

"I believe in one only God in three divine Persons, distinct from, and equal to, each other—that is to say, the Father, the Son, and the Holy Ghost."

How often he had heard Uncle Miles tangle himself up in the labyrinthian mazes of this incomprehensible "three in one" business—as if it mattered; as if anybody knew.

"I believe in the true, real and substantial presence of the Body and Blood, together with the Soul and Divinity, of our Lord Jesus Christ, in the most holy Sacrament of the Eucharist."

That's what the little jewelled case was about. The Lord Jesus Christ was in there. They took Him out, and then put Him back in again.... Uncle Miles had some queer ideas, too; but—

The rest of it Dinny merely glanced at.

"I believe in the seven Sacraments...

"I believe in Purgatory...

"I believe in the Primacy, not only of honour, but of jurisdiction, of the Roman Pontiff, successor of Saint Peter, Prince of the Apostles...

"I believe in the veneration of the Saints and of their images."

"And"—the book was closing now, and in an instant it would be shut with a sharp slap—"I believe in everything else that has been defined and declared by the sacred Canons and the General Councils, and particularly by the Council of Trent—"

Dinny didn't know what the "Council of Trent" was, but it was with the "Council of Trent" that his spiritual exploration terminated. It was seven years before he smelled incense again.

He undressed, and went to bed with the book Mr. Brophy had lent him at midnight. Mr. Brophy had asked him along to lunch, for on Thursday nights he always worked overtime, ads being heavy in the Friday morning edition of *The Star*.

They went to Clancy's, which closed at eleven, in accordance with the law, and remained open until one to accommodate the Fourth Estate, certain other discreet, and Sergeant O'Shane, who paused at Mr. Brophy's table to exchange the customary:

"Annything new, Misther Brophy?"

"More fighting in Ireland, Sergeant; that's all."

"And that's not news, Misther Brophy."

"Dinny," said Mr. Brophy, when Clancy, himself, had put down on the bare table a plate of Swiss cheese, rye bread, and two steins of beer, "did you ever read Hardy's *Jude the Obscure?*"

Dinny, his mouth full, shook his head.

"I'll lend it to you," said Mr. Brophy, taking the book from his pocket and pushing it across the table.

"Thanks," mumbled Dinny. "What's it about?"

Mr. Brophy made up a cheese sandwich, painstakingly.

"It's about a tremendously ambitious youngster who wanted a college education, so he could be somebody, and threw a wrench into the machine by marrying out of his class."

"And so he didn't get to be anybody?"

"He didn't even get a college education."

"Why do you want me to read it, Mr. Brophy?"

Mr. Brophy shrugged a shoulder.

"It will do you good to get acquainted with Thomas Hardy... vigorous style... sound workman."

In bed, now, with the book, Dinny became absorbed in the tribulations of Jude's boyhood—strikingly like his own, in spots. He read until four, lowered the book, stared for a long time at the wall, sighed deeply, and turned out the light. It had been a long day. Dinny had grown much older, since sunrise.

CHAPTER VIII

MAGNOLIA students, unable to return to their homes, were welcome to the seven o'clock dinner at the President's house on Christmas.

That no bones were made about the purely philanthropic nature of this affair was blandly certified by the technique of recruiting its guests. The bulletin boards, a few days in advance, announced that if these stranded would make themselves known to the Y.M. and Y.W. secretaries, they would receive personal invitations.

It was easily to be deduced, from the character of the agencies thus serving as a clearing-house for this social function, that its guest-list would consist largely if not wholly of barbs; for, almost without exception, the fraternity and sorority element had no truck with the Y.M. or Y.W. beyond the dollar perfunctorily disgorged during the early October campaign for their maintenance. The Greeks were not, as a rule, religious.

Tradition held that these Yuletide festivities, however praiseworthy in their altruistic intent, lacked brilliance. Indeed, when a seasoned Magnolian—whether Greek or barbarian—was hard pressed for a simile adequate to bound some experience of boredom *in extremis,* he was apt to liken it to the Braithwaites' Christmas Party, even if he had never attended one himself and might have added but little to its incandescence if he had. Dinny had missed the affair, a year ago, truthfully offering the excuse—though he could have invented one—that he was obliged to work at that hour.

Nothing was more remote from his intention than attendance at this year's Christmas conviviality in the big, square, dormer-windowed, brick house which dominated this end of Sunnyside Avenue, dignifiedly aloof from the long row of Greek chapter houses—for it was set in spacious grounds—but obviously mothering them and sharing with them the same Strozzi lamp-posts in the broad green parking, four to the block, on either side, as if the Old Lady, upon installing hers, had said they might as well provide similarly for the children.

But it now turned out that Dinny was to be one of the guests at the annual barbarian spread.

Encountering President Braithwaite, whom he sincerely admired, Dinny impulsively pledged himself to attend the feast. They had met in the almost deserted hall of the Administration Building on the morning of the twenty-second. The college session had closed.

"Not going home, Brumm?"

"No, sir; not this time, sir."

Dinny did not feel it necessary to add that he was done going home; never expected to go home again; had, in fact, no home to go to since the receipt of Angela's astounding letter, a month ago, easing her burdened soul of a confession that, while rummaging in her father's desk, she had discovered evidences of long-continued misappropriation of funds rightfully Dinny's—a defalcation in which Aunt Martha was a silent but culpable accomplice. Angela, deeply stirred in a revival staged by the celebrated "Buster" Brown and the incomparable song-leader, "Merry" Merriweather, had experienced "the third work"—an altitudinous degree of sanctification involving the wholesale confession of sins, venial and mortal, in which salutary enterprise she had, after a manner of speaking, spilled the beans.

"The money," wrote Angela, in an affected back-hand on reeking pink paper, "must have stopped coming about two years ago.

"I think my father must have begun to be scared, about that time. Your father probably wanted to arrange to send you to college, though I couldn't find that letter in the package.

"The only one on that was dated more than two years ago. It was written on a New York Central train. It said, 'If it is true my son has no inclination to go to college and has a good job and bitterly resents any further help from me, there is nothing more to do.'"

Savage with indignation, Dinny rapidly composed and destroyed a half-dozen letters—three to the rascally old Uncle Miles; two, slightly less ironical, to pious Aunt Martha; concluding with a real masterpiece of shocking sacrilege to the thrice-blest Angela. Having thus documented his sentiments in regard to the elementary decencies, and the mysterious ways of Providence in delegating the propagation of sweetness and light to ambassadors so nonchalant on the subject of common integrity, he screwed the cap back on his fountain-pen, and called it a day's work.

Presuming, correctly, that Angela's purgation demanded her having it out with Uncle Miles and Aunt Martha, Dinny thought he would wait until these unctuous defaulters had had time to concoct some ingenious explanation. But they, judging by their silence, were waiting for his offensive; so, communication was cut off. As Christmas neared, it occurred to him that, aside from the greeting cards he meant to mail to Mr. Brophy, old Peter Andrews, and the Fagans (whom he rarely visited now, Kitty having impatiently transferred her affections to young Mike Slattery, a handsome and promising department manager in the Crystal Laundry), he had no occasion for shopping. Dinny hoped Aunt Martha would not trouble herself to send him anything. But it would be quite like her to do so—a sappy book of preachments, perhaps, written, published, and peddled by the Reverend Bouncing Bilgewater, or some such moron.

"Then you will be coming to our Christmas dinner," said the President, genially.

"Oh, yes, sir," declared Dinny, with grateful enthusiasm. "Thank you very much, Doctor Braithwaite."

Almost from his first day, Dinny had found himself wondering how little Magnolia, so narrow and reactionary, had invited a man of President Braithwaite's broad sympathies and urbanity to direct her affairs. And how had Doctor Braithwaite ever persuaded himself to lead a cause so unpromising?

It was common knowledge on the campus—even the freshmen chattered it—that the President was in hot water, the conservatives furnishing the fuel. The President had been elected for his skill as a money-getter. But for that he would have been ousted long ago. But for that he would never have been called from the Financial Secretaryship of little Minton, in Wisconsin, a despairing toy college that he had rescued from the grave. Minton had called him to that job in the very nick of time to save him from a heresy trial at the instigation of his Conference. As a minister, he had been too modern, nobody but the young people following him.

"Everybody knows—" Orville Kling, still Dinny's dormitory neighbour, and now President of the Y., had come over, last week, to borrow a pot of mucilage; for, as Religious Editor of *The Blossom,* he was always out of paste. "Everybody knows," declaimed Kling, fresh from a meeting of his cabinet, in which Doctor Braithwaite had been put in the pan, "that he's an out-and-out higher critic!"

"Critic of what?" inquired Dinny, absently, intent on the trail of an irregular verb in his Greek lexicon, "Critic of *what?*" he repeated, "and higher than *who?*"

"You wait!—"

Disdaining the persiflage, Kling slowly closed one eye and tipped his head far back, hinting at inside information he dared not reveal.

"You just wait until Braithwaite has finished this two-year drive for the Half-Million Endowment Fund. The Board will give him his walking papers!"

"Not very sporting, I should say," observed Dinny.

Kling hooked a leg over the corner of Dinny's table, rested an elbow on his knee, and beat time to his oracle with an impressive forefinger.

"The conservation of Christian faith," he intoned, "is not a sporting proposition."

"I had noticed that," drawled Dinny, not very pleasantly.

"What I say is," continued Kling, warming, "if Braithwaite wants to make a dash for this so-called liberty of religious thought, let him do it—but not while he's on the pay-roll of an orthodox institution."

"Like Martin Luther, for instance?" queried Dinny.

"That's quite a different matter," growled Kling, pacing to the window and backing up defensively against the sill, "Luther, as it happened, was right!"

"But the conservatives didn't think so," amended Dinny, "or did they? I'm not very well posted on that."

"No—I don't suppose you are," muttered Kling, meaningly, "though you ought to be, considering your background."

Dinny impetuously pushed back his chair, and was on the point of offering a sarcastic discrimination between "background" and "back-fire," but thought better of it, and turned again to his lexicon.

Kling strode heatedly toward the door.

"Here," said Dinny, "you've forgotten the mucilage."

"Thanks," said Kling, stiffly, "I think I can find some."

"Sure you can find your scissors?" teased Dinny, grinning.

"I suppose you think that's witty, son." Kling had his hand on the knob.

"I think it's a scream, Brother Kling," retorted Dinny, *"all of it!*—the Board of Directors, Christian faith, home background, the Y.M.C.A., *The Blossom's* Religious Column, and—and the paste-pot and the scissors!—"

The door banged with a resounding wallop.

"—and you, too," finished Dinny, addressing the infuriated footsteps in the hall. "You're a scream, too!"

* * * * *

At three, still uncomfortable over his promise to attend the Christmas party, which was going to be dull with an exceeding great dullness, no matter how the Braithwaites might tear their hair to make it interesting, Dinny went skating in the park.

There was nothing he enjoyed so much. The day was perfect, air crisp, tonic, the sky turquoise, the sun bright.

He recognized no one on the pond, but it required no company to complete his satisfaction.

With long, lazy strokes, he traversed the quarter-mile longitudinal stretch of the steel-blue lagoon, delighting in the ease of a locomotion that always gave him the sensation of flying. There was a unique exhilaration in the ability to let oneself go; to lean back confidently on the promise of that strange centrifugal energy developed by "the outer edge roll"—a confidence more exacting, and better rewarded, than the faith of the floating swimmer.

He glanced without much interest at the indifferent skaters as he swept past them. Most of them were huddled in small parties, hacking away with short, stumbling steps, what time they were not clawing at each other for support, or spilling themselves, or shrieking hysterically over the misfortunes of their neighbours, or fussing with their straps. Magnolia was a bit too far south to breed able ice-skaters.

Presently Dinny sighted a tall girl, apparently alone, who knew what she was there for. My word!—what a competent young eagle she was! He wheeled, and followed her at a respectful distance.

She was slender, but beautifully formed; exquisite from the top of the brown fur toque that matched her curly hair to the flashing blades of the high-laced skating-boots which intriguingly disclosed attractive segments of gleaming silk between them and the short brown skirt. Her gauntleted hands—long, strong hands—were outspread at the tops of her hips as if they signalled the measured strokes like a coxswain. She clasped them behind her back, now, as if they had nothing whatever to do with it.

The girl had leisurely slowed down, at the end of the pond, finishing the lap with a series of incomparable "eights."

Observing that she was quite absorbed in her own affairs, Dinny did not linger to join the admiring circle that collected rapidly to view her skilful manœuvres, but drifted negligently away toward the farther end of the lagoon. Turning, there, he noticed with satisfaction that she had detached herself from her little theatre and was again on more extensive flights. He hoped she would come on. Pursuing a small orbit, in reverse, Dinny waited. His heart gave a hard bump as she swept closer. Her face was radiant with vitality—a patrician face, thought Dinny; a portrait face, finely modelled brows, sensitive nostrils, red lips curved like the bent bow of a medieval arbalest. Little curls peeped from under the fur toque, softening the lines of a gallant forehead.

She smiled, as one artist to another.

"Very good ice," she said, casually, in a tone that made Dinny think, if she sang—and surely she did—it would be contralto.

"You skate beautifully," said Dinny.

Her slightly raised brows and parted lips accepted the candid tribute.

"You should know," she replied.

"But you didn't learn it in Magnolia," Dinny hazarded, flushed a little by her bland compliment. He held out his hands, invitingly.

"Shall we?"

"Why not? I'd like to."

She had hardly consented before they were beginning to drift, crossed hands clasped, into a long, indolent roll that inclined their tall, lithe forms so far off balance none but the expert could have trusted to it.

Their wake was a double row of graceful fern-fronds, laid down almost end to end on the glassy lagoon. At first the fronds were twenty feet long and sixteen inches apart. Then they lengthened to thirty feet and narrowed to thirteen inches, for Dinny had drawn her closer, and she had instantly responded.

They moved as one body, their rhythm perfect. Sometimes the long twin fronds seemed pointing directly toward a mighty collision with a group of wobbly-ankled gigglers; but, without signalling each other by so much as a pressure of the fingers, the welded pair of ice-artists would bend the arc of the fronds and sail past with the grace of a yacht acknowledging the sudden puff of a capricious breeze. Preferring to sense to the full the ecstasy of reckless swallows, they had not attempted conversation, but their thoughts had been active.

It had required no deduction on Joan's part to identify her overtowering companion as a Magnolia athlete, for there was a huge pink *M* on his white sweater. Dinny was still in the dark, his curiosity mounting.

"What's the letter about?" she asked, when they idled to the first stop at the eastern end of the pond where they had met.

"Football—but this is a lot more fun, don't you think?"

"Yes," she laughed, "but I never played football.... You must live here—or you would have started home."

"No," replied Dinny, "do you?"

"Yes.... Are you coming to our Christmas party?"

"I certainly am!" said Dinny, fervently. "Whose party?"

"I'm Joan Braithwaite."

"I should have known," said Dinny. "But you're always away. University of Wisconsin—isn't it?... I'm Ferdinand Brumm, Miss Braithwaite."

"Oh!" Joan's pretty mouth rounded in happy surprise. "So you're the lad that galloped the sixty yards with all Camford hanging on to you! I read about it.... You're 'Dinny'!"

"Thanks!... But it was only the last three or four yards that they all got on.... Like to do it some more?"

"How many of them were there—actually?" laughed Joan, taking his proffered hands.

"I believe they had eleven on their team, that day," said Dinny, thoughtfully. "It may have been a few more. Camford is frightfully unscrupulous, you know."

They chatted, amiably.

Yes—she loved Wisconsin, but her father was insisting on her coming to Magnolia, next year. Dinny expressed his sincere regrets.

"I mean, of course," he amended, "I'm sorry for *you,* having to leave your friends... and Magnolia will be quite a change, you know.... Not much doing here."

"Oh, I won't mind—much," said Joan; adding, after a considerable pause, "The Gammas gave a nice party for me, last night—that's my sorority, you know.... By the way—where were *you?*"

"I'm a barb," drawled Dinny.

"Oh... I didn't know.... Pardon me, won't you?" She endeavoured to cover her confusion with a contrite little laugh as she added, "I didn't know the—the non-fraternity men called *themselves* 'barbs.'... I thought they quite bitterly resented the word."

"Why should they?" asked Dinny, dryly. "We know that when the fraternity men call us 'barbs,' it's just a bit of friendly chaffing—same as when we call them 'Greeks.' We haven't the courage and vitality to be barbarians, and they don't know any Greek. Why—if their badges weren't of different shapes and colours, they'd never know when they met a brother."

"Frightfully satirical, aren't you?" Joan's tone was crisp.

"It's the best thing I do," boasted Dinny, in mock seriousness. "I've been commended for it by Professor Grover, a couple of times. In fact, he gave me $E,$ last semester, in Creative Composition. E stands for Excellent, doesn't it?"

"Oh, yes," consented Joan, "and it stands for some other things—when it's grading satire and sarcasm."

The twin fronds on the ice behind them widened a little.

"What—for instance?" Dinny wanted to know.

"No matter," said Joan, idly. "Forget it."

"But I quite insist. You had something you wanted to say."

"I'm afraid it isn't very polite," ventured Joan, "but doesn't E stand for Enraged—and Embattled—and Embarrassed— and—"

"And—what?—"

"Envious."

"You're quite frank," said Dinny, after an instant of recovery.

"Well—you would have it, you know.... I told you I didn't like irony."

"But—you like humour, don't you?... and if there's anything funnier than a bunch of college students taking on airs because they're 'Greeks,' I'm sure I don't know what it is. You'd think they would tumble all over themselves getting into old man Appleton's classes. We barbs have Homer all to ourselves. Oddly enough, old Appleton is a barb, himself!"

Joan disengaged her hands, a little before they reached the end of the pond. Her face showed disappointment.

"Does it make you happy," she asked, soberly looking him straight in the eyes—"to be... that way?"

"I've had very little occasion to be happy," parried Dinny.

"You mean here?... at Magnolia?"

"I mean everywhere... and always," said Dinny, suddenly sincere. "If I were to tell you—"

"Do you want to?" Joan's tone deepened, and her dark brown eyes searched his rugged face.

"No," he answered, brusquely, adding, suddenly contrite, "Thank you—all the same. I think I'd—I wouldn't mind telling you—if it weren't such a dull story."

They simultaneously felt that their little visit was over. Joan glanced at her wristwatch. Dinny squinted at the declining sun.

She reached out her hand.

"I'll be seeing you, then, on Christmas?" she said.

Dinny felt very lonely as she glided away. She was the most superb creature he had ever seen.

* * * * *

President and Mrs. Braithwaite were warmly effusive as they welcomed him in the wide doorway of their spacious parlour.

Joan was standing a little to one side, within the room, talking animatedly with Barney Vaughn, who seemed in unusually high spirits. Dinny had forgotten that Barney, who had passed a dozen universities en route from Phœnix, Arizona, to Magnolia—to the never-flagging curiosity of all, unaware that his father was a Magnolian—might be a guest tonight.

He had not talked with Barney since last May. They had briefly informed each other about the weather, when they happened to pass on the street, unless they sighted each other early enough for one of them to cross over and avoid even this laconic exchange of cool civilities.

The constraint that stiffened their previously close friendship dated from Dinny's refusal to become a Sig.

The Sigs had not bidden him promptly. Within a week after his first appearance on the athletic field, the Delts had spent two hours with him, reciting the honoured names of alumni (none of them Magnolians, as it happened) who had gone forth to hold aloft the good old banner, and the Pies had offered to share their refined salt, but he had politely declined. Barney had urged him to wait.

The Sigs were a good while getting around to it. His work at *The Star* kept him occupied, and made it difficult for him to be sociable. The preliminary overtures of the Sigs were made somewhat listless by the fact, which developed in casual conversation when Barney had him in as his luncheon guest, that he would be unable to conform to many of their regulations for the disciplining of "the frosh." The Custer Cottage was already crowded to capacity with their pledges.

The bid was not issued until early December, Dinny learning, later, through an outburst of confidence on the part of Barney, who had had it from Curly Sprague, a soph, that Spike Davis had held out for some time, threatening to blackball Dinny, if it came to a vote. Spike had been talked into consent on the night after the Thanksgiving game with Camford in which, as fullback, he had kicked the goal that tied the score and rent the sky. He was feeling very much at peace with all mankind, and a bit drunk; so he waived his objections, and agreed to Dinny's election.

196

Dinny was unsure whether he wanted to accept the belated invitation. He confided his dilemma to Mr. Brophy, one night.

"You'd better, I think," counselled Mr. Brophy. "Otherwise you're rated a barb, and that will be awkward for you, not only while you're in college, but—always."

So—Dinny had accepted the little button symbolic of the tardy honour the Sigs conferred, and merged into the pack, to his considerable inconvenience, for the new relationship levied irksome requirements. He bolted his six-thirty dinner at "th' House," dashed for a street-car, and arrived at *The Star* usually ten minutes late, requiring double-measure overtime at his own expense. He never had time to eat a dessert, except on Saturday.

The fraternities initiated their freshmen during the first week of June. The Sigs did not initiate Dinny.

Each candidate, according to custom, was assigned a special test of his nerve, or an earnest of his eagerness to become a Greek. Barney was to stand in front of The Palace Theatre, one night, from eight to eight-thirty, with a hand-organ and a monkey—a salutary lesson in humility, though he had been cuffed about almost enough to have cured him of any uppishness. Chuck Rawlins was to present, on the occasion of his initiation, a live sparrow, the Sigs offering no suggestions for its capture, but insisting that his approach to the classic shrine, minus a live sparrow, would be undesired. Porky Bennet was to attend the Pan-Sorority tea, that afternoon, as Carmen, the Sigs volunteering to furnish the tambourine from their property closet.

Spike Davis was chairman of the committee on initiation. Most of the stunts had required no imagination on his part, having been bequeathed, through many generations of Hellenic forbears.

Dinny's special assignment had cost Spike several contemplative hours. Cocky young Brumm had taken his honours too lightly; had dodged too many disciplines on the ground of his employment in town. Furthermore—though this factor Spike would have denied with fists and fangs—Dinny had played exceptionally good football at fullback on the frosh team. The local sports writers had made no riddle of their belief and hope that next autumn, when he was eligible, he would add lustre to the varsity. Even Woods, reviewing the season in *The Cincinnati Times-Telegram* (recently popularized and circulation-boosted through its absorption by The Craig Syndicate), had remarked, of next year's prospects, "Magnolia has an excellent chance at the Conference pennant, what with her strong line, and the long-legged Dinny Brumm, who will have reached the age of responsibility."

All these things being as they were, Spike had something unique for Dinny to do as proof that he was worthy to wear a Sig pin.

"What's eatin' you, Spike?"... "You can't have him do that!"... "Snap out of it, old son. That's much too thick." Thus did the seniors try to talk him out of it. But Spike held his ground. It was his show, wasn't it? He was running this affair, wasn't he? Brumm had it all coming to him, didn't he?

Dinny was to carry a football under his arm, to all his classes, for a week. It was to be the one monumental pigskin on which Jim Faucett, the frosh captain, had vaingloriously inked the scores of their games with other classes—most of which triumphs had been freely conceded to Dinny's fleetness and ruthlessness at fullback.

"I can't do that, Spike." Dinny shook his head, determinedly.

"Very well," said Spike, loftily. "That's that, then! If you want to be a Sig, you know what you've got to do. Think it over."

Barney Vaughn came to Dinny's room, that afternoon, troubled.

"Dinny—you've got to, you know," pleaded Barney. "They've talked to him, but he won't budge."

Dinny sat toying with a paper-knife, his brows knitted in a brown study.

"He told me to find you." Barney's voice trembled a little. "And come back with an immediate reply."

Dinny rose, presently, tossed the paper-knife on the desk with a clatter, thrust his hands deep into his trouser pockets.

"No, Barney; there isn't anybody at Magnolia who can give me such an order—and if there was anybody who could, it wouldn't be Spike Davis."

"But—" Barney was half-frantic. "What am I to do?... What shall I tell him?"

Dinny took the little button from his lapel, laid it in Barney's hand, and said, slowly, but without heat:

"You can give this to Spike, with my compliments, and tell him to go to hell."

"Do you realize, Dinny, what this is going to do to our friendship—no matter how I feel about it, personally?"

"I'm afraid I do," muttered Dinny. "That's the worst part of it, of course."

"Want to sleep over it?"

"No—that's final. I shan't change my mind."

"Awfully sorry, Dinny.... Good-bye."

* * * * *

Mrs. Braithwaite, buxom, black-gowned, maternal, proceeded to adopt Dinny, who had been the last to arrive, engaging him in a conversation which she endeavoured to pivot around himself, somewhat to his anxiety, for any discussion of his home and his people was distasteful.

Joan and Barney had moved away, joining the group clustered about Miss Gresley, whose parents were missionaries in India. She would rejoin them, after her graduation in June. Miss Gresley was always an object of interest, frequently appearing at missionary teas and church affairs in Hindu costume which became her more than the clothes she wore now.

Dinny wanted very much to speak to Joan; hoped she would presently welcome him. But dinner was announced at that moment. Tall, genial, handsome Doctor Braithwaite excused himself to find Miss Gresley, who, as the farthest away from home, was clearly eligible to sit at her host's right hand.

"I am going to take you with me, Mr. Brumm," said Mrs. Braithwaite. Dinny offered his arm.

It was not until they were all standing with their hands on the tops of their chairs, waiting for whatever of ceremony was in order, that Dinny noticed the position of Joan at the right of Barney, who sat next to Miss Gresley. Their eyes met, briefly, and Joan accorded him a little nod of recognition.

The President suggested that they sing a verse of "Holy Night," after which they sat, fully three fourths of the score of shy guests immediately and concertedly helping themselves to a nervous sip of water, as if to say that they knew what *that* was for, anyway, whatever baffling dishes might challenge their social experience later.

"You met our Joan, didn't you, Mr. Brumm?" Mrs. Braithwaite had dipped a spoon into her fruit cocktail. "She told me. So nice you could skate together. She quite enjoyed it. See—she's looking this way now—"

Dinny glanced in Joan's direction, not quite sure whether the smile was for him or her mother. Barney, at the moment, was speaking to Miss Gresley.

"Of course you know Mr. Vaughn. You are classmates, aren't you? Joan met him, last night, at the Gammas' reception. I'm so anxious for Joan to make some good friends, for she's coming to Magnolia, next year. Her sorority sisters were so kind to her, last night."

"Yes—they would be, I should think," assented Dinny, hopeful that the conversation might soon veer away from the reception. Apparently it occurred to his hostess, at that moment, that Hellenic activities might not be of interest to him.

"The Y.M. and Y.W. have just lovely parties, too," she said, "don't you think?"

"So I'm told," replied Dinny, in a tone that evinced about as much personal knowledge as if she had remarked on the exceptionally large pineapple crop grown last season on the Island of Oahu.

"You're a naughty boy," chided Mrs. Braithwaite, smiling. "I don't believe you go to them, at all, and they're really very pleasant affairs."

"I work nights, Mrs. Braithwaite," explained Dinny; and, when she had inquired for particulars, he told her, their conversation broken, now and then, by her brief exchange of talk with Orville Kling—though he was mostly occupied with Miss Naylor, the Y.W. secretary—and Dinny's futile efforts to find some mutual interest with sallow, little Miss Upton. His eyes roved about the table, and when he reached Joan, they exchanged a steady look of inquiry, as if she still asked, "Does it make you happy—to be—that way?"... and as if he countered, "Why should you care?"

"But you have almost no social life at all, Mr. Brumm," lamented Mrs. Braithwaite. "What a pity you are tied up to such an exacting schedule."

"It's no great matter, Mrs. Braithwaite." Dinny lightly dismissed the dilemma with a slight shrug. "I rather enjoy my work on *The Star*. And—as for society—well, I'm not eligible to it, you see. As a matter of fact"—he lowered his voice, confidentially—"I came into this town in a day coach."

Mrs. Braithwaite laughed a little, glanced about the table, fleetingly, and replied, "But so did most of us, I fancy."

"I dare say," agreed Dinny; adding, "You understand." Again his eyes wandered toward Joan, who met him with a level gaze that continued to ask, "Does it make you happy?—"

"I do understand," said Mrs. Braithwaite, as if they were done with riddles, "and I'm sorry, and something ought to be done about it—but I'm sure I don't know what."

After dinner, Kling announced—bouncing up and down on his experienced toes—that, at the request of the President, they would sing a few songs. Miss Noble, invited to the grand piano, carefully put her handkerchief down on the ledge of the key-board, and accompanied "On, Magnolia," to Kling's encouraging direction, all joining with loyal enthusiasm. Then they sang "America," with unusual heartiness, for patriotism was in the air, and "God Save the King," as a second verse, for the "neutrality" of early autumn had been buried under the falling leaves and the snow. Kling suggested "The Marseillaise," which they hummed, uncertainly, no one knowing the words very well.

Dinny was not quite sure which wing of the party he belonged to, after the dinner. Mrs. Braithwaite had signed him to remain by her, just a little to his discomfiture, for perhaps she was making an effort to pay him special attention, in atonement for the indifference of her sort toward the social redemption of day-coachers. But Dinny felt remote. On the other side of her, the President, Joan, and Barney represented the kindly condescending element that viewed the party as finely bred settlement workers look on at the games promoted for the uplift of slum brats.

In all fairness, Dinny reflected that he was super-sensitive on this subject; told himself that what appeared to be conscious superiority on their part was nothing but an acknowledged inferiority of his own. But the situation was awkward, and he wished himself well out of it. He felt like an overgrown child, sitting with adults, at a children's party.

Kling, who appeared to be the spokesman for the guests, ventured upon a little speech of gratitude on behalf of them all. Pleased with the success of his remarks, he pulled out the tremolo stop, and, gradually increasing the tempo of his teetering up and down, jambed his stubby hands deeply into his coat pockets, achieving the posture and meter that presaged an early outburst of emotion.... Of course, none of us was forgetting, in the midst of our Christmas gaiety, the bereavement and suffering of our hard-pressed neighbours beyond the sea, waging valiant warfare to protect civilization against the ruthless selfishness of The Hun.... Kling was roundly applauded.

"Terrible—isn't it?" Mrs. Braithwaite turned to Dinny, her brows knitted in painful reflection.

"You mean the war?"

"You're a bad boy," said Mrs. Braithwaite, reproachfully.

Kling now suggested that they have a few words from the President, and sat down, smiling expectantly.

Doctor Braithwaite rose, rather soberly, thanked them for coming, invited them to drop in when they liked, through the lonely vacation days.... It was true, as Mr. Kling had indicated, that our happiness should be tempered with sympathy for the millions defending themselves in an unnecessary war. We would be justified in extending sympathy, also, to the millions who, through no fault of their own, were being pushed into a conflict, as aggressors, for which they had no personal inclination.

"The thing we want to avoid—or postpone as long as possible—is the attitude of hatred toward the Germans," went on Doctor Braithwaite, deeply earnest. "Germany has contributed too much to the enlightenment and beautification of the world to be dismissed, lightly, as an enemy of civilization.... These lurid tales of atrocities may, or may not, be true. I, for one, do not believe them!"

Dinny pounded his hands, the others tardily and rather doubtfully joining in the applause for politeness' sake.

"I see you agree with Doctor Braithwaite—about the war," said his hostess, upon the conclusion of the President's brief address. "It's not the popular thing, I'm afraid."

"I'd agree with Doctor Braithwaite—no matter what he said!" declared Dinny, fervently. "He's always right—and I know he's right about this."

"Thank you, Dinny!" she said, softly, adding, "You won't mind if I call you 'Dinny'?... I'm afraid Mr. Braithwaite will find only a minority willing to share his views."

"He doesn't need to care—a man like him!" declared Dinny, with assurance.

Mrs. Braithwaite shook her head, uneasily.

"People are growing more and more militant," she said.

The party was breaking up, now. The Braithwaites attended to their duties as hosts. Joan was shaking hands with the girls, as they filed out and up the stairs to recover their coats. Barney had escaped. He and Dinny had not exchanged a dozen words.

"Going up the hill?" inquired Kling, breezily, still under the influence of his success as an impromptu speaker.

Dinny assented, without enthusiasm.

Joan moved toward him, her eyes troubled. Overriding the antagonism that had developed between them there was a curious intimacy in their attitude as he bent to listen to her swiftly spoken confidence. It was as if they had known and trusted each other for years.

"Don't say or do anything to encourage my father in his—his attempt at suicide!" pleaded Joan. "He's dead wrong, and he's going to get into trouble! Don't lead any more applause that might make him think he has backing. Please!"

"How do you know he's wrong?" Dinny's grey-green eyes challenged her brown eyes with a steady look.

"Indiscreet, then," she compromised, impatiently. "My father—" Joan lowered her voice almost to a whisper. "My father has quite enough problems on his hands, just now, without incurring any more. You like him, don't you?"

"More than any man I ever met!" said Dinny, with fervour.

"Well—so do I," murmured Joan, "and I'm not going to let him ruin himself if I can help it."

Dinny offered his hand.

"Good-night—Miss Braithwaite.... Sorry my little gesture of loyalty to your father has distressed you."

Joan's brown eyes fired, angrily.

"I don't like sarcasm," she muttered, "and I think you're perfectly hateful, Dinny Brumm!"

Dinny's hand was still extended. She seemed determined to ignore it. Her hot eyes winked rapidly as she faced the faint traces of a conciliatory smile—half-reproach, half-indulgence—on Dinny's lips.

Impetuously, she took his hand, for a fleeting instant, and turned away.

* * * * *

"What did I tell you?" exhorted Kling, as they trudged up the slope toward the dormitory. "The man's positively dangerous! You'll find"—Kling measured his syllables with a didactic hand—"that when a man's religious faith breaks down, it isn't long until his patriotism isn't much good, either!"

"Looks like it's going to snow again," observed Dinny, with exasperating unconcern.

"And *you* want to be careful, too, young fellow," warned Kling, ominously.

"Meaning *what?*" growled Dinny, dangerously, with a savage clutch at Kling's sleeve that flung him almost off his feet.

Amazed at this unexpected onslaught, Kling was speechless for a moment, and then said, nervously, "I'm not going to fight you, Dinny, if that's what you want."

"Oh—so you are a pacifist, after all," taunted Dinny. "Well—you needn't fight, this time, if the idea of it alarms you, or violates your convictions; but"—he clutched Kling's overcoat collar in the strong grip of his long fingers—"if I ever hear of you dishing out any more of your damned impudence about Doctor Braithwaite—ever again—in public or private—I'll beat hell out of you, whether you defend yourself or not! Have you got that, now, so you can remember it?"

He left Kling standing there on the path.

Without turning, he proceeded on up the hill, climbed to his room, slammed the door, disrobed, and wrote two letters, the second addressed to the Reverend Miles Brumm.

Dear   Sir:

I have instructed the Speedway Moving and Storage Company of Indianapolis to call at your address for a small walnut desk of mine, formerly the property of my mother.

You will be good enough to let the moving people have the desk for immediate shipment to me, at my expense.

This, I think, will terminate our business and other relationships.

Any fear you may entertain relative to the possibility of an effort on my part to recover the money you stole from me, can be safely dismissed.

In view of the fact that my contempt for Mr. Alexander Craig is all of a piece with my contempt for you, I would not press the claim.

No reply to this letter is expected or desired.

Yours   truly,
FERDINAND BRUMM

CHAPTER IX

MAGNOLIA COLLEGE was considered good copy during the academic year of 1915-16.

It was a period when any recognition on the front page, crowded with heavy artillery, marine disasters, massacres of millions, and the multisonous clangor of a world on fire, required more racket than small church schools were accustomed to add to the cosmic din.

Even the Associated Press, sated with sensation, conceded, at the close of her second semester, that Magnolia—for sixty-three placid years an earnest little violet, staking her last shy petal on the nobility of diffidence—had done her bit in leaded black-face.

In the autumn, Magnolia spectacularly won nine smashing victories on the gridiron with scores that dizzied her competitors, no one of whom got within ten yards of her goal-line. Egged on by sports writers, she tentatively booked an exhibition game with Harvard to be played the next September, an engagement which was cancelled in the spring, Harvard having lost interest, Magnolia having lost Dinny Brumm.

On New Year's Eve, the Recitation Hall burned to the ground, unquestionably the work of an incendiary, public opinion agreeing that some ardent "preparedness" fanatic had thus expressed his sentiments toward a college so spiritless as to permit an uncompromising pacifist to direct her destiny.

On March tenth, the most widely known member of the undergraduate body, whose long legs and reckless courage had been primarily responsible for Magnolia's brilliant achievements in football, was expelled for adorning the President of the college Y.M.C.A. with two black eyes and a split lip.

The prosecution, appealing to the increasingly popular cause of patriotism, made large capital of the fact that the plaintiff had come by his injuries as a result of an impassioned address in behalf of his country's injured pride. The defendant's spirit of disloyalty was further evidenced by the recent appearance of his article in *The Iconoclast,* a discordant organ of protest, in which the author had heaped contumely upon his Alma Mater, and shown a disposition to bite the hand that fed him.

The defence endeavoured to show that the attack on Mr. Kling's person was an honest, albeit over-enthusiastic, reprisal for certain damaging remarks made in reference to Doctor Braithwaite. It further ventured to prove, politely as the circumstances permitted, that the statements of Mr. Brumm in *The Iconoclast*—though admittedly phrased in the pardonable superlatives of rampant youth—were unfortunately true. The faculty jury, Professor Grover, chairman, was out only five minutes.

Had it been Kling who was being fired, the press might have passed over the matter with negligent observation. The expulsion of Dinny Brumm was quite another affair. *The Cincinnati Times-Telegram,* in particular, wanted to know all about it, and set forth Dinny's cause with so much unction that the Magnolia Board of Directors was deluged with letters and telegrams inquiring, in varying degrees of indignation, whether the college had lost her mind.

On March thirteenth, a student mass-meeting was held. The use of the college chapel—Magnolia's only adequate assembly hall—having been denied for this purpose, the auditorium of the City Building was secured. Unwittingly, the promoters of the event thus recruited not only the attendance of almost the entire student body (the Sigs refusing to participate), but augmented the audience by several hundreds of interested towns-people whose concern for Magnolia's welfare was largely based on her athletic activities.

Mightily cheered and heartened from the packed galleries, which included not only ardent football fans with nothing at stake beyond their own enjoyment, but anxious representatives of the Chamber of Commerce, the Better Business Association, and scores of influential resident alumni, the undergraduates, after an accelerating tempest of fervid oratory, voted as one man for the rescinding of the faculty's action and a prompt reinstatement of Dinny Brumm.

A few of the more audacious wanted a trailer affixed to the peremptory resolution, threatening a general strike in the event of refusal on the part of the faculty to conform to student opinion. This, however, was voted down, the Magnolians, as a whole, recovering their habitual prudence even in the tumult of revolution vociferously fanned by the town.

On March twentieth, after an all-night session of the faculty and the Board of Directors, Dinny Brumm was restored to his previous rating. A mild proviso was attached demanding that Mr. Brumm settle for Mr. Kling's personal repairs and the mending of sundry articles of furniture which had impeded the celebrated fullback in his task of chastising his neighbour—it having leaked out that Dinny had already made these reparations.

On March twenty-first, Dinny left Magnolia to accept the position offered him by wire from Mr. Steinberg, the Managing Editor of *The Cincinnati Times-Telegram.*

The Athletic Association, getting wind of Dinny's offer and acceptance, hastily organized plans to see him off with a procession led by the college band, but he had already gone when the committee rushed to his room to disclose the nature of the vindication they had arranged for him; was, in fact, sitting in Mr. Steinberg's office, listening to the latter's expectations of him, at the very moment when the committee was scouring Magnolia in quest of him.

The bone of contention having been thus providentially dragged from the arena, the Board of Directors again assembled to focus its attention upon the President and inquire diligently of itself whether, in view of all the controversy stirred by his pacifistic opinions, it might not be better to set him free to preach his unpopular gospel of non-resistance on his own hook, undetained by any further obligations to the college.

The Board split squarely in two on this issue, the objectors maintaining that a considerable number of important "prospects" whose contributions to the Endowment Fund would depend upon the retention of Doctor Braithwaite, were awaiting the outcome of this affair with a concern that might affect Magnolia to the tune of a hundred thousand dollars, or so.

Notwithstanding this meeting was conducted *in camera,* every member under pledge to give out no interviews, the discussion, the decision, and the underlying cause thereof, were good for a first-page column with a throw to three, next morning, in the public prints.

On May nineteenth, President Braithwaite delivered the address to the graduating class of the Theological Seminary, in which he lost the support of the well-to-do conservatives whose influence had previously fended off the attacks of the swashbucklers.

Later, at the funeral, it was remarked on all sides that Doctor Braithwaite was not quite himself while delivering this "unfortunate" speech. He should have been in bed; was running a temperature of 101°.

At the hour, however, no alibis were offered, and the address was judged on its demerits. Doctor Braithwaite proceeded vigorously to reappraise the preacher's job for the edification of the fledgling prophets.... We were entering upon a Reformation of the Church comparable to that of four centuries ago. The bulk of the old beliefs were irrelevant. The oncoming generation would be so disinterested in them that it would never even glance in their direction. The old credos were as dead as Queen Anne.... We had done with musty metaphysics, at least for the epoch with which we would have to do, and would concern ourselves so exclusively with kinetic energies that speculative philosophy could safely retire to the sanctuary of the museum.... The only service any longer possible for the old theology would be rendered in the capacity of an ancient landmark from which explorers might plat the curve of Christian progress.

The Board went into conference, late that afternoon, and passed a resolution requesting Doctor Braithwaite's resignation. But he was too ill to be handed the document, next morning, for he had developed a grave pneumonia.

On the following Friday, he died. It was quite obvious that the minority who agreed with him would say he died a martyr. It was equally obvious that the majority, who had thrown him out, would refer to him as a sincere, misguided radical whose disaster was easily to be accounted for: he had broken loose from the old moorings. Let this be a lesson.

A few of the elderly invincibles muttered that it was a judgment of God. One bushy-haired apostle, large of lung and expansive of gesture (eight years later elected Sublime Cyclops of the Ku Klux Klan in that region), ventured to preach, the following Sunday, on "Vengeance is Mine: I will repay, saith the Lord." Hopeful of riding into public notice on the shoulders of a corpse, he sent his manuscript to *The Star,* which, on the indignant Mr. Brophy's orders, was printed exactly as written, inclusive of all the bad spelling, bad grammar, and bad temper which distinguished it as a flagrant example of passionate ignorance.

It was an eventful year at Magnolia College. Hitherto it had been her proud boast that in her quiet corner she had preserved the faith once delivered to the saints. Having bred no speedy hares, she had gone in for steady tortoises, promising that great merit occasionally accrued through a race won by the plodder whose brilliant competitors had gone to sleep, on the course, overcome by sheer boredom. The highest mark ever accorded the winner of a Rebecca Winters Dutton Medal had been scored by an essay entitled "Obscure Martyrs."

Little Magnolia, in the fierce glare of the spot-light, felt stark naked, and was ashamed.

* * * * *

But if the college year was a succession of dramatic events so interesting to the public that Magnolia's carryings-on were fetched in, every morning, off forty thousand doorsteps, along with the milk—events in which Dinny Brumm continuously figured either as an active principal or an unwitting accomplice—the season was replete with unpublished episodes vastly more upsetting to this junior's peace of mind.

Having worked full time on *The Star* through the three months' vacation, Dinny's economically administered savings were augmented to the point where he felt safe in launching upon his junior year without a job.

With more leisure in prospect, he had accepted the associate editorship of *The Blossom.*

Had the barbs been able to move concertedly, they might easily have had their way in all the college elections relating to non-academic activities, for they outnumbered the Greeks three to one; but, lacking such unity, they were usually trounced by the sophisticated minority. This time, the Sigs and the Pies had failed to get together on a slate for *The Blossom* staff, each offering a favourite son. The sororities took sides, the Gammas, as usual, lining up with the Sigs, the Lambies throwing their vote to the Pies. The barbs elected their ticket.

Gates, the impecunious senior editor, less concerned about becoming famous as a journalist than for the commercial success of his paper (the staff receiving a modest rake-off, if the year's business justified a bonus), encouraged Dinny to assume unrestricted liberty on the editorial page.

Faithful to its innocuous name, *The Blossom* had ever been a frail and shrinking organism, a mere amplified bulletin of collegiate announcements and uncritical comments. Its platitudinous editorials roused no breeze. Such spoofing as it indulged in usually applied to budding romances on the campus, calfish persiflage worthy of a high-school "annual."

Grinning with satisfaction, Dinny milled the college paper into a giant cracker that went off, every Thursday afternoon, with a loud bang. After the first issue, *The Blossom* sold on the news-stands over in town, and was warmly discussed in the faculty meetings. Gates raised his advertising rates on unengaged space.

The Cincinnati Times-Telegram reproduced, in its Sunday supplement, *The Blossom's* first long editorial entitled, "What Every Freshman Ought to Know."

Satirically featuring the unsurpassed spirit of friendliness, democracy, and smug insularity of Magnolia College, which rejoiced in its self-containment and its ability to make of its student-body "one happy little family," the editorial proceeded to explain the fraternity system for the benefit of bewildered newcomers.

"Less than one fourth of our students," continued the editorial, "are domiciled in large, imposing residences on either side of two sacred blocks at the western end of Sunnyside Avenue. Here dwell the Greeks in dignified sequestration from the raucous shouts of the proletariat.

"On each massive front door there are secrets carved in classic Greek, and on each roof is a mortgage presumably printed in the baser argot of the contemporary banking-house.

"You are advised to ask no questions about these institutions or their tenants. If they recognize you as a Greek, they will tell you. In that case, their secrets will be entrusted to you, and you may be assured that they are secrets, and no mistake; for when a senior who knows no Greek confides a Greek secret to a freshman who knows no Greek, it is guaranteed to remain a mystery. You will also be encouraged to carry with you to your ancestral home a generous portion of the venerable mortgage and drape it a-straddle your father's chimney. If he is of a grateful mind, he will realize the honour thus brought to your tribe.

"If, unfortunately, you are not of the stuff instantly identifiable as Hellenic, make no struggle to simulate a virtue which cannot be achieved by personal effort. In almost any pawnshop in town you will see jewelled fraternity badges on exhibition. To purchase and wear one of these emblems would not improve your rating.

"Neither will it aid you, in this endeavour, to enrol in Greek courses with the hope of promoting your eligibility, for the tongue of Olympus is a native gift with our fraternity and sorority people, and you will rarely meet one of them in the inquisitive groups that cluster about the feet of Professor Appleton.

"Pass quickly through the Delphian groves, when you must needs venture upon Sunnyside Avenue, lest you be blasted by anathemas from some Corinthian portico.

"And when—as sometimes happens—you are snubbed and snooted by the Greeks, because you are a barb, if it so be that the gods have blest you with even the atrophied vestigial remains of any sense of humour, permit yourself the luxury of breaking forth with wild spasms of 'inextinguishable laughter.'

"If you are a co-ed barb, so much the worse for you. It ill becomes a girl to be a barbarian. You are not built for it. Submissively accept your unkindly fate. Defer to your more sophisticated sisters when you encounter them on the campus. Step off the path, and humbly address them in their own language. Many of them have never learned to speak English correctly, and it will be a pleasant courtesy if you salute them in Greek.

"While it may be superfluous, perhaps impertinent, to suggest a suitable amenity, *The Blossom* will cheerfully furnish upon request, a brief salutation to be employed on such occasions. We do not guarantee, however, to provide applicants with the English translation."

* * * * *

Of all the people who relished Dinny Brumm's sour diatribe, nobody more keenly enjoyed it than Professor Ernst Martin, for eighteen years master of Geology, Archaeology, Anthropology, and sundry other brittles.

Professor Martin's odd gait, due to a club foot, and amazing tricks of facial expression, acquired through diligent dealing with a stammering tongue—(sometimes he hung on a dead centre in the middle of a sentence, and whistled himself out of it, to the utter devastation of persons unacquainted with his slight disability)—amply explained why, at fifty-two, he was a dry old bachelor.

Long-time faculty wives could well remember when "Ernie" had lain frank and futile siege to every good-looking girl within hobbling distance.

Convinced, at length, that he was at his best when in pursuit of inorganic objects of nature, Professor Martin had reluctantly renounced romance in so far as it related to himself, but he had never relaxed his interest in the heart attacks of other people. His library shelves were crammed with love stories, the more ardent of them re-read until he knew them by rote. He was a devotee of the movies, and at least twice a week followed the sinuous grace of his favourite stars with hungry eyes.

But nothing afforded him more pleasure than to observe the brief and covert exchange of wistful, exploring glances in his class-room. He had become so adept as a heart-diagnostician that he believed he could tell, almost the first day of a new semester, what pairings-off were likely to develop.

It was the shy ones who interested him most, the pairs who sat farthest apart, never entering or leaving the room together, until—one day—oh, joy!—the tortured stag would manoeuvre to the side of the flustered doe, as the herd filed out of the room, and Ernie's secret forecast had come true.

Sometimes he would mate a pair so sluggishly moving toward each other that he was exasperated beyond endurance.

On one occasion, he had waited a whole year for signs of advancement on the part of two diffident young things, who were forever looking at each other, and, caught at it, would quickly busy themselves in some other quarter. Unable to be patient any longer, Ernie contrived an errand that would speed their affair.

His class in Anthropology was taken to "the mounds," near Pinckney. The gate was locked. He sent the timid pair to the owner's house, a half-mile away, over a narrow, rocky path, and through a tangle of uncleared forest, for the key. They were gone an hour, and when they returned, they were no longer on foot, but floating in a gossamer golden cloud. The stag's shoulder was white with powder, and the doe's ears were pink with embarrassment. But they had remembered to bring the key. It was a great occasion.

By far the most baffling problem that had yet engaged Ernie's attention was the annoying current case of Joan Braithwaite and Dinny Brumm who were now members of his junior section in Anthropology.

In Professor Martin's expert opinion, if ever two handsome thoroughbreds had been destined from all eternity to find each other—even if they had to meet halfway round the globe—these tall, proud, self-sufficient personalities were that privileged pair.

It was a small class, seventeen in all, accommodated by the first semi-circular row of chairs in the room whose walls were eventful with high glass cabinets stuffed with meteorites, stalactites, fossils, pottery, and plaster casts of extinct animals and approximate humanity of uncertain date.

"If my l-lectures bore you," Ernie was accustomed to say, at the opening session of a class, "there are p-plenty of interesting trinkets to look at, a c-ca-casual inspection of which would do you no dis-s-s-service."

Joan had chosen the chair at the extreme end of the curved row, Dinny had taken the seat nearest the door. The intervening chairs were occupied by average examples of *Homo sapiens* in its commonest variety, worthy and well-meaning young persons, no doubt, but clearly of a different biological category from the two who, at opposite ends of the row, were so definitely of a higher species of primate. The amusing, the infuriating thing about it was that neither of them seemed to know what anybody should have been able to observe at a glance.

There was that good-looking young cub, Barney Vaughn, for example. *He* knew it. Vaughn was pathetically infatuated with Joan. Anybody could see that. But Vaughn avoided Brumm. Once Ernie thought Vaughn had purposely snubbed Brumm in a brief clash of opinion in a class discussion.... Why did Vaughn have an aversion for Brumm? Obviously—Vaughn knew, by instinct, that Joan Braithwaite was Dinny Brumm's property!... Ernie was furious.

After a few sessions of this class, Professor Martin became increasingly excited over his secret discovery that the calm disinterest of Joan and Dinny was more calculated than a mere mutual indifference. There was something between these two. Their avoidance of each other was intentional. They were not strangers, but enemies.

At ease in his woollen dressing-gown, with his bad leg outstretched on a neighbouring chair, Ernie read the editorial, that Thursday night, in *The Blossom,* and laughed aloud. It was Brumm, of course. None of the others would have risked it. None of the others could have done it, had he been as audacious as the devil. It was Brumm! My Uncle!—what a savage disposition the young beast had!... Then the corners of Ernie's mobile mouth drew down, and his thin brows met.... The surly piece was funny enough, God knew, but Dinny shouldn't have done it. Wasn't Joan Braithwaite the acknowledged queen of the whole sorority outfit? What did the chap mean by jumping up and down with his big feet on the soft white neck of Joan's exclusive social tribe?

205

For a full hour he sat tugging his lip, relighting his pipe, occasionally grinning, faun-like, sometimes shaking his head despairingly. At length he arose, limped to the gate, poked the fire, and muttered, grimly:

"D-a-a-a—dammit... I'll t-t—try it! It w-w-worked w-w-w—once!"

* * * * *

On the following Wednesday afternoon, the class in Anthropology made the annual excursion to view the mounds.

It was a comforting late October day, hazy and lazy, blue and white on top, purple around the edges, brown underfoot. Blackbirds were noisily mobilizing for the southern expedition. Grey squirrels were working overtime storing their warehouses. Red-headed woodpeckers were drilling deep for drowsy hide-aways. The woods glowed with smouldering embers of a summer, and the narrow black stream that had carved a rough toboggan through the limestone cliffs ran swift and cold.

The seventeen budding scientists, conducted by Professor Ernst Martin, were glad to be out in the country. At one they had met for the twelve-mile trip on a jerky, jangling, little accommodation train to Pinckney. The sexes had segregated in the dusty coach. Barney Vaughn, seated proprietarily beside Joan, made himself agreeable to the cluster of girls. Some of the men read newspapers, others stared out at the windows.

Dinny sauntered to the rear platform, where, watching the grass-grown ties and rusty rails squirm through the hills, he was presently joined by his preceptor, who nodded amiably and seemed, by the companionable twinkle in his sharp little eyes, to be threatening an intimacy. They stood for some time, swaying with the motion of the train, eyes intent on the reeling hills.

"B-Brumm," shouted Professor Martin, against the racket, "as a s-sour old barb, permit me to c-c-congratulate you. It was very c-c-clever."

"Thanks." Dinny grinned down into the bright, beady eyes. "Great scenery, down this way, isn't it?"

"Especially at this season.... B-but it would have been even more c-c-clever if you hadn't done it."

"Somebody had to," defended Dinny, suddenly clutching the thin arm of his master as the train whip-cracked around a hairpin curve. "It was long overdue."

"T-too bad it had to be you," shrilled Martin. "Y-you might have c-c-capitalized your p-popularity.... N-n-no use baiting the d-d-damn frats.... And there are some m-m-mighty fine girls in the s-sororities.... T-t-take a g-girl like Mmmm-iss Braithwaite, for example. W-well w-worth c-c-cultivating, I should say. N-n-not mmm-any like her!"

"Plenty of nuts, this year," observed Dinny, pointing to a clump of tall hickories, vanishing around the screeching bend.

"Y-y-yes... j-just what I was s-saying!... N-not all of 'em on t-trees!... I'm g-going back inside. T-too c-c-cool out here for me."

Dinny turned, and regarded his professor with fresh interest.

"It's a rough road," he said smiling.

"I-i-it always was for m-me," rejoined Martin, meaningly. "B-but it ought to be easier f-for you." One little eye winked, sardonically.

Dinny felt that something was expected of him, though if the fantastic little geologist thought a confidence was in order, he was going to be disappointed.

"You're fond of riddles; aren't you, Professor Martin?"

Martin chuckled, nodded vigorously, and shouted over his shoulder as he retreated:

"Y-y-yes—and I've s-solved a f-f-few!"

Now what did the uncanny little devil mean by that?... Something up his sleeve, no doubt.... Had women on his mind.... Unhealthy imagination.... Meddling matchmaker.... Damn fool.

Arrived at the dingy wooden station in Pinckney, they straggled off toward the path that led a mile toward the grove of the Indian mounds, Martin hobbling ahead, cane-whisking at brittle milkweed pods, the girls single-file behind him, Barney Vaughn leading the male contingent, occasionally pressing solicitous attentions upon Joan as if she needed assistance on the rugged stone ledge of the ravine. Dinny brought up the tail of the procession, quite conscious—he had had one fleeting glance from her, as they entered the train—that he was in high disfavour with the only person in this party that mattered.

At length a path diverged from the ravine and ambled toward the left, through a seared meadow strewn with huge boulders. In groups, the expedition crossed leisurely toward the high-fenced grove. At a considerable distance, keen young eyes learned that the place of interest was somewhat lacking in hospitality.

NO TRESPASSING! THIS MEANS YOU!

"W-w-what's this?" exclaimed Professor Martin, indignantly, as they gathered in front of the padlocked gate. "Mr. B-Bowers assured me it would be left open for us. I m-must g-g-go for the k-key. The sh-short way to his house is d-d-down the ravine. N-n-no—I shall deputize a c-c-couple of you to go. It w-would take me too long. W-we must not be delayed."

With the critical air of making a momentous decision, he deliberately took a careful invoice of the company, obviously contemplating the appointment of an important committee. His little eyes shone. They devilishly rested, for an instant, on the expectant face of Barney, wistfully posing for an Eagle Boy Scout who had not yet had a chance, today, to do a good turn.

Dinny could hardly believe his ears. What had possessed the ugly little jackass to hurl them at each other's heads in this ruthless fashion? He glanced apprehensively at Joan, but she had quickly recovered. She smiled, graciously enough, left the group of girls, and joined him. Professor Martin had suggested that Mr. Bowers might be glad if the President's daughter and the 'varsity's best-known star were sent to ask the favour. If they had no objection, would they go and get the key?

"Martin's a nice little arranger," said Dinny, when they were out of earshot.

"Yes," returned Joan, frostily, "charming idea."

"You don't have to talk to me, you know," explained Dinny, indifferently.

"That's good," returned Joan, quickening her steps.

In sullen silence, they retraced to the ravine. Joan briskly led the way along the narrow ledge, bending forward the stiff branches of intruding shrubbery, and not caring what became of them.

"Perhaps you'd better let me go first," called Dinny.

There was no reply. Joan hurried on.

"And look out for those loose stones!"

It happened, presently. Joan, with a startled exclamation, disappeared over the edge. She was attempting to rise from her knees in the shallow, rock-strewn stream, when Dinny reached her.

"Now you've gone and got yourself in a mess, haven't you?" scolded Dinny, reaching out both hands toward her. She ignored them, and tried to scramble to her feet.

"You needn't bother," she protested, hotly. "I don't want your help—a bit!"

"Yes, you do," he drawled—"and quite a lot of it. You've hurt yourself. Haven't you?"

She nodded, reluctantly, like a defeated child, and reached up for Dinny's hand.

"Help me over to that flat rock, won't you?... No—not that way!" Dinny was gathering her up in his arms. "Take my hands, please. I can manage, if you steady me."

Joan took one short step and unsuccessfully tried another, shook her head, held out her arms. Her lips were white. Dinny lifted her clear of the water and deposited her gently on the little limestone island.

"It's my knee.... It hurts dreadfully." She was trying to keep her voice steady, but she was trembling.

"Think it's broken?" Dinny knelt beside her, anxiously. "Can you bend it? Try."

Her eyes were tightly closed, and her face was drawn. She began slowly unrolling her stocking.

"Rather I'd go away?" Dinny swallowed, nervously, and felt foolishly helpless.

Joan eased back on both elbows, dizzy with pain, too sick to inspect the purpling bruise. Dinny wet his handkerchief in the cold stream, and was about to lay it on her forehead. Anticipating, she took the handkerchief, and dabbed at her temples, clumsily.

"Does it—look broken?"

Dinny carefully examined the damaged knee, resolutely telling himself he was a cad if he failed to concentrate his attention on the immediate field of Joan's injury. It was not broken, he reassured her, but it was frightfully bruised. Perhaps the sharp pain would ease up, presently.

"But you mustn't stay here any longer," he decided promptly. "I'll take you to this Bowers place, and we'll have a doctor."

"You can't," objected Joan. "Better leave me here, and get some help.... Oh—what a beastly nuisance!"

Had anyone been watching, thought Dinny, the pair of them must have made an amusing spectacle as he waded downstream, carrying Joan—huntsman fashion—on his back, her head drooping forward over his right shoulder, her curls tickling his ear, her warm cheek close against his. His left arm circled under her knees, his left hand firmly clasped her right. With difficulty he repressed a grin, and wondered if she was too uncomfortable to realize the absurdity of it all.

For the first fifty yards, nothing was said, Dinny picking his steps, deliberately.

"Am I jolting it too much?" he inquired.

"I can stand it," said Joan, "if you can.... I'm sorry.... I was hateful."

"You were going pretty fast," reproved Dinny. "It was rather reckless."

"I was furious!" Joan's voice registered directly into his ear a justification of her imprudent speed. "He had no business asking me to go... with you."

"Well—why did you?" growled Dinny, sourly. "I'm sure I made no bid for it. I was surprised when you came along."

"Couldn't make a scene—could I?" demanded Joan.

"Of course you could... I don't believe you're above making a scene.... I never knew a woman who didn't like a—like a chance to exhibit her resentments."

Dinny plodded along for several steps, conscious that he was carrying an explosive, and wondering how long it would be until the detonation occurred.

"Yes," mocked Joan, acidly, "I expect it's a lot you know about women—as irresistible, and polite, and—"

"You see that little bridge ahead?" interrupted Dinny. "I'm going to put you down, if you can stand on one foot, and try to hoist you up.... Pardon me—you were saying—"

"I was saying"—Joan bit her words into hot little shrapnel—"that you're a beast... and I don't like you!"

"There's no reason why you should," muttered Dinny.

Hostilities were briefly suspended during the process of mounting over the rocks to the foot-bridge. Joan independently made her way alone to the end of the railing, and looked wistfully in the direction of the stone house, a hundred yards away.

"Well—here we go again," said Dinny, cheerfully, ready to resume his burden. "It won't be far now."

"I can't see why you wanted to write that mean thing," complained Joan, after Dinny had lifted her to his back.

"Just for devilment."

"Sure it wasn't for revenge?"

"No."

"'No,' it wasn't?—or 'no,' you're not sure?"

"I'm not sure it wasn't."

There was a long silence Dinny was almost to Mr. Bowers's little lawn, now.

"I wish you weren't... that way," murmured Joan, in a tone of genuine regret.

"Why should *you* care?" drawled Dinny, with cool indifference.

He carefully lowered her to the porch steps, where she slumped down, spent with the fatigue and strain of their trying half-hour. Dinny stretched his arms at full length, drew a deep breath, readjusted his scarf, ran his long fingers through his damp hair.

Late that night, as he sleeplessly reviewed the afternoon, alternately glowing with the memory of Joan's physical warmth and chilled by her hostility, he wondered what he might have said in reply to her tardy rejoinder had the front door not opened, at that moment, with Mrs. Bowers hurrying out, all sympathy and concern.

"Why should *you* care?" Dinny heard himself saying, in a tone of sarcastic self-depreciation.

Joan had looked up, wide-eyed, lips parted, searching his face with the undisguised candour of a child inspecting a total stranger.

"I—don't—know," she said, slowly, her lips trembling a little. Then she glanced toward the opening door. "Thanks, Dinny, for helping me."

Mrs. Bowers had rung down the curtain on this disturbing scene, murmuring solicitous little cries of motherly interest, and Dinny felt his immediate responsibility transferred to her competent hands. He waited until the telephone conversation assured the early arrival, by motor, of President Braithwaite and a physician.

The men were playing ball in the meadow, when Dinny returned with the key. The girls were seated in the shade. Martin was consumed with curiosity, the brief explanation failing to satisfy.

He endeavoured to corral Dinny into a corner, later, on the train. When all hints and subtleties of inquiry had been adroitly parried, he threw delicacy aside and asked a direct question. "D-d-did you have to c-c-carry her?"

Dinny's eyes narrowed as he stared absently into the questing little grey beads that flashed a hungry wish.

"Miss Braithwaite said she needed no assistance," he replied, dryly.

Ernie gave it up then, mumbled something about the stuffiness of the atmosphere, and hobbled aimlessly out to the sooty back platform, where he hung on to the begrimed iron railing and gazed moodily into the gathering dusk. "H-h-hell!" he muttered. "D-d-damned ungrateful c-c-cub!"

* * * * *

So few swans had fledged in the Magnolia duck-run that the approaching visit of Congressman Philemon Bascom, '98, resident of Washington and Dubuque, was an event demanding celebration.

The Honourable Mr. Bascom had consented to deliver the principal address at the formal opening of the new Science Building on the afternoon of March thirtieth.

That the reception in his honour, on the night previous, might be loyally backed by undergraduate interest, the faculty had appointed a student committee of five to co-operate with their elders and betters in making arrangements.

Wesley Tinker, President of the Hellenic Council, was to represent the fraternities. Dinny Brumm was easily the most conspicuous figure among the barbs. Sophia Wise, temporarily in the public eye as winner of the recent essay contest, would speak for the girls who knew no Greek secrets. Joan Braithwaite naturally epitomized the sorority element at its best. Orville Kling was asked to appear in behalf of the theological students.

At the committee meeting, held in the library at the President's Mansion, lent to Joan for the occasion, an hour and a half was spent, that first Thursday night of March, in a rubber-stampish approval of the "tentative suggestions" sent from the faculty "as a basis of discussion."

Hopeful of enlivening the stupid and perfunctory chatter of obsequious acquiescence, Dinny ventured the opinion that a reception was no place for a long programme of speeches. Would it not be sufficient for Doctor Braithwaite to welcome the honoured guest, briefly, and let the guest say "thanks." Why all these amateurish student harangues. There would be plenty of oratory touched off next day, at the impressive dedication.

Kling, whom Dinny suspected was over-eager to represent the seminary on the reception programme, promptly sustained the policy of offering the student body a chance to express itself.

"Speaking for the theologues," he declared, determinedly, "I think the faculty's wish in this matter should not be questioned."

Unable to resist the temptation to tease, Dinny soberly remarked:

"One might imagine the theologues would be quite relieved if they were not pressed to participate."

"How so, may I inquire?" demanded Kling, bristling.

"Well"—explained Dinny, with a nonchalant gesture—"this reception impinges on the opening of the Science Building, doesn't it?"

Kling truculently protested that he didn't care to enter into any controversy, but could assure Mr. Brumm that the Church was heart-and-soul in sympathy with Science—"of the right sort."

Dinny wished, a moment later, that he had been content to let the matter rest there; but, resentfully remembering Kling's impudent attacks on Doctor Braithwaite's liberalizing beliefs, he decided to jab the harpoon a bit deeper.

"How do you mean—'the right sort of Science'?—the kind taught in Genesis, maybe?"

Kling's ears were red, and he folded and refolded his note-paper, angrily.

"I did not come here, sir, to debate theology with a—an atheist."

"In that case," said Dinny, conciliatorily, "I withdraw my suggestion.... Let the theologues express themselves, by all means.... I would like to propose that Mr. Kling be asked to speak on 'The Contribution of Orthodoxy to Scientific Research.'"

"You're trying to be funny.... Aren't you?"

209

"Of course—*I* think it is funny. But I wasn't sure that *you* would. May I apologize for underrating your capacity for humour?"

Tinker, the chairman, rapped on the table with his knuckles.

"Now—if you two will hire a hall, sometime, the rest of us will be happy to attend. For the moment, you're both out of order, I think. Let us proceed with our business."

The meeting adjourned, presently. As Dinny passed Joan, who stood in the doorway of the parlour, she whispered, "Wait."

When the others had gone, she returned to the parlour, where Dinny, standing by the table, was leafing a magazine.

"Dinny—I wish you wouldn't."

"I'm sorry," he said contritely. "But the chap's always needing a trimming... and never getting it... not properly."

"Oh—I think I know why you feel that way." Joan motioned toward the divan, and they sat. "Mr. Kling has been very annoying in his attitude towards my father.... I think you like my father, don't you?"

"You know I do, Joan. I would do anything for him!"

"Then—don't try to fight his battles. I don't want this to sound ungrateful, Dinny, but it won't help my father for you to be on his side.... Because—well, you see, you're too often on the *wrong* side! And you are so dreadfully savage and sarcastic that you infuriate people!"

"Very well," said Dinny, slowly, "if you think it annoys your father... for me to be loyal to him, I'll not intrude again."

Impulsively Joan laid her hand on his, and exclaimed, impatiently:

"Now—there you go!... That's just what I mean... that ironical... cruel—" Hot, angry tears welled in her eyes.

Dinny rose, glanced at his watch, smiled.

"We won't quarrel," he said, indulgently.

Joan stood, facing him, eyes flashing.

"Yes, we will, Dinny Brumm! You've been perfectly hateful! I don't know what all's happened in your life to poison you so, but if you don't get rid of it—somehow—you'll be wretched forever!... And so will everybody else that... that's interested in you... at all."

Unable to think of an appropriate reply, and stirred to frank admiration of her militant pose, Dinny grinned, appreciatively.... Gad—she was a superb creature!

Joan turned away, utterly exasperated.

"I won't keep you!" she snapped out, hotly. "Good night.... The maid will show you out."

Dinny followed her toward the doorway.

"Joan," he called, "please—don't be angry."

She hesitated, turned, waited.

"I didn't mean to hurt your feelings," he said, gently.

He reached out both hands, and looked down repentantly into her reproachful eyes. She took his hands, and regarded him with an expression of pity.

"Why do you do it—Dinny?" she said, pleadingly.

"Because"—Dinny was serious, sincere, contrite—"because I can't help it!... I was started—all wrong.... The world's full of—full of bunkum, and I can't help laughing at it.... I fancy I shall keep on laughing at it, until I die.... That's the way I'm made.... I'm sorry, sometimes, and wish I wasn't that way.... But—you mustn't trouble yourself about it."

She loosed her hands, slowly, and stood looking down at the floor.

"Good night, then," she said, huskily, with a wan little smile.

"Good night—Joan—dear."

Very tenderly, Dinny drew her, unresisting, into his arms. She laid a soft palm on his cheek, and looked up into his face.

"Oh, Dinny," she whispered, "please... please!"

He bent to kiss her. She shook her head, buried her face in his breast. Dinny gently touched her hair with his lips. His voice trembled a little when he spoke.

"I'll try, dear, to be good," he said, sincerely.

"Honest?" Joan was smiling through her tears. She raised her head slowly, rather shyly, cheeks aflame.

"Honest!" promised Dinny, tightening his embrace.

Joan closed her eyes. The hand that was laid against his cheek moved slowly upward, caressed his hair, circled his neck.

Very gently, Dinny's lips sought hers. It was a chaste, comradely kiss that he offered her, symbolic of a resolution to cultivate a more amicable spirit. Only on such terms, he felt, would Joan permit this intimacy. Passionately in love with her, it was difficult to discipline that kiss.

To Dinny's amazement and exultation, Joan met the endearment in quite another attitude than that of a pleased reformer enheartening a penitent to keep his vows. At the touch of his lips, she responded as to an electrical contact, drew a long, convulsive breath that confessed the depth of her emotion, and the kiss she gave suffused him with an ecstasy he had never known.

They clung to each other for a full minute before Joan, her lips still on his, shook her head ever so slightly, and then, with a contented sigh, laid her cheek affectionately against his shoulder.

After he had gone to his room, that night, Dinny sat for a long time on the edge of his bed staring straight ahead, trying to reconstruct each separate instant of that exultant experience. Had any other girl than Joan Braithwaite consented to—much less joined him in—a kiss like that, he might have wondered a little about her.

But, because the girl was Joan, the warm, tingling memory of it carried a peculiar possessive, protective tenderness. His eyes were wet. Joan belonged to him! He walked to the window and looked out, down the hill, at the big house, loving it because it sheltered Joan. ... Dear Joan!

* * * * *

The next afternoon at the Athenian Literary Society, which Dinny rarely attended, believing it worth a fifty-cent fine to spare himself the irksomeness of sitting through a protracted session of parliamentary wind-bagging, Kling made a patriotic speech.

As an alumnus, he was there on invitation, and glad to be back in the spacious room, where, he averred, he had learned to speak on his feet.

His attacks on Doctor Braithwaite were ostensibly cryptic, at first, but as he warmed to his theme, the clumsy devices of indirect accusation were abandoned. It was an insolent address. Dinny hotly scowled through it, promising himself that Kling would have to pay for his surly impudence.

That night, he executed the threat he had held over Kling, so blind with indignation he gave no thought to consequences. What Joan might think of it did not occur to him.

Next day, the campus hummed with the story. Dinny called up Joan, but she was not at home.

On Monday, current copies of *The Iconoclast* were in circulation. Dinny had sold it many weeks earlier; had almost forgotten it. But Joan, without considering how much time must have elapsed between the composition and publication of this brutal effrontery, avoided him when they met in the hall; ignored him in the class-room.

He dropped her a note, attempting explanation, but was indiscreet enough to jest about the article as "a hang-over" from his "unredeemed estate." The note, plus the spreading rumour that Dinny had made savage war on Kling, so distressed Joan that she was at a loss to know what to reply. While she debated, the faculty moved in the direction of punishment for Dinny. Her father's affairs were already sufficiently complicated. Any attempted reconciliation with Dinny, at this moment, might add to the President's problems. She waited.

Almost before she realized the swiftness with which Dinny's case had become a *cause célèbre*, he had left town. He telephoned to her. Mrs. Braithwaite answered.

"May I speak to Miss Braithwaite?"

"Who is speaking, please?"

"This is Dinny Brumm."

"Miss Braithwaite is not in, Mr. Brumm."

Her voice was not unkind, but Dinny interpreted.

Considering how much variegated disaster menaced Doctor Braithwaite, from all sides, it was obvious that the family was better off without any further traffic with Dinny. He appreciated the situation, and felt almost sympathetic with Joan's mother. She had done the right thing.

CHAPTER X

LOUNGING with athletic arms negligently disposed along the back of a slatted, sun-drenched iron seat in Central Park, overlooking undulous acres of verdant velvet, the prosperous young creator of the column capped "Green Cheese" absently twirled an inventive pencil between thumb and finger-tips; but he was worried.

His deep-set, grey-green eyes, shaded by a brim-turned felt hat of the same colour, were half-closed against the bright distractions, the tiny crow's-feet at their outer corners registering an habitual, detached amusement which he daily sent to market in forty newspapers.

On the broad gravel path immediately before him, perambulators that had cost thrice the price of Uncle Miles's jump-seat surrey leisurely trundled smug, superior kewpies whose interest in the narrow ribbons dependent from their lace bonnets seemed an earnest of future adroitness in the fingering of ticker-tape.

A hundred yards down the slope, kneeling around the lip of a gigantic concrete saucer, small scions of the well-to-do alternately righted unseaworthy sloops and wiped April noses on monogrammed coat-sleeves. Farther down and to the left of this mimic ocean, clumps of tourists, undistressed by the discomforts of their caged kin, idled from the monkey-house toward the bear-pits, pausing briefly to glance up through the untidy steel netting of the squawking, acrid aviary.

Sometimes—as today—the manufacturer of Green Cheese glumly wished he had chosen another vehicle for his syndicated satires than these fantastic "conversations in the moon"; but they had proved immensely popular and profitable—even more so than his earlier, riskier series of "Unfrosted Persimmons," whose astringent quality had so unexpectedly piqued the public palate, jaded by a quadrennium of sentimental superlatives ranging all the way from lush and morbid pathos and the agony of hair-tearing despair to the loud and hysterical hallelujahs of Utopianism at its ultimate peak of drooling idiocy.

Still young in years but prematurely seasoned by cumulative disillusion, Dinny Brumm had been among the earliest to venture a bit of whimsical spoofing, indulgently phrased in the soothing "Now, now; there, there; come, come," of the psychiatrist making his afternoon rounds in a genteel madhouse. Dinny approached his increasing constituency gently, regarding them as convalescing victims of a pestilential neurosis superinduced by a long debauch under potent emotional stimulants.

At the outset, his covert fun-poking at the perfervid apostles of idealism who, watch in hand, galloped to catch trains that hurled them from platform to platform, where daily and nightly, they beckoned and bellowed—saving the world for democracy, for civilization, for altruism, for our children and our children's children, for God the Father and Christ His Son—had been as shocking as a ribald joke told in a funeral address at the expense of the corpse.

But presently it began to appear that a considerable section of the public—weary unto death of the unconscionable nonsense brayed and bleated from ten thousand pulpits, lecture halls, luncheon clubs, women's clubs, open forums, and whithersoever the tribes of salvation-hucksters went up—found itself grinning over the audacities of a youthful cynic who, with no reputation to lose, offered comic relief in the midst of the wearisome epilogue following the final act of a tragedy that had spun itself out overlong.

Two years later, there was none so timid for whom it was not entirely safe and righteous to damn war and invent wry jokes to caricature the apostles and slogans of the noble cause that aspired to world-brotherhood and the Golden Age; but, at the hour, only the venturesome dared apply for such hazardous employment.

Dinny had promised himself the luxury of sweet revenge. Plenty of times he had staggered under the garbage and scoured the latrines for failing to wear the right expression of empty-eyed awe when stiffening to salute the self-conscious lieutenant who, only last winter... or was it the year before?—no matter... used to mince, limp-wristed, to the light of the department-store door, a bolt of silk under his arm, trailed by the plumber's haughty spouse, murmuring, meekly:

"It's a real mauve, madame, as you shall see—and prettuh, very prettuh."

But the lieutenants and the captains and the majors were not permitted to come to bat every day in the column of "Unfrosted Persimmons." The civilian orators had their innings. Dinny was at his best when pitching them a fast one.

The ubiquitous civilization-savers, to whom everybody had listened spell-bound, in a desperate state of finger-gnawing fright, as they luridly depicted the crash and clatter of a blown-up world, were now become somewhat of a nuisance. With the arrogance of Jonah they had howled disaster into the ears of the populace until they, themselves, were fallen afoul of a nasty psychosis unpleasantly akin to sadism.

The war was over that had been so great a Godsend to the large of mouth and small of faith, but the frantic ink and screech of the calamity-merchants was unabated.... Ethical journals of opinion wagged an ominous pen. Prophetic fists pounded verbally inspired Bibles, and cited Jeremiah the empty-umpth chapter beginning at the orty-erth verse. Journey-man seers stamped the rostra of village chautauquas pointing bamboo fish-poles at the seething hot spots on the reconstructed map of Yurrup.... Could civilization survive?... Was not the whole social order on the rocks?... What shall we do to be saved?... (What's become of the treasurer who was supposed to hand me my cheque?)... Let us humble ourselves before God!... Socialize! Evangelize! Fraternize! Organize! Do your bit! Till it hurts! The ushers will now distribute the pledge-cards. Dinny had a good time.

It pleased his whim, one day, to set the clock back to the closing hours of the fifteenth century. Indulgences were on sale at the tail of a cart.... Step up, terror-stricken, and bail your bloody brothers out of hell!... Yesterday, with valour shining in their eyes, they went forth to make the supreme sacrifice for you and yours.... Christ leading on... who had come not to bring peace, but a sword.... Come, now, wipe out this stain... for war is crime, and soldiers are murderers—shame on them!

The more devastating of these ironical gas-bombs, charged from the corroded coils of Dinny Brumm's bitter laboratory, were thrown from the pages of the candidly caustic magazines of protest, the sour humour of the "Unfrosted Persimmons" being somewhat less diabolical. "Green Cheese" was even more gentle and conciliatory.

Dinny yawned, and resharpened his pencil. He was tiring of his product. However—one could endure a certain amount of drudgery and boredom over the daily output of Green Cheese, seeing its present market value was two hundred and fifty dollars a week, just as one had endured the tedium of plucking and hurling the Unfrosted Persimmons whose spontaneous acceptance at the hands of the disenchanted had liberated him from his nightly desk at *The Philadelphia Ledger,* and set him loose to live where and as he pleased.

He was not a conscious apostle of common-sense. Had anyone asked him if, in the spirit of a crusader, he were not aware of his mission to a public whose emotions had been scarified and cauterized by the lancets and blisters of the sensation-smiths and calamity-quacks until there wasn't another kick left in them, Dinny would have denied it with a scowl.... "Crusade?... Mission?... Me?... Hell!"

Nevertheless, he daily polished the mirror so that the people might see themselves almost exactly as they were—a pitilessly honest glass it was, that neither convexed to them a reflection of cherubic amiability nor concaved them to misanthropy.

In these genially mocking "Green Cheese" columns, synchronous in two scores of widely read papers, the Man in the Moon, ancient, wise, sated as Solomon, drowsily replied to the imbecilic queries and comments of Luna, the Lady of the Moon, an effervescent flapper.

A few experimental lines, raw material to be fabricated for today's output, had been scribbled on the bulky wad of paper reposing on Dinny's lanky knee.

"Lookit, Gramp!" pointed Luna, wetting a finger and setting a curl. "Lookit what they got now!"

"More progress, I dare say.... Another epoch-making invention. ... Civilization at the cross-roads... now marching on, eh?... Heads up... nothing to fear... *altus et altior.*... What's this, Luna; an electric banana-peeler?"

"Don't be ridiculous, Gramp!... It's a new cigarette-lighter. They're all quite mad about it!"

"Out of matches?"

"Certainly not!—but this automatic lighter's so much more convenient.... It's a little metal lamp—all the way up to sixty dollars. You unscrew at the bottom and pour in a special kind of oil. When you want a light, all you have to do is snap a small iron wheel a few times with your thumb—it doesn't seem to hurt the thumb very much unless you have to do it too often—and it scratches a flint that quite frequently strikes an electric spark that sets off a little wick that's soaked in the oil, and—"

"How do you mean—it's more convenient?"

"Don't be so grumpy, Gramp!... Aren't you interested in progress, at all?"

*****

Very shortly after Dinny Brumm, fresh from the pandemonium that was Magnolia, had walked into the office of Mr. Steinberg to inquire what *The Cincinnati Times-Telegram* expected him to do, interesting things began to happen.

The first month—he had been told to "sub" for Clint Mitchell on "police and fires" until he learned at least the points of the compass—was too routinish and uneventful for his liking; but presently life was galvanized by the enlivening hubbub stirred when it was announced there would be a visitation from Zandy Craig—*the* Craig, of the Craig Syndicate—first week of May.

The "T-T"—employees of *The Times-Telegram* always abridged the name—was in a grand state of excitement. Everything was speeded up, soaped, scraped, scoured, scrubbed, sponged, shined. High efficiency prevailed.

Reporters put fresh ribbons on their machines (it was in the uncoddled days when reporters were still able to do that for themselves), cleared their desks, bought a new hat. The girls at the Want Ads counter stopped doing their nails in the presence of customers. Linotype operators tried valiantly to break themselves of the reprehensible habit of tossing pied slugs back into the pot. Windows were washed in the composing-room. The devil wore a clean shirt.

For Zandy Craig saw everything; eyes of a hawk and nose of a hound.... Last time he was here, the entire Circulation was fired in a body, every man-jack of them. Forty salaries were raised. *The Enterprise* was bought in and swallowed up. A new off-set press was installed. Four pages of funnies were added.... The very building had rocked on its bricks for six dizzy days. God only knew—certainly no one else, not even Mr. Steinberg—what might happen this time.... You just kept out of the way, and hoped for the best. If what you were doing satisfied Craig, all he wanted out of you was silence—and damn' little o' that!... So went the tribal chatter out of apprehensive mouth-corners.

It had not occurred to Dinny that the omnipotent Zandy Craig could be of more intimate concern to him than as the Dread Jehovah of Journalism, his absentee boss. He was related to the great Craig as a blade of grass to a forty-acre meadow. The dim, far-away figure of the contemptible fugitive who had left in the lurch an unsophisticated, over-trustful, little school-teacher, had never been spoken of in his presence as "Zandy" Craig. He did not even reflect upon the unlikelihood of his unknown parent's achievement of so great prominence. The name roused in him no curiosity, at all.

Everybody spruced up for the big dinner at the Barstow, with Zandy Craig as both host and guest, and all hands present, as was the custom, from the Managing Editor's office down to the coal-bins. The dinner was always an inspiration. Besides, Craig was not niggardly with the fare. You heard what was good for you, and what you'd—By God—better do if you wanted to work for *The T-T,* but you also ate the food of a gentleman, and plenty of it.

Dinny sat by Mitchell, whom he easily liked, far down the T-shaped table seated for six score. The common herd had been settled and was fussing with its spoons.

"You never saw him," remarked Mitchell, offering a cigarette; "quite strikin' personality."

"No," replied Dinny, furnishing a light. "He would be, of course."

"Straight as the scales—and hard as hell."

A slight commotion at the door of the banquet-room signalled the arrival of the important guest and his retinue. Dinny followed with intent, inquisitive eyes the progress of the tall, dynamic, early-frosted figure, as he strode to the seat of honour, preceded by the Mayor and Mr. Steinberg, and trailed by Mr. Latimer, the City Editor, and Mr. Orton, of the Circulation Department. A genuine outburst of applause acknowledged Zandy Craig's advent. Chairs were pushed back and the company stood, still pounding its hands. Dinny joined in the clapping, through sheer animal reflex to the racket, hardly conscious of what he did.

The big man signed to his slaves with a downward push of the heel of his long, strong hand, and they sat. The orchestra was off at full gallop. A battery of white-jacketed waiters trooped in, with soup aloft, a buzz of conversation broke out, and the dinner was in high gear.

"Dinny," oracularly observed Mitchell, who was short and chubby, "it takes beef to make a big man. You've gotta be tall if you're ever goin' to look down on 'em."

"Napoleon was rather—brief, wasn't he?" suggested Dinny, encouragingly.

"Not on a horse," defended Mitchell. "Napoleon never hollered at his tall grenadiers unless he was walkin' on four legs."

"How about us getting a horse, Clint?"

"Us? Me—you mean. You're rangy enough. Tall as Craig, himself.... Damned if you don't look a little like him. Same eyes; sort o' navigator eyes—if you know what I mean."

Dinny, leaning far forward to gaze down the long table, was only half-conscious of Mitchell's prattle. Tugging suddenly out of his mesmerism, he returned to Clint with an abstracted stare, apologizing for his inattention.

"Beg pardon, old man; you were saying something—"

"Yeah," drawled Clint, indifferently, "you better come to, and munch your fodder."

Handsome Bob Moore, Municipal Building and The Courts, leaned across Dinny to inquire: "Know if he brought the angel along, this time, Clint?"

"Haven't heard. She's probably in school, some place." Then, for Dinny's enlightenment, Mitchell added: "Craig's got a girl, seventeen or eighteen, that left a trail o' destruction behind her, last July. Moore's never been the same man. They told him off to show her the finish of a dramatic lawsuit in Circuit Court—she'd never seen a trial—and he was so stampeded by her amazin' pulchritude that he forgot where they were goin' and took her to a ball-game. It was reported the old man asked her, that night, who won the case, and she said, 'The Sox.'... But, even at that, Bob had his pay raised, when he thought he'd be fired."

Young Welland, Clubs and Theatres, nosed in from Mitchell's left.

"Yeah, she's here, all right. Saw her in the lobby with Mrs. Steinberg, Mrs. Forsythe, and some other swells. All dolled up to kill and cripple. Very easy to look at.... Guess they were going to a show."

Dinny was having difficulty keeping his eyes away from the head of the table. It was a curious, unaccountable fascination. Never had he been so engrossed by a personality. He wished he could be close enough to hear Craig's voice as he turned from one to the other of his immediate companions, occasionally putting down his fork to make short, expressive gestures with both hands.

Successive courses came, and clattered away on sagging white shoulders. Coffee arrived, smoke curled upward, chairs diagonalled.... "Pardon my back, old son."... Legs crossed, comfortably. Eyes roved to the gavel-zone.

Steinberg hitched about, stroked his chin, rose slowly, pulled down his waistcoat, told an old yarn about Henry Watterson, teased the Mayor discreetly, waited for the polite chuckle, waved a John-Baptist hand toward Craig, and backed out of the picture.

Craig was on his feet quickly.... No stories, no felicitations, no preamble. He strode swiftly, confidently, to the end of the plank and dived off. Dinny never forgot that first sentence—crisp, curt, cold, impudent, kinetic, arresting! With bushy black brows contracted, and narrowing his grey-green eyes, Craig bit his opening sentence into five ragged chunks and spat it, growled it:

"The only chemicals—imperative to evolution—are water, blood, and ink—and the greatest of these—is ink!"

Craig talked for an hour, his voice rarely rising from the deep, searching, commanding, dynamic diapason of the dogmatic credo with which he began.

He was speaking to a hard-boiled, blasé crowd, not only fully aware of its thick hide, its cynicism, its fish-eyed challenge that dared any man to speed its heart, tighten its throat, or flush its temples; but unafraid of it. Dinny viewed him as a reckless lion-tamer, stalking arrogantly into the cage, blacksnake whip confidently flicking bristling manes into a corner.... Shades of Nietzsche—but Craig was hard!

Now he had eased up on the old brutes with the long, yellow fangs, and was growling at the cubs; trying to make lithe lions of them... . Dinny responded to the tug. Gad—but life seemed potential, the way Craig talked about it! In his hands, a driving, obsessing ambition seemed august! You wanted to thrust out impatient elbows, crackle your chrysalis, and take wing!

One life!... One chance!... One enchanted youthtime!... Make it pay!... Hurl into it!... Take the cash, and let the credit go!... Be something—quickly!... Let the dead bury the dead!

Dolts and dawdlers, pull up along the right kerb and let the unscared strong go by. If you haven't the nerve to pass your sluggish leader, don't hog the middle of the road, but clear the way!... Live precariously!—and like it!... Be sportsmanly; gamble with Life; play for big stakes!... Choose now—whether to scoop or be scooped—all the way to the box that latches on the outside!... My God—but Craig was cruel!

And yet—and yet—Dinny Brumm was drawn to him with an uncanny yielding. Craig had the idea. Craig was a superman, made of superstuff. It was impossible to withstand the attraction of the man's kinetic energy. Dinny's pulse pounded with an admiration close to idolatry.

He shuffled along with short, impeded steps, thick in the ruck that jammed the exits, and cramped with a chunk of the pack into the noxious elevator. The passengers were silent, a bit constrained. Dinny wanted only to hurry to his room, twenty blocks away and up the hill, to beat out a few hot resolutions while they were still malleable with the glow of the Craig forge.

The lobby swarmed. The revolving, leather-lipped street-door spun—plop, plop, plop, plop—as the animals, in line, left for the kennels; the grizzled and mangy, the playful and cocky, the yawning and gamboling.... Dinny squared his shoulders.

Mitchell was calling from the rear, somewhere. Annoyed, but complacent, he left the line, sauntered back, inquired.

"Moore's met the Craigess, Dinny.... We're asked to watch her nibble a rarebit in the grill, and do her a little genuflection. Want to?"

"Sure.... Thanks, Clint."

The princess was already at court, and presiding uncommonly well. No need to have her identified as the daughter of Craig; it was on her face, in her eyes, in her hands. She was Craig—young Craig, drawn to about three-fifths scale. The Craig *savoir faire* pleasantly veneered what promised to be—when it matured—a ligneous substratum of will-to-power. She was not haughty, not arrogant, not vain; but consciously assured. Whatever-it-was-she-had seemed to be saying: "It's mine: give it me: thanks."

Nobody needed to guess which was the head of the round table, seated for six. All were standing, for the moment, surrounded by twice as many more, half of them collected by Mitchell, en route to the grill. In the polite bedlam of introductions and renewals of acquaintance, Dinny, with no responsibilities, stared appraisingly at the self-possessed blonde, frankly envying her birthright to a magnetic personality that dominated from her grey-green eyes and firm, red mouth, and pink palms.

"How do you do, Mr. Brumm?" She gripped his hand like a man, and gave him a steady, smiling look of honest welcome, same as she had done for young Fitzgibbon, who had come along with *The Enterprise* since her last visit.

"It must be nice to come back," said Dinny, "and find everybody so happy to see you, Miss Craig."

She had not released his hand. Her smile had vanished. Her eyes had contracted slightly, and shuttled from his brows to his chin, as if attempting to recover a long-forgotten acquaintance.

"You're new, too; aren't you?" she said. "I'm sure I never met you.... Did I?" She shook her head, still searching his eyes. "Funny," she added, half to herself.

He made way for the others behind him. She released his hand slowly.

"Auntie Alison, Mr. Brumm would like to meet you. Mrs. Forsythe, Mr. Brumm." Her eyes momentarily dropped to the hand he extended, and again swept inquisitively to his face, before she turned to listen to Mitchell's next presentation.

"My son—Mr. Victor Forsythe, Mr. Brumm," murmured the tall, rather imperious lady in mourning.

"Mrs. Steinberg, this is Mr. Brumm," reiterated Victor, whose sleek, black hair was extraordinarily long. The tip of a white handkerchief peeped from the sleeve of his dinner-coat.

Mitchell's recruits were insisting that the diners resume their seats, and most of them, waving good nights with smiles, were drifting away. Dinny followed, laggard, ostensibly lingering a little for Mitchell and Moore, in the process of tearing themselves away from the girl who paid flattering attention over her white shoulders. Something she was saying now made them glance in his direction.

"Dinny!" beckoned Moore.

He obediently joined them, inquiry in his eyes.

"Miss Craig wants you," explained Clint, adding, with pretended pique and as if the remark were *sotto voce,* "lucky devil!"

"Mr. Brumm," she asked, almost inquisitorily, "did you ever work for any of my father's other papers?"

Dinny shook his head, regretfully.

"Should I have?"

She did not join in the chuckle with which his colleagues rewarded his naïve query.

"Do you mind telling me where all you have lived?" she persisted, as to a witness under cross-examination.

"Well—we'll leave you now," interjected Mitchell, breezily, laying a propelling hand on Moore's shoulder. "It would be like you, Dinny, to discover that you and Miss Craig had been schoolmates, or something.... This chap has more lives than a cat, Miss Craig.... Got fired from college for knockin' the steeple off the Y.M.C.A., and made 'em take him back and pay him for lost time.... Good-night!... See you some more, I hope."

"Nowhere you're likely to have been," said Dinny, when the clamour had subsided. "Indiana—and Magnolia College.... We never met before, Miss Craig.... But"—recklessly—"now that we have, let's pretend we're old friends."

He had laid his hand on the back of her chair, and when she looked up with still serious eyes to reply, her warm, supple body glowed against his fingers.

"I have never seen the Rookwood Pottery," she said.

"Would tomorrow be convenient?"

"About eleven, preferably. You work at night, don't you?" She was looking squarely into his eyes, sheltering her voice a little from her table companions.

"And luncheon?"

"Yes—I think so."

She held out her hand, like a man, without coyness.

"Good-night—Miss Craig," said Dinny, deferentially, as became an obscure employee taking leave of the magnate's daughter.

"My name is Alison." Her lips barely moved, as she spoke, making no effort to disguise the fact that their conversation was private. Slowly she disengaged her long, strong hand, gave him another swift, serious scrutiny that circled his face and came to rest, for an instant, on his lips; and rejoined her company.

* * * * *

Alison was amazingly direct. The bland candour with which she ignored all the age-old subtleties of her sex, proclaiming in every look, tone, and gesture that Dinny Brumm was hers, by priority claim, all but took his breath away.

It was not brazen, but transparently ingenuous. Dinny was neither amused nor annoyed. Her attitude was that of a wilful child daring all-comers to dispossess her of a toy. She had lost no time defining her convictions, indifferent alike to their possible effect on Dinny or any who might discover them.

Even on that first morning, strolling beside an impressed executive, who, learning her identity, had volunteered to guide them through the celebrated pottery, she put herself to no bother of pretence that their interest in art accounted for their visit.

Mr. Dabney would reverently hold up an exquisite vase, turning it, slowly, kaleidoscopically, inviting her to luxuriate in its mellow, parti-coloured translucence; but, with a nonchalance so unconcerned that Dinny was half sorry for the fine old pagan, Alison's eyes—briefly, abstractedly regarding the treasure—returned to search his face. She held tightly to his arm. Employees grinned, slyly; exchanged an appreciative wink.... Honeymooners... second day out... utterly dippy... at least, the bride was.

They lunched downtown at the Hofbrau, where Alison expressed no preferences when their fingers touched on the menu-card, and seemed unaware what she was eating. Dinny was surprised to find himself quite unembarrassed by this devotion. It was too genuine to provoke a smile.

When she talked of herself, it was of herself and Geneva, herself and Montreaux, herself and Paris, as if she hadn't had an existence prior to her school-days in Switzerland, begun at fifteen, a few months after her parents' separation. When she talked of Dinny, it was all in the future—hot burning fires of ambition for Dinny. She all but suffocated him with it.

The goal of success was leisure to live, write, and play in Europe. That's what Dinny must live for, look to, as the reward of genius multiplied by hard work. That's what she lived for, looked to—Europe! She implied they were both going there, one day. She did not say they were going on the same ship, but she described moonlit nights on the boat-deck in a dulcet tone and ecstatic mood whose implications were almost shockingly direct.

217

Whether Zandy Craig was so confident of his dynamic daughter's self-sufficiency or so infatuated with his own business affairs that he gave her no thought, Dinny Brumm could not divine. It was enough to know that Alison's society, for ten memorable days, was not only accessible to him at all hours but flatteringly urgent.

She casually disclosed that Mrs. Forsythe, who lived in New York, was visiting in Cincinnati, hopeful of interesting the well-to-do music-lovers of the city in the budding talent of young Victor, whom Alison catalogued, briefly, brutally, as "a bit of a cad, too dumb to succeed, and too lazy to bluff"; though she spoke almost tenderly, for her, of Tommy, the eldest, and Grace, who were forever stepping aside to make way for the callow prodigy in whose thin, listless fingers their ambitious mother had placed a fiddle almost before he was able to stand alone.

Alison's disgust and distaste for Victor apparently had wrought somewhat of constraint between her and Mrs. Forsythe. In view of this circumstance, and also the exigent desire of her aunt to promote Victor among Cincinnati's art-patrons, perhaps it was natural that the girl should be independent of much restriction.

After three crowded days in Cincinnati, almost constantly tied up in business conferences, Craig had scurried to Louisville. If Alison had been mistress of her own fate before, she was now even more completely in charge of her time. That time was Dinny's.

At Alison's suggestion, they procured saddle-horses and rode all day in the hills. They ferried to Covington, and strolled in the country. She even had the audacity to call up Mr. Steinberg, late one afternoon, from some undesignated outpost, reporting that she had asked Mr. Brumm to entertain her for the evening, and he would not, therefore, appear at six, as was his custom; to which information Mr. Steinberg replied, dryly, that he hoped she would return him, eventually, to *The T-T,* unspoiled by the honour.

Mulling over the whole tragic affair, later, Dinny found a little comfort in the fact that he had made no effort to capitalize Alison's devotion to the discredit of either of them. Nor was it easy to maintain his attitude of chivalry in the face of her quite abandoned, ruthless, reckless disclosure of a fascination for him to which she had yielded utterly.

Every day tightened their intimacy. Often she hinted of a story she meant to tell him; he would be "quite frightfully" interested in it, as a scribbler, she knew; a long story, it was; she would let him have it when there was time. Dinny did not press her for it. She had implied that the tale impinged somehow on her family affairs.

* * * * *

It was Saturday afternoon.... Craig had wired he was returning that night. Alison was to be packed and ready to leave with him for New York, next morning, at ten.

They had tied their horses at the edge of a grove; had sauntered to a favoured rendezvous on the rocky lip of a glen; were promising each other more happy days when she returned with her father in the autumn.

"I'm going to tell you that story, now, Dinny," she said, snuggling close to him, and childishly tracing patterns on his lapel with a possessive finger.

"Do," said Dinny. "Don't leave anything out."

They leaned comfortably back against the warm rock, his arm around her, and the story began; just a bit diffidently, at first, for the story was not hers, really, but her father's.

After ten minutes of Alison's calm narrative, paving the way for the most pleasant possible interpretation of her father's youthful tragedy by recalling many of his college experiences, the story abruptly shifted to another locale.

Dinny relaxed his affectionate hold, and fumbled awkwardly in his coat pockets for cigarettes and matches.

"You smoke too much, dear," said Alison, rather petulantly, annoyed at the distraction. "It isn't good for you.... Your hands are trembling.... Look!" She gripped his fingers. He did not reply or smile, but obdurately lighted the cigarette.

"And then," continued Alison, sinking back against the rock, with a little sigh of disappointment not to find his arm there, "the most natural thing happened.... You know my father.... He's always been that way.... What he wants, he wants—that same day!"

Dinny sat with eyes half-closed, listening, smoking; lighted another cigarette off the hot end; averted his face, savagely ran his fingers upward through his hair.

Too disconcerted over his unaccountable mood to continue without some explanation, Alison broke off, presently, in the midst of a sentence, groped for his hand outspread on the rock between them, and asked, anxiously: "What is it, Dinny?"

He did not turn to her or respond to the pressure of her fingers.

"Dinny!" she entreated, pressing her face against his shoulder, "tell me, dear!... What did I do?... What's come over you?"

"I'm afraid"—he said, hoarsely, after some delay—"I can't tell you."

She sat for a moment half-stunned and silent; then, with a little sob, she wrapped both arms tightly around his neck, and murmured, thickly: "I can't bear it, Dinny. You must be good to me. You've made me love you. I'm mad about you!"

She raised her face, eyes closed, and offered him her parted lips.

Suddenly haggard, Dinny gripped both her hands and drew them down, holding them vice-like against his knee. He swallowed, convulsively, and when he spoke, his voice was hollow.

"You mustn't, Alison," he muttered.

"Don't you love me—even a little, Dinny?" she pleaded, with brimming eyes.

"I mustn't!... We can't!" he whispered, staring into her face, the muscles of his cheeks twitching.

"Why?" she asked, inaudibly, her lips forming the query.

He drew her head tightly to him, with a gesture of protection, as if to shield her from a blow, and, after a long minute, measured out the words, dully, one at a time:

"You—are—my—sister."

* * * * *

Dinny never pretended this was the reason for his almost immediate decision to join the artillery unit mobilizing at Gettysburg, where the only artillery to be had, at that moment, was in the cemetery, slightly outmoded, as such things went.

Neither did he ever explain to himself—much less to others—that he had waived the exemption Craig had provided somehow for "necessary members of editorial departments" (meaning everybody on the payroll) out of a sense of patriotic duty.

He wryly, profanely, squirmed into an ill-fitting, ludicrous suit of khaki solely to save his face, and because he was quite too fit a specimen of physical vitality to be at large in civilian clothes at a time when so many hundreds of thousands of inspired patriots were rushing about extolling "the supreme sacrifice" as a noble privilege dangled before the enchanted eyes of "our valiant boys."

Most of this exultant talk was offered by prophets and soothsayers of forty-five and up, who, albeit unable to make such renunciation themselves, were obviously uplifted by the thought that they were not standing in the way or taking the place of some other brother, hungering and thirsting for such righteousness as might be had by blowing a Teuton's head off with a handful of blasting-powder.

Dinny's long, monotonous months in camp never benefited his native land by so much as a feather's weight; and, as for what he himself got out of it, either in discipline, experience, or stimulating friendships, the total result was exactly nil; unless his increasingly bitter cynicism, later capitalized to a monetary advantage, might be said to have fermented a little more through those hateful days.

Even with unpleasant memories as his chief stock in trade, memories fetched to market and savoured by the similarly disillusioned, Dinny did not like to cogitate too much about his life at Gettysburg. The revulsion made him ill.

As for "heroism," the most heroic act anybody in that camp was expected to perform consisted of the valiant refusal to commit the half-dozen murders for which Justice clamoured. Uniforms played weird tricks on people who, in civies, must have been halfway decent. It seemed to make very little difference about a man's previous character or relation to society, once he had been required to perfect the debasing art of revolving himself stiffly on one heel, by some reflex to a growl that brought the flat of his hand smack against the brim of his cap, the only way he could square with his own soul, for this indignity, was to look promptly for somebody else, even more debased than he, who might be rank-badgered to do him a kow-tow.

Nobody ever saluted Dinny Brumm. Nobody would have saluted Dinny Brumm had he remained in the army until the Dawn of Everlasting Peace. He wasn't the type.

According to the letter, he went through all the motions, which largely consisted in offering sustenance to the vanity of suddenly ordained Plattsburgers and surly non-coms; but Dinny's spirit—such as it was—refused to participate. His contempt glared in his eyes, against his will. It was chiselled in the deep lateral cleft between his lower lip and chin, quite beyond his control.

They nearly let him die, during the flu epidemic, for offering frank comments, when half-delirious, relative to the institution with which he was connected, and the important members of its personnel. Before he was able to pull his trousers on again, he had learned a disheartening thing or two about the only profession for which he retained the slightest degree of respect. Always had he venerated the medical profession. Now he had discovered, regretfully, that a few metal buttons, a squeaking new belt, and a pair of spurred boots would frequently play the same amount of hell with the Hippocratic oath that they so incomprehensibly wrought in the disordered minds of formerly gracious grocery clerks and collegiate sons of honest farmers. He saw many a competent, generous, integrity-loving physician degenerate into a pompous, puffy, arrogant ass.

Even the nurses went about, stiff-necked and consciously professional, mouthing the phrase, "War is no tea-party!"

Dinny Brumm never went over the top, in France, at four a.m., but he spent six weeks in a military hospital, during the flu contagion, which called for almost as much patriotism, and lasted longer.

On the day he went back into civilian togs, he promised himself he would get even with eight anthropoids, to wit; one captain, one lieutenant, two sergeants, two doctors, one orderly, and a nurse. He expected to hunt them down, in their postwar haunts, and pummel them to a jelly—all but the nurse, who was to be enticed to some public place and spanked in the presence of a large, appreciative audience.

The determination to do these animals physical harm cooled, after a while, to an acidulous contempt which he occasionally tapped with a pen for the approval of demobilized thousands who, with ungodly glee, found in his devastating satires a vicarious vengeance.

Alison wrote to him almost every week while he was "in the service."

"I am not going to tell father," she stated, in her first note. "Poor man couldn't do anything about it, could he?... But, Dinny, darling, it is a frightful thing he's done to us."

In sober truth, Dinny was incapable of viewing their tragedy with the same despair. Much as he admired Alison, their brief and unfortunate affair had not been of his own contriving. As for permanently linking his life with hers, he would as soon have married a hoisting-engine. Indeed, he had already begun to wonder, before discovery of their blood relationship, by what pleasant, painless process he might adroitly excuse himself from an impending attachment brimful of agony.

He replied to her letters at the rate of one to three, painstakingly shifting their mood, by a calculated katabasis of affection which, within three months or so, had—at least so far as he was concerned—placed their relations on an approximately normal and sound footing.

Angela wrote from the midst of a great revival in Hamilton that the Lord was blessing her labours in a miraculous way. It was not her first important revival, but the first in which she had starred. From now on, she expected to be at the head of her own company. Angela made no effort to disguise her natural gratification over the material features of her success. Dinny was pleased at this honest, albeit unintended, confession, and thought a little better of Angela. She didn't mind admitting that she was in the show business... on behalf of The Lord, to be sure, but—well—the show business.

Joan Braithwaite was much in his thoughts. Upon the death of her father, he had written her a note. Her reply, some six weeks later (though he had promptly received a black-edged card from her mother, acknowledging his flowers), was postmarked New York. Whether she was there temporarily, or to stay, he did not know. That she expected no further correspondence was implied by the absence of a specific address. There was no one of whom he cared to inquire.

Mr. Steinberg occasionally wrote to him, as became the employer of a volunteer hero, and there was a letter from his father, shortly after he enlisted, commending him on the splendid thing that he had done. The letter was dictated, and signed in a feminine hand, doubtless the same hand that had done a score of them.

"Take this, Miss Rabbit, and make twenty originals for our enlisted employees. Miss Hare has the list of names."

"Wish to see them, sir?"

"No—you can sign 'em."

Dinny had chuckled while composing samples of conversation between his father and the stenographer, relative to the issue of Craig sentiments *in re* the war to end war, and save civilization.

The T-T confidently expected Dinny to come back and resume his place, wrote Mr. Steinberg, immediately after the Armistice; but there was to be no more of the family salt eaten; starve first!

With surprising ease, he found a place on *The Philadelphia Ledger*. And then, with no more effort, the bright idea came, the "Unfrosted Persimmons" offered to be plucked, the mounting wave of prosperity rolled in, and Dinny was at liberty from clocks, bells, and whistles.

He resolved to live in New York. Why not? It was the mecca of journalism and such as do syndicated columns. He did not go there saying to himself that Joan might be accidentally encountered; but, every bus that passed him, as he strolled Fifth Avenue, was thoroughly raked with a questing eye, the roll was swiftly called in the subway-train, traffic-blocked taxis were peered into with undefended impudence, the peacock-alley of the hotel, stuffily scented, was daily, gravely, tallied off—for Joan.

Sometimes, though he was not given to worrying, naturally, Dinny found himself distressed over imagined predicaments in which she was posed in a tragic rôle. He was not quite able to reconstruct the face of a sad or beaten Joan; but, annoyingly often, he had a vision, at night, of lovely shoulders slumped in grief or pain, and the back of a curly head bowed in serious trouble.

It became a mild obsession. He had no use for telepathy, and the slightest hint of any mystical thought-conveyance was, in Dinny's opinion, the sign of a weak mind. But—he was looking for Joan, and the longer and farther he looked, the more deeply he felt that when he found her she would be vastly in need of help.

Dinny wished her well, but honestly wondered whether his anxiety might not be the product of an undefined hope that he could find Joan in a mood to accept his affection, even if at the price of some substantial favour of which she stood seriously in need. Indeed, he brooded so much over the matter that it became a definite fixation. Joan was in some kind of a scrape. Joan was hungry. Joan was walking the streets, looking for a cheap lodging-house. Joan was being imposed upon by some predatory rascal who controlled her rations.

He even tortured himself with fears of which he was ashamed. Joan was, he had discovered, possessed of a pretty active "temperament." Could she take care of herself if ruthlessly stampeded?

Today he was weary of the job that almost anyone might have envied him; wearied and worried.

He interlaced his long fingers behind his head, closed his eyes, and re-canvassed all the expedients he had contemplated for the recovery of his Joan.

Budding April in Central Park left him unstirred. Life was stale, flat, and unprofitable.

He began to toy with the idea of a vagabond trip through some foreign country.

CHAPTER XI

"HAD it ever occurred to you," elaborated Dinny, as the speakeasy waiter made off with their luncheon order, "that my gifted cousin Victor comes perilously near being an ass?"

Tommy Forsythe traced a brief design on Joe Lombroso's white tablecloth with the tip of his spoon, and grinned wryly. It was not the amiable smile that so readily curved Tommy's lips. The grin threatened a bit of irony.

"I've known that," he said, slowly, "for a long time; but—I hadn't supposed *you'd* ever find it out."

"Thanks," returned Dinny, dryly, not a little surprised at the satirical come-back. Tommy was always so direct, so honest, so transparently sincere.

"And may I inquire," pursued Tommy, with an excellent imitation of his cousin's calculated ridicule, "just when and how you contrived to make this belated discovery of my brother's asshood?... He arrived home only yesterday. You haven't seen him, have you?"

Dinny nodded, sipped his cocktail.

"Last night—down in the Village.... Tommy, he was just a little this side of unbearable."

"'This side'?—looking from where?" Tommy's sour query rasped and crackled.

"Who's been feeding you raw meat, Pollyanna?... My God—I didn't know you had it in you!" Dinny stared at his cousin with honest amazement.

The Damon-and-Pythias comradeship of Dinny Brumm and Tom Forsythe, which was to rake fore and aft the whole gamut of emotion, from high delight to frantic misery, dated from the latter's receipt of a letter from Alison Craig, written from Seattle in June.

Reticence impulsively discarded, Tom's dynamic young cousin had told him everything, even to confessing an affection for Dinny out of all proportion to their blood relationship; declared she "never expected to be the same woman again"; urged her beloved Tommy to lose no further time in hunting down this attractive collateral to their tribe.

Before sunset, that day, telephone communication had been established between Tommy's office in the huge department store on Thirty-Fourth Street and Dinny's bohemian three-room suite in Greenwich Village, the shabby equipment of which—save for his sturdy typewriter-table, and his mother's little walnut desk—consisted of ill-related rubbish that had passed from one impecunious artist's keep to another's, each piece with a story to tell of battered ambitions, pitiful frugalities, and somewhat of despair.

They spent the evening together in Dinny's rooms; and when, at midnight, they parted at his street-door, each felt the other an old friend.

From the first, they were conscious of having little in common, as to temperament and outlook, Dinny finding his steady-going cousin amusingly naïve, boyishly enthusiastic over the elementary simplicities, a "typical case of arrested adolescence," though Tommy was nearly four years his senior, and had been extraordinarily successful in business.

Tommy, encountering for the first time a determined cynic, obviously proud of his versatile collection of disbeliefs, distrusts, and disenchantments, regarded his new acquaintance with fascinated interest. Dinny Brumm didn't appear to belong to this world, at all. He had merely dropped in, as a spectator. He stood on the side-lines, paper and pencil in hand, watching the human race plod by, making ironical notes and grinning when it stumbled.

In general appearance, the two were strikingly alike; of approximately the same height, weight, carriage, and pigments. They had the Craig eye, deep-set, searching, flanked by innumerable, faintly traced crow's-feet. They shared many an odd little trick of gesture and posture.

Alison's suggestion that Dinny's relation to their clan should not be disclosed was approved by both of them. Tom promptly took his handsome new acquaintance home with him, the next Sunday evening, to the Forsythe apartment in White Plains; was pleased to observe how easily his mother accepted him; was surprised at Victor's enthusiasm, for Victor rarely had any use for Tom's friends; was anxious over the eager Grace's frank display of admiration.

"Why—you two things actually *look* alike!" commented Grace, with the half-impudent candour she had learned at the feet of Victor. "Aren't you afraid you'll quarrel?"

Victor—at that time temporarily home from Italy at the suggestion of his mother, who, as his *impresario,* thought it prudent to have the talented violinist back, occasionally, "to conserve his contacts," and give the papers a chance to stir his potential public to remembrance of his existence, progress, goings and comings—instantly attached himself to Dinny with a proprietary air that threatened to elbow Tommy out of the picture.

He couldn't conceive how his unimaginative old dray-horse of a brother, who knew everything about leather baggage and nothing about the creative arts, had captured the friendship of this sophisticate. He must see more of this Dinny Brumm. Brumm had the good sense to live in the Village, too, where everybody who was anybody in the field of the arts found freedom, stimulating companionship, encouragement, inspiration. It had taken Dinny only ten minutes to discover that the Forsythe establishment operated exclusively to serve the high destiny of Victor.

Grace—dark, swarthy, shiny, with a button popped and loose hairpins—lived solely for the talented fiddler, fetching and carrying for him like an earnest retriever. Tom, nearing thirty, had apparently accepted it as his manifest destiny to devote the bulk of his salary to this lofty emprise.

Once, after three months of increasing intimacy had broken down all reserve, Dinny ventured an expression of his feelings on this matter. He and Tommy were dining together at The Astor. Victor had sailed, that morning, returning to Ghili in Milan, bon-voyaged by a score of friends from the general vicinity of Washington Square, the family, and not quite enough inquisitive reporters to satisfy Mrs. Forsythe.

"If I were you, Tommy, and Victor my brother, I'd request him to unstraddle himself from around my neck, and try walking on his own feet."

Tommy had been tardy with a reply, shook his head, slowly.

"Victor," he said at length, deliberately, "was born without feet. ... Victor's all soul."

"But he eats!" persisted Dinny, indignantly.

"You don't understand. It's a long story. You see—my mother—God bless 'er—managed to make quite an important personage of my father. She married him to make him, and succeeded. She was so ambitious for his success that for thirteen years she gave him twenty-four hours a day; became just a bit obsessed, maybe.

"He died early—as you know—just as her hopes had been fully justified, and the rewards were rolling in.... It nearly finished her. I was only eleven, at the time, but her condition was serious enough to worry me, dreadfully, though just a kid. I'll not inflict you; but—she was in a sanitarium for six months.

"Then—with the patience of a spider, she began all over. With a kind of fierce determination, she set about building Victor up for a career with a fiddle. Father had left practically nothing but the royalties on his phonograph records. This income was pretty good, at first; large enough to warrant expensive foreign study for Victor.... Afterwards, when the records of my father's voice began to slip—well—I couldn't let my mother down; could I?

"Besides"—added Tommy, brightening—"Victor might put it over.... I sincerely hope so—for my mother's sake."

* * * * *

That had been in late September. It was November, now, of the succeeding year.

Tommy Forsythe had just returned from a month in Mexico, full of interesting experiences, though not of the specific business errands that had taken him there. They rarely discussed Tommy's business. His phenomenal rise at Lacey's, from the shipping department up to the leather goods, and from successful salesman to assistant manager of the department, and from assistant to Department Chief, had been achieved in seven years; but Tommy did not often talk about it.

Dinny rather regretted now that he had spoken his thoughts about the asininity of the parasitical Victor. Tommy had enough to bear. It would have been more gracious to keep off it. However, the subject had been pushed into the open: it would have to be discussed.... The picture of last night's affair in the Village drifted unpleasantly across Dinny's memory.

He had been surprised to find Victor at the midnight arty-party in the untidy kitchen of The Red Bear. He had not known Victor was back. But, of course, he would lose no time coming to collect adulation from the art colony to which Dinny, at his fervent request, had earlier introduced him.

Victor—still boastfully giddy from eight nauseous days of hurdling home over a shrieking sea which, he was averring, had put the doctor to bed in his cap and boots, and shattered not only a thirty-year Atlantic storm-record and the captain's elbow, but all the *Vendome's* crockery (not—he languidly chortled—that the latter had been much missed after the first twelve hours out)—had come to The Red Bear in tow of Diane Wimberly, a lanky, pink-haired, lower-case poetess who needed a dickey and a thousand dollars' worth of dentistry.

Dinny had gone late to Felice's party. Once he had thought Felice quite interesting; but, in recent months, she had begun to weary him. In fact—the whole outfit, now that their novelty had worn off, lacked the originality and sparkle he had earlier imputed to the Villagers when, as a lonely stranger in New York, he was in need of quick and easy friends.

Last night's bizarre affair had palled on him. The thing had been carried on in murky gloom feebly tinctured with magenta by a sooty lantern suspended from a peg in one of the massive, ancient, weathered-oak rafters—made of half-inch pine, and installed the previous summer.

Victor—whose voice Dinny instantly recognized, even before his eyes had adjusted to the thick fog into which he groped—was seated in the dilapidated wheelbarrow intended for the "fagots," when there were any—The Red Bear, with reckless leanings toward Communism, pretended to be a Russian peasant's hovel—loathsomely detailing his recent discomforts at sea.

Dinny's tardy arrival had not interrupted the undulating flow of his cousin's obnoxious reminiscence, nor was the company much distracted from its wan interest in the nautical narrative.

Felice (Mamie) Manners (Johnson), the hostess, seated on the floor near the doorway, on an outspread newspaper, moved over a little to make room; and, pursing her scarlet mouth in apology for the humble offering, handed him, with her fingers, a large, pallid cream-puff which she ruefully extracted from the bottom of a brown-paper bag wherein the dessert course had been served.

Dinny gingerly surveyed the gift, in the manner of a fastidious dowager examining a freshly exhumed skull, to the considerable amusement of Felice, who, a little drunk, was finding Victor tediously verbose, and wished to be playful.

Wanting Dinny to know that she shared his carnival attitude toward her party, Felice strangled the empty bag, put the neck of it to her blood-red mouth, and with many long, cheek-distending, eye-bugging exhalations, proceeded to the task of its inflation; or nearly so, the final blast proving abortive due to her sudden conviction that her employment was ridiculous enough to merit a shocking explosion of suppressed mirth.

Victor reproachfully glanced in the direction of the disorder, but calmly continued his monologue in a marcelled, affected baritone that inspired Dinny—a little drunk, also—to nudge Felice to attention while he feigned to take careful aim at the self-infatuated minstrel with the soggy token of her vanished hospitality.

"Dare you!" whispered Felice, cupping her mouth with her hand, but Dinny reprovingly shook his head, pretending shocked regret that she would entertain the thought of such an effrontery.... Then he had stretched out his long legs, and tried to listen.

Victor had finished with his disgusting *mal-de-mer* and was now in a messianic mood concerning the martyrdom of all true artists, and the tribulations of cat-gut and horse-tail artists in particular. Evidently somebody with a bit of money had recently stepped on Victor's slim, expressive fingers, for he was swishing about with a bare rapier that threatened to annihilate the well-to-do.

Dinny wondered if this were the formal opening of Victor's campaign to impress his friends that he had a good excuse for failure; wondered if Victor was frightened, now that he had finally caught up with his exceedingly bright future, and had it to demonstrate.

"Old Victor," reflected Dinny, as he sat listening to the makings of an alibi—"good old Victor knows time's up. He's either got to catch fish, or cut bait, or bail the boat."

Abstractedly, Dinny had let his heavy eyes rove about the room while his blasé cousin deprecated the necessity for living in a world propelled by the almighty dollar.

He was acquainted with all but two—the youth with the black velvet jacket and negligent Windsor tie, and the thin girl beside the youth, a blue beret drawn down over one eye, and a limp, home-made cigarette dangling precariously from her lip. The rest of them he knew quite well. Gregory, thirty-five and tuberculous, had confided freely. Gregory was writing an important novel; quite a bit daring, it was; might have to be privately printed. He had been at it now for upwards of three years. It was his first novel, though there had been a slim, mauve, deckle-edged (Gregory was ashamed of the deckle—but Aunt Agatha, of Phoenix, Arizona, who was financing it, quite insisted) volume of unpunctuated verse. Dinny had one of these, a presentation copy, autographed with a scrawl that beckoned the beneficiary to consult the title-page for verification of the little book's parentage.

Vivacious Anne Pelham, who, to better her credit at the expense of her artistic integrity, had confessed her degeneration to drawing for commercial purposes—though what or for whom she drew Dinny had never learned—caught his vagrant eye, smiled, twinkled friendly fingers. The salute would cost him five dollars, thought Dinny. Anne already owed him thirty, not that he cared: the poor little fellow was always hungry.

Sylvia (what the devil was her other name?—He had always thought of her as Carmichael) sang, or was going to... in opera... once she got a chance. Squat and shaggy Carmichael, next her, did portraits—quite atrocious ones, Dinny thought, though it was out of his line—which Sylvia, who lived adjacent on the fourth floor of a cheap and dirty, gas-

224

reeking, bug-infested tenement house, and shared the bow-legged painter's kitchen, bath, studio, and fatuous ambitions, considered masterpieces.

They had never struck Dinny Brumm quite this way before. He had sympathetically appraised them as a wistful tribe of aspirants to success in creating something interpretative of their thoughts. They had become suddenly ridiculous. There wasn't one of the dozen present, he reflected, who had ever done anything worth a second look. With the possible exception of the gloomy Victor, whose career was unpredictable, not a man or woman of the lot was likely ever to get to first base in the game whose lingo they prattled with such glib familiarity.

At long last, Victor's monotonous harangue was concluded. The audience untangled its legs, milled about the room, yawned toward the door. Felice led Dinny to the little group still clustered about the wheelbarrow.

Victor extended a limp, soft, slim hand.

"'Lo, Dinny.... So you're here.... Who told you I was home?"

"Nobody... I didn't know you were back."

Somehow—the raw impudence of the chap annoyed him. His egotism was insufferable.

"In fact," drawled Dinny, "we've ventured to have several little social affairs much like this, in your absence; just to keep our spirits up until you returned.... Hope you don't mind."

No—Victor didn't mind. He smiled, indulgently, and said it was quite the proper thing to do, he was sure; and turned to luxuriate in the twitter of the new girl with the blue beret.

Dinny had slipped out, presently. The Village was beginning to bore him.

* * * * *

Tommy impatiently shattered one of Joe Lombroso's crusty rolls with his fingers, a bit heated by Dinny's spoofing.

"Ordinarily," replied Tommy, "I don't permit myself to become disturbed over anyone else's damned foolishness besides my own; but, now you've invited it, I'd like to tell you something that will be good for your soul—if you still have one."

"Attaboy, Tommy!" applauded Dinny, merrily. "Skin 'em alive!"

Tommy drew a heavy frown that Dinny had never seen him wear before.

"This isn't going to be funny," he muttered. "After lunch, we're going over to your squalid hole in Daubville, where you're to listen to something I've got for you.... And here's hoping you won't get sore."

Dinny threw back his head and laughed.

"I'd really like to see you on the war-path, Tommy."

The subject was not resumed until, having climbed the dirty stairs, and tossing their hats on the littered table, Dinny, amused and expectant, lighted his pipe, and signed Tommy to "turn it on."

"As I understand it," began Tommy, didactically, "you are one of the most venomous—certainly the noisiest—of all the animals now in revolt against everything your betters have built up over a period of five thousand years, or so.

"You've distinguished yourself as a kicker, knocker, scorner, spoofer, and snarler. Your sour comments on faith, piety, and patriotism are worth a dollar a line.... And, incidentally, I bet you anything you care to put up that the time will come—not long from now—when you've repeated, over and over, all the smart and surly words you know—your stuff won't be worth ten cents a garbage-pailful.... Some of it's beginning to run a bit thin already, Dinny, if you don't mind my speaking of it. I just noticed in the last issue of *The Emancipates* that you used the word 'moron' nine times. Better get yourself a new thesaurus.... You're writing too much, anyhow, my son. Your rhetorical disbursements are so far ahead of your intellectual income that you'll be bankrupt, presently. However—that's your affair.

"You've been the great champion of sincerity. You've thumbed your nose at the hypocritical Bible-whackers, and the gavel-swingers, and the sword-toters. Everybody's an ass but you—and the Villagers; you—and your little hand-picked minority of freedom-fanatics.... Parsons and professors, doctors and lawyers, senators and judges, philanthropists and missionaries—you've had 'em on the grill in a dozen contemptible magazines. You've roasted 'em whole, brought 'em back in a stew, served 'em cold in a salad with sulphuric acid dressing.

"And yet—you'll live down here in this poisonous rat-hole, chumming up with a bunch of third-rate, would-be artists, yodelling about liberty to express themselves!

"You rant about hypocrisy! Hypocrisy!... My God!... Can you imagine anything more utterly rotten with pretence than the rubbish that's written and daubed and sculped by these—"

"Have a light, Tommy," interrupted Dinny, offering a match, "and don't yell so loud.... It's Sunday."

"You wipe that smile off your face, and sit down! I'm not through yet. I mean to tell you some more, and if you don't like it you can go straight to—"

"I know, Tommy, what you have in mind.... Proceed.... I'm liking it."

"The new art! Bah! I've been supporting art since I was a youngster; missed college to become an art-patron; had the house littered with artists for years.... Ninety per cent of 'em too incompetent to hold a job, too lofty to earn a living, and too lazy to wash their ears.

"The new literature—realism! Tripe! A lot of dirty stories dignifiedly told by dirty-minded little shrimps, and solemnly discussed by pretenders who make-believe they are enduring the dirt so they can capture the beauty of the 'style,' when it's plain they're only enduring the 'style' for the sake of the dirt.... Kidding themselves!

"Modernism—modernistic painting!... Cubist stuff!... Nobody can tool me, any more, about that.... This latest whelp of modernism is nothing but an idiot begotten of Gin and Geometry.

"And *you*—cramming the magazines full of high-browed sarcasm about the dull slaves of superstition!... chanting about freedom!... yowling about the unpardonable sin of stupidity! Haven't you any sense of humour, at all?... These birds have imposed on you, down here. They've made you believe they were artists—most of 'em clumsy dubs who couldn't draw an honest picture of a long-tailed rat.... Try it out, if you don't believe me. Ask one of these paupers to draw you a picture. Offer this Felice person a hundred dollars to draw—not paint—but *draw* a picture of those two hats on your table, and see what you'll get.... Hypocrisy—hell!"

"Tommy—I've an idea!... Just came to me.... I'm going to write a novel... about the Village.... It's marvellous! Wonder I never thought of it before."

Tommy scowled, relighted his pipe, puffed moodily.

"What you'd far better do is to let up on mean and surly criticism for a while. There ought to be some kind of a mental laxative on sale for chaps like you. Why don't you treat the world as if you weren't too superior to live in it? Pity there isn't some neighbouring planet for you scoffers to go to, once in a while, for a vacation."

Dinny suddenly recalled himself from the absorbing reverie into which he had drifted. Tommy had been chiding him pitilessly, and he had missed much of the latter part of it. He reproached himself for his wool-gathering at such a moment.

"You're quite outspoken, Tommy.... But—Boy—you've given me a whopping inspiration... for the novel, you know. I mean to do it, without delay.... It will be a wow!"

There was no further withstanding the contagion of Dinny's enthusiasm; no use bristling against Dinny's conciliatory smile. Tommy capitulated with a sigh. The chap was incorrigible, utterly inaccessible to reproof.

"Let's go do something," he said, restlessly, reaching for his hat.

"Young Vladimir Polovsky's talking at three in the Village theatre," suggested Dinny. "Shall we hear him?"

"Rot!" exploded Tommy. "Hell of a lot of amusement that would be! More dribble about Communism; eh?"

"It might improve your mind," exhorted Dinny, paternally. "I'll bet you never heard a real Communist talk?"

"Don't you believe I haven't. Just got done firing one—a female one—from the store.... Talk? That girl could talk down a Senate filibuster!"

"Yes," Dinny wagged his head, knowingly, "that's the answer of capital... big business... to any independent opinion offered by the slaves!... Poor girl airs her theories—and gets fired!"

Tommy chuckled, reminiscently.

"Well—this happened to be the answer of big business to a young slattern who refused to act on the broad hint that she'd be improved by a shampoo. Nobody at Lacey's cared a damn about Sophie's bad opinion of the capitalistic system. It was her revolt against soap."

Dinny remained loftily sceptical, but willing to grin.

"Lacey's may have pretended that was the reason, but Sophie would probably have been given the sack, just the same. Sophie"—Dinny feigned a sympathetic tear—"Sophie wanted to be a little candle of liberty—and you snuffed her out!"

Tommy shook his head, laughing.

"We sniffed her out."

"You've a mean tongue, Tommy.... Suppose we go up to The Capitol and see Hollywood canonize some racketeer who's just come home with his pockets full of money to lift the mortgage off his widowed mother's cottage.... That's about your speed."

* * * * *

Dinny began to work on his novel, that night. It was his first long story, and he meant to spread it on a huge canvas that would provide plenty of room for the minutiæ of detail.

He knew he could draw Victor—to the life—and meant to make him lead the ludicrous procession of enchanted bums across an elaborate stage set for Art passionate with Revolt.

He believed he would let Victor succeed, at least measurably, and return from time to time collecting laud, honour, and glory from his satellites. As an affected, arrogant ass, Victor would be hard to beat.

There would be room in the story for a bit of honest pathos, too, he thought. These people's ambitions would be vapid enough, and their pretensions no end silly; but there was nothing fictitious about their hunger and heart-break. Dinny paused in his swift typing of the rough memorandum for the first chapter, and wondered if he would be able to do the *lento*movement, when he came to it. Hadn't he debarred himself from any such excursions into the "human interest" zone of sincere yearning mixed with tears? He had so consistently mocked at everything savouring of the sentimental that he doubted his ability to write about the deep emotions without inviting a hilarious "haw-haw" from his cynical constituency.

He settled back in his chair, long hands dangling inert over its arms, and gave himself to sober reflection on this dilemma.

His field had always seemed so pleasantly inexhaustible. Why—a man could keep on spoofing current movements forever! There was positively no limit to the materials at one's elbow. So long as there was an absurd human race, competing in silliness, there would be daily something new to grin at. The satirist's mine had barely been scratched.

Tonight, Dinny's ironically amusing profession seemed suddenly to have walled him in. His field of exploration was quite restricted, after all. Tommy Forsythe had given him an anxious moment, that afternoon, hinting that certain pet phrases of ridicule and contempt, which had served him well, were in danger of becoming tarnished ornaments.

Perhaps he had better stop using the words "moron" and "imbecile." It was a fact that he had called them in to explode disparaging comment rather more frequently than he should.

For a long time he sat meditatively tugging at his left ear-lobe, absently fingering the key-board with the other hand.... Nonsense! He couldn't do a novel! He had had so much highly lucrative sport in ridiculing every phase of tender sentiment—the sickly slobber of penitence, the mawkish drool of the meddling doers-of-good, the exultant imbecility of idealism, the owlish asininity of philanthropic fuss-budgets and sniffling uplifters who loped about crying aloud over the plight of carefree people who desired only to be left alone—that he seriously doubted whether he dared risk a forthright invasion of "heart issues."

Viewed from a slightly different stance—Dinny, adroit in metaphor, was fond of considering his problems in the algebra of his craft—the section of the woods where he claimed the right to swing his axe was limited to a very small tract of the forest. It was his job to cut down, chop up, stew, and distil astringents, bitters, and lethals from henbane, hemlock, and wormwood—a sophisticated employment. He would only seem ridiculous tapping maple trees, or sawing down hollow sycamores for their wild honey.

Who would have thought that staid old Tommy would pip off like that?... Talked a little like Joan.... Tommy and Joan would have a good time together, if ever they met.... Dear Joan!

Slowly disrobing and easing himself into dressing-gown and slippers, Dinny recapitulated the strategic might-have-beens of his arrested romance with Joan; relived that passionate half-hour when he had sat, fists clenched, in his dormitory room at Magnolia, debating whether to punish the insufferable Kling.

Suppose he had cooled off, and decided to let Kling go unrebuked. ... Suppose the piece in *The Iconoclast* had not appeared at that unlucky moment.... Suppose Doctor Braithwaite had been secure enough in his position for Joan to risk a response to his honest overtures of reconciliation.... He might have had Joan!

And then—what? Joan would have insisted on his living in a Fool's Paradise, no doubt. She would have coaxed and nagged him into a pretence of sharing her ingenuous optimism. He would have spent his life driving spikes into maples, and boiling the sap down to syrup and selling it to the fudge-makers. Ye gods—what a career!... Thirty-five or forty dollars a week, riding up and down elevators, interviewing candidates, magnates, and redeemers who would impressively keep him waiting in their outer offices while they sat hungrily watching the clock, lusting to let him in for a padful of their oracles.... No—it wouldn't have done. There would have been no "Unfrosted Persimmons." Joan would have seen to that. The "Persimmons" would have been brought to market ripe—sticky—sicky sweet—rottenly soft.

And yet—

Dinny sighed, turned on his bed-lamp, rolled in, and tried to read the current Lawrence; pretty clever dirt, that.... Rather amusing—Tommy's appraisal of erotica. Tommy was more than half right, of course. Previous to the recent emancipation from superficial prudery, the male youths had climbed up into the haymow to exchange convictions on the ever-exciting subject, and the girls, in three-somes, their arms twined around each other, had taken a nice long walk, whispering with red cheeks.... Something unhealthily furtive about that, of course.

Now the talk was all out in the open.... Lecturers packed hotel convention-halls with rosy-faced, eager, wide-eyed customers who owed it to themselves to post up on psychology as it related to the old, old problem.... No longer was it necessary for the inquisitive youngster to hide his nasty little paper-backed shocker in a corner of the oats-bin.... The subject had been milled up into "literature," now.... There need be no further hypocrisy or furtiveness about this matter. Dinny audibly expelled a contemptuous "Pish!"... Old Tommy was dead right!

All these college boys and girls swarming into classes on "Abnormal Psychology"... all these altruistic women elbowing into the Court of Domestic Relations... all these questors of culture, hunting for rhetorical gems in the new, breathtakingly frank, censor-baiting literature of libidinousness!... Same old story... same old furtiveness. But—while the earlier crop of curious youngsters had deceived their parents, the new outfit were deceiving themselves!

Dinny turned a few pages, and pushed the book off the bed on to the floor; snapped the light, closed his eyes, scowled.

And yet—

Whatever Joan might have been able to do to him and his literary aspirations, it might have been worth the sacrifice.... Gad—what a thoroughbred!

Vivid pictures of her came, lingered, and made way for others even more luminous.... Joan—radiant, supple, agile, tantalizing, generously blending her splendid body with his, that first afternoon on the ice... Joan—demurely eyeing him, and denying it with an indignant toss of the head when he caught her, in silly little Ernie's fussy museum... Joan—warm across his shoulders, her cheek against his, scolding into his ear and hating him with all her might while she drove him nearly mad with her rampant vitality... Joan—gently chiding, tenderly, wistful, in his arms!... Joan's kiss. He must find Joan. Suddenly, the slumbering, half-hopeless, half-abandoned yearning for her almost suffocated him. Whatever it might cost—even to the ruinous price of degrading himself to the maple-sugar business—he must see Joan. They were made for each other. How often he had said "Rot!" in comment on some such observation made in reference to a congenial pair. But, it wasn't rot. Joan was his—and he meant to have her.

Item by item, Dinny recovered her in every remembered posture, expression, mood, each delicious recollection confirming his decision to track her down and have it out with her.

He reinvoiced all the tentative projects that had occurred to him, earlier, for quests of the vanished Joan. This time he would see it through. He would pocket his prudence, and ask questions of people who might know.

A light suddenly broke. Dinny grinned, nodded, rose, went across to his mother's desk, and began to scribble. For a half-hour he wrote and tore and flung away. At length he was determined to be satisfied with his production, addressed an envelope to *The Times,* Want Ads, enclosed his copy and a five-dollar note.

Dressing hurriedly, he went downstairs, telling himself he was silly to be so precipitate, seeing there was nothing to be gained by posting his letter at two-thirty a.m., but eager to relieve his impatience, somehow.

Wide-awake, mentally turbulent, he walked all the way to The Battery, seeing nothing en route but a stuffy little coffee-shop where he stopped and gulped a cup of scalding brown stuff that had been stained by the original grounds described in the lease.

Now that he had made the adventure, Dinny wondered if he could wait until Tuesday. His ad would appear then. Joan would probably read it before the day was out.... And then what?

Time dragged very slowly, all Monday. It was impossible to concentrate. Dinny was thankful he was a few instalments ahead of the game in the manufacture of his "Green Cheese."

At seven, Tuesday morning, he rushed over to The Brevoort, bought a *Times,* went in to breakfast, rummaged deep in the advertising pages, found the column of "Female Help Wanted," and searched for his request.... It looked a bit crazy.

RESEARCH SECRETARY—by feature writer. Applicant must be at least casually interested in Indian mounds, preferably of southern Ohio: graduate small college, member sorority; native Wis.; 26, ht. 5:7¼; wt. 125; brown hair and eyes. Experienced ice skater preferred. Excellent salary. Reply in handwriting to Times X29008.

CHAPTER XII

HIS decision, a fortnight later, to see Angela in action was one of the most unaccountable caprices to which Dinny Brumm had ever yielded.

The sudden resolve to go to Dorchester, New York, and watch Angela heal the sick and cast out devils, was arrived at one Wednesday evening shortly after a casual little dinner with four neighbours at the Purple Pig.

Indeed, the first insistent bleat of desire to do this eccentric thing had whimpered from the depths of Dinny's mind during the dinner conversation when Felice Manners had moodily mooned over her early adventures with religion back in Gimmel, Illinois.

Felice, to judge from the blue circles under her heavy eyes, and the smeary elisions of her thick talk, had been steadily tippling all day. She was now making a muddy landing from her ascension into the upper ether of Bacchanalia.

On such occasions, Felice shamelessly turned her soul inside-out for the edification of whosoever happened to be within range of her appalling self-disclosures.

This time, a brief—and, to Dinny, unwelcome—conversation about Angela, now well on the way to becoming a national figure, had set Felice going about the ponderous piety of Grandfather Johnson's home in frowsy little Gimmel where, at nine, she had been dutifully taken in, after the death of her mother, and had remained until, at sixteen, she had fled unfounded and unpursued.

And while Felice rumbled heavily on, recovering fugitive scraps of a stormy girlhood that had creased the brow and whitened the whiskers of Grandfather Johnson—"and Grandmothersh, too," she had added, with an irresistible touch of realism—Dinny, possessed of memories not dissimilar, twirled his own reel back to weedy little Zanesdale.

Now and again, and at briefer intervals, Dinny had been aware of momentary surges—something very like nostalgia. Increasingly given to self-analysis, as life became more and more stale and unpromising, he found this the most singular of his mental phenomena.

It was quite natural, reflected Dinny, that a fortunate man who, in youth, had lived in a congenial home from which he had emerged, at length, reluctantly, would so cherish his memories that there would ever be a strong tug in that direction. It was easy to understand how, across a widening chasm of miles and years, such a man might so long for home and a recovery of its endearments that the yearning would obsess him.

But—as in his own case—for a man who, in youth, had fretted in his home, counting the days which must elapse until he could escape its intolerable irksomeness, eventually rushing out of it without one backward glance, asking nothing but to be spared the necessity of a return, these occasional tidal-waves of homesickness were inexplicable.

Dinny found himself wondering if it might not be true that the homing instinct is universal, omnipresent, inevitable; not very much conditioned by any individual's immediate reactions to his native environment while in it. Why, he even had fleeting seizures of desire to see frumpy old Aunt Martha!

Frequently he told himself that the next time he had an errand in Chicago, he would start a day early and drop off in Zanesdale; he would sit on the fence at the corner of Harsh's melon-patch, and watch the Erie "fast-lines" whiz by.

These attacks did not last long, however, and when he had regained his sober senses, Dinny would accuse himself of a growing tendency toward weak-mindedness. It would be entirely consistent with his unhappy career, he thought, if at about forty, he would have to be carted off to a funny-house.

He had rarely thought of Angela for several years. Lately she was much on his mind. Angela was becoming famous—or notorious—the choice of an adjective depending on the mood of the reader who found her startling exploits, at the behest of Heaven, demanding larger space in the newspapers.

The first important tidings of her spectacular ministry had broken from Spottswood, Pennsylvania, where for six hectic weeks she had had that smoky mill-town by the ears.

The revival had begun in the custody of the biggest church in Spottswood; had rapidly outgrown its quarters and migrated to the city auditorium; and, because it was September, had swarmed to the County Fair Grounds where the Holy Ghost had obliged Angela with a recurrence of Pentecost.

Hundreds—screamed the big black headlines—had rushed about, babbling "tongues" which sounded strangely even in the ears of a polyglot foundry-town composed of a little of everything all the way from Mesopotamia and the parts of Libya about Cyrene to the uttermost jungles of Siam and the suburbs of Babel.

Still other hundreds, unblest with tongues, had ecstatically rolled in the sacred sawdust, popping out of one trance into another. In the hilarious "after meetings," happy converts milled up and down the aisles, affectionately embracing their fellow-lunatics without regard to age, sex, or colour.

After a short interval of recuperation, Angela was reported at Wrayville, Tennessee, from whence the news proceeded of a miraculous restoration of sight to an elderly woman, nine years blind. A local doctor had verified the miracle, though there had been some difficulty verifying the doctor, who, the Wrayville Medical Association insisted, was not an oculist, but a specialist in botts and glanders.

Presently Angela was again on the hook in twenty score of composing-rooms, this time at Stillman, Iowa, whither excursion trains from neighbouring towns hurried with yearning cargoes of sick and afflicted.

"Thish Ashula Brumm"—Felice had thickly inquired, that Wednesday evening, at the Purple Pig—"sisher o' yoursh, Dinny?"

The Carmichaels, and the Strothers boy who played Sylvia's accompaniments, laughed.

"Do I strike you as having come from a family of deities?" countered Dinny, rather annoyed that the question had come up.

Felice nodded, thoughtfully.

"Such ash you, Dinny, alwaysh come f'm holy hillsh."

"Perhaps Dinny's a fallen angel," suggested Sylvia.

"No—I mean 't," persisted Felice, with an expansive gesture. "If all th' atheish and agnoshish in thish rotten villish were honesh, nine out o' ten would shay... born pioush home."

"Let's begin with you, then," proposed Strothers, indulgently. "You're an atheist, aren't you, Felice?"

"Ever' mornin'," went on Felice, woodenly, "Grandfa'r took twenty-poun' Bible on hish lap, an' read long chapter f'm Deuteromony er Ebeneesher—"

"No such book as Ebenezer," corrected Dinny.

Felice grinned, cannily, over having scored a point.

"Uh-huh!—jushesh I sushpected, Dinny Brumm.... You were brought up on 't. You're f'm holy hillsh—jush like me."

"Go on, Felice," urged Carmichael. "What did Grandfather do next?"

"Well—after he had read longesh chapter he could find, 'bout th' Amalekitesh an' th' Stalactitesh, all eight o' ush schwoop' faish-down into our chair cushionsh, an' tied an' untied an' retied th' yarn knotsh while our Heav'ly Fa'er wush thanked that He had shpared ush to shee th' light o' 'nother day... hell of a compliment f'r Heav'ly Fa'er... Heav'ly Fa'er hadn't murdered ush all in our bedsh."

Aware, from previous experience, that Felice, at such moments, was very sensitive, Dinny had done his honest best to keep a straight face during this recital; but, having clamped down a bit too hard on his feelings, he now regretfully blew up with a loud report which sent Felice into a pitiable drizzle of maudlin tears.

Dinny had never been party to an event at once so tragic and so devastatingly ridiculous. Felice, barely intelligible, poured out a story that might have made the angels weep while they laughed. As a child, the lonesome little thing had gone out by herself into a far corner of the garden and looked bravely up into the blue, telling God she didn't believe a word of it, and hoping He'd please excuse poor old Grandfather Johnson, who didn't know any better, and meant all right.

"An' God ushe t' talk t' me... Nosshir, I mean 't!... He would jush grin, and shay, 'Thash all ri', li'l' Felish. You run an' play!'"

Sylvia had taken Felice home when it was generally agreed that she had talked enough, and was attracting too much attention.

Leaving the mussy little restaurant, Dinny had gone to his room somewhat depressed. Felice had stirred some quite vivid recollections of his own boyhood. There had been a time when he, too, had been acutely conscious of something—something winged, inside himself—looking up inquiringly, hopefully. Felice had apologized to God in behalf of Grandfather Johnson. Dinny remembered having had much the same feeling as a little boy. God had been maligned. God was their Father... and they had gone down on all fours, twice a day, grovelling like heathen.

But, strangely enough, Dinny wanted to see what was this peculiar energy that Angela had laid hold on. Angela might be no end a mountebank—probably was nothing less or else than that—but thousands were finding something at her hands. Surely she hadn't inherited anything from his smug and stupid Uncle Miles that would stampede city after city into orgies of repentance and hysterias of joy.

At ten-thirty, that night, he was in his berth, listening to the trucks pound the rail-ends as his train scampered up the right bank of the Hudson, and wondering what had possessed him to spend any time or money on such a silly adventure.

* * * * *

Thursday afternoons—Dinny learned at *The Dorchester Sun,* where he had been cordially welcomed when applying for a press ticket to the Angela Brumm Revival—were set aside for the healing of children.... Lucky, he thought... couldn't have struck a better day!

He lunched with Fred Channing, the editor, after having met a few of the boys at the office, where, as was inevitable, he had been chaffed about his gifted "relative."

Channing had slowly closed one eye, impressively, in the midst of the banter.

"You wait!... Some woman!... May be a quack and a faker—but, you take it from me—Angela's got a lot o' *It!"*

They went to the stage door of the big public auditorium at two-thirty. Literally hundreds of people stood about the entrances, hopeful of crowding in to secure standing-room after the ticket-holders had been accommodated. In tow of Channing, Dinny followed through a long concrete corridor, swarming with the surpliced choir, busy functionaries, reporters, parsons, and up the stairs to the large stage, set for three hundred.

The auditorium was packed to suffocation. A tense feeling seemed to pervade the place, as if some astounding event—some sickish tragedy, perhaps—were imminent. Dinny's eye swept the huge hall; raked the galleries into a vertiginous smear of wide-staring, open-mouthed, morbidly curious expectants. Then he analysed the crowd—small sections of it—item by item; nervously thumbing their paper-backed hymn-books with mechanical fingers, gnawing their lips, apprehensively, as if they had come to a hanging.

The great choir filed in, confident and conscious of its importance, and stood, as in a tableau, until the celebrated Maurice Manwaring, lithe, athletic, leonine of head, an extraordinarily handsome brute, strode on, raised both modishly white-flannelled arms, and with a commanding gesture that seemed to reach far forward and grab the first triumphant note out of their obedient open mouths, he summoned them to the great declaration that the affair was on, and Heaven was being called in to witness. The piece was Gounod's "Unfold, Ye Portals." Dinny had not been so stirred to the depths—ever! He had come as a spectator; rather a cold-blooded spectator, too. Now he felt himself vigorously pushed into the crowd.

"Un—fo-o-o-o-l-l-ld!... *Unn—fo—o-o-o-ol-l-ld!...* UNNN-FO-O-O-O-OL-L-LD!!—YE POR-TALS EV-ER-LAAAST-ING!"

The great crowd couldn't resist the pull of it another minute; came up out of its seat in response to something gripping that reached out, and took hold, and lifted up. Dinny found himself on his feet, his heart pounding, his eyes smarting, his throat dry.

Angela came on, passing him so nearly he could have reached out a hand and touched her black velvet gown. She was an insuperably regal figure, exquisitely formed, incredibly beautiful, with the carriage of a goddess and the rapt eyes of a mystic. Except for the white silk stole which depended almost to her knees, she wore no ornament. Walking confidently to the centre of the stage, she rested an expressive white hand on the pulpit and gazed over the multitude with a sort of inspired compassion. Dinny would have given his all for a faithful picture of what was actually going on, at that instant, in Angela's mind.... It was utterly impossible, preposterous, that this woman could stand there, before this yearning crowd, swept by the nerve-tingling influence of such music—and be calmly plotting a hoax!... Angela should have the benefit of every doubt. *Angela was not a fake!*

The anthem rose to a great *crescendo.* The multitude sat. Angela stood. There was a heavy hush. She prayed. It was a quiet voice, but commanding. Angela maternally gathered up the three thousand in her soft, strong arms, and, having affectionately held them to her ample breast and wiped their tears and fears away, tenderly handed them over into the infinitely stronger arms of their Father. It was not God's wish that any of these little ones should suffer, or face life unable to savour its sweetness.... Dinny remembered it was a "Children's Healing Day," and, glancing about, became aware of babies in arms, little cripples in arms, big-headed, empty-headed, pallid, grotesque *monsters* in arms. Never had he seen such a conglomeration of juvenile misfortune. They seemed suddenly to spring into existence. He had not noticed them before.

God did not want these little ones to suffer.... By faith, they would be healed.... God had promised.... It was enough. We could take Him at His word.

Spontaneously, the choir, as if unable to restrain its pent-up emotions, quietly hummed the old hymn-tune which Dinny recognized as "My Faith Looks Up to Thee."

Angela, face uplifted, blue eyes wide, enraptured, called upon her Father, these little ones' Father, to keep His word with her—with them—with us.... Then there began to come from the depths of the auditorium a surge, a sobbing surge of questing song, as if it was welling up out of hearts rather than throats. Dinny's eyes filled. He didn't sing; couldn't have sung; but he was conscious of being in and of that longing multitude whose honest faith—or whose desperate hope, at least—was reaching up.

Dinny never liked to remember, afterwards, the procession that came down the aisles, and up the stairs to the stage, bearing its pitiable freight to the Lamb of Calvary and His calmly confident representative.... Pale, twisted, little children... blind babies... hare-lipped... club-footed... hunch-backed.

Angela laid her potent hands upon each of them, raised her eyes, murmured a prayer, and a motherly woman in white gently propelled them on, across the stage, to another stairway leading back into the auditorium.

At the foot of this stairway, a huddle of young women, also in white, were receiving the bewildered mothers with encouraging smiles, distributing gifts to the children—gay trinkets, oranges, little dolls for the girls, mechanical toys for the boys.

Dinny began to understand the reason for this quite dismaying anti-climax to Angela's wholesale conferment of God's grace. It was a shock-absorber to provide distraction of the hapless victims' minds from their disappointment in case the power of God was not immediately manifest. There was no question about Angela's excellent intent. Her faith looked up to the Lamb of Calvary. She sincerely hoped—more than hoped; expected—that the Lamb of Calvary would take pity on these wretched. But if, for some baffling reason unknown to Angela, the Lamb of Calvary let her down, there would still be dolls and oranges and toy automobiles, and a red, red rose for mother.

The long procession kept coming on. Dinny was seated where he could observe the faces of the mothers at the moment Angela was in the act of bearing their anxieties to the Throne. He winced as if witness to surgery performed without benefit of anæsthesia. The faces of the mothers seemed strangely alike, the tense, stiff, open lips showing tips of teeth in half-open mouths, as if expectant of sharp and sudden pain; as if Angela were a surgeon, and they had come to have her lance some deep, dangerous infection; waiting, now, for the plunge of the knife. The faces were all set in masks—masks through whose stiff vents, round, wide eyes, and open, straining mouths—the mothers were prepared to shout for joy or scream with despair.

Not often did the mothers immediately inspect their children, after the supplication. They dared not tarry to do that. The thing was to hurry on, as bidden. Dinny suspected the management did not encourage any loitering on the stage, any looking to see.

One mother's trembling hand ran swiftly down the thin leg of her six-year-old boy, and felt for the crooked little foot. The crooked little foot was still there, just as she knew it would be, her tightly pursing lips seemed to say. Perhaps her faith had not been very robust.

One young mother paused, momentarily blocking the traffic, while she lifted her blind baby shoulder high and gazed hungrily into the child's opaque eyes. All the sickening grief of a sickeningly grieving world spread across her face as she slowly turned her head and made a pitiful little sucking noise with her lips as if she had been stabbed. A compassionate hand was laid under her elbow, and she resumed her tramp to the stairs, consulting each step for safe footing as she descended from Calvary's Fountain to have pressed into her trembling fingers an amiable, smiling, wide-eyed, blue-eyed, china doll—the gift of the white-organdied angels, and the black-velveted Angela, and the blood-red Hands, nailed to a Tree. They also handed her a red rose-bud. Dinny hoped the management had had the forethought to snip off the thorns.

A bit of unusual stir about Angela detached his gaze from the retreating figure of the blind baby's mother. A nine-year-old boy, with steel braces on his emaciated legs, was being gingerly put down from his father's arms, at Angela's command She prayed—audibly, this time—in a tone of assurance, of gratitude, as if the boon she asked was already a *fait accompli.*

The silence was absolute, as Angela unbuckled the boy's braces. The clatter they made, as she cast them aside on the floor, had the effect of heavy chains dropped by a prisoner freed. She took the child by the hand, and bade him walk.

He walked! There was a sudden, concerted intake of breath in three thousand open mouths. The father of the boy, an embarrassed farmer, smiled self-consciously, smoothed his tawny moustache, and followed along. The mother stooped and picked up the braces. Angela darted a swift glance, noting the act. She betrayed a faint, fleeting trace of annoyance, but instantly regained her grateful smile, put the skinny little hand of the lad into the big red hand of his unstirred father, and quickly returned to her post beside the pulpit.

Dinny's quick intuition suggested that the little drama had gone bad. The boy's father was a dolt, and his mother was a woman of little faith. Doubtless both of them knew the boy could take a few faltering steps without his braces if someone held his hand. To the vast crowd, however, the miracle was genuine enough. Anyway—the crowd had come to see miracles, and was definitely on Angela's and the Lord's side.

The meeting was drawing to an abrupt close now. The choir had risen and was leading the congregation in praising God From Whom All Blessings Flow, with an unction that certified to the complete success of the demonstration of grace outpoured.

Angela, with face a bit drawn, evidencing that the neural strain of the hour had cost something, raised a graceful, hand, pronounced a brief benediction, and left the pulpit. As she passed Dinny, she glanced straight into his staring eyes, stopped, searched his face, and spoke:

"Ferdinand!"

Dinny extended his hand soberly, almost deferentially. Angela did not take it.

"Come to the hotel—the Savoy—at five."

She did not pause for a reply to her command. When Dinny turned, somewhat disconcertedly, to observe what Channing might have made of this revealing episode, his friend had taken prompt advantage of the priestess's exit, and was rapidly escaping. Channing glanced back over his shoulder, drew a quick, non-committal smile, and pointed significantly in the direction of the stage door, as if indicating they would meet there.

He had vanished, however, when Dinny, thick in the exodus, reached the pavement.

* * * * *

They did not call her "Miss Brumm," but "Angela Brumm," as if it were a four-syllable word accentuated on the ultimate.

When the girl at the Information Desk turned to the switchboard operator, relaying Dinny's request to see "Miss Brumm," she said.

"Mr. Ferdinand Brumm has an appointment with Angela Brumm."

She did not say, "Mr. *Ferdinand* Brumm has an appointment with *Angela* Brumm." There was only one authentic Brumm, and that Brumm was Angela *Brumm*.

The bell-hop, whom he trailed to the elevator and over the padded carpet of the seventh floor, did not ring, but opened the door to the first room of what proved to be an extensive suite. This first was a very business-like reception office where Dinny stated his errand to a white-gowned secretary.

"Angela Brumm is expecting you, sir. Come with me, please."

They passed through another room, equipped for secretarial purposes and occupied by three typists zealously tapping noiseless machines. The large sitting-room adjacent was brightly appointed, clearly the boudoir of a woman who knew how to surround herself with the indispensables of the well-to-do; everything in excellent taste, Dinny thought, as his conductress signed him to a rust-silk davenport, and retired.

Angela sauntered in presently, from the opposite door, her shimmering gold hair plaited down her back, dressed in a flowing négligée of unrelieved black silk, black silk stockings, black silk slippers. The high heels added a touch to her regal carriage. Dinny stood, wondering what manner of take-off this conversation might have, after a lapse of more than eight years. Would Angela begin with something conventional—"unexpected pleasure"—and that sort of thing?

"People call you 'Dinny,' now; don't they?" she asked, negligently, as she approached. "I would have told you to come at once, dear," continued Angela, putting both hands on his broad shoulders and lifting her face for the kiss which speeded his heart a little—"but I'm frightfully uncomfortable until I've had a bath and a mauling by my masseuse."

Dinny understood and expressed his amazement that she could go through so much nerve-wrecking business, daily, without breaking.

"But you're the picture of vitality," he added, honest admiration in his eyes. They sat, at her inviting gesture, on the luxurious davenport.

"Well?"—Angela glanced up brightly, smiling inquisitively—"now you've seen it, what do you think?... Is the Man in the Moon disgusted, or amused, or—amazed?"

"He hasn't quite made up his mind yet, Angela," returned Dinny thoughtfully. "He's always reserved, you know; probably a bit over-cautious.... Maybe due to his age."

Angela puckered her full, red lips into a playful tease.

"I presume Luna thought it a good show," she ventured, blue eyes widening roguishly.

"Luna leaps at conclusions, of course," parried Dinny, Angela's woman-of-the-world air and tone mystifying him: he hoped he was keeping his surprise out of his voice. "However"—weighing his words—"instinct maybe more trustworthy, in such matters, than shear intellect.... If you don't mind leaving the Moon out of it, for a moment, I'll admit I was never so uplifted, and—expectant, and—"

"—and shot down, tumbling, wings broken, scattering a trail of bloody feathers—" prompted Angela, when he paused, groping for the right word.... "Am I right?"

Dinny soberly studied her face, somewhat perplexed by her candour.

"Not quite," he said, indecisively. "Not shot down, exactly, a little more as if one had risen rapidly, dizzily, in a balloon—and it had sprung a leak.... One had to come down, then."

"And it was a rough landing," sympathized Angela. "I knew by your face."

"Quite!" admitted Dinny—"but one still has the balloon. Whether it is beyond repair remains to be seen. I'm afraid I haven't had the courage to look.... Anyway—there's been no time. This sort of thing deserves some—some thinking over."

She nodded, comprehendingly.

"You may find you've lost nothing by your cruise, Dinny.... Judging from the things you've been writing—and I follow them closely, dear, laughing and crying, laughing at them and crying for you—it seems you haven't even known you *had* a balloon.... Perhaps it's been worth a trip to Dorchester, just to find that out."

Which of his sardonic, satirical cronies, thought Dinny, would have had the effrontery to predict that, some day, he might sit in a confessional, unreservedly pouring his sincere wistfulness into the dainty pink ear of an itinerant woman evangelist and miracle-worker! His mood amazed him.

"Honestly, now, Dinny!" Angela had murmured, intertwining her fingers with his. "Let yourself go—a bit.... It'll be good for you."

"It has come—only twice"—said Dinny, dreamily—"in about fifteen years—this strange, brief, uncanny tug; this afternoon, and another time, in a Catholic Church, when I was a freshman.... But—when I was a small boy, Angela, I frequently experienced big, suffocating waves of—of exultation. They never came in winter, as I recall, and never except when I was alone."

Dinny reclined, staring at the ceiling, and reflected.

"Yes—go on," said Angela, quietly, patting his hand.

"Only on summer afternoons, flat on my back, looking up into the blue and white, a gentle breeze stirring, bees humming, birds singing, squirrels scampering about—I used to get it, then—just a big wave of it, and it would be gone.... I didn't know what it was, and I can't describe it now, but—I suppose brave old Walt came about as nearly—"

"Walt?" queried Angela.

"Whitman."

"Oh—I never knew him that well," confessed Angela. "Somebody gave me a book of his poems. I've always meant to—"

Dinny glanced in the direction of a well-filled book-case.

Angela, following his eyes, rose, and crossed the room.

"Maybe you can find the place, Dinny, and read it to me. I think I'd like to hear it," she said, returning with the book.

"It's pretty long," warned Dinny, leafing rapidly. "I'll try to give you just an idea of it.... Of course"—he laid the open book face downward on his knee—"I'm not meaning to say that I had precisely these thoughts when I was a little chap, but the thoughts I had have never been put into words more adequate to describe my feelings than these."

Angela impatiently took up the book, and confronted him with it, nodding her head.

"Just a minute, Angela—and then I'll read some of it for you... . I think I hated religion, from the start. As I try to recover my boyish opinions, I think I always knew that religion was a selfish, ignorant, hole-in-a-corner affair perpetuated by small people.... God had instantly fallen out with the world, soon as He'd made it. But He was glumly allowing the Whole Thing to go on, despising It, deploring It, enduring It, and wondering how long it would be yet until all the people became Baptists; and the Baptists, aware of His impatience, shouted back, 'How long, O Lord, how long?'... Previously—ages before the Baptists—God had wondered how He was going to put up with everybody but the Jews, who seemed to have caught His fancy.... I knew, by instinct, that all such stuff as that was rubbish!... Adam!—and Adam's 'fall'!—I think I knew, even as a freckle-nosed, barefooted, little boy, that it was nothing but a fairy-tale, and not a very pleasant one, at that. It didn't ring true.... And all that tiresome story of early Jewish magic left me cold. I hated it!

"But—sometimes—on summer days, a wave-like surge of—gladness, of—of understanding, would sweep over me. I would suddenly *belong!*—if you get what I mean. The Whole Thing was all of a piece, and I was part of it, and—"

Dinny took up the book.

"Whitman says he had heard a great deal of talk about the beginning and the end; and he writes—

"There never was any more inception than there is now,
Nor any more youth or age than there is now,
And will never be any more perfection than there is now,
Nor any more heaven or hell than there is now.

In all people I see myself, none more and not one a barley-corn less,
And the good or bad I say of myself I say of them.

I know I am august.
I do not trouble my spirit to vindicate itself or be understood.
I see that the elementary laws never apologize.

I think I could turn and live with animals, they're so placid and self-contain'd.
I stand and look at them long and long.
They do not sweat and whine about their condition,
They do not lie awake in the dark and weep for their sins,
They do not make me sick discussing their duty to God.

They show me their relations to me and I accept them,
They bring me tokens of myself...

I wonder where they get these tokens.
Did I pass that way huge times ago and negligently drop them?"

Angela sat, with brooding eyes, venturing no comment, when Dinny paused.

"Just for a moment—today—I had one more strong, quick *tug* of that... whatever-it-is! Perhaps you know. Of course you know!"

"Exactly when—Dinny?" murmured Angela, scarcely above a whisper.

"Well—I'd like to say—it would be the most gracious thing to say—that I got it through something you said or did; but that wouldn't be quite true.... It came while your choir was singing that opening anthem—the Gounod thing—'Unfold!'... Angela—did you ever catch a big, fighting trout?—I mean a huge, muscled, determined, *savage* trout?... No?... Well—you've been casting for three hours; quite confidently, at first, having been told there's trout in the pool; rather impatiently and exasperatedly, after an hour; and then dully, unhopefully, mechanically, half-inclined to quit, scorning yourself for going to the bother—"

"I'm following, Dinny," prodded Angela. "Do catch one!"

"And then—suddenly—there's a *strike!*... I don't mean there's a timid little nibble of some sluggish, grubby four-inch blue-gill.... I mean a swift reaching and grabbing and a *tug* that bends the rod to a horseshoe, and the reel goes 'Zzzing'!"

"Great!" shouted Angela, eyes shining.

Dinny stilled her enthusiasm with an outspread palm.

"And then—the line falls limp—and whatever-it-was had given you that instant's exultant thrill—is gone!... But"—pursued Dinny, meditatively—"just to know you're still capable of a fleeting exultation like that, even if it's only for an instant—well, as you say, it's worth a trip to Dorchester."

"Can't you stay a few days, Dinny?" pleaded Angela.

"No—I'd probably not get it again. In fact, I'm quite sure.... The physical healing—you know.... It was—do you mind if I speak plainly, Angela?... It was the most shockingly cruel affair I ever saw.... My dear—*how can you?"*

Angela's voice trembled when she replied.

"Sometimes I help them," she said, hoarsely. "I—I thought I could at first. I was honest, Dinny... And then—they just expected it, and insisted, and there'd been so much talk about it... But, Dinny, sometimes I do help them... a little... Really!"

He shook his head, with a faint, incredulous smile.

"I didn't come here to rebuke you, Angela. You know your own business, and you handle it—*superbly!* God knows I've no right to offer you any counsel—but—" He hesitated.

Angela gripped his hand in both of hers.

"Say it!" she commanded, soberly.

"Very well—I think you're making a cheap and grotesque thing out of a mystery that's too big for you—too big for anyone!... It's a great pity."

Dinny rose, laid his long hands under Angela's elbows, looked her squarely in the eyes.

"I'm quite proud of you—all but *that!"*

"Must you go? Have dinner with me. I don't eat—much—but I'll watch you. Please?"

When she saw he was quite determined to leave, Angela gave him her hand, gave him her lips, smiled, pushed a bell. Dinny left without a further word.

* * * * *

In the morning, he found among the many letters waiting in his box, another package—they came daily—from *The Times.* He opened them without interest, tossing them aside, half-read. Here was one addressed from Pine Hill, Wisconsin. Dinny's curiosity was stirred.

Dear *Sir:*

This is in reply to your recent advertisement for a "Research Secretary." I formerly worked in New York, and the clipping was sent me by a friend.

As to age and physical dimensions, I could qualify for your position, if it is still open.

I know almost nothing about Indian mounds, but am willing to learn from you.

Very *respectfully,*
JOAN *BRAITHWAITE.*

P.S.—I do need a job, Dinny, quite frightfully! JOAN.

CHAPTER XIII

IN the pursuit of his singular trade, Dinny Brumm's requirement of a "research secretary" was about as urgent as his professional need of a trap-drummer or a tea-taster.

At the moment of his frantically impetuous decision to advertise for news of Joan, it had not occurred to him that he might soon be put to the necessity of inventing an occupation for her.

As for the expense involved in taking on an employee, the prospect of assuming such a responsibility, with Joan as the incumbent, filled Dinny with proud delight. He had plenty of money. His residence in cheap Bohemian quarters and his association with friends mostly of simple tastes and meagre means, while not an intentional frugality, had made but small demands upon his mounting income.

He had preferred that manner of living. Had he possessed a fortune yielding a million a year, his sense of humour would have stood in the way of its distribution by any of the customary tactics employed by the gilded whose alleged exploits in quest of pleasure would, he believed, have bored him to an early and welcome grave.

With the exception of mild extravagances for books, theatres, and clothing—for while Dinny always dressed conservatively, he dressed well—his personal outlay was so trifling that for more than two years his disbursements per month had rarely exceeded his income per week; nor was that quite all of the story, for he had been very fortunate in his discreet speculations.

Tommy Forsythe, whose natural flair for prognosticating movements in the stock market had been capitalized to his own very considerable advantage, was generous with timely tips. Without making much more than an interesting avocation of his investments, at Tommy's canny suggestion, Dinny had been doubling his income. If, therefore, he should find himself disposed to take on a "research" or any other kind of a secretary, it would be no inconvenience.

It was quite evident from the plaintiveness of her little distress-signal that Joan was in straitened circumstances. Dinny tried to imagine the glorious satisfaction he would experience at sight of the superb creature, exquisitely groomed, smartly gowned, happily independent, with pride in her eyes and money in her purse—himself responsible for her well-being.

For the first hour after his receipt of her letter, Dinny's entire attention had been devoted to the pleasant daydream of wrapping a probably half-starved Joan around an expensive collation of Vitamins A, B, and C, to the accompaniment of haunting melodies dispensed by the Hungarian orchestra at Dexter's. Joan, stifled and staled by who knew what drudgeries out in little Pine Hill, Wisconsin, should have a sunny, gaily equipped apartment, high up, somewhere on Riverside Drive, with a beautiful view. He would show her how a successful young syndicate writer thought his secretarial help ought to be treated. It would be great fun.

But when he tried to construct a tentative portrait of Joan's patrician face, in its response to a detailed statement of his happy plans for her comfort, he found himself dismayed. Joan would not fit into that picture. Joan would not consent to become his beneficiary, nor would she accept a penny more than such secretarial services were worth on the open market.... And, by the way, just what would be the nature of such services? Any flimsy subterfuge he might ingeniously invent would only invite Joan's indignation, once she discovered herself in a mere sinecure.

Only one tenable suggestion offered itself. Dinny, as an ardent student of Pepysian lore and the Restoration which he considered the most interesting period of English history, had lately amused himself by tinkering with an idea for a magazine article to be entitled "Pepys on Lord's Day." His only reason for not proceeding to the first draft of it, at once, was explained by his own distaste for the considerable drudgery involved in digging out of the diary all of Samuel's chronicles in reference thereunto.

He could set Joan at that. Surely she need not suspect that such employment was mere make-believe. By Gad, he wanted that information. Dinny found himself becoming rather indignant in his imaginary debate with Joan, who had looked him squarely in the eye and accused him of giving her something to do that nobody in his proper senses would ever want done.... What do *you* know about what I want? Maybe I'll ask you to mole out some further data about other people's observance of the Sabbath. Maybe I'm going to write a book—two or three books—on this subject. Maybe I'll want to know how all the characters in Dickens, Scott, Thackeray, Hawthorne, and a lot more, entertained themselves on the Lord's Day.... That's what a research secretary is about! Funny you didn't know that!

By evening, Dinny felt himself prepared to answer Joan's letter. His manner of approach was friendly but dignifiedly businesslike. He needed secretarial help, and it had occurred to him that Joan, if footloose and attracted by such employment, would admirably adapt herself to that position.

He didn't mind admitting—this sheet had to be torn up, several times, before it carried just the right degree of restraint—that it would give him more personal pleasure to be working with Joan than with anyone else of his entire acquaintance. (Joan mustn't be frightened off by hints that he hoped their association might be a bit closer than the business relationship contemplated.)... And he was looking forward with keen anticipation to her arrival; and when might he expect her—for the Pepys matter would not stand much putting off—and might he hand her the enclosed draft to cover travelling expenses?

Eight days elapsed before there was a reply. Dinny's face fell when the money he had sent her dropped out of the letter.

She had not expected, she said, that Dinny would personally engineer a job for her on his own staff. She had written that she needed work, hoping that if Dinny happened to know of anything he would tell her. Her reply to the advertisement in *The Times* "really couldn't be resisted." It had so pointedly signalled her out as its object.

You have kindly inquired what I have been doing. Shortly after Father left us—we were quite out of funds, mother and I—it seemed best for me to apply for work. That was not so easy, for I had not been trained for any specific kind of employment.

Barney Vaughn's father—he was very kind to mother and me through all that dreadful time—

Dinny scowled, wondering apprehensively what might be the nature of the obligation Barney's father felt he owed to Joan.

—knew a man of influential position with Minch & Grimsby's in New York. I got my position that way; started as a saleswoman; was soon advanced to the Personnel Department. I liked that very much.

How I came to leave there is too long a story, but you will know it wasn't because I stole anything or slighted the work in which I was greatly interested. Is it sufficient to say that I walked out, late one afternoon, nose in air, on receipt of a significant hint that I might have a much larger income by assuming other tasks than I had bargained for? (Now please don't go plunging into Minch & Grimsby's waving a hard fist and offering to kill somebody.)

Mother was far from well. She had gone to live with Aunt Patty and Uncle Jim at Pine Hill, Wisconsin. Uncle Jim Bailey has a furniture store and is the town undertaker. He had wanted me to help him in the store.

So I came to Pine Hill. Mother continued to decline. She was never well after father's death. Three months ago, she passed away.

Since then, my life here has seemed almost unendurable. There is nothing to do that interests me. Uncle Jim and Aunt Patty are very kind and want me to stay, but know that I am restless and consent to my going to New York.

"By Gad!" shouted Dinny. "She's coming! She's coming!"

I am returning the money. It was good of you to offer it. I have saved enough to pay my expenses. If you really think I can be of use to you as a member of your organization—

"My organization," chuckled Dinny, a bit worried. "Wait till she sees it! What could I have said to make her think that?"

—I'll do my level best. If it doesn't work out, maybe you can help me find something else.

I expect to leave here about the middle of next week. I shall call you up about ten o'clock Friday morning, and get my orders.

Gratefully,
JOAN.

* * * * *

She did not expect to be met at the train, but he would surprise her. Deducing from the time-tables, Dinny hypothetically routed Joan to arrive at six-thirty on Thursday evening. Short of funds, she would not patronize an extra-fare train. Neither would she linger in Chicago. Six-thirty was the time.

Thursday was the longest day he had ever spent. In the forenoon he went up to The Roosevelt and reserved a room "for a lady who is to be my guest for a couple of days, at least," the clerk, recognizing Dinny's name, promising every attention and giving definite assurance that the bill would not be presented to Miss Braithwaite. Yes—and he would personally see to it that the flowers would be in her room when she arrived.

A few moments after six o'clock, Dinny was wandering about the huge concourse of the Grand Central, nervous as a cat. He tried to kill time by inspecting the various wares at the news-stand; bought an expensive box of chocolates and the latest *L'Illustration.* At the quarter-hour, he strolled toward the gate. As the minutes slimmed down to four, three, two, Dinny found his heart beating rapidly. The suspense was eating him up.

The straggling group of welcomers began lining up along the ropes. The gate was open now. The train was in. The vanguard of the day-coaches plodded up the incline, bumping their legs with their fat, frumpy luggage.

Here came Joan!... She was carrying her own bags. She looked weary. Now they had found each other's eyes, and her half-reproachful, half-pouting little smile seemed to be saying, "You really shouldn't have gone to the trouble. I didn't expect it."

Dinny reached for her baggage and passed it along to a redcap. Joan put both her hands in his, as his welcoming gesture invited, and lifted her brown eyes inquiringly.

"How did you know?"

"Oh—I meet all the trains," said Dinny. "Sometimes people come to New York alone—and appreciate a little friendly greeting."

"Taxi, sah?" inquired the red-cap.

"No," snapped Dinny—"The Roosevelt."

"Yassah... At the desk, sah."

"But—Dinny!" protested Joan, as she watched her bags bobbing away through the crowd, "I can't afford to go to The Roosevelt—even for tonight."

"We're going there for dinner." Dinny took her arm, and signified by his manner that there was to be no debate about this.

"Oh, but I've had my—really, Dinny, I'm so mussed and the train was so dirty. All I want is to go some-place where I can clean up." Joan halted, obdurately.

So—she had made this long journey in day-coaches, and was worn to a frazzle!

"Where had you thought of going?" demanded Dinny.

"Out to the place on Eighty-Sixth—where I lived before."

"You come with me, and do as I say.... You're my employee, now, and this is an order." Dinny tried to be very stern.

"I don't begin work until tomorrow."

"Nevertheless... Let's have no nonsense. You're tired."

Rather confused and reluctant, Joan demurely consented to be propelled through the throng in the brightly lighted station. Dinny paused at the desk, spoke to the room-clerk, and, turning to Joan, said, in a tone that expected her prompt compliance:

"Follow the boy... Give yourself plenty of time... If there's anything you want, ask for it... I've an errand. I'll meet you here in the lobby at eight."

Joan shook her head.

"I don't want to, Dinny." Her eyes were troubled.

"It would be quite embarrassing—if you didn't."

She stood for a moment, debating, and then said, her voice lowered almost to a whisper—"I can't pay for it... I'm sorry."

Dinny looked her soberly in the eyes.

"Please do as I tell you!" he said, biting his words into a crisp command.

She drew a tired little smile, and followed the boy.

"Strike *one!*" said Dinny, triumphantly, to himself, as he watched her enter the elevator... "The darling!"

* * * * *

Joan's hour and a half had done wonders for her. When she came down, Dinny, who had been pacing about, restlessly, watching the clock and counting the minutes, quickly joined her, wondering if other people were not thinking him a lucky dog. She was simply dressed in black crêpe, but carried herself with all the poise and confidence of a queen in ermine.

Dinny's admiration shone in his face. He was recklessly ecstatic.
"Haven't you grown some more, Dinny?" she asked, taking up her napkin.
"I hope not.... I wasn't exactly frail before, if you recall.... Remember the trip we took through the ravine, the time Ernie sent us for a key?"
Joan smiled, nodded, flushed a little.
"I'm afraid I wasn't a very pleasant companion," she said, regretfully.
"You had good reason, Joan... I had been behaving very badly. You'll find I've changed... Vastly improved—"
Dinny broke off to order their dinner, consulting her wishes, but making it evident that her negatives were not taken seriously when she demurred against unnecessary items.
"What's the nature of this vast improvement, Dinny?" queried Joan, when the waiter had retired. "I've been reading your articles."
"Have you?" Dinny's eyes sparkled, appreciatively. "Then that means you like them!"
Joan pursed a doubtful smile.
"Not necessarily... One doesn't always have to like what one reads .. But—I'm an optimist, you know. I keep on hoping you'll write something I'll like, sometime."
"For instance?"—Dinny was too happy to be dashed by her criticism—"If you'll tell me what sort of thing you'd enjoy, I'll make a special effort, dear."
There was a considerable delay before Joan replied, and when she lifted her eyes they did not immediately meet his own.
"Dinny"—she said, as if announcing a resolution that had required some debate, and might not be warmly received—"let's start right... I've come here to work for you... Please dont make it awkward for me. Or—I'll not be able to do it, you know."
"But you *are* my dear, Joan!... You needn't try to reciprocate, the least bit. I'm not expecting it. I'll not worry you with it. You're to think of me as your employer, and you can be assured of the sort of treatment that would be desirable by an employee... But—you will be my dear Joan... just the same!"
"Thank you, Dinny," she replied, respectfully grateful. "Now let's talk about something else... Where is your office? Do I come at nine? Are there other—help? How much of my work will be done in the library? I hardly know what you want me to do, you know."
Neither did Dinny know. He suggested that they eat their dinner untroubled by dull care: plenty of time for that. Her hours would be of her own choosing. There was no office. There were no other secretaries. Joan was to make the researches for him, and report "from time to time."
"Once in the morning—and once in the afternoon, maybe?" guessed Joan, vaguely.
"Something like that—or once a week, anyhow," agreed Dinny, indecisively—"unless, of course, you were working on an assignment like this Pepys affair, which will probably take you a month, at the least."
"Then I won't see you for a month—after you've told me exactly what you want?"
Dinny made a quick gesture of protest.
"See me! Of course! Every day! We'll be having dinner together, and there are at least a dozen good shows you'll have to see without delay.... You didn't think I would let you perish of loneliness, did you?... Shall we dance?"
Joan was thoughtful for an instant; bit her pretty lip, and reflected, seriously. Then, apparently coming to an impulsive decision, she nodded brightly, rose, and offered herself to his arms. Dinny held her very close, and whispered: "You precious darling!"
She brushed his cheek lightly with her hair, and murmured, entreatingly, rather breathlessly:
"Oh, Dinny—please—let's don't—I mustn't."

But her fingers tightened on his shoulder, and Dinny's happiness was almost more than he could bear.

"You *are* my darling... aren't you, Joan?"

She did not reply, but glanced up into Dinny's eyes, searching them soberly—and smiled.

* * * * *

Dinny was aroused at eight from sleep, profound because belated, and felt a great wave of happiness breaking over him.

The messenger at his door handed in a letter bearing the device of the Roosevelt Hotel.

Dear *Dinny:*

I've been thinking things over. I don't see how I can work for you. Maybe you will help me find something else to do. Please don't try to dissuade me. I'll meet you in the hotel lobby at one, as we agreed. Would you like to take me to the Metropolitan Art Museum after luncheon? I'd love it. Thanks for everything.
JOAN.

So—that was that. Joan insisted on having something else to do. Perhaps she was right. He would consult Tommy. He would tell Tommy all about it—everything! No—Joan wouldn't like that. He would approach Tommy as if the applicant for work were a casual acquaintance.

At ten, he had Tommy on the telephone. Would Tommy do him a favour? Very capable young woman, daughter of the late president of his little college in Ohio, was in town seeking employment. Yes—she had had good experience at Minch & Grimsby's. Did Tommy know of an opening anywhere?

"Might possibly place her here with us, if she's all you say," replied Tommy, obligingly. "Tell her to come in at once. I'll talk to her."

Splendid! Dinny called Joan, who was in—and delighted. She would go over to Lacey's at once. Mr. Forsythe? Thanks!... Dinny should hear all about the interview when they met. Yes—at once. She'd be waiting. Thanks again, Dinny!

"Such a busy morning!" exclaimed Joan, breathlessly, when he joined her. "I'm moving back to my old place on Eighty-Sixth, where I lived before. My trunk has gone out there already."

"How did you make out with Tommy Forsythe?" queried Dinny.

"Beautifully!" Joan was radiant. "He was so friendly. I'm to be in his department for a month, beginning Monday; and then, after I've learned my way about, as he put it, I'm to be given a chance in the Personnel... I'm so happy... What all did you tell him, Dinny?"

He gave her a proud smile.

"Just that you were an acquaintance, daughter of my college president, fine girl. I didn't add that you were an adorable, lovely—"

"Tut, tut!" cautioned Joan, softly.

"The taxi-driver won't tell—and, as for Tommy, he'll discover it. Tommy's one of the best there is, Joan. I hope you'll like him."

She was sure she would. Tommy had treated her as an old friend. She was going to like it at Lacey's.

"And so"—regretted Dinny, dolefully—"you're not to be my fair employee, after all. I'd quite counted on it, you know."

"Perhaps I can help you, anyway. I wouldn't mind digging out the story of what Sam Pepys did on Sundays. I might do it, evenings... Any more work on the novel, today?"

242

"Very little... No composition; just a few more rough notes, and a short cross-section of conversation between Cecil and Margery, who've got themselves in no end of a scrape."

"You mean *you've* got them into a scrape," accused Joan. "You created them; didn't you?"

"It's a fairly accurate picture of real life, I think," said Dinny, defensively. "Such things happen every day."

They had arrived at a little French restaurant on Forty-Fifth, a favourite of his, and were investigating—Joan with curiosity—their variegated assortment of *hors d'œuvres.* She had insisted on knowing something more about the new story which Dinny had begun to tell her last night. Throughout the luncheon he talked and she listened attentively, without more comment than little murmurs of encouragement and interest.

When, however, he had brought the narrative up to date with the stark outline of an episode considerably to the discredit of his principal characters, Joan frowned—a little flushed.

"It had never occurred to me before," remarked Joan, when their taxi had reached Fifth Avenue and had turned north en route to The Metropolitan, "what a heavy responsibility rests on the shoulders of a story-writer."

"In what way, dear?... Let's have your theory."

She hesitated, groping for adequate phrases.

"Perhaps I can't express it, but it's something like this: when a man builds a bridge, or a tower, or paints a picture, or composes a song, he really isn't a creator in the sense that a novelist is a creator.... You—for example—created Cecil and Margery, just as Jehovah created Adam and Eve—"

Dinny laughed, teasingly.

"That Garden of Eden affair points no moral, Joan. That was just a story—about Adam and Eve."

She nodded, victoriously.

"Exactly!—and so is this just a story—about Cecil and Margery. Who's ever going to estimate the wholesale damage done to human personality, through the ages, by that Eden tale?.... No—I don't believe it, and I know you don't, but millions have believed it, and do believe, at this moment! Think of the centuries of unfair, unjust, belittling appraisals of God—all derived from some ancient shepherd-minstrel's fantastic story, told at an evening camp-fire on some desert oasis!"

"Bravo—Joan! Proceed! God!—that's good!"

"One of the best things you've done, Dinny, is to sneer and scowl at that old story, and its monstrous implications. Many times, in your ridicule of orthodoxy, you've pointed the finger of scorn at a crafty Jehovah who would bring an innocent pair of inquisitive people into the world, and immediately direct their attention to some experiment brimming with tragedy.... But aren't you doing the same thing to Cecil and Margery?"

"How absurd!" laughed Dinny.

"It's too serious to be absurd," persisted Joan, soberly. "Your new book will be on the stands in a few months. It will have a great sale among all the restless, scornful, idol-smashers in the land. They follow you as if you were a new messiah. You've never done a novel for them, and they'll grab at this one while it's still damp from the binders."

"Laus Deo!" exclaimed Dinny, fervently. "I hope you're right!"

"It's a very pretty picture you draw of Margery, innocently yearning for an expanded life. Little Glenville, Missouri, offers security, three meals a day, and a minimum of struggle; but Margery isn't quite satisfied with her easy Eden. She wants a larger life. Well—why in Heaven's Name, don't you give it to her?"

The taxi drew up at the kerb. They sauntered up the steps, momentarily diverted from their serious theme, traversed the spacious foyer, and continued through to the huge chamber of replicas and models of classic buildings.

"Let's sit here for a moment, Dinny... I think I want to finish what I was saying... It's quite important—to me, at least."

She laid her hand lightly on his arm, and swept his face with an entreating query.

"This Cecil—he was so discontented, too, in Sparrow, Minnesota; wanted to go places and do things. Why didn't you let him?"

"Didn't I?" protested Dinny.

"What makes it all seem so pitifully tragic," Joan went on, unheeding, "is just the fact that a hundred thousand young Cecils and Margerys, fretting and steaming in their little Glenvilles and Sparrows, are sure to identify themselves with this pair of revolutionists. Can't you think of some better destination for these people of yours, who are sure to be trailed by a nondescript army of admirers, than this degrading wallow you've planned for them?"

"Oh—it isn't quite that bad, Joan... Come now!"

"Dinny—you've a great chance! There isn't a priest or a preacher or a poet or a professor in the whole world who has the opportunity that you have.... You haven't gone in for sentiment. You haven't had any use for religion. You've been a fire-eating iconoclast. Every cynical young fellow, bent on freedom from the old frustrations, is hanging on your words. There isn't one single idealist, in the whole crew of modern apostles, able to command the attention of these discontented people—people like you and me.... Why don't you capitalize this peculiar grip you've got on the imagination of your—your Cave of Adullam, and show them the way out!... *What a chance!"*

"Nonsense, Joan!" scoffed Dinny, superiorly. "What sort of a figure d'you think I'd cut? I'm not writing Rollo books. There'd be a laugh go up that you could hear to the poles!... Besides—I'd rather draw honest pictures of life as it is, no matter how ugly, than to paint frescoes and friezes of the heavenly host. I'll leave that job to the parsons."

Joan smiled a little, her expression reminding him of the gentle dejection she had shown, one eventful night, in her parlour at Magnolia. She snapped the latch of her bag, absently, a few times, and rose.

"Let's forget it—then," she said, strolling over to the model of the Acropolis.

Dinny joined her, silently, and not a little troubled.

* * * * *

He had not seen Joan for five days. She had begged off from engagements on the ground of fatigue. Her hours were long, her new work was exacting because unfamiliar, a great deal depended upon the record she might make for herself at Lacey's, especially through these probationary days. The excuse was valid, and Dinny had tried to be patient.

Tonight they had dined at Dexter's and were now en route to a musical show at The Strand.

"Been seeing much of old Tommy?"

"Of course—every day.... We lunched together, yesterday."

"I didn't know that was customary," commented Dinny, with a surprised little chuckle. "You might as well have worked for *me.*" He tried to make this sound like a pleasantry.

"Don't be silly. Tommy thinks I've the makings of a buyer, and wanted to tell me a lot of things there's no time for, when we're working. It was very interesting."

Dinny pretended interest in the traffic-jam, ahead.

"That's quite reasonable. Tommy can do a great deal for you, if he wants to—and evidently he does. You've got on well with him.... Calling him 'Tommy' now, eh?"

"He's just a big boy." Joan's tone was maternal. "It's awfully easy to call him 'Tommy,' don't you think? It was you got me into it. ... Rather I'd not?"

"Why should I care?" Dinny's magnanimity was almost militant. "I just asked out of curiosity. I had hoped you two would like each other.... Well—here we are, dear."

The show was good; tuneful, colourful. Joan seemed to enjoy every minute of it. Gad—how vital she was! Dinny tried to share her enthusiasm, but had to confess to himself that the piece was dull and tedious. Annoying little dissonances rasping from deep inside him, shrilled the ensemble until the clamorous yelp of it tore at his nerves. He was glad when it was done, and inhaled the first tonic draught of the outer air with reinvigorated spirits.

Joan was graciously remote, almost too interested in her distractions to be giving much thought to the new phase of their comradeship. Whether she was still sensing the slight constraint which had slowed them up, on that afternoon at The Metropolitan, or had some other reason for mentally fending him off, Dinny could not make sure. They were on the way to her quarters, now—she had insisted, because of her work—and within another five minutes Dinny would be headed for home tormented by forebodings.

"Can't we take a little spin in the park before we put in?" suggested Dinny. "It isn't late."

"If you like."

He spoke to the driver, who nodded, and slackened the speed.

"Life has become very important, darling, since you came." Dinny's voice was tender. He reached for her hand.

"I'm glad I came, too, Dinny," she responded, promptly. "I never was so happy before... almost as happy as I'd like to be."

"I wonder if I'm supposed to know what that means—about your—your wish to be happier.... Is it—anything I can do?"

Joan did not immediately reply.

"I—don't—know, dear," she said, at length, doubtfully. "I rather hoped you could, but—maybe not."

He drew her to him.

"Joan, dear—we do belong to each other, you know."

"Sometimes—I've thought that, too, Dinny." There was a weary little sigh. "But—you see—I have to live. I need air, light, sunshine! You don't seem to require it. Sometimes we really do belong—just for a moment... and then... well—we don't belong any more than—than rocks and petunias belong!"

"But, darling, we needn't try to be alike! That's the real beauty of a comradeship like ours. Neither has to sacrifice personality, opinions, or individuality of outlook."

"No—we needn't try to be alike," repeated Joan, thoughtfully, "but it would be preferable if we belonged to the same kingdom of nature. I'm for the world! I like it! It warms me, and I respond to it.... You're at war with it, Dinny."

"Oh, Joan, dear—can't you forget this silly little difference in our viewpoint.... I love you, darling."

"I know," murmured Joan, laying her cheek lightly against his shoulder.

"And you?" he whispered. "You do care—don't you, Joan?"

"Yes—Dinny—I care.... I care so much that I simply couldn't bear to live that close to perfect happiness—and—and be robbed of it."

"I'll try—very hard—Joan," promised Dinny, sincerely.

"Do—please—Dinny!"

Joan's cheeks were wet with tears when he kissed her. He was stirred to an almost painful ecstasy by her response to that kiss.

For a long moment she clung to his lips; then, nestling her face against his arm, with a tremulous little sigh, she said, with passionate insistence:

"Don't fail me, Dinny.... You know—now—how much I love you."

CHAPTER XIV

JOAN, who had been crying, was mechanically collecting the remains of their picnic; the mockingly gay paper plates, the paper cups, the half-emptied little bottles of olives, artichoke hearts, anchovies, the sandwiches, the devilled eggs, the chicken, the ingenious French pastries.

"Don't bother, Dinny," she said, pensively, as he ventured to assist.

He put down the salad plate and made quite a task of lighting his pipe, uncomfortably wondering if Joan felt herself not only an object of compassion but of chagrin, too, as she sat, tousled and swollen-eyed, gathering up the pitifully absurd litter of the feast she had spread, an hour earlier, with such a bright, confident air, archly mystifying him with the delicacies she conjured from her wicker basket.

It was rather debasing to Joan, wasn't it, to sit here and owlishly watch her attend to these little drudgeries? Perhaps it was even more humiliating to her if he tried, awkwardly, to share them.

"Go take a stroll and smoke your pipe," she suggested, divining his perplexity. "I'm not very nice to look at, anyway." She smiled, with a sort of childish contrition. "I'm sure my nose is red.... Awfully sorry, Dinny."

"It was a crime for us to quarrel on a day like this," growled Dinny. "All my fault, Joan."

She shook her head, preoccupiedly.

"I'll divide the honours with you.... Run along, dear. I'd so much rather you did... And we won't talk about it again—ever!... Anyone would think we might have learned better—by now."

"My God—yes! We're a couple o' fools!" Dinny unfolded his long legs and scrambled to his feet. "I'll be back presently, then. You've the book.... Think I'll saunter down and see the chap's sailboat."

They had left shortly before eight, that June morning, bound for the country in Dinny's new sport roadster which he had bought with just such excursions in view. They had had the streets to themselves. Dinny had called the tubby old Hoboken ferry their private yacht.

Shady, lawn-clipped Montclair was still asleep when they rolled softly through. Except for an ambling group of little girls with long curls and short skirts, three of them walking backwards, obviously bound for Sunday School, and a slim, sedate lady of forty-plus, carrying a black parasol loftily over a high-perched black hat, who was being overtaken and passed by a square, craggy, determined man with a Bible, the residence streets were deserted.

Joan had furnished most of the talk, gaily offering an unpunctuated flow of light persiflage, undaunted by Dinny's silent and studious attention to the road, for he was still far from a competent driver. It was clear, though, that he had something on his mind besides his responsibility at the wheel.

Greenwood Lake, their objective, was all that Joan had hoped it might be when, last night, they had touched heads over the road-map in her little parlour.

The shiny blue car was parked in the grove, at eleven.

Suddenly shaking loose from his dourly reflective mood, Dinny made up for his taciturnity on the road by exhibiting a noisy hilarity as he unloaded their festival cargo and spread the new motor-rug on the grass, fifty yards from the lake-shore. But his impetuous jollity bubbled by artifice, thought Joan. It was not quite spontaneous... Perhaps he would tell her.

They were nearly finished with their luncheon when, Joan having come to a full stop in her narrative of recent events at Lacey's, Dinny, who had been fixedly staring at her face without hearing a word she said, suddenly blurted out:

"I've some news for you."

Joan nodded, understandingly.

"I knew you had," she said, playfully, but a little anxious.

"I'm not sure you will approve," he warned, "but I've accepted the editorship of *Hallelujah*...Begin in September."

She recoiled as if he had struck her.

"Oh, Dinny—how could you—after what you'd promised? There isn't a magazine in the whole lot of them that's been so mean—and cynical—and fault-finding... It has hurt me when you even contributed to it. Now you're to operate it!... I'm sorry you told me."

Dinny did not meet her eyes, but gazed glassily at the lake, scowling.

"Don't my feelings count, at all, dear?" persisted Joan, tenderly reproachful.

He recalled himself, then, as from a distance, and regarded her critically.

"I've never undertaken to discipline your thoughts, Joan," said Dinny, crisply, "and—I hope this isn't going to sound too surly—I dispute your right to regulate mine."

"In other words—it isn't any of my business."

Dinny leaned back on one elbow, toying with the fringes of the rug.

"I wouldn't have thought of using that phrase, Joan, but—is it?... You see"—Dinny's brows contracted as he felt for his words—"it's very difficult to refashion another's mind, even if both the—the redeemer and the sinner are—"

"I don't think that's very kind, Dinny... And I dislike being talked to that way," interrupted Joan, her lips trembling.

"Well—putting the mere choice of words aside—you've honestly and lovingly wanted to make me over into something other than I am.... And I have honestly and lovingly tried to accommodate you. But it's no good. It won't work. I can't do it. If our difference of taste were—Look here: if I hated golf, and you liked it, I would go with you and play it—just because it brought you pleasure. I'd learn to like it for that reason. But this is a different matter, dear. This is a problem of work and wages, bread and butter. I'm a journalist. That's my profession. I'm not omniscient, and I can't write about just anything and everything. My line is criticism. And when you ask me to leave off criticism, and go in for hymn-writing and sappy little twitters set to the score of 'Buttercups and Daisies,' you've asked too much!"

Joan, with mounting indignation, made an impatient little cry, but Dinny raised a hand, briefly, and went on doggedly:

246

"There's a whole battalion of sugary smilers, rocking and knitting and purring on the front porches of 'Houses Built By the Side of the Road.' I doubt if there's room in the journalism of loving-kindness for one more dulcet coo; and, if there were, I'm mighty sure I haven't the voice for it. I know you've set your heart on my doing it; and, because I wanted to please you, I've made some sincere experiments in that direction; bought a little volume of verse entitled 'Just Folks,' and tried to set my big feet in those dainty tracks, but it was hopeless, darling. I put on my starchy white pinafore, tied my little pink sunbonnet under my chin, and went skipping merrily down the road with a nice basket of pansies for rheumatic old Granny MacDoodle, but before I had gone very far I found myself grinning again. I can't help grinning, Joan. You'll either have to get used to that grin—or—"

"Or—*what?*" queried Joan, soberly.

Dinny was tardy with his reply.

"I'm afraid the alternative is—up to you."

"May I talk now?"

"Please do. It's your turn."

"Well—I never asked you to scribble soft sentimentalities. I hate them, too. There's been too much of it. But there's a pretty wide gap between 'Pollyanna' and *Hallelujah*. It's easy enough to understand why people crowd about the news-stands to buy *Hallelujah*. They've been fed up to the throat on the other thing.... But *Hallelujah* isn't the right answer to their demand for something more sturdy and sensible than mawkish slush.

"There are a few things that deserve better than to be ridiculed. I looked through the last issue of *Hallelujah*—because you asked me to. One article was a reprint of a little booklet some man had written for private circulation among his friends and neighbours. It was dedicated to the Kiwanis Club. He was its president in Littlegrass, or somewhere, Oklahoma. He and his wife had just returned from a six-weeks' trip to Europe, and he wanted to tell his friends what they had seen. It was badly written, and full of childish comments; but the man hadn't prepared it for the smart young spoofers who read *Hallelujah*. It was intended for simple-hearted, inexperienced people who own the houses they live in, and pay their bills, and go to church on Sunday, and have only one wife.... And *Hallelujah*—that's always ranting about the bad manners of yokels who eat with their knives, and don't know whether Chekhov won the last Irish sweepstakes or swam the Channel or designed the dome for Saint Peter's—printed that friendly little booklet—mistakes and all—to fetch a chuckle from the really cultured people, the smart people who've been about, and know which spoon comes first—and who wrote 'Ulysses.'... I don't believe I could bear it to see your name at the top of the staff in a magazine so—so—"

"Yes?"

"—so self-consciously clever! So pompously superior! So insolently vulgar!... If that's the kind of company you find yourself at home with, Dinny Brumm, I'm sure you'd never be very happy with me!... You've said you aren't 'omniscient,' and mustn't be expected to write about everything. That's just where we disagree. You *do* think you're omniscient! *Hallelujah* is omniscient! There isn't anything that *Hallelujah* doesn't know, far better than anyone else. It cackles at theology for being dogmatic, and calls all the preachers idiots and all the creeds rubbish—and after it's through ridiculing them, the all-wise *Hallelujah* proceeds to be just as dogmatic and arbitrary as the people it reviles.... It's always poking fun at Jehovah.... You'd think, from the way it hands down sublime oracles about Art, the Drama, Music, Literature, that it expected the whole world to reserve its opinion about any art-form until *Hallelujah* had spoken.... After that, the wise would know just what it would be safe for them to think.... And now you're going to be the Solomon who supervises the schooling of the sophisticates.... No—Dinny!—I don't believe I could live comfortably quite that close to the summit of Olympus. I'm afraid the bright light would hurt my eyes. I'd always be at a terrible disadvantage!"

"Very well, then," rasped Dinny, "that's that—and now we know where we stand.... It would be tragic for us to go on with it."

"I'm glad you see it, at last," agreed Joan, in the same tone.

Dinny's lip curled, unpleasantly.

"By the way," he drawled, dryly, "speaking of sarcasm and ridicule, you're fairly good at it yourself. I may be bitter enough, but I'd never talk that way to anyone I loved.... And I don't believe you could, either."

Joan hung her head, and put both hands over her eyes, and wept like a little child.

"Oh, Dinny, forgive me," she pleaded, brokenly. "I didn't mean to hurt you."

For an instant, he was moved to join her with assurances, but still smarting under the sharp raps, he delayed; and the longer he delayed the harder it was to conciliate.

Joan's little storm of emotion cleared. She wiped her eyes, and tried to smile. Dinny stole a quick glance, and solemnly looked away, heavy-eyed. With a long sigh, broken by little sobs, she began to gather up the fragments, Dinny watching her automatic movements dully. She was a typical picture, he thought, of Woman—instinctively carrying on with the tasks Nature had assigned to her, regardless of what tragedy might rake her heart.... No man would have done it. A man would stalk away—and let the damned dishes go to hell!

He pitied her, and his pity was tinctured with a trace of vicarious mortification. He could have wept, himself. He picked up the smeary little paper plate on which his salad had been served him, and was in the act of passing it across to her.

"Don't bother, Dinny," she said, pensively.

He walked down to the shore where a tanned youth was untangling some new white ropes in his little sailboat, and was surprised at the steadiness and nonchalance of his own voice as he chatted, amiably, with the young stranger. Here he was—only three minutes and one hundred and fifty feet away from a disaster that had pulled his very house down about his ears—calmly puffing his pipe and inquiring whether the yacht's ropes were the same thing as sash-cord.

Did that mean, he asked himself, that his love for Joan was of less consequence to his happiness than he had thought? Or was his quick recovery due to the fact that he was taking the instinctive course of Man? Woman, anchored to dishes and brooms and beds and babies, always had had time to think—to grieve, to regret, to mope and grow morbid. Man, whacked over the head with a battle-axe, had had no chance to sit down and nurse his hurts. He must instantly be on the alert for another wallop from some other direction.... He and Joan were faithful to their respective atavistic responses to their mutual disaster. She was sitting there on the grass, crying softly, and telling herself her world had gone to smash. He was smoking his pipe, and talking to a stranger about different weights and weaves of rope.... But that didn't mean his little Paradise hadn't been hurled to Purgatory— same as Joan's.... Odd—reflected Dinny.... Elemental forces!—he had never felt their grip, or appraised their long reach, quite so discriminatingly before.

She joined him, after a little; sauntering down to the shore with all the evidences of her grief discarded. While he had been philosophizing over the easy resilience of the male— the quick, decisive rebound of the male who, no matter how straight the gate, how charged with punishment the scroll, would remain the master of his fate, the captain of his soul— the moody, brooding female had deftly repacked the hamper, stowed it in the car, combed her hair, adjusted her swanky little hat at a jaunty angle, powdered her nose, reshaped her lips, donned a smile, and had now slipped a hand through his arm as much as to say to the boy in the boat, "I've tamed this Animal to drive single or double; rack, pace, trot, run—or what gait would you like to see him do?... I've been training him for fifty thousand years.... He doesn't know it, of course. The silly ass thinks he's the warden of the asylum instead of a patient."

Dinny wasn't sure he liked to have his theories tossed about in this reckless fashion.

"I've been thinking," he said, after they had driven a mile without much talk. "I've had my nose to the grindstone for a good while—in my work, you know—and I believe a change of air would be good for me. I'm going abroad for a few weeks."

"Splendid!" enthused Joan. "I wish I could."

He laid a hand gently on her arm.

"Very well—I'll take you."

"No, Dinny—we've settled that!" Her voice was casual now.

"I'd be glad to, you know."

"I believe you would—but it's quite impossible."

The long silence that followed gave her words a chance to chisel their way quite deeply into her memory. She recalled them, with a start, one September evening, when, in response to a similar invitation as sincerely offered, she used them again, *verbatim*.

A swarthy gypsy girl, one afternoon, last summer, had padded softly back to the little office in Uncle Jim Bailey's dimly lighted, varnish-reeking furniture store, and, pausing before Joan's high desk, had said:

"Your fortune—for four bits?"

Joan had declined.

"Please—I'm hungry."

The girl had slipped the half-dollar into a dirty, beaded purse attached to her belt, and reached for her client's hand.

"Make it short," advised Joan. "I'm busy."

The girl had stooped over the extended palm, scrutinizing it intently, Joan, with equal interest, marvelling at the black, straight, coarse hair on the bowed head, seeming to belong to a well-groomed horse rather than a young woman.

"You are going on a far jorney... on a beeg boat... with a tall man."

"Is that all?" asked Joan, as the girl moved off, with the slinky gait of something born in the woods.

She paused, spread one brown hand high on her hip, tossed her head arrogantly, and retorted, her white teeth gleaming in the twisted, half-envious smile:

"Ees that not enough?"

* * * * *

According to Dinny's weekly letters, the cynical amusement he had expressed in his first laconic, staccato, dash-sprinkled note, scribbled on his return from viewing the changing of the guard at Buckingham Palace, was giving way to an unexpected admiration for monarchy.

Joan needed never to have been in England to guess what might be Dinny's instant reaction to the ancient shrines and tombs of the departed great. He had a flair for making history vital, and was extraordinarily well posted on the lives of British sovereigns.

As for the bronze and marble memorabilia of departed kings and queens, Dinny's interest was assured, and Joan confidently expected him to relay observations faithfully, interestingly reflecting the half-dreamy mood in which he would saunter through the gloom of the cathedrals.

She was quite unprepared, however, for his comments on contemporary pageantry.

"It will have to go, of course," ruminated Dinny, in mid-July, writing from the Victoria Hotel in London. "The general drift is toward republics, and the last of the kings have already been born. There will be no revolution, no choppings-off, no slow tanning of royal heads on iron-spiked towers. The British manage to express themselves with but few gestures. They are not a yelping, mobbish, excitable race. When the time comes, the king will be retired on half-pay and allowed to keep his horses, dogs, and grouse-gun.

"But it will be a great pity when 'the captains and the kings depart': especially the kings, though I presume you couldn't very well have kings without captains. They'll leave the stage together.

"I'm afraid I've become quite a tory, Joan. I have had time and opportunity for a lot of thinking about this. Humanity hasn't evolved out of the king phase. It's a wise, practical government. Republics sound promising enough in their constitutions, highfalutin slogans, apostrophes to 'liberty,' senatorial oratory, and patriotic verse, but it's no good in practice.

"I'm for the king! I'm for the divinely ordained king who can do no wrong, no matter what capers he cuts. America would be vastly better off topped by a real, honest-to-goodness king, with twenty million dollars' worth of diamonds in his hat, bells on his fingers and rings on his toes, than a harried, worried, temporary president whom any sleek-haired little squirt, paragraphing and cartooning for some impudent, wisecracking editor, can smear with his smartaleckisms."

"Why—Dinny!" exclaimed Joan, happily, to his photograph on her table. "Whatever's happened to you?"

"The whole king business is on the skids, no doubt; but it's a great misfortune. So's the Established Church close to the end of the last inning. Nobody on bases, two men cut, and two strikes already called on a feeble bat.... But it's a pity. The thing's had a sort of majestic dignity. It's never been in a suppliant attitude, penhandling the brethren and sisters for sixpences to pay the parson's coal-bill. It has been guaranteed by The State, okayed by The Crown. It's been lofty, confident, time-worthy!

"Maybe it hasn't been quite so fussily, busily, frantically energetic, and maybe the rank and file of the people have accepted it rather perfunctorily—about the way they accepted breathing and the circulation of their blood—but it has stood there calmly certifying to an Eternal Fact (or at least an Everlasting Wish). It will be voluntarily supported, pretty soon, I suppose. And that will be the end of its greatness.... Oh—it will still go through the motions; but its dignity will have departed.

"That's what ails the nine score different sects in the States. No dignity; because voluntarily financed by people whose Sunday dime has given them the right to dictate its policies. Even they—especially they—who presume to manage the thing have no respect for it. How could they? Don't I know? Didn't I grow up in it?

"Wormy, shiny-elbowed, little Jonas B. Pring, lifetime errand-boy and cuspidorian for some fusty old firm of lawyers, snubbed by his betters, henpecked at home, hectored by bill-collectors, a measly little nobody, contemptuously snooted by his own dog—he's quite a tremendous fellow at The First Church of Christ.... Only place in the whole world where Jonas can let himself go, and be somebody... . Gets up at the annual business meeting and tells the thirty-six women, nine old men, and four little girls, that the Reverend Blubb is no executive and had best be asked to move along.... And on what meat hath this our nasty, contemptible, little Jonas fed? How came he so important?

"Jonas was a subscriber. For fifty cents a week, Jonas had bought the right to swagger up and down the aisles, distributing hymn-books, himself yelping the tune at the top of his lungs. At the small cost of twenty-six dollars annually, Jonas B. Pring, who everywhere else was dodging sharp elbows, shoe-tips, snarls, and skillets, could fold his important arms high over his inflated chest, tuck in his forceful chin, draw a sagacious frown, and tell 'em all where to get off at when the Lord's business was under discussion at The First Church of Christ."

Odd, reflected Joan, Dinny's concern about the Church of England. The only comment she'd ever heard him make about the Anglicans was a sour remark to the effect that their chief job was "to apologize for the Reformation."

She did not commend him for his slightly altered attitude toward "institutions," fearing her approval, however casually phrased, might sound I-told-you-so-ish; evaded discussion of his new ideas; filled her letters with current news, and doings at Lacey's.

There was a great deal in her letters about Tommy, inevitable because her busy life was now bounded by Lacey's, and Tommy was Lacey's so far as Joan was concerned.

She wrote much too much about Tommy without realizing what conclusions Dinny might come to. Tommy's luggage department had been augmented by a line of motor-rugs and other whim-whams relating to cars. Tommy had had a raise. Tommy had been to Chicago, but was back now.

Tommy's brother Victor hadn't been at all pleased with the reception he had received on his Western tour, and was thinking of giving up the fiddle and studying voice. Someone had told him he could sing. Tommy had said he wasn't sure yet whom the joke was on, but suspected it might be on himself.

Tommy had a new eight-cylinder car, very pretty and very easy riding.

After she had mailed her longest and last letter, the second week of August, and recalled what an inordinate amount of Tommy had found its way into her chronicle of current activities, Joan heartily wished she could have it back for revision. However, Dinny would understand. Besides, he liked Tommy; didn't he?

But it was an unfortunate letter to be her last to Dinny, seeing he was so far away, and alone. Joan had expected to write at least once more.

Then the September issue of *Hallelujah* appeared. She bought it hoping to find nothing in it about Dinny's accession to its tripod. The announcement was there—on page one. *Hallelujah* stated, with a swagger, that, from henceforth and until further notice, the increasing success of the magazine was assured, and gave the reason that had all but broken her heart.

Leafing with distaste and disgust through the condescendingly superior titles, Joan presently came upon Dinny at his worst in a venomous attack on a certain great newspaper syndicate.

It was capped "Greck."

Soon after her coming to New York, Dinny, in a mellow moment, had confided his story to Joan. It was not told to solicit her sympathy, or to interpret his maladjustment to the normal ways of viewing human relationships; but, with the whole picture of Dinny's frustrated, disillusioned, and embittered childhood, she had tried to understand the savagery of his cynicism.

Sympathetic as she was, however, toward his disaffection in regard to his father, there was no excuse, she thought, for this unconscionable onslaught.

It seemed that some prominent editorial writer in the employ of "The Greck Syndicate" had caustically criticized *Hallelujah* on much the same grounds as she herself had based her disastrous comments on the magazine in discussing it at Greenwood Lake.

The Craig Syndicate, as everybody knew, had in its employ, at the top. a considerable number of keen, clever, high-powered Jews. They were forever playing to the prejudices of the vast, unintegrated, dissatisfied, general riff-raff.

Hallelujah was in the same business, of course, but bidding for the interest of a different clientèle. *Hallelujah* and the Craig Syndicate were as nearly alike as identical twins, except for this: *Hallelujah* appealed to the prejudices and dissatisfactions of some fifty thousand self-confessed intelligentsia; the Craig Syndicate appealed to about the same invoice of aversions possessed by ten millions of illiterate... How natural that they should hate each other!

Some editorial writer for "Greck"—Joan presumed it must have been the chief incendiary, Enoch Birnbaum—momentarily forgetting, according to Dinny, that he had been divinely ordained to minister unto the feeble-minded, had remarked of *Hallelujah* that it suffered of "grandiose paranoia in the penultimate phase of that malady, with paresis indicated as the unhappy sequela."

Dinny, breathing out slaughter, had assumed championship of the besieged *Hallelujah*. Joan, who knew him as well as or better than he knew himself, could easily picture with what lip-smacking, demoniacal glee he had hauled up the drawbridge, dropped the portcullis, and heated the oil he meant to pour down upon the haughty head of "Greck."

She did not read it all. Undeniably clever, fantastically cruel, Dinny's indictment of "Greck" described him in terms of Moses; Moses the law-giver, Moses the sea-cleaver, Moses the manna-man, Moses the medicine-man.

"Greck," assisted by all Israel, and trailed by millions of uncircumcised, untutored, and largely unwashed hicks and yokels, was headed for the Promised Land. True, he hadn't got any farther than the wilderness, but Jehovah would doubtless look after His People, as was His pleasant custom.

The last paragraph—the one that gave Joan a sickish feeling as if she had witnessed parricide—was a masterpiece of brutality.

"If the great Greck ever made a mistake, he does not recall it. This, too, was a Mosaic gift—forgetfulness. In his youth, Moses ran away and hid himself after having killed a young neighbour; but if he ever remembered, or was regretful, the Good Book—which almost never omits anything resembling contrition—fails to document his misgivings. It is said that Moses' victim was a young man. Had he killed a young girl, he would of course have forgotten the incident utterly, and remembered it against himself no more."

Joan tossed the nasty thing into the waste-basket and washed her hands.

* * * * *

Tommy Forsythe was sailing tomorrow for Lisbon on the *Vulcania*. It was a business trip. He would go to Italy, also returning to New York in late November.

Joan had lunched with him at Dexter's. He had seemed distraught, probably due to his anxiety that all the last-minute duties should have attention. He had little to say, Joan furnishing most of the talk.

At six, he bade her good-bye as she left the store. It was a casual farewell; a brief handclasp, a bit of banter.

At eight-thirty he called her on the telephone. Might he see her for a moment about something rather important?... Would she object to a short drive?... He would call in ten minutes.

They headed for Central Park. Tommy was nervous and moody. Joan's curiosity mounted.

"What's on your mind, Tommy?... Anything I can do?"

He was a long time finding words.

"Joan"—the car slowed down to five miles an hour—"I'm to be away quite a while. There's something I'd like to know before I leave. I have become very fond of you, as you can't help knowing.... Are you engaged to Dinny Brumm?"

She shook her head.

"Then I've a right to tell you that I—"

"No, Tommy, please don't!"

"Will you think about me sometimes, Joan?"

"You know I will, Tommy. You've been such a dear friend. And I hope you're going to have a wonderful trip."

"I wish you were going along.... I'd take you if you'd go, dear."

"I believe you would—but it's quite impossible."

There was a long silence.

"Joan—tell me this much. Are you in love with Dinny?"

"Must I say?"

"No—you needn't say. I understand."

Joan patted his arm gratefully.

"Tommy—you are a dear."

He drove her home then, as he had promised, and soberly said good-bye again at her door. Joan felt very much depressed. Early in the evening one of the girls where she lived had suggested their going to a movie. She should have gone. It was too bad—about Tommy. She had known he liked her, but she hadn't been prepared for this.

Now she could not work for Tommy any more. She would have to leave Lacey's. It was rough sledding... for a girl... in business; difficult to retain the proper balance. If you were up-stage and untouchable in your attitude toward your employer, you had no chance of promotion. If you were friendly, he made love to you.

Old Mr. Abercrombie, of Denver, with business at Lacey's in July, had spent an hour with Tommy. Evidently something pleasant had been said to Mr. Abercrombie about her, for when Tommy introduced him, he said:

"If you're ever tired of New York, and want to live in a really good town, where the air is pure and the wages are right, wire me."

"Maybe I'll do that, Mr. Abercrombie," she had said, accepting it as a gracious little courtesy.

Then Mr. Abercrombie had met several others of the department, and was about to leave, but had returned to her, saying, seriously:

"I meant that, Miss Braithwaite.... We would like to have you at Abercrombie's.... Here's my card."

By midnight, Joan had dismantled her room of everything that belonged to her, and was ready to be off, pending instructions. She called a taxi at midnight and went to the nearest Western Union branch on Broadway. After dispatching the night-letter to Denver, she returned to her room and slept—badly.

At ten-thirty, next morning, there was a wire telling her to come at once. The telegram expressed delight. Joan was cheered.

"Where shall we send your mail, Miss Braithwaite?" asked the mystified Mrs. Higgins.

Joan hesitated, and impetuously resolved upon a bit of bridge-burning.

"I'm not looking for any," she said.

"Are you going far?" inquired Mrs. Higgins.

"Very—and I shall not be back for a long time."

The train left at noon. Joan, feeling like a fugitive, was glad when it was in motion. Once through the tunnel and out into the sunshine, she had a pleasant sensation of freedom from an accumulation of perplexities. She dallied long over her lunch. They had passed Poughkeepsie before she had finished.

* * * * *

The *Berengaria* docked at ten on Friday. Dinny, who had never asked himself whether he felt at home in New York, was glad to be back. England had done his mind a few small services. The passionate impatience with which he had viewed nearly all the traditional reliances—now that they were outgrown, outworn, and anachronistic in a new, mechanized era—had tempered considerably.

There was an assuring solidarity in the massive grey stones of England, poise in the recumbent, armoured effigies that lay in single-file through the vaulted transepts of her quiet cathedrals, peace in her tranquil greensward.

On the homeward voyage, with much time for thinking, Dinny had determined upon certain changes in his manner of living. He would take life a little more comfortably, for one thing. He would live less feverishly, as became a balanced mind. The thought of returning to his shabby little suite in the Village was distasteful. He would move uptown, equip his bachelor apartment with a few solid comforts, and make a less hectic and hurried thing of his life.

Now that he was actually home again—his light baggage had been quickly inspected by customs—he was eager to carry out his resolution. He would proceed to it without delay. Joan would be happy to see him well out of the Village and its associations. How pleased she would be when he told her!... He had quite abandoned his novel. Joan would be gratified.

The rooms were shabbier than ever. The few pieces of furniture that were his should be sent out for redressing. His mother's walnut desk had had no attention ever, for all that it had been knocked about from pillar to post for a quarter-century. Its legs were scratched and scored and its body bore many scars. He must not trust its rehabilitation to any but an expert in such matters.

Why not get going on it at once? He called up Becker's, who dealt in antiques, and inquired for Mr. Becker himself; explained who he was, what he had, what he wanted. The elderly Becker, with an errand in the vicinity of Washington Square, said he would run in and have a look at the desk himself.

Dinny was sorting over his books when old Becker arrived, having found it important to occupy his mind with such diversion as was to be had. He knew Joan did not like to be called to the telephone during business hours. It would be a long day.

Old Becker was a thin, wiry, little man with a grey beard and pale blue myopic eyes that peered at you in an absurdly childish fashion.

"Lofely!" murmured Becker, caressing the rich wood with an appreciative palm.

"My grandfather made it a long time ago for my mother, when she was a young girl," explained Dinny. "The old fellow was quite handy with tools, I've been told; though, of course, the value of the desk is largely sentimental."

Becker drew down the lid, almost reverently.

"Handy mit tools!" he muttered, ironically. "Handy mit tools? Mein Gott! A greadt ardtist! Und you say—handy mit tools; hein?"

He peered inside the desk.

"Vas iss dat?... Mueller?... Mueller!" His pale little eyes searched Dinny. He poured out a torrent of queries. Where did this grandfather live? Was that his name—Mueller? Indiana? Gott in Himmel—no!... Where had he lived before that?

Dinny said his grandfather had migrated from Dresden as a youngster.

"Ah—so!" Becker wagged his head and tugged at his straggling whiskers. "Der Muellers made no desks... but your grandvadder Mueller—he made a desk for his childt.... It iss very lofely!"

So—Aunt Martha's occasional vague, proud references to the glory that was Mueller, back in "th' old country," had some substantial basis of fact. He had always thought the story an exaggeration—one of Aunt Martha's pipe-dreams.

Old Becker was grinning mysteriously, and Dinny regarded him inquisitively.

"Leedle secret, too; hein?" He significantly tapped the exquisitely crafted little pilaster between the centre pigeonholes with an understanding thumb.

"I'm afraid I don't understand," said Dinny, stooping to inspect the pilaster critically. "Secret?"

Becker's expression was a study. He had stumbled upon two secrets—a secret drawer—a mystified owner.

"What makes you think so?" inquired Dinny.

The old man was slow with his reply; looked Dinny up and down, searchingly, as if wanting to satisfy himself that his client was really entitled to know what an owner of such a treasure should have known. Apparently assured on that point, he explained that the central pigeon-holes were an inch wider apart than any of the others. Back of the ornamented pilaster there was a narrow drawer.

Dinny was on the point of suggesting that they experiment, but on second thought decided to make the exploration alone. He quickly came to terms with Becker about the expense, and the old man left, saying: "Ve vill treadt it vell.... Mein Gott!... a *Mueller!*"

With the point of his knife-blade, Dinny endeavoured to loosen the pilaster and start the alleged secret drawer. The little pilaster was unbudgable. Doubtless something else had to be pushed, pulled, moved, before the drawer would open. He inquired of every nook and cranny for a suspicious knob, button, or unexplained gadget. The desk remained calmly innocent of any duplicity. He would have to fall back on old Becker, after all.

253

Tommy Forsythe would hardly have gone out to luncheon by now. He wondered if they might not go together. Perhaps he might find Tommy free to do so. He called Lacey's and connected with Tommy's department.

No—Mr. Forsythe was not in. Mr. Forsythe was out of town. Who was this—please? Oh—Mr. Brumm. Mr. Forsythe sailed for Europe on Wednesday. Yes—Wednesday noon.

Dinny decided to risk asking for Joan, so long as he had the connection.

"May I speak to Miss Braithwaite?"

There was quite a little pause.

"Miss Braithwaite isn't with us, any more, Mr. Brumm."

"You mean she's not with Lacey's? Since when? Where's she gone?" Dinny tossed his prudence aside, and fired his questions as if he'd the right to ask them.

"She's not been here since Tuesday—closing time. We do not know where she is."

"That's strange!"

"Yes, sir... Is that all, Mr. Brumm?"

Dinny's hands trembled as he hunted for the telephone number of Mrs. Higgins. His voice was unsteady when he asked his questions.

No—Miss Braithwaite wasn't there any more... Yes, she had taken all her things and left shortly before noon on Wednesday.... No—she hadn't said.... No—they positively did not know!... And who was this, talking?

Dinny slammed the receiver back on the hook, and sat for a long time, lost in moody thought, wondering if it were really so. He brought both long hands down with a despairing slap on his knees, rose with a sigh, caught up his hat, went downstairs, and strolled down the street, hands deep in pockets, his mind in a tumult. He had lost Joan!... Damn Tommy Forsythe!... Damn Greenwich Village!... Damn *Hallelujah!*... To hell with Everything!

CHAPTER XV

A RAGGED, rumpled, yellowed scrap of paper, solidly printed on both sides in nonpareil, fluttered to the floor.

Dinny picked it up and held it between his fingers while he unfolded the bulky letter from which it had fallen. The fragment could wait. He laid it on the desk. It had taken him an hour, that night, to open the narrow little drawer faced with the miniature Corinthian pilaster.

In the afternoon he had dragged the desk to the window and painstakingly inspected every square inch of its surface. Nothing had come of it. At nine he had laid aside his coat, emptied the desk of its meagre contents—for he almost never used it—and set about his task determined to see it through.

The long, shallow drawer below the lid which, when let down, was the writing-table, he removed. This operation promised little, for the drawer was a full fifteen inches below the pilaster and clearly unrelated, but he had done everything else and had now arrived at the phase of his exploration where the incredibilities were being examined.

Taking up this skilfully mortised drawer in his hands, Dinny scrutinized it, inch by inch. In the centre of the back panel there was a notch in the top, half an inch deep and three-eights of an inch wide. It excited his curiosity. Perhaps there was some small projection in the depths of the desk, at the rear of the aperture from which this drawer had come, something articulating with the unobtrusive little notch.

Aware of his inability to thrust a well-muscled forearm into this shallow drawer-space, he inserted a walking-stick and probed about with the tip of it until he found a small, squared, wooden tongue. He pushed up on it gently. It instantly responded with a sharp metallic click that seemed to come from higher up in the region of the pigeon-holes. The quick, decisive tap, unquestionably the release of a spring, startled him; for upon having reached the path of discovery, Dinny's nerves had keyed to the sensitiveness of fiddle-strings.

Lowering the hinged writing-table, which he had been supporting on his arm, he glanced toward the little pilaster. It was protruding about three inches. Attached to it was a narrow upright drawer. He drew it farther out. It contained a thick letter which all but filled its limited space.

With rapidly beating heart, Dinny held it closer to the desk-lamp, for the writing on the sealed envelope was faded almost to illegibility, and read the words written in a sprawling feminine hand: "Confidential—to my child—from Julia Miller Craig." The letters were so large, and growing larger as the end of the sagging line was reached, that there had been no room on it for the "Craig," which was written below "Miller," almost as if it were an afterthought.

Dinny drew up a chair to the desk, sat down, and, with a strange sensation of having stepped into the presence of a disembodied spirit, he carefully opened the brittle old envelope with his paper-knife. A ragged, crumpled fragment of paper fell out. He picked it up from the floor without regarding it closely. Doubtless the letter would explain.

It was not easy to read even the first page on which his girl-mother had clearly spent the best of her waning energy. This fact she recognized at the outset. She was writing in bed; she was very ill; she would do her best. She was burning up with fever, and things were all "out of drawing."

"God!" muttered Dinny.

She had seemed rather remote—a mere sacred symbol—until he came upon that little phrase.

Why—that was exactly the way he would have said it, himself! He and this girl, nearly ten years his junior, were not only of the same flesh and blood; they were mentally, temperamentally kin!

For the first time in Dinny's life, his mother assumed definite reality. She came alive in this letter—in this single phrase—and spoke as clearly as if she were at his side. He had a curious feeling that he was not alone. He drew a quick breath, and slowly turned his head, glancing up over his left shoulder. Then, pulling himself together, resolutely, he returned to the letter. A wave of tenderness swept over Dinny; something other than a feeling of filial reverence; rather the sense of desire to lend her his strength, as if she were a young sister in dire need of his protection.

Things were all "out of drawing" because she was so hot and weak. Yesterday she had been quite excitable from the fever, and had wandered a little. She would speak of that, later, if her strength held out, she said—

I'm not out of my head now. In fact—my wits seem to be speeded up by the fever. Everything's so much brighter and louder. Father is working, out in his shop, and when he lays his chisel down on the bench, I can hear it drop, both ends of it, the wooden end and the iron part. Each leaf on the maple—I see the three through the window—is twins, after I have looked awhile. One of the twins is blue, the other yellow. At first, when I look out, each leaf is green. After I have looked hard, for a minute, the leaves are twins, like I said, one blue, one yellow. Then my eyes hurt, and I stop looking. At noon I heard the cracked school-bell over at Hinebaugh's. That's four miles. You can't hear it this far. That's how sick I am, and that's how this kind of sickness sharpens you till you're sharper than you want to be, and it hurts. You don't hear things with your ears, when you're this way, but with your eyes. Every tiny noise is big, and pounds in your eyes, deep behind them.

So, if I say anything queer, you will know why, if you're old enough. But I'm not crazy, and I know what I'm doing. I hope you believe this, for I'm going to tell you something very important before I am through, if I can still hold my head up that long. It's pretty dizzy.

"God!" muttered Dinny, half-sick.

If I only knew how to talk to you, dear, it would be easier. I can't quite place you. You're not a baby. I know that. I'm never going to have a baby. One minute, you seem a boy about fourteen that looks ever so much like Zandy, and next minute you're a girl about my age, and look a little like me. I expect they will put me by mother, near the fence, close to where Zandy first told me. There will be some comfort in that—at least there is now.

Dinny's eyes were smarting; his throat ached.... "God!—what a cruel thing for the dear little chap to endure!" He read on.

The Dresden part of it was difficult to interpret. It demanded hours of study, later, and the utmost concentration, for Dinny to disentangle the crashed and telescoped detail of the jumbled memories. The narrative resembled nothing so much as a cyclonded house, with the refrigerator upside-down on top of the piano, and a large, ragged chunk of identifiable dining-room plastering—wall-paper holding it together—in the kitchen-sink alongside a gift copy of Maeterlinck's *The Life of the Bee* and an old wreath of immortelles. The stuff was all there, but out of normal juxtaposition, by no means easily put to rights.

But for the fact that Dinny had already been given reasons for respectful credence in the Mueller tradition, his mother's confused reference to Dresden would have been too fantastic. The things he most wanted to know about that were absent. The superficial detail was highly elaborated; the garden, the garden-wall, hollyhocks, the door in the wall and the wrought-iron hinges on the door, the grassy-banked river, the boats, and a punt with a red-and-blue canopy—but almost nothing about the life of the place.... The cushion on the window-seat in father's room was of rose velvet, but there was not a word about father's reason for running away from home to America or what had become of the people left behind.... There were lily-pads on the pool in the garden and goldfish under them.

The part about his own father was in keeping with the lyrical quality of the Dresden story—a girlishly romantic reminiscence of tender things said and done. Dinny felt, at this point, that the letter had drifted slightly away from the original intention of confiding to a child, and had taken on the style of a personal journal quite too private for any other eyes than the writer's. He was reluctant to read certain parts of it.

Dinny found it very difficult to reverse the career of the spread-eagle, dictatorial, dominant Zandy Craig, of the Craig Syndicate, and return him to the bewildered, gentle, downy fledgeling that had been the "dear, dear Zandy" of his mother's memoirs.... He would have given ten thousand dollars for the unpublished manuscript of "Greck."

Perhaps he had misjudged his father. After all, Zandy—Dinny found himself thinking of this man as "Zandy"—had been but a youngster when it happened. If he had had it to do over again, five years later, he might have shown up better. There was no doubt Julia—Dinny was thinking of her as "Julia" now—loved him, trusted him. Surely that was worth something. You could mark that up to Zandy's credit.

But—all the same—By God!—Craig had killed her! You had that to remember, too.... Well—we could think that over—later.

Dinny turned to the next page, and continued. The writing was even less legible now. What with the cloudiness of the composition, and the almost indecipherable script, his mother's attempt at a discussion of an apparently bizarre theory she had arrived at, in her dishevelled mental condition, was not a thing to be read with full understanding.

The curious metaphysics she seemed trying to express, phrased in whatever naïve terms a country school-teacher might catch up hastily in the exigency of her fatigue and fever, was still further enshadowed by the increasing uncertainty of the nervous pen. The faded letters were so ill-formed that a given character might be *h, n, u, r,* or *v,* with the adjacent vowel offering you your pick of *a, e,* or *o.*

* * * * *

It was nearly three o'clock before Dinny had reached the reference to the little scrap of crumpled paper which, in the stress of translating the letter, he had all but forgotten. He took it up, and read it now, but it seemed strangely irrelevant to the matters his mother was treating with such a valiant struggle to make herself understood.

Dinny went back a few paragraphs, and re-read. Julia had written this at mighty cost. She deserved his best efforts to interpret it.

Long before this trouble came to me... don't feel badly, child, it wasn't your fault... I had been frightfully bitter about lots of things. I was lonesome, and didn't belong in this house. I had never been taught anything worth knowing. I didn't even know how to eat. If it hadn't been for the books I read about the habits and little courtesies of refined people, I would have known no more about how to do at the table than old Florrie.

I got so I hated the sight of them. Father, poor old darling, I loved him with my pity, but that was about all. The girls—Martha never was a girl—were so silly and coarse and ignorant that I despised them with all my heart, hating myself for feeling better than they were. For I was not naturally conceited. I am shy and bashful, really. But I was always ashamed that I was related to Susan and Greta.

I hated Martha. I got so I hated everything she said and did. Since I've been sick—up to yesterday... I'll tell you soon about that, dear... I couldn't bear even to have her touch me. The sound of her voice, down in the kitchen, made me want to get up and shout that she was nothing but a sour old simpleton, even when I couldn't hear a word of what she was saying—nothing but the nasty noise.

I hated the boys. I think I had always hated them. They were dirty, inside and out. They were exactly the same as the rest of the loafers that sat along the porch at Baber's store, and got all quiet when you came, and, after you had passed, there would be a rough rumble of a dirty voice, and then they would all spit and laugh a dirty laugh. If you're a girl, maybe you'll know what I mean, though I hope not much. If you're a boy, and you ever laugh like that, I hope there'll be no chance for me to hear it wherever I'm going to. I'd rather die like a dog, and stay dead forever, than endure such shame.

I don't know what's going to become of you, child, but I do hope you'll never have reason to hate things and people the way I have.

Then—when this trouble came, and lately when it's seemed pretty doubtful—I got to hating the whole world until I was just as sick from that as this other trouble. It was just like a poison that was eating me, burning me on the inside. My hate hurt clear up in my throat. I hope you'll never know what that kind of hate feels like.

"God!—don't I know?" muttered Dinny. "You poor little thing!"

Well—yesterday a queer thing happened. Part of it was awful, and I hope you won't think less of me. Martha came and wanted to read the Bible to me, and I wouldn't let her. She put it under my pillow then, and went away. I was so angry at her and it that I tore it up. Maybe you'll be shocked. It was too bad, and I'm sorry. But I tore it up because it was full of what Martha called "precious promises"—and look what had happened to me! This was God's Book, and He had been mean to me. So I tore up His Book. I'm ashamed to tell you this, but it gave me a kind of terrible pleasure to do it—a kind of hot joy that I used to think the Devil had when I was a little girl and believed there was a Devil.... You don't believe there's a Devil do you, child? I'm thinking of you as a little girl, now, about the size I was when they used to frighten us at revival meetings. I hope you're not living with ignorant people who believe in hell and devils. Surely you've a right to a little better raising than that. I couldn't bear it if I knew you were that poor and degraded.

I quit tearing at the Bible only when my hands were so tired I couldn't move a finger. Pretty soon I fell asleep. Father found the awful mess I had made and cleaned it up before anyone else saw. But there was a little piece left. The next time I was alone I read what it said, and it seemed so different, maybe because it was all there was left.

It seemed to be intended for me. Maybe it won't mean just the same thing to you, because you're not all full of poison and hate and mean feelings toward almost everybody and everything, the way I was. At least I hope you're not, for it's dreadful and worse than any sickness. It really is a sickness!

This little piece that I read wasn't like religion at all. I hated religion. You did something wrong, and had to go crawling on your hands and knees to be forgiven for it. You had to cry and beg and whine like a dog. But this wasn't like that. It wasn't anything to sniffle about the way they have to do in church when they are sorry for hating people who have wronged them. I always despised whiners. They said in church that God wanted you to whine, for He liked to hear sniffles from scared people. So I despised Him for that. He wasn't my sort.

Dinny put down the letter, rubbed his tired eyes, and shook his head. His mother's reminiscences were his own. Again he felt that strange kinship between himself and this unhappy girl who had given him birth. Her blood coursed through his veins. Her queries were his. His criticisms were hers. It was in the blood-stream! His temperament was a biologic inevitability. You grew figs on fig-trees. You grew thorns on thistles. Didn't you? Well—there you are, then! Nothing to be done about it! Is there?

Julia had despised whiners. God liked whiners. "The sacrifices of God are a broken spirit." God liked broken spirits; liked to hear 'em wail; liked to see 'em wring their hands, and pour ashes on themselves. That had been his own chief objection to the whole structure of traditional theology. He wanted to be a man. He wanted to stand upright and face the sun. God wanted him to grovel like a cowed animal. Dinny knew now how he'd come by his passionate aversion to such self-abasing, personality-destroying, soul-defiling ignorance! He wanted to reach across the Border and clasp the hand of this fearless, unfettered spirit. He was proud of his Julia. His eyes were wet with emotion.

This little piece of religion that I had left, lying under my hand as if it was meant for me, doesn't whine at all. It doesn't ask you to whimper for mercy.

It's just a business proposition same as if you owed a thousand dollars to Mr. Smith, and ten other people owed you a hundred dollars apiece, and Mr. Smith said, "Pay me that thousand dollars," and you said, "I can't—with all these people owing me."

And Mr. Smith said, "I don't need the money so much, but I like you and want to be friends with you, and as long as you are owing me you'll be keeping away from me for fear I'll ask you for it and make you ashamed. And it won't do any good for me to tell you just to keep the money and forget it, because that would make you ashamed, too, and you would always feel in debt. So—I'll make you a proposition. If you will cancel all the debts of these people who owe you, and are afraid to face you, so that they can afford to cancel the debts of the people who owe them, I'll call it square with you. Then we can all be good neighbours again, and nobody will be afraid of anyone else, or shy, or ashamed."

This all sounds so much more sensible to me, dear, than the way they talk about it at the meetings. It's just as if God wanted us to do business with Him about these things that have kept us strangers.

Maybe this will sound silly to you, but I closed my eyes and said, down inside myself where there seemed a little spot that brightened up, "Please forget that I tore up Your Book, and help me to forget it too, for it makes me very sorry to remember." And God said, speaking from down inside of me, just as plainly as anything I ever heard, "Will you forgive your father for drinking up the opportunities you might have had, and Susan for refusing ever to come into your room on account of the desk, and the boys for being rude, and Martha for not wanting you to have any fun?"

And I said, "Yes—I will."

And then He said, "Will you forget everything they ever did that has made you disappointed and sorry—just as I'm going to forget everything you've done to disappoint and sadden Me?"

And I said, "Yes—I will."

Of course I can't expect you to understand the strange feeling that came over me, but it wasn't like anything else that ever happened. Please don't think I'm telling you something I dreamed. I was quite wide awake. The queer thing that happened was just as if some wonderful doctor who knew how to cure any disease instantly had given me a powerful medicine that cleared out all the poison! I felt all <u>clean</u> and <u>new!</u>... Then I found myself smiling, and I laughed. And—this was because I am so weak, I suppose—I cried a good deal; but not for being unhappy or afraid or ashamed. Maybe I can't explain this very well, but I felt proud, just as if I had been promoted or had won a great prize, or had discovered I was a princess or something!

It's awfully hard to try to make this sound the way it actually was. For I don't know whether I'm talking to a little girl with a doll in her hand, or a big boy old enough to go to college, but this thing that I've got is a sort of <u>power!</u>

That's the best I can do to explain it. When you get it, you'll know. I want you to have it, for there's no other feeling like it. I believe that if I could get well, now, I could do almost anything!

It's great to be able to talk to God, now, any time you want to, and say anything you like, and know that you're fast friends. It would be wonderful to get well, and see Zandy again; but if I don't, I'll see God exactly as He is; and I'm not afraid.

I thought about it nearly all night—and kept talking to Him, and He would answer me. Please don't think I'm out of my head. I'm awfully tired. That's what makes the writing so bad. And I said I was dreadfully sorry I had misunderstood Him so, and he said, "Well—Hiram and Elmer misunderstand <u>you.</u> They think you consider yourself too nice to have anything to do with them. And Susan and Greta think the same thing, that you're above talking to them about their little troubles."

This morning Susan came to the door and looked at me. She seemed so shy and scared, as if she had never seen me before, and I motioned to her to come in, and she sat down on the little chair by the bed. And it was just about as easy as it had been, last night, when God and I made up. I just reached out my hand and rubbed my fingers over Susan's face, softly. It was the first time I'd intentionally touched her for years, and we almost never had anything to say to each other, not for years and years. And Susan slipped down on her knees by the bed, and put her arms around me, and we both cried, but I was happy, and I loved Susan for the first time in my life.... Dear Child—the poison is all out of me now. Of course, I'm too sick of the other trouble to get well—but it doesn't really matter. I'm happy. I love the boys, too, and I'm going to let them know. And poor father—he does feel so badly about everything.

Dinny put down the letter, and paced the room, unable to endure another line of it. Of course, poor Julia was labouring under intense emotion, terrific neural strain. A great deal of her experience could be charged to an hallucination easily explained. Naturally, the whole family would be wrought up. Susan would have been a beast to remain cold and aloof under the pitiful little tender of affection. Nobody was normal at the time.... But—God!—suppose such relief and release were real! Suppose that for the mere act of unloading one's memory of all the bitter hatreds and cankered grudges, one might feel free to lift one's eyes and smile into the face of God—as dear Julia had—and be cleared of all the "poison!"

Suddenly there came a definite surge of such painful wistfulness to lay hold upon some strength beyond his own as had never possessed him—not even for the instant when Angela's choir, bursting forth with an exultant "Unfold! Unfold!! Unfold!!!" had tugged at his soul—not even in that brief, boyish quest of The Mystery when he had sat in church with the Timmy Fagans.

In those fleeting experiences Dinny had glimpsed the possibility, resident in him, for rapture and radiance. For these ecstatic instants, the Light had broken through, certifying to two facts: there was a Light, and he possessed the spiritual retina to see it. The shutter clicked—and for that one little split-second the Light poured in; but, afterwards, the darkness settled again.

Maybe Julia had found the way to a permanent possession of that spiritual illumination which, rarely, he had sensed with a brief ecstasy that stirred him to the depths, and promptly left him cold.

If Julia had found it, and in such high degree that she was undaunted even by the impending tragedy that stared into her girlish face, might he hope to capture that strange magic for himself? Why not? They were the same sort of people; weren't they? Julia and he were kin. Her queries were his queries. They had shared much the same dilemmas of frustration, disillusion, disappointment. They had shared the same hot hate of a world that had consistently let them down... . Julia had never "belonged," but, at last, *she had "belonged"!*

* * * * *

Slumping down in his chair, taut with the emotional tension of the past half-dozen hours, Dinny covered his face with his outspread hands, and muttered, half aloud:

"I'll give it a trial!... God!—I wonder if I'm losing my mind. ... I'm going to make the experiment, and see what comes of it."

He reached for the crumpled scrap of paper, and sat staring at the well-remembered words which he had heard Uncle Miles read, monotonously, scores of times, words now highly charged with energy. He felt himself studying a formula in Physics. Again Dinny returned to his mood of deep meditation.

God!—suppose the thing were real!... But, if it was real, why didn't more people know about it? If there was anything to it, surely the religious would have practised it. A man who possessed this dynamic joy that Julia had found—why, you could spot him at a thousand yards by the light in his eyes!

That was the appalling obstacle in the way of Dinny's confident belief in the reality of the mysterious "lifting power" that had caught Julia up, and held her, in an hour of crisis.

Would she have discovered it, at all, had she been well, mentally sound, physically fit? According to her own documented testimony, she was upset to the point of having to plead with her child for belief in her sanity. Was she any too sure of it, herself?

Sane people had no capacity for permanently possessing this uncanny spiritual strength. They had brief experiences of ecstasy. He had had them. Doubtless everyone, according to his temperament, had felt these occasional tugs from Otherwhere. Perhaps every inquisitive person nourished the vague dream of making lasting connections with this strange energy of exultation. That's what the religious were out after. They wanted to "fix" their idealisms on the highly sensitized plate, and make them permanent... But—with what success?

Dinny found himself recalling instance after instance, in the little churches he had known as a growing boy, when the activities of a congregation of alleged Christians seemed actually to interfere with the personal peace of the individuals thus brought together. Not only did their religion fail to illumine them: it quite definitely got in the way of their self-confessed aspirations.

He remembered his own grinning, as a lad, over the celebrated rumpus that had rent Uncle Miles's little church at Zanesdale. Mrs. Bilger wanted the Sunday School chairs for the Eastern Star banquet on the same night that Lida Kronk had promised them to the Modern Woodmen of which her Claude was the Chief Axe-Swinger, or whatever it was. And before they had done with the acute phase of the battle, not only was the whole congregation lined up in two hostile camps, but the town itself was involved. Uncle Miles had raced frantically back and forth across No Man's Land, pleading for arbitration, meanwhile being himself potted from both sides. Even as a small boy in short pants, Dinny had considered the affair a howling farce.

Now—in the light of what Julia said she had found, Dinny knew that the vulgar and noisy controversy over the church chairs hadn't been funny, at all. The whole matter had been tragic beyond the telling. Was it not just such small-minded jealousies and stupid little exhibitions of egotism brazenly flaunted by persons conspicuous in the business affairs of country and village churches that had made the general public laugh the whole institution to scorn? Surely, thought Dinny, he had done his bit toward making such *gaucheries* ridiculous. Conventional religion, in the custody of the typical church of his own acquaintance, was not merely banal, farcical, impotent. By Gad—that sort of thing was definitely blocking our evolution! It was shutting off even such fugitive glimpses of the Light as a man might find for himself if left to his own devices as an untaught pagan!

Of course, reflected Dinny, here and there, even in the stifling antagonisms forever on display in Uncle Miles's little churches, a rare spirit contrived somehow to grow.

There flashed across his mental screen the picture of "old man" Houk. They never referred to him in any other way: "old man" Houk, who kept the light hardware and notion store near their church on the edge of Fort Wayne. There was a peculiar light in the old fellow's eyes. There was the quality of thermo-dynamics in his smile. How good God was to him, "old man" Houk was always saying in that gentle voice of his. How "blest" he had been. And sometimes the people laughed a bit when they talked about "old man" Houk's gratitude, for if ever anybody had his nose to the grindstone with nothing tangible to show for it, Houk won the prize. The two girls had married early, one bringing a worthless husband home to live; the other had abandoned hers, returning with three small children. As for the boy, he was no end lazy, impudent, and always in trouble. But "old man" Houk had something!... However—he may not have been quite all there. Even Uncle Miles had said that the old chap had a loose screw.

Now the question arose, in Dinny's mind; was "old man" Houk a bit unhooked mentally, or had he managed to "lay hold" on the energy that Julia had found? Were these occasional mystics inspired or demented?

Pursuing his recollections of Uncle Miles's ugly little churches that seemed bent on nothing but trivial expedients to pay their insignificant bills, in the course of which silly endeavours—rummage sales, ice-cream socials, and shockingly dull home-talent plays—they generally stirred up fresh rows, Dinny's honesty forced him to concede that you really couldn't expect much fineness to develop in the weedy Zanesdales and Ungers, where there was nothing to think about but one's treadmill and the callosities worn thick and hard by one's ill-fitting harness. It wasn't quite fair to judge religion, as an institution, by what one observed of it in Zanesdale.

But then—there was Magnolia! Magnolia had been the mecca for a religious cult whose constituency in that zone numbered well into six figures, a cult that regarded its neighbours with sour pity. Had not smug and pious little Magnolia excoriated and discharged the only Christ-like personality on her staff—the only man in the whole outfit who had had the valour to stand up and say that the Master he followed was an uncompromising apostle of peace?

Dinny remembered how they all used to laugh over the perennial feud between the factions that backed Professor Strickler, who taught Hebrew, and Professor Munger, who taught Homiletics, each of whom had been trying for years to discredit the other in the opinion of the parsons over a region five hundred miles in diameter.

But here, again, fairness demanded that Dinny take account of all the facts in the case. Magnolia, after all, was but a little tea-pot. You couldn't appraise religion at large by the disgusting envies that stood out awkwardly, like sore thumbs, interfering with everything the college and seminary aspired to do.

Who were Professors Strickler and Munger—for all their unctuous mouthings and frock-coated pomposities—but grownup farmer lads, innocent of any experience whatsoever in an outer world of urbanity and culture? Dinny knew their story. Having graduated from the seminary, they had been fortunate enough to marry the daughters of well-to-do lay members of the Board. After a few years of inconspicuous paddling about in the mud and dust of small-town parishes, their fathers-in-law had engineered them into seminary chairs (rocking-chairs), where, between venomous thrusts at one another, they had taught the young fry what they ought to know about the Old Testament in the original, and the theory of preaching the gospel of peace and salvation. Admittedly, that was pretty bad; but you mustn't judge all institutionalized religion by the performances of fat and furtive little Stricklers or lean and malicious Mungers.

No—to be decently fair, you had to look at The Thing higher up. But what results did you get from such investigation? What spirit had actuated the organization of the greater sects in Christendom? What ghost had haunted the passionate conclaves in which reformations, reappraisals, and re-evaluations had taken wing? Surely not the Holy Ghost! Which one of them had walked out of a Mother Church because it wanted a better chance to believe and exemplify the theory of whole-hearted forgiveness, tolerance, sympathy, and "second-mile-ish-ness," which had constituted the very solar plexus of the Galilean gospel? Stand 'em up in a long row and demand their reply to this question, and see what you get: "Do you believe in the celestial commerce whereby you, yourselves, come into the possession of permanent power and radiance, in exact proportion to your ability to condone and explain and forget other people's 'trespasses'?"

And yet—here stood this Ancient Thing.... By Gad—everything else in the world, by comparison of age, reeked of fresh paint, green lumber, hot rivets, and perspiration. It had outlived every other institution on earth, despite the fact that its early death had been forecast by the wiseacres of each generation for nearly two millennia. A new day had come. The arm-wavers were saying that more had happened in the past twenty years than in the preceding five thousand. Radical changes were tearing down yesterday's customs, mores, laws, dogmas. Religion was on its last legs. But was it? Not so you could notice it. The Thing had as much vitality as ever.

What, actually, did it stand for? You had to explain its enduring life somehow, didn't you? Had it arrived at this apparent guarantee of perpetuity by virtue of its high achievement in promoting the world's peace?—Nonsense. It had been a notorious fighter.... Had it offered notable service in encouraging scientific progress?—Ha! ha! Now you tell one!... Had Rome shown much inclination to walk a second mile? Had Calvinism presented the other cheek? Had Wesleyanism handed over its cloak when sued for its coat? Had the Anglicans agreed quickly with their adversaries, "whilst in the way with them?" ... Hosts of them were unquestionably excellent people, the majority wanting to improve themselves; occasional individuals, in all the cults and sects, contriving to "lay hold"; but, considered as institutions—considered as An Institution—exactly what did it stand for? How, in the face of all the dismaying facts, had it earned its evident immortality?

It had always done a bit of philanthropy, yes; but so had the "unredeemed," for that matter. Its sporadic efforts at charity were always being outranked in volume and administrative acumen by secular agencies. It had always pretended to educate, but was without caste in the opinion of high-powered schools. Sometimes the parsons made a great to-do about the imposing array of North American Universities, all of which had been founded by preachers, and backed by churches. Even so, at the beginning; but such of these institutions as had actually won high recognition had long since lost their original religious affiliation.

In short—what was religion good for? What did the Ancient Thing stand for? What made it last? Dinny thought he knew. Organized religion stood for the people's *yearning!* It was a costly monument to the people's *wistfulness!* All the people, considered as individuals, felt occasional little clicks of the camera shutter: the Light poured in on them for an instant: they kept hoping to make these fleeting surges of ineffable luminosity permanent, good for all weathers!

But, in the face of this testimony of religion—intolerant, irascible, pig-headed, hair-triggered—was it really worth the effort for a person so materialistic, so critical, so unsentimental as himself, to hope that he might find the spiritual dynamics which had come to the rescue of his disappointed and embittered girl-mother?

Dinny looked at his watch. It was four o'clock. He had exhausted the last tag-end of his mental resources. Any further thought about these matters, in his present condition of fatigue, would be merely exasperating. He threw off his clothes, snapped out the light, and slept.

* * * * *

Street noises roused him at nine from a deep sleep, and he sat up dully trying to remember where he had left off. There was an odd sensation that the day promised to be eventful, though in what manner Dinny had no definite idea. The best he could make of it was a nervous tension of expectancy, anticipation, novelty, somewhat as he had felt when he awoke on the day he had sailed to England, and on the day Joan was to arrive. Something was going to happen.

Tuning himself up with a cold shower and ten minutes of vigorous callisthenics, he dressed carefully and walked over to The Brevoort for breakfast. There were several important things he had planned yesterday to do today. He must go up to the *Hallelujah* office for a bit of conference, for one thing.

On his homeward voyage, Dinny had looked forward to this new position with interest; hardly with pleasure, for it had been difficult to feel quite satisfied over it while haunted with the memory of the hurt look in Joan's eyes. And even now that she had run away, and didn't belong to him any more, and was probably pacing the deck of the *Vulcania*, at this very moment, fondly arm in arm with Tommy Forsythe, Dinny still sensed a feeling of unrest and dissatisfaction over the whole *Hallelujah* business, heartily wishing he had never gone in for it. Perhaps tomorrow would be soon enough to report there.

He had planned also to go uptown and look at a few bachelor apartments somewhere in the west eighties, but there was really no hurry about it.

Well—then—what *was* the important thing he had on his mind?—this something that had to be done without delay.

Dinny never wearied of analysing his own mental processes. He had learned that it was no longer considered scientific to speak of one's "subconscious mind." The new Psychology said there wasn't any such thing. "Subconscious mind" was as obsolete as "Soul."

But you could call it what you liked, or refuse to call it at all; the fact remained that two distinct mental processes could be carrying on at the same time in one individual's head. Dinny often marvelled at this queer phenomenon. Here he was, this morning, rumpling his hair with his fingers and trying to remember just what it was that so urgently demanded his attention, and, all the time he was wondering, his subconscious mind—which was mere nonsense, of course; for he didn't have a subconscious mind, there being no such organ now recognized by science—was quite certain that he would return promptly to his room and attempt an experiment based on Julia's letter.

While he was drinking his second cup of coffee, Dinny rather reluctantly admitted to his subconscious mind—which he didn't have—that such had been his intention from the moment he had wakened, an hour ago, and that if it would just have the decent courtesy to wait until he had finished his breakfast, he would do as he had planned to do, anyhow, without benefit of such counsel. In these occasional interior conferences, Dinny's subconscious mind always seemed much older and more mature than the rest of him, which he was inclined to resent. There was something a bit too paternal and hortatory and all-wise in the advice offered from that quarter.

This morning, the distinct identity of his two minds seemed more clearly defined than ever in his experience. Perhaps he had been thinking about that one matter, bringing both his conscious and subconscious minds to bear on it, until they had temporarily lost their capacity for integration, like the green leaves on Julia's maple tree that she had stared into twins—one blue, one yellow. It was almost as if he, himself, were facing a battle with a very mature and omniscient ghost who, normally benign and approximately acquiescent, had suddenly decided to say: "Yes—you will!... And I'll see to it that you do!"

Dinny was determined, however, not to give in too promptly. On his way back to his rooms he decided not to take another look at the gripping letter until he had done at least one "Green Cheese" essay. He always tried to keep about three weeks ahead of the release date, and was now four days behind his schedule, due to indolence on shipboard.

Taking every advantage of current and seasonal topics, Dinny's theme for this morning's composition would relate somehow to the national observance of Columbus Day. He had scribbled a few rough notes, yesterday; nothing of value, however. All he had was:

"Lookit, Gramp!... They got the flags out again!... Some festival or other."

263

"That doesn't mean anything, Luna. The Ku Klux have terrified them into buying flags. They're flying almost every day now. Hadn't you noticed?"

"Yes—but the Knights of Columbus have run one up on their buildings."

"Humph!—it must be something else, then. What happened on October twelfth, Luna? You wouldn't be likely to know, would you?"

Dinny typed this much, and, thrusting his hands deep in his coat pockets, appraised it with a critical eye. What was the good of it? Many people would grin, no doubt. Some of them would be sore. All of them would again be made aware of the widening rift between the "One Hundred Per Cent Americans" and the field, embracing other pigments, other creeds, other nativities, than the increasing organization of sheeted patriots who had bought their right to hate their neighbours for Ten Dollars and the price of a white cotton disguise.

He drew the paper out of the machine, and crumpled it in his fist. Why not try to do the thing constructively once. Surely the readers of his "Green Cheese" column would forgive him a wee digression from his habitual spoofing, scoffing cynicism. They might even enjoy just a touch of sincerity; not too sentimental, of course: that would spoil everything.

Why not try it? It would be in line with the experiment he hoped he was going to make, wouldn't it?

Dinny inserted a fresh page into the typewriter, and wrote the opening phrase which always distinguished his feature article. "Lookit, Gramp!"

And then he sat for full five minutes, absently toying with the keys, utterly unable to proceed.

But—I can't do anything like this, reflected Dinny. If there's any substantial fact in what Julia says, there are a few things you have to do first before you can take an affirmative position. You've got to "un-bitter" yourself. He grinned, rather foolishly.

"Very well, Mr. Smith," he soliloquized, half aloud, "we'll say I've owed you a lot of money; and Zandy Craig, and gloomy old Aunt Martha, and the Reverend Miles Brumm, and Spike Davis, and Major Clemens, M.D., and Barney Vaughn, and Orville Kling, and—and Tommy Forsythe—owe me. And you're prepared to call it square, and sweeten me up, if I stop despising these other people.... All right, sir, I'll take you up!" Dinny made a sweeping gesture of dismissal to the imaginary company of his enemies.

"I'll forgive the outfit at one swoop. Or, if you'd rather, I'll forgive 'em one at a time. Here they go. I'll forgive Uncle Miles, first—the damned old embezzler."

Suddenly the sardonic grin left Dinny's face, and a wave of self-disgust swept him. What a cad!—to let his chronic cynicism defile a situation that had been brought about by a farewell message from the dear girl who had died to give him his life! There would be no more of this vulgar sacrilege, he could promise himself that much. He would give up all attempts to do the impossible thing, of course. It was not for people of his type. He had carried his load of aversions too long. It had grown fast to him. But, at least, he could honour Julia's faith by refusing to make a travesty of it!

That much settled, then, Dinny lighted his pipe, and drew up to his machine, quite confident that he had shaken off this strange temporary psychosis that had been playing the devil with his thoughts. The page wasn't quite straight, and he made himself a great deal of bother adjusting it. The machine needed a drop of oil, and it took quite a while to find it. The ventilation in the room wasn't very good, and he opened both windows. Having sat down again, ready now to go at his task in earnest, he felt a draught and got up to close one window partly. His coat cramped him, and he took it off.

And then—from far in the depths of himself, where his subconscious mind might have been, had he had one—there welled up a solid, substantial, mature thought, as definite as if it were actually phrased in a spoken command: "You may as well proceed with the thing you are going to do. You're wasting your time. You've lost your knack at Green Cheese. There'll never be any more; not from you. You've gone into this liberty-quest too far to back up! Admit you're beaten—and see what you can make of the other thing."

Dinny rose, with a sigh, went to his mother's desk, and sat for a half-hour with his elbows on the writing-table, his head in his hands.

Rousing, at length, with an air of determination, he went to the telephone, called a familiar number, and was almost startled by what he found himself saying.

"Hallelujah?... Mr. Brumm speaking.... Is Johnny Keaton there?... Please.... Johnny?... Dinny Brumm.... Very good. How are you?... I'd rather expected to be in, today, but I've just had word that I'm required to make a business trip West. May be all of a couple o' weeks. Wish you'd carry on without any co-operation from me until you hear from me....

That's fine.... And Johnny—how would you like to do my Green Cheese stuff for a while. You can, you know. Better than I.... If you like it, and can get away with it so everybody's satisfied, it'll be a nice thing for you. I'm tired of it. And I may have to do quite a little travelling for a few weeks. Might even have to go to Europe. You take over all the editorial responsibility up there until you see me again.... No—this is something sudden; more or less personal business; emergency stuff.... Thanks, Johnny. I'll write you more in detail.... Yes—tonight; if I can get a reservation. Just now learned that I had to go.... Goodbye."

Dinny turned to his clothes-closet, reached to a high shelf and threw down the bags he had put away yesterday.

"There may be nothing in it," he muttered, as he began peeling his clothes off their hangers and tossing them on to the bed, "but I'm going to give it an honest work-out.... God!—if the thing should be true!"

CHAPTER XVI

"I'M a-goin' out that way myself soon as this here gol-darned loafer changes my oil," volunteered the middle-aged farmer, who had taken his foot off the hub and sidled up to help answer the query about transportation to Oak Grove. "Yuh c'n come along, if yuh don't object t' ridin' with a hawg."

"Bet you'd raise hell if anybody else called yuh thet, Jase," drawled a voice that apparently belonged to the pair of legs protruding from beneath the truck's engine.

Jase spat, nonchalantly, grinned, and rubbed a stubbly chin; then winked companionably.

"If yuh ever wants t' take one o' them slow movin' pitchers," he advised, elaborating a confidential air, "yuh can't do better 'n t' come t' Larwill. These here fellers in Lije Hinebaugh's garage has been a-practisin' till they's purty good."

"Thanks for the offer of a lift. I'm wanting to go out and see my Uncle Miles Brumm. That's my name, too—Brumm."

The obliging farmer left off his bantering attitude, stared hard from under his shaggy brows, and rubbed his palm on his blue denim pant-leg before presenting it.

"Yer Julia's boy, mebby?"

"Yes. Did you know her?"

"Reckon I did. My name's Schrofe. We was neighbours like. She taught our school fer a winter—er a part of it. You ain't never been out here afore?"

"Once," said Dinny, shoving his bags out of the way, as the legs began to wriggle out from under the engine, followed by a large pan of spent oil. "I was about seven. Aunt Greta was being married. We were here only for a day. How long have my Uncle Miles and Aunt Martha lived up here? I'm afraid I had almost lost track of them, for a while."

"Well—it's about two years, come Christmas. I've owned th' little place fer quite a spell. Angela writ a-askin' could her folks come back 'n' live there. 'Pears like th' ol' man 'd had a stroke, er somethin'."

"How's he now?"

"Oh—he gits about."

"And Aunt Martha?"

"She's well as common. Makes a little garden, 'n' that. Chickens, 'n' that.... Yuh ain't seen 'em lately?"

Dinny shook his head, waiving the opportunity to explain.

"Guess we c'n go now," said Jase, pulling out a fat roll of soiled money. "Here's yer filthy lucre, Lije. I'll be gol-darned if that ain't what it is. Time a dollar bill's made a dozen trips t' one these here little garages—"

"We don't have no trouble a-gettin' people t' take 'em," drawled Lije. 'Better have an understandin' with this feller, Mr. Brumm, afore yuh start north, er he'll charge yuh th' price of his dang truck fer th' ride."

"Any time I'd take a dime offen Julia Miller's boy—" said Jase, soberly. "Climb in, won't yuh, and we'll go down t' th' express office fer that Berkshire shoat. Bought 'er last week over at th' fair in Wayne. Wasn't fixed t' take 'er home with me. Had th' family along—pap 'n' th' girls. Ain't got none o' my own. I'm a old batch."

They were rattling down the dusty street toward the railroad station, Jason waving a hand to the hicks idling in front of the implement store.

"I s'pose yer married, this good while, eh?" he shouted.

"No," replied Dinny, adding, "The only girl I wanted wouldn't have me."

Jason made a careful job of backing the truck up to the station platform, turned off his engine, and climbed down.

"Same as me," he said, grinning mysteriously. "The gal was yer maw."

There was a little surge of resentment in Dinny's mind over the impudence of this untutored old yokel. He didn't like the idea of Julia's having been admired to this extent by a person so far beneath her. What right did this fellow have to cherish the memory of Julia?

The rough wooden crate scraped into the truck with a screech accompanied by the pig's shrill squeal of alarm. Jason climbed up, started the rackety engine, which added to the pig's consternation, and they rumbled through the village, and out upon the highway, driving at a snail's pace.

"This damn pig cost four hundred and twenty-five dollars," explained Jason, "'n' she's got t' be handled with care. I spect yer quite anxious fer t' git up there, too, seein' it's been so long since yuh heared from 'em."

"I hadn't supposed pigs were so expensive," commented Dinny, hoping to distract attention from his obvious lack of knowledge about his relatives. "How much is pork worth now?" He tried to make the query sound as if he had at least a passing interest in such matters.

Jason guffawed loudly.

"Well—pork ain't a-bringin' much, just now; but this here shoat ain't pork, 'n' when she has pigs, 'bout a year f'm now, they ain't a-goin' t' be pork, neither. I got a Berkshire boar over t' our place that I'd like fer t' show yuh. By Golly—nobody's ever called that feller pork. Say—if yuh was t' slit that there big boy's belly up intuh bacon, I guess it 'd cost yuh 'bout fifty dollars a slice. It's easy fer t' see yuh ain't no farmer."

Dinny listened with a pretence of interest, but conscious of an uncomfortable irritation over the fact that his Julia, once upon a time, had been the object of this crude old chap's attentions. Somehow it pushed Julia farther away from him, even if she had been unaware of this devotion. This pig-fancier had unwittingly thrust his rough, unrefined bulk between him and the idealistic image of his mother.

"I've saw pieces o' yourn in th' papers," Jason went on, grinning broadly. "Seen 'em in *Th' Tribune,* when I've went t' Chicago. Our papers 'round here don't seem t' take t' 'em like. I brung a couple o' 'em home once f'm Chicago, 'n' I thought pap 'd laugh hisself t' death. Pap says, 'Gol-darned if that ol' feller in th' moon ain't about right.' I mind one time yuh writ a piece 'bout them flossy automobiles a-splashin' mud on people 'long th' sidewalk when there wasn't nothin' in th' car but a poodle dog a-ridin' by hisself in th' back seat. Yuh oughta heared pap holler 'n' laugh. He likes 't when yuh git 't on 'em, 'specially th' tony folks. Pap's always a-braggin' 'bout yuh, 'cause yer Julia's boy, 'n' he set such store by her. He says, 'Gol-darned if Julia's boy ain't a sharp feller that they's got t' leave alone, fer he's got a mean tongue, 'n' enough pizen in him t' start a bran' new hell.'"

"Was that what he said—'poison'?"

"Yeah... 'Course pap was only a-foolin'. He likes yer pieces. Pap didn't mean 't harmful. It was just a joke, 'n' that."

"It's no joke with me, Mr. Schrofe." Dinny was surprised to find himself saying this. He had blurted it out, impulsively. Now he would have to explain, best he could. "Your father's quite right. And he meant what he said as a friendly joke. I know that. But—there's been too much poison in me, and it's not good for me. I don't mind telling you that I'm taking a little treatment for it."

"Pills—'n' that?" inquired Jason, interestedly.

"The equivalent of pills—yes. I'm going to look up a few of the people I've had occasion to despise, and see if I can't come to terms with them. Perhaps that will do the trick. Just confidentially—I haven't seen my uncle and aunt for many years; not since I started away to college."

"Forget 'em—mebby?"

No—Dinny hadn't exactly forgotten them. It was not easy to explain, but he had gone away to school, and then the war had come along, and then he had gone East, and always his time and mind had been occupied.

266

"Yeah—I reckon," agreed Jason, indulgently. "But I bet there's more to 't than that. We always thought Preacher Brumm was a kind o' slippery ol' cuss. Mebby he done somethin'. As fer Martha, she prob'ly wouldn't a-done nothin', a-bein' what she is, so pious 'n' that."

"I thought it would be good for me to see them again."

"Yeah—that's proper—'n' let bygones be bygones, eh?"

"Exactly."

"Well—that's proper like, if yuh can do 't. Pap's always a-sayin', 'Fergive 'n' fergit, 'n' like th' ol' Indian says, "Always remember!"'"

Dinny indulged in the first hearty, spontaneous laugh he had had for several days.

"That's the only brand of forgiveness I've ever carried in stock, I'm afraid."

"Well—there's only just one feller in th' world I ain't never a-goin' t' feel right about, I guess. They's lots o' people what I don't care fer, not special, but this here feller I hate. I ain't never got over 't. Long time ago, come winter, 'n' nothin' much t' do, nights, but set 'n' think, I used fer t' do a little plannin' how I c'd go out West where he lived, 'n' stick a knife in him."

"I don't suppose I could guess his name," ventured Dinny, half-suspecting Jason would not be averse to a confidential chat on the subject.

"Reckon yuh could. That's th' feller, all right. He prob'ly never done nothin' fer t' help yuh. Gol-darned selfish brute! By Golly—I'd like t' kill him!"

"It's been a sore spot with me, too, Mr. Schrofe, though I think it's only fair to say that he made an honest effort to show an interest in me. I suppose it was my own fault that his generosity was unrewarded. I didn't care to take anything from him. However—"

"By Golly—I honour yuh fer 't. So'll pap." Jason idled the truck to a stop on the grassy roadside, and pointed across the highway to a barbed-wire gate fronting the dense woods. "Mebby yuh'd like t' see th' ol' path. Let's git out, 'n' I'll show yuh."

They ambled across the road, and Jason hooked an elbow over the top rail of the gate.

"Julia used fer t' leave th' road, right here, 'n' take that there path through th' timber, when she was a-teachin' th' Schrofe school. It used fer t' b'long t' ol' Squire Craig, damned ol' hawg." Jason drew a bunch of keys from his pocket and unlocked the gate.

"Apparently it belongs to you now," observed Dinny, as they entered the woods.

"Yeah—I bought 't. Didn't rightly have no use fer 't, er nothin', but ol' Craig was purty hard up afore he died, 'n' was willin' t' sell."

Jason stooped and picked up a dead branch that had fallen across the almost obliterated trail.

"Right along here she come, ev'ry day."

Dinny felt sobered in the chilly shade. Hardly conscious of his act, he removed his hat. His resentment over Jason's attitude toward Julia was quite gone now.

"Yeah—yer Julia's boy, all right," muttered Jason, candidly studying Dinny's face. "That there little point where yer hair sort o' grows down like, right in th' middle."

"You have asked me several personal questions today, Mr. Schrofe," said Dinny, seating himself by Jason on a fallen log beside the grassy path. "Would you object to my asking you one?"

Jason's eyes crinkled with understanding.

"Yeah—I guess that's the reason I bought 't. That's what yuh was a-goin' t' ask, eh? I kep' 't secret from pap fer awhile. But when he found out I'd bought 't, he said, 'Glad yuh done 't, Jase. No use fer ev'ry Tom, Dick 'n' Harry to be a-trampin' through them woods.'"

Dinny impulsively laid a hand on Jason's knee.

"Julia would have appreciated it, I know," he said, a bit unsteadily. There recurred to him certain fragments of adroitly crafted ridicule he had hurled at the insensitiveness and general stupidity of the hicks and yokels who composed so large a percentage of America's population. What could you expect, he had often queried, of people who never went anywhere, never saw anything, never read anything? What did a ballot amount to in their hands? What did they know about the type of government that speeds the spread of culture?

Here was a hick, sitting beside him on this log. He talked like a hick, dressed like a hick, and was on the way back from a hick town with a pig in a crate. The hick was just now in the act of rummaging in his overall pockets, with clumsy fingers. His big brown thumb had a purplish-black discoloration at the root of the nail. Now he was bringing up in one hand a huge jack-knife and in the other a soggy plug of chewing tobacco. Typical hick! Cow-companion! Pig-comrade!... But he had bought a twenty-acre tract of second-growth timber that he didn't need or want, because there was the faint trail of a path through it that a neighbour girl had travelled on the way to her school, more than a quarter-century ago... Ignorant hicks! Country full of them! And what could you expect—Dinny had often inquired, superiorly, in the smart journals of sophistication—of a civilization so loaded down with dull dolts who spent their lives wading about through the ooze of the barnyard?

"Want a chew?" inquired Jason, hospitably.

"I've never been quite brave enough to do that," grinned Dinny. "I'll smoke a cigarette. Would you like one?" He tendered his gold-lined, monogrammed, silver case.

Jason chuckled quietly and shook his head.

The unexplained chuckle was just a bit disquieting. Dinny had long been of the opinion that yokels possessed no sense of humour, at all. Evidently this one had what passed for that, though it was odd what things amused him.

"I want to tell you a secret," said Dinny.

For ten minutes, he reviewed the peculiar circumstances which had concealed Julia's letter from him, until now. Jason's eyes interestedly followed Dinny's long, slim, well-kept hands as they brought out the leather wallet containing the precious legacy. He took the letter, rather timidly, and turned it over and over in his calloused palms, before handing it back.

"I'm going to read you some of it—all of it, if you wish. I believe Julia would want me to."

"I'd like fer t' hear 't," replied Jason, huskily. "That is," he added, admonishingly, "if yuh don't think she'd mind—my knowin'. We was never close like, yuh unnerstand. It wasn't her, yuh unnerstand. It was just me. Julia never knowed, not proper like, 'bout my feelin's 'n' that."

Dinny nodded, comprehendingly... Hicks and yokels couldn't be taught good taste, he had said, in the ultra-refined pages of *Hallelujah*. All these silly attempts to add anything to their culture were wasted time. You only made them restless, self-conscious, and ridiculous. They didn't have the *savoir-faire!*

"I know Julia would want you to share this secret, Mr. Schrofe," reiterated Dinny, impressively. "Some of it I found just a bit difficult to understand—but you're the kind of a person to see through it... Much more clearly," he added, "than I."

* * * * *

An hour had passed. They had been dimly conscious of dinner-bells. Through the latter part of Dinny's reading, Jason had made no further effort to conceal his emotion, trumpeting into his voluminous red bandanna with an abandon of restraint. It was as if Julia's tragedy had occurred only yesterday.

"I s'pose there must 'a' been somethin' to 't, like she says," he remarked, thickly, as Dinny folded the letter. "She c'd forgive 'em all, and get th' power like, 'n' that. But Julia wasn't just ordinary folks. You 'n' me, we couldn't. 'Tain't in us. Leastwise—'tain't in me. D'yuh think yuh c'd do 't?"

"I don't know," said Dinny, soberly. "That's what I'm trying to find out."

The wrinkles around Jason's eyes deepened as he candidly studied Dinny's face.

"Not meanin' any offence," he ventured, "but I sure w'd never 'a' picked yuh fer th' part. Yuh don't 'pear t' be th' kind o' feller that c'd make a go of 't." He rubbed his knee and grinned, broadly, hinting that a new idea had struck him amusingly. "Say—if yuh do get this here big power t' be free 'n' happy like, yuh'll sure have a hell of a time writin' them sassy pieces, won't yuh?"

Dinny stared, amazed at the old chap's quick deduction.

"You've touched a mighty live wire. I'll tell you something about that. It's a queer story."

"No—I don't think that's s' gol-darned queer," decided Jason, after Dinny had spent some time explaining how, since finding Julia's letter, he had been unable to get himself into the mood for composition of "sassy pieces."... "Yer handlin' dynamite, by Golly! Julia said 't was a sort o' power, 'n' yuh c'd always count on what she spoke. She's put this stuff in yer hands, 'n' told yuh how t' shoot 't off. Gol-darned if yuh hadn't better do 't th' way she says."

"You're joking. It's serious with me. I've ruined myself for my work. I've lost a taste for the only thing I know how to do."

"Like hell I'm a-jokin'!" protested Jason. "It's just like I said. Julia has handed yuh some high explosive! Yuh c'n either blow stumps with 't, 'n' clear yer ground so yuh c'n raise somethin'—er yuh c'n leave 't a-lyin' around, and take th' risk o' a-blowin' yer brains out... Ain't there nothin' else yuh c'n do b'sides make snoots at people in the papers 'n' that?"

This last was too much for Dinny, and he laughed, Jason joining, apparently well pleased that he had lifted his young friend from his gloomy mood.

"I learned to handle a chisel, a little, when I was a lad," said Dinny, reminiscently. "I think I could make a living."

"'Pears like th' more sensible thing t' do is t' carry on, now yuh've started out t' experiment with Julia's idear. Mebby, if yuh git that there power, what she talks about, yuh c'n write anything yer a-mind t'."

"I'm afraid I've a long way to go."

"I know I couldn't do 't. That there one feller'd always be in th' road. I'd fergive 'n' that—but I wouldn't stop a-thinkin'. What he done t' our little white stone, what pap 'n' me put up—I'd never fergit that, not in a thousand years."

"What was that?" asked Dinny, sympathetically.

Jason busied himself for some time, breaking a handful of dead twigs into little pieces of equal length. "'Twouldn't do yuh no good t' know 't. Yuh got a big job afore yuh, anyways. 'Twouldn't help yuh none—yer knowin'."

"Very well—if you'd rather not tell me."

"Julia's name really was Mueller, after all," soliloquized Jason. "We thought they'd made a mistake on th' big stone what he had made fer her. But this here letter looks as if he was right. We always thought 'twas Miller... Well—sh'll we go now?"

Jason had leaned forward to turn the ignition key, after they had boarded the truck, but, apparently impressed with a fresh idea, straightened to offer a further comment on Dinny's problem.

"Just now come t' me—somethin' mebby yuh hadn't thought about much. If yuh did grab on t' this here power o' Julia's t' be steady 'n' happy like, 'n' begun a-writin' afterwards, yuh c'd write about that! By Golly—I bet lots o' folks 'd read 't. Gol-darned if they wouldn't eat th' paper 'twas writ on, a-thinkin' 'twas medicine. 'Course—if yuh'd been a parson, always a-snifflin' 'bout fergiveness, 'n' that, 'n' a-gettin' paid fer bein' friendly with God like, that'd be differ'nt. Th' people'd all say, 'Aw—hell!'—'n' turn over t' th' funnies... But if ever a feller like yerself took t' a-writin' that he'd rech up 'n' got some power f'm on high what had cleaned out all his pizen 'n' made him happy 'n' that, fer keeps, by Golly, there'd be a million folks a-wantin' th' recipe fer 't!"

Jason felt satisfied with this long speech, finishing it with vigorous nods of his head and convincing smacks of his brown fist on the steering-wheel. He drove the truck back on to the road, and began making up for lost time without concern for the comfort of the indulged shoat. Dinny was thinking. The old fellow might be a hick, but he possessed extraordinary native sense.

In a few minutes, they had turned to the right, and were nearing the little white Baptist Church. Jason pointed it out, as they approached, but did not slacken speed, nor did he turn his head as they passed it and the quiet cemetery that lay to the rear. Dinny suspected that the treasured path through the woods had come to be the hallowed ground in Jason's opinion, rather than the grave where, apparently, some misunderstanding about a monument had seriously embittered him.

"Not very fer now," he shouted. "Just b'yond that there little holler. Yuh c'n see th' chimbly. There's yer Aunt Martha, a-pickin' up them winter pears... Well—I'll set yuh down. Wish yuh c'd come over 'n' see pap, whilst yer here. I c'd come 'n' fetch yuh."

"I think I would like to," said Dinny, gratefully. "Could you come over in the morning? I want to see your father."

Aunt Martha was shading her eyes with both hands, her inquisitive grimace distorting her face into an expression of naïve perplexity. The vanished years spun like a top. Dinny felt eight, as he lifted his bags down, and started toward the house. Uncle Miles, shaggy, seedy, and minus the short burn-sides of yesterday, appeared in the doorway. He had drawn the well-remembered, benevolently patronizing smile.

"Well, well, well!" boomed Uncle Miles.

* * * * *

"Would yuh care fer another piece, Ferdinand?" Aunt Martha was saying primly.

"By all means, Ferdinand," heartily seconded Uncle Miles, taking up Dinny's purple-stained pie-plate. "Abso*lute*ly!"

It had been amazing to Dinny with what ease and dispatch he had fitted back into the environment he thought he had outgrown.

Aunt Martha was a little greyer, and laid her thin hand on the backs of the familiar chairs as she moved about. There were nice new teeth, but she still shielded with the corner of her lip the area where once there had been a missing right upper canine. One of Uncle Miles's legs was not quite so up and coming as the other. The shoulders sagged, the least bit, making the shiny black coat a size too large. Otherwise, they were the same people; mellower, perhaps; a little more subdued.

Dinny had feared a painful constraint. As he had neared the house, bags in hand, his heart had pounded. For the moment he would have given much to efface himself from this awkward reunion. But there had been no dilemma. Uncle Miles was as openly cordial as if he were welcoming home a son in whom he had invested his all. Aunt Martha murmured little tendernesses as she nervously clutched at his sleeves.

He had lied effortlessly when they inquired whether he had had his dinner, and responded with enthusiasm when they wanted to show him "th' place." He was shown the chicken-coops, the barn, the little shop that had been his grandfather's. Dinny lingered there for a time. It was long since it had been in use, but it smelt of good, sound wood in process of fabrication, as if fuddled old Ferd had just stepped out of it.

They did not hint to know why Dinny had come. So far as he could observe, they were not craftily concealing that query. He was not asked where all he had been, or what he had been doing. They made no comments on his success. The fact that he had withdrawn to another world with which they were totally unacquainted, and now belonged to it as he had never for one moment belonged to them, gave them no apparent sensation of diffidence.

Uncle Miles rigged two cane fishing-poles, later in the afternoon, and invited Dinny to go with him down the hill to the little stream where they caught a few small perch and talked freely about Angela, of whose celebrated exploits her father was gratefully proud.

At supper, served shortly after five, to Dinny's high satisfaction, Aunt Martha accounted for the scattered family whose ghosts vaguely hovered about the well-worn door-steps, the old-fashioned thumb-latches, the paths to the shop, the pump, the barn. Poor Susan, of course, was dead. Ferdinand knew that, didn't he? Yes—she had worked fer the Squire Craigs, and died there. Greta was still out in Californy. They had an orange farm and three fine boys. Yes—Greta wrote, about twice a year. No—she had never came back. It was purty fer. Elmer was still down at Lafayette in "th' Home." Hiram was up in "th' Thumb," a-workin' at a sawmill... Dinny followed the Miller saga, at a distance, interested mostly in the fact that these people and their affairs were as remote as if Aunt Martha had reported on the goings and comings of a family in Zanzibar.

He waived his proffered right to a second helping of huckleberry pie, and, having easily gained the floor in the process of graciously declining their hospitable entreaties, Dinny ventured, without preamble, to account for his unexpected visit.

He had become convinced, he said, that his life was not being very well lived. The phrase struck him oddly, once he had uttered it. Doubtless it had been shaped by this environment. It was the way Uncle Miles might have said it, had he been in a mood of confession. Life had lately seemed to lack fulfilment, he said. He had felt a desire to make peace with the few people whose relations to him had been a source of "disquiet" to himself—and doubtless to them also. He paused.

"So yuh've been 'n' got converted, Ferdinand," murmured Aunt Martha, sanctimoniously. "Bless th' Lord fer that!" She lifted the corner of her white apron, and, raising her spectacles, wiped her eyes. "Miles," she said, brokenly, "our prayers has been answered. Our wandering boy has at last saw th' light. Praise t' His Blessed Name!"

"Abso*lute*ly!" ejaculated Uncle Miles, smiling approvingly, and hitching his chair back to cross his legs. "And your aunt and I are very glad you came. How long can you stay, Ferdinand? Hope you won't have to hurry away. There'll be lots to talk about, now you're here after such a long time."

"Thanks, Uncle Miles," returned Dinny, in a brief aside. "As I was saying, it has recently distressed me that I had permitted certain misunderstandings to—"

"That's all right, Ferdinand," broke in Uncle Miles, "and there's nothing to forgive. You're as welcome as—as the flowers in May."

Aunt Martha was crying now, noisily. A sudden wave of distaste for the whole adventure flooded Dinny's spirits. His old repugnance claimed him. He might have known there would be just such a calamitous scene. It had been his hope that there might be a calm, conciliatory talk. The tension would be eased. But clearly it was hopeless. Uncle Miles wished only to dodge the issue that had hurled them apart, offering an effusive and blustery hospitality as an alternative to the air-clearing discussion which the situation so urgently called for. Uncle Miles was extravagant with his tender of huckleberry pie, but winced at the thought of an honest invoice of their disaffection. It was somewhat like Angela's gift of an orange and a doll to the baby whose eyes she could not open. Aunt Martha, as usual, had taken refuge behind a tear-drenched apron.

"I shall be leaving, in about an hour," said Dinny, calmly, "and it would please me greatly if we three could have a quiet talk."

Aunt Martha left off sobbing, wiped her eyes, and listened. Uncle Miles broke out with vigorous protests. Dinny raised a hand, insistingly, and the old man subsided, rather crestfallen.

"I don't mean to make a long story of it," pursued Dinny, "but something has happened to make me quite seriously anxious to be on the very best of friendly terms with everyone. You have wondered, Aunt Martha, if I had been converted. Probably not—in the way you mean. I don't feel any more religious than before. It's only that I have discovered myself to be thoroughly poisoned with aversions, disgusts, and bitter memories, which are making a sorry mess of my life. I want now to rise above all that, if I can."

"But that's conversion, Ferdinand!" exclaimed Aunt Martha, fervently. "It's th' workin' of th' Spirit! Blessed be His Holy Name!"

Uncle Miles nodded, sagaciously, and his lips formed the large word that denoted unqualified endorsement.

"And so—I'm here to ask you to forgive me, my dears, for putting myself completely out of your lives. I would like also to be forgiven for all the hot, hateful thoughts I have had in regard to you both—especially toward you, Uncle Miles, and for the bitter contempt that has swept through me whenever I thought of you. I'm asking for your pardon. I want to be at liberty. I'm weary of carrying that load."

Aunt Martha was crying softly. Uncle Miles's face impulsively brightened, wreathed with an absolving smile. He cleared his throat, and stretching out a hand, patted Dinny assuringly on his coat-sleeve. Dinny took the old hand in his, and, observing that Uncle Miles was in the very act of booming out a volley of gallant "abso*lute*lys," leaned far forward, stared questioningly into his uncle's eyes, and slowly, meaningly, shook his head.

"No, Uncle Miles—not that! It's your turn to talk—but not that! Say what you're thinking! You'll feel much better afterwards—I can promise you!"

The old fellow slowly withdrew his hand, and with the back of it rubbed his forehead, beaded with perspiration. Then he swallowed hard and essayed a grisly yawn. Dinny had once seen a man die who, after the exhalation of his last breath, had yawned just that way—a yawn with no breath either coming or going.

They waited—and Uncle Miles spoke, hollowly.

"Well—it was like this, Ferdinand. At first, you were only a baby, and had no use for the money. Our salary was too little to live on, comfortably. What came in for you was a great help—a great help. Your income was larger than mine—than ours. I suppose I must have had a worldly pride, and dreaded to see the time come when you would be better off than the rest of us." He hesitated, rubbing his eyes with his knuckles.

"I can understand that perfectly, Uncle Miles," declared Dinny. "It must have been a very real problem."

"Well—then I saw how you felt toward your father, and knew you would never accept any help from him. That's when I should have—"

Dinny nodded, comprehendingly.

"It was a great temptation, I am sure, Uncle Miles."

"Yer Uncle Miles kept a-sayin', when he went into that Holstein cattle business, out in Ioway—and lost ev'ry cent to that rascally, thieving—" Aunt Martha's voice was growing shrill.

"Yes—I had the thought that perhaps I could invest your money so you could—" Uncle Miles groped for the right word.

271

"Don't spoil it, Uncle Miles," admonished Dinny, hardly above a whisper. "It's a great sensation, let me tell you! I hope you can have it! You'll find it's worth it, sir!" Dinny's voice had risen to his exultant words. Aunt Martha murmured, "Bless th' Lord!"

"No!" shouted Uncle Miles, in a tone that explained how much effort that one agonized little bark cost him. "The fact was—I wanted to put away something. I wasn't saving it for you... Now—you know all about it!... God—help me!" The brave old head sank, lower and lower, there came a sort of inhuman guttural cry from his tight throat.

Aunt Martha rose, with a little whimper of alarm, and put her arm around him, pressing her cheek hard against his.

"Miles—my *dear!* Yuh done it—at last! Bless th' Lord! Bless th' Lord!... Oh, Ferdinand, you've been sent f'm God to help your poor uncle—'n' me."

Dinny was deeply moved. He did not attempt to analyse his strange sensations, but, eclipsing the surge of sympathy for these repentant, broken-hearted old people, there rose in him a consciousness of an almost uncanny vitality—the "will-to-power" consciousness, as nearly as he could define it at the moment. He felt suddenly matured! It was as if his permanent mind—what he was always thinking of as his "sub-conscious mind" in spite of anything the new Psychology might say—had not only ceased complaining at the decisions and intentions of his "conscious mind," but had actually taken charge of the whole enterprise! He knew now what Julia meant, though he had fresh reasons for understanding her lack of words to explain her strange sensation. She had called it a *power!* Well—that's what it was. It would sound trite and sentimental if he attempted to elucidate. But—what he had come by was not a sentiment—any more than the roar of the turbines beneath Niagara is a sentiment. Julia was right! *This was a kind of power!* God only knew what all you could do with it—but here it was!... Power!

Uncle Miles rose, his old face twisted in a pathetically tearful smile, and offered Dinny his hand, Aunt Martha still hugging his arm.

"Seems like we ought to have a word of prayer," suggested Aunt Martha, when they had passed through the doorway to the little sitting-room.

"We've just had that, Aunt Martha," said Dinny—"the real kind. Now—suppose we sit down and talk a little more about this. Did I understand you to say that some man, out in Iowa, had defrauded you of—of that money?"

They told him the story in relays. Uncle Miles becoming so excited over the rank injustice they had suffered that Aunt Martha tried to calm him.

"Yer uncle gets almost sick, sometimes, a-thinkin' and a-talkin' about it. I do wish he could ferget it."

"That's why I asked," said Dinny. "Uncle Miles—whatever became of that fellow? Do you know?"

"The last I heard," growled Uncle Miles, "he was back on a rented farm not far from Unger, where I first met the dirty skunk. He broke up, out there, as he deserved."

"Broke up—did he? Perhaps he did not intend to cheat you. Probably he was a poor business man. Chances are he's burning up his insides hating the people who took his property away from him. Knowing what I do now, Uncle Miles, if I were you I'd write him a friendly letter—you and he were once good friends, weren't you?—and ask him to come up here, this autumn, and spend a Sunday. Tell him you and Aunt Martha have a big, fat hen that ought to be stewed. Noodles, too, and huckleberry pie.... Treat yourself to a thrill! Set yourself free!"

"Ferdinand," said Aunt Martha, smiling pensively, "it sure does sound queer—yer a-talkin' like this—when yuh look so worldly like 'n' all."

"It doesn't sound a bit queerer than it feels, I can assure you, Aunt Martha."

"You'll stay the night with us now, won't you, Ferdinand?" entreated Uncle Miles.

* * * * *

Old Abner was leaning on both elbows, his boot on an inverted three-gallon tin swill-pail, gazing down into one of the pig-pens. He turned his head as Jason and Dinny approached. His jaw sagged, and chopped up and down, nervously, as he stared. The worn tabs of his ancient coon-skin cap lopped his ears. Had Dinny seen a faithful photograph of him, a week ago, he would have identified the subject as the patriarch and original founder of The Hicks.

He came slowly to meet them, rubbing his gnarled hand on his short, stuffy, leather coat. There was no introduction.

"Take off yer hat," requested Abner. "Jase says yuh've got that funny little point o' hair, like her'n."

Dinny obliged.

"Powerful funny 'bout that, Jase," drawled the old man, pointing a crooked forefinger at Dinny's head, as if inspecting an animal. "Her pap had that there, same as her, same as him. The old feller always had his cap on, mostly, 'n' I never rightly noticed 't until he was a-layin' on th' coolin' board, next mornin' after he hung hisself. Gol-darned if he didn't have 't, too! Danged if he didn't look like a 'ristocrat, a-layin' there!... Well—come in t' th' house, son, 'n' be welcome."

"I never knew before that my grandfather had taken his own life." Dinny became aware that many mysterious silences and evasions of Aunt Martha's had now been explained.

"Well—it won't hurt yuh none t' know 't. Yuh c'n be proud o' your grand-pap, son. Gol-darned if 'twasn't purty fine 'n' brave o' th' old codger. I sure never'd a-thought he had 't in him. Ev'rybody was a-moonin' around, that night, a-feelin' scared like, 'n' kind o' shamed fer the Millers. Gol-darned if I wasn't proud o' th' old cuss!"

"You have some unusual ideas on the subject of—suicide, Mr. Schrofe."

"Well—o' course—I wouldn't 'xac'ly recommend 't t' nobody, but, all th' same, if I'd knowed yer grand-pap had 't in him, I'd 'a' had a lot more respect fer him whilst he lived."

They drew up their chairs before the grate—stiff, prim, narrow rocking-chairs that had a tendency to creep about on the worn rag carpet—and spent two hours talking about Julia's monument.

Old Abner's bitterness about Craig's shocking discourtesy in having their little stone cast aside had obviously become an obsession. Once he had launched upon the painful topic, there was no distracting him.

"Guess we'll have t' start now," admonished Jason, consulting his big nickel-cased watch. "I'm a-drivin' him over t' Wayne, pap, to ketch a train fer Cincinnati."

"'Pears like I done all th' talkin'," regretted Abner. "Lot o' things I wanted t' ask yuh, too. Seems like when I get a-goin' 'bout that there feller, I can't stop."

"Yes," said Dinny, "it's too bad. I'm sorry. I am on my way to see him, and I mean to ask him about it. I don't believe he ever knew the particulars. It must have been a terrible mistake. Would you be glad if you found out it was a mistake, and that he was not really to blame?"

The old fellow slowly nodded his head.

"Gol-darned if I wouldn't give ev'ry one o' them Berkshires, out there in them pens, t' hear that feller say he hadn't knowed, 'n' was sorry 'n' that!"

"Like hell yuh would, pap! Half o' them hawgs b'longs t' me!" Jason, vastly pleased with his joke, gave the old man an affectionate whack between the shoulders.

"All fun aside, Mr. Schrofe," said Dinny, seriously, taking his hand, "I hope to find out that my father never meant to do you generous people this harm. I believe it would hurt Julia, terribly, if she had known about the misery it's caused you."

As they sauntered toward the sedan, standing by the old hitching-rack, Jason said, "Would yuh mind if I told pap?"

"About the letter?"

"Yeah—th' letter 'n' that."

"I believe Julia would want him to know about it, don't you?"

"Yeah—I'll tell him."

CHAPTER XVII

ALTHOUGH aware of the curious phenomenon of familiar streets narrowing, during one's extended absence, to about three fourths their previous width, and tall buildings shrinking to a mere travesty of their former stateliness, Dinny Brumm was unprepared for the shock when, at midnight, he followed his bags from the taxi to the desk at The Barstow.

Even allowing for the fact that when he had first timidly ventured through its spacious, shriekingly ornate lobby, as an untravelled youth, The Barstow was vain-gloriously, self-consciously new, it seemed impossible to believe that a few years could have so tarnished its gilt and frayed its cushions.

The once impressive gargoyles still reared on their hind claws to support massive old-worldish lamps, but the awe-inspiring challenge of their "How dare you, worm?" that had darted from their shocked, staring eyes, was now replaced by a simpering, apologetic servility. Their orbs were dull, their flanks were lean, their talons had straightened out as if to ward off a slap.

The desk, formerly to be approached hat in hand and with regret that one had not brought a joss-stick, had had its stinger pulled, too, its smile resembling the conciliatory smirk of the urgent driver upon invitation to pull up at the kerb and state his name and address for the augmentation of certain statistics in process of assembly at Police Headquarters.

And yet, barring the normal wear and tear of a half-dozen prosperous years, The Barstow, Dinny knew, had not altered appreciably. The change was all in himself.

But whatever of modified outlook had been gradually coming to pass in his mind, due to the liberating experiences of the years, to the tarnishment of earlier glosses and glitters, and the reduction of once astounding dimensions, it was nothing compared to the uncanny magic that had suddenly recreated him into something so different from the self whose habitual deductions and reactions had been stabilized—so utterly different that he found it difficult to recognize his attitudes and opinions as his own. His habitual responses were inactive, as if he had been smitten with an amnesia.

Yesterday's experience of complete reconciliation with Uncle Miles and Aunt Martha had performed some queer tricks on Dinny's mind. He had not been surprised at the sound of his own words soliciting pardon for the bitter animosity he had nourished in regard to them. That was what he had gone there to do, and he had meant to see it through, hoping for no further results than the satisfaction of getting it off his chest. Down inside himself, whatever he might say to Uncle Miles, there would unquestionably remain the private opinion that the pompously pious old fellow was a piker.

All that Dinny would have to show for his strange adventure in the voluntary enterprise of crow eating would be a sense of having made an honest experiment with Julia's theory for the purgation of poison. He did not expect that his estimate of Uncle Miles would be in any way reappraised.

But when he had finished with them, last night, he had not only told Uncle Miles that he fully forgave the wrong he had done; he really had forgiven the old man and was in a mood of sympathy for him. Uncle Miles had faced an odd predicament as custodian of a child's annuity exceeding his own salary.

Dinny could understand how his uncle had postponed doing the thing that required to be done, saying to himself, "Next year I must tell him," but always fearful of the consequences. What indeed would become of a small boy, living in a frugal home, were he suddenly handed an allowance in excess of the family's total income? Uncle Miles had drifted into an unhappy perplexity, but not because he had the instincts of a thief. And Aunt Martha had consented to it, ruefully, no doubt, believing that Uncle Miles knew best.

Once upon a time Dinny had felt that if ever the occasion arose when he could back the old weasel into a corner and force him to confess himself an unmitigated fraud the sensation of seeing his despised pomposity shrivel and peel off like snake-skin would be worth all the mental torture he had suffered.

Uncle Miles had crumpled to a degree surpassing the most extravagant hopes Dinny had sourly cherished, but there was no diabolical pleasure afforded by it; Dinny had shared the old man's sorrow with an understanding that seemed to enhance the value of his own personality. He began to appreciate what Julia had written concerning her altered estimate of herself, after sincerely making peace with Susan. She had felt "promoted." It was as if she "had won a prize." It was as if she had discovered herself to be "a princess."

Throughout today Dinny had reviewed last night's strange experience in Julia's room where he had slept.

At ten, Aunt Martha had lighted the way up the steep, narrow, uncarpeted stairs, piloting him with a reeking kerosene lamp.

"Almost nothin's been changed in here since it was her'n," said Aunt Martha, turning down the patchwork quilt. "Hiram had a sale cried when him 'n' Lucy moved to Michigan, but Jase Schrofe, who had previous bought the house, bid in these here things o' Julia's and

274

had 'em left where they was. Exceptin' fer the desk, it's the same." Aunt Martha patted the pillows. "Yes," she sighed, reminiscently, "dear Julia died in this here old bed."

So it was here that Julia had summoned her slimming strength to write the letter that was "promoting" Dinny to something of the lofty dignity that she had won ' like a prize."

Ordinarily, he thought, it would not be much of a recommendation for a bed to say of it, five minutes before one climbed in, that someone of far-reaching posthumous influence had died in it, in a lugubrious tone hinting that the departed spirit might be within earshot; but if Julia's ghost haunted the room, so much the better, thought Dinny.

He was a long time going to sleep, and even when, from sheer fatigue produced by the emotional strain of the day, he drifted into semi-consciousness, there was a strange sense that Julia was coming along into his dreams.

There never had been a photograph of her except a cheap little tintype of a group of girls taken at the county fair. The cheeks had been tinted to an unhealthy flush, and the mouth had been drawn into a prim little pucker. It was unfair to Julia, of course, as even Aunt Martha admitted, to whom beauty was but skin deep.

In his half-somnolent state, Dinny conjured a portrait of Julia, the radiant. It was a satisfyingly clear picture, and, as he half-consciously brought it alive and put it through a variety of moods, he felt he was recovering his girl-mother.

The dream, if it was a dream, was not altogether pleasant, however. Julia seemed to proceed into an attitude of entreaty as if he had done something to make her very unhappy. And when, at length, sitting opposite him on the grass, her feet folded under her short skirt, she began pensively gathering up the little paper cups and plates, her eyes downcast and swollen with crying, Dinny roused with a painful recurrence of the one tragic mistake that could not be mended.

He had made peace with Uncle Miles to their complete mutual satisfaction. And tomorrow he would have an interview with his father who, he had learned by wire before leaving New York, was in Cincinnati for a week on one of his periodical inspection visits; doubtless that interview would lift the burden of misgiving he had carried in respect to Zandy Craig. He had it in mind to stop at Magnolia also, and attempt to revise his opinions of that institution, in the light of his new flair for sympathetic understanding.

But there was nothing to be done in the case of Joan. She had made it quite impossible for him to repair the damage he had done to an affection which, instead of relaxing its grip, seemed to be mounting!

He tossed about for an hour, worrying over the utter hopelessness of his longing for Joan. Conceding that their romance was a closed incident, what might still be done to insure her happiness? For, surely, Joan could not feel satisfied with the manner in which she had left him without a word when she had decided—quite impulsively, he presumed— to run away with Tommy. What a dismal honeymoon for Joan! And for Tommy, too, who couldn't be expected to be pleased with himself.

If they weren't on the other side of the Atlantic, reflected Dinny, he would go to them with his comradely congratulations and the assurance that he not only bore them no ill will but sincerely wished them great and lasting joy. It would be worth almost any length of journey to replace, in his memory, a contented and joyful Joan for the torturing image of her tear-stained face as she collected the pitiful little remains of their picnic luncheon. It would be a quite dreadful thing to have that picture of Joan's dejection and disappointment increasingly menacing his peace.

His decision to mend matters with Joan in so far as might be achieved through a friendly interview with her and Tommy involved a long series of imaginary circumstances in which they were brought together now at a little dinner he would give for them at Dexter's, now at their own table in an apartment somewhere up town. But—by Gad!—why wait? Lacey's had said Tommy was to be in Europe until early November, hadn't they? Why shouldn't he slip over there, directly, and give the poor things a chance to enjoy their honeymoon, undistressed by the remorse which Joan would inevitably feel? By Gad!—he would do it! As soon as he had finished with his father, and the intended visit to Magnolia, he would sail. He would make his relations to Tommy and Joan so pleasant for them and him that they could expect to be comrades for ever! That would take but a day. Then he would go to London for the winter, and try to write. He had no notion what he would be writing, but there was a sensation of desire. That was good: he had quite lost it.

It was a great idea! He would sail next week. That would solve the problem. He couldn't have Joan back, but he could do his utmost to make her happy. Dinny had gone to sleep constructing scenes and dialogue for the little play that was to dispose of the paper dishes.

* * * * *

At ten, next morning, Dinny telephoned up to the suite which Zandy Craig occupied on the ninth floor, requesting an interview.

A male secretary informed him that Mr. Craig's day was entirely engaged. If Mr. Brumm wished to confide the nature of his business to Mr. Craig's assistant, Mr. Effelbaum, an appointment could be arranged.

Dinny sensibly refused to be irritated over this slight delay. It was consistent with good business that Zandy Craig should not be open to the importunities of any bore or beggar who happened to drift in. He said he would be glad to see Mr. Effelbaum and explain his errand. The time was set for eleven. That was excellent. Mr. Effelbaum would quickly clear the way for him. Perhaps he and his father might lunch together.

With keen anticipation, and not a little nervous excitement, Dinny dressed carefully, and, at eleven sharp, took the elevator to the ninth floor, where he was shown into the suite, the secretary taking him immediately into the presence of the bright-eyed, urbane, little Jew who served as the last barricade between his exalted master and the public.

"So you would see Mr. Greck?" began Mr. Effelbaum, tapping his desk lightly with a long steel paper-knife.

Even making due allowance for Mr. Effelbaum's Hebraic handling of gutturals, there was something rather ominous in the manner of his pronunciation of "Greck."

"Mr. Craig is my father," replied Dinny, suddenly, resolved to make his story short and come to the point without circumlocution.

"Mr. Greck has no son," said Mr. Effelbaum, stiffly.

Instantly Dinny understood. Effelbaum, resentful of the "Greck" article in *Hallelujah,* was treating himself to a helping of revenge.

However, Effelbaum was acting according to his best knowledge, no doubt. He was honest in his belief that Zandy Craig had no son. Dinny was a mere impostor, so far as Effelbaum's information went.

"Perhaps you had better ask him. He is in, I presume?" Dinny was patient, respectful.

"There is no needt I should inquire, Mr. Brumm."

Dinny reached in his pocket for a card, scribbled a line on it, and handed it across the desk.

"Would you mind giving this to Mr. Craig?"

Effelbaum read the brief message and returned the card with a crooked smile.

"Mr. Greck will nodt see you, sir. You may tell me whadt you want."

Dinny flushed uncomfortably, and leaned forward with an elbow on the mahogany desk.

"Is he in?" Dinny's tone hinted at an impatience that was rapidly getting out of hand.

Effelbaum, savouring the situation, grinned sardonically and nodded.

"Budt not to you—Mr. Brumm."

Impetuously, Dinny rose, and observing that Effelbaum's hand was moving toward the row of ivory buttons on the left corner of the desk, quickly grasped him by the wrist.

"You may think you're doing your duty," he growled, "but this time you're exceeding it. I came here to see my father, and I mean to! Understand? Which of us takes that card in—you or I?"

To Dinny's surprise, Effelbaum glanced up with a taunting distortion of lip, and laughed.

"You take idt in to Mr. *'Greck!'*" He wagged his head in the direction of the adjacent door and shrugged a shoulder, self-absolvingly. "I haf triedt to spare you a bainful moment. You are determinedt to haf it... Go—and haf idt!"

Dinny released his grip on the unresisting hand and searched Effelbaum's sneer with eyes suddenly nonplussed.

"Do you mean to infer that my father has given instructions I am not to be admitted?"

Effelbaum's brows, lips, shoulders and palms raised, concertedly, in a gesture that wished himself well out of the awkward *contretemps.*

"Mr. 'Greck' toldt me he had no son. If you can convinze him to the contrary, I shall nodt detain you." He rose, opened the door, and bowed Dinny in, with an elaborate gesture.

"Mr. *'Greck'*—Mr. Brumm."

The stenographer at Zandy Craig's elbow rose and retired. Craig pushed in the slide on which her notebook had rested, leaned back in his opulent swivel-chair, folded his arms, and regarded his intrusive caller from under lowered brows.

"You may sit down, if you like," he said, coolly, dashing Dinny's intention to offer his hand. "I assume you are my son. In fact—now that I see you, I know you are. There is a certain likeness. And you have something of the facial lines of your mother."

Dinny smiled, half-heartedly, wondering, as his father paused, whether it was time for him to speak.

"May I inquire why you came, and how I may serve you?" continued Craig, steadily.

"I came to ask your pardon." Dinny's voice was sincerely contrite.

The big man slowly raised both long arms, clasped his hands behind his leonine grey head in a pose that Dinny recognized as a natural posture of his own when in a quandary, and closed his eyes.

"I am sorry I have waited so long," added Dinny.

"Yes—I'm afraid you waited... too long!" Craig looked squarely at the tardy prodigal, his expression severe.

Dinny nodded.

"I never thought I wanted to see you, sir, until lately. Something quite important has altered my opinion. I would like to tell you about it."

"That can wait," said Craig, folding his arms on the desk. "I'll talk first, if you're agreed. I've probably thought more about this matter than you have; and, anyway, I'm your father. It's my right to speak first, is it not?"

Dinny smiled approval.

"When you were a lad, young fellow, I made many efforts to show you that I meant to do everything I could for you, in face of the circumstances that kept us apart. I could not hold it against you when you resisted my attempts to—"

"I did not understand, sir. I had been led to think that—"

Craig signed that he did not wish to be interrupted. "Yes—I know, or can surmise, what you were led to think. Your Aunt Martha would have seen to that. And as for your parson uncle, I dislike to think of him. But—to continue—I did indulge the hope that once you were away from that atmosphere, it might please you to reflect that you had a father who had tried to do what is customarily thought of as the right thing.

"After Mr. Brumm had informed me you had a job and were on your own, I still waited. Sometimes I hoped that you would be moved to write me at least a note of appreciation. I disliked to think that I had bred a child who, in his later teens, had not managed to develop as much common courtesy as would have seemed to demand some sort of response."

Dinny's chagrin and remorse were painful. He lowered his eyes, and nodded, slowly.

"Through that period when you would have been going to college like a gentleman, and backed by the full support of your father, I happened to be heavily worried by a variety of cares, by no means the least of which—though I'm damned if I know just why I'm telling you this, for you have no right to my confidence—was my wife's separation from me. She had found me incompatible, though I was very fond of her. My duties required a great deal of my time. I was much away from home. We drifted apart. She left me.

"My daughter Alison was shortly sent abroad to school. Had you come to me, in those days, informing me that you had been an ass and an ingrate, I should have attempted to dissuade you of that estimate of yourself, I think, just from sheer loneliness and a natural wish for a reconstruction of my family ties.

"Eventually, Alison comes home, and accidentally encounters you here, though I was not informed of that until much later. Why she did not tell me, at once, I do not know, though I have surmised, and if that unfortunate accidental meeting brought either of you unhappiness—and I rather suspect, from chance remarks of Alison's, that it did—I am sorry. She did not tell me until the appearance of your assault on me in that damned dirty little rag which, I am told, you are now editing."

Craig's voice had risen, indignantly, with the last few words. His eyes were full of pain and his big fists clenched. He pushed back his chair, and rose, thrusting his long hands deeply into his trouser pockets.

"That day," he shouted, savagely, "whatever desire I still had for a sight of you—my son—was utterly abandoned. God knows which one of your ancestors you may resemble, but you're not like your charming mother, and I have the self-esteem to think you're not like me!"

Craig had flung the chair back against the wall, and was pacing up and down behind the desk, biting his words into hot bits.

"If you had come here shabby and broke, I would instruct my secretary to draw you a cheque. That would be for the relief of my own mind. You do not appear to be in want. You are well dressed and apparently have had your breakfast. I presume your position as the editor of a filthy magazine devoted to sophisticated blackmail and parlour socialism puts you beyond the necessity of my alms.... So—there is nothing you are likely to want that I can give you. As for this belated request for pardon, suppose we don't go into that, at all. I am not a sentimental person, either by instinct or practice. Neither are you, if I have correctly interpreted your temperament as reflected in your writing. Whatever made you come here, I don't know—and I don't care to know! If you have any remorse run along with it! If I have any regret, it's my own business.... Now—I think that's all, and if you're sure you are in need of nothing but my pardon, may I ask you to excuse me. This is a busy day, and, as you know, this interview was unsolicited by me.... Mr. Effelbaum will show you out."

He pushed a button, and Effelbaum appeared as if he had been waiting, hand on knob, for his cue.

This sudden move of his father's had been so unexpected, so ruthlessly conclusive, that Dinny was at a loss to know what, if anything, to do.

The door was wide open, Effelbaum was in the room waiting, Craig had readjusted his gold nose-glasses and was busying himself with the papers on his desk. Dinny had been definitely dismissed, and nothing remained for him to do but leave. He felt himself chastised like a half-grown boy. This man was his father, in very truth. Dinny's complete breakdown of self-possession was obviously an automatic response demanded by filial instinct suddenly recognizing the paternal authority of this man who, a stranger, had now loomed large as the sire.

For a moment only Dinny hesitated, took one step forward, was on the point of entreating for a chance to be heard. His father did not look up. Effelbaum fiddled with his watch-guard. Dinny turned slowly away. At the doorway he paused.

"I am very sorry, sir," he said, respectfully.

There was no reply. Effelbaum was at Craig's elbow, receiving a handful of opened letters. The trim stenographer was waiting for the retiring caller to make his exit. Dinny's interview with his father seemed to be over.

* * * * *

Magnolia was only fifty minutes away, but in those fifty minutes Dinny carefully examined his own mind in respect to the adventure on which he had launched, a few days earlier, and was delighted to discover that the unfortunate meeting with his father had not dashed his interest and belief in the thing he had set out to do.

A week ago his mind would have been tempestuous with bitter hate and stormy schemes for reprisals. He could easily picture the nature of his burning thoughts as he rehearsed, item by item, the progressive phases of his defenceless humiliation in his father's office. No!—By God! There wasn't a man alive who could put Dinny Brumm into such a debasing predicament and expect to get away with it unscratched! Least of all the man who had been responsible for so much of his mental torture, all through the years! Craig should have his pay with usury! Damn him! *Damn him!*

Dinny was surprised, this afternoon, at his mood; not surprised so much over his attitude of sympathetic understanding for Zandy Craig who had waited and hoped for some manner of response from his disaffected son—waited until the wound had healed and left an impermeable scar. The thing that amazed Dinny was the nature of this new serenity. It was not a mere hand-folding inertia. He tried vainly to define it in a phrase, and could arrive at nothing more adequate than "dynamic peace."

As he sat looking out at the window of the club car which served as a hub for the revolving wooded hills, faintly tipped with early autumn tints, Dinny's mental state was a novelty to himself. Whatever description his mood deserved, it was certainly not apathy. There was something vital, vibrant, kinetic in it. Jason Schrofe had not been far afield when he thought of this peculiar energy as "dynamite."

Always Dinny had entertained varying degrees of contempt for the unworkable theory of non-resistance. Sometimes he grinned when he saw the word in print. What sort of people were advocates of non-resistance? Strong men—likely to make some constructive contribution of skill or genius? Not at all. The non-resisters had had their frail, other-cheeking, boot-licking programme of life handed to them at birth. It was less a sublimity of soul than a feebleness of body.

As for organized warfare, that was quite another matter. That was a mass-madness inspired by predatory bankers and swashbucklers, diabolically unconcerned about the cost of their greed and pomposity to the drafted and driven who were herded into the tragic hoax by the stimulating rattle of brave drums, stampeded into indifference to the likelihood of their being ushered out of it to the depressing tune of scalpels and saws and forceps tinkling metallically on glass-topped, rubber-castored tables. That was, indeed, another matter!

But non-resistance, attempted practised by an individual, was sheer cowardice. How idiotic—for a church full of people to stand up, of a Sunday morning, and bellow their lungs out for a theory that none but the sick, crippled, and undersized actually believed in to the point of practical demonstrations.

How deliciously absurd—when some hollow-cheeked, hollow-chested, dreamy-eyed, five-foot-four, one hundred and nineteen pound Christian boosted himself up at prayer-meeting to declare, in a thin, piping squeak, that, as for him, he believed in non-resistance.

The only sane answer to that, offered by the people who really had the world's work to do, was a laughing "By Gad—you'd *better!*"

"But," shrills the altruistic little fellow, "this is my honest conviction! I sincerely believe that it's more sensible never to fight back!"

"Doubtless," grins the ham-handed six-footer. "You would! You're a wise little man. You just keep on thinking that, if you know what's good for you!"

Invoicing his own feelings, today, Dinny marvelled that the hymns and liturgies and homilies of Christianity had taken so little account of the fact that non-resistance, far from being a state of supine lethargy, was a dynamic of high potentiality.

Why didn't the Church leave off singing, "I am Jesus' little lamb," and recognize the very substantial and demonstrable power of *the spirit in action!* Dinny had never felt so alive, so alert, so energized in his life. His compliant understanding of his father's rudeness and refusal to conciliate was accompanied by a rising tide of personal poise and power. Perhaps this serenity was at least approximately denoted by the ancient phrase—"the peace that surpasseth understanding."... By Gad—it was a fact!

For a moment there was a flash of belief, as if he had discovered a universal cure-all for every possible anxiety, that the potent sentence printed on Julia's salvaged scrap of scripture was possessed of magical properties. But, of course, even this formula for power was conditioned somewhat by circumstances. He could forgive Joan for running away from him without a word of regret or explanation. Doubtless he deserved it. She had given him his chance. By what right could he expect her to live interminably on the hope that he might wear himself out with hateful cynicism, and, having eventually burned up all his carbon, ask her to take charge of the ashes! The girl had her life to live; hadn't she?... Oh, yes—all that was plain as a pikestaff; but the fact remained that no length of his love, no depth of his understanding, no dynamic of forgiveness could restore Joan to him. Some mistakes were irrevocable!... He could forgive—had forgiven—his father for the savage rebuff, but that would not give him back his father.

* * * * *

Magnolia was a mere pocket-edition. The clangor of the gong on which the motorman cleared the track, as the Sunnyside Avenue car demanded her right of way at the corner of Main and Broad—busiest spot in town—was surely redundant, seeing how little traffic she coped with. All activity on the streets had been slowed down to the tempo of Zanesdale and Unger.

Dinny watched the familiar shops amble by, smiling unconsciously at their decrepitude. Had the town built nothing new? Yes—here was an important replacement; a full half block of glossy yellow brick six storeys high! The car had stopped on the red, and there was ample time to read the names of the businesses that occupied the imposing new building. Some of the names he recognized. There was Hunter the Hatter which he had always considered a choice bit of alliteration, often wondering whether Hunter's selection of a vocation had been influenced thereby. Some of the names were unfamiliar. The whole

279

transparent corner of the ground floor was occupied with swagger motor-cars—"Spencer Davis, Manager."

Was it possible that this was "Spike"? That was his name—Spencer. It would be interesting to see what manner of man Spike had evolved to. Dinny impulsively strode to the rear platform as the car started forward, and swung himself off. He had all but forgotten Spike. Once upon a time, he had hated him with all his might, but in recent years nothing had been left of it but a dulled, dispassionate aversion.

The place was empty except for the display cars, a workman with a chamois-skin, and a neat girl with an adroit nail-file who was advertised as ready to furnish "Information," in case—as appeared unlikely—anyone should desire it.

"Yes, Mr. Davis is in," replied the girl, indifferently, as if the fact could scarcely be expected to interest anybody. "Through there," she added, pointing over her shoulder with the nail-file, and resuming her occupation.

It was Spike; no question about that. There was a symmetrical bald spot on his crown about the size of a tonsure, but it would hardly have been mistaken for that if the picture of it had included the ears which, viewed from the rear—he was bent over a desk telephone—were built rather for enduring combats than confessions.

Dinny waited, just inside the door, for Spike to finish and greet him. Becoming aware that the conversation was embarrassingly private, for Spike was in an attitude of frantic supplication, he quietly backed out, but in that moment he had accidentally heard enough to inform him that his erstwhile opponent was in difficulty.

"Yeah—but see here, Mr. Amberly, I simply can't do it today! Maybe I can by Monday or Tuesday, if I can make some collections. Give a fellow a break, can't you? Yeah—I know it's a sight draft, but I can't raise seventeen-fifty this afternoon, and that's all there is to it!... Hell! It's impossible!"

The receiver had banged back on the hook, and Spike, considerably shaken and distraught, was moving toward the open door. Dinny was occupied with reading a large bulletin pasted on the glazed partition setting forth the merits of a new oiling system that had just made over the whole motor industry into something theatrically other than it had been. Spike looked his age—plus.

"Do you remember me?" asked Dinny.

Spike stared hard for a moment; then grinned as amiably as his perturbation would permit, and nodded, extending his hand.

"Y-e-a-h!" he marvelled, as the light slowly filtered through. "Dinny Brumm! I'll be damned! What are you doin' here?"

"A little business trip, Spike, and"—a sudden impulse prompted Dinny to rush on into an unintended remark—"I have decided to buy a car here and drive back to New York. Thought you might be willing to talk it over with me."

"That's what we're here for, old-timer," rejoiced Spike, noisily. "About what are you looking for, Dinny? You're turning something in, I suppose."

"No—I disposed of my car some time ago when I was to be out of the country for a while."

"That's good—and unusual."

They stepped out into the show-room, where Spike, who knew his business, proceeded without delay to an energetic sales-talk, utterly oblivious of their earlier antagonism and the marked changes wrought upon each of them by the intervening years.

Dinny was only a half-hour making up his mind to purchase the dark blue coupé with the grey whipcord upholstery. It was, he said, about what he wanted.

"How soon can it be ready for the road, Spike?"

"It's ready now!"

"How about plates?"

"I'll get 'em for you. You can take it along with the demonstration tags; they'll be all right for today."

They returned to the office desk and sat down.

"The usual terms—over ten months?" Spike straightened the carbon in his order-book and prepared to write.

"No—I'm going to pay cash for it." Dinny produced his cheque-book, and unscrewed the top from his pen. "Seventeen hundred and fifty—right?"

"Yeah—that's right," repeated Spike, with a combination gasp and sigh that struck Dinny as one of the most startling expressions of surprise and relief he had ever heard.

"There you are," said Dinny.

Spike fanned his shoulder with the unblotted cheque, and laughed nervously.

"By God, Dinny, you don't know it, but you've damn' near saved my life. I don't mind telling you that if I hadn't sold you this car—right now—for cash—I likely would have lost my agency!"

"Glad I happened in, then, at the opportune moment." Dinny tried to make the comment sound casual.

Of a sudden, Spike's face grew serious and he gnawed his lip, reflectively.

"Just when did you come in, Dinny?" he asked.

"Two-forty—from Cincinnati."

"Yeah... No—I mean, how long had you been here when I found you outside the door?"

"Only a moment... It's quite all right, Spike. I can use the car. I had expected to buy one, sooner or later."

"Well—it's pretty damn' decent of you—I'll say," muttered Spike, in a tone of mingled gratitude and contrition.

"You would have done the same thing, doubtless, if you had accidentally stumbled in on me and found me in a jam."

"I doubt it!" confessed Spike, brusquely. "What's come over you, Dinny? You sure weren't that sort of a chap when we were in school, and"—he chuckled, dryly—"nobody would think you were a Fairy Godmother, to read your—"

"It's all happened just lately, Spike. Like to hear about it?"

"Yeah—if it isn't private. I sure would... Wait till I tell that boy to put on a new spare. The one she's carrying has had couple o' hundred miles about town."

It was not an easy task to confide the secret to Spike. He was quite unprepared for such thinking, and he had important matters on his mind. He had first to talk to Mr. Amberly. Dinny could not help being amused at the vast alteration of tone with which he informed Mr. Amberly, crisply, that he would be over presently to take up "that little matter" in full. It called to mind the story about the rabbit that found the whisky.

"Well—I'm damned if I ever thought you'd get religion," observed Spike, after listening, rather absently, for some minutes. "You're the last man in the world."

"I don't think it is that," said Dinny. "I've discovered that it's impossible for a man to be healthy and up on his toes with his system poisoned by old grudges. I suppose it's like arthritis. The poison's all through you, though the focal infection may be in one place and the pain in another."

"Yeah—I see. You've got an infected back tooth, and a pain in your shoulder. Is that what you mean?"

"Precisely! You've an old grudge against your uncle, and—and take it out on your girl."

"Married—Dinny?"

Dinny shook his head without looking up.

"You must have had a grudge against your uncle. Have you fixed it up?"

"Yes—but I waited too long."

"Lost the girl, eh?"

"Quite definitely." Dinny rose, and they went out to the kerb where the new car was parked.

"I suppose you'll be driving over to the college," wondered Spike. "Lot of changes over there since you—"

"Since I was fired," assisted Dinny, smiling.

"Yeah—I wouldn't blame you if you never wanted to see it again. They sure did give you a rotten deal."

"I thought that, too, until just lately."

"By God!—I believe you're in earnest! Do you honestly think that it would make a fellow more efficient in his business if he made friends with all the people he despised, and everybody that had got his goat, and not given him a break?"

"Well—if he went into it for the sole purpose of selling more cars—that's what you mean, don't you?—I doubt it very much. But if he made an honest stab at it, with the hope of cleaning out his poison and promoting himself to a higher class of animal, his increased efficiency would inevitably follow, don't you think?"

"It sure sounds sort o' moonshiny. God!—I'd feel silly going into old man Kennerly's place, for instance, to ask him to be friends. Couldn't, if I wanted to, now," added Spike, with apparent relief that a good excuse had occurred to him. "The old double-crosser's laid up at home, I understand, with some kind of a heart attack. Damned if I knew he had one!"

Dinny smiled broadly.

"Maybe he's poisoned. Why don't you go and help the doctor pull the old bird through?"

"How would that help *old Kennerly* get rid of his poison, if I went to see him with the idea of getting rid of *mine?*"

Dinny shook his head, admitting his perplexity.

"Funny thing about that," he said, thoughtfully. "It's true, though: this stuff's contagious, Spike.... You know"—he went on, after a momentary reflection—"I didn't come here today to do anything for *your* poison. I'm trying to be free of *mine.* If you go to old Kennerly to be free of *yours,* I dare say that before you're done with it, Kennerly will have unloaded *his.* Might save his life! Or—if it didn't, he might at least be able to die like a gentleman."

Spike stood staring.

"My God!—Dinny! Do you believe there's anything in this?"

Dinny took Spike's coat lapel lightly between thumb and fingers, looking him steadily in the eyes. "Yes—and *so do you!*"

He opened the car door, and climbed in. The engine responded smoothly to the starter.

"You remember the way, don't you?" called Spike.

"Yes... But I'm not going out there, just now. How's the road down to Pinckney?"

"Perfect! And pretty, too. Remember the cliffs and mounds, down there?"

Dinny nodded, let in the clutch, rolled slowly down the familiar street. In his present state of mind, he wondered if he was really competent to drive. His hands were trembling. Old Jason was right. This stuff—whatever it might be—was like dynamite. You had to handle it with care... Sentimental moonshine? My God! The stuff acted like radium! It didn't go off with a bang—but you had to look out! There was no question but it would destroy a man who trifled with it! He decided he would think twice before he told anyone else. A conviction was taking form in his mind that hadn't occurred to Dinny before. An energy as potent as this mustn't be trusted in the hands of people without definite instructions concerning its nature. He must find out a little more about it before he passed it on any further. Canny old Jason had seen the dangers at a glance. *Anybody who tried to use this dynamic for his own material advantage would almost unquestionably burn his fingers!*

* * * * *

"Yes—poor old Clancy had to give up the battle," drawled Mr. Brophy, pushing the mustard-pot across the table. "The beer was no good, any more, and cost too much, and, anyway, the old chap had a certain self-respect; didn't care to be associated with the young crop of bootleggers. So—he closed up."

"If they could have had Clancys dispensing beer, all over the country, perhaps we would never have come to this pass," observed Dinny. "But the thing had got out of bounds, most places. The Clancys were in the minority."

"But there were enough Clancys to justify a bit of steady thinking on that subject before the whole liquor industry was turned loose to be operated by pick-pockets and safe-crackers!... Well—it's too late to be owling over that tragedy. It's done; we're in for it!... Let's talk about *you!* What brings you here?"

Dinny had strolled into *The Star* office at midnight, finding Mr. Brophy taking his coat off the peg preparatory to going out for lunch. After a warm welcome, or as warm as was to be expected of the unexcitable editor, who was not given much to hysteria, Dinny went back into the composing-room and renewed old acquaintance with the four or five who remained. Old Timmy Fagan had died.

"Shall we go over and see Clancy?" asked Dinny, when they were out on the street.

"No—that's a speakeasy now," growled Brophy. "I don't like the people who run it. They'd sell you a stroke of paralysis for a dollar. We'll drop in here at Ketolphus's place. You like Greeks, I recall."

"I came out this way on several errands," said Dinny, replying to Mr. Brophy's inquiry. "I'm on a sort of peace commission."

"Didn't suppose you went in for that kind of thing, Dinny."

"No—it has been rather out of my line."

Brophy grinned.

"Out of your line!... You've been a young hell-cat! Whoever sent you out with the impression that you were a cooing dove? You've been a storm centre so far back as I can recall... Well—let's hear all about it."

It would be interesting to try it out on Mr. Brophy. The chances of his accepting it, to his damage, were as nothing is related to everything. Dinny, somewhat obscure and hesitant with the preliminaries—for his auditor's impassive face held out no promise of sympathetic comprehension—reported quite fully on his strange legacy and his recent experiences in so far as he could without violating confidences.

Brophy had smoked, stolidly, and listened.

"My son," he said, gravely, when the narrative had reached the point of highest ecstasy for Dinny, and highest density for the white-haired Brophy, "you've been working too hard. It's a natural penalty for philosophizing. You've made it your job, for years, to find out how much is the matter with the world. You never tried to treat it for its diseases; you just diagnosed, and shook your head, and telephoned for the undertaker. Now you've tired of that and are looking for some kind of a patent medicine. I think you're crazy as hell, and ought to be in a sanitorium."

Dinny laughed, heartily, and tapped the end of another cigarette on the table.

"I never felt so well in my life, Mr. Brophy."

"Any lunatic will tell you that. You'd better have a nice, long talk with a reputable psychiatrist. What do you suppose Beaton and those other chaps on *Hallelujah* would think if they knew you were cruising about in this state of mind? Why—you talk like this what's her name... My God!... she's no relation of yours, is she?"

Dinny's attempt to defend himself and his theory was not very satisfactory, chiefly for lack of time. Brophy had pressing work to do before *The Star* was put to bed, and made no disguise of his urgent necessity to be off.

When they parted, he was not only cordial but rather disconcertingly solicitous. Dinny must have a bit of rest. It was clear he had been working too hard, and had let things get on his nerves.

Back in his room at the hotel, Dinny suffered a moment's reflection that people victimized by psychoses are usually unaware of their misfortune. However, Spike Davis didn't think him crazy... or did he? His father didn't think him crazy, or he would hardly have thrown him out so indifferently. Old Jason didn't think him crazy. By Gad—he was never so sane in his life! Of course Brophy couldn't see it. Suppose Brophy had come to *him,* a month ago, with a similar story: what would he have thought of *Brophy?*

* * * * *

It was an exquisite chapel, the gift of Mr. Joel Day in memory of his mother. Expense had not been considered. It was a work of art.

Recalling the general stampede of the old days when the ten-fifty bell summoned all Magnolians to compulsory prayers in the barn-like, taffy-coloured assembly-hall, Dinny was amazed at the apparent reverence with which the students filed into the beautiful Gothic structure, dimly lit by mellow tints sifted through windows of unquestionable æsthetic value. He was struck by the fact that the current crop of Magnolia students was vastly superior in appearance and bearing to the hicks of his own collegiate generation; then promptly decided that the change was probably within himself. His appreciation of almost everything was on the rise; why not his respect for Magnolia? There was a rightful place for the little college, after all. His long-time disdain of it had been unjust.

But, even allowing for his own alteration of outlook, Magnolia had broadened. There were candles on the altar, and when the college choir appeared in the stalls it was appropriately vested. The organ, concealed behind chaste grillwork, was playing *Ein Feste Burg* with skilfully conceived variations. It was a good place to be. All the old feeling of antagonism toward everything that was Magnolia had vanished. She had suddenly become Alma Mater.

A tall chaplain in academic robes had followed the choir into the chancel, approaching the lectern where he stood for a moment with bowed head. Even in the uncertain light, Dinny recognized him at once. Doubtless Kling was a professor in the Seminary now; a commanding figure, obviously deserving of the confidence they had in him. After the service, Dinny would seek him out, and the old constraint would be lifted.

The *a cappella* choir sang, very impressively, one of Tschaikowsky's haunting anthems. With dignity and feeling, Kling began to read the last chapter of Ecclesiastes.

It was as if Dinny listened to the majestic thing for the first time. Often he had made some ribald joke that played on "the grasshopper" who, perhaps through over-indulgence, had become a "burden." That this ancient confession of a cynic was great literature had never occurred to him. What a superficial, heady fool he had been! What insufferable impudence! Speaking of hicks and yokels, who but an ignoramus could have been guilty of impertinences so raw?

Here was an incomparable pen-portrait of the penalties of such sophistication as had all but quenched the springs of Dinny's life. In this drab picture, the shutters had been closed, the garden had dried up, the porters at the gate sat dully oblivious of the world's activity. In the adjacent mill, the sound of the grinding was low. Things were so quiet that the voice of a bird startled one. The great palace was all but dead.

Once upon a time, fountains had played, flowers had bloomed, the spacious corridors had been flooded with music. The whole institution had throbbed with vitality. The joy of life had been drawn up from the inner spring of the luminous spirit as if by a silver cord attached to a golden bowl.

But the magic elixir had not been valued for what it was worth. The silver cord had slipped through unheeding fingers and *the golden bowl had been broken!* It was necessary now to go outside one's own gates and seek the fountain for one's water-of-life, using the communal pitcher that served other unfortunates who had broken their golden bowls. One day *that pitcher was found broken beside the fountain!* There was nothing left, now, but to go to the public cistern and stand waiting one's turn; and finally there came a day when *the wheel was found broken at the cistern!*

It was at that exact moment in Orville Kling's sonorous reading of this ancient cynic's lament—as Dinny often confessed, later—that the inspiration suddenly came which produced his monumental story, *Thirst*—a book so gripping that it was carried to the farthest corners of the literate earth; laughed over, wept over, prayed over by hundreds of thousands who, though hosts of them may have broken their golden bowls, or had been so unfortunate as to have found the pitcher broken at the fountain, resolved they would see to it that the wheel was not broken at the cistern!

When Kling had finished his reading, and closed the Book, he prayed. Every head was bowed; Dinny's, too. He found himself simple-heartedly grateful for the mental guidance of the man for whom he had long nourished a sullen hatred. There was a benediction while they sat in reverence; then, after a moment's absolute silence, the congregation stirred, rose, and quietly departed. But Dinny was too deeply moved to lift his head. A feeling of great exultation swept the strings of his soul. There had been laid on him a commission. He had been appointed an apostle to them whose gardens were wilting, whose silver cords were slipping, whose golden bowls were in danger of breaking.

The organ had returned to its versatile adventures with the courageous score of "A Mighty Fortress is Our God." Dinny's eyes were suffused with a rush of hot tears. His heart was pounding. His consciousness of his new responsibility was almost more than he could bear.

"Lookit, Gramp!... at *Dinny Brumm!*"

"What's the matter... Did he upset his vinegar jug?"

"No!... Lookit!... *Lookit!*"

CHAPTER XVIII

IT was not an ideal evening for a stroll. The air was damp and uncomfortably chilly. Apparently it had been raining very hard, a little earlier, for the wet leaves on the sidewalks were laid in semi-circular festoons as if swept there at the turn of a tide, and the gutters were filled with tight-packed, soggy piles of them.

But Dinny wanted to move about under his own power. The rough voyage had been tedious, and the trip from Cherbourg had tried his patience, for now that he was nearing his journey's end he was eager to have done with it and proceed to the singular errand that had brought him so far.

It was too late to locate Tommy and Joan tonight. To-morrow, pursuant to the advice he had secured from Lacey's, he would endeavour to connect with Tommy through their Paris office. If lucky, he might have the contemplated visit with the honeymooners before the day was out. Next morning he would run up to Calais, and so to London, where he had already engaged a room at the Victoria.

Descending the steps of the Continental, Dinny sauntered up and down the arcaded block, strolled over to the Place Vendôme and back again to Rue de Rivoli, wondering how he might amuse himself for the remainder of the evening.

On impulse he took a taxi and drove across the river. On Raspail, a little below Saint-Germain, he decided to get out and walk. After ten minutes of aimless rambling, he sighted a café that seemed more active than any he had seen.

Pleasurably recognizing its name, for he had often heard of "The Dome" and its popularity with Americans, he turned in among the little iron-legged tables that cluttered the sidewalk, found one unoccupied, ordered a glass of sauterne to ensure his welcome, and leisurely took stock of the amiable crowd, most of whom were youthful, many of whom were reminiscent of the Greenwich Village habitués, and all of whom—with one single exception in sight—appeared to be in a more or less festive mood.

The unaccompanied woman who sat facing him, a little distance away, took no interest in her neighbours. She did not appear to be in acute trouble, but was downcast, meditatively toying with a half-empty glass of something that looked like cognac. Hers was not a problem of poverty, for she was the best-dressed person there. She could have pawned the silver mesh handbag on her table for enough to put her up at the Ritz for a few days, and the price of her black fur coat would have kept her in good comfort for six months.

In a moment their eyes met briefly, and, because hers were unmistakably American eyes and full of loneliness, Dinny was faintly conscious that his face must have reacted a bit to his recognition of the fact that they were fellow-countrymen. If she noticed the fleeting smile in his eyes, she made no response to it, abstractedly returning to her pensive fingering of the glass.

Dinny found it difficult to detach himself from her, and studied her face with interest. In her depression, she looked forty. Later, when she smiled, five years vanished magically. She was a lady—with a story; no doubt of that. But it was not necessarily a sordid or discreditable story, for though her face was sad, it was not hard and it was not ashamed.

She glanced up now, smiled faintly as their eyes momentarily met again, drained her glass casually, and drew the collar of her fur coat more snugly about her neck. Doubtless she was on the point of leaving now, and Dinny was half-glad. Her dejection was dampening his own spirits, already low enough, for, as the distance lessened between him and the courage-testing event that had invited him to Paris, the more sensitive he became to his irreparable loss. He had moments when he wondered whether he would be able to go through with it.

Rising slowly, she took up her expensive bag from the table, and, with eyes regarding him inquisitively, came over to Dinny, paused, laid a black-gloved hand on the back of the vacant chair. He rose instantly, and invited her to sit down. She did so, with entire self-possession, folding her arms on the table.

"Were you surprised, Dinny, when you found my note?"

"Janet!—my dear!"

He reached out both hands to hers.

"You didn't recognize me," she said, ruefully. "I must have changed more than I had thought."

"But it has been so long, dear, and of course I wasn't expecting to see you, and—you've bobbed your hair, haven't you? It's quite becoming, Janet."

"No—I've changed. I know that, Dinny. The game I've been playing alters one."

"How does it compare with—wheel-barrow?"

"Less exciting. Much slower than chess; and if you win, there's no prize."

"It wears the players out, you mean?"

She nodded, with just a faint recovery of the Janet look of quick understanding.

"Exactly. The players are worn out, and it's after midnight, and finally one of them makes the last move, which both had seen coming for an hour, and—the game's over. The guest yawns and goes, and the drowsy host calls in the cat and puts out the milk-bottle. And that's all. Not very stimulating, would you say?"

"Where is he now, Janet? Want to talk about it?"

"As for wanting to—no. But I'll tell you. We separated more than a year ago. Oscar returned to the States for a while. He is in Florence now; or was, the last I heard from him."

"Who won the game?"

She shrugged slightly and dismissed the query with a lazy little flick of her fingers.

"I believe I made the last move, but by that time we were both too indifferent to care, or to remember—certainly not with any pride of victory, or—"

"Humiliation of defeat," assisted Dinny, comprehendingly.

"I'm not so sure there wasn't some humiliation," confessed Janet, after a pause, "even for the winner—if I won."

"The money part—maybe?" Dinny wondered.

Janet nodded.

"Why do you ask? The story will surely bore you, and it makes me unhappy to remember."

"Sometimes it helps a little to talk things over, dear."

"Well—I fancy you know that Mr. Day divorced me, as of course he should. Along with word of that came notification that he had made over a great many valuable securities to me. I declined them, through our attorneys, but Mr. Day's decision remained unchanged. You may recall that Mr. Day's temperament was not to be described as—as vacillating, or volatile."

Janet's drawling understatement left so very much unsaid that Dinny laughed, appreciatively. She had not changed, after all.

"The dividends kept coming along," continued Janet, in an even tone, "and I used them, reluctantly at first.... And then, when Oscar and I parted—it was mostly my fault, for I think I was the one who remarked that we both knew we were weary of each other—he gave me his blessing and three thousand shares of T. and T."

"You're well provided for, dear."

"Oh, yes—I have almost everything anyone would want except self-respect, and I've been doing without that for so long I hardly miss it." She had tried to make this last sound dryly cynical, and ended it with a twisted little smile.

"Janet," said Dinny, soberly, "you've broken your golden bowl!"

She lowered her eyes, and nodded; then glanced up, inquiringly.

"What's this—about a golden bowl, Dinny?"

"It was attached to a silver cord," he explained cryptically. "And whenever you wanted happiness, you drew it up from the spring. I'm afraid you've let the silver cord slip through your hands."

"Is that what that means—'Or ever the silver cord be loosed, and the golden bowl be broken'? I never knew." She laughed, quietly. "Since when did you go in for such philosophy, Dinny? I've read enough of your hellish satires to know that you're not in the golden-bowl business."

"I'd like to tell you all about it, Janet. You say you've changed. I wonder that you recognized me! It's quite a long story."

She pushed back her chair.

"Suppose we go over to the Crillon—I live there—and sit in the lounge. And you can begin at the beginning, and tell me everything.... But you won't scold me; will you, dear?"

* * * * *

Dinny's heart was beating furiously, and his mouth was dry, as he paced nervously to and fro near the little elevator. The shaft of it, rising from the lobby, was a mere skeleton of ornamental wrought-iron curlycues, and one could see the descending occupants long before they arrived on the ground floor.

At any moment now, Tommy would be coming down, and Joan, too, more than likely, for it was nearly ten and she would undoubtedly be up and dressed for the day.

They would greet him with a brave show of cordiality, trying hard to cover their mystification with a rapid fire of questions. "Why—of all things!—Dinny Brumm!"... "How lovely to see you here!"... "Where are you stopping? When did you come? How nice of you to look us up!" But underneath all the friendly racket, how much of constraint would there be? It had not been difficult to locate them. At nine-thirty, Dinny had telephoned Lacey's office. Yes—Mr. Forsythe was in town, stopping at the Regina.

Perhaps he had not left yet; might catch him there. It was only a step over from the Continental.

"Down in two minutes, old chap!" Tommy had answered, on the house telephone. "Powerfully glad you're here! Delightful surprise!"

Was it, really? Dinny wished he could be more certain of that.

The little elevator had again slipped slowly upward through the gold ceiling. And now—a few frantic weeks of waiting having elapsed—it was coming down, bringing Tommy's long legs, broad shoulders, expectant smile. Dinny was steadied and comforted, a little, by the smile.

"This is certainly a great treat, Dinny!" Tommy gave him a comradely thump on the shoulder, and beamed.

"I'm on my way to London," explained Dinny, hastily, as if his train were waiting. "It occurred to me I'd like to have a glimpse of you and Joan—for old sake's sake—"

"Joan?" echoed Tommy, happily. "Is she here, too?"

"My God—Tommy! You don't mean to tell me—"

Tommy stared, uncomprehendingly, for a moment, and then grinned.

"You didn't think we were here together, did you? The last I saw of Joan was the night before I sailed in September."

They were standing near a little gilt and scarlet divan; and Dinny, whose knees were shaky, sat down, Tommy joining him, much amused by his sudden collapse.

"The fact is," resumed Tommy, "Joan has been much on my mind, these past few weeks. She vanished, the same day I left. She did not show up at the store, next morning. They made inquiries without results."

"Had anything happened," inquired Dinny, huskily, "to account for it? Do you suppose some harm has come to her?"

"I'll tell you all I know," said Tommy, soberly, after a moment's delay. "I suppose you've a right to all the information there is."

* * * * *

"Her Uncle Jim ought to know where she is!" shouted Dinny, excitedly. "Perhaps she's there! She went to him once before when she was in trouble. I'll cable!"

"I'll go along. You're not fit to be at large, Dinny. You'll get yourself run over. Buck up now! You look like a ghost. We'll find her. Uncle Jim will know—if you can get it out of him."

* * * * *

He knew that Janet and Tommy were amusing themselves at his expense, as the boat-train started. Tommy had said something funny to her, and nodded toward him, as he waved from the window of his compartment. She had laughed, gaily. Had anyone ever heard of so good a joke? A round trip from New York to Paris for information about his girl!—information he might have had for ninety cents if he had queried Uncle Jim in the first place.

The three of them had lunched together. Dinny well satisfied over the prompt congeniality of Janet and Tommy, whose amiable chatter left him without much responsibility for the talk. He had never been in such a state of utter rout, mentally. Uncle Jim's cable had not arrived until nearly four. After that there had been a great panic about getting Dinny aboard the first ship. The *Olympic* was due to call at Cherbourg at eleven. He could just make it.

The train was increasing its strides now. Dinny's hands trembled as he took the cablegram from his pocket. Bless old Uncle Jim! He had come through without a moment's delay. The message was brief, but illuminating.

Tommy had fortunately been able to fill in the details. He remembered Mr. Abercrombie's call at Lacey's, and his unusual interest in Joan.

It was a long trip to Cherbourg, and the *Olympic* was exasperatingly slow getting herself persuaded to draw up the anchor and amble on toward the west. Dinny wondered, as he stood at the rail, whether it would help things along if he volunteered assistance.... What? Another big netful of mail-bags? What did so many people have to write about that was so important?

* * * * *

There was a telegram from Janet at the purser's office when he called to arrange for his passage.

TOMMY TELLS ME MUCH TO DO FOR SHOP GIRLS IN NEW YORK STOP PERHAPS CAN USE MONEY MENDING BROKEN BOWLS PITCHERS CISTERN WHEELS STOP THANK YOU DEAR FOR COMING STOP KISS JOAN FOR ME STOP TOMMY ADJACENT SAYS ME TOO STOP LUCKY DEVIL

* * * * *

Every day en route Dinny composed radiograms to Joan by the dozen, informing her he was on the way and hurrying as fast as possible. None of them was sent. He couldn't explain, by radio, that he was ready now to keep his promises, several times broken, nor dare he risk frightening her away from Denver with the announcement that he was about to press his claim.

The *Olympic* might have been an old square-rigged three-master from the way she wallowed and plodded as if it was of no concern to her whether she ever reached New York or not; but one morning, after ages and ages, she nosed her way into her berth, and at two Dinny was on the train, composing speeches for Joan... The *darling!*

* * * * *

He had firmly decided, after much debate, that he would not attempt to see Joan at the store. He would call on Mr. Abercrombie, briefly explain his mission, and Mr. Abercrombie would give him Joan's street address. From what Tommy had said about the fine old fellow, that seemed quite reasonable.

The train arrived shortly after three, and Dinny went directly to the big store. Mr. Abercrombie listened with interest.

"We should be very sorry to lose Miss Braithwaite," he said. "But I'm afraid I couldn't stop you, even if I tried. So—find her, my boy, and good luck to you."

He sent a message to her house from the Blackstone, asking her to give him a ring at the earliest moment, and waited in a state of near-lunacy. Six-twenty!—twenty-five!—thirty! Joan should be at home by this time. He sat near the telephone, ready to leap to it.

At seven, unable to endure another minute of this torture, he called her house. The voice replied cheerfully, "Hold the line, please," and a little later said sympathetically, "Sorry—but Miss Braithwaite is out."

He sat for a long time with the telephone in his hands, wondering what next to do. His hopes were tumbling to pieces.

At eight, he resolved that nothing was to be gained by moping in his room, and was putting on his coat to go down when a letter was delivered by messenger. He opened it, in a panic of apprehension.

Dear Dinny:

You and I have caused each other a great deal of misery. And nothing could be easier for us to do than keep on making ourselves and each other utterly wretched until one of us died or ran away.

I'm not going to pretend that I'm happy, but I'm busy, and I like my work. It cost a good deal to decide that it was better for us never to see each other any more. But, having made that decision, I know it is to your best interest, and mine, that I stick to it. You know I would love to see you; but, Dinny, I can't go through it again!

Please don't try to persuade me. Here is once when I'm certain that I know what's best for us.
Ever yours,
JOAN

After a half-hour of suffering, Dinny resolved to play the last card in his hand. He went to the desk, and wrote:

Dearest Joan:

I'm not asking you to renew friendship with the Dinny Brumm of the Green Cheese and "Hallelujah." It may be hard for you to believe, but I'm definitely done with all that. I am just learning to walk. I need you as never before, and I love you desperately.

You will find enclosed a letter that I found secreted in an old desk that was the property of my mother. Please read it, dear. I have made the experiment that Julia recommended to me. And it has worked!

Do let me see you, if only for a moment, tomorrow!
Loving you dearly
DINNY

Having dispatched the letter to Joan's address, he went down and walked the streets for an hour. He remembered that he had had no dinner, but was not hungry enough to care. Returning at length to his room, he went to bed, and, utterly exhausted with the long strain, drifted off into a troubled sleep.

How long the telephone had been ringing he could only guess. The insistent demand had been punctuating a series of dreams in which he was being entreated, urged, belaboured, to respond to some desperate situation. Half-awake, he groped for the instrument, noting, as he turned on the light, that it was half-past five.

"Dinny!" Joan's voice was very low, and broken.

"Yes, darling."

"Dinny—I'm afraid I can't wait till morning."
"Come on down here, then... I'll meet you in the lobby."
"Would that be too dreadful?... What would people think?"
"Hang the people!... Oh, Joan!... My dear!"
There was a considerable pause.
"Very well... I'll come... Half an hour... Good-bye."

Dinny found himself laughing aloud, half-hysterically, as he dressed. He bet his last dollar nothing like this had ever happened before. His fingers were clumsy as he wrestled with his collar. Joan was coming! He glanced out of the window. There was a faint dawn-glow.

The lobby of the hotel was deserted except for a sleepy clerk at the desk, and two old fellows with damp mops scrubbing the tiled floor.

Dinny stood just inside the revolving door, and waited.

A taxi drew up. He rushed out to meet it, opened the door, stepped in.

After a while the taxi-driver closed the door with a bang, but whatever hint it was intended to convey had been too subtle for his passengers.

Five minutes later, he opened the door again, and said:

"I'm goin' across here for a cup of coffee and a doughnut. And if the cop gives me a ticket for parkin', I'll expect you to pay for it!"

* * * * *

There was a very simple little wedding that afternoon at five. Joan had made no objection to its immediacy. She was beside herself with happiness, and whatever Dinny wanted to do, no matter how impetuously arrived at, was acceptable.

At breakfast, Dinny said:
"What would we be waiting for, I'd like to know, if we waited another day?"
"That's so," agreed Joan. "It would be silly, wouldn't it?"
"This afternoon, then?"
She nodded, enthusiastically.
"And go away—directly afterwards."
"As you like, dear."
"Far off... somewhere on a ship... around the world, maybe. That's a great thought, Joan. We'll go 'round the world... Want to? We can, you know."
"I'd love to, Dinny."
"Why are you smiling?"
"I'm happy."
"No—it was something more than happy. Tell me."
"I was just remembering," said Joan, "what a gypsy girl told me, a few months ago. I was soon to go on a long 'jorney' with a tall man on a 'beeg' ship."
"By Gad, Joan, I was afraid you had!... We'll take the first train out, after we're married. Right?"
"Yes—we couldn't go any sooner than that."
"To San Francisco... and sail! Agreed?"
"Let's!"

* * * * *

The lobby of the Saint Francis was astir with dinner guests arriving for a banquet when Dinny and Joan came down from the room they had occupied for an hour. It was a newspaper affair, they learned. Zandy Craig was meeting the entire *Enquirer* outfit and a score of prominent citizens.

"There's Alison, darling," exclaimed Dinny, as a half-dozen modishly gowned women stepped out of the adjoining elevator. "We must speak to her."

She turned as if she had overheard her name spoken, and joined them with a little ejaculation of happy surprise.

"Dinny!... You don't mean to tell me you've managed to persuade this lovely—"

"Joan, please meet my sister." Dinny was ecstatic.

290

"I would give anything for a couple of minutes with you, Alison," murmured Joan. "But you're going to the dinner, and I mustn't detain you."

"No—I'm not. Father couldn't be bothered with mere women at his parties. Do you want to tell me something that won't keep another minute?"

"We're sailing in the morning. I may not have another chance." Joan seemed much disappointed.

Alison searched her eyes with an inquisitive glance, and fleetingly regarded Dinny with a similar inspection.

"Very well. I'll talk to you now. We'll step over into the lounge. ... Will you wait for me, a few minutes, Mrs. Baumgarten? I'll not be long."

They disappeared, Joan's hand tucked under Alison's arm. Dinny was very proud of them. They were thoroughbreds!

Ten minutes later, when they rejoined him, they were smiling as if the interview had been mutually pleasant. Alison collected her party and hurried away.

"Big secret, Joan?" queried Dinny, consumed by curiosity.

"Don't try to make me tell you, dear; not yet."

"I'll wait, but don't keep me at it too long!"

* * * * *

Returning from the theatre, which they had found rather tame, for it had concerned itself with the tribulations of a pair who were put to tremendous bother and expense to find each other after a long misunderstanding, they went to their room and were bending over an array of cruise literature, outspread on the table, when the telephone rang.

"It's for me," said Joan, taking up the instrument... "Yes, Alison... That's wonderful!... Now?... Nine-sixty-seven?... I'll be up in two minutes!" She put down the telephone on the table, and smiled into Dinny's eyes. "I've an engagement, dear, for a little talk with—can you guess?"

"That's marvellous, Joan. Hope you'll not be disappointed."

"May I take Julia's letter along?"

"I don't know who has a better right to it."

* * * * *

Joan had been gone for more than an hour. Dinny had tried to pass the time by studying the itinerary of the long journey on which they were about to embark.

Utterly unable to command his thoughts or concentrate his attention on the gaudy promises of the illustrated prospectus, he sat staring at the wall, wondering how Joan was making out with her strange adventure. It would be quite a monstrous pity if anything had happened to distress her. She had been barely touching the ground with her toes. Never had he seen anyone so radiant!

There was a peremptory summons from the telephone. Joan's voice sounded as if she had been deeply stirred.

"Come up here, dear, please... Room nine hundred and sixty-seven; I'll wait here for you."

Joan and Alison met him at the elevator, when he arrived. They had both been crying recently, he thought. They parted as he came toward them and, turning, each took an arm. He waited for them to speak, but they had nothing to say as they piloted him down the long corridor.

At the door they stopped, and released him.

Dinny looked inquiringly from one to the other.

Alison turned the knob, pushed the door open a little way, patted Dinny affectionately on the arm, and stepped aside.

"He is waiting for you, Dinny," she said, softly.

Joan put her arm about his neck, and, standing on tiptoe, whispered, brokenly:

"Be very tender, dear."

THE END

Doctor Hudson's Secret Journal

BRIGHTWOOD HOSPITAL, DETROIT, MICHIGAN
October sixth, 1913, 11 p.m.

THIS has been an eventful day. We formally opened our new hospital this afternoon. The city's medical profession was ably represented and many of our well-to-do philanthropists came for tea and a tour of inspection.

Everybody commented on our astounding luck in disposing of the shabby old building in Cadillac Square for a quarter of a million. Lucky, they said, that our site had been chosen for the new skyscraping office building. And what a lucky dog I was, added the mayor, that this exquisitely landscaped four-acre tract came onto the market just as we had begun to look for a new location.

I nodded an appreciative assent to all of these pleasant comments on my good luck, but felt rather traitorous; for it wasn't luck. Nothing that has happened to me since June of 1905 could be properly called luck. I am in the grip of something that I don't understand; but, whatever it is, there's nothing capricious about it.

But if I had blurted out some such remark to the mayor or good old Mrs. Arlington, or Nick Merrick, there would have been a lot of explaining to do (or dodge) so I cheerfully agreed with them that I was lucky. Had I told them the whole story about our acquirement of the new hospital, they would have thought me stark mad.

Billy Werner called up from New York, about four, to offer congratulations and regret he could not be here. He said, "We're square now, Doc, except for the interest on that loan." And I said, "Don't ever try to pay that back, Billy. It might upset the apple-cart."

Frequently, during these past few years, I have fairly burned with desire to confide in someone. The weight of my secrets has been almost crushing at times. But I have this load to carry alone as long as I live. The strange events which have come to pass through my private investments do not permit of an airing: their good results might be jeopardized. I know a few other people whom I suspect of bearing the same sort of burden, but we can't discuss it. I often wonder if it is not more difficult to suppress a great exaltation than to conceal a secret sorrow.

An hour ago, Nancy Ashford paused at my office door to say good night. She was drooping a little with fatigue from the day's unusual excitements.

"Well," she said, wearily, "you have put over a great project."

I wanted to invite her in and tell her how we got this new hospital. It wouldn't have taken very long. She knows the beginning of the story. I needed only to say, "Nancy, do you remember the woman we had with us for six months, the one with the broken neck?"

And Nancy would have replied, "Of course—Mrs. Werner—and her husband was sore about the bills."

I would have gone on from there. Mrs. Werner had had the best room in the hospital and a deal of extra attention, much of which was unnecessary but expensive. Everybody assumed that the Werners were wealthy. He had a big store downtown, and they lived in a beautiful home. There was a rumour that they were extravagant. She was always travelling about, and he was reputed a gambler.

It wasn't my job to supervise hospital statements, but Werner's must have been pretty high. When he was billed for the surgery, the amount was not excessive, but it was in the same general bracket with the other expenses of his wife's illness. I was not informed, until some time afterwards, that when he paid the bill he made quite a scene, protesting that he had been overcharged.

About that time there was a story afloat about town that Werner was in serious straits financially. He had offended the president of his bank and had been unreasonably cocky with almost everybody else. He had no one to turn to in his emergency. Perhaps his irascibility, in his dealings with us, was all of a piece with his other blunders. But—once upon a time he had been able to build up a fine business. Something had happened to him. He needed to be rehabilitated.

One morning, in *The Free Press*, I noticed a conspicuous advertisement of Werner's home for sale at a cruel sacrifice. On impulse, I went down to his office immediately. He was reluctant to see me and greeted me with a glum grunt and a surly scowl. I told him I had come to lend him twenty thousand—the amount he had asked for his house. He could put that into his business, and perhaps save his home. He was suspicious, and wanted to know what rate of interest I expected. I said I didn't want any interest because I intended to use it for another purpose. He asked me if I was feeling well, and brought me a drink of water.

Of course, that small loan wouldn't have been a drop in his dry bucket, considered as mere dollars and cents. But the fact that I had volunteered to let him have it when he was all but on the rocks, and it seemed like pouring so much money into a rat-hole—and he knew that I knew it—had the effect of a shot of strychnine.

He paced up and down the room, for a minute or two, and then snapped out, "Thanks, Doc. You'll not regret it."

"Not if you keep it a secret," I replied. "This must not be told."

I made no effort to keep track of his activities but it was evident that Werner had gone at it again with tremendous energy. Perhaps he plunged recklessly. I do not know the details of that story. But soon he was enlarging his store and in command of his mercantile field. Three years after that, he organized the company that put up the new office building. Because he had conceived the project, his board of directors deferred to his judgment in many matters including the selection of a site. He urged the purchase of our old hospital.

So—that's the way we got the new hospital. But I couldn't recite any of this even to Nancy, who would have been stirred and mystified by the story. I can hear the way she would have murmured, "Well—of all things!"

I did not detain her. I simply smiled, nodded, and told her to go to bed; that she had earned a good night's rest. A remarkable woman. Sometimes I wonder how much she knows about my odd investments. She has witnessed my signature, occasionally, on papers that must have excited her curiosity. Perhaps she thinks I am living a double life. I should like to set her mind at ease about that. But it is impossible. My lips are sealed. She will have to draw her own conclusions.

* * * * *

I suppose I should be content with the rewards of my dynamic discovery, even if not permitted to disclose it to others. It has brought me innumerable satisfactions; an excellent rating in a difficult field of surgery, a position of influence in civic affairs, a comfortable home, and—above all—the enduring gratitude of a large number of persons whose lives have been reconditioned through these investments.

But it is a lonesome sensation, sometimes, to feel that one is in league with a catalytic force as versatile as electricity, prompt as dynamite, stirring as a symphony, warm as a handclasp—but available only on condition that one does not tell. To confide what one has done to achieve this peculiar power might be very costly, not only to oneself but to others whose welfare is integrally related to one's own success.

Not to confide it, especially to one's close and trusted friends, seems unconscionably selfish; yet there is no way—so far as I know—for confiding the theory unless one divulges the practice, which would necessitate a narrative of specific events.

But for a long time I have had it in mind to record at least a few of these facts for the guidance and encouragement of someone who might wish to experiment with this thing after I am gone. To record some of these events in a private journal and deposit the book in my safe would seem entirely feasible, except for the risk that the book might fall into the hands of some person who would read it without imagination or the slightest glimmer of sympathetic understanding. Hence my decision to write the book in cipher. I do not think that anyone will go through the drudgery of decoding it unless he is interested in the contents. Whenever he finds that the job isn't worth the bother, the reader can quit. And the sooner he quits, the safer the secret.

I would give a good deal to know—at this writing—what sort of person will have the time, patience, and disposition to translate this book. I hope he will not be in too much of a hurry to learn the secret. I intend to approach the matter with a deliberation that may exasperate my reader. But if he isn't concerned enough to persevere, he probably would not know how to use the secret even if he discovered it.

If you have got this far, my friend, perhaps you will have decided that I am crazy. This will be incorrect. I have contrived to lay hold upon a principle that has expanded my life and multiplied my normal energies. I have a consuming curiosity to know more about this thing; and if you are still engaged in deciphering this book you share this curiosity. If I am crazy for writing it, you are equally crazy for reading it. I warn you that if you go much farther, it will get you, as it got me. But I am not crazy.

Eventually the time may come, though I shall not live to see it, when mental aberrations are regarded with the same sympathy now bestowed upon physical disabilities. As the matter stands at present, while it is no disgrace to have an ailment of the heart, you are viewed with aversion if there is anything wrong with your head. I understand this feeling; and, to a considerable extent, share it myself.

Of course, when I am dealing professionally with a brain tumour, my patient's mental disorder does not offend or annoy me, for I have a scientific interest in his dementia as an inevitable concomitant to the pressure on his brain. Indeed, the phenomena of his lunacy sometimes aid me in defining the field of the pressure.

But—professional curiosity aside—I am very uncomfortable in the society of people whose minds are upset. I dislike hysterics. I have a strong distaste for exhibitionism in any of its manifestations. I have no use for the mentality that hankers to be unique. I have no patience at all with eccentrics who go chasing about after ridiculous isms and fantastic ologies. I like normal people and I should like to be considered normal myself.

When a man tells me that his Aunt Alicia roused suddenly in the middle of the night, dressed, packed a bag, and took a train, at the behest of some esoteric hunch that her bankrupt nephew was on the brink of a tragedy, and arrived at the nick of time to talk him out of his revolver and into a new resolution, I instinctively add this fellow's name to the list of those with whom I shall not be going on a canoe-trip around the world.

I try to avoid the balmy, the monomaniacs, the religious fanatics, the obsessed, except in my hospital where it is my business to see them. I would walk a mile to escape a conversation with somebody who had gone in for spiritualism, astrology, yogism, or an expectation of the return of Christ by a week from Tuesday. I take no stock in magic. Belief in the supernatural comes hard with me. I automatically shy off at reports of miracles, both classic and contemporary.

And the reason I am so tiresomely insistent upon the orderly and conservative nature of my own mind, and my distaste for persons with odd kinks, quirks, maggots, crotchets, hallucinations, and various benign psychoses, is that I want the reader of this journal to believe that I am as sane as anybody he knows. I insist on this, at the outset, my friend, for I shall be documenting some very strange events.

It is broad daylight now, and we are both weary. I have to be in the operating chamber at ten, and I assume that you, too, have something important to do. It is unlikely that an idle person would have access to this book.

AT HOME
October tenth, 1913, 9.30 p.m.

IT all began on a fine June morning in 1905. Nothing has been the same since. Life took on a new meaning, that day.

It was the first anniversary of my wife's death. I had found it hard to reconcile myself to that loss, and the recurrence of the date revived in sharp detail the whole pitiful story of Joyce's unwilling departure and my unspeakable desolation.

For some time it had been in my mind to order a suitable marker for her grave. I had been tardy about it, hoping that my financial circumstances might improve. But there was no sign of such improvement. My affairs were growing more dismaying.

Restless and lonely, I resolved to visit some concern dealing in memorial stones and see whether I could afford to honour my dear girl's grave with a little monument. It was while engaged in this errand that I came by the secret of personal power.

Joyce and I had been very companionable. Not only were we naturally congenial, but her long illness had bound us together in a tender intimacy hardly to be achieved under any other circumstance. During the last year of her life, which we spent in Tucson, I made no attempt to do anything but keep her comfortable and amused. I tried to stand between her and all the little jars and irks and shocks. When the baby cried, I promptly found out what she wanted and got it for her. I have been doing that ever since, and if she isn't a spoiled child she has every right to be.

I loved my wife no more for her devotion to me than my own sympathy for her. I think we love best those whom we serve most zealously. It is an ennobling experience to love anyone in need of tender ministries. The time comes when nothing else matters much but the happiness of one's beloved.

There are plenty of afflictions more difficult to deal with than pulmonary tuberculosis. The patient is usually hopeful, cheerful, wistful. As physical vitality ebbs, the psychical forces flow with the strength and speed of a harvest tide.

If it ever becomes your destiny to entertain an invalid over any considerable length of time, it will be to your advantage if the patient's disability has not struck him below the belt. Your heart and lung people are optimists.

Of course I couldn't help knowing that Joyce was doomed. Had she been only one-tenth as sweet and patient, my sense of obligation to her would have kept me by her side. But I sincerely enjoyed that final year with her. We read innumerable books, lounged in the sun, swam in the pool, played together like children; and all this at a period of my career when—under normal conditions—I should have been working eighteen hours of every twenty-four to get a start in my profession.

Once in a while I would be swept by a surge of dismay over my inability to do anything at all when it was so obvious that I should have been going forward with my vocation. But these misgivings gripped me less frequently and more feebly as the days passed. The sunshine was genial, the air was sedative, my excuse for indolence was valid. I almost forgot I wanted to be a doctor.

Even now, after more than nine years, I cannot bring myself to the point of relating the events of Joyce's last hours, the sad and all but interminable journey home, the funeral, and—afterwards—the enervating depression; the feeling that life was barely worth the bother; the almost sickening aversion to the thought of resuming the old routine in the clinic.

The people at the hospital were very kind and forbearing. I must have been a dreadful nuisance. It should have been easy enough to see that my heart wasn't in it. But they seemed to understand; Doctor Pyle, especially. Pyle had always been a bit crusty, and I hadn't known him very well. They used to say of Pyle that if you could let him do all the abdominal surgery with the understanding that the patient would never see him again, he might become popular. Next morning after removing a kidney or a gall-bladder, Pyle would call on his uncomfortable victim and offer him some such amenity as, "What in hell are you making so much racket about? Lots of people in this hospital with more pain than you have."

But it was good old Pyle that helped me—roughly—back into the harness. I still hated it, and it galled me, but I wore it. Pyle fitted it on me again, muttering many a what-in-hell, but apparently bent on making something of me—a very unpromising project. One day I told him I believed I had better give it all up and go into business.

"What kind of business?" he growled. "If you went out as grim and glum and licked as you look to-day, you couldn't sell silver dollars for a nickel apiece. You stick to your job, young fellow."

So—I stuck to the job; but I didn't like it.

It was in that state of mind that I went to look for the little tombstone. I told the manager it would have to be something inexpensive. He was quite obliging, treated me as considerately as he might if I had come to spend a thousand dollars. We agreed upon a small block of granite at what I thought was a merciful price. Then he asked me what I wanted engraved on the stone. I wrote Joyce's name and the dates.

"Would you like a brief epitaph?" he asked.

"Is it necessary?" I wondered.

"It is customary," he replied.

I told him I had nothing in mind, and he suggested that I go out into the production room where many monuments were in process. Perhaps I might see something suitable. It was a good idea.

He opened the door and considerately left me to explore on my own. Several stone-cutters glanced up and nodded as I paused to watch their work. I wasn't very much impressed by the various texts they were carving. None of them sounded much like anything Joyce would have been likely to quote.

Presently I came to the half-open door of a large studio where a man was at work on an amazingly beautiful piece of statuary. High above me on the catwalk of the scaffolding, and intent upon his occupation, the man did not notice me standing there until I had time to survey his creation deliberately. This fellow was not a mere stonecutter; he was a sculptor, and an uncommonly good one, I surmised.

The piece he was working on seemed to be nearing completion. It was a triumphant angelic figure, heroic size, gracefully poised on a marble pedestal, altar-shaped; an exquisitely modelled hand shading the eyes which gazed into the far horizon, entranced by some distant radiance. It occurred to me that no man could have invested those eyes with such an expression of serenity and certitude unless he himself was convinced, beyond all doubt, that something was to be seen Out There. The statue was august in its simplicity. It had all the combined delicacy and strength of a Canova. On the face of the altar-shaped pedestal there was engraved, in gothic lettering and in high relief, a text which was not decipherable from where I stood. My movement for a better view caught the sculptor's attention. He must have seen that I was impressed.

"Come in," he said, cordially. "My name is Randolph. Anything I can do for you?"

"My name is Hudson. I have been looking about for a suitable epitaph to have engraved on a tombstone."

Randolph leaned over and pointed down with the handle of his mallet.

"How do you like this one?" he asked.

The inscription read, "Thanks Be to God Who Giveth Us the Victory."

"Means nothing to me!" I remarked, rather testily, I fear. "If there is a God, He probably has no more interest in any man's so-called victory, which can always be circumstantially explained, than in the victory of a cabbage that does well in a favourable soil."

"Then you're related to God same as a cabbage," chuckled Randolph. "That's good." He resumed his work, deftly tapping his chisel. "I used to think that," he went on, talking half to himself. "Made a little experiment, and changed my mind about it." He put down the mallet, leaned far forward; and, cupping his mouth with both hands, confided, in a mysterious tone, "*I've been on the line!*"

He did not have the tone or stance of a fanatic; spoke quietly; had none of the usual tricks by which aberrations are readily identified; talked well, with absolute self-containment. "Victory? Well—rather! I now have everything I want and can do anything I wish! So can you! So can anybody! All you have to do is follow the rules! There's a formula, you know. I came upon it by accident!" He took up his chisel again.

He was a queer one. I felt shy and embarrassed. Clearly, he was cracked, but his manner denied it. I tried to remember that he was an artist, with permission to be eccentric; but this was more than an eccentricity. He made me shivery. I wanted away. So—I was backing through his doorway when he called, "Doctor—do you have victory?"

"Victory over what?" I demanded, impatiently. I had not told him I was discouraged; hadn't mentioned I was a doctor... I never did find out how he guessed that—the question being eclipsed by more important mysteries.

"Oh—over anything—everything! Listen!" He climbed swiftly down from his scaffolding, and gliding stealthily toward me as if he had some great secret to impart he whispered into my ear—his hand firmly gripping my coat-lapel, somewhat to my own anxiety—"Would you like to be the best doctor in this town?"

So—then I knew he was crazy, and I began tugging myself loose.

"Come to my house, to-night, about nine o'clock," he said, handing me his card, "and I'll tell you what you want to know!"

I must have looked dazed, for he laughed hilariously, as he climbed up again. I laughed too as I reached the street—the epitaph matter having completely left my mind for the time. I had never heard so much nonsense in my life. "Like hell," I growled, as I started my car, "will I waste an evening with that fool!"

AT HOME
October nineteenth, 1913, 8.30 p.m.

AT nine o'clock I was at Randolph's door... When these words are read I shall be unable to answer any queries as to my motive in going there that night. And that will be fortunate; for I have no explanation further than to say (and this will unquestionably be regarded with distrust and disappointment) that I was propelled there against my wishes. I had no thought of going; went in response to some urge over which I had no control... I was downtown to dinner, that evening; returned home at eight; went immediately to bed—quite contrary to my custom, for I never retired before midnight—and began reading a book, unable to concentrate on a line of it. I could not keep my eyes off the clock. It ticked louder and louder and my heart beat faster and faster until the two of them seemed synchronized. At length, becoming so nervous I could no longer contain myself, I rose, dressed hastily, dashed out for my car, and drove to Randolph's address without regard to boulevard stops or angry traffic officers. My mouth was dry, my heart thumping.

"You had not intended to come, had you?" inquired Randolph, taking my hat.

"No!" I replied, sourly.

"That's what I feared," he said, gently, "but I felt so sure you needed to have a talk with me that I—"

"That is what I want to know!" I demanded. "*What did you do?*"

He grinned slyly, rubbed his hands together softly, satisfiedly, and said, "Well—I earnestly wanted you here; and, as I told you, this morning, whatever I earnestly want—*it comes! I wanted you here! You came!*"

He motioned me to a seat—I was glad enough to accept it for my knees were wobbly—in a living-room furnished in exquisite taste. His daughter, whom he had gracefully presented, promptly excused herself, and left us alone. Offering me a cigar, he leisurely filled a long-stemmed churchwarden pipe for himself, and drew his chair closer. In his velvet jacket, at his ease, he was all artist; quite grizzled, wore a short Van Dyke beard; had a clear, clean, gray eye that came at you a bit shyly and tentatively, but left you no way of escape.

He lost no time in preliminary manoeuvres. Reaching to a small book-table, at his elbow, he took up a limp-leather Bible. I knew then that I was in for it. Impetuously, I resolved upon an immediate, if inglorious exit. Savagely, I put up a protesting hand and said firmly, "Now—if it's that, I don't care to hear about it!"

To my surprise, he put the book back on the table, and calmly puffed at his pipe, thoughtfully, for a while; then replied, "Well—neither do I—except as it's really an important history of a great religious system. Quite useful, I presume; but I'm not specially interested in it—except one page—" He blew a few smoke rings, his head tilted far back against his tall chair, "—And I have cut that page out... I just wanted you to see this particular copy of the Bible. I was about to say—when you plunged in with your impatient remark—that this copy of the Bible lacks the secret formula for power. I keep that one page elsewhere!"

"What's on it?" I inquired, annoyed at my own confession of interest.

"Oh—" he replied casually, "it's just the rules for getting whatever you want, and doing whatever you wish to do, and being whatever you would like to be. But—you're not interested in that; so we'll talk about something else."

"What is on that page?" I demanded—my voice sounding rather shrill.

"Do you really want to know?" he challenged, leaning forward and fixing me intently with his gaze.

"Yes!" I barked.

His next words came slowly, incisively, single-file.

"*More - than - you - have - ever - wanted - to - know - anything - before?*"

"Yes!" I admitted—and meant it.

"Say it!" he commanded.

I repeated it: "*More - than - I - have - ever - wanted - to - know - anything - before!*"

His manner changed instantly.

"Good! Now we can talk!"

He went down into an inside pocket and produced a morocco wallet. From the wallet, he extracted a folded page. I did not leave Randolph's house until four o'clock, and when I finally went out into the dark, considerably shaken, I was aware that my life would never be the same again. Whatever of success has come to me in my profession dates from that hour and can be explained in terms of the mysterious potentiality which Randolph communicated to me that night. I had reached out my hand greedily for the page Randolph unfolded, but he shook his head.

"Not just yet," he said, smiling at my eagerness. "I mean to let you see it; but I must tell you something about it, first. This page contains the rules for generating that mysterious power I mentioned. By following these instructions to the letter, you can have anything you want, do anything you wish to do, be whatever you would like to be. I have tried it. It works. It worked for me. It will work for you!"

Combined impatience and incredulity brought a chuckle from me which he did not resent.

"You saw that piece I was working on when you came in this morning?"

"Beautiful!" I exclaimed—sincerely.

"You liked it that much?" He was pleased with my enthusiasm.

"Nothing short of a masterpiece!"

"Perhaps I should be more grateful for that compliment. doctor; but I really have had very little to do with it... You may be interested to learn that I was an ordinary stonecutter until about three years ago, hacking out stamped letters with a compression chisel. From my youth, I had cherished an ambition to do something important in stone. But there was never any money for training; never any time for experiment. Such crude and hasty attempts as I had made, from time to time, had netted nothing but discouragement.

"One day I went to the church my little girl attended, and heard a preacher read what is on this page. It evidently meant nothing to him, for he read it in a dull, monotonous chant. And the congregation sat glassy-eyed, the words apparently making no impression. As for me, I was profoundly stirred. The remainder of the hour was torture, for I wanted out where I could think.

"Hurrying home to our bare little house, I found—with considerable difficulty, for I was not familiar with the Bible—that page from which the minister had read. There it was—in black and white—the exact process for achieving power to do, be and have what you want! I experimented."

With that, Randolph handed me the magic page. Some twenty lines of it were heavily underscored in red ink. In silence he puffed his pipe while my eye traversed the cryptic paragraphs, and when I looked up, inquiringly, he said:

"Of course, you will not realize the full importance of all this, instantly. It seems simple because it was spoken dispassionately, with no oratorical bombast or prefatory warning that the formula he was about to state was the key to power!"

Edging his chair closer to mine, he laid a long hand on my knee and looked me squarely in the eyes.

"Doctor Hudson—if you had a small, inadequate brick house, and decided to give yourself more room, what would you need for your building?... More brick... If you had a small, inadequate steam-engine, you would want more steel to construct larger cylinders—not a different kind of steel to house a different kind of steam, but merely more room for expansion... Now—if you had a small, inadequate personality, and wanted to give it a chance to be something more important, where would you find the building materials?"

He seemed waiting for a reply, so I humoured him.

"Well—according to the drift of your argument, I presume I would have to build it out of other personalities. Is that what you're driving at?"

"Precisely!" he shouted. "But—not 'out of'!... *Into!*... Glad you said that, though; for it gives me a chance to show you the exact difference between the right and wrong methods of making use of other people's personalities in improving one's own... Everybody is aware, instinctively, that his personality is modified by others. Most people go about imitating various scraps and phases of the personalities that have attracted them—copying one man's walk, another's accent, another's laugh, another's trick of gesture—making mere monkeys of themselves... This theory I am talking about doesn't ask you to build your personality *out of* other personalities, but *into* them!"

"I'm afraid all that's too deep for me," I admitted befuddledly.

He rose and stamped back and forth in front of the grate, shaking his shaggy mop of grizzled hair, and waving his long-stemmed pipe as if trying to conjure a better explanation.

"See here! You know all about blood transfusion. That's in your line. Superb!... One man puts his life into another man.... Doctor—how do you accomplish a blood transfusion? Tell me in detail!"

I explained the principles of transfusion, briefly, and Randolph seemed mightily pleased, especially with that feature of it which concerned the problem of coagulation.

"You will notice there," pointing to the page in my hand, "that this first step toward the achievement of power is an expansion—a projection of one's self into other personalities. You will see that it has to be done with such absolute secrecy that if, by any chance, the contact is not immediate and direct—if, by any chance, there is a leak along the line of transfer—the whole effect of it is wasted! You have to do it so stealthily that even your own left hand—"

Randolph returned to his chair, and went on, in a lowered voice:

"Hudson—the first time I tried it—I can tell you the incident freely because nothing ever came of it, although it had cost me more than I could afford, at the time, to do it—the chap was so grateful he told a neighbour of mine, in spite of my swearing him in. He had been out of work and there had been a long run of sickness in the family, and he was too shabby and down at heel to make a presentable appearance in asking for a job. I outfitted him. He told it. A neighbour felicitated me, next day. So there was more than sixty dollars of my hard-earned cash squandered!"

"Squandered!" I shouted, in amazement. "How squandered? Didn't he get the job?"

Randolph sighed.

"Oh, yes," he said. "He found a job. I was glad enough for that, of course. But—that didn't do *me* any good! You'd better believe—the next time I made an outlay I informed the fellow that if I ever heard of his telling anybody, I would break his neck."

He laughed merrily at the remembrance of the incident.

"The man thought I was crazy!" he added, wiping his eyes.

"And you weren't?" I inquired, in a tone that sobered him.

"Really—it does sound foolish, doesn't it? I mean—when you first hear of it. I don't wonder you're perplexed."

"I am worse than perplexed," I admitted, bluntly. "I'm disgusted!"

"You might well be," admitted Randolph, "if I were trying to get power, that way, to stack up a lot of money for my own pleasure. All I wanted was the effective release of my latent ability to do something fine!... And, as for being disgusted because I requested the man not to tell anybody what I had done for him, if that offends you, you wouldn't like the Lord himself!... For he often said that to people he had helped."

"I'm sure I don't know," I said... "Not very well acquainted with what he said... Go ahead with your story."

"Thanks... But, first let me lead you just a little farther into the general philosophy of this... On the night of the day I made my first successful projection of my personality—I cannot tell you what that was—I dare not—I went literally into a closet in my house, and shut the door. That's the next step in the program, as you have read there on that page. You see—I was very much in earnest about this matter; and, having already bungled one attempt, I was resolved to obey the rules to the letter... Later, I discovered that the principle will work elsewhere than in a closet. Just so you're insulated."

"Oh—Randolph—for God's sake!" I exploded. "What manner of wild talk is this?"

"I confess I can't understand," said Randolph, impatiently, "why you find this so hard to accept! Why—it's in line with our experience of every other energy we use! Either we meet its terms, or we don't get the power. What did Volta's battery or Faraday's dynamo amount to, practically, until Du Fay discovered an insulation that would protect the current from being dissipated through contacts with other things than the object to be energized?... Most personalities are just grounded! That's all that ails them!

"So, I went into a closet; shut the door; closed my eyes; quietly put myself into a spiritually receptive mood; and said, confidently, addressing the Major Personality—*I have fulfilled all the conditions required of me for receiving power! I am ready to have it! I want it! I want the capacity to do just one creditable work of statuary!*

"Now—you may be inclined to believe that I experienced a queer delusion, at that moment. As a scientific man, you may think that my mental state can easily be accounted for by principles well known to psychology. If you think that, I have no objection. The fact that a process of achieving power by the expansion of the human personality admits of an explanation, in scientific terms, does not damage its value at all, in my opinion. I dare say the time will come when this matter is made a subject of scientific inquiry.

"But—whether it is explicable or not, I can truthfully assure you that upon finishing my experiment in that closet, I received—as definitely as one receives a shock from an electrode, or a sudden glare of light by opening a tightly shuttered room—a strange inner illumination!

"It was late in the night. I came out of that dark, stifling little closet with a curious sense of mastery. It put me erect, flexed the muscles of my jaw, made my step resilient. I wanted to laugh! I tried to sleep; and, failing of it, walked the streets until dawn. At eight-thirty, I approached the manager of the factory and asked for six months' leave. When he inquired my reason, I told him I had it in mind to attempt a piece of statuary.

" 'Something we might use, perhaps?' he asked.

" 'I am confident of it,' I said, surprised at my own audacity. It was enough that I had determined to survive somehow, without wages, for six months; but now I had made an extravagant promise to the manager. He was thoughtful for a while and then said:

" 'I'll give you a chance to try it. For the present, you are to have your usual pay, and a studio to yourself. If you produce something we can place, you will share in the sale. Your hours will be your own business. I should be glad if you succeeded.'

"I began work at once in a flutter of excitement. The clay seemed alive in my hands! That first day was a revelation. It was as if I had never really lived before! All colours were more vivid. I want you to remember that, Hudson. See if you have the same reaction. Grass is greener; the sky is bluer; you hear the birds more distinctly. It sharpens the senses—like cocaine.

"That night, I went into my closet again, and was immediately conscious of a peculiar intimacy between myself and That Other; but it was not so dynamic as on the previous night. I decided that if I was to get any more power that way, I would have to make some further adjustments of my own spiritual equipment.

"That was on a Friday, the tenth of June. On the first day of September, I invited the manager in to see the cast I had made. He looked at it for a long time without any remark. Then he said, quietly, 'I have some people who may be interested in this.'

"It was the figure of a child, a chubby little fellow about four years old. The boy was posed on one knee. He had just raised up from his play with a little dog that stood tensely alert, in front of him, with a ball in his mouth, waiting for the child to notice him. The boy's shirt was open at the throat. His tight little knickers were buttoned to broad suspenders. The legs were bare to the knee. He was looking straight aloft, his little face all squinted up with baffled amazement, wonderment, curiosity. His small square hand shaded his eyes against a light almost too bright for him, the head tilted at an angle indicating that he had heard something he could not quite understand and was listening for it to be repeated.

"The next afternoon, the manager's clients came in—a man and his wife. She was in black. They had recently lost their little boy. She cried at first, heart-breakingly. But, after a while, she smiled. It made me very happy when she smiled. I knew then that I had been able to express my thought.

"I was told to go on with my project and put it into white marble... Quite incidentally, the people adopted the boy I had used for a model."

AT HOME
October twenty-sixth, 1913, 10 p.m.

IT was about four o'clock when I left Randolph's house that night. I was in a grand state of mystification. I went home resolved that I would make an experiment similar to his. Before I went to bed, I tried to project my thoughts to some remote spiritual source, but was conscious of no reaction whatsoever. In the morning I decided that I had been most outrageously imposed upon by an eccentric and scowled at my own reflection in my shaving-mirror. Nobody but a visionary could do these things with any hope of success, and I was, by training and temperament, a materialist and a very cold-blooded one, at that. All that day, however, I was aware of being on a quiet, unrelenting search for some suitable clinical material to be used for an experiment in the dynamics of personality-projection... The strangest feature of my mood, however, was the fact that the power I had begun, rather vaguely, to grope for—under Randolph's urging—was not the mere satisfaction of an ambition to make myself important or minister to my own vanity... For the first time, my profession seemed to me not as a weapon of self-defence but a means of releasing myself!

The last thing Randolph said to me, at the door, was this caution: "Be careful how you go into this, my friend! I do not know the penalties this energy exacts when misused... I've no notion what dreadful thing might have happened to the Galilean if he had turned those stones into bread!... But, I warn you!... If you're thinking of going into this to feather your own nest, you'd better never give it another thought... I'm not sure—but I think it's terribly dangerous stuff to fool with!"

My own experiences are hereinafter set forth as possible aids to whoever has had the curiosity to translate this journal. I trust I have made it quite clear why I have chosen this peculiar method of passing it along. Had I ventured to report my experiments, it would have been at the expense of my reputation for sanity. I do not know of a single friend to whom I could have told these things without putting an unpleasant constraint between us. It has been a hard secret to keep. It is equally hard, I am discovering, to confide—even with the realization that these words are unlikely to be read during my lifetime. I dislike the idea of being thought a fool—dead or alive.

You—whoever you are—may be inclined to read on;—perhaps personally interested in making an experiment; perhaps just curious. I wonder—would it be asking an unreasonable favour—if you would not consent to stop, at this point, if you are smiling?... You see, some of these experiences of mine have meant a great deal to me, emotionally. I don't believe I should want them laughed at... If the thing hasn't gripped you a little by now, put it down, please, and think no more about it... If however you seriously wish to proceed, let me counsel you, as Randolph counselled me, that you are taking hold of high tension! Once you have touched it, you will never be able to let go... If you are of the temperament that demands self-indulgence to keep you happy and confident enough to do your work—and many inestimably valuable people are so built and cannot help it any more than tall men can help being tall—leave all this alone, and go your way!... For if you make an excursion into this, you're bound! It will plaster a mortgage on everything you think you own, and commandeer your time when you might prefer to be using it for yourself... It is very expensive... It took the man who discovered it to a cross at the age of thirty-three!

AT HOME
October twenty-seventh, 1913, 2 p.m.

I WAS required to stop writing last night because of a summons to the hospital and now I find that I cannot go to bed without finishing what I had meant to say. This subject is not to be taken lightly and I hope to safeguard you against any misdirected experiments.

It is important that you should know how serious are the conditions to be met by any man who hopes to increase his own power by the way of the technique I pursued under instructions from Randolph.

I must mention them at this juncture, because it is quite possible these words may be read by some impulsive enthusiast who, eager to avail himself of the large rewards promised, may attempt experiments from which he will receive neither pleasure nor benefit; and, dismayed by failure, find himself worse off in mind than he was before.

Indeed, this was my own experience at first, Randolph having neglected to warn me that certain conditions were imperative to success. I learned them by trial and error.

It must be borne in mind, at the outset, that no amount of altruistic endeavour—no matter how costly—can possibly benefit the donor, if he has in any manner neglected the natural and normal obligations to which he is expected to be sensitive. Not only must he be just before attempting to be generous; he must figure this particular investment of himself as a higher altruism, quite other than mere generosity.

Every conceivable responsibility must have had full attention before one goes in search of opportunity to perform secret services to be used for the express purpose of expanding one's personality that it may become receptive of that inexplicable energy which guarantees personal power.

My own life had been set in narrow ways. I had had but small chance to injure or defraud, even had I been of a scheming disposition. There had been a minimum of buying and selling in my program. I had lived mostly under strict supervision—in school, in college, and as an interne—with no chance to make many grave or irretrievable blunders.

Once I began to discharge my obligations, however, it was startling to note how considerably I was in the red. For example: I found that there were a good many men, scattered here and there, who had been scratched off my books. Either actually, or to all practical intents, they had been told to go to hell. In some cases, there had been enough provocation to justify my pitching them out of my life, I thought. But, more often than otherwise, they were to be remembered as persons with whom I had sustained some manner of close contact—close enough to make a disruption possible. I discovered that almost without exception the people I had pushed away from me—consigned to hell, if you like—were once intimately associated with me... So far as I was concerned they had gone to hell taking along with them a very considerable part of me!

To lose a friend in whom one had invested something of one's personality was, I discovered, to have lost a certain amount of one's self.

The successful pursuit of the philosophy now before you demands that you restore whatever of your personality has been dissipated, carted off by other people. If any of its essential energy has been scattered, it must be recovered.

The original proposer of this theory, aware of the importance of insuring against such losses, advised that all misunderstandings should be settled on the spot. When an estrangement takes a friend out of your normal contacts with him, he leaves with part of you in his hand. You must gather up these fragments of yourself, by some hook or crook, so that you have at least all of the personality that rightfully belongs to you, before you attempt its larger projection.

In the next place: you may make the mistake of seeking far and wide for opportunities to build yourself into other personalities through their rehabilitation. A happy circumstance kept me from doing that. Strangely enough, the first really important service I was permitted to do, prefatory to experimenting with this mysterious dynamic, was for the daughter of the man who had shown me the way to it... I risked what small repute I had, and put a mortgage on whatever I might hope to acquire, by the performance of an operation that saved her life, and, quite incidentally, brought me three pages of comment in the next edition of the *Medical Encyclopaedia*.

BRIGHTWOOD HOSPITAL
Sunday Night, November ninth, 1913

THAT operation on Natalie Randolph's fractured skull marked the beginning of my specialization in brain surgery, and because of its importance in determining the nature of my professional activities, I feel that the events which immediately preceded it should be recorded here. If you prefer to consider them as coincidental rather than causative, you are quite at liberty to make that deduction. In my own opinion, my investment in Tim Watson and the success of my operation on Natalie Randolph were integrally related.

On Wednesdays and Saturdays, that summer, I was on duty in the Out-Patient Department of our Free Clinic. This assignment was extremely distasteful. Ailing indigence, bathed and fumigated and in bed, clad in a sterilized hospital gown, was one thing; sick poverty, on its feet—with black fingernails, greasy clothes, a musty smell, and a hangdog air—was offensive to me. I was not a snob. I was born poor and brought up in a home where the most rigid economies were practiced. The first new suit of clothes I ever owned (it cost sixteen dollars) was purchased when I entered high school. But—all the same—I thoroughly detested those long, hot, midsummer afternoons in the dingy Free Clinic, and I am afraid I made very little effort to disguise my aversion to the dull and dirty patients who grimly applied for its benefits.

For the most part, it was a thankless task. Not many of them co-operated with us. They wouldn't take their medicine according to directions; complained that their treatment did them no good; the majority of them were surly, stupid, and stubborn. Many of the men stank of cheap liquor and tried to wheedle you out of a half-dollar to buy more.

Perhaps if there had been only a few patients to deal with, during an afternoon, one might have been more disposed to analyse their disgusting infirmities with more sympathy and listen to their assorted misfortunes with more interest; but they came too thick and fast for painstaking attention. In my own defence I must insist that it wasn't their poverty that exasperated me, for God knows I was having a struggle to make both ends meet, myself. My salary was small, and it was difficult to economize. Little Joyce required the attention of a full-time practical nurse, who served also as my housekeeper. Those were difficult days, and I was in a position to be sympathetic with any man whose pockets were empty.

But I hated that clinic. Our elders and betters on the hospital staff pretended to believe that it was good practice for us young fellows; but it wasn't. It was the worst training imaginable, tending to make a doctor cold-blooded and careless.

One afternoon in latter August, within a few minutes of the closing hour, a young chap was shown into my cramped cubicle with his left hand bound in a dirty rag. He was about eighteen, six feet tall, lean as a bean-pole. He had a good head, thatched with a tousled mop of the reddest hair I had ever seen. His eyes were blue and edged with premature crow's-feet which gave them a defiant hardness. If it hadn't been for the pair of boyish dimples in his tanned cheeks, he would have looked decidedly tough. He was bareheaded and badly sunburned; wore a soiled gray suit that wasn't big enough for his rangy frame, a blue shirt with a rumpled collar, and a pair of cheap and dusty sneakers.

I pointed indifferently to the other chair. He sat down and began unwrapping the hand.
"Pretty bandage," I remarked. "What was it, originally, a shirt-tail?"
He drew a sardonic grin, dropped the rag on the floor, and extended his injured hand. It was badly swollen and there were deep abrasions across the knuckles.
"Looks as if it's broken," I guessed.
"Yeah," he agreed, "right there: those two metacarpals."
"Know your bones, eh?" I glanced up and met his eyes.
"What's that called?" I revolved a finger-tip lightly on his wrist.
"Sesamoid."
"Would you say that was a bone?"
"Umm—well—it's partly cartilage."
"Want to tell me how you got hurt—and when? This hand has been neglected. It's in bad shape."
"Last night. The freight was pulling out of the yards and picking up speed faster than I thought. I missed my hold, and fell on my hand."
"You must have had something in your hand, or you would have met the gravel with your palm down."
He liked my deduction and his eyes lighted a little.
"That's right," he said. "Handful of chocolate bars."
"You swiped them," I announced casually.
He nodded and asked me how I knew. And I told him he must have been very hungry to have hung on to the candy when he might have broken his fall more safely with his open hand.
"And if you had had the money to buy the chocolate bars," I continued, "you would have bought a hot dog or a hamburger instead."
"I didn't have time to think which was the safest way to land."
"That's true," I agreed. "When you are very hungry, your stomach does your thinking for you. Are you hungry now?"
He nodded, adding, "But if you're going to set this hand, I'll need a little ether, won't I?"
"What do you know about such things?" I inquired.
He grinned.
"My father was a doctor," he said, "and I've read a lot of his books." He made a self-deprecatory little gesture. "About the only books I ever did read. I hated school."
Having confided that much, he responded to my encouragement and told me some more. His name was Watson. His father had died when he was ten. His mother had married again. The stepfather had resented his presence in their home. After a while, his mother—unable to defend him without a constant battle—began to take sides with her husband, in the interest of peace.
"But I don't blame her," the boy went on. "I wasn't very easy to get along with. I played hooky pretty often. And once I operated on a cat. I got licked almost to death for that."
"How about the cat?" I couldn't help asking.
"He got well. I didn't hurt him. Doped him with chloroform."
"You'll have to tell me about the operation when we've finished with yours," I said, rising. "Come on. I'll fix you up. What's your first name, Watson?"
"Timothy. Tim."
"All right, Tim. Follow me. No—don't put that rag on again. You're in enough trouble without that."
As I led him into the operating chamber, he was interested in everything but his injury. I think he would have been willing to undergo an amputation rather than miss the experience of seeing our preparations to reduce his fractures and clean up his cuts. The last thing he said before the anaesthetist put the cone over his lean face was, "Gee—it must be great to be a doctor!"
They renovated him and put him to bed. I was under no obligation to look at him again that evening; but I went over to the hospital about nine. He was awake—and smiled.
"How does it feel, Tim?" I inquired.
"About the way it ought to, I think."

"In the morning you may have some ham and eggs for breakfast."

"And then—I'll be discharged?" he asked, a bit anxiously.

"No—I think we will keep you here for a few days; make sure those scratches heal safely. You hadn't any other plans, had you?"

Tim chuckled.

"Plans!" he echoed. "Hell—no."

I surprised myself by saying, "Well—maybe we can make some. We'll see. I'll drop in again in the morning."

He reached out his good hand and I took it. At the door, I paused to say, "Good night." But his face was turned away, and he did not reply.

BRIGHTWOOD HOSPITAL
November 14, 1913, 8.30 p.m.

THE lacerations on young Watson's knuckles showed no signs of infection when I examined him the next morning, and the fractures would take care of themselves. He could have been safely discharged at once. Under ordinary procedure we would have sent him packing without delay. But I couldn't bear to turn him out into the street.

My own early experiences in Detroit had much to do with my interest in this chap. At his age I had wanted to study medicine; an absurd aspiration, for I had no resources at all. My chance came through what seemed at the time to have been a lucky accident. In recent years I have had reasons for changing my mind about "accidents." I do not mean that there are no accidents: I mean that many unexpected events, classified as accidents, deserve to be called something else.

My thoughts on this subject are still in a fluid state, but I shall share them with you, my friend, and you may make of them whatever you like.

I am not inviting you to believe (or to believe I believe) that everything occurs by design and decree. Such a theory—if pursued to its logical end—would destroy human freedom and make mere puppets of us all. But I do think that if a man is suddenly interrupted by some unheralded event—not of his own contriving—and is thereby deflected for a time from the course he had been pursuing, he would be well advised to keep his eyes open for some new and valuable opportunity which this circumstance may provide. Even if the so-called accident involves a great deal of pain and hardship, the victim may have a right to suspect that he has been very far off the track leading to the full development and expression of his powers; that severe discipline may be necessary to recondition his mind for a discovery of his unrecognized talents and capacities.

Every day, here at Brightwood, where so many victims of accidents put in for repairs, I see patients who haven't the slightest notion that their experience might be turned to good account. They whine and growl and fret over the discomforts of a tedious convalescence; and, after a few restless weeks of uncapitalized apathy, they pull on their pants and leave, with nothing to show for their time but a receipted hospital bill.

Once in a blue moon, somebody gets the idea that he may have been laid up for a purpose, like a ship in dry-dock getting her barnacles scraped off. To such as these, who have confided to me that they have found comfort in this supposition, I have lent some encouragement; but I have never taken the initiative in such a discussion. In my capacity as a surgeon, I can't go about telling people they have been whacked on the head to give them a chance to reorganize themselves and find out what they are good for. Such talk would quickly discredit a man in my position. His colleagues would crack jokes at his expense. He would soon be regarded as some sort of faith-healer; a quack, at heart; a fellow who plays around with the angels. No—if I'm serving as a surgeon I must be respected as a sound scientist; and there is no room in science—at present—for a theory of this character.

And, curiously enough, everything in me naturally revolts against such notions. Even in the face of my own experiences and observations, if some friend of mine should break down and confide to me his belief that almost nothing happens by accident; that Fate, or a busy-body Providence, or some such other-worldly Mr. Fixit trots about banging misdirected people on the topknot, or laying them low with a lumbar tumour, to the excellent end that they might have time to orient themselves in regard to their gifts, their duties, and their destinies, I should think him a little bit unhooked.

To save his face, I should probably concede that strange things do happen; that many an apparent misfortune has turned out to be a blessing. I might tell him about an eminent lawyer of my acquaintance, whose father owned a planing-mill and wanted his boy to learn the trade; and the boy collided with a saw and lost three fingers, ruining him for a career in the mill. But—all the same—I should privately rate the man an eccentric, who maintained that our seeming accidents are planned for us and our ultimate good, and it wouldn't surprise me if he turned up, some day, with the confidential report that he had just lunched with some prominent member of the Heavenly Host.

* * * * *

You see, my friend, I am trying to be honest with you about all this. It is a dangerous subject to talk about, and surely no man dares be dogmatic when he expresses an opinion on it.

In the laboratory, many an experiment that is utterly bewildering to the layman is clear enough to the chemist. If you pour water into sulphuric acid the effect is far different than if you had poured sulphuric acid into water—a startling phenomenon that baffles the uninformed, though the chemist knows the secret.

But this thing that we have been talking about—you may experiment with it as long as you like, and not know much more about it than when you began. In this field, nobody is an expert; everyone is a layman. And when any man sets out to prove, by his own experience, that we are all in the grip of spiritual forces, he will demonstrate nothing but his mental untidiness.

Doubtless there are plenty of real accidents which shouldn't have happened; involve no hidden purpose; hold no possibilities for good. Almost anybody could compile a few cases in which painful events opened a way to happiness—if not to greatness. I know a woman who broke her leg and wrote a highly successful novel while she was convalescing, but I have seen many women with broken legs who did not write novels or discover any other opportunity to make capital of their enforced leisure. I once amputated an infected arm that had got into trouble with a rusty fish-hook. The fellow was a loafer, with no interest in anything but fish and fishing. It was all he could talk about. We had him with us for weeks, and to entertain him we ransacked the libraries for books about fish. He went out, at length, and found a good job in a government fish-hatchery; and, to the amazement of everybody, distinguished himself as an expert in the disabilities of salmon, or something like that. But I have cared for many a loafer who never amounted to anything afterward.

You can't afford to be doctrinal when you consider accidents as the work of Providence. One man accidentally burns some rubber on the kitchen stove and discovers vulcanization; another fellow has much the same sort of accident and merely sets the house on fire. One man accidentally spills some camphor into a pan of collodion and gets celluloid; another man accidentally upsets a bottle of something into a pan of something else, and goes out through the skylight. One redoubtable reformer gets tossed into jail, and whiles away the time by writing *Pilgrim's Progress*. Another equally good and zealous martyr goes to jail and merely gets lousy.

But the ways of Providence are well worth thinking about, if one can do it in a spirit of inquiry rather than with a determination to organize a cult and enlist disciples. This thing will not stand the strain of being woven into a creed: I am sure of that.

* * * * *

Something tells me, though, that all persons in trouble should be exposed to a consideration of this subject, even if it doesn't obey a formula.

I have often wondered if it might not be an interesting experiment, in a hospital, to hand each patient—on arrival, or as soon as he is able to read anything—a little manual of advice.

As the matter stands, it's nobody's business to offer counsel on this subject. A few stark injunctions are tacked to the wall. Don't clog the plumbing. Don't throw banana-skins out of the window. And so forth. All the advice the patient gets presupposes that he is a destructive fool whose previous experience in public institutions has been limited to the calaboose and the poorhouse.

There is a wide-open market here for some friendly talk to these unhappy guests. The little booklet might run something like this:

We are honestly sorry for people who, through no fault of their own, are obliged to undergo discomfort, pain, and boredom, in this hospital. But it is not our fault, either, that you encountered the illness or accident that brought you here.

This is not a hotel. Hotels must pay their own way or close up. Hospitals do not pay their way, but they do not close up; for, at the end of the year, the deficit is absorbed by a company of kind-hearted people who believe that we are trying to do our best. We hope you will share in this belief; for it is important to your comfort—and perhaps also to the promptness of your recovery—if you consider this place as a friendly refuge; not a mere money- making repair-shop.

Our nurses are well-trained. Part of this training is in the control of their personal feelings. If they do not seem very much upset over your gas- pains, that does not mean they are indifferent: it means only that they are disciplined. They have many distasteful tasks to perform, and they do them without showing how they feel on the subject; but that does not mean they are insensitive. They are just as human as anyone else; have their own little frets and forebodings; their days of disappointment and depression. Sometimes a patient's cheerfulness will help a nurse to a fresh grip on herself.

Your doctor wants you to get well as rapidly as possible. In this matter, you and he share the same wish. He will appreciate your full co-operation. Some morning when you are feeling unusually well, you may offer him a little witticism, and be dismayed to note that he fails to respond to it. But that isn't because he is indifferent. More likely it is because he has just put in an hour and a half of tense and trying service in the operating-room; and he doesn't feel jocular. If he can sense your sympathetic understanding of his mood, your attitude will be of much benefit to him.

In short—if you want to get the largest degree of satisfaction out of your experience in this hospital, join hands with us, almost as if you were a member of the organization. If you believe in the hospital, and in the skill and sincerity of the doctors and nurses, you will not be troubled by the little vexations and irritations which menace the peace of many patients.

Perhaps we, who are devoting our energies to the care of the sick and injured, should be contented if we were able to dismiss you fully restored and sound as you were before.

But we have an ambition still higher than that. It would gratify us immensely if—when you leave us to resume your activities—you might go out not only repaired physically but reinvigorated in mind and heart.

In the normal ways of an uneventful life, people do not often have a chance to find out how much pain they can endure, or how long they can wait. Here they can take their own measure, and discover their strengths. Many a man, in peace- time, has wondered how stalwart he might be on a battle-field, facing danger, risking agonies. Circumstances may provide him a chance to learn, in the hospital, whether he has what it takes to be a good soldier. We do not conduct these examinations. The patient examines himself, and marks his own grade. Ever afterward he will be pleased and proud if he passes with credit. No matter what may happen to him, in the future, he will always know exactly how much disappointment, anxiety, inconvenience, and pain he can stand. It's worth something to a man to find that out. So—if you have been informed that the doctor is taking out your stitches to-morrow, you can do yourself a good turn—that will last you all your life—if you face up to this in the morning without flinching. You have always wondered, when you saw others in trouble, whether you could take it. Now you know. It's a very gratifying thing: almost everybody finds out that he is braver than he thought he was. It's worth going through a lot of perplexity and pain—just to be assured on that matter.

Sometimes people who hadn't succeeded in making anything very important of themselves—either inside or outside of themselves—have discovered, during the enforced leisure of a convalescence, certain neglected gifts which they have thereafter exercised to their immeasurable satisfaction.

In many instances, this self-discovery has resulted in such a marked expansion of interest and success in after-life, that the beneficiary has wondered whether Destiny had not shunted him off his course in order to let him take stock of his resources.

We suggest, therefore, that you give a little thought to this subject while you are with us. Was it an accident? Was it a misfortune? Was it a mishap that brought you here? Think this over. We think about it a great deal.

* * * * *

Young Watson's case vividly recalled my own first acquaintance with Detroit. It was in mid-August. We had threshed the wheat, the day before, and my father and my uncle were starting, that morning, on a few days' fishing trip. I had strongly hinted that I should like to go along, but there seemed no room for me.

Barnum and Bailey's big show was to be in Detroit that day. I knew better than to ask if I might go. I had saved something like six dollars, which would be ample to cover expenses; but I knew I should be reproached if I squandered my money in this manner. But, having been left out of the fishing excursion, after a hard summer's work, I felt that I was badly treated and would be quite justified if I helped myself to a day's outing.

Father and Uncle Jim were to start at five. I quietly sneaked out of the house at four, walked three miles to the little station at Wimple, and waited for the milk-train to come along. Arriving in Detroit at noon, I took a street-car to the circus grounds where I spent one of the most exciting days of my life. I saw it all; the menagerie, the demobilization of the garish parade, the circus and spectacular pageant "The Burning of Rome." I also patronized several units of the side-show. It was six-thirty before I left the grounds and boarded a crowded street-car for the business district. My train did not leave until nine-thirty.

After a long ride, we were clanging through brighter lights and heavier traffic, so I got off and sauntered along the edges of the crowd on the broad pavement, staring into the shop windows. Besides my return ticket, I had a little money left, and decided to look for a cheap restaurant. There didn't seem to be one on this street, so I turned the corner and walked a couple of blocks, looking for an eating-place that might fit my resources.

Presently I came to a café that had a very imposing front. Several very elegant turnouts were drawn up along the curb, the drivers lounging near their horses' heads. I ambled past, inspecting them with admiration. A tall, handsome man with a flushed face lurched out of the café and walked unsteadily down the street, pausing before a pair of beautiful roans harnessed to an open stanhope. One of the drivers called to his neighbour, "Doc's pretty well oiled."

I followed along slowly, though it wasn't much like me to take a curious interest in anyone's humiliation. The near horse, tied to the hitching-post, had tugged his bridle off and seemed about to bolt. "Doc" was making an unsuccessful effort to put the bridle on.

"Let me do it," I said.

"All right," he said, thickly, "if you think you can."

It wasn't easy to do, for the horse was nervous, but I managed.

"You know how to drive?" asked Doc. "I'll give you two dollars if you drive me home."

I told him I had to take a train at nine-thirty, but if he thought I could drive him home and get back in time, I would do it—adding that I didn't want to be paid for it. My attitude seemed to please him; for, shortly after we started, he professed an interest in me. I told him where I lived; that I had come to the circus; that this was the first time I had ever been in the city alone; that I wished I could stay in the city; that I didn't like to work on the farm; that I wouldn't stay on the farm if there was any chance to get away. All this was in reply to questions, for I was not naturally garrulous.

Then it was "Doc's" turn. He told me he was Doctor Cummings. My heart gave a hard bump. We often read of Doctor Cummings in the papers. He was said to be one of the finest surgeons in the country. It was hard to believe that I was sitting by his side, driving him home. And he was talking to me as if I really was somebody. He told me that his hostler had been away for two days on a spree; couldn't depend on the fellow any more; wondered if I could stay and look after the horses until he could find another man.

I did not pause to consider what my father might think of this, nor how much my mother might worry if I failed to show up at home. All I could think of was the fact that I should be working for a doctor—one of the greatest doctors! I said I would stay.

"And so you don't like the farm," remarked Doctor Cummings. "Anything else in mind?"

"I'm afraid you'd laugh, sir," I confessed, adding, "I have never told anybody."

"But me," encouraged Doctor Cummings, "and I won't tell."

"I want to be a doctor," I confided, "but I'm afraid it's no good. We haven't the money. I'm not even sure my father can afford to send me to high school."

He didn't say anything for a while. Then he asked me my name and I told him. Then there was another long silence.

"So—you are not interested in anything but medicine; is that right?" he said, rousing from what must have been a little nap.

"That—and swimming," I replied.

"You like to swim?"

"Yes, sir."

"Then I suppose you must swim pretty well."

"Like a water spaniel," I boasted. "If I can't be a doctor, I'll have to be a professional swimmer."

There was another long pause.

"Well—you stay here for a while, Wayne, and look after my horses," said Doctor Cummings, "and we will see what we can do. I don't think there's much of a future in swimming."

So—that was how I got my chance to study medicine. I began it by being Doctor Cummings' shadow. I was his hostler, errand boy, and diplomatic agent. Drunk or sober, he was always kind to me. And he gave me my opportunity to go to school. If it had not been for my meeting him, that night, when he needed someone to look after him, my whole life might have been set in a different key.

Perhaps that circumstance was accidental; but I don't think so.

AT HOME
November twentieth, 1913, 9 p.m.

DURING that summer I frequently spent Sunday evenings with Randolph. On these occasions I would finish at the hospital about four and drive home in the primitive but expensive Cadillac that Joyce had bought before we went to Arizona—an extravagance we could not afford, but it was her money. And I didn't have the heart to tell her how low we were in funds. She was not to be here long, and it was no time to be economical.

After making sure that my little girl was being properly cared for (it would presently be her bedtime), I would drive out to Randolph's sequestered home on the north side, where there would be a light supper and some good talk, with my host usually initiating the conversation. I think it was these serious but stimulating chats with Randolph that sustained my spirit through that perplexing period. But for him I fear I might have found my professional duties too irksome to be borne. I had very little work to do that presented any challenge. The nearest approach to it had been an emergency case—a pretty bad concussion—that had come in, late one night, when the only ranking surgeon available was Doctor Pyle, who, though a very able abdominal man, never tackled a head if there was anybody else at hand competent to do it. This operation wouldn't wait; and Pyle, remembering that I had been much attracted to brain surgery while in school, summoned me in. It was not a difficult operation—as such things go—and the patient made a prompt recovery, as he should have done. I lived on the thrill of that experience for many days. But events calculated to stir my interest and professional pride were few and far between. It was Randolph who held me up.

Looking back from this distance, I think Randolph was wise in not pressing me too urgently with his strange theory. After the first few days' enchanted wistfulness, following the night when Randolph confided his secret for more important living, the sheen faded perceptibly from this promising prospect. This was, of course, inevitable. It is very difficult to endure an unabating emotional storm, even if that were desirable. And I want to call your attention to this fact, before it is overlooked.

If you, my friend, are moved to a deep interest in this subject, keep it in mind that your resolve to pursue it does not insure you against the inescapable sag that follows an unaccustomed emotional exaltation. If this thing really lays hold upon you, it is likely that you will feel—for a few days, at least—as if you had come into the possession of some magic, good for all weathers; and, when you find the same old rain dampening your spirit as usual, you are very apt to say, "Oh— what the hell!" Let me assure you that this witchery does not guarantee against any further experience of boredom; neither does it pledge that from henceforth you will enjoy all your routine tasks and smile steadily at your disappointments.

In other words—don't consider this thing as a Pullman car in which you have engaged a berth, with the understanding that it will carry you forward—waking or sleeping—toward your desired destination.

Randolph made no effort to fan the flame he had lighted in me. To the contrary, he counselled an exercise of cool common-sense in accepting the theory that had literally transformed his life.

"Some day," he would remark placidly, "you will find a project, and then you can attempt an experiment. But don't go feverishly sniffing about for a beneficiary. That would certainly put you into the wrong state of mind. It would mean that you wanted to do someone a service with the expectation of material reward."

And I needed this counsel, too; for that's what I had been doing. For example: there was an old orderly at the hospital who had been there for a long time, and couldn't keep up with his job. They let him out, and I promptly nosed into his affairs to see if I could do him some little kindness. I was emphatically snubbed by the family, for they considered me a part of the heartless hospital organization that had tossed the old man out onto the scrap-pile for the relatives to gather up. He was a surly old codger, and before I had finished my proffered ministration I realized that I had picked the wrong fellow for clinical material. I told Randolph about it and he grinned.

"Better let the family attend to such matters," he advised. "It is their responsibility and it will be good for them to accept it. It is quite possible, though," he added, with a twinkle, "that the family's haughty repudiation of your interest in papa will require them to take much better care of him than they might have if you hadn't welded them together with their own outraged pride. So—perhaps it isn't a total loss—what you did."

And we had a middle-aged nurse who was worried over the truancy of her twelve-year-old boy. This problem had provided the woman with so many alibis that I decided to look into the case. The boy was indeed a problem. While I was trying to think of something to do about it, I observed that the incorrigible's silly mother—utterly mistaking my motives—coyly conceived the idea that I was interested in her. When it became clear that she was even more eager to help me than I was to help her obnoxious son, we both dropped the matter by mutual consent.

Randolph was amused. "Don't grow impatient for an opportunity," he said. "Doubtless you will recognize it when it comes."

* * * * *

Young Watson had been in the hospital since Wednesday afternoon's clinic. I think he knew I should have discharged

him, for he was bright and uncommonly well versed—for a youngster and a layman—in medical procedure.

On the Sunday of which I am writing now, he had said, when I called in the morning to see him, "You have been very good to me. Doctor Hudson. But I shouldn't stay much longer."

"Want to go?" I asked.

"It isn't that," he replied, "but I am well now."

"Have you any place—in particular—to go?"

"N—no," he confessed, "but it doesn't matter much—does it—whether I go out bumming it to-day—or Tuesday?"

"We'll make it Tuesday," I said, reproaching myself for implying that there might be a solution to his problem in a day or two. There was nothing I could do for him. I might

310

have tried to find him some menial job, but even that would have been impossible with his broken hand. It would be five or six weeks before he would have any practical use of it. I couldn't support him until he was able to work at starvation wages. I had no room for him in my apartment. No—it was quite out of the question.

That evening, Randolph and young Natalie and I had supper under the big maple on their secluded rear lawn; and, after the girl had excused herself, we sat smoking our pipes. Randolph wanted to know, after a considerable pause in the conversation, whether anything interesting had happened in the hospital. It had been a fairly typical, fairly tiresome week, I said. The clinics had been about as drab and dirty as ever.

"Just one enlivening, and rather perplexing incident," I went on. "A young fellow came in the other day with a broken hand; hurt it falling off a freight-car; quite an unusual chap, for a tramp; very likable boy; left home on account of family trouble; the old stock story of a beastly stepfather and a mother who is badgered into being a stepmother; deceased father a doctor; the boy had access to his medical library; pretty well posted on Physiology. I could have discharged him, almost at once, but I didn't like to turn him loose."

Randolph blew several smoke-rings, but made no comment. "I'll have to let him go, in a couple of days," I continued. "He can't work with a broken hand; and, in any case, he has no training for a city job. Eventually—after he is sick of tramping and riding on freight trains—he'll have to stop somewhere and work on a farm. Might amount to something, I think, if he were taken in hand. But I can't see it as my job." I paused to give my host a chance to make some rejoinder. Randolph, with his eyes half closed and his head tipped back, continued to blow smoke-rings.

"He's probably a bum—at heart," I went on. "Probably couldn't settle down to anything. requiring perseverance." I puffed meditatively on my pipe for a while, and asked, "What do you think?"

Some moments elapsed before he gave any sign that he had heard what I had been saying; just sat there blowing rings and staring into the darkening sky and the arriving stars. Then he slowly turned toward me, drew a short sigh, smiled apologetically, and said, "Forgive me, Hudson. I'm afraid I was wool-gathering. It's such a glorious night! Shall we go in? The dew is falling. Besides—I want to beat you at chess."

I felt rebuffed. It was not at all like Randolph to be so inattentive. We rose and walked toward the house, his hand in the crook of my arm, as if to reassure me of his comradeship. On the doorstep he paused, detaining me, and said-just above a whisper, "I didn't mean to be so rude."

It miffed me a bit to have Randolph binding up my babyish bruises, and blotting my tears and blowing my little nose for me; and I replied, crisply, "I didn't mean to be so uninteresting."

He refused to be annoyed; chuckled a little; gave me a friendly slap on the shoulder, and said, "You were not uninteresting, Hudson; you were just unimpressed.'

"By the sky—you mean?"

"Well—the sky is impressive, to-night; that's a fact."

We played chess until eleven. Randolph came along out with me to the gate. As I climbed into my car, he said, "Be careful now, Hudson. Good night. God bless you!"

It was an odd thing for Randolph to say. Be careful. God bless you. Almost as if he was giving me farewell advice. In the guarded, urgent tone of one sending another forth on some sort of hazardous mission. Be careful now. God bless you. The words resounded in my ears.

* * * * *

That night I went through my modest wardrobe, remembering that Watson was about my height, though lacking fifteen pounds of my weight, and selected a suit of clothes for him. And a couple of shirts and some collars.

There was a small room in the apartment which had been used as a "den." I had my books in there, a desk, a couple of chairs; but the room could be spared. I dragged everything into my bedroom. Next morning, on the way to the hospital, I stopped at a furniture store and bought an inexpensive cot.

I wasn't sure that Watson would be willing to avail himself of my hospitality, but I had decided to put it up to him. He was up in the solarium when I called on him at ten.

"Tim," I said, "I am going to let you go now."

"Yes, sir," said Tim. "I'm ready."

"But—I should like to have you stay with me, at my home, for a few days. You are well enough to be out of the hospital, but not quite well enough to be on the road. Will you do that?"

Tim shook his head.

"It wouldn't be fair," he said. "I'm not going to impose on you. You don't owe me anything. You've done enough."

"But I'm afraid I should fret about you—and you don't want me losing sleep on your account. Better do as I say. You will be at liberty to go—any time you like."

He drew a quizzical face and did not reply for some moments.

"All right," he agreed, reluctantly. "But I don't want to be a panhandler. Maybe there's something I could do to help myself."

"We'll see," I said.

I drove him home at noon.

"I can wash your car," said Tim. "That's good," I said. "It needs it."

* * * * *

When I got up, the next morning, I found Tim running a dry mop around the edge of the rugs, holding the end of the handle under his left arm, and making a very satisfactory job of it, too.

I had a notion to tell him he needn't try to do any work under such conditions, but fortunately thought better of it. If he wanted to make an effort to show his gratitude, he had a right to do it.

I have had many occasions to meditate on this subject. Anyone who has had experience in giving—and getting—knows that it is much easier to be generous than grateful. Generosity expands you; builds you up; stiffens your spine. But if you are on the receiving end of this philanthropy, you either have to do something to earn it and demonstrate your gratitude, or the gift is likely to tear you down. It is indeed more blessed to give than to receive.

And I think that what passes sometimes for ingratitude is an insurmountable feeling of chagrin. It should be kept in mind that any gift—no matter how much it may seem to be to a man's immediate advantage—can do him a permanent injury if it has the effect of damaging his pride. Persons who find delight in helping others should exercise the greatest of tactfulness.

Of course any sensible person will agree to this, for it is so obvious; but it is not easy to practice. One time I gave a fairly good suit of clothes to a fellow; and, because he looked hungry, I put a dollar into one of the pockets. He had no opportunity to find the money, in my presence. I had found a box, so that the chap wouldn't have to go down the street with his new possessions over his arm. Early the next morning, he showed up at my door with the dollar, and I told him to keep it, which he did with honest reluctance. Afterward it occurred to me that I had made a serious mistake. The man thought it quite possible that I had overlooked the dollar. He wanted to demonstrate his integrity. If I had permitted him to do this gracious thing for me, it would doubtless have gone a long way toward repairing his self-esteem which had suffered when he accepted the clothing.

My proper move in this affair was to receive the dollar— and without making too much fuss about it, which would have been equivalent to saying that I was amazed to find such nobility in a man who looked so crooked. Had I merely thanked him respectfully for the money, in the same way I might have thanked my neighbour for restoring something I had lost, my dealings with him would have been perfect. He would have had the clothes, and the consciousness that he had also my esteem, which might have meant a great deal more to him—at that stage of his unfortunate experiences—than the clothes. There's a lot of very careless, thoughtless, injurious charity. It takes more brains to give something away than to sell it.

I let Tim Watson do anything he wanted to try to do, about the apartment. He dusted all of my books, he cleaned and refilled my pens, he answered the telephone with all the dignity of an experienced butler. You would have thought he was in the employ of some very important person. This may sound silly, but I think Tim did me and my professional standing a great deal of good on the telephone—even if my young colleagues at the hospital did tease me about it.

"This is Doctor Wayne Hudson's residence."... "May I ask who is speaking, please?"... "Thank you. I shall see if the doctor is at liberty to come to the telephone."

I know that Tim's technique was ever so much better than mine. I had been in the habit of scurrying to the telephone and saying, "Hullo." Tim cured me permanently of that careless, self-damaging method of answering a telephone call. It seemed to please him greatly when I thanked him for the favour. I think he grew a couple of inches. He replied, tactfully, that "a scientific man, with lots of important things on his mind, couldn't pay much attention to such small matters."

It did Tim a vast amount of good to contrive an apology for me that would save my face.

Soon I discovered that it was one of the most fascinating games I had ever played—this casting about for occasions which might build Tim up. And I think that his gratifying response to my constructive efforts in his behalf assured me that any sacrifice I might have to make for him would be justified.

It delighted me to see that what I was doing for Tim had not only done his personality no damage, but was rapidly calling out good talents which he had never been given a chance to exercise.

Little Joyce helped, too. She immediately became devoted to him. If she needed any spoiling, at that early period of her life—which I can't believe possible—Tim slavishly attended to it; and the undisguised affection she showered upon him must have made him feel exalted. Sometimes a man will get much the same quality of spiritual uplift from his dog. Dogs make good evangelists because they overlook so many obvious imperfections. One can't say as much for cats, who seem to have no capacity for concealing their contempt.

BRIGHTWOOD HOSPITAL
November twenty-fifth, 1913, 10.30 p.m.

NANCY ASHFORD and I have been holding an informal conference in my office for the past hour. Sometimes I wonder how I could get along without her uncommonly wise counsel. I'm afraid I have come to take Nancy too much for granted. If anything were to happen to her, I might find out how heavily I had depended on her business efficiency and loyal comradeship.

The past few days have been exceptionally trying. I should not have thought it possible for a nine-year-old child to stir up so much excitement. It seems clear enough now that a public school is no place for Joyce; at least, not yet. So we have gone back to the nurse-governess idea. Nancy found the new teacher—a Miss Wingate—who gives promise of being a good choice. She is considerate but she will be firm. She is well-balanced and has the instincts of a lady. Joyce likes her—so far. One has to make allowances for my child's wilfulness and instability. We have had too many different types of people working on this job. But I couldn't be both father and mother.

It has often struck me as a peculiar thing that so many people, who have been able to redirect and improve the lives of comparative strangers, are helpless when they try to do something beneficial for their own flesh and blood.

I raised this question with Nancy to-night, and she offered an explanation. Persons living restless, unhappy, undisciplined lives are so because they are in a battle with themselves. Their conscience gets after them for their misdemeanours, and shames them until they resent any counsel from their "censor mind." Nancy thinks it a fallacy to believe that conscience is always a wise counsellor. She holds that a conscience is just as likely to be defective as a thyroid gland. That is to say, an over-active thyroid can throw one's whole emotional machinery out of balance; and an over-zealous conscience can be so brutally intolerant and tactless that it destroys what little self-esteem you have left, after committing some indiscretion.

I couldn't help showing my amusement over this fantastic theory, but Nancy stood by her guns.

"That's why some children resent parental advice," she continued. "They are constantly besieged by an abnormally energetic conscience; and they are so integrally blood-related to their parents, and have so many quirks and kinks in common, that father's admonition is just another annoying harangue of the sort that the conscience delivers."

"I gather, then," said I, "that a child's unwillingness to heed her father's advice is not because she lacks a conscience—but has too much of it"; and then added, "Nancy, sometimes you have the foolest ideas—but I'll admit they satisfy, even when they haven't a leg to stand on."

"I'd rather hold on to a legless idea that had the makings of consolation in it," she replied, "than a sound idea that makes you unhappy."

"But you have given up Santa Claus," I drawled.

"Yes—and that was a mistake. I was much happier when I believed in Santa Claus," she said, pensively, "—and better, too."

"You couldn't be any better than you are, Nancy," I said. "I never knew anyone with a sweeter soul."

She shook her head a little, smiled, rose, said "Good night," and closed the door softly behind her. That's the way it always is when I express some appreciation: Nancy thinks of an errand she has to do without delay.

I wish I could obey the dictates of my own heart. Maybe Nancy shares that wish. We have never discussed it. She is absolutely indispensable to this hospital. She is its brain and soul. She has an important ministry here. Everybody leans on her; the staff, the nurses, the patients. I have no right to disrupt this relationship. Sometimes I have almost permitted my desires to get the better of me in this matter. I think I know how she feels. Perhaps I could break her down and override her convictions about her clearly appointed duty. If I told Nancy that I needed her more than Brightwood, she might agree; but she would never be happy about it—and neither would I.

Once, a couple of years ago—we were still down in the old building in Cadillac Square—she came into my office with an open telegram in her hand and the tears running down her cheeks. Her father was dead. I impulsively drew her into my arms and she pressed her forehead hard against my white coat; then laid her cheek against my heart and clung to me tightly for a long moment. I was much moved. Presently she released herself, glanced up, dabbed at the corners of my eyes with her handkerchief—an act very like the one she had performed almost every day in the operating-room when she was a surgical nurse and would wipe the perspiration from my face—and said, softly, "Thanks—for the tears." But there has never been a repetition of such mutual affection, and it has not always been easy to be restrained.

* * * * *

On several occasions I have observed that it has been comparatively easy to finance an investment in somebody else, when it would have been difficult to do as much for myself. I do not pretend to understand this; much less explain it. I simply state it as a fact, and you may appraise it for whatever it seems to be worth.

On the tenth day of September, 1905, I was so hard up that it was doubtful whether I could pay the month's current bills in full; yet, on that day, I decided to make arrangements for Tim Watson to enter the university at my expense.

I sold the Cadillac for seven hundred dollars, a good price. The car had cost a great deal more, but that was all it was worth now, and I was lucky to get that much. It would be a long haul to sponsor Watson through college and the medical school. And I wouldn't have a car to fetch to market every September. But I was ready to take the risk, and see what came of it.

I asked for the next day off, and went to Ann Arbor. Everybody was gracious and cooperative. I engaged a room for Tim, and found a place where he could work for his board; had a conference with the Registrar; even had the audacity to call on President Angell, and came away feeling that I amounted to something. It was a great day for me. When I walked down to the station to take the train home, I wore a broad smile. People whom I passed gave me a second look, and sometimes they grinned. I remembered what Randolph had said about his own sensations. He had declared that the grass was greener, the sky bluer. It was a fact! One became acutely conscious of the birds. All colours were more vivid. The people on the street seemed more friendly, more alive. I had done something to myself: there was no doubt of that.

I had not told anyone where I was going. During the day, several calls had come in at the house inquiring for me, and were informed that I was at the hospital, and called back to say I was not there. Tim was getting anxious. I found him pacing the pavement in front of the apartment house when I arrived at seven.

"Hope I haven't worried you," I said. "I have been to Ann Arbor, arranging for you to enter college, a week from Wednesday. It's all settled—your pre- medic course."

Tim said nothing. He seemed stunned. He held his red head on one side, quizzically, staring at me with a stupefied incredulity that made me laugh. I led the way in, and he followed me like a sleep-walker. We went up to the apartment where the middle-aged maid met us saying that dinner was ready and drying up.

*If you'll excuse me," mumbled Tim, "I don't want any." He went to his little room and shut the door.

"What's the matter with him?" asked Lizzie, grimly.

"He'll be all right," I said. "Keep something warm for him."

About nine o'clock he came into our small living-room and sat down close beside me.

"Doctor Hudson—" he began, nervously.

"Don't try to make a speech, Tim," I interposed. "You're going to be a doctor; and doctors aren't often very good speech-makers. I know how you feel. You are very happy— and so am I. I have never been this happy before."

"I'll do my best," gulped Tim.

"I know you will," I declared. "Now—I want you to promise me that you will never tell this to a living soul. It is nobody's business but ours how you got a chance to go to the university. It is our secret. I have a reason—and a very good one—for wanting this to remain private. Will you promise?"

Tim promised—and we shook hands on it.

* * * * *

Two Sundays elapsed before I went out to see Randolph again. I had phoned what time I would be there and he was waiting for me at the gate. I had gone out on a street-car, getting off at the nearest point, two blocks away.

"I see you're afoot," said Randolph, extending his hand. "Car laid up?"

"Sold it," I said, casually. "Hadn't much use for it. Street-cars go everywhere and are less expensive."

It was too chilly to have supper on the lawn. A table had been set up in the living-room near the fireplace. The maid was off duty and Natalie served us. I had not noticed before how rapidly the girl was blossoming into a young woman. She was becoming very pretty.

Ordinarily, when Natalie had supper with us, she made no effort to participate in the conversation and excused herself promptly when the coffee came on. To-night she was willing to talk. Randolph seemed surprised and pleased. I drew her out, and she chattered about her school, her teachers, and the thrill she was having—every afternoon—at a riding academy. It was her first close acquaintance with horses, and she was having the time of her young life. Natalie seemed a different person. She had never before paid me the compliment of showing the slightest interest in me. Now she looked me squarely in the eyes and talked animatedly, as if we were long-time comrades and contemporaries.

When she left us, for a moment, to bring on the salad, Randolph chuckled a little, and said, "I don't know what you've done to Natalie."

"She's a charming girl," I said. "I'm glad she wanted to talk."

"I think," said Randolph, slowly, "she has just discovered something in you that she had not recognized before; a high capacity for friendship, maybe."

It was a delightful evening. Natalie went to her own room, about ten, shaking hands with me before she left and saying, very prettily, that I must come again soon. I was much stirred and a little bewildered, too, over this unaccustomed attention.

Randolph and I discussed almost everything of current interest. I surprised myself by taking the lead in most of our conversation. When I rose to go, he said, "You're in uncommonly high spirits to-night, Hudson. Perhaps your work at the hospital is growing more pleasant."

"Yes," I replied. "I have really enjoyed it, lately."

Randolph looked me steadily in the eyes and drew a sly smile, accompanied by a slow wink.

I grinned, in spite of my effort to be poker-faced. He reached out his hand and I took it. He laid his other hand on our warm clasp and affectionately patted my fingers.

"I am very happy for you, my friend," he said, softly. "It is easy to see that life has taken on a new meaning for you."

And that was true. I had begun to live!

* * * * *

Perhaps I have been tedious in my presentation of the circumstances which preceded my operation on Natalie Randolph's head; but, to an understanding of my state of mind in that event, it is important that you shall have had the whole situation laid before you.

The investment I had made in Tim Watson might or might not be the making of him: but it had already begun to appear that it was going to be the making of me.

My relation to the hospital changed, almost overnight. The new vigour I felt within myself must have shown through, for not only did I approach my tasks with an entirely different attitude, but it was easy to see that the personnel of the hospital had noted the change in me. These observations were, for the most part, inarticulate, but they were certified to in various ways. By some I was regarded with wide-eyed curiosity; by others with unusual displays of personal interest and friendship.

On the following Wednesday morning, Doctor Shafter, who was then considered the best brain surgeon in town, asked me if I would assist him in an operation that afternoon. I replied that I should like to, but that I was on duty in the Free Clinic. Within a half hour. Doctor Means—our superintendent—sent word that I was to be relieved at the Clinic so that I might be with Doctor Shafter. I felt very proud of this assignment. Incidentally, I was never sent to the Free Clinic again.

It would be difficult for me to explain what were the outward manifestations of my new relation to life and work. Perhaps my recognition of this new and vital force had found immediate expression in my manner and behaviour. The old indifference was gone. I had acquired—without conscious effort—a confident stride, a more erect carriage, a capacity for making every motion count. The thing—whatever it was—had actually deepened my voice and given it a new resonance. When I gave an order, people hustled; not as if they were scared, but anxious to serve.

However much my colleagues and the nurses may have been bewildered over my strange metamorphosis, they weren't any more bewildered than I was. Crusty old Pyle came the nearest to voicing what must have been the general consensus about my case when he stopped me in the corridor long enough to remark, dryly, "They say that even a blind pig will find an acorn once in a while. Congratulations!"

Natalie Randolph was brought into the hospital at four-thirty in the afternoon of November twenty-seventh. She had been thrown from a horse, striking her head on the hard asphalt pavement. The nearest available physician—a Doctor Juniper (since deceased)—had made a hasty examination and prompt arrangements with the hospital. The ambulance made a quick trip. Doctor Means, locating me by telephone in the Men's Surgical, told me of the accident and said that Mr. Randolph wished me to be on hand when Natalie arrived.

She was quite a pathetic little figure in her trim riding habit. Her face was scratched and already purplish; her corn-yellow curls were matted and stained with blood. Frequently, in such cases, there is a brief revival of consciousness before the coma settles in; but Natalie had not roused. Her respiration was irrhythmic, almost undetectable in its declensions. The injury was a compound parietal fracture, the deepest one I had ever seen.

My afflicted friend Randolph hovered close to the table. His face was ghastly white but he had himself well in hand.

"How about it?" he whispered. I shook my head, and told him it looked very bad. "But you'll do something; won't you?" he asked, desperately.

"Perhaps not immediately," I replied. It was going to be hard to tell Randolph the truth.

Doctor Means, assuming that Doctor Shafter would be called in, had telephoned his house immediately upon hearing of the accident, only to learn that the surgeon was on a train *en route* for Chicago where he was to spend the next day—Thanksgiving—with his daughter.

But after a brief consultation it was agreed that an operation was impractical.

"I don't think Shafter would touch it," muttered Pyle. Then he turned to Randolph and said, "I'm afraid there is very little to be done here, sir."

Randolph clutched at my sleeve and tugged me a little way apart.

"Hudson," he whispered, "will you try? I know that some life-giving energy has come to you, lately. Perhaps you will be able to accomplish a great act here. I trust you completely. May I tell them that you will operate, at my request?"

It was a terrific responsibility, and for a moment I was at a loss for words. I wondered what my elders and betters would think of my audacity if I consented to attempt something that even the experienced Shafter—in Pyle's opinion—would not venture upon. While I debated this serious problem, Randolph stepped back into the group about the table and announced, in a firm voice, "Gentlemen, I have asked Doctor Hudson to operate." Nobody looked up. I could feel their reaction.

Doubtless if Natalie had been less gravely hurt, there might have been further deliberation; perhaps a suggestion that we had better wait until Shafter could be returned; perhaps a protest from Pyle that it wouldn't be fair to commit so difficult a task to a young surgeon with no more experience than I had had in the repair of head injuries. But no one protested. In this case it really made very little difference what was done or by whom.

Pyle's only comment to me was, "It's too bad, my boy, that you are expected to do this. But we all know the circumstances, and we'll see to it that it does you no damage. Mr. Randolph thinks you can do it, and his wishes should be served. You haven't the ghost of a chance, but Randolph will have the satisfaction of knowing that an attempt was made."

I consented to try, but decided to wait a few hours until we had suppressed the haemorrhage by introducing a hypertonic solution. It was almost three o'clock in the morning before I felt that the surgery might be attempted.

Curiously enough, my hope began to mount from the moment I started the operation. Perhaps it was Randolph's amazing faith that I could do it; perhaps my awareness of the new strength I had lately found gave me confidence. It surprised and delighted me to find myself working with steady hands, and not a trace of nervousness. And when, at last, I made the final suture, I had a feeling that Natalie might recover. I went to Randolph, as soon as I had washed up. He was keenly anxious, but bright with hope.

"You have saved her—I think," he said, questing my eyes for assurance.

"We must wait—and see," I replied, prudently; but Randolph knew, by my tone, that I was not disheartened. He wrung my hand, and murmured, "God bless you!"

If you are interested in the history of this case, from a professional standpoint, you will find it fully documented in the *Medical Encyclopaedia* (edition of 1907). You will note that this was the first occasion when depressed fragments of bone were approached by a rongeur through a burr-hole opening in the adjacent normal skull. This technique is quite common practice now, but it had never been tried before. And it wouldn't have been attempted then if the case had been less desperate.

It was indeed a very close thing—our saving Natalie. And the operation was by no means the end of our dilemma. We had a post-traumatic haematoma on our hands that required the most vigilant watching and care for the next three weeks. But Natalie slowly recovered. Her appreciation of my solicitude was very sweet, and our friendship became one of the most precious experiences of my life.

One night in early February—we had taken her home that day—Randolph said, "You remember, Wayne, my telling you of my earliest experiment in sculpture, and my earnest request—to Somebody or Something Outside—for a chance to do just one creditable piece of statuary?"

I remembered—and thought I knew what he was leading up to.

"Now you have had your big chance," he continued, "to do a monumental thing in brain surgery. It has already directed attention to you. You will have many opportunities, in the future, to test your faith as well as your skill. Never forget how you came by it. Don't ever let yourself believe, when you have become eminent as a brain surgeon, that this new technique you hit upon in Natalie's case was something that you invented in a time of emergency. *I say it was handed to you—from the Outside!*"

"I believe that," I said, sincerely. "I don't understand it; but I believe it."

And I still believe it.

AT HOME
February eighth, 1914, 9 p.m.

YOU will observe, my friend, that some time has elapsed since the last entry was made in this journal. The interruption has not been due to negligence, but indecision whether to continue.

As I stated, at the outset, the purpose of these memoirs was to give my reader—whoever he might be—a glimpse of the cause-and-effect relationship between private investments in other people's upbuilding, and the rewards of such investments accruing to the donor and empowering him to accomplish things otherwise impossible.

I wanted to go on record with my belief, arrived at by experience, that if an act of human rehabilitation is secretly wrought, the development is manifest not only in the life of the beneficiary but the benefactor. In other words, if I do something for you that builds you up for increased usefulness, my own capacity is augmented by that much. I do not mean that if I do something of value for you on Thursday I may expect to exercise some new power by Saturday at the latest; for this thing doesn't always operate on a cash-and-carry basis. But I do insist—and I have consistently demonstrated this to my own satisfaction—that you cannot add to another's personal power without increasing your own.

Having finished my narration of the peculiar experiences of 1905 when, under the direction of Clive Randolph, I tested this theory and found a new and promising way of life, it occurred to me that either I had made my case—in the opinion of my reader—or would be unable to do so, no matter how much additional evidence was piled up. I debated whether it would serve any good purpose to offer more testimony of the same sort.

But something has happened lately which throws light on this subject from another angle. I think you should have your attention called to it.

In my previous entries, I have tried to give you a brief but fairly comprehensive account of my own adventures in this strange field. I want now to tell you what little I know—knowledge achieved mostly by deduction and guessing—concerning another person's experience in self-investment. You will note, as you proceed, that there are a couple of open gaps in this story of Dorothy Wickes which will never be filled in. At these intervals you are at liberty to exercise your own imagination as I have exercised mine.

And now that I have decided to resume work on this journal, perhaps it will be well if I carry on a little farther with some of my experiences subsequent to the operation on Natalie Randolph, an event that promptly gave me a new rating in my profession and set me going toward a larger success than I had dreamed of.

It may interest you to learn something more about Tim Watson and his reaction to college life. It is quite possible that you may be acquainted with Watson. Indeed it is possible that Tim may be reading these words himself. If so, he will suffer no chagrin in perusing my report of him; for, from the very first, it was evident that this loyal young fellow meant business. His marks were exceptionally good—better, on the whole, than my own grades in college—and his conduct, so far as I know, was above reproach. I was never given one minute's anxiety about him.

At the close of his freshman year, he returned to Detroit, found a job in the Olds Motor Works, where he was quick to learn, made good wages, and saved his money like a miser. When it was time for him to go back to school in September, while he did not have quite enough cash to see him through the entire year, it was unnecessary for me to do very much for him; though by that time I was able to aid him without making any sacrifice. I had discontinued work in the field of general surgery, and was giving full attention to diseases and injuries of the brain. Patients, in increasing numbers, were being referred to me from considerable distances. Sometimes they were brought into the hospital; sometimes I made long trips. Brain surgery is not the most pleasant vocation in the world. You do very well if you can hold your mortality down to fifty per cent. Most of the cases that recover have a long and tedious convalescence, the patient growing more crotchety and fretful every day. I mention this only because the burden rested heavily on me, and I was very thankful to sense the increasing devotion of Tim Watson.

I had not altered my habits of living, to any appreciable extent. We had moved to a more commodious apartment, had found more efficient household help, and I had bought another car. Otherwise, our manner of life had not been affected by the improvement in my income. It would have been impossible for Tim not to observe that I was now in a position to make things easier for him, but there never was the slightest hint that he would lean on me. Quite to the contrary, he began mothering me in a manner that was a bit embarrassing at times. He was so solicitous of my comfort that I began to feel quite elderly in his company, though there were but fifteen years between us. One evening, in summer, when he had dragged a big chair across the room for me, so that I might read under what he thought was a better light, I said, rather testily, I fear, "Damn it; you don't have to fag for me as if I were a hundred!"

"I like to do little favours for you," said Tim. "It isn't that I think you're old. Certainly I wouldn't think that after yesterday."

The day before, I had come off with some kudos in an aquatic tournament—my chief recreation was had in the water—and Tim had been much impressed.

His affectionate comment made me feel quite contrite; and, if anything, a bit older.

I had occasion to be very proud of him. In 1908, he graduated with a *cum laude*. His courses, during the Junior and Senior years, were definitely pre- medic, leaving him only two more years to do in the Medical College after achieving his A.B. I took Joyce along with me to the Commencement exercises. He led the child about, afterward, showing her off to his friends. She was very pretty. I was proud of them both. Tim deferentially asked permission to take Joyce with him to luncheon when he learned I had been invited to lunch with a half-dozen of my professional colleagues. He did this in the presence of my learned friends, and his filial attitude—plus the fact that when he left with Joyce he addressed her as "sister"—evoked a natural curiosity which I ventured to appease by remarking, dryly, "This young man is not my son, gentlemen. He is my grandson."

Of course I have always felt sure that it was my investment in Tim—at a time when the expense of it was considerable—that put me in a state of mind to work at my job with the highest possible efficiency. The investment had been amply justified. It had paid out handsomely. Now that it was reasonably clear that Tim was going to be a success, my satisfaction was complete.

He wanted me to get him a job, that vacation, as an orderly in the hospital, or an ambulance driver, or almost any sort of labour that would keep him in the hospital atmosphere with which he had become somewhat familiar; but I wouldn't consent to it.

"You will probably be back here as an interne after you have finished with the Medical School," I said, "and it will be much better for you if the nurses haven't made your previous acquaintance by ordering you to empty the slop."

"But I shouldn't mind that," he replied. "If an orderly does his job efficiently and obediently, he ought to be respected."

"Yes, yes," I agreed, impatiently, "and so he is. But the orderly defines his position, in relation to other natural objects, and he mustn't try to come back later as a doctor."

Tim nodded, not very enthusiastically, and said he supposed I was right. But I could see there was something on his mind that needed release, so I said, "Well—what's the rest of it? Go on."

"It's about this caste idea," said Tim, feeling his way. "I don't like it. From what I hear and see, there's too much of it in the medical profession; experienced nurses doing the wrong thing, and knowing they're doing the wrong thing, simply to obey a bad order that some doctor has issued through ignorance or mistake; and aware that it's doing the patient harm. Everybody afraid of everybody else, all the way up the line, from the man with the mop to the man with the scalpel, including the student nurses, who are afraid of the graduate nurses, and the graduate nurses, who are afraid of the superintendent of nurses, who is afraid of the interns, who are afraid of the older doctors. It's the bunk! It's a crime!" Tim's long speech had grown a bit shrill toward the end.

I tried to explain that while there were probably occasional unfortunate occurrences connected with hospital discipline, in the long run it was better for everybody to understand the limits of his own authority and initiative. Otherwise, everything would be on the loose, with nobody in particular responsible for what happened.

"Oh, I see that," agreed Tim. "But I also see a lot of red tape that doesn't do anybody a service. I'd like to see a hospital proceed on the theory that it's there to accommodate the patients rather than the doctors and the nurses. I've been looking into this thing a little, and asking questions. In most of the hospitals, the business office is entirely too fussy. A patient comes in sick as a dog and deserving every consideration, but the business office has to devil the life out of the fellow with questions that have no immediate bearing on his case and could be asked, just as well, a week later; and all this cruel nonsense practiced to accommodate some brittle little clerk who wants to keep his index-card system in order."

"I don't believe they do much of that in our hospital," I protested. "I'd look into it—if it was any of my business. I'm not on that end of the machine."

Tim stood up and waved a long arm, energetically.

"There you are!" he shouted. "That's what I mean!"

I couldn't help being amused over the youngster's indignation. It wasn't like Tim to pop off like that; so I knew the matter went pretty deep with him. I told him I thought he was on the right track, to have the patient's welfare at heart. I also promised to ask a few questions, quietly, in our hospital.

As a result of that investigation, which I pursued deliberately for a month or more— considerably to my dismay— I began to nourish the idea of a private hospital in which common-sense discipline would take precedence over a growing tendency to mechanize the healing arts. It was for this reason that we organized Brightwood, and I have Tim to thank for unwittingly launching a project that has been a great satisfaction to us all. I realize that the disciplinary measures which are required in a very large hospital have to be more exacting than in a small one. But when I discovered that patients were roused at five a.m., from a deep sleep, to give some student nurse a chance to practice reading her clinical thermometer, I resolved to lay plans for the establishment of Brightwood.

Tim again spent the summer working in the automobile factory where he had been employed before. He must have been rather good at it, for his wages were excellent. I often wondered, through those days, whether he wasn't tempted a little to carry on in that game; for it was the coming profession, if a man wanted to make money; incomparably more promising, in that respect, than the practice of medicine.

It gratified me that he wanted to be with me as much as possible week-ends. I found him increasingly companionable. A couple of times I took him with me on Sunday evenings at the Randolphs. He and Natalie were immensely congenial. I rather thought— and hoped—that he would make an effort to cultivate that friendship, for it was easy to see that the girl had attracted him. So far as I know, he made no attempt to enlist her interest in him. But I nourished the hope that something might come of it later.

*****

One of my earliest cases at Brightwood was a brain tumour operation on a Mr. James Wickes. They were poor people, Wickes having been out of employment for more than a year in consequence of his illness. There was a twenty-two-year- old son, also unemployed, for some unspecified reason. Accompanying the sick man to the hospital was his wife, a discouraged, taciturn little mouse, and a daughter Dorothy who was eighteen, bright, and uncommonly attractive. Her clothes were of inexpensive stuff but modishly cut and she wore them with confidence.

They made no bones about their poverty.

"My daughter is the only one working now," explained Mrs. Wickes, nervously. "Fifteen dollars a week—in a store. And I must say she is a good girl. She gives us all of it, she does." My glance wandered over Dorothy's stylishly made ensemble, and Mrs. Wickes defensively added, "She makes all her own clothes."

I reassured them about the financial problem, told them there was a fund available for hospitalization; that there would be no charge for surgery, if an operation were required. After a few days' observation, it was evident that the patient had a very slim chance. The case was operable, but practically hopeless. Dorothy had come alone, that Sunday afternoon. I took her into my office and told her that while I intended to operate, the next morning, I seriously doubted whether I could save him. She was grieved, but not surprised. I drew a little diagram for her, outlining the appallingly large area involved. She drew her chair closer to my desk and seemed avidly interested in the pencil- sketch.

"Can you draw?" she inquired. Her blue eyes were wet, but they lighted as she asked the irrelevant question.

"That much," I admitted, with a shrug. "Can you?"

She nodded, confidently.

"I have had no chance to take lessons," she said, "But I can draw."

It seemed to me that the conversation had taken rather an odd turn, in view of the fact that I had been doing a rough sketch to show the girl how little hope I could offer that her father might survive. And then it occurred to me that Dorothy had been casting about for something she might do to earn the money required by her father's hospitalization. If that was it, I reflected, her attitude deserved encouragement,

"What sort of things do you draw?" I asked.

"Boats," she answered, decisively.

"Just boats?"

"Boats and docks—and that's the trouble. I can't draw boats well enough to hope ever to sell a picture. Maybe, if I knew the principles of drawing, I could get a job as a dress designer. I have ideas for dresses, and I believe I could make some money that way."

"I should like to see your sketches sometime," I said, non-committally. "You tell your mother what I have told you. Don't upset her with a report that this is definitely hopeless, but give her warning." I rose, and Dorothy considered herself dismissed. That was about three-thirty. At five, she was back at the hospital. The girl at the information desk, remembering that she had called earlier, told her to go into my office and sit down. I found her there, waiting for me.

"You said you wanted to see some of my drawings," explained Dorothy, laying a portfolio before me.

"But I didn't mean to cause you a special trip," I protested.

She drew out a marine sketch and held it up. I had seen wetter water in pictures, but it was obvious that the girl was a keen observer and had talent. The shadows of the ropes and spars rippled in rhythm with the choppy swells of the breeze-swept harbour. It wasn't a great picture, but it held out great promise.

"Did you draw that?" I inquired. She nodded. "Didn't copy it?" I asked. "Sketched it from life?"

"Yes, Doctor. Is it any good?"

"Good? Of course it's good!"

* * * * *

Well—we had to let James Wickes go from the hospital to a mortuary, as I had ruefully anticipated; though, had he lived, I suspect that his survival would have been of small satisfaction to himself and his family. The next few days were so heavily weighted with serious duties that I had but little time to think about the Wickes family. On the next Sunday afternoon at five, when I was about through with the day's work, I found Dorothy waiting for me, just outside my office door. I invited her to come in. She sat down on the edge of her chair and tugged nervously at her gloves.

"It's about one of my girl friends in the store," she began, without preamble. "I'm so dreadfully sorry for her. She is almost crazy with worry. I want to ask your advice."

"Is this what I'm afraid it is?" I asked.

Dorothy nodded, and flushed a little. "But she's a very nice girl—just the same," she declared loyally.

"Not you—by any chance," I suggested, looking her squarely in the eyes. But the eyes did not flinch. She shook her head. "That's good," I said. "I believe you. Well—go on. Tell me anything you want me to know; though I hope you're not going to ask me to think of a quick way out of this for your friend, because I am quite definitely not in that line of business."

"N-no—I wasn't going to ask that, exactly," said Dorothy reluctantly, "though of course it would be just awfully sweet of you."[1]

[1] Among Doctor Hudson's papers I found the notes of an address he had delivered before the State Medical Association on March 9, 1914, the subject of which may have been inspired by this conversation. In his address. Doctor Hudson states it is his belief that many young persons, confronted by this problem, do not always realize the gravity of their efforts to escape from their desperate predicament. They cannot see farther than the immediate threat of disgrace. Doctor Hudson advised that when a medical man is approached on this matter by people half-insane with worry, instead of treating them with cold anger, it would be to his credit if he viewed the circumstances in a spirit of sympathetic understanding, and tried to suggest some ethical procedure which would not only safeguard the life of an unborn child but shield the mother from a ruinous collapse of personality. This is, I think, an interesting side-light on the man's nobility; and on his courage also, for this is a ticklish subject. (R. M.)

I couldn't help grinning, though I suppose I should have been indignant. She was as transparent as glass, with no more realization of her unpleasant implications than a six-year-old.

"No," I reiterated, firmly. "Sometimes these cases are very sad, indeed; but—there's nothing we can do about them."

"It's too bad," sighed Dorothy. "I read a story once about the older sister of Jairus' daughter; you know, the little girl that Jesus raised from the dead?"

I remembered the narrative, but said I hadn't recalled that the child had an older sister.

"Not in the Bible, she didn't," agreed Dorothy, "but in this story that I read. Shall I tell you—or haven't you time?"

"Tell me—if it isn't too long."

"Well—after Jesus had brought back the little girl to life, he left the house and was on his way up the road and pretty soon a beautiful young woman stepped out of the shrubbery and asked if she could speak to him. So—they sat down, and she told him that she loved a young Roman centurion, but her people would not consent to their friendship—much less their marriage. And now she was in trouble. And she would be disgraced; likely driven from home.

" 'You gave my little sister her life back,' she said. 'Can't you speak a word that will save mine?'" Dorothy paused.

"So—what did he do?" I inquired, with sincere interest.

"The author of the story didn't say. He just stopped there— and left you guessing—like in *The Lady or the Tiger*."

I observed that it was a prudent way to finish the piece, even if it did leave you a bit curious over the outcome. She nodded agreement, and remarked that the problem must have put the Master in an embarrassing position. "For he was always so kind and helpful to everyone," she murmured, meditatively. Then, after a little pause, she searched my eyes, and asked, "What do *you* think he would have done?"

I glanced at my watch—an ignoble trick—and replied that I shouldn't be impudent enough to make a decision for the Lord; adding that perhaps we'd better proceed now with the main story.

"Millie—that's my friend—" said Dorothy, settling to her task, "—can't stay in the store very much longer. And she can't stay at home much longer, either."

It was a fairly long narrative of a selfish aunt's too exigent attentions. After Millie's mother had died and their home was broken up, she had been taken in, at the age of twelve, by her mother's sister Susan, a half-psychopathic woman of forty, with a bare subsistence income, a lame foot, and a weak heart.

She was too sensitive about her lameness to venture out of the house, except on short errands to the near-by grocery, and her erratic heart was much on her mind. One of the first things Millie had learned, upon coming to live with her, was that Aunt Susan mustn't be upset.

Shy, reticent, and self-conscious. Aunt Susan lived the life of a hermit, unsparing in her stifling affection for the unhappy child, but dreading the intrusions of Millie's young friends. So Millie gave up trying to entertain any of her girl companions; and, when she was invited to parties. Aunt Susan was distressed over what might happen to her ward. As Millie grew older, this cruelly strict supervision became more and more galling. If she was five minutes late in getting home from school, full explanations were in order. Aunt Susan, sitting at a front window, gnawing her thumbnail, would meet Millie at the door, shrill and shaky and scared.

"And that's the way it went," continued Dorothy, "All through her high- school days. She never had any fun. Sometimes we said, 'Come on! Let your old lady worry a little, if she wants to.' But Millie couldn't risk a heart attack; and, anyhow, she wouldn't have a good time, knowing that her Aunt Susan was hobbling about through the house, half crazy with anxiety."

I nodded my understanding, and said, "Too much devotion."

"That has been the hard part of it," Dorothy agreed. "The good old lady has simply strangled Millie with her love and kisses; never lets her alone for a minute; fusses with her hair, pats her on the cheek, stuffs her with home-made chocolates, insists on reading aloud, in the evenings, the sappiest, sloppiest, goody-goodiest stories, out of funny old books, about sweet and obedient girls who took care of grandpa until he died of it. And—"

"And so Millie finally broke through the fence," I suggested, feeling that I now had the picture fairly well in hand. "Any chance of a marriage? That might help quite a bit."

"I don't believe he could stand it," doubted Dorothy. "He would have to live there. Auntie's heart would go back on her if Millie tried to make a home elsewhere."

"Yes—I know about those hearts," I said, "the kind that cave in whenever their custodians can't have their own way about everything. There's an awful lot of heart disease that's just one way of putting on a tantrum."

"They're really worse than tantrums," declared Dorothy.

"That's right," I agreed. "You can spank a tantrum—but you're afraid to paddle a defective heart." We sat there in silence for a minute; then I said, "I'm afraid Millie will have to figure this out, herself. Perhaps her best course is for her to make a clean breast of it to her Auntie."

"I suppose so," said Dorothy, regretfully, "but Aunt Susan will have a fit."

"Well," I said, not very helpfully, "people have had fits— and got over them. By the way—have you been drawing any more pictures?"

She shook her head.

"I think I should like to make a little investment in you," I said. "Your boats are pretty good, and they would be ever so much better if you had some lessons. And perhaps you would be able to do one for me. I, too, am very fond of the water."

Her blue eyes widened and her pretty lips parted.

"Do you think I could—really?" she said, just above a whisper.

"It's worth trying. I know a man who is well posted on local art schools. I want you to go and see him. He will give you good advice. I shall tell him to expect you."

"Now?" asked Dorothy.

"When you get anything on your mind, you certainly don't waste much time; do you?" I teased.

"But this is so important," "she replied soberly.

"Very well. I'll call him up. Perhaps he will be free to talk to you this evening."

I stepped back into my private office, closed the door and telephoned to Randolph, finding him at home as I had expected. I told him I had been talking with a young woman who thought of taking a course in drawing. Would he give her some counsel? Might she come out to-night? I omitted to say that I had any further interest than that in this art course.

"He will see you this evening," I announced to Dorothy, writing Randolph's address on a card. "And now I have an urgent request to make of you. You are not to tell Mr. Randolph that I am having anything to do with this matter. I don't care what else you tell him about yourself; but you're not to tell him that."

"But—I'd *like* to tell him," insisted Dorothy. "If he is your good friend, wouldn't he be glad to know that you were being kind to me? And what you did for us—about father, too."

"Well—maybe—but that's not the point. The point is that I do not want this told. I don't want it told about your father, either. I'm very particular about this. Tell your mother never to talk about any of this—not even to her closest friend."

"That's funny," said Dorothy, bewilderedly.

"It isn't funny, at all!" I replied, bluntly. "It is an investment. And investments aren't funny. They may be foolish, but they're never funny."

Dorothy blinked her long eyelashes a few times, and shook her head a little, dizzily; then she said, "I hope you won't lose too much by—by investing in me; but what about father?"

"Now don't worry me," I commanded, rising. "You're too young to understand. I couldn't explain this to you, if I tried. You wouldn't know what I was talking about."

"Maybe I'm not as dumb as I look," she said, smiling.

I was anxious for her to go now. I had had a long day, and needed some relaxation. I opened the door for her.

"Of course you are!" I declared.

"I hope," she said, gently, extending her hand, "that I can pay it all back, sometime. Doctor Hudson."

"That's all right." I waved a large overhand dismissal. "I don't want any of it back; not a nickel of it; do you understand? I'm expecting to make use of it."

"Well—good-bye!" she said, dazedly, fingering her cheap beads. Then she backed out through the door, regarding me with an odd expression such as one sees sometimes on the faces of people visiting a zoo.

Pyle came in, a few seconds later, and wanted to know what was so funny.

I said, "You wouldn't think it was funny if I told you."

"Maybe not," he growled. "You aren't—may I venture to inquire—losing your mind?"

AT HOME
February twelfth, 1914, 11 p.m.

I HAVE just returned from the annual banquet of the Lincoln Club where the commemorative speeches were, I thought, a little better than usual; perhaps because they were briefer.

One journeyman soothsayer predicted the early outlawry of war, on the ground that with modem weapons available to all nations, no one of them could resort to arms without ruining itself.

The nations, he deposed, had proved "again and again" that war is a futile waste of men and property. I couldn't help feeling that the good man's spirit was ever so much better than his logic. Anything that has been proved "again and again" might have to be proved yet again—and again. I sincerely hope that his forecast is more sound than his reasoning.

Pyle arrived home from Munich yesterday. We have been taking considerable interest at Brightwood in the rapid improvement of X-ray apparatus; and Pyle was sent over—financed chiefly (and not very enthusiastically) by Nick Merrick—to investigate Lilienfeld's new adaptation of the hot cathode ray tube. Strangely enough, while Pyle was abroad. Doctor Coolidge of Schenectady perfected a tube that implements the ray much more effectively. This amuses Merrick, who is intensely patriotic and hoots at the idea that we have to inquire of Germany for the latest tricks in applied science.

Pyle seems more than a little disturbed over what he thinks is a dangerous interest in militarism over there. Of course, we have had some inkling of this in the press, but Pyle says it has a more sinister appearance in Berlin than it has when we read about it over here. He thinks England is apprehensive.

But if our wiseacres, who talked at the dinner to-night, have any notion of the seriousness of the situation in Europe, they kept their frets nicely concealed. The general consensus seemed to indicate that the world had beaten its spears into pruning-hooks, and that lions and lambs may now frolic together in a state of amity.

* * * * *

You will recall that I had sent the Wickes girl to Randolph for advice about lessons in drawing. I had volunteered, without giving the matter any deliberation, to finance this undertaking. It couldn't cost very much. The lessons would probably be taken after Dorothy's working hours; in the evening, perhaps. I was to learn more about that, presently.

At half-past ten, that Sunday night, Randolph called up to say that my young friend had spent the evening there, and thanked me for the privilege of her acquaintance. I chuckled a little over this odd remark and assured him the thanks were all mine to offer, adding, "Bright girl; don't you think?"

"Better than bright," declared Randolph. "She's got something."

I waited a few seconds for him to add a few decorations to this cryptic comment; and, when he didn't avail himself of the opportunity, I inquired whether she had shown him her sketches.

"Yes," he replied, "—and a few glimpses of her soul."

"Sounds as if you might have had a fairly serious conversation," I remarked, with mounting curiosity.

"Same sort of conversation that you and I had, the first time we met. Remember?"

"Of course. But this is quite interesting. I should have supposed she would be too full of art talk to take much stock in your personal investment theory."

"The two subjects," said Randolph, tutorially, "aren't so very far apart. I told her how I happened to do the piece of memorial statuary that gave me standing as a sculptor."

"And Miss Wickes wondered whether a brave experiment in secret philanthropy might make a painter of her," I surmised. "Is that it?"

"Well—she was mightily impressed. It seemed to me that she caught the idea with remarkable promptness, almost as if she had heard about it somewhere else." Randolph paused a moment, and then asked, "You haven't been talking to her about it?"

"No. But Dorothy is a very intelligent young woman, and you probably did a neat job of expounding your theory. She needn't have heard it before. At least, she did not get it from me. Well—did you arrive at any conclusions about the sort of instruction she should have?"

"Tentatively—yes. There's nobody here who could do much for her. The girl has an instinctive flair for movement, composition, perspective. I shouldn't like to see her in the hands of some schoolmasterish artist who might recommend a change of technique. There's an authentic talent here that's far too valuable to be fooled with. What she needs, above everything else, is release from her job; a change of atmosphere; association with gifted young people in some art colony, perhaps; and the guidance of a teacher who will offer her inspiration and encouragement rather than the mere bare bones of planes and contours and— "

"Hi! Wait a minute! Hold everything!" I pleaded. "I'm in over my head."

"So you are," agreed Randolph, apologetically. "I hadn't meant to inflict so much trade-lingo on you. What it all boils down to is that your friend needs emancipation, for a while, from everything that distracts her mind. If she can raise the money—we didn't talk about that—I think she should go to one of the coasts and pursue her special interest, which seems to be ships and wharves. She might go to California. A couple of months might be sufficient to demonstrate what further study she should do, and under what type of master."

"Thanks," I said, "for the attention you have given her. I hope she can find some way to follow your advice."

I refilled my pipe, and walked about through the house, trying to accommodate myself to this project. I got out my pencil and added up a row of figures. The thing had sounded a little more formidable than it really was. Say three months in California. That's the travel expense and modest living costs. Then, there's the equivalent of her wages at the store, which the family will require. That isn't very much. The whole job might run to six hundred and fifty dollars. Doubtless worth doing.

Dorothy called me up, the next evening, at dinner-time, to inquire when she might see me. I told her to come at once to my house.

She was somewhat flustered, when I showed her to a big chair in my library, and her excitement accented her vitality. I had thought her a very pretty girl, but had not credited her with as much character as I now saw in her face. It was more mature than I had thought.

For a while we discussed the suggestions Randolph had offered.

"I'm afraid," she said, "that this must seem to you more like financing a nice vacation than a project to make a real artist of me. It's so different from the plan you had in mind for me that I shall not blame you if you don't think well of it."

I assured her that Mr. Randolph's opinion on such a matter as this should have precedence over anything I might think, and added that it seemed entirely reasonable to me.

She seemed very reluctant about accepting my proposal to cover her wages at the store while she was gone, but consented when it was pointed out that the whole proposition was otherwise impracticable.

"Mr. Randolph's belief is," I reminded her, "that what you need now is a period without drudgery and without care. But you couldn't have a free mind if you had left your mother without support."

Then I asked her if she had given any thought to the place she might go to, and she shook her head. I thought this very odd. It seemed to me that if somebody had made me a proposition of this sort, I should have made haste to investigate travel literature, consult maps, and secure data about the best locations for the purpose.

"But you are decided on Southern California?" I said. She smiled a little, nodded—but not very convincingly, I thought. Then I began to put two and two together and thought I would add them up and see what they totalled. "I suppose you will be too much absorbed by your work, out there, to write to me," I said, casually.

Her eyes brightened, quickly, as I went on.

"I don't think you should have any distracting obligations on your mind—not even letter-writing. So—I shall not feel bad if I do not hear from you until you are back home again."

Dorothy was radiant. She said I was very considerate. She hoped she could prove her gratitude, some day.

So—then I knew she wasn't going to California. She was going to use this money for something else—and I thought I knew what this something else was. Very well; if that's the way it is, it is still a fine investment, I thought; a finer investment than the other.

I moved over to my desk and wrote her a cheque for the full amount I had felt would cover the project, and as I handed it to her I said, "Now, I think this will do it. You need not make an accounting to me. I don't care to have a detailed report. What we are trying to do is to give you a chance to improve as an artist. You are to spend this money as you like; whatever will contribute to our hope for your success—that's what we want."

She drew a quick little sigh of combined relief and gratitude, and said, softly, "Oh, thank you! I am so hopeful!"

At the door, I said, "I'll expect to see you, then, in May."

"And I'll be thinking about you—and your wonderful kindness," said Dorothy, holding on to my hand. "And I'll give you the first important picture that I paint."

And she did. I can see it from where I sit, as I write these words. It won a prize in an art exhibition put on by the Architectural League of New York.

But she didn't paint it in California.

* * * * *

Of course I never asked her, and she never told me, how she invested that money. I do know that she didn't leave town. One day, Nancy Ashford remarked, "By the way, I saw that lovely Wickes girl, this afternoon, when I was shopping. What a charming young woman she is getting to be!"

"That's nice," I replied, trying to make it sound casual. "Did you talk to her?"

"No—she was busy. I don't think she saw me."

I had a notion to say, "That, also, is nice," but checked myself in time.

One Sunday afternoon in May Dorothy showed up at the hospital. She was carrying the picture. It was indeed a lovely thing—and so was she.

"Well—" I said, "you've done it! Have you shown it to Mr. Randolph?"

"Of course not," she declared, coyly. "Think I'd show it to anybody until you had seen it?"

"I'll tell you what we will do," I said. "I had expected to go out to the Randolphs' to-night for dinner. I'll call him up and tell him I am bringing you along—you and the picture."

She was delighted. On the way, I ventured to ask how California was—in a vague sort of way—so she wouldn't suspect, by my silence on that subject, that I had discovered her secret. She replied, with equal indefiniteness, that California was very nice indeed, and added that Detroit was very nice, too. I could find no fault with either of these remarks, and pursued my inquiries no further.

Randolph was excited! Of course, I thought the picture was a magnificent piece of work; but I was no artist. Randolph knew what he was talking about—and he didn't talk about anything else that night. Natalie was sober, as she looked at the painting. Then she said, quietly, "Now you can do anything you want to do; can't she, father?"

* * * * *

I did not see Dorothy again for a month. It was at the hospital, Sunday afternoon. She was aware of my usual schedule of work on Sundays, and I found her waiting for me. I was sincerely glad to see the girl. She had matured, surprisingly. She was now at work on another marine sketch, she said, and felt sure she could sell it. It was most gratifying to see the firmness of her self-confidence.

She was on the point of leaving when I said, "Oh—by the way; you never told me how your friend Millie made out with her little problem."

Dorothy was tugging on her gloves. Her eyes drifted to the window and she replied, slowly, "She went to a sanatorium somewhere, away up in the Adirondacks. Her lungs weren't very strong. Her Aunt Susan consented to her going, when Millie told her that the money was provided for people with that trouble." Dorothy paused, but did not meet my eyes. Then, cautiously, she proceeded. "It must have been only a slight touch of T.B. She is well again—and back in the store, with a little better position."

Perhaps I should not have pressed this inquiry any farther, but I was too sorely tempted.

"Well—as I recall the story," I rejoined, "Millie also had a slight touch of something else. Did she get over that, too?"

Dorothy's lips tightened in a reluctant little grin, but she did not risk facing me.

"Yes," she replied, after some hesitation, "and it was adopted, by very nice people. It will have a good home."

"I am glad," I said. "Very glad."

Dorothy's face lighted and she looked me squarely in the eyes. She gave me her hand.

"Well—good-bye—for this time," she said, sweetly. "And—thanks—for—for everything. You've given me such a wonderful chance to be what I want to be."

I held her hand for a moment, debating a reply. It would have been very pleasant to me if I could have risked saying I had guessed the secret, and was proud of her. But I felt that any such comment might damage the joy she had found. These are things you can't talk about.

I simply smiled into her eyes and said good-bye. She waved a hand as she went through the door, and her lips were parted in a radiant smile. I know that she knows that I know—and she is glad that I wouldn't venture a word about it.

Dorothy and I now belong to a strange little fraternity that makes no signs, speaks no pass-words; but has a mutual understanding that is rich and deep and full.

* * * * *

These are crowded days. We are having an increasing number of emergency cases. More people are driving automobiles. The roads are being improved. Everybody is driving faster. Last year there were sixty-six persons killed outright in this country; double the number for the preceding twelve months. I wonder how this reckless destruction of life is to be checked. No one seems to be doing anything about it. Perhaps the lawmakers would be more alert to this problem if they could spend a day in our hospital and see the mangled people brought in for repairs.

AT HOME
June nineteenth, 1914, 10 p.m.

Watson and his young protégé Leslie Sherman were here for dinner to-night and have just left for the hospital where Tim had a post-operative case to see. Sherman was keen on going along, for he begins his internship with us next week and is bursting with curiosity over his new duties.

Yesterday morning, Tim and I drove over to Ann Arbor to see Sherman get his M.D. I was much amused over Tim's motherly concern and undisguised pride. You would have thought him an elderly relative. There are, I believe, four years between their ages.

I have been suspecting, for some time, that Tim was helping this handsome young fellow through his medical course; and now I feel sure of it. Perhaps this accounts, in no small measure, for the amazing progress that Watson has made in his work at Brightwood.

I have forgotten whether I reported, in this journal, that Watson received his medical degree in June of 1910. One of the difficulties of keeping a journal in code is that once the entry is made, and a few weeks have passed, the author himself can't find what it contains unless he goes to an enormous amount of bother. If my reader thinks this is funny, he is welcome to his amusement.

If I did not mention Tim's graduation from the Medical School, I should have done so; for it was an event of much importance to both of us. Of course, even if I had not provided a way for him to attend college, he might have contrived to do it by some other means; but it has been of immense satisfaction to me to have had a part in this brilliant chap's unfolding. It has been my privilege to witness this evolution—almost hour by hour—since that midsummer afternoon, ten years ago, when a rangy, red-headed, penniless young tramp showed up at the dirty old Free Clinic on Fort Street with a broken hand and an astonishing fund of medical patter.

Immediately after graduation from the Medical School, he came to Brightwood for his internship, but I am not sure that he ever was an interne. Nobody on the staff blamed me for the preference I showed him. They all knew I was deeply interested in his future, and I think they felt it was justified. Had he been my son, Watson could not have received more attention. He not only stood in at my most interesting operations but was as welcome to watch Pyle at work and McDermott and Harper.

Nancy Ashford, who has an unusual capacity for attaching herself to promising people, flattering and cajoling and badgering them so that they work like dogs rather than disappoint her, pretended from the first that she was Tim's aunt—a relationship he has always played up to with effortless skill.

Had he been but one-half as intelligent and industrious, he could hardly have avoided success; for all the ways were greased, and everybody gave him a push, no one—not even Tim, himself—knew exactly when his "internship" was over and his work as a junior on the staff began. He certainly had an early start. To the best of my knowledge, he was the youngest surgeon of my generation ever to have full responsibility for a major operation.

You will credit me, I hope, with a fair attempt to explain Watson's youthful arrival at a high rating in his profession, on the ground of his exceptional opportunities—plus his alert mind and indefatigable diligence. My own belief is, however, that all these fortunate factors in combination could not have made Watson what he is, to-day, without the additional inspiration of some personal investment in another's upbuilding. Tim unquestionably has the inner glow—or whatever this peculiar radiance may be called—that is to be had by one means only.

This strange motivation began to show up in him about a year ago last September. He never confided anything about it to me, but I think he knew that I knew that he knew, judging from chance remarks that tumbled accidentally into our intimate conversations. That he was making sacrifices on somebody's behalf was apparent. His modest stipend from the hospital was going somewhere; for he never had any money, never went any place, had no social life at all; yet seemed smugly satisfied to live on nothing, and could stand any amount of chafing about his parsimony.

Through his college days, Tim had a very small part in my own social life—such as it was. Naturally we saw but little of him while he was in Ann Arbor, and during vacations he worked hard at jobs which made a considerable demand oil his physical energy. He saw very little of the Randolphs. After he came to Brightwood, I suggested occasionally that it might be pleasant for him to renew this acquaintance, but he was prompt with excuses; appreciated my thought, but had something else to do.

One Sunday evening, about a year ago, I prevailed on him to accompany me to their home. I knew he was having a good time. I knew also that he had been more than pleasantly stirred by Natalie's fresh young beauty and grace. This delighted me. It was what I had secretly hoped for. I have never sought any prizes as a matchmaker, but I thought it would be interesting if Tim and Natalie should find each other as attractive as I had found them both to be.

It seemed to me that Natalie was at her very best, that night, and I couldn't help feeling that they were congenial.

On the way back, I clumsily remarked, with a pretence at playfulness, "I'm afraid I have started something, Tim, by letting you and Natalie see each other again."

"You must never be afraid of anything," drawled Tim, tossing back one of my pet clichés.

Perhaps I should explain, at this juncture, that I had latterly become convinced that fear plays a very conspicuous role in most of the diseases of a psycho-physiological character; and I have been saying—perhaps too frequently—that many people would be able to build up their resistance to disease and increase their vitality if they identified their various phobias and went bravely to the mat with them. I have been contending that any sort of fear—no matter how apparently inconsequential—filters through all of a man's thought processes. He had better grapple with his pet fear, whatever it is.

Take insomnia, for example: here we find, very frequently, that the difficulty isn't rooted in a physical disability, but can be accounted for by a little phobia. The victim goes to bed wondering whether he will be able to sleep to-night. He is afraid he can't. He lies there fretting over the possibility that he may have this thing to contend with, all the rest of his life.

My counsel is that the man should turn on the light, open a book, and assume that he doesn't need any sleep at this time or Nature would be attending to it. He doesn't get scared if it happens that he isn't very hungry, some day at noon; nor is he so silly as to force food down his throat simply because he has been accustomed to eat at this time of the day.

Let him talk himself out of his fear of insomnia, on this common-sense basis. I have done it, myself. Plenty of nights, after I have spent a crowded day of perplexing duties—involving life-and-death decisions—I have gone to bed fairly sure that I should mentally reconstruct the whole string of dilemmas, hour after hour. I learned to handle that problem by going forth to meet my insomnia, more than halfway. And I have conquered this fear. I believe I have done a fairly good job of conquering *all* of my fears. The only thing I am really afraid of now is fear. Perhaps I talk about it too much. I didn't blame Tim for teasing me with it, especially when I had invited such a retort by my facetious comment concerning him and Natalie.

"She is a lovely girl," I declared, fervently.

Tim agreed to this, in such a forthright manner that there was but little left for me to say on the subject unless I wanted to be impudent enough to ask him whether he was likely to be seeing more of her.

After a studious silence, he said, "I think you would like to see me try to get Natalie interested in me; isn't that so?"

"I had not realized that my hope had been quite so transparent," I replied.

"If a high school boy," said Tim, irrelevantly, "likes a girl, but has only ten cents in his pocket, he can buy a bag of peanuts for her entertainment, and they can sit on the steps of the library and swear that they belong to each other. And no harm is done. They both know that it would be a half-dozen years before this decision could lay a real obligation on either of them. My own attitude toward heart affairs," he continued, deliberately, as if he had thought it all out and composed his speech with care, "is conditioned by the fact that I shall be twenty-nine years old on my next birthday. I am not in the fortunate position of the youngster who can—without any impudence—offer a girl everything when he has nothing to offer. Any man of my age, who encourages a young woman to believe that he has an interest in her, is something of a cad, I think, if he has no means of seeing it through to an honest conclusion."

"Naturally—I agree to all that," I broke in. "But—young women have been willing to wait patiently until their men have accumulated something—especially in the case of professional men, whose early income is small."

"Yes, yes, I daresay," responded Tim, half-impatiently, "but—well—let's suppose a case. So long as you have been thinking about Natalie Randolph, let us talk about her. I imagine that she is about twenty-three. She enjoys an active social life. Her friends are pairing off. They go to the theatres, and downtown to dinner, and for drives in the country. They play golf and ride. Now—I cannot do any of these things. My work is exacting and my funds are meagre. But I have some pride. And I shouldn't accept the gift of Natalie Randolph's time—not an hour of it!—in my present situation."

"Well—if it's money, Tim—" I ventured.

"No; thank you, sir," said Tim, promptly. "I'm getting all the money I'm worth."

We thought it better to change the conversation then, and we have never renewed it. But I think that Watson is in love with Natalie Randolph. And I think also that if he had the use of his income, he would be seeing something of her. Of course, that makes his investment infinitely more valuable. I hope young Sherman turns out to be something. His chance has been well paid for.

* * * * *

Yesterday noon, after the Commencement, Tim and Leslie invited me to have lunch with them and I gladly consented. We found my car, parked several blocks from the auditorium, and Tim drove. Before we had gone very far, I began to be a bit nervous. We were headed toward the Michigan Central station, and I knew there was only one restaurant in that vicinity worth patronizing. I should have been glad enough to go to Tony's by myself, and had done so many times; but I did not like the idea of going with anyone else.

It would have been very awkward, however, for me to have raised an objection, now that we were almost there.

"Tony's will probably be crowded," said Tim, as we got out of the car, "but it's the best place in town to eat."

At that point, I should have said I knew that. I should have added that I had been here. It would have been much better, too, if I had said I knew Tony. There was no reason why I couldn't have admitted that much; but I didn't want to discuss Tony with anybody. Tony and I had a secret that was several years old.

The restaurant was full, as Tim had threatened; full of students, alumni, young faculty men, tobacco smoke, miscellaneous noise, and the tempting aroma of broiled steaks and chops. Tony, himself—rotund, deliberate, and unrattled—was moving ponderously about, making room for his clients.

Sherman remarked that Tony was becoming a snob; wearing a white coat; just because it was Commencement, and there were out-of-town guests.

"Doesn't he generally wear a white coat?" I was hypocrite enough to ask, feeling that I ought to contribute something to the conversation.

"Doesn't wear *any* colour of coat," obliged Tim. "Polo shirt; no sleeves; big white apron. I don't think it improves him to put on style."

Presently Tony ambled our way and caught sight of us. His enigmatic old face lighted as he approached. He extended two big fat hands, palms up, fingers spread, grasped me warmly, and said, "Doc! Eet ees too long since you come!" He shrugged a massive shoulder and gave a despairing glance around the room. "Now what shall Tony do with you?"

I told him we were quite willing to wait until there was an available table.

"Aren't we?" I said to my hosts, whose faces registered about as much inquisitiveness as they could hold. Tony, noting my company, bobbed a little bow to each of them, and said, considerably to my embarrassment, and doubtless to their further mystification, "You are dam' lucky yawng fellows!"

A table was cleared, presently, and we sat down. Tony asked if we would let him arrange for our luncheon, and we were glad enough to trust his expert judgment. After the old chap had paddled away, Tim drawled, "I take it that you and Tony have met before." It was quite funny, and we all laughed. I was glad something had been said to ease the tension.

"It's a rather long story," I remarked, after a while.

"Whenever he says a story is long," said Tim, pretending to offer a confidence to Leslie, "he just means it's a story you couldn't blast out of him with dynamite." »

I recognized a former classmate at an adjoining table, and went over to shake hands. When I returned, it was taken by consent that we wouldn't be talking any more about my acquaintance with Tony. And I observed that when the good old chap came with our incomparable steaks—which he insisted on serving, himself—he seemed to have sensed that it wasn't the right time for him to make any more allusions to our friendship. He was standing behind the cash register when we came up to settle our account.

"I'm afraid you didn't give us a cheque," said Tim. "How much is it, please?"

Tony's face grew very stern.

"Doc Hudson—he settle hees bill! Gooda-bye, Doc. Come again. You come—too," said Tony, slowly wagging his head to my young companions.

We thanked him, and when we were outside, Tim—who is a fairly competent mimic—said, ostensibly for Sherman's benefit, "Doc Hudson—he settle hees bill. Dam' lucky yawng fellows—to be with Doc Hudson!" And then he added, "Any other place. Doctor, you'd like to visit? You don't happen to have a secret with a good tailor, do you?"

But we dropped the matter there, and Tim has never referred to it since.

It is growing late and I am tired. Perhaps I shall tell you the story about Tony, some other time.

BRIGHTWOOD HOSPITAL
October fifth, 1914, 10.30 p.m.

NANCY ASHFORD has been spending the past hour in my office. There is only one thing to talk about now, so we talked about that.

330

For two months the war has driven every other current topic into total eclipse—and no wonder. You pick up the morning paper and distrust your own eyesight, though goodness knows the type is big and black enough to be read by the born blind. Every hour more people are being swept into this thing; and, once in, they can't get out.

Without asking for them you can get cocksure opinions, in any club lounge or Pullman smoker, on the scope, duration, and outcome of this incredible affair; and the editorials—quite indiscreetly, it seems to me—are already defining our national sympathies and antipathies. Surely, if our attitude as a nation really has to be documented, it should be expressed by the State Department. It is certainly not a job for the journalists.

I find myself growing more and more dissatisfied with the manners and morals of the public press. It has become the most potent influence on the thought of our people; and, fully conscious of its power, it has about left off appealing to the reader's calm commonsense, apparently feeling that it can do a more flourishing business by pandering to prejudice and fear.

I shocked Nancy by remarking that general literacy is a dangerous accomplishment.

"What a silly thing to say!" hooted Nancy, who takes much stock in modern progress and grows dewy-eyed when she talks about the recent inventions.

Forced to defend my statement, I maintained that it is a good thing for people to know how to read if what they read is good for them to know. If their reading inflames their aversions and fans their slumbering hatreds; or, by insidious propaganda, teaches them aversions they had not previously held, their ability to read does them damage and makes them a menace to the public peace.

I had never thought this through carefully, and in any other company than Nancy's I might have hesitated to air my unconsidered views. I admitted as much to her, and she drawled, "Go right ahead. Doctor, and see how far you can wade before you get mired."

With this encouragement, I began to expound. And I am recording our conversation here because I want you to think about this matter earnestly. Of course it may be that when these words are read, there will have come a complete change of conduct—if not of character—on the part of the papers. As the matter stands, the very large majority of them are definitely on the side of degradation. When sternly queried, they reply that they are giving the public what it demands. My own opinion is that they developed the public taste. And bad taste it is, too.

I reminded Nancy that the people of the world—until recent times—believed what they were told to believe, without much independent thinking.

"They lived on their prejudices," she assisted, slyly.

"Yes—but that word needs to be examined. It has come to mean stupidity and stubbornness, but a prejudice isn't necessarily a bad idea. For example: nobody ever tried to murder me and I have never tried to murder anyone else. I never saw a murder committed; never knew anybody who had committed a murder. Neither by experience nor observation do I have direct knowledge on this subject; but I am uncompromisingly against it. I have a prejudice."

"You and me both," laughed Nancy. "But where do we go from here?"

"Before printing was invented," I continued, undistracted, "back in the benighted old days when people lived almost exclusively on their prejudices—"

"And boiled turnips—and polluted water—" interposed Nancy, who is standing firm for our modern civilization.

"That's irrelevant," I complained, crisply. "They lived on their prejudices; but these prejudices were authorized by established institutions. They had dignity. You weren't yelled at, from every corner, by discordant voices. The prejudices weren't peddled around on the street. The Church handed you a creed. It may have contained some statements that a contentious individualist might disavow; but this creed was a respectable product of earnest thinking by many wise and sincere men. It may have had its imperfections, but it had solidity, maturity, sanction. At least, it wasn't something that an unlicensed hawker served, smoking hot, for a penny! It wasn't something that a newspaper man had pounded out on his typewriter, between nine-thirty and ten, with a boy at his elbow waiting to grab each article of faith as it climbed out of the machine.

"The State," I went on, gathering momentum, "provided the unlettered public with a pattern for patriotism. This patriotism was a prejudice, if you like; but it had roots. It had stability. You didn't have to be told—by some paragrapher or free-lance columnist—what patriotism was, and how it worked, and what it expected you to do. The State taught you your loyalties. You didn't derive them from the yipping and snarling of the scribes."

"Well—that's a pretty long speech," observed Nancy, when I had run down. She struck a match to indicate that I might be benefited by a cigar. I regarded her gesture with reproach, but drew out a cigar and she lighted it for me. "Has some particular newspaper man made you mad?" she asked.

I shook my head. As individuals, they were fine fellows. I had had the most pleasant relations with them. They were bright, congenial, obliging. I couldn't remember ever having asked a favour that they hadn't granted. No—it wasn't personal.

But the papers were a bad influence. To begin with, they had a mighty low regard for the people's intelligence, imputing to them a sort of brutishness that isn't a normal characteristic of the average citizen. They assumed that the people had no respect whatever for private griefs; no sensitiveness about pushing themselves in to gaze upon another man's misfortunes. The press would risk its very life and limbs to take photographs of mourners weeping at the grave of an accident victim. It would force its way into a hospital to torture an interview out of the next of kin, in some sad circumstance. Only half-witted and mentally diseased persons would have the morbid curiosity to flatten their noses against the windows of homes afflicted by tragedy; but the newspapers did it, on the assumption that the public is psychopathic. Their arrogant impudence knew no limits. They had utter contempt for the dignity of the courts, and taught the public to share their rude defiance.

All that being true, what could you expect of the press at a moment when the public needed to be kept steady and dispassionate in their attitude toward a world-cataclysm crowded with menace?

Nancy reminded me that we believed in free speech. But I think it is to the people's serious disadvantage that they are able to buy, for two cents, a stimulant to hatred, morbidity, savagery, and scorn for the elementary decencies.

If it is illegal to peddle heroin, cyanide, and nitroglycerine on the street, what excuse is there for the general distribution of printed matter that debases the mind? If a manufacturer is required by law to state on the ketchup bottle that it contains benzoate of soda, the newspaper should be made to say—at the top of page one—"This edition contains stuff that whets the appetite for ghoulishness, sadism, and similar psychoses."

Nancy said I was getting excited again, so we agreed to wheel out the newspapers, and discuss a few other agencies dealing with the public's thought. According to report, some inspired ass on the local Board of Education had inquired, yesterday, whether it wasn't about time to discontinue the teaching of German literature in the high schools. I wonder if we are going to allow our prejudices to unbuckle our reason. Here pops up a glowing patriot, who—only thirty days after a European war begins—wants his children sheltered from the sinister influence of Goethe and Schiller. I suppose the next thing to expect will be a frantic attack on Mozart. Perhaps they'll ban the performance of *Parsifal*.

"Maybe I'll have to go to the calaboose," I growled, "for using a Zeiss microscope."

"You'd better be careful where you make such remarks," advised Nancy. "They'll say you're pro-German."

"Well—I'm not," I muttered. "Far from it!"

* * * * *

Nancy bade me good-night at that point, sweetly suggesting that I go home and sleep it off, which I mean to do presently. But I want to add a reflection or two before I stop writing.

I wonder what manner of influence, if any, the churches may exert in this bewildered time. If they were able to unite on a policy calculated to steady the public mind, it might produce good results. I do not know much about the churches. I do not attend their services. Sometimes, on Saturdays, I have glanced over the sermon topics announced for the next day. I regret to say that I do this largely for entertainment, and it does me no credit to be amused by these irreverences. For the most part, the topics imply a gift of omniscience, on the part of the clergyman, which reflects sadly on his mental housekeeping. The out-and-out lunatic always has a disturbance of the ego. In some instances his ego atrophies, and he develops an inferiority complex. In many more cases his ego becomes inflamed and distended, resulting in "hallucinatory omnipotence." Sometimes he thinks he is Napoleon. Sometimes he is Moses. Not long ago I saw a sermon-topic, "What God Thinks of Detroit." I wonder just what is the difference between the mental condition of the cracked old man who says he is Moses, and the up-and-coming prophet at the Holiness Tabernacle who knows what God thinks of Detroit. Very sad business, this. And the saddest feature of this humourless state of mind is the assumption that people will come to listen.

I presume that in the dignified old churches a more reasonable policy is pursued. I know that my good friend Dean Marquis, of the Episcopal Cathedral, isn't going to get off any such balderdash; nor is Doctor Spence likely to make himself ridiculous in the presence of a churchful of conservative Presbyterians. I daresay there are a dozen or more who wouldn't countenance the sort of thing that obviously goes on in the big wooden tabernacle.

But—that's exactly where the trouble is, you see. Reverends Marquis and Spence and Rossman and the other intellectuals are dealing with a clientele largely composed of privileged people, who—it may be assumed—have learned how to think calmly. They cannot be easily stampeded.

The enormous crowds that gather in the big tent, where "Buster" Beecham, the saxophone-playing evangelist, holds forth, and in the wooden tabernacle, where "Bob" Somebody thinks for God, are not people of privilege. They are excitable and more reliant upon their emotions than their intelligence. It is absurd to hope that the Gospel of Peace— as interpreted in these places—will have a steadying effect upon people's minds. That's where the trouble is: the very people who are most in need of steadiness are the least likely to have it offered to them.

Last Saturday I noted that one howling sensationalist was going to preach on "When a Christian Should Fight." Doubtless he is getting ready to rattle the sabre.

As I understand the original message of Galilee, it was distinctly pacifistic, whatever may have been the shocking history of Christianity as a militant force. In peace-time the churches are for peace. In time of war they join the army. Indeed, they mobilize a little ahead of the army!

I wonder whether there is, to-day, any powerful influence at work in this country that may keep the public on an even keel. I doubt it; and I am very unhappy about it.

The papers say, to-day, that three hundred and fifty thousand people jammed the churches of Detroit yesterday to pray for peace, in response to the President's nation-wide appeal. I wonder how much good such prayers accomplish. It has been my experience that before a prayer for a great favour can be offered with any hope of success, one has to put up some security; some valuable collateral, to attest one's sincerity and willingness to toss into it everything one can assemble. I expect our people would have to bring forward a mighty fine record for internal and privately possessed peace, before they could hope to do much with their petition for Europe.

BRIGHTWOOD HOSPITAL
May sixth, 1915, 4.30 p.m.

IT has been a long time since I wrote anything in this journal. Many events, which in less tempestuous times might have been worth mentioning here, have seemed utterly insignificant in the face of the general stress.

To be quite honest, I had almost forgotten about this little book. And I doubt if I should be writing in it now had it not been for the fact that I stumbled upon it, a little while ago, while searching in my office safe for a deed to some country property.

Of course I might have set down in this journal a day-by-day commentary on the appalling things that are happening overseas and their repercussions on this side; but this project was not conceived as a history of contemporary movements in the world. It had but one motive: to record my own experiences in self-investment and the rewards accruing from such adventures into the lives of other people.

When you read these words, the Great War will undoubtedly be over; for it will reach its end by sheer exhaustion, one of these days, if not by a decisive victory. You will have more information than you want on this subject. You may be bored by any reference to it here. But it is a live issue, I beg you to believe; and one can't think or talk or write about anything that doesn't swing on this one pivot.

The President has had an unenviable job; trying, on the one hand, to serve the wishes of the majority who want us to be kept out of it, at almost any cost of national dignity, and the passionate patriots who strongly counsel him to put an end to the temporizing with something that we will have to do, pretty soon, whether we like it or not.

Most of the men with whom I associate are feeling that the President's diplomatic notes of protest to Germany have now reached a point of futility where they are beginning to seem a bit ridiculous.

Last Wednesday night, at a Chamber of Commerce dinner, one militant speaker satirized this situation rather cleverly. I doubted whether it was in very good taste to do it, but it was undeniably amusing. He illustrated by taking off an exasperated mother issuing requests, entreaties, and commands to her incorrigible nine-year-old brat. The monologue began in a comradely mood, and moved on through dulcet cooing to indignation and hysteria.

"Johnny—please be mother's fine little friend—and don't do that: that's a good boy."
"Johnny—mama is going to be offended."
"Mama doesn't want to scold her little boy."
"Must mama tell papa?"
"Johnny! Now you listen to me!"
"Now—you do that once more, young man, and you'll see what happens to you."
"*Johnny!* Stop that—this minute! This is the last time I am going to speak to you!"
"*Johnny!*"

* * * * *

It sounded funny, at the moment; but it isn't really very funny. The President is in an awkward position. He is probably as anxious as anyone else to preserve the national honour, and it must be a bitter dose to have oneself reviled for spineless cowardice when one's big hope is to save our people from avoidable bloodshed. And there's another question, too. Far as I can learn, we haven't much of an army to send over there, even if we should decide that our patience is exhausted. One hears all manner of conflicting opinions on how long it would take to mobilize, equip, and train an army strong enough to be effective.

The typical speech, urging a declaration of war, is amusingly illogical. The harangue usually begins on a highly altruistic note, demanding that we plunge into this mess "to save civilization," and ends by threatening that if we don't the Germans will come over here and lick the pants off of us, after they have finished with France and England. So—we have two excellent reasons for going in. We can help save civilization; and, incidentally, save our own skins. I feel that these two appeals—so divergent in motive—instead of being placed in the custody of a single orator, should be handled by specialists. One man could present the idealistic appeal, accenting our selfless interest in humanity at large; and another man could present the more practical aspects of our case in particular.

I have a lot of sympathy for the President. Many people think—and I find myself sharing this view—that Mr. Wilson would ease his own strain somewhat if he took advantage of the statesmanly counsel to which he has access. He seems to be trying to do it all himself. I said that to Pyle, the other day, and he replied, "Well—Lincoln didn't have any very valuable advisers; did he? And there was a time when George Washington seemed to be playing a lone hand."

I had to admit that these things were true; but, all the same, I think a lot of the responsibility, that now seems concentrated in one man, might be shared. After all—the President does have a Cabinet.

But it is easy to criticize. I know that if I were placed in such a perplexing position as that of the President, I should find the gravity of it insupportable. Even without any such crushing cares, I am neurally fagged by this long-continued tension. Perhaps it might not afflict me so much if I were in a less depressing occupation. More and more I am confronted with brain surgery in which half of the cases are potential funerals before I see them. Maybe, in normal times, my task would not weigh on me so heavily. Maybe, if my job were not so dreadfully serious, I could view the world's predicament—and our own national perplexity—with less fretting. The combination of the two is very wearing.

When the news broke, to-day, about the sinking of the *Lusitania*, yesterday afternoon, I felt that we had turned a sharp corner on the road that inevitably leads to war. In the event that we go into it, I may be needed; and, if so, I shall go, of course, and "do my bit," as the saying goes, these days.

But, in the meantime, I realize that I must try to find some quiet retreat where I may spend a day, occasionally, apart from the racket and strain. I asked Carter to give me a going over, the other day, and he thinks there is a slight aneurism; advised me to take it easy. How can I take it easy? He might as well suggest to the Fire Department to take it easy! The cases I deal with won't wait until the surgeon has himself a two months' vacation.

A couple of years ago I inadvertently acquired a little ten-acre tract of untamed scrub-oak and briars on the rocky east shore of Lake Saginack. There was a decent old chap named Baldwin, who had brought his wife into the hospital for an abdominal operation that revealed a malignant condition. It was Pyle's case. He advised them not to go back to the country; to remain in town, if possible, close to medical attention. Baldwin got into conversation with me about his problem. It developed that he had very little to go on. There was this unpromising tract on Lake Saginack (the wrong side) which he could put up as security for a loan. I knew he needed the money in a good cause, so I let him have it, and took a deed to the land. His wife died, and he followed her, not long afterward. One of these days, I shall build a little cottage up there, and sneak away from town, week-ends. Meantime—I think I shall pitch a good tent, and try camping out. I have never done anything of the sort, and I daresay it will be deucedly uncomfortable.

Perhaps I forgot to say that I built a commodious home, on the north side of town, two years ago. Joyce spends most of her time in a girls' school, but she entertains her friends at home during vacations, and she needed something better than an apartment. The money was well spent, I think, though I can't see that Joyce is any the less restless in our more attractive quarters.

Of course I cannot expect to get her interested in going out with me to the lake. She would be bored to death. I am not sure what the solitude may do for me, if I attempt this. But if I don't arrange for something of the sort, I may get into trouble. At least, that's what Carter said, and he is a very good heart man.

* * * * *

I have just come from another wearisome interview with Maxine Merrick—Cliff's widow—who has been under observation here for a week; thinks she is going crazy; and so do I. Far as I can determine, the only thing that ails her is self-pity and too much concentration on the bad treatment she has had. It is true that Cliff treated her like a dog, and broke her spirit; but now that he is out of the picture there seems no reason why she should not brace up. There is nothing physiologically wrong with Maxine's head. Her trouble is emotional instability. I feel sorry for her, and sorrier for good old Nick, who has been trying to compensate for Cliff's neglect. It is a pity that Nick couldn't have had a son for whom he might feel some pride. He has built a huge country house—a costly mansion—on the west shore of Saginack, and is living there alone with a battery of servants. I doubt if he gets much pleasure out of it. If I were in his place, I should travel. But Nick wouldn't know what he was looking at, if he did travel, unless it had something to do with machinery; and he can see more machinery here in Detroit than anywhere else in the world.

Maxine has now developed into a typical hypo. She has pains. She has pains in her inner ear. She has a pain in her neck. Watson, who has examined her, says she *is* a pain in the neck. She also has much discomfort in her left shoulder, in her lower abdomen, and in her heels. Not that she hasn't been diligent in trying to find relief. She has been to Carlsbad and Aix-les-Bains; she has been to Lourdes. Every so often, in the past three or four years, she has packed her trunks and a maid or two and her badly spoiled son, Bobby, and has galloped away for another sort of treatment. She has had violet rays, mud packs, and Hindu philosophy. She has tried Battle Creek, Theosophy, Arizona, Christian Science, White Sulphur Springs, the Wisdom of the East, and enough colonies to sap the vitality of an army mule.

At present, her anxiety over her own disabilities is somewhat distracted by the untimely arrival of Bobby from the Culver Military Academy where, she said, he had been getting along so nicely. Bobby came to see her yesterday, carrying a huge armful of red roses. You can't help liking him; neither can you help feeling that he must have missed a large number of spankings to which he was justly entitled.

Maxine sent for me to come to her room and meet Bobby, whom I had not seen for a long time. He conversed, without reticence, about his recent retirement from Culver. I rather expected he would try to throw the blame for his expulsion onto the school, but he didn't; was entirely unabashed in reporting that they had "put up with a lot," and declared that the Colonel was a mighty fine man. Bobby was very tender in his attitude toward his mother, but I don't see how he can have very much respect for her, in her unbalanced condition. I sympathize with the boy. His father was no good, and his mother is a damn fool. I wonder what will become of him. He's bright enough to be anything he wants to be.

When I dropped in to see Maxine, this afternoon, she was sitting up in bed, attractively jacketed in something made of pink satin and white feathers, and intent upon a little book. Without preliminaries, she asked me what month I was born in; and informed me—after a good deal of leafing back and forth—that I was very firm, very strong, and very stubborn, as indicated by my astral control which, she had discovered, is Alpha of the Nebulae Andromeda. I thanked her for assigning to me such of these attributes as might be considered complimentary, and asked her if her bowels had moved well, to-day, which she seemed to feel was irrelevant.

"Right while I'm telling you," she complained, "about your horoscope, you ask me a rude question that shows you weren't paying the slightest attention."

I assured her that the two topics were not so incongruous as they seemed; that her defective elimination and her interest in Astrology might be more closely related than she thought. Maxine laughed a little, which I considered a good sign. It has been a long time since she has exhibited any appreciation of humour.

But it was only a fleeting promise. Pretty soon she was back on one of her pet subjects: what to do next in the great cause of her health and what she calls "mental rearmament." Most of our current clichés have a military flavour.

What Maxine really needs is something constructive to do, but I hesitate to suggest a philanthropy. I am sure she would be an insufferable nuisance on the board of a charity, and she would unquestionably make a mess of any attempt to befriend an individual.

Before I left, she showed me some literature she had received from a goofy colony in Southern California where you study what Maxine says is an eclectic derived from Rosicrucianism, Bahaism, and Buddhism, in combination with a vital diet, cosmic breathing, and systematic meditation. I told her it was just the place for her, and I hope she goes. I don't like to see the hospital taking her money. I should like to have given her a stern lecture about her amazing silliness, but it wouldn't have done the slightest bit of good. [1]

Had Doctor Hudson foreseen that it would fall to the lot of Maxine Merrick's son to transcribe this journal (a most unlikely circumstance when viewed from the date of this entry), his comments on her eccentricities might have been less severe. I suppose he was sorely tried by my mother's hypochondria and general instability. At this period of her life she was indeed difficult and pitiably unhappy. (R. M.)

As I was in the act of locking the safe, there was a tap on the door, and to my surprise and delight Natalie Randolph breezed in. It has been a long time since I have seen anything so pretty. Natalie certainly knows how to dress.

She was very animated, very much on tip-toe.

It was the first time she had ever honoured me with a voluntary call, and I was curious to know what her errand might be.

"It's easy to see," I remarked, "that you haven't come to consult me professionally. You never looked healthier in your life."

"I had a few minutes to wait," she explained, "and I thought I'd run in and say Hello—if you weren't too busy."

I assured her that I would never be too busy to talk to her; inquired about her father; answered questions about Joyce; asked whether she had come to see one of our patients.

She flushed a little, most becomingly, and said, "I have driven over to carry off one of your doctors for dinner. Do you mind?"

I tried not to seem too foolishly pleased, and had sense enough not to press any questions. Mind? Of course, I didn't mind!

"It's going to do Brightwood Hospital a lot of good," I said, "if one of our doctors is seen in the company of such a charming young woman. What we need over here is a little more class."

She made a puckery little mouth at me, told me to be careful what I said to impressionable young women, offered her hand, and dashed away.

I hope this thing comes off. Tim deserves a girl like Natalie. He has been pretty sly—keeping this a secret from me.

BRIGHTWOOD HOSPITAL
May tenth, 1915, 9.30 p.m.

LATE Friday afternoon I had a telephone call from my friend Doctor Russell in Chicago asking if I could run up and attend a consultation the next day. I asked him what it was about and he said it was a glioma. I might have suspected as much, for whenever I am called to a medical centre as well equipped as Chicago the case is almost sure to be one of the forty-nine gliomas.

If it should happen that you do not know anything about this, it may be sufficient to tell you that a glioma is an intracranial cyst—and it is no picnic, either for the patient or the surgeon.

If you do know anything about it—and it is indeed quite probable that the person who comes into possession of these memoirs is well informed on medical matters—it may have come to your attention that it has been my good fortune to have experienced a considerable success with these gliomas. Until nearly six years ago, I tried to content myself with the usual procedure.

The customary technique was to empty the cystic cavity, and let it go at that. I assume that every surgeon suspected there was a localized tumour nodule responsible for the secretion of the fluid that caused the pressure and set up the general derangement and degeneration of the brain; but it is very serious business to go exploring in a cystic cavity, in a blind search for something practically indistinguishable from the convolutions of normal brain tissue.

My own practice was to drain the cavity, and hope for the best; and I think that almost every other neurologist believed in the same procedure.

On the first Saturday of July, 1909, I operated on a young woman who, three years earlier, had been hospitalized elsewhere with a cerebellar cyst. The surgeon had done what I should have done in that instance. He had emptied the cystic fluid. There was nothing unusual about the history of the case, after that. The patient made a fairly satisfactory recovery. That is what one might expect. Customarily, a gratifying convalescence promptly ensued. In the course of a year—possibly up to two years—you would begin to find the same old symptoms showing up again; early morning headaches, nausea, faulty vision, and an ataxic gait.

This erratic and violent nausea, by the way, frequently misled medical men, formerly, who were disposed to look for the trouble in the gastro-intestinal tract. But I suppose you know that.

On the occasion to which I am referring, my patient had all the stock symptoms that had been exhibited immediately prior to her previous operation. I did the only thing that was indicated; drained the cavity; and would have stopped with that.

But I was having a few peculiar symptoms that day, myself. I'm afraid I can't describe this sensation very well, but I felt something that might almost be defined as prescience. I don't mean prescience in relation to a divining of future events, but something like prescience in respect to a sensitivity a little beyond one's reach. Am I making myself clear, at all? Well—it was as if the nerves in my fingers extended to the end of the probe; as if the probe were an integral part of my hand, alert as the antennae of a bee.

Of course, if you want to think that one acquires this faculty by constant exercise, backed by the utmost concentration, you are taking a very commonsense view of the matter. You have a good deal of testimony on your side. Blind persons, who read Braille, offer an excellent example of what diligent training will do to make a fingertip cognitive. I hope you will not object to this word cognitive. The intelligent blind man will tell you that he can read Braille with the tip of his right index finger, almost as rapidly as you can read a newspaper by sight. If he uses the tip of the second finger of his right hand, he has to spell the words—letter by letter. If he runs the tip of his little finger over the raised letters, he can't read Braille any better than you can. It might—by accommodation—be said that this blind man's little finger, in respect to literacy, is still an infant. His second finger, in respect to literacy, is five years old. His index finger is adult. Does that help any to illustrate what I am trying to say about this "cognitive" quality that came into my hand? I believe that I could read, with the tip of my probe, where the tumour nodule was located!

Let me repeat—if you want to think this had come about through practice, all very well; but the fact is that I had never been so acutely conscious of that faculty before, or so confident that I could exercise it with any hope of success. So—I went after that nodule. Hunting for a needle in a haystack, compared to this quest, is merely child's play.

I was very fortunate, that day. After the removal of the tumour, my patient's recovery was rapid and decisive. She regained her health and there has been no recurrence of her trouble. Since then, I have approached these cases with a great deal of confidence. They are still serious enough, but we have cut down our operative mortality from fourteen per cent to four, which is a nice gain.

There are a few other men, in my specialty, who have had much the same success. How they came by their faculty of prescience (if you can endure that not very adequate word in this connection), I do not know. But I know how I came by mine. And I'm not ashamed to admit it, no matter how crazy it sounds.

I performed that epochal operation on a Saturday afternoon in July. On the Tuesday before, I spent six hours with Tony Bontempini, shopping for a kitchen range, assorted pots and pans, stone dishes and steel cutlery, so that he could open up a little restaurant. There is no doubt in my mind but I found there were nerves in my probe, in my lancet, in my scalpel, because I made something important of Tony.

* * * * *

Tony Bontempini had been a patient of mine. A railroad surgeon had brought him in, one afternoon in April, with about the sorriest-looking head I ever saw, which is saying quite a bit. The railroad doctor hadn't the slightest notion that Tony would survive any attempted repairs, and neither had I. It was one of those cases that make a cold shudder run down your spine, no matter how accustomed you may be to compound fractures. Nancy lost her lunch.

I asked the doctor why he had gone to the bother to bring this man away out to Brightwood, and he said he wanted Tony to die in some institution, where, it might be conjectured, everything had been done for him. The doctor didn't even wait to consult; said we could 'phone him when it was all over, and he would attend to the rest of the job.

In other words, Tony Bontempini was a pretty sick man. I wouldn't have bet ten cents on him.

Before leaving the hospital, the railroad doctor—a very good fellow, but quite inured to the sight of bad accidents—remarked that it was rather a pity, for the affair was no fault of Tony's. Tony hadn't been careless. There was an old chap in the section-gang who was very hard of hearing. Tony saw him about to be mowed down by a shunted freight-car; had grabbed him to drag him to safety; and was himself struck a crushing blow by the protruding end of a coupling-rod.

When the doctor was gone, I went up to have another peep at Tony. He was breathing stertorously, but with fairly steady rhythm. Watson drifted in, and after watching for a while, remarked that Tony must have some good stuff packed away. At nine, Tony was still pumping along at the old stand.

"He seems to be practically indestructible," I said to Tim. "I'm going to get in there and see if anything can be done."

I have seen people die, who might have been saved if they had been a little bit sicker. So long as there is a ray of hope, a surgeon is likely to be prudent; sometimes too prudent. If the patient is going to die, anyhow, and it doesn't matter what you do to him, you are likely to be audacious. Once in a while that audacity will do the trick. I've seen it happen. It happened to Tony. He must have had the constitution of a horse, or he couldn't possibly have survived what we had to do to him. Tim muttered, "I've never seen this much of the inside of a head since I studied Anatomy."

Little by little, Tony came plodding back from wherever he'd been, and I wondered whether we had really done him a service. All he was good for was a pick-and-shovel job. It was obvious that he could never do anything like that again. And he seemed to realize that the outlook was most unpromising. You couldn't get a rise out of him. He was glum, torpid, incommunicative. I think he understood English much better than he pretended; responding to questions concerning his appetite, his discomforts, his physical wants, but becoming dumb as a moron if you tried to interest him in anything that might distract his mind and lift his depression.

The railroad doctor began to call up, with increasing frequency, to learn how Tony was getting along and when he might be discharged. I do not think that the doctor was positively annoyed by Tony's recovery, but it would have been a much less complicated situation if Tony had confirmed the early forecast.

Every afternoon, the nurse would wheel Tony up to the solarium where he sat staring at the sunshine, taking no stock of his fellow convalescents, and pretending not to understand them when they tried to be pleasant. Finally I got an order to discharge Tony as soon as he was able to be released. I couldn't keep him any longer. I went to his room and told him; expressed my hope that he would find something to do. The railroad was going to arrange some sort of compensation, no doubt. They were always quite decent about such things, I had found. But Tony didn't want to be kept in idleness. The prospect of a pension was merely another cross to bear.

After a protracted silence, he made a weary, despairing little gesture with his bony hand, and said, in a dull monotone, "Eet ees no good, Doc. You are a dam fine feller. Fix Tony's head. But Tony ees no good—no more—no good."

"Perhaps there is something else you can do, Tony," I said, not very hopefully. "You mustn't work with a shovel, any more, and you mustn't work in the hot sun. But there are indoor jobs. Is there anything you know how to do?"

"I cook—mebbe. Aw—not so good," he shrugged, self-deprecatingly, "—just—what you call plain cook. But—nobody want poor, seeck wop for cook."

I grabbed at this straw as we were going down for the last time.

"Cook!" I exclaimed, happily. "Now we've got something."

"Aw—no, Doc," protested Tony. "Mebbe—in soma poor leetle dump—by myself—but not to work all day."

I had an inspiration.

"Tony," I said, brightly, "over in Ann Arbor there is a big college. You know what I mean?"

Tony nodded, comprehendingly, and muttered "Footaball," which made me grin a little, so accurately had he hit the thing smack on the button.

"Many hungry boys," I went on. "Eat all day; eat all night; eat anything, everything; eat on stools, eat standing up; eat out-of-doors—in the rain—in the snow—" Could I believe my eyes? Tony was pulling a reluctant grin. It was the first one he had ever put on in my society. I continued, with enthusiasm. "Good place for little restaurant. I want you to go there and start one. I am going with you! We are going to-morrow! I shall set you up in business. It won't cost very much. We will find a little room somewhere and buy you a skillet."

Tony grinned, and rubbed his jaw hard with the palm of his hand, like an embarrassed child. Then he rubbed both fists in his eyes; and, after a good deal of swallowing, muttered that I was a damn fine feller. I couldn't take any more of that, at the moment, so I went away.

Next day, I went head over heels into an adventure that I knew nothing about; but Tony seemed to know what we wanted. You wouldn't have recognized him for the same fellow, as we drove to Ann Arbor; chattered like a magpie; understood everything I said to him—all but my earnest request that he must never, never tell.

He couldn't get this through his head, but he consented. He warmed genially to my suggestion that if—sometime—some cold night, maybe—a hungry chap came in, looking pretty hollow, perhaps it would be well to feed him—and forget the loss. I wasn't quite sure how Tony would feel about that proposal, but he nodded, emphatically, and said, "Alia right, Doc. Tony will turn no one away hungry."

He proved to be a good bargainer. I was doubtful of his wisdom when he selected his location. It was a long-abandoned, shabby storeroom, about a block from the railroad station.

"You won't be able to catch a very profitable class of trade down here, Tony," I protested. "This is off the beat. The students won't come into a place like this—so close to the racket and dirt of the railroad."

Tony grinned, superiorly.

"College fellers," he declared, "same as any other yawng fellers. Lika de railroad, lika de noise, lika de dirt. Homeseeck—come down to seea de railroad. Tony feed 'em. Gooda place."

I gave in, and we rented the storeroom from an old codger who let us have it at our own figures and almost kissed us when we made an advance payment. Then we bought the range, and the rest of the stuff. I took Tony to the bank I knew best and introduced him, placing some money at his disposal.

"Gooda-bye, Doc," said Tony, when I was ready to go. "I paya you back—soma day."

"I don't want it back. I have other plans for that money. Do you understand, Tony?"

"Hella, no!" said Tony, scratching his head, and regarding me anxiously.

"No matter," I called after him. "Good-bye, Tony!"

"Gooda-bye, Doc," he said, waving his hat.

That was Tuesday.

On Saturday I did the first of that long string of gliomas with which I have had such gratifying success. Maybe these two matters have no relation. Maybe they occurred coincidentally. My own opinion is that my investment in Tony Bontempini made me aware of what I had in my cognitive hand. Sometimes my friendliest colleagues have pleasantly remarked that I am "a good guesser." But I am not a guesser. I wouldn't say this anywhere else than in a private journal that will not be read while I am living: I have what might be called a prescient hand.

And I know how I got it!

* * * * *

It was pleasant to hobnob with Clark Russell again. We were classmates in the Medical School. I always considered him a brighter and more responsive student than myself, and admired him greatly. We meet frequently. He was very fortunate in marriage. Clara Russell has an excellent mind, shrewd wit, and an amazing capacity for developing lasting friendships. Whenever I go to Chicago on a professional errand, if I have an hour or two to spare, I see the Russells. Sometimes I go out to their home. If the time is short, we meet down-town for dinner.

I arrived in Chicago Saturday morning. We went into consultation over Russell's glioma at nine. I said, "I can't see why you called me in. You knew what it was." And Russell replied, amusingly, like a small boy caught in the jam-pot, "I thought perhaps you'd like to take it out." So—I operated, though it isn't going to do very much good, for the growth was a glioblastoma multiforme, which will presently reinstate itself, and fully a third of them are malignant. Our patient was a woman of fifty. She will be free of her bad headaches for a year or two. It's worth an operation. One of these days, she will die. So will Russell and I. And you. But, in the meantime, we have a right to be relieved of our aches and pains, if we can find a way. I think this sort of surgery is justified, even if it doesn't hold out much promise of permanent recovery. What is permanent recovery? How permanent do you think you are?

I dined that night with the Russells: and, because I had planned to take a ten o'clock train for home, we had our dinner at the Blackstone. We talked about the war. Russell is sure we are going to be in it presently, and I suppose he is right. At all events, we had no debate on the matter. I aired my recent reflections on the deplorable lack of steadying agencies at a time when the public needed reliances in which the people might place their trust. I was pretty stern about the newspapers, and I had some unflattering things to say about the churches.

Clara conceded my points, in the main, but wanted to call my attention to at least one church—the one she attends— where this matter is receiving proper attention. I inquired about it, and Clara said it was Trinity Cathedral. Then she went on to quote generously from some of the recent remarks of the preacher there. Dean Harcourt. I had occasionally seen his name in the papers.

As I have said, I have a great deal of respect for Clara Russell's intelligence. Anything that she thinks is sound is likely to be worth consideration. I listened attentively to what she had to say. She believes that if the people at large had access to Harcourt's august philosophy it would brace them up.

"The intellectuals, you mean," I remarked.

"Not exclusively," she said. "That is the triumphant thing about Dean Harcourt's sermons. They appeal to the intellectuals, but are understood by people who have never learned how to think straight. They learn it there. I wish you could hear him."

The Russells went home at nine-thirty. I went up to pack my tackle, expecting to go to my train, only a ten minutes' taxi-drive. Then I decided, impulsively and to my own surprise, that I would stay over and hear this man Harcourt in the morning. For I needed some bucking up myself.

* * * * *

Nancy Ashford, whom I had not seen since my return from Chicago, has just been in to tell me I have been working long enough and should go home to bed. This is good advice, and I shall defer a report of my visit to Trinity Cathedral until my next leisure hour. All I care to say about it now is that I was strangely moved by that event and I believe that if this man Harcourt could be harnessed up somehow to a wide-spread channel of communication he could do a great deal for the public.

I asked Nancy if anything interesting had happened, and she said, "Your attractive young friend, Natalie Randolph, was here again this afternoon."

"Came for Tim, likely," I remarked, with satisfaction. "That affair gives promise. It will be good for both of them. I hope they make a go of it. Couple of thoroughbreds."

"It isn't Tim," said Nancy. "It's Leslie Sherman."

AT HOME
June twenty-fifth, 1915, 11 p.m.

JOYCE is at home again for her summer vacation. I think twelve years must be a difficult age for a girl. She isn't a mere child, and has a long way to go before she is a young woman. I am not quite sure how we are going to amuse her here.

She says she doesn't want to study during vacation, and one cannot blame her for that. She has no very serious interest in the piano or any other music. Having been out of town for so many months, she seems to have lost connection with her former friends here. I asked her if she would like to invite a couple of her school companions as house guests for a while, but she thinks they are all spending their holidays with their families; many of them at the seashore. Joyce wonders why we can't go to the seashore, too; but it is quite impossible for me to get away now. I suggested a girls' camp, but she doesn't like the discipline; admits that she is too lazy to keep up with the various activities.

I am afraid I have not done a very good job in bringing up this child. Joyce has fleeting seizures of demonstrative affection for me, interspersed with longer periods of detachment. She is restless, and I cannot contrive anything to occupy her mind. Everything will be all right when she returns to school in September. She has a good many of the erraticisms of her Grandfather Cummings; not all of them, I devoutly hope.

* * * * *

In my last entry in this journal I referred to the interesting experience I had, a few days ago, at Trinity Cathedral in Chicago. I was much impressed by some remarks made by the preacher. Dean Harcourt. I judge him to be a little east of fifty, though his manner is more venerable, due, no doubt, to the fact that he is a victim of infantile paralysis, seriously crippled, and bearing the deep criss-cross lines about his eyes which certify to the pain he has endured. There is tracery around the mouth, too, that tells its own story; though there isn't the slightest indication of self-pity, rebellion, or despair. Quite to the contrary, it is a reposeful face. I never saw a man whose outward bearing seemed so well deserving of the word "spiritual." He inspires confidence. You have a feeling that nothing could shatter him or make him afraid or quench his inner glow.

I tried to analyse the whole event, that Sunday morning. I was deeply moved, yet curious to discover the predominant factors which had stirred me; whether the organ, the choir, the architecture, the solemn reverence of the place, the sermon, or the man himself. I suppose it was the perfect harmony and complete integration of all these persons and properties.

In the very first place, you had a sense of the solidarity and sureness and effortless self-confidence of the building itself. It was massive and it was sincere. The walls not only looked like stone: they were stone. I thought a little about this as I approached. Some of our churches are built of concrete blocks, in imitation of stone. And some of our wooden steeples, fussy with jigsaw ornamentation, are painted gray to resemble stone. I had never considered this matter, but it occurs to me now that a church should never be an imitation of something. If the people cannot afford to build their church of stone, let it be made of wood; but, in that case, let the wood be wood.

This may seem to be cavilling over a very small matter. The more that I think about it, the more important it grows. If the church wants to have a steadying effect upon the people, it must begin the task by being absolutely honest. The individual may not pause to ask himself why it is that the church he attends does not compose his spirit, but I think it must have a disquieting effect on him if the building itself is an architectural fraud. If he can't believe in the integrity of the structure, how is he going to believe in the soundness and sincerity of the institution?

I hope I am not making too much of this, but I think the feeling of repose, reliance; the feeling that I was, for a little while, in the custody of something substantial, enduring, and impeccably honest, had a lot to do with my mood, that day. Everything was genuine. The candles on the altar were candles; they were not electric lamps fashioned to resemble candles: they were candles.

There was something about that stately music that had the essence of permanence. It was elemental stuff.

In the village church that we attended, when I was a youngster, the minister—a kind, well-meaning man, with an obsequious smile but no dignity either of speech or bearing—would open the service with a short prayer in which Deity was verbally patted on the shoulder after the manner of a genial greeting between a couple of lodge brothers, and then the good man would announce a song, such as—"Only an Armour-bearer, Proudly I Stand." Or—"Let the Lower Lights be Burning." The announcement of the song was always accompanied by an informal—sometimes jocular—admonition urging the congregation, whom he habitually addressed as "folks," to join heartily in the singing. Often he would add, playfully, "If you can't keep on the tune, try to make a joyful noise."

I realize that this may be an exceptional case of irreverence; or perhaps "gaucherie" might be a less severe and more accurate designation. But from what I can learn about the prevailing habits of the majority of our churches in this country, I strongly suspect that the difference between that village church procedure and the current customs of our churches is a difference of manner rather than mood. The idea seems to be that the church is a social club; and, as such, should avoid anything like formality. Let us all loudly sing now, folks, and make whoopee for the Lord.

As I sat there in Trinity Cathedral, waiting for the service to begin, I felt conscious of an other-worldly environment. This was not a club. An usher had quietly shown me to a seat. He had not pawed me. Nor had his manner indicated that I was doing Trinity Cathedral a very good turn by honouring it with my presence. I gathered that Trinity Cathedral hadn't been fretting about the possibility of my non-attendance. The place was very quiet. Everybody faced the thing alone.

Presently the organ began. One couldn't see the organist at work, and one couldn't see the organ. It gave the swelling music a chance. The vested choir came down the broad, stone-flagged aisle. The people stood. The choir filed slowly into the chancel, singing. Two young men in vestments supported on either side the tall, white-haired, crippled man, who came into the chancel from an adjacent door. There were prayers, chants, readings from the Bible, stately hymns. I confess I was almost suffocated with emotion when the august hymn began—"O God Our Help in Ages Past; Our Hope for Years to Come." I had been so dreadfully upset; so beaten down with worries; so riddled with anxieties—in my professional work—and anxieties over the stunning deeds of violence abroad. My eyes burned and flooded while that confident hymn confessed its faith in the everlastingness of the Divine Guidance. "A thousand ages in Thy sight are like an evening gone." Here was permanence for you. "Time like an ever-rolling stream." The hot tears rolled down my cheeks. It was the first time my neural tension had been relieved for a long, long time.

* * * * *

When I began to write this, I had it in mind only to record a few of the things that Dean Harcourt said, that morning; but it occurred to me that you might be a little more impressed by them if you realized the mood I was in when I heard them. As I have said, I was deeply moved, that day. I suppose almost anything the man might have said would have found me wistfully receptive.

I don't think there had been a sermon topic announced, and I am not sure that the Dean began by stating his theme, but what he talked about was the insured life. It was a tribute to our spirit of co-operation, he thought, that we had been able to insure so many of our interests. Once upon a time, if a man's house burned down or his horses were stolen, he took his loss alone. We had now reached the point in our socialization where we were bearing one another's burdens.

The Dean digressed a little here to remind us of the great progress we had been making in this field. Only a little while ago, as Time is counted in terms of epochs, the social order was hardly aware of itself as an integer. The handful of kind-hearted men and women in a community did what they could to aid their neighbours and kindred in distress, but the kindness was sporadic. There was no enduring momentum to it.

"May one suggest to the dismayed," said the Dean, "that instead of deploring the long way we must yet go until we have reached an era of universal amity, we rejoice over the immeasurably longer way we have come from an era of universal suspicion, distrust, and fear. This is not a single day's march—from the jungle to the city of light—but we are much closer to the light than we are to the jungle. We are not there yet, but we know which way we are headed. There have been many detainments, many detours. It has not been—and may not be—a straight and steady course toward the Golden Age, but the general direction is forward; the general movement is upward. We cannot afford to be patient, if patience—in our opinion—means apathy; but we can well afford to be patient, if patience means poise. We are not indignant with our ancestors because they moved no faster, nor should we be too critical of ourselves if, in our time, we have days of plodding with leaden feet."

All things considered, thought the Dean, we had not done so badly. One of the evidences of our increasing willingness to befriend one another was manifest by the widespread interest in insurance. If a man's house burns down, the community builds another.

"It will not build him another unless he has previously given evidence that he, himself, would help restore another man's house; but if he has declared his willingness to assist in defraying the cost of another's accident or illness or death or the care of his helpless survivors, he can expect that the age he lives in will do for him whatever he stands ready to do for others. There are many imperfections and inequities in our social order which need correction, but our present system warrants our optimism. We have a right to be hopeful—and hope, I think, is the first requisite of courage."

Perhaps these words that I am trying to quote, and I believe I am recording at least the substance of them, may sound trite and obvious; but, in the solemn stillness of that place, they had a peculiar steadying quality. The world—in spite of its problems—wasn't galloping a tam-o'-shanter to the devil. The world was operating on a long-term schedule. Its defects were many, but they were not as many as they were a hundred years ago. We were too close to this movement to observe its progress. Did William the Conqueror come forth from his tomb, and survey the world, he would observe the course and distance we had come. Sometimes it is difficult for us to note the world's advancement—but William could see it, if he came back.

So much, then, for progress, of which insurance was a good sign. It had come to pass that we could insure almost anything; insure an outdoor pageant against the loss occasioned by rain; the pianist could insure his hands and the dancer her feet.

But there were still some possible losses which a man must bear alone; some risks he would have to carry without aid.

Here the Dean remarked that it would be indeed a great comfort if one could insure one's memories so that they would ever bless him, and never burn.

"You can insure your memories," said the Dean, "but you will have to do it by yourself. And they are very real property, too. Some of them are assets; some of them are liabilities. Be careful what kind of memories you store up to live on in a rainy day."

Let me repeat: perhaps this sounds commonplace, apart from its setting. But everything was so strangely hushed. It seemed as if you were getting a direct message from Headquarters!

"Be spiritually thrifty!" advised Dean Harcourt. "Put aside some memories that will nourish you in your declining years. Be mindful not to stock memories that will keep you awake nights. It will be too bad—too bad—if, every time there is a little cessation of the noise and confusion, you hear the sound of people sobbing—people who loved you. It will be very good if, when the noise about you subsides a little, you can remember the words and tones of gratitude—gratitude of people who lived more abundantly—because of *you.*"

This whole affair made a profound impression on me. I do not think that I shall live long enough to forget it. I hope my reference to it may be of benefit to you.

I went out of the Cathedral feeling that I had been fitted with a new balance-wheel. I wish everybody had access to such an inspiration in these troubled times.

* * * * *

I am driving up to my "estate" on Lake Saginack to-morrow. The idea of pitching a tent up there is, I feel, absurdly impractical. But perhaps I may want to build a little cottage there. It is not so very far away. I might have a good deal of satisfaction in a quiet place like that. I am taking Joyce along, but I fear she will not find it very entertaining. I do wish I could think of something that might give pleasure to this restless child.

BRIGHTWOOD HOSPITAL
December fourth, 1915, 9 p.m.

HENRY FORD'S peace ship sailed this afternoon from Hoboken and the papers are amused. Perhaps they cannot be blamed, for this excursion does seem a bit fantastic.

But it isn't much harder to believe that a dozen unauthorized pacifiers could hope that they might stop the war than that such a war could have been precipitated. The whole thing is an incredible nightmare!

Of course the main point of weakness in this well-meant adventure is the conspicuous absence of anyone officially empowered to represent the United States government. Assuming that this party of altruistic cruisers voices the thoughts and hopes of many millions of American citizens—and I think it does—it has no recognized standing. Governments—not private citizens—make wars. And when wars come to an end, the governments end them.

Ford's project is put on by laymen. It is very doubtful whether the governments of the countries involved will pay the slightest heed to it; except, perhaps, to sneer at it. But it is by no means an ignoble gesture, however futile. I was glad to see that none of the spoofing paragraphers has insinuated that Henry might be doing this to show off; for that wouldn't have been true. Henry does not hanker for front page publicity. He is not a vain man. Nobody can accuse him of exhibitionism. He has gone into this thing sincerely.

And in spite of all the editorial snickers, I'll bet there are a lot of people, throughout this country, who are earnestly hoping, perhaps expecting, that something may come of this expedition.

I am mentioning this event here because it is likely that when these words are deciphered the Great War will have passed into ghastly history, and I want you to realize the mental condition of our people in these closing days of 1915. If a man as bright and cold as Henry Ford will charter a ship, at the instigation of a not very thoroughly credentialled Hungarian woman, and sail for Europe with a little group of newspaper men and parsons, intending to stop the war "and get the men out of the trenches by Christmas," you can get a general idea of the dishevelled state of mind in which the less bright and more volatile find themselves. We've got to the point where we think that nothing short of a miracle can save civilization. And if the Ford expedition accomplishes anything, the feat will prove that our surmise has been correct.

* * * * *

Dorothy Wickes has sold two more pictures for excellent prices. She has stopped working in the store; has moved her family to better quarters.

Somehow I had gathered that her older brother Harry was not passionate on the subject of work. But a chance remark of Dorothy's, a few months ago, gave me a better impression of the chap, and I exercised myself a little to find out what he thought he could do.

Harry said he believed he might be useful in a shop handling art supplies. I liked this. It has been my observation that when some member of a family exhibits a special talent, the brothers and sisters are likely to be jealous. Their favourite method of showing how they feel about it is to manifest a cool indifference—if not positive contempt—toward everything related to the fortunate one's art or trade.

Harry Wickes not only didn't have a trace of this sulkiness in him: he was exultant over the honour that had come to the family; proud of his sister and intensely interested in what she was doing. He had no artistic talent himself, but it delighted him that Dorothy had it. His enthusiasm and glad surprise must have meant a very great deal to her in those days when she was trying so hard to express herself. Now he wanted a job selling drawing-boards, pencils, easels, paints, canvas, and brushes, because they were the implements of Dorothy's success.

When I learned this, I made an effort to find him a place in an art shop. He has done very nicely. I think there is a pleasant future for him in this trade. I see him frequently.

More and more I am believing in what someone has styled "the contagion of character." And I make a deliberate endeavour to expose myself, whenever possible, to the influence of people who possess some peculiar nobility.

I venture to call your attention to the importance of this. Of course, it would be the very supremacy of selfishness if one were to pick one's friends on a basis of what they had to give forth. There are plenty of people, in need of our attention, who have very little with which to repay us. But I feel that we are well within our rights if we cultivate the acquaintance of persons whom we have discovered to be in possession of specialized talents in the field of character-building. One such acquaintance may serve as a stimulant to us; another as a sedative. One man laughs his fears and frets away and another growls at them. It is fortunate for us if we can recognize the exact effect that other people have on us. Then we know when to seek or avoid them.

These persons may or may not be of our own social stratum. I find that I get a good deal of solid satisfaction from people who seem to live narrowly restricted lives. Some of them are like beavers. They don't know anything but how to build dams; and, if their dams are torn down, they begin immediately to build again. So—if you find you are no good at building dams, or get too easily upset when the dams you have built are torn away, you can learn much by observing the beavers; provided, of course, that you do not frighten them away.

There is, for example, an orderly at Brightwood named Blake. He has a fourteen-year-old daughter at home with the mental age of four. He is quite devoted to her and insists that she is going to be all right. I listen to him, with sincere interest, whenever he wants to talk about Dolly, whose name, I think, is singularly appropriate. No amount of persuasion has succeeded in convincing him that he should place Dolly in a school for backward children. He thinks she is better off at home, and—in the circumstances—I agree with him. It may come to pass, some years from now, that the child will be too grave a problem for Mert Blake and his wife to handle; but there is plenty of time to decide on that matter. For the present, the child may as well stay where she is.

Mert tells me that Dolly is getting on nicely with her spelling; especially with the names of animals that are not too difficult. She spelled "mouse," the other day.

Now I don't want you to leap to the conclusion that Mert Blake is a soft-headed sap with a mentality not much more advanced than Dolly's. Down inside himself, Mert knows that Dolly hasn't really grown an inch or gained a pound mentally since she was a mere tot, and he knows as well as I do that she is never going to know any more than she knows now. There is a constant ache in Mert's mind that never eases. It is aching when he wakes up in the morning, and it is still aching when he goes to sleep at night. He sees the neighbours' budding young girls, ready for high school.

And Mert—who is no fool—knows that I know all about Dolly; for I have gone through her with a lantern; and, if there was anything to be done for her, Mert knows that I should have had a go at it.

And—all the time that her is chattering away, with an optimistic smile, about Dolly's fine progress—and all the time that I am punctuating his lively reports with little exclamations of pleased surprise—Mert knows that we are both playing relief parts in a heart-breaking tragedy. I like Mert because he has the stuff in him that enables him to do that. Not everyone has an authentic talent for it. I wouldn't exchange a half hour's chat with Mert Blake for a dozen dinner engagements with as many brilliant intellectuals.

I have thought that this might be worth mentioning to you. It has become my practice to nourish my own character by exposing it to the influence of specially endowed personalities who, by sublimating their griefs or by inventing ingenious compensatory devices, have—unwittingly, perhaps—made themselves very important.

It's quite easy to miss chances to improve oneself in this way. I might have skipped the blessing of Mert Blake's friendship if it had not been for Tim Watson's remarks to me on the subject of caste in a hospital. Once upon a time, I should have considered it the wrong thing to do—from a standpoint of good discipline—to encourage Mert to come into my office and sit down and talk about Dolly. I have happily graduated from all such nonsense. And I strongly recommend to you the policy of establishing close and comradely connections with people who have something of spiritual fineness in them, regardless of their social rating. Don't be misled by the fact that the man may use very faulty diction, and have uncouth manners, and be in need of a thousand dollars' worth of dental attention. If he is a spiritual athlete (Can you bear this phrase?), you can afford to watch him do his tricks.

Most people of our sort pick their friends on a sheer basis of propinquity, congeniality, and social equality. If you want to build character, you must not be content to know only persons who are no stronger than yourself.

Young Wickes' range of interests is not very wide. You couldn't load what Harry doesn't know about almost everything into the largest moving-van on the road; but he has got something in him that I should like to have more of.

I do not believe that I am, by nature or habit, a jealous or envious person. That is: I do not think that whatever jealousy or envy I may have tucked away in me is virulent enough to show through in my bearing and conversation. But—not to be envious is, after all, a negative virtue. Wickes has moved over into the positive zone, in respect to this matter.

He asked me, point-blank, one Saturday night when we were at dinner together downtown, why I "bothered" with him. And I told him, with equal candour, that he had been given a clean-cut talent for magnanimity (which I had to define for him), and that it built me up, quite a bit, to be in his company. He blinked a little, but got the idea. I daresay he later examined this gift of his, in his mirror, and decided to give it a little more air and light.

Next time I met Dorothy, she said, "What have you done to Harry?"

"Have I done something to Harry?" I countered.

"You know you have." Her tone was intimate. We were the same age now. She searched my eyes from under long lashes. "Harry is a precious darling—and you are making him more precious, every day."

"That's nice," I replied. "You ought to know. When a fellow's sister thinks he is a precious darling "

"I'd like to swap a few stories with you," broke in Dorothy. "I don't see why we can't. If you'll tell me what you've been doing to Harry, I'll tell you what I did for—"

"Stop!" I pointed my finger directly into her pretty face, and grew very stern. "*Do you want to spoil it?*"

* * * * *

Randolph tells me that Natalie and Leslie Sherman are engaged. I wonder if Leslie knew that Tim was interested there. I hope he did not.

If Tim has been hurt, you wouldn't know it by his manner. But he always did have himself well in hand. You could skin him alive without getting an outcry. I like this about him, though I think that in order to achieve such distinction a man has to sacrifice a lot of emotional sensitivity which is really imperative to normal living. I can't help admiring stoicism in other people, but I think the overhead charges on its maintenance come pretty high. You bottle up too many urgent wishes and you can't be sure whether the chemical reaction is going to make a saint or a sourpuss.

Whenever a person espouses a martyrdom, he needs to be mighty careful about the mood in which he goes to the stake. I have known a lot of fried prigs.

BRIGHTWOOD HOSPITAL
June seventeenth, 1916, 10.30 p.m.

NATALIE and Leslie Sherman were married this evening at the Randolph home. There were only about twenty guests, but the affair did not lack distinction, the house beautifully decorated and the excellent dinner served expertly by the best caterers in town. Natalie, who grows more winsome every day, was dazzling in white satin and orange blossoms. She had wanted a church wedding, but economy is in the air just now and such pageants are not popular.

But while this restriction may have been slightly disappointing to Natalie, I daresay Leslie was not annoyed by the fact that he assumes his new obligations at a time when frugality is fashionable; for, so far as I am aware, he has no resources beyond his small income at Brightwood.

Tim Watson was Leslie's best man. His athletic figure showed up to great advantage in his evening clothes. I observed that the bridesmaids were pleasantly impressed. Whether Tim consented to stand up with Leslie because (a) he really doesn't care, any more; or, (b) wanted to prove there was no constraint between him and his long-time chum; or, (c) thought he would be healthier if he cauterized his wounds—nobody is going to know. Tim keeps his own counsel. Perhaps he is part Indian.

On several occasions in the past few months I have been on the point of writing something in this book, but most of the things I might have recorded will be accessible to you elsewhere.

What part we intend to take in the European war has been the one burning question that monopolizes all conversation. The controversy between the preparedness advocates and the peace-at-any-pricers grows more acrimonious; or, rather, the onslaughts of the militant group against the pacifists are becoming more savage. The latter are on the defensive; and, I think, on the decline.

Anyone who would have risked saying, a year ago, in the conservative atmosphere of St. Paul's Cathedral, that "a pacifist is an anarchist," might have found himself criticized; but it was said there, a month ago, and it does not appear that the statement has been challenged. Thus far have we moved toward a warlike mind.

Many solidly substantial men, whose normal attitude toward debatable questions has testified to their sound judgment and sportsmanly tolerance, have lately given themselves to expressions of opinions so hot that they sizzle and sputter. A man can hardly believe his ears. Conservative old codgers, some of whom have never been notorious for any other extravagance, are now quoted as making wild remarks utterly foreign to their training and temperament.

There is manifest, on every hand, a pious lip-service to patriotism. The theatre orchestra always plays the National Anthem now, with unprecedented vigour; standing in a row, facing the audience, and blowing itself pop-eyed and purple, perhaps to give assurance of its own loyalty, for the names and personal architecture of many of our professional musicians are unmistakably Teutonic.

With the unleashing of the brasses and tympani, everyone bounds to his feet and assumes what feels like a military posture; stiff, severe, statuesque. Out of the tail of our patriotic eye, we invoice our neighbour's behaviour in regard to this solemn rite; and should he be detained by so little as a split second in displaying a zeal that matches ours— perhaps while retrieving his hat from under the seat—we furtively analyse his physiognomy to see if he is something other than pure Nordic.

We have also learned to salute the flag more ceremoniously. which is doubtless good for us. We were always a bit too casual toward the sacred emblems of our patriotism. But we have been well cured of that apathy. We now not only pay our own devout tribute to the Stars and Stripes with deep fervour; we also scrutinize the other fellow pretty carefully to make sure that his obeisance has the sanctioned form and substance.

Any man with a German name is out of luck. The fact may be that Fred Schroeder (unfortunately nicknamed Fritz) is of the fourth generation of his family since its migration to this country, and it may be that his grandfather's brave old bones rest in the National Cemetery at Gettysburg: but nobody is going to listen to Fritz while he explains that America is his native land. Fritz is regarded with suspicion. If—alarmed over his unhappy situation—he seeks to mend matters by spelling his name "Shrader," we conclude that he did have something to be frightened about, and a self-deputized committee of super-patriots visits his meat shop to challenge his loyalty. Children on the school playground boo and catcall at his hapless little Gretchen.

It has occurred to me that a few of these minor tragedies of the war might well be mentioned here. As for the more epochal events, you will learn them from other sources. But perhaps history will not bother to reconstruct the atmosphere in which we are living now. Here we are, riddled by factional disputes, angry and distrustful; humiliating honest people with whom we never had a quarrel and for whom we had respect, all because of a war four thousand miles away.

If we can contrive to get ourselves into such a mental state as this—before taking up arms—I wonder what may happen to our skittish brains in the event we decide to toss ourselves into it.

* * * * *

The American is not a very good hater, perhaps for lack of time. To be a really competent hater, you have to give yourself to it with earnest diligence. You can't hate efficiently and get much else attended to, for you have very little nervous energy left over. A man will burn less carbon while sawing wood than while maintaining a steady, glowing hatred.

Our people have always been anxious to succeed in their business undertakings. To make money, acquire property, equip for a rainy day, and have something to bequeath to the children, has been of more importance to us than the relative superiorities of races and nations. We are all comparatively recent imports from ancient lands. Most of us rejoice that it is our happy lot to have escaped from worn-out soils and age-long feuds. If we could sell a man something, at a profit, we didn't care what language he spoke; nor did we inquire into his former loyalties and inherited antipathies. It was our boast that these things were so. It was our first point of national distinction—the ability of all these polyglot, polychrome people to live together in neighbourly fashion. We are now in the process of tossing this unique merit to the winds, and—whether or not there is to be war for us—we are going to regret this tragic blunder!

Now that it is popular to disparage our own citizens of German extraction, we have gone into it with a thoroughness that is no more cruel than ridiculous. We are calling sauerkraut "liberty cabbage." This, in my opinion, practically completes our recent struggle to achieve a finished asshood.

But no man, if he values his reputation at all, can afford to speak his mind on this matter. He mustn't laugh. Indeed— however absurd these things are—he doesn't want to laugh. It has passed the point of being ludicrous. It isn't funny any more.

* * * * *

The dispatches concerning the German army's inhuman atrocities continue to come, growing in volume and appalling details; mutilations, crucifixions, eyes gouged out, hands dismembered. Belgian refugees are coming over; most of them small children. It is said that some of these unfortunate little things are without hands, though it has been difficult to locate anyone who has, himself, seen these cases.

Many of our preparedness orators say that they have talked personally with people who had seen such mutilations, but I have not heard any man say that he saw such things with his own eyes.

Yet the dispatches, reporting such atrocities, come to us with what appears to be official sanction. While it is very difficult to believe that any nation in this modern world would resort to such frightfulness for the sake of terrorizing the enemy, it is absolutely inconceivable that the high officials of a nation would deliberately concoct and disseminate such stories about another nation unless there were properly attested facts to warrant it.

If Germany has actually committed these crimes, she will have to pay dearly for them. And if the other people have been maliciously lying about this, that too will have to be paid for. No cause can be worth very much that has to win its way by mutilating civilians and prisoners; nor can any cause be worth very much that has to win its way by a campaign of wilful defamation of a nation's character. If it may be assumed that these premises are sound, I think it is of great importance that we find out, pretty soon, whether the atrocity stories are true or false. If true the barbarians should be crushed, no matter what it costs to do it; if false, any further talk about our side as "a righteous and holy cause" is, of course, a lot of hypocritical nonsense; though it would ill become us to criticize anyone else for hypocrisy—much less nonsense—in our enfeebled mental condition.

My friend—if I were to hand these pages to a newspaper, to-night, I should unquestionably spend to-morrow at police headquarters, trying to give an account of myself. But I want to document my thoughts about war—as of this date—and put them away for safe-keeping. I have no notion what mood our nation will be in when you read these words. If the war is over, and the public's sanity has been approximately restored, you may not find my opinions on this matter differing very much from the prevailing thought of your time. If the war is not over—or another war is in sight—you will realize how imprudent it would be for me to express my feelings publicly. I am a very unhappy man. I have taken pride in my practice of living above fear. I have held that if a man is afraid of anything, his fear filters through everything he thinks and does. And now I think that I am afraid to stand up and say to my neighbours that I think war is a degrading thing, that war soils everything it touches, that no war can be truthfully considered "holy."

* * * * *

The American Medical Association has been in convention here since Friday. A couple of distinguished army surgeons have made speeches; but, in view of our theoretical neutrality, neither Surgeon General Rupert Blue nor Assistant Surgeon General Rucker adverted to the war, which I thought was in excellent taste and a commendable pattern of speech and behaviour.

Doctor Blue said that the physician's greatest enemies are ignorance and intemperance. I couldn't help wondering, while he spoke, whether—when he referred to intemperance—he wasn't thinking of intemperate talk as well as intemperate habits.

Doctor Charles Mayo made a statement that I find difficult to understand. He was tracing the progress of the race, particularly stressing the advancement in medicine and surgery. It was a very thoughtful address. The conclusions he arrived at, however, were a bit startling.

"The Slavs," he declared, "will be the coming nation of the earth."

Surely this is not the logical outcome of the scientific progress that had been laid before us in such a masterly array of facts. If the Slavs are to dominate a world that has been blest by scientific discovery and invention, one naturally gathers that these people have been and are in the vanguard of this evolution, and may be expected to rule as a reward for their superior contributions to our advancement. But I can't recall any outstanding service that the Slavs have performed in this field.

The doctor further went on to say that we ourselves are destined to be a commercial nation of the meanest type. I can't agree with this, either. Just because we have become temporarily upset mentally, and have been showing up at a disadvantage, it does not follow that we have permanently lost our souls. We have pounded ourselves pretty hard on the subject of our greed, our frantic grab-and-get ambitions; but I think it should be remembered that we have been quite soft-hearted toward other peoples in distress.

I think it was a generous act when we returned the indemnity to China that had been paid to reimburse us for our losses in their revolution, asking them to spend the money on scholarships for their boys. Whenever there has been a great catastrophe affecting the people of cities and nations thousands of miles away, we have subscribed huge sums for their relief, without any other motive than human kindness. I wonder if the Slavs are to take the lead in world philanthropy. If so, they should get themselves going in this direction. At present, they do not seem to know whether they are afoot or horseback.

As a cosmic prophet, I think that Doctor Mayo is one of the most brilliant surgeons in this country.

* * * * *

I had a few sketches drawn for a cottage on Lake Saginack, but the time is not propitious. I doubt if I would use it, even if it were built. Besides, it will be prudent to economize now. If we have to get into the war, it will be very costly.

HOTEL PONTCHARTRAIN, DETROIT
December second, 1917, 8.30 p.m.

I GAVE up housekeeping a week ago, drained the plumbing, locked the shutters, and moved to this hotel. It wasn't worth the bother to maintain my establishment, under existing conditions.

Joyce is at school in Philadelphia—or I hope she is, the management having reluctantly consented to let her remain, on probation, with the understanding that she is to be more obedient. I have had a merry time, these past few weeks, with this mischievous young lady who has a gift for getting into scrapes.

Nate Swihart—who for the past three years has been my man of all work—is at Camp Custer, marching twenty miles per day with full equipment which, he writes me, includes everything but the piano. Gladys, his wife and my cook, has been threatening to die of loneliness and worry, so I have packed her off to Owosso where she will live with her parents "for the duration."

My decision to retire from the irksome farce of keeping my house going was precipitated by the alarming coal shortage. I have suspected that a good deal of the country's noisy economies, in recent months, was part of the phenomena of our patriotism; but the resolve to save coal is certainly not an affectation. The fuel situation is so grave that unless it is relieved promptly the factories will have to shut down.

We are all on a war basis now, with everything regimented. Heatless Mondays, lightless Tuesdays, meatless Fridays. Save sugar, save butter, save flour, save coal, save peach-stones, save democracy. Posters everywhere, advising, challenging, prohibiting, threatening. It is a hell of a way to live, after one has gone one's own gait for more than two score years.

And yet, if one can endure this temporary sacrifice of personal liberty, without too much irritation, it has its commendable points. There is nothing that this country has needed more than discipline. We have had plenty of laws, but very spotty enforcement. The average good citizen has fallen into the habit of obeying such laws as he finds convenient. For the present, everybody walks the chalk. Unquestionably this gives us more respect for the government, and for ourselves too.

This generation of children has had a minimum of supervision, either at home where their parents are too busy or too pleasure-loving to oversee their conduct, or at school where the new psychology encourages Junior to express himself. It is the first unspanked generation in the history of the world. Now that military mores have the right of way, even the little children are readjusting their ideas to fit the time.

One would have thought that our soldiers, suddenly tugged out of their civilian freedom to be barked at by cocky young sergeants, might have resented such treatment; but they seem to have accepted it as good sports, and when hard put upon they sing, "We're in the army now." And so are all the rest of us in the army now—or what comes to the same thing. Little Junior eats his oats without grousing, having been sharply informed that he should be mighty thankful he has oats to eat, seeing what the Belgian children are living on. And Junior's erstwhile bridge-playing mother works all day at Red Cross Headquarters making bandages and other hospital necessities, while Junior's father is losing his excess fat as he gallops about selling Liberty bonds. The whole family is invigorated.

I find democracy a more comfortable form of government, but there is no denying the fact that this temporary autocracy has been beneficial to most of our people. The majority of us indulged ourselves too much. We have overheated our houses in winter. We have eaten too much meat and sugar and white bread. Moreover, we have lacked a unifying motive to stimulate our herd loyalty. Many people were too individualistic for their own good, striving for some manner of uniqueness which often resulted in mere silly posing.

You might be amazed at the difference all this has made in the public health. Fully a third of the rooms at Brightwood are unoccupied. My own business has not been affected, one way or the other, diseases of the brain not seeming to discriminate much between peace-time and war-time; but Pyle's days are not so crowded, nor Carter's, nor Jennings's.

Perhaps it has not been such a bad thing for us to have had a sniff of dictatorial, militarized government, after so long an experience of an easy- going democracy. Of course, the thing is a novelty now, amply justified by an emergency. We might fret under it if it were permanent. We might even fret under it now, if we feared it might become permanent.

And it might easily become permanent, I think. The federal government has discovered how simply and promptly it can get whatever it wants. The states have largely waived their accustomed rights to exercise their individual prerogatives, willing to conform to orders from The Top, for the sake of expediency. To-day, if the national government resolves upon some drastic action at ten o'clock, it publishes the decree at eleven, and by noon the thing is in full operation in high gear.

This naturally pleases the government, whose power is now concentrated, and it must be of immense gratification to be able to shout an order to a hundred million people and hear an immediate "Aye, aye, sir!" I surmise that the federal government will be very reluctant to hand this privilege back to the states, after the present emergency is over.

I do not pretend to know very much about the philosophy of history. I am not sure that anyone knows much about it, judging from the wide divergence of expert opinion on the subject. But I think it is generally agreed that democracy is not a hardy perennial. Even a temporary compromise of democracy endangers its life. It wouldn't surprise me if— when the war is ended—we never fully recover the liberties we have given up. Whether it would be a good thing to have a permanent concentration of more power in the national capital would depend, of course, upon the manner in which such power was exercised. If the leadership was wise and just, you might get a better government than was had under the old system. There is something to be said for a benevolent despotism. The trouble is to find your benevolent despot.

I should give a good deal to know how all this is coming out. Washington is packed and jammed with government employees. When the war is over, I wonder whether these extra thousands will be willing to go back to their homes and resume their former occupations.

* * * * *

Shortly after war was declared, I presented myself for service as a surgeon, and was promptly rejected—as I had anticipated—on account of the faulty heart. Owens, of the Medical Examining Board, kindly attempted to condole with me over my rejection, but I assured him that I was quite contented to remain in my hospital and do my accustomed work.

I could afford to be entirely honest in making this statement, for the question of a doctor's courage in enlisting for service was not at issue. The army doctor's personal risk is negligible. He is not a combatant. He is probably as safe in the camp hospital as he is at home.

Pyle registered as willing to go, but the board put him on the reserve list, on account of his age, and he will not be called. They have plenty of doctors.

Tim Watson was promptly accepted and is at Fort Sheridan where his duties are light and not very interesting. Tim has always been very ambitious, especially in developing his surgery. At present he is mainly occupied with administering cathartics and looking at lame feet. If he is sent abroad, it will be a different story; but, until now, he is doing nothing that couldn't be done as well by a trained nurse. When he wrote me this, I requested that he be released on leave, for important work at Brightwood. It was thirty days before I had a reply, but when it came it was a most impressive document—an assembly of printed forms, duly stamped and signed by a dozen officials located in district, regional, and national headquarters. The upshot of the voluminous communication—which I did not take time to read in full—was that my request could not be granted; so Tim stays by his castor oil bottle and acknowledges the salutes of tired youngsters who have stubbed a toe.

Leslie Sherman is at Camp Custer. I don't think the war has discommoded him seriously. Natalie is living at the Post Tavern in Battle Creek, and Leslie sees her every day or two. Randolph has closed up his house and is living in New York.

* * * * *

It is of much interest to me, in these days, to note what the sudden imputation of military authority is doing to different types of men.

For many years I have preserved a delightful friendship with a man named Zimmerman, who lives in Ann Arbor. We were quite comradely during our freshman and sophomore years. Dan got into the manufacturing business and became very well-to-do. He was a fine executive.

He has always taken a vital interest in military affairs, and has ranked high in the National Guard. When the Officers' Training School was opened at Plattsburg, Dan was early on the ground. Then he was sent to Texas, during our difficulty with Mexico. Now he is at Camp Custer, a major.

I was called over there a few weeks ago on a professional errand which concerned a young non-com in Dan's outfit, and learned that his men were sincerely devoted to the major and proud to be under his command. He came into the room, while I was in the camp hospital, and exhibited the same concern for the young patient that he might have shown toward a nephew. Everybody had stood at attention when Dan strode in, tall, bronzed, physically fit. I liked the gentle tone with which he said, "Please be at ease." I don't think he lost a mite of prestige.

Now—Dan Zimmerman, I happen to know, is not much of a back-slapper. He is essentially an aristocrat, lives in a palatial home, moves in an exclusive social set, and has the general bearing of an English squire. At a hasty glance, you might have guessed that there would be a pretty wide gap between this major and the rookies. But Dan, without the sacrifice of his authority or any negligence in discipline, had his men welded into one solid chunk—and all of them ready to follow him anywhere.

It is going to be good for these chaps to have this sort of association with aristocracy at its best. They can't help being finer men after having observed the effortless sportsmanship of Dan Zimmerman. He wore his uniform as if he had been born in it; and, because it came naturally to him to obey and command, he inspires not only confidence and loyalty, but affection.

A few blocks from Brightwood Hospital there is a high-class food store. The manager is an amiable and hard-working fellow named Brink. Jim Brink has grown up with the business, and knows all about it. His clientele is composed mostly of wealthy people who know exactly what they like in the way of delicacies and are able to pay for them; or, at least to order them and consume them, though I suspect that Jim carries on his books a good many assets which would make a banker laugh.

I shouldn't think of envying Jim his job. All day long, for years, he could be found saying—to customers quite too valuable to be handled by a mere sales- person—"Yes, indeed, Mrs. Northby, if we haven't got it, we will find it for you."—"Yes, yes, Mrs. Highwall, we will make a special delivery, of course. Thank you! Thank you—very, very much!"

It was difficult to imagine Jim in any other setting than his snobbish shop; but, to the amazement of everybody, he decided that the government needed him badly. He went to Grayling to train. He is at Camp Custer, now, with the rank of second lieutenant.

Not very long ago, a private in his company, on leave for a day to visit a sick relative, got into a trolley accident a few miles from here and was seriously hurt. Because it was thought he had a skull fracture, they brought him to Brightwood. The head injury did not amount to much, so Pyle put him together again, a tedious job, for the young fellow was broken in a half-dozen places.

Yesterday, Lieutenant Brink showed up at the hospital. Announcing at the desk that he had come for the private, whose name I have forgotten, he was referred to Doctor Pyle, who at the moment was with me in an operation. Informed that he would have to wait a little while, the lieutenant became very much annoyed; came up to the operating-room, pushed the nurse out of the way who told him he must not come in, and stalked—booted, belted, spurred, and bright-buttoned—to the side of the table.

Pyle, half-stunned over this amazing impudence, glanced up and said, "Why—Good morning, Jim."

"Lieutenant Brink, sir, if you please," snapped Jim. "I have come for Private (whatever-his-name was)."

"You had better leave him for another week or ten days," advised Pyle, swallowing his indignation. "He isn't able to travel yet."

"I shall be the judge of that," growled Jim. "Where is he?"

This was too much for Pyle, who is not accustomed to this kind of talk, and he exploded.

"You get out of here, Brink! You know better than to invade an operating- room in street clothes. Just because you've harnessed yourself up in leather— "

"That will do!" broke in Jim, shrilly. "I want my man—and if you don't take me to him I shall put you under arrest."

"Very well," said Pyle, breathing hard, "you arrest me— and we'll see what comes of it."

Jim stiffly consented to wait until the operation was over, but insisted on taking his cripple away with him in a taxi; had to have him lifted in, though he himself did not assist. Pyle thought he might have to go to Battle Creek and make explanations, but heard no more about it.

So—here we have a pretty nice little problem in psychology. It doesn't require very shrewd deduction. Jim Brink is compensating for years and years of boot-licking. A few months ago, he was the most obsequious little yes-yesser in this town; a grinning, fawning, stickily sweet toadier who always seemed to be saying, "No bother at all. Glad to do it, I assure you. And you may kick me if you want to." Now he is a disgusting type of the *brute in buttons!* I suppose it is one of the hazards of war that impressionable young men have to be exposed to close-up contacts with freshly hatched officers who are trying to mend their damaged personalities after long and bitter experience in some relationship where they have played expertly the role of whipping-boy.

I am told that cases of this sort, while far from being in the majority—thank God!—are frequent enough to constitute a menace to the efficiency of the army; for a contemptible fellow like that couldn't hope to enlist the honest loyalty of his subordinates, and wouldn't dare lead the way for his men in battle where so many accidents have been known to happen to officers who had earned the hatred and contempt of their troops.

* * * * *

It has been interesting to note the predictions of our local prophets in respect to the ultimate good that is to result from the World War. They seem generally agreed that civilization will take a fresh grip on itself and march forward into a new day.

I haven't been to any of the churches, but I read reports of the sermons in the papers. They are very heartening; perhaps a bit too optimistic. I have clipped a few of these pulpit observations, and am going to record them briefly here. When you read this, you will note that we are fairly hopeful of the future, and justify the savage means by the noble end to be achieved.

One prominent minister said, not long ago, "There are signs now which indicate that every autocracy will be driven from the earth through the agency of this war, and that government of the people, for the people, and by the people will be established everywhere. At the close of the war there will be a greater brotherhood of individuals and nations than the world has ever known." Perhaps this is a pretty tall order, but it seems to meet with general approval. Everybody thinks the war should do us all a lot of good. I hope so.

Another preacher declared, "This great conflict is hastening the coming of Jesus in his reign over mankind. It will end in his crowning as King of Kings and Lord of Lords." This strikes me as being a bit hysterical, to say nothing about its being illogical. I can't think that a world-wide acceptance of the Galilean teacher would be the natural outcome of a general war. War doesn't seem to be the right build-up for it. Of course it is conceivable that everybody will be so weary and hurt and remorseful, when it is done with, that we will all resolve to follow a different program in the future. But it is certainly a hope that has little encouragement from history. All sorts of special interests are banking on the war to solve their assorted problems. One preacher sees the complete abrogation of class distinctions, another forecasts the end of disputes between capital and labour. Life in the trenches, where rich and poor have mingled their blood in a common cause, will bring about an enduring brotherhood. Maybe there is some sound sense to this. At all events, we are taking much comfort in the thought.

I see that a Mrs. Kohut—a prominent leader in Jewish education—speaking at the Temple Beth El, said, "The war will develop an international psychology which will end forever the persecution of our race." This, I feel, is worth looking forward to; for the Jew has surely taken an awful lot of beating, in the past dozen centuries, and I expect he will be right thankful to get some sound insurance against any more of it in the future.

There are a good many howls for revenge and punishment which, it seems to me, would be more fitly spoken in camp than in church. One parson is quoted as saying, "The war must go on until Germany is on her knees begging for mercy and the militarists are punished in their persons for their hellish wrongs." This chap is probably not a bad fellow when things are normal, but his value as a leader of people's thinking—in a time of excitement—is questionable. I surmise that he is the sort of chap who, when the house is on fire, would throw the baby out the window and carry its cradle downstairs in his arms. As a spokesman for Christ, who said to his enemies, "Father, forgive them for they know not what they do," this brother seems to be slightly off the old reservation.

New York papers quote one of their eminent clergymen as shouting in his pulpit, "To hell with the Kaiser!" I have, often wondered whether, with all the accumulated inhibitions of speech and conduct laid upon him, a preacher might not sometimes wish that an occasion would arise permitting him to let himself out a little. Doubtless it was the irksomeness of a steady devotion to piety that led the medieval sculptors—at work on stone angels, apostles, martyrs, and such things, for the great cathedrals—to have each his own pet rock, out in the back yard, on which he operated for amusement, off hours. These sculptors probably got so damn sick of the uprolled eyes and penitential smirks of the saints that they had to do a grotesque and sinister gargoyle to restore their emotional balance. This war has given the preachers a chance to yell "hell," "damnation," and "filthy swine!" It is in questionable taste, but probably provides a sort of much needed neural laxative, human nature being such as it is.

I do not possess a monopoly of this thought. Last week I attended a luncheon in Ann Arbor, of doctors and University executives. In the course of general talk about the table, somebody referred to the wild intemperance of speech in the pulpits, and President Hutchins dignifiedly observed, "Yes—the war has been a Godsend to the preachers."

I should have liked to hear him express his opinions on the subject a little more fully. Hutchins is one of the wisest men I know. The University has been very fortunate in her choice of presidents. Everyone feared, when Doctor Angell retired, that it would be difficult to find anyone who could so widely command the love and esteem that he had earned. Hutchins has it. It does me good to be in his presence. This man has ballast! It is a great blessing that a person of his august mind directs the University in these trying days.

BRIGHTWOOD HOSPITAL
October sixteenth, 1918, 2 a.m.

I HAVE not been outside for three days. This hospital is a pesthouse. Every available inch is filled with influenza victims.

It may seem odd to you that I am taking time, in this distressing situation, to make an entry in my long neglected journal; but, utterly fagged as I am, I cannot sleep. Neither can I think about anything else but this catastrophe. So I shall briefly record what is going on here—and everywhere—all over the country.

This is by far the worst scourge that our people have ever known. We have had sporadic epidemics of "flu" for many years, but not this type. Usually the disease, in its primary stages, has been hardly distinguishable from a stubborn cold. It would drag along for weeks, leaving the patient a depleted prey to whatever he was naturally vulnerable; arthritis, sinus and mastoid troubles—or, indeed, almost anything; heart, sometimes. Now and then a pneumonia developed. It was a tedious thing; particularly hard on elderly people and others with low vitality.

The influenza we have now is swift and savage. One of its peculiarities is the high rate of mortality among young people. The better equipped they are with physical resources, the more promptly it consumes them. It is mowing down the young doctors and nurses in appalling numbers. You may use your imagination on what is happening in these big cantonments where—even at their best—the camp hospital is more or less makeshift and not rigged to care for a large-scale pestilence.

The disease gives very brief warning. It strikes a hard blow. The patient melts like wax under high temperatures, while you stand there helpless. Nothing does any good. If it was smallpox, we would know what to do.

In any other circumstance, I should have gone to Battle Creek to-day—yesterday—to be present when they shipped Leslie Sherman's body back to his family home in Bay City. He was sick, in the crowded camp hospital, only four days. I couldn't leave Brightwood. There was nothing I could have done for him, anyway. The doctors over there know as much about this deadly stuff as I do; more, maybe; certainly no less. You can't subtract anything from nothing.

I have just been talking with the Battle Creek Sanatorium. They say Natalie is holding her own; perhaps rallying a little, though you can't count much on the usual signs for encouragement. Your patient will seem to have passed a crisis; temperature begins to recede; you begin to take heart. In an hour or two your patient is subnormal; other customary warning-signs absent; no cyanosis, no Cheyne-Stokes respiration. Now your man is alive; now he is dead. Just like that.

Randolph had just arrived from New York; quite unfit to travel. They had put him to bed. Natalie has not been told about Leslie. I shall call up again in the morning.

We are growing seriously short of help here. We have five nurses in bed. I know that McDermott was running a temperature to-night, though he denied it and got almost peevish when I accused him of it.

The papers are quoting various persons as believing that the flu germs were released in several regional centres in this country by enemy agents. I suspect that this is a precious lot of poppycock. We have been imputing to the Germans a great deal more ingenuity than they possess.

I had a comforting telegram from Joyce to-night. She has spent her first month in Capital Seminary; and, from early reports, I honestly believe we have struck the right place for her. It is the first time she has ever seemed to be contented in school.

Recent letters extol the charm of the teachers and the comradeliness of the girls. Joyce writes that each new girl is assigned a Junior adviser, who gives her helpful hints about her studies, her manners, and her adjustment to the school's regulations. This seems a desirable arrangement, especially in our case, for we have had a difficult time in as many as three reputable schools, and if we can contrive to keep our footing now it will be a great comfort to a lot of people—including the young lady's papa.

During the past couple of weeks I have been hearing much about Joyce's beautiful mentor. My child's description of this Miss Brent involves a string of adjectives not often used except in services of worship. I hope Joyce's infatuation is not a mere passing fancy. If she will hang on to the Brent girl, and accept her counsel, for love's sake, perhaps we will have solved our problem. I hope so. It's about time!

The teachers at Capital Seminary have had the good sense to prohibit the girls from going into any public places, since the epidemic set in; and, so far, they are free of it. I am mighty glad that Joyce is fairly well insured against it. This is, at least, something to be thankful for, in my distress over conditions here with which I cannot cope.

I must resume my too great burden now. I have rested for an hour. Nancy Ashford consented to go to bed at midnight. She is completely tuckered out; but, so far, unaffected by The Thing.

HOTEL PONTCHARTRAIN
November eleventh, 1918, Midnight

THE war is over. We thought so last Thursday, but the announcement was premature. This time the news seems to be authentic.

The celebration began long before daybreak and still continues with remarkable vigour. It is growing hoarse, and a bit rowdy, but it has a good deal of vitality left; enough, I think, to keep everybody in this hotel awake all night.

We are calling what has happened the "armistice." I'll bet there aren't forty people in Detroit who had ever used that word in a sentence until a few days ago. I'll bet also that ninety-five per cent of the population had never heard the word before. Two thirds of them don't know now what it means. All they care is that it stands for Peace. Germany has asked for an armistice, which means that the war is over! Nobody has bothered to look up the word, which means "a truce; a temporary cessation of hostilities."

There will be a conference of the powers to determine what manner of peace terms are to be offered to Germany, and it is expected that such terms—whatever they are—will be accepted, for Germany is not in a position to put up much of a debate on this subject. If the Allies want to, they can strip Germany clean to the hide. And I suppose a great deal of pressure will be put upon the council to do that. In their present temper, the people of the Entente will not be very magnanimous.

Personally, I think there is something to be said for the old Chinese doctrine of "face-saving." So often I have seen how nicely this works out in man-to-man relationships. I wonder why it might not be practicable in the settlement of difficulties between nations.

There is nothing worse that can be done to an individual than the destruction of his self-respect. Of course, if he wrongs you, it is just and right that he make amends. But I think great care should be exercised that his personal pride is not destroyed. In the heat of passion, you may get some satisfaction from seeing him down on all fours with his chin in the mud, confessing that he is a lousy scoundrel, unfit for association with decent men. But the trouble is that after you have done that to him he has nothing more to lose; and a man who has nothing to lose makes a very mean antagonist.

I think that when Grant told Lee to keep his sword, thus implying that he had been at war with a brave man, a gentleman whom he respected, his act was of priceless value in the unprecedented rapid healing of the wound between the North and the South. Grant had a chance that day—and I daresay he would have had a lot of applause from short-sighted people, clamorous for a long-term vengeance—Grant had a chance to humiliate Lee by a display of cocky arrogance, and make the South sore forever and ever! I never realized how much was at stake there until I began to speculate on the present problem abroad. Grant was a great man, that day!

Then he told Lee that the Confederates could take their horses home with them, and whatever other equipment was needful on their farms, as to say that the South—far from being ruined—would now be resuming the usual activities.

Looking back on it from this safe distance, I think we have been disposed to minify the enmity generated by that war. It was a hard-fought thing, and the mutual hatred it developed was fierce, passionate, virulent. But it was not contemptuous. That was what ultimately saved the Union. People can fight and hate each other, and get over it, so long as they concede gallantry.

I hope this magnanimity may be observed when the peace is made in Europe. Otherwise, "armistice"—in this case—may eventually mean no more than it means in the dictionary.

* * * * *

The flu, which strikes fast and hard, has eased up appreciably, at Brightwood, anyhow, where the number of new cases is falling off. Things are by no means normal, but they are so much better that we are beginning to breathe more freely. Doubtless this diminution of the epidemic may be attributed to the city's strict quarantine enforcement, and the closing of theatres, churches, and other places of public assembly where the contagion operated at a deadly advantage.

* * * * *

Dorothy Wickes came to the hospital this afternoon to tell me that Harry, who is in France with the Rainbow Division, was well and in good spirits when she last heard from him, a letter dated October thirteenth. Naturally, she was rejoicing over the peace, and the prospect of having her brother back home in the near future.

"Of course," she admitted, suddenly shadowed, "some terrible things could have happened to him since that letter was written; but"—brightening quickly—"I have a feeling that he is safe." Then she asked, soberly, "You believe in hunches; don't you?"

"Well," I replied, cautiously, "I believe in my own hunches."

"Did a hunch ever let you down?" she asked, childishly.

'Yes," I confessed. "Occasionally."

"Do you have a hunch that Harry is coming home?"

"Yes," I said, adding that I hadn't really laid hold on any deep convictions about it; but, now that she asked me, I felt quite confident I should be seeing Harry again.

"I have that hunch too," said Dorothy. "Don't you think that two hunches are better than one?"

"Twice as good," I declared, reasonably enough, I thought.

There was a little pause before Dorothy inquired, with blue eyes wide, "Where do hunches come from?"

I toyed with my watch-chain and smiled ineffectively.

"I've noticed that whenever you're stuck," drawled Dorothy, with the bland impudence of a five-year-old, "you begin to wonder what time it is. Does that watch trick of yours mean that you want to get rid of me; or, do you do that when you're alone—and stuck?"

Never having examined myself on this matter before, I hesitated in replying, a chink she promptly filled with "But maybe you're never stuck—when you're alone." And when I failed to answer quickly she added, "Are you?"

Now, ordinarily, I should find this sort of impertinence very annoying and would make an effort to discourage any more of it; but Dorothy Wickes and I are close friends, in spite of the disparity of our ages. I like her immensely, partly because she is such a lovely creature, and mostly because she is so sensible.

"Yes," I said, "I get stuck when I am alone. Just at the moment I am feeling quite jubilant over the prospect of being unstuck from a problem that accounts for much of this gray hair."

"Hunch?" asked Dorothy.

"A little better than a hunch."

"Want to take your hair down?" she inquired, companionably.

"Beg pardon?" I said—unfamiliar with the phrase which appears to be a recent device when inviting a confidence.

"I mean," explained Dorothy, with a puckery-lipped grin, "do you want to tell all? If so—I have plenty of time."

"It's about my daughter," I said. "She has been away, nearly all of the time, for years, in girls' schools, because she has no mother and I could not give her the attention she needed."

And then I proceeded to give Dorothy, who was most attentive, a fairly comprehensive sketch of my anxieties—through the years—winding up happily with my recent assurance that things might now be much less troublesome.

"Of course," I added, "I cannot expect this Miss Brent to be at Joyce's elbow twenty-four hours of the day. There's the Christmas vacation, for instance. Joyce will come home. This young set that she was training with, last summer, may upset everything."

"Perhaps this Miss Brent could come home with her as a guest through the holidays," ventured Dorothy.

"Not very likely," I said, doubtfully. "All of two years difference in their ages. This girl probably has her own home and friends. But—it's well worth looking into."

"I should think," said Dorothy, "that if Miss Brent has had such an unusual influence on Joyce, she might be willing to make a little sacrifice of her own holiday pleasure. Maybe it could be put up to her on that basis."

"You are about her age," I said. "What would you think if somebody made such a proposal to you?"

"Well—if I was aware of all the circumstances, and believed that I might help, I think I would do it. And"—she added—"I've a hunch that Miss Brent will do it—if she can. She must be a pretty good sort, or she couldn't have had this effect on Joyce."

I said I would take her advice, and see what comes of it. I wrote to Joyce this evening, asking her if she would like to invite her friend here for the holidays. Joyce will undoubtedly consent. I hope it works out. I should be glad to see this interesting girl, myself.

I said as much to Dorothy, before she left, this afternoon, and she grinned impishly.

"But I suppose you haven't any hunches about that?" she teased.

"If you are implying that I might become interested in Miss Brent for any other reason than the one you know," I said, "it may clear the air for you if you remember that I am twice as old as this young lady."

Dorothy poised her head on one side, wisely, and said, "Even so—there's no—"

"No fool like an old fool," I assisted.

"Suppose I had said that," chided Dorothy.

"It would have been true," I declared.

"But you wouldn't have liked it."

"Well—no; perhaps not."

AT HOME —
January twenty-eighth, 1919, 10 p.m.

FOR quite too long a time my entries in this journal have been a dismal record of tragic events.

I am not by nature a morbid person and I have had no pleasure in reporting these various frights and frets, but they have bulked so large, during these past few years, that it was impossible to ignore them.

I have made sketchy notes on the war, or such aspects of it as might be remarked by a remote spectator. I have dragged you through at least the edge of our devastating pestilence. I have occasionally adverted to my personal perplexities, chief of which was my worry about my wilful child.

It will gratify you to learn, after wading through this almost interminable wilderness of woe, that my mind is now more at ease than it has been for a quadrennium.

Of course the one overpowering torture that had dwarfed all other agonies was the war. We are done with that now, and a sort of peace has been arranged for. You will have been fully informed about that, so I shall add nothing farther about the nature of this peace, except to say that many thoughtful people are wondering whether it gives promise of durability.

It seemed to be taken by common consent, the world over, that our President would guide the deliberations of the Peace Conference. This seems rather strange, too, for Mr. Wilson made no bones about his hope that this parley would establish a working agreement for international amity in the future, rather than to conduct an autopsy over the late German Empire.

It must have been a serious disillusionment to this lonesome idealist when he discovered that the delegates had not assembled primarily to implement a practical peace, but to punish a beaten foe. If correctly reported, that Conference must have resembled nothing quite so much as an avaricious group of expectant brothers and sisters, cousins and second cousins, nephews and nieces, in-laws (and outlaws), convened to divide among themselves the realty and personal effects of a stricken relative who had died intestate.

Once this division of property is amicably agreed upon, and everyone has made off with his share, it may be presumed that the peace has been concluded. This arrangement, however, is shakily founded upon the belief that our belligerent relative is indeed deceased. Should it turn out that he is not dead but only in a deep coma from which he may emerge some day, it is not inconceivable that he may insist upon a restoration of his goods.

With customary generosity, the United States has not asked for so much as an old brass hat, for a souvenir; and, in token of their appreciation of our magnanimity, the other surviving relatives have voted us the privilege of financing a good deal of the expense incident to the last illness, until such time as our kinfolk can conveniently liquidate.

Mr. Wilson has found himself in the awkward position of having proposed to the enemy peace terms which he is now unable to confirm. I suppose the main trouble here grew out of the fact that he made this tentative offer on his own hook, without making doubly sure that his proposals would be approved at home and abroad. If this was a blunder, I can see how a man might easily make such a mistake with the very best intentions in the world. Because it was a time of great stress, everybody had been willing to confer unprecedented power upon the President. The only way you could insure a solid front and a steady drive was to let the President hold all the reins.

I surmise that almost any man, empowered with such authority, might come to feel that suggestions and queries and counsel—however well meant—were distracting annoyances which shouldn't be added to his already crushing load. Of course, his attitude—in that event—presupposes that this one man—and he alone—can provide the necessary wisdom and direction. Any practicing psychiatrist will tell you that no man can carry a burden like that very far without crumpling under it.

* * * * *

As for the epidemic, it has been considerably relieved. I don't think we learned much about it. I'm sure I didn't. When fatal, it almost invariably wound up in a swift pneumonia. Whether these pneumonias were all of the same type, I do not know. They were similar in their deadly effectiveness.

My most grievous personal loss, during the worst of this plague, was occasioned by the death of my valued friend Clive Randolph. He practically reorganized my life. He helped me to whatever I am and have. It is difficult to believe that he is gone. His spirit was so bright with light and energy that one can't consent to its being extinguished. Nor can one be quite contented with the thought that Randolph will continue to speak through the lives he has illumined. Perhaps this sort of immortality should suffice for any man. But—even so—it is not easy to dispose of Randolph by declaring him henceforth an inspiring memory in the minds of grateful friends. Personal survival is a baffling doctrine, hard to accept. But, for me, it is more worthy of credence than the thought that Randolph, as a person, has readied the end of his life. I have no convictions about heavenly harps, streets of gold, or any celestial properties or employments. I have no guess to offer concerning Randolph's present abode or manner of living. But I strongly suspect that—somewhere, somehow—he is alive. If this seems unscientific, and lacking in sound evidence, keep it in mind that until you have stood by the open grave of a cherished friend the testimony in favour of immortality is not yet all in.

* * * * *

Natalie's convalescence was naturally retarded by the shock of her bereavement. To have lost her husband and her father within a few days, and in circumstances which made it impossible for her to be with them, was an almost insurmountable grief. It must be said for her, however, that Natalie's acceptance of this tragedy was a credit to her training and her personal character.

By the middle of December she was sufficiently recovered to leave the Sanatorium. I had visited her there several times. She had told me of her intention to go to Denver for a few weeks with an uncle and aunt who lived there. But shortly before it was time for her to start, Natalie had word that her uncle was ill. Realizing that she would be only an additional burden to her relatives at this time, she accepted my invitation to come to Detroit and remain through the holidays.

I reopened the house, sent for Gladys, found some additional help, and prepared—not without some uneasiness—to entertain three young women; Natalie, physically frail and emotionally upset; Joyce, who might or might not manage to adjust herself to the mood of a recently bereaved guest; and Miss Brent, whom I had never seen and whose reaction to this delicate situation was indeterminable, though—from what Joyce had written of her—I was willing, in advance, to give her the benefit of the doubt.

Natalie was with me for three days before the school girls arrived. I brought a lively young nurse over from Brightwood, rather for my unhappy guest's entertainment than any need of professional care. It was natural, I think, that Natalie should have talked quite freely to me, almost as if I were a relative. She seemed eager to discuss future plans. Her father had confided to her the general nature of the estate she would inherit. It was pleasant, but not surprising, to learn that Randolph had amply provided for her. There was some valuable real estate, besides their home which would be easily marketable in case Natalie decided to give it up—as she undoubtedly would; a respectable list of conservative stocks and bonds, and fifty thousand dollars worth of life insurance.

So—we didn't have that to fret about. Natalie's future, considered from an economic standpoint, was safely guaranteed. She doubted whether she could be contented to live with her uncle and aunt, even if that were agreeable with them. She had seen little of them in recent years and had very few friends in Denver. She wasn't sure that Detroit was the place for her, with its inevitable reminders of her former happiness and present desolation. New York might provide distractions, but it sounded pretty lonely without her father. As for going to live with Leslie's people, that was definitely out. "I hardly know them," she said. "It wouldn't be fair to them—or me, either.

"Sometimes I have thought," she went on, "that foreign travel might help me; new things to see; new acquaintances who wouldn't be talking to me about my trouble. I could take a long trip; around the world, maybe; be gone a year."

I let her prattle on, without interruption, about an extended tour. Apparently she had been thinking about it a good deal; for she seemed well posted on the subject. Only half attentive to her recitation of possible itineraries, I found myself reviewing some of the cases I had known of bereaved people who had fled from their loneliness at home to experiment with loneliness abroad.

My opportunities for observations in this field have been fairly frequent. As has often been remarked in this journal, brain surgery is not always successful. In the past dozen or more years I have been invited to counsel with many bewildered persons—women, mostly—who, having lost their husbands, wonder what to do with themselves. If they are left with meagre resources, the problem is to find something profitable to do. This isn't always easy, but it is easier than to deal with the widow who has been well provided for. A typical case finds the widow possessed of more ready cash than she has ever seen before. Plenty of times—in cases where the death was the result of an accident, and I see my share of them—the life insurance carries double indemnity, which materially increases the inheritance.

I know at least a score of widows who, to-day, would be much happier and in better health—mentally and physically—if they hadn't been left a nickel. People do not often look for work unless they need to do so, and sometimes the only insurance they can get that will defray the emotional expense of a serious bereavement is to be found in some responsible job, a job with a lot of wear and tear to it, one that demands an alert mind and a dextrous hand.

When Natalie had disembarked at Singapore, or somewhere, to give me a chance to comment, I surprised her by saying, "I wish I could be a little more enthusiastic over this, my dear."

Her eyes widened inquisitively.

"Don't you want me to?" she asked.

"I'm not sure," I replied, slowly. "If you had been left penniless, I know that your friends would think it a great pity. They would say, 'Poor Natalie! As if it wasn't enough to bear a double bereavement, she will now have to go to work!' But, however sympathetic and kind, these friends will be missing the point exactly. They would be thinking, 'If Natalie had not suffered such frightful blows, it might not be so terrible for her to have to go to work.' Such reasoning is incorrect. It is *because* Natalie has been dealt these exceptionally hard blows that she *should* find work to do."

"You mean that—seriously?" she asked.

"Yes, dear; seriously. I don't believe you are going to find an anodyne for your sorrow aboard a ship, or in the Alps, or on the Riviera. I don't think it is going to help you, the least bit, to make casual acquaintances on a voyage or in foreign hotels."

"But perhaps you do not care for travel?"

"Indeed I do, and I hope the time may come, before long, when I may be free to do it. And you, too. Some day you will travel with enjoyment. But I think you'd better reorganize your life first. You see"—I went on, encouraged a little by her show of interest—"the chief ground of your distress at present is the loss of your motive for living.

You had two important employments; loving and cherishing your husband and your father. Of course, you are dreadfully lonely without their love and care for you; but the most serious feature of your bereavement is not the loss of what they were doing for you, but of what you had been doing for them. You had a responsible job, and now you have lost it. Do you see what I mean? If you sit down now with folded hands, to brood upon your loss, you are ruined. And you're too young and sweet and capable to be wasted. We couldn't afford to lose Leslie, and we couldn't afford to lose your father; but we can't solve these problems by losing You!"

"I couldn't do anything," muttered Natalie, half to herself. "What could I do? I ride horses, but I couldn't show anyone else how. I play the piano, but I couldn't teach it. I trained Scotty to do some clever tricks, but I don't believe we could go on the stage."

"Yes, yes, I know," I growled. "And you bake nice angel food cakes. You couldn't earn enough money to keep yourself in shoelaces, doing any of these things. But—if you honestly want a job, we'll find you one."

"Well—I certainly don't want to go through the motions of doing something, aware that I wasn't earning my wages," said Natalie. "It's worth thinking about. I'll be open to suggestions."

Perhaps I have made too long a story to account for Natalie's present employment in the Winslow Art Store. It was easy enough to arrange. They were short-handed. Young Wickes, whose division is still retained with the Army of Occupation, may not be home for some time yet. Mr. Winslow was glad enough to avail himself of Natalie's services. He and Randolph were long-time friends, having so many common interests. I think he assumed that Natalie, having grown up in an atmosphere of applied arts, might come fairly well informed about the implements of these professions.

Natalie went to work on the sixteenth. She came to see me last Sunday. I was amazed at the change in her face and manner. She was positively radiant. I have often marvelled at what blood transfusions will do. That's what the new job had done for our girl. Almost back to normal was Natalie. She bubbled with enthusiasm over her new interests. They were paying her twenty dollars a week and she had resolved to live on it.

"Just to show myself that I'm capable of paying my way," she explained proudly. "And—anyway—it will be interesting to find out how people manage on small incomes. Maybe I'll get tired of it," she added, "but—so far it has been like a new game. I've never had to study the luncheon menu before, with economy as the main consideration."

I found myself deeply interested in Natalie's adventures. It had been a long time since I had done much skimping. As she rattled along with her droll story of the joys and excitements of her self-imposed frugality, I vividly recalled the days when the new suit of clothes—albeit not made of very good stuff—brought me pride and confidence. I know I got more profit from the book that I couldn't buy in September, and had to wait for until another cheque came in. One's purchases, in those days, were made with care. Natalie was valuing what she owned, for the first time in her life, she said.

"It's really amazing," she went on, "what very nice things you can get at the ten-cent stores. They have almost everything." She fondly patted a glittering brooch at her throat. "How much do you think I paid for that?" she asked, lowering her tone, confidentially.

"Well—if it's real," I replied, judicially, "I should think it must have cost about two million, five hundred thousand dollars."

"A quarter!" confided Natalie.

She had taken a room in a private house on a once fairly prosperous residence street, lately grown shabby and cluttered with little one-man shops. Her neighbour on one side was a locksmith. Natalie had already got acquainted with him, through the Horner family with whom she lived.

"Jim makes keys while you wait," she remarked, in passing.

"Do you call him Jim?" I couldn't help asking.

"Why not? That's his name."

There was no Mr. Horner. We hadn't learned what had become of him, but we guessed he wasn't dead or Mrs. Horner would have said so. There was a son, about twenty-two, who worked in a factory. His name was Ethan but everybody called him Jack.

"I can see how they might," I said.

"But he doesn't sit in a corner," observed Natalie. "Soon as evening dinner—or supper, rather—is over, Jack hurries down to a bowling alley. I'm afraid he doesn't contribute much to the family's upkeep. But his mother idolizes him and is always quoting the funny things he used to say when he was little. I think he outgrew that." Natalie was stripping her gloves onto her fingers.

"No, no, no," I protested, "not yet. Tell me some more about the Horners. By the way—is your room comfortable?"

"It isn't what the movies show you when they do an impressive boudoir scene," admitted Natalie, "but it is warm and the bed can be slept in if you're pretty tired. People who work all day don't require expensive mattresses. Same thing goes for food. Pot roast is quite tasty if you have worked hard enough to be hungry. The rest of the Horners? Well—Winnie is seventeen and in high school. She has a beau who doesn't look any too good to me; and I'm afraid the affair is rather serious, for he helps Winnie with the dishes almost every evening."

"Sounds to me," I put in, "as if this boy's heart is in the right place."

"It isn't his heart," explained Natalie. "His heart's all right."

"Well"—I persisted—"any young fellow who will wash the dishes for his gal must have something to him."

"No, sir!" declared Natalie stubbornly. "He is going to be doing that for Winnie, all their lives. He'll wash the dishes, and Winnie will have to go out and earn the living."

I was amazed at the versatility of her new interests. I don't suppose Natalie knows a nickel's worth about domestic-relations problems as comprehended by the group-lingo of Social Science experts. But she has her eyes open, and it is going to be of great value to her to have discovered a few facts about the way people live who are not of her social rating. It's a new life for her. It has taken her mind off her trouble.

"Any more besides Winnie?" I wondered.

"I have been saving Sammie for the last," said Natalie. "Sammie is ten. He belongs to me. Very lovable little fellow."

"Sickly?" I asked.

"Well—he isn't very strong. How did you know?"

"You said he was lovable—and ten years old."

"What do you suppose he wants to be?" asked Natalie, mysteriously.

"I wouldn't know. Fireman, maybe?"

"Doctor!"

My thoughts were busy for a moment with several reels of reminiscences.

"We will always need doctors," I said.

"You know—" murmured Natalie, dreamily. "Now that Leslie's gone—and so early in his life—"

I tapped my lips significantly with my finger-tips, and shook my head.

Natalie's eyes were thoughtful and her lips presently parted in a slow smile. She nodded her head, understandingly. I wonder how much Randolph may have talked to her about such things. It is evident that she knows the principles. She gave me her hand, at parting, and said softly, "Funny. That's what Father would have done—if I had started to tell him what I had been thinking." Then—after a pause—she had slipped her arm through mine, affectionately—"You and Father had a lot of secrets; didn't you?"

"Yes, dear," I replied, "but we never shared them."

"I often wondered," she said, just above a whisper. "I knew how devoted you were to each other. I knew Father had secrets. His life was full of little mysteries. I always thought you had some, too." She looked up into my face and shook her head inquiringly, as she went on, "But you never told each other—about your secrets?"

"No."

"Did any of your secrets leak out—just a little—around the edges?"

"Just a little, I'm afraid. But we always pretended we hadn't noticed."

"The way one does, before Christmas, when one stumbles upon a parcel—in a closet—on a high shelf?"

I thought it was time we terminated this conversation, and accomplished it by remarking that one rarely stumbled over things on high shelves.

I think Natalie is in a fair way to make her life mean something very important. How glad Randolph must be—if he knows!

* * * * *

It had been my intention to write something here, to-night, about the gratifying change in Joyce's disposition and behaviour—all of which is to be accounted for by the quiet influence of Helen Brent. I had thought also of recording a few of my impressions of this charming girl who has so singularly stirred my heart. I am too tired to do this adequately.

Indeed I am reluctant to do it at all. I have discovered that if you want to remember something, there's no better way than to write it down. Perhaps I should not write anything about this girl. It may be much better sense if I try to forget her. Did you ever try to forget anything? A tricky job, that. [1]

[1} Yes, sir! (R. M.)

AT HOME
January twenty-ninth, 1919, 9 p.m.

WE have been *en route* to National Prohibition for some time and now we have got it. Enough states have ratified the Constitutional Amendment to make it effective, and the Secretary of State announces to-day that it is so ordered.

The Drys are ecstatic, as they have every right to be, seeing how long and zealously they have battled for this, and are in a mood to chant, "Rest, soldier, rest, thy warfare o'er."

I have seen this prohibition movement in all its phases: township option, county option, state option. When the township was the unit, the enforcement was nearly perfect. It was everybody's business, and the officials had no alternative but to be lily white. When the county attended to the enforcement, it was still pretty well done, though infractions of the law were more frequent than when the township carried the responsibility. When whole states went dry, it didn't work quite so well. Many of the close observers thought the county had done a better job.

Now the whole country is dry, and Washington is going to see to it that the law is enforced. I surmise that there is trouble ahead, but I wouldn't risk saying so where anyone could hear me; for I might be considered a Wet. I am not a Wet... I have had plenty of opportunities to know what strong liquor has done to a great many people. It has been responsible for much poverty, illness, violence, and humiliation.

Being a surgeon, I have had no choice whether or not to drink. For many years there has not been one moment when, waking or sleeping, I might not be summoned immediately to perform some delicate, life-or-death operation requiring the utmost precision of eye and hand. So, I couldn't drink if I wanted to, and am therefore disqualified to regard my own abstinence as a virtue.

For this reason I have tried to avoid seeming self-righteous on the subject. And I shouldn't presume to regulate another man's habits.

Of course, in my professional capacity I frequently warn gluttonous patients against digging their graves with their teeth, and I advise the hard drinker that the human liver—however sturdy and obliging—is not rigged to deal happily with copper and fusel-oil. But never, as a citizen at the polls, have I had the impudence to vote that my neighbours shall not have a gin-fizz or a third helping of pickled tripe and fried onions.

Privately I wish that strong liquors could be abolished by common consent. So very many people drink who do not know how, and what a pestiferous nuisance they are when they have overdone it. Too many youngsters have had easy access to it at a period of their immaturity when surely they are lightheaded enough without seeking any artificial devices to numb their wits. Not many adolescent brains are important enough to be preserved in alcohol. I fear that my Joyce has a tendency to experiment with it. I hope she has not inherited her eminent grandfather's proclivities in this direction.

Now that enforcement is in the hands of the Federal Government, I suspect that it will be handled clumsily, with a minimum of effectiveness and a maximum of expense. The issue will probably be regarded as another political football. If I were a captain in the Dry Army, I wouldn't unlace my boots yet.

* * * * *

As I was writing here, last night, I briefly alluded to the satisfaction I had in Joyce's visit home, during the holiday vacation. I had not supposed it possible for so great a change of attitude and disposition in the course of a few weeks.

To be sure, Joyce is getting to be a young lady now and she is aware that a little more dignity of decorum is expected of her. But one would think she might have been somewhat impressed by that fact a couple of years ago.

No; there is only one way to account for the new Joyce. She has been completely carried away by the charm of her student counsellor, whom she worships with full devotion.

And this I can readily understand; for Helen Brent is indeed an adorable creature. From the first moment, I felt that she belonged to us. Not to me; to us.

My sober judgment warns me against dwelling too much on my impressions of this endearing person, but I shall indulge myself, for a moment, and then avoid any further reference to my own feelings toward her.

I met them at the train. It was a bright, crisp morning. The station was crowded, because holidays were at hand and everybody was going somewhere or meeting friends. The gate-man reluctantly let me go through. I did not know what car my people would be in. By the time I arrived on the platform, there was much confusion. I tramped hurriedly back and forth, trying to watch several vestibule-exits where emerging passengers were gathering about their baggage.

Presently I identified Joyce's corn-yellow head. She was pointing out their tackle to a red-cap. I began threading my way through the crowd when this lovely girl gave me both hands and a comradely smile. I have never seen such vivid contrasts of colour; hair so black it was blue, with an even fringe framing a close-fitted toque on an extraordinarily white forehead; dark, long-lashed eyes, set wide apart; expressive lips—and dimples. When she spoke, her voice was of a deep contralto quality; a very unusual timbre; it makes everything she says sound like a confidence. Perhaps that helped to create the illusion that we were old friends.

"You're Helen," I said, a bit rattled. "So glad you've come."

She tucked a hand under my elbow and we moved on to join Joyce.

"I knew you by your picture," she said.

Joyce was all over me for a moment, and we three started down the platform, arm in arm. I was immensely proud of them. I couldn't help being amused by the almost startling difference between them; Joyce such a striking blonde, Helen as brunette as something Latin. I don't think they will ever be mistaken for sisters.

There was a wave of almost poignant tenderness swept through me, as we marched along; not only toward my own dear girl, who was clinging tightly to me, but toward the new one too, hugging my arm as if she belonged to me. It was quite exhilarating.

After we had gone a little way and were about to descend the steps, Helen, wanting to make sure the boy with the bags was in tow, slowed our gait and turned halfway round to look back, but she did not relax her tight hold on me. She was so close that when she turned, her face brushed my sleeve. It was almost a caress, and it warmed my heart. I hope I am not making myself ridiculous in your sight. It stirs me deeply to recover that enchanted moment.

* * * * *

Many persons are distrustful of themselves when standing on the edge of high precipices. The possibilities of the situation seem to exercise a sort of hypnotic urge. It isn't that they have a temptation to destroy themselves; but there is a strange infatuation here that startles persons who become suddenly aware of their unsuspected phobia.

I found myself a little bit unsure of myself in the close presence of Helen Brent. I believe and hope that she did not realize the effect she had on me. I know she did not, or she would have gone to more pains in avoiding chance contacts offering opportunities for a caressing touch.

Joyce is lazy and took advantage of her liberty to breakfast in bed. Helen had hers with me. It is my habit to glance over the telegraph news in *The Free Press*, in my library, before breakfast. On the next morning after the girls arrived, Helen sauntered into the library, came to my chair, took my hand, and said, "Breakfast. I'm hungry. Take me to it, please." She had on some sort of lounge costume; black velvet skirt and a high-buttoned chartreuse smock belted with a heavy cord and tassels. It was such an exquisite outfit, and so uncommonly becoming, that I told her she shouldn't ever wear anything else.

"If you feel that way about it," she replied, in that husky voice of hers that will be always getting her into trouble, I fear, "I'll never wear anything else. But"—she added—"it will look funny sometimes—at the theatre, and ball games."

I liked the way she made friends with Natalie, who—to my surprise—wanted to talk with her about Leslie; his good humour, his kindness, his diligence as a doctor. I hadn't thought Natalie would open up that way to a stranger. But Helen isn't a stranger. She has some peculiar faculty of—belonging to you. I'm afraid I can't do any better than that. I know this will sound silly unless it should happen that you meet this woman, some time. Then you will know what I mean. [1]

[1] I know what you mean. (R.M.)

We three made the most of the holidays; went to see *Aida* and *Pirates of Penzance*, put on by the Chicago Grand Opera Company, had dinner downtown at The Pontchartrain and the Statler and the Cadillac; saw Charlie Chaplin in a rollicking farce in which—attending a show—he climbs back and forth over outraged people seated in the same row and gets embroiled with the orchestra; one of the silliest, one of the most devastatingly ridiculous things I ever saw. In one of the more riotous moments, when we had all laughed until we were half hysterical, Helen pushed her forehead hard against my arm and said, "I'm not going to look, any more. I've got a pain in my side." I took her hand, and she held it tight, like a little child.

―――――――――

AT HOME —
February twenty-fourth, 1919, 10 P.M.

YESTERDAY noon Nick Merrick called up to inquire whether I could conveniently dine and spend the evening with him at his country place on Lake Saginack.

It was an unusual request. I had never been invited there except on a couple of occasions when Nick was having a large dinner party. When he wants to talk to me about anything, he suggests luncheon at one of the down-town clubs. It wasn't like him to invite me out to his home on such short notice, and when he added, "There will be no one else," I concluded that he wished to consult me about something of importance.

I had made other plans for the evening, but felt that I owed it to Nick to comply with his request, so I promised to go. About three he called up again to suggest that I plan to stay the night and avoid a late drive back to town. I felt sure then that Nick's confidences promised to be somewhat extensive.

I had often wondered why he wanted to build that palatial twenty-room mansion away out there in the country. Mrs. Merrick was long since dead, and Cliff, too. Maxine was an inveterate traveller, and when in the States she lived mostly in hotels and sanatoria. Nick is essentially a city man. His whole life has been spent in the clatter of big factories and the amiable buzz of the Columbia Club.

Once I tried to sound him out a little on his pastoral interests, and discovered—what I had already suspected—that he didn't know a dahlia from an aster or an azalea from an hydrangea or a hawthorn from a flowering crab.

He maintains a herd of pedigreed Guernseys and a staff of trained dairymen to look after them, but I doubt whether there is anything in this project that amuses Nick beyond the fact that his milk costs about five dollars a quart. It is good milk.

Nick also raises fancy Berkshires. One day he told me some of the distinguishing marks of a Berkshire. The undercarriage of the hog's head should be shaped like a rocker. This tilts up the snout. The forehead should overhang, leaving almost no face, at all. A really damn good Berkshire hog, said Nick, should be barely able to see out between his eyebrows and his nose. The legs should be short and slim. There had been a movement to breed for slimmer legs, Nick explained, but the thing had gone too far. The improved legs weren't strong enough to carry the hog, so they had been obliged to breed the sturdier legs back on again.

These genetic phenomena amuse Nick, but I can't believe that he gets very much entertainment out of it; for he has nothing to do with it aside from looking at his expensive pigs, occasionally, when someone visits him. I saw them, one afternoon, couple of years ago. They are clean as cats. At precise intervals, in their recreation yard, lathe-turned and rope-wrapped posts are planted for the accommodation of the hogs when they want to scratch.

There are also pens of highly bred poultry, cages of pheasants, and a green-tiled duck-pond with a little fountain in the middle.

Every morning, weather permitting, Nick takes a stroll, inspecting his livestock. Then, if the day is bright, his poker-faced Powell drives him into town where he has an office on the top floor of one of the new skyscrapers and an ancient secretary who shares alone with God the knowledge of Nick's reasons for coming in; for he is done with business and makes no pretence of keeping himself informed about the dizzying progress of the industry which he helped to inaugurate. I understand that the stock market reports, and a succinct summary of the previous day's business in the Axion Motor Company are always laid on his desk, and the inkwell is kept filled.

Last night I found out why Nick built the big house he calls Windymere. It is intended for Bobby. Bobby is unlikely ever to do anything but play, and this will be just the place for him. He will undoubtedly do a great deal of travelling about. His appetite for going places was acquired early. He had made seven round-trips to Europe before he was eighteen. But Windymere is to be his permanent address, and he will be here at least every four years to vote the Republican ticket. It takes six men to keep the lawn in order that slopes a quarter-mile to the lake shore where there is a commodious boat-house containing a high-powered speed-boat, a cabin cruiser with a capacity of ten passengers, and a couple of sail-boats. It was to talk with me about Bobby that Nick invited me out. I was so sorry for the old man I could have cried.

* * * * *

I arrived about half-past six. The day had been quite spring-like, but after sundown it was snappy. Nick had a comforting fire in his big library and the welcome he gave me was as warm. He had been reading a new detective story, and queried me about my taste in such fiction. When I confessed that I wasn't up on the subject, he informed me—and quite soberly, too—that if a man really needed a time-killer, there was nothing equal to it. His library shelves are loaded, almost floor to ceiling, with crime and mystery tales. I daresay these shockers are diverting, but it seems a pity that Nick's range of reading is so restricted. There are so many other things in which, one would think, he might find enjoyment.

After dinner—a man's dinner, oxtail soup, superb steak, baked potato, head lettuce salad, cheese, and coffee—we returned to the crime-and-mystery museum. Our table talk had dealt mostly with the peace, which Nick thinks is impracticable, and with prohibition, in which he has even less confidence. He gets it from his men on the farm that liquor in plenty is coming across the Canadian border, and believes it will not be long until a systematic evasion of the law will develop a new industry; says we will have a bootlegging profession, same as we have wholesale fish dealers.

In the library we settled into luxurious leather chairs, before the grate, and lighted our cigars. They were good cigars; much too good for me, because I do not often set fire to anything that costs a dollar.

"I had a rather distressing letter, this morning," began Nick, puffing industriously. "Thought I'd like to talk to you about it."

But first, he announced, he would have to tell me something of the circumstances which had produced it.

"My grandson, after several years of getting kicked out of one prep school into another, finally struck his stride at the University. He is a junior now. I haven't had any complaints about his conduct over there. Of course, boys will be boys, and you can't hold too tight a rein. Bobby spends a good many of his week-ends over here, always brings three, four, half a dozen of his fraternity chaps along. Naturally, they are a bit noisy. They take over the house and raise hell with it. They drink and play poker and sleep late in the morning and upset the servants. But I suppose they're not any worse than other high-spirited young fellows, enjoying a couple of days away from the grind of college work."

I nodded, comprehendingly, and remarked that such festival occasions must bore him.

"Not any more," explained Nick. "This is the third year of it. I used to try to play host, but I gave that up. When the racket begins, on Friday night, I pack a bag and go into town." He paused, for a moment, and added, "Maybe that wasn't the thing to do. They might have behaved a little better if I had been on the premises."

"Anything special happened?" I wondered. Nick reached into his breast pocket and produced the letter. He did not open it at once; just sat there slowly tapping his thumb with it.

"I had this by special delivery early to-day. It is from an old friend of mine in Grand Rapids, Knute Larson. Knute was with me in the Axion Company for many years; retired now. His family is pretty much scattered. Only one left in whom he has any particular interest: his grandnephew. This boy is one of my Bobby's closest friends. He has been over here so often that we feel quite well acquainted with him. Several times Knute has dropped me a line or two, thanking me for hospitality to his youngster. I had gathered that Knute liked to have the boy visit us." Nick drew the letter from the envelope and adjusted his nose-glasses.

The contents of the Larson communication did not surprise me very much, after the introduction Nick had given it. Mr. Larson was more than grateful for the many kindnesses shown to young Knute at Windymere, but it was becoming more and more evident that the boy would be much better served if he could be induced to pay serious attention to his university work.

" 'I have heard from the dean,' " read Nick. " 'He happens to be an alumnus of the same fraternity to which our boys belong. I hope this is not going to worry you, but the dean says your Bobby is not good for young Knute.' "

"I should have thought," I put in, "that if the dean felt this way about Bobby, he might have hinted as much to you, and given you a chance to counsel with Bobby about it."

Nick puffed vigorously, for a while, before replying.

"I was afraid you'd ask me that. Doc," he growled. "Fact is; the dean has spoken to me about it, a couple of times."

"And how did Bobby feel about it when you talked to him?"

Nick shook his heavy mop of white hair, and made a jabbing little gesture of futility.

"Oh, he just screwed up his face, the way he has always done, ever since he was a baby, when someone tries to correct him—and said the dean was a prissy old sissy. 'His trouble is,' Bobby said, 'that he has to live on college wages—and he's jealous. Always dragging me in to pan me for showing the other fellows a good time.' "

"Maybe the dean has a case, Nick," I suggested. "Perhaps you might solve your problem if you reduced Bobby's allowance."

"I would," agreed Nick, promptly; "I have! But this damn-fool mother of his makes it up to him. I can't forbid him the house! And I can't stand here and play policeman every week-end!"

We were both silent for some moments, and then I inquired again whether anything in particular had happened to provoke the Larson letter. Nick scowled and nodded.

"They celebrated Washington's birthday over here," he said glumly, "and drove back to Ann Arbor late in the night. Seems they got into a little accident on the road; hit a farmer's market-cart."

"Sounds as if it might have been early, rather than late," I remarked, grinning a little.

"Yes—I guess so," grumbled Nick. "They were all asleep but this young Knute. He was driving. They tried to settle with the old man, but he had them arrested. Knute spent the forenoon in the calaboose."

"And your friend Larson thinks it's time to change the program a little."

"Exactly—and so do I. But I don't know where to begin," admitted Nick, helplessly. "Can't take him out of school. No use sending him somewhere else. He probably wouldn't go, anyhow. He's not dependent on me. Has plenty of money of his own."

"Bobby has never struck me as the sort that would stand up and defy you," I said.

Nick promptly rushed to his grandson's defence.

"No, no," he exclaimed. "He wouldn't be mean about it. Bobby's polite enough. Picked that up in France. He would just grin and pat me on the back—and do as he pleased."

It occurred to me that if Bobby had had a little less money and a few more spankings his prospects would be brighter. Without taking second thought, I said that aloud. Nick shook his head.

"Bobby is a fine boy," he said, half to himself. "It isn't his fault that he hasn't been brought up like other boys. His father died when he was a mere child; and you know how unstable his mother is. And I never felt it was my job to be his nurse."

"Well—" I said, "something will have to be done." I was glad Nick didn't take my comment for more than it was worth, and ask me what I had in mind. "Does he ever talk as if he wanted to do anything—in particular?" I asked, to chink the long pause.

It was at this point that I could have wept for good old Nicholas Merrick. He leaned forward—sagged forward—in his chair, with his elbows on his knees and his chin in his mottled hands, silently shaking his head.[1]

[1] This thing has nearly broken my heart. I wish I had known how deeply Grandpère had grieved about me. I am glad he has lived to see a little brighter prospect for me. (R. M.)

After a long, agonizing minute, he straightened up slowly and said, "Doc, my boy Cliff disappointed me, poor chap. I was too busy, when he was young, to give him proper direction. I have hoped that Bobby might find himself and amount to something. He has some very good traits, a fine mind, a nice disposition. Everybody likes him. He makes friends easily. Why, sometimes, when he is here alone with me, he goes to the piano and plays for me by the hour; things he knows I like. But—mostly—he's whooping it up with his rake-hell friends. What would you do—if you were in my place?"

I have never been at such a complete loss for adequate words. I tried to console Nick with the empty surmise that Bobby might come to his senses; mumbled something about his being young yet; that he might tire of loafing and carousing, and give himself to a worth-while job. But, all the time, I felt that Nick was assaying my hollow phrases at their exact value.

"If we could get him into a little different atmosphere" mused Nick.

"Yes," I agreed, woodenly, "different atmosphere. That's right. That might do it." A very silly rejoinder. Bobby carries his own atmosphere along with him. "What he needs," I went on, "is the influence of some sound young friend who isn't a mere playboy."

Then it occurred to me that I might as well give Nick a glimpse of my own problem, and its happy solution, so I told him about Joyce. And the amazing change that had come over her through her devotion to Helen. Nick was very attentive. His deep-lined face brightened.

"Now that is fine!" he said, momentarily dismissing his own perplexity to rejoice with me. "All the girl wanted was proper direction. And there weren't any rules or regulations that would keep her in line. What she had to have was the inspiration of somebody she liked. Think it will last—when she gets out of school, and away from this other young woman?"

I could only tell him that I hoped so. Our conversation lagged a little. Perhaps that was my fault. Nick's comment about the time to come, after Joyce's school days are over, when she may be seeing little or nothing of Helen, depressed me.

For I have responded, as gratefully as Joyce, to the tenderness and radiance of this exquisite girl. She is much in my thoughts; much too much.

Nick and I played three games of Russian Bank in which I was so decisively licked that his victories could hardly have brought him any satisfaction. I'm afraid my mind wasn't on it. The good old boy dragged out his watch, about ten-thirty, and considerately observed that I had to work next day. He took me to my room with a graciousness of hospitality that would have done credit to a prime minister bedding down his king, patting the pillows to make sure they were the right ones. Poor, rich, old Nick!

Ever since I was a lad, I have read and heard about the inadequacy of wealth to provide happiness. Mostly, I have let all such platitudes in at one ear and out at the other; for these reflections were usually offered by parsons and professors whose knowledge of money was limited to the fact that they didn't have any. I suppose the typical essay on "What I Would Do with a Million" is usually written by some poor devil who hopes to sell his piece for enough to pay an overdue gas-bill.

But, last night after I went to bed, it occurred to me as a solemn and somewhat startling fact that large wealth is really about the most feeble resource anyone can lean on who is in search of happiness.

Take Nick's wealth, for example. It made a rotter of his only son. It induced Nick into an early retirement that has made him utterly wretched. It is going to ruin his grandson.

Bobby is Nick's last stand. Everything else has palled on him. Nothing left but Bobby.

And now Bobby is no good.

It is too bad.

I wish there was something I could do, but I'm sure I don't know what it would be.

* * * * *

This was Pyle's birthday and I invited him to dine with me at The Pontchartrain. Tim Watson and Natalie came in, and tarried a moment at our table. It pleased me to see them together. I hope something may come of this, eventually. I must try to have sense enough not to seem too much interested.

BRIGHTWOOD HOSPITAL
June twenty-sixth, 1919, 10 p.m.

HELEN came home with Joyce two weeks ago, expecting to spend at least a month with us, but upon receiving a summoning letter yesterday from her uncle, left for Philadelphia this morning, greatly to our disappointment.

I have been blue and restless all day. My saner judgment tells me it is probably for my own good that Helen has been called home. More and more I have been looking to this girl for my happiness. And the fact that I find myself, to-day, distrait and day-dreamy and indifferent to my tasks, surely should be enough to warn me against this tug at my heart. It will not be long until there will be no occasion for Helen's present relation to Joyce, and then I shall have to give her up.

She hasn't talked very much about her home life, but one gathers that it is pretty bleak. Doubtless that accounts for her tender attitude toward me. Her uncle, with whom she has lived for years, is a taciturn, frugal, small-time lawyer, whose clientele is limited to a group of elderly people—widows and spinsters, mostly—living on incomes derived from conservative bonds and rentals of small business houses. Mr. Brent paddles about, collecting rents, overseeing repairs, ousting undesirable tenants and haggling with the others. It is that sort of legal practice. I infer that it is not very lucrative, and I suspect that the nature of it has made the old man mean.

It seems that Helen has a little income from a trust left by her deceased father, which accounts for her ability to go to a fairly expensive school. I hope the uncle is dealing honestly with her in the handling of this money. And I have no reason to suspect that he is not, aside from my own observation that penurious people—adept at driving hard bargains and pinching pennies—sometimes find it difficult to release their grip on money that rightfully belongs to others. If this old man has worn the same derby hat for seven years, which Helen has humorously reported in mentioning Uncle Percival's eccentricities, I think it is not improbable that he would consider himself morally justified in withholding from his niece the full payment of funds to be spent on what he might consider unnecessary fripperies.

It certainly is none of my business to be making these deductions, and the very fact that I am mentally sticking my nose into their affairs means nothing more or less than that my personal interest in Helen has grown out of all proportion to my slim claim on her friendship. It's not my habit to mole into people's private lives.

But—though I suppose I should despise myself a little for these petty sleuthings—I have been thinking a great deal about Helen's probable home life, since she left here on such short notice this morning, and I have constructed a picture of old Percival Brent which certainly does not flatter him. Helen says that her Uncle Percival's patron saint is Noah, his main interest in life being preparation for a rainy day.

When I was a boy, in the country, there were stories about stingy farmers whose policy it was to eat the spotty apples first, from the barrels in the cellar. By the time some more were needed for the table or for cooking, there would be another batch of apples which had become defunct in the meantime. So—the family ate half-rotten apples all winter. I think the same psychology prevails with the inveterate rainy-day economist. It is always a rainy day. It begins to rain on such people when they are thirty, and the sun never shines again.

Not much wonder that Helen responds to a little brighter home environment. I know that is why she snuggles close to me. I have to repeat that to myself, over and over, to keep my head.

Uncle Percival's son Monty, who lives at home, is in a brokerage house. Probably posts the board. Unlike his papa, Monty is not fretting much about a rainy day. Helen seems very fond of him, probably because of her concern over his improvidence rather than in admiration of his virtues. Father and son do not have much in common, naturally, and they can eat dinner together at the family table without a syllable of conversation. I suspect that when this Monty goes broke, he wangles some money out of his cousin. When Helen refers to him, it is usually with a quick little sigh and an anxious shake of her head. "Poor, dear Monty," she calls him. It wouldn't surprise me if it was some scrape of poor, dear Monty's—may his tribe decrease—that rushed her off to Philadelphia to-day.

I realize—you needn't tell me—that I have made a dismaying self-disclosure in the things I have said here. But it frets me to know that Helen is unhappy, and I can't help mulling over the obvious causes of it. I think that between sour old Percival and slick young Monty the girl's life is deucedly unpleasant. It would be a god-send to her if she could be emancipated from such a dreary and stultifying atmosphere.

Perhaps some cold-blooded psycho-analyst would suggest that my wish to get Helen out of that glum and frustrating home is not quite so altruistic as I have been making myself believe. He might inquire if I wasn't more concerned about rigging some good excuse to get her into our home. Very well, professor, I'll admit it, if that tickles your vanity. If Helen were in straitened circumstances I could propose that she come to us as Joyce's companion and counsellor, when her school days are over. As matters are, it would be an impertinence to hint at such a thing. But I cannot think of anything else that sounds the least bit plausible. I must put this enchanting creature out of my thoughts.

AT HOME
June twenty-eighth, 1919, Midnight

JOYCE, lonely without Helen, went down to the Winslow Art Store this afternoon for a glimpse of Natalie. At dinner this evening she reported having met Harry Wickes, who has just arrived from France. She raved about him with shrill, boarding-school enthusiasm and accused me of having tried to conceal him from her.

"You might have told me about him," she said, reproachfully. "You must have seen a lot of him, from the way he talks about you."

"Sorry," I said. "You're almost always away, you know. And Harry has been abroad for a long time."

"I asked Natalie to come to dinner next Saturday evening," said Joyce. "And I invited Harry too. Hope you don't mind. I think he's marvellous!"

I agreed that Harry is a fine fellow, and said I was glad she was having him here, provided it would be agreeable with Natalie. Joyce felt sure about that. How could Natalie help liking him?

"Harry has an uncommonly bright and pretty sister, too," I said. "Perhaps you might enjoy meeting her. Would you like to ask her to come with Harry?"

"Next time," said Joyce. "How about asking Tim? You said he and Natalie were friendly."

I grinned and Joyce made a nose at me.

"Of course you may ask Tim," I said. "He hasn't been here for months. And that will leave you free to back young Mr. Wickes into a corner and get acquainted." I had never teased Joyce about a young man before, and apparently I hadn't done a very neat job of it, for she scowled a little as she stabbed at her salad.

"I can't see why you are saying that," she protested. "I'm not in the habit of making war on every good-looking boy I meet."

"It was in fun, you know."

She drew a conciliatory little smile and said she knew that; then added, "But I don't like to be teased about such things—any more than you would."

I glanced up to meet her eyes, and said, "I?"

"Sure! You would turn a cartwheel, right out through the window, if I teased you."

"What about?" I asked, indiscreetly.

"What about!" she echoed hollowly, and then, in a tone of elaborate irony, mumbled, "As if you didn't know."

I was considerably shaken by this unexpected challenge. Surely if anybody ever made an earnest effort to sublimate his feelings, I had been doing so. And this mere child had seen through me. I told her I should like some more peas, and she rang the bell. My failure to make a rejoinder didn't help my case very much.

"It's all right with me," said Joyce, maternally, when the maid had retired. "I'm sure I don't care. You know how very fond I am of her."

"Helen?" I asked, rather unnecessarily, perhaps.

"Don't be silly, darling," recommended Joyce.

"Well—" I said, not quite sure that it was well, "I certainly hope you haven't been imprudent enough to discuss with Helen whatever ideas you may have on this subject."

Joyce shook her head and pursed her pretty lips.

"No," she said, crisply, "I haven't mentioned it. I wouldn't need to. She can't very well help knowing. She's pretty bright—for her age."

I winced a little over that last phrase. We were about through with our dinner while this distressing conversation was going on. I suggested that we have coffee in the library. It seemed that complete candour was in order now. I couldn't leave this matter dangling. It was too important.

Joyce drew up a low stool in front of my chair, refused the coffee, and folded her arms across my knees.

"I've hurt your feelings, Daddy!" she murmured. "I was horrid."

"No—you weren't horrid," I said, "but—you bewildered me a little. I've made no secret of my fondness for Helen. She is one of the most charming girls I ever knew. But—I haven't been romancing with her, if that's what you mean."

Joyce put her face down into her folded arms and shook her head. Then, without looking up, she mumbled, "I know you haven't, darling; but you're in love with her." And when I did not reply promptly, she added, "You know that."

"My dear," I said, "it isn't always easy to supervise your feelings toward people. Some you dislike, for no very good reason, and they seem to sense it—no matter how much pains you take to conceal it. And some people you like, perhaps without knowing exactly why, and—"

"Daddy, don't!" said Joyce, thickly. "If you aren't going to talk honestly about it, let's drop it."

"Very well," I declared. "If it gives you any pleasure to put your father on the grill, I'll admit that Helen is very dear to me. If I were fifteen years younger—ten years younger—I should try to win her love."

"Try to win her love!" repeated Joyce. "Are you blind? Or are you trying to spoof me?"

"Are you attempting to make me believe," I demanded, "that you think Helen Brent is fond of me—in that way? It couldn't be!"

Joyce straightened up, clasped her slim hands around her knees, and looked up steadily into my face.

"Are you being truthful, Daddy?" she asked, soberly.

"Never more so!" I declared, sincerely. "Helen has never given me the slightest reason for thinking that she considers me otherwise than as a devoted friend—old enough to be her father. Doubtless it is because she has no father that she treats me with such tender solicitude."

"She likes to be close to you," said Joyce, reminiscently.

"Let's analyse that," I suggested. "When she was with us, last Christmas, and we were starting out to spend the evening, you probably saw Helen tuck my scarf closer about my throat; but that was the sort of attention a young person shows toward an elderly person. In fact, it defined our relation."

Joyce smiled knowingly.

"But you are not an old man, Daddy. You swim, and golf, and drive like the devil was after you, and go everywhere performing tricky surgery. Helen doesn't think you need your throat bundled up."

"You're on the wrong track, my lass," I said, condescendingly.

"Well—maybe," she conceded, arching her brows. Rising, she kissed me lightly on the forehead and sauntered toward the door. "Have you read *My Antonia*?" she paused to inquire. And when I said I had not, she suggested that I do so. "I am in the middle of it now," she said. "If you'll excuse me, I'll go back to it. You know how it is—when you're in suspense about a story."

"Run along, dear," I said, cheerfully enough. "When you are through with it, I'll read it—if you can recommend it as a book that keeps you in suspense."

"I didn't know you cared much for such stories," drawled Joyce, a bit slyly, as if she were inviting me into a commitment. "I thought you liked stories that put you to sleep."

"Not always," I replied, gratified over the change of conversation. "Suspense is good for you, sometimes; helps to keep your blood in circulation. I don't object to a story that keeps me awake."

"Well—I'll tell you one then," said Joyce, slowly sidling through the doorway. "Helen carries your picture in her card-case."

I'm afraid my heart gave a strange little bump that wasn't the fault of my aneurism; but I decided not to be left sitting with Joyce's half-malicious valedictory.

"And what if she does?" I retorted. "That doesn't mean a thing! If she carries my picture—and it's mighty sweet of her—she has about the same reason she would have for carrying the picture of her philosophy professor—or Uncle Percival, if he wasn't such a grim old icicle. For the present, Helen considers me as an anchor. She wants something substantial to lean on." I realized, too late, that this final remark had not been happily selected.

Joyce, framed in the doorway, slowly nodded her head several times, in mock acceptance of my speech.

"Something to lean on," she repeated. "I've seen her do it."

"Jealous?" I asked.

Joyce ambled toward me, her lips twisted into a pout.

"No—I'm not jealous," she said, defensively. "I think I'm rather glad. You've been lonesome—for years and years. I'm crazy about Helen. It would be gorgeous to have her here— always! Only—what peeved me was your taking this hoity-toity attitude, as if you were Moses—and I was nothing but— but— "

"The Ten Commandments," I suggested, when she failed to complete the pass. "Come here." I wiggled a finger. She sat on my lap, and dabbed at her eyes. I pulled her down into my arms.

"I ought to be slapped," she muttered, huskily.

"Me, too," I admitted. "I should have been more generous with my answers to your questions. But, darling, I really don't know the right answers. All that I can tell you is this: I do love Helen, and—that's the end of it. I'm never going to tell her, and I sincerely hope you won't. Because, if you do, we can never have her here again. Promise?"

Joyce raised up to look me squarely in the eyes.

"You mean—you don't intend to ask her to marry you?"

"Of course not!"

"But you two would be enormously happy!"

I shook my head.

"It wouldn't work," I said.

"Poor Daddy!" Joyce patted my cheek.

Her tender words and the caress added several more years.

* * * * *

I deeply regret that this conversation occurred. It is very doubtful if Helen and I can retain the sweet relationship we have had. I should like to believe that Joyce will have sense enough to keep my secret, but I wouldn't bet much on it; and I shall not know—certainly—that she hasn't confided it. This doubt will make me self-conscious. Helen will sense it, and wonder why. Even if Joyce doesn't tell, Helen will feel this constraint. The situation troubles me.

I hope I'm not indulging in self-pity. But this precious woman has been good for me. It has restored my youth to have her close to me and be aware of her dear companionship. Aside from my work, my life—for many years—has been lonely. Surely no one would have begrudged me this beautiful friendship.

And now my child has unwittingly ruined it. If Helen comes here again, she will find me remote, austere, casual. I won't be able to resume our friendship freely.

When the tact was passed around, my daughter must have contented herself with a very modest serving.

Here goes for another sleepless night.

Joyce knew a story that would keep me awake.

BRIGHTWOOD HOSPITAL
July fifth, 1919, 9.30 p.m.

LATE this afternoon McDermott and I were together in an operation. It turned out to be a fairly simple mastoid, and I did little but look on. Mac had thought he might run into something deeper. We were both glad his suspicions were groundless, and so was the patient who seemed almost as much interested in the case as we were.

It was a tedious affair and by the time we were into our street clothes it was six-thirty. Mac suggested that we have dinner here. It has been a long time since I have done that. We met Tim Watson, on our way down, and invited him to join us. Our table conversation was of considerable interest to me, and I am going to recapitulate it briefly. We were discussing the increasing disregard for law and order, and the probable outcome if this tendency is permitted to go on unchecked.

The subject arose as a corollary to our unanimous indignation over yesterday's inexcusable racket. There is a city ordinance prohibiting the sale or shooting of firecrackers, but for the past week all sorts of noisy and dangerous fireworks were to be had almost any place in town. The patients at Brightwood—and we are far out in a residential zone where you would think we should be protected—were kept awake and on edge all night of the third and all day and all night of the fourth.

At the four corners of our grounds, which occupy the entire block, there are conspicuous signs reading "Quiet—Please—Hospital." It was generally agreed that there was more shooting in our block than anywhere else we had been, during this period.

McDermott insisted it was the signs, requesting quiet, that accounted for this annoyance. Mac thinks the rowdies see the notices and growl, "To hell with your rules!" And light a cannon-cracker the size of a rolling-pin, and toss it into the hospital grounds.

We asked one another, "Who are these people? Where do they come from? Who breeds this stock?" These queries set us going on our serious talk about the mounting inconsiderateness of our time. It would seem that a certain element of our population is utterly callous to the fundamental claims of common decency. Tim thinks we are rapidly becoming a nation of boobs.

I do not think that I am personally acquainted with a man or boy who would deliberately throw a nerve-splintering explosive onto the lawn of a hospital. But there are such people. Who are they? How did they get that way? Do they derive from any particular species? Or are they just unclassified halfwits and hoodlums?

McDermott, who is I fear slightly prejudiced in favour of persons speaking something that resembles the English language, thinks we have been far too lax with our immigration restrictions; says the public's bad manners have been imported. While I do not share his certainty that this fully explains the growing impoliteness and disregard of the ordinary amenities, I do believe that the country is too heavily stocked with aliens who have no interest in the American way of living.

Now that bootlegging is rampant—as might have been expected, with the Federal Government in charge of prohibition enforcement—it is significant that the very large majority of the men arrested every day for liquor-smuggling and liquor-peddling are foreigners bearing other than English names.

Mac had an evening paper along with him, which he proceeded to spread out over the table and into the hollandaise sauce, and began drawing little circles around the names of persons figuring in to-day's crime news. "Look!" he said, "See what I mean?"

It really was amazing! It appears that we are supporting an imported underworld composed of people who arrogantly defy our laws. In what other nation, inquires McDermott, would such a thing be permitted?

Tim thinks the war had a lot to do with the prevailing rudeness; says the demobilized soldiers, released from rigid restraints, are eager to exercise their liberty; thinks they enjoy the distinction of being "tough guys."

I ventured the opinion that the automobile has had much to do with making people inconsiderate. A naturally rude fellow will impose on other people, when he is behind the steering wheel of a car where they can't get at him. The bigger coward he is, on foot, the more bravely impudent he is, on wheels.

We still don't know what sort of people touched off the firecrackers around the hospital. But we do know that there is being developed, in this country, a contempt for law and the elementary civilities. I wonder if the big factories haven't something to do with it. Until the recent techniques of mass production came in, men in industry found joy in their work. The cabinet-maker produced a bureau; all of it. He designed it, fitted it together with skill, applied its hardware, varnished it, fetched it to market. Now, his son's contribution to the five thousand identical bureaus that the big furniture factory has contracted for, is limited to the job of feeding an automatic machine that dowels the boards with a punch—and a whack. You can't expect this young fellow to find any joy in that sort of occupation. He has to find his pleasure apart from his work. And he doesn't know how. He goes out looking for excitement. Firecrackers, perhaps.

I have made some notes on our conversation, to-night, because the problem we discussed is likely to grow more and more serious. Unless this increasing contempt for authority and indifference to the public welfare is effectively dealt with, the tendency may become a grave menace to the very life of this nation.

Evidently it is an easy step from impoliteness to vandalism, and from vandalism to disregard of life and safety. If we are not vigilant, there may come a day when life in this land will be cheap, and property rights insecure.[1]

[1] Deaths by automobile accidents in 1919, 11,154; in 1922, 15,326. (R. M.) In 1938, 32,400. (Editor.)

When the hoodlum class has become sufficiently important, numerically, to be aware of its united power, it may either decide to make war on honest and industrious citizens at the polls, or stage a revolution.

* * * * *

For the past hour I have been in my office, talking with Nancy Ashford, who returned this evening from a two weeks' vacation in the country near harbour Beach on Lake Huron.

One of our pet nurses, Cynthia Bates, hails from that neighbourhood and is forever extolling the peace and quiet of the shore farms. Nancy, physically and emotionally worn by her heavy responsibilities, thought it might be good for her to escape into such a tranquillizing environment.

Her report was amusing. Nancy had the usual experience of the city dweller who, battered by the rasp of traffic and the suffocating contacts with the urban pack, seeks repose in the open spaces and among persons of simple life. The first day of this serenity is so delightfully healing to the bruised spirit that one doubts whether one will ever be able to return to the racket. And the first night, one sleeps like a baby—probably because well done up from a long journey. The next night—but I'll let Nancy describe it.

"The next night was mosquito night. They had a fiesta. And I was in the front row. Martha was sorry they didn't have electric lights—I mean the house; not the mosquitoes—and so was I; for that meant I couldn't read in bed. There was a two candle power kerosene lamp on the table. I couldn't see to read by it, but it was just right for the mosquitoes to find their way about. And—so far as the peace and quiet went—I never heard so much noise; noises I wasn't used to. The katydids! My word! And the frogs! And the bugs!"

"Bugs?"

"Oh, no—not that kind. Martha is clean as a pin. I mean gnats and various things that fly around and sing—and carry hypodermic kits."

"How was the food?" I inquired. "You can generally get some very nice saddle-leather, at these country places, served with brown gravy."

"The food was wonderful!" replied Nancy, fervently. "Martha is a grand cook. I wish we could induce her to come to Brightwood. I've had about all I can take from Emmons."

"Drinking again?"

"And surly—and impudent—and untidy."

"Very well: get Martha."

"She would like to come. I talked to her about it. But she lives with her brother. They're twins. They've never been separated. We would have to find a job for Perry."

"That might not be hard," I said. "What can he do?"

"I don't know," said Nancy, with a little sigh. "Perry has a stiff knee that's gone to his head. It has made him sour as a pickle. He might be taught to help with the furnaces and mow the lawn and—odd jobs. He is handy with tools. Made his own motor-boat. Took the engine out of an old flivver."

"Did you take a ride in it?" I asked.

"He didn't invite me. Perry's about as companionable as a—a porcupine. But Martha is a darling! And I can't see how she endures that lonely life up there with nobody to talk to but this sorehead." Then Nancy went on to eulogize Martha's wide range of domestic accomplishments, and repeat her wish that the frustrated woman might be given "a chance to live."

"All right," I agreed. "Bring her on. We can find something for Perry. Maybe the change of scenery would be good for him too."

So—we left it at that. Nancy hopes it will work out happily; and, for her sake, I do too; though it won't bother me very much, if it doesn't; I'm not responsible for what goes on in the hospital kitchen. It's Nancy's job.

* * * * *

I fear I have forgotten to report on the dinner party we had, a little while ago, attended by Natalie and Tim and Harry Wickes.

It was expected, at least by me, that Natalie and Tim would consolidate and leave Harry to the mercy of Joyce. From the first it was evident that Natalie and Harry have discovered their mutual indispensability.

If Tim has been in doubt whether to pursue his interest in Natalie, I think he may now set his mind at ease on that subject.

About nine, he put in a call to Brightwood, and regretted to learn that he had to leave us at once. I hope Tim is not going to fret, and I don't believe he will. I should like to see him in a home of his own. I wonder if he might like Dorothy. We must arrange to have them over together some evening.

Joyce heard from Helen to-day. Uncle Percival insists on her spending the rest of the summer at home. It's a very drab life for her. I wish we could do something about it.

AT HOME
August twentieth, 1919, 10.30 p.m.

ON several occasions, during the past year or more, I have talked vaguely with my good friend, Fred Ferguson, about a small cottage I thought of building on my few arid acres overlooking Lake Saginack.

Fred has always made a little joke of it. As the best-known architect in town, he doesn't waste his time on such insignificant projects, and he has doubted whether I would make much use of a house in that uninviting region.

Last night, we found each other at the Columbia Club, and had dinner together. Mrs. Ferguson was out of town, and Joyce is a guest at Windymere over the week-end where Bobby Merrick is entertaining a dozen young friends from town. I wasn't keen on Joyce's accepting the invitation, but I didn't care to have a row with her.

Fred, as usual, wanted to know how the little house was coming on; and when I assured him that I still had the thing seriously in mind he said, "Why don't we drive out there to-morrow and look the place over—and make a few pencil-sketches."

I picked him up this morning about ten and we arrived shortly after one. The last two miles are off the highway on a narrow gravelled road. I must say that the country round about is anything but attractive; a lot of dwarfed pine and brambles. Of course, everything is seared now with the usual midsummer drought. I felt a bit chagrined over the general appearance of my untamed property, as we turned into the ill-conditioned lane and proceeded slowly toward the unfenced west boundary of the tract which overhangs the water at an elevation of some eighty feet. Fred was saying nothing as we got out of the car and sauntered through the briars to the ledge. I rather expected he would remark, presently, that the situation was bad and that I had better not waste any money on it. He looked for a long time at the lake and the land, and then said, "If you really want a little hideout, Doc, where you can rusticate in peace, I think we can build something suitable. It's a great view. And all you need, to make a lovely setting for your house, is a good job of landscaping, a deep well, and some competent person to keep up the grounds."

We sat down on the parched grass and Fred continued thinking aloud. I might as well make up my mind, he said, that there would be a nice little item of expense—at the outset—for the engineering. There should be a low stone wall fronting the lake, and some grading and excavation necessary to make a safe and comfortable way down to a boat-house and swimming-wharf.

"But it will not be of much satisfaction," he went on, "if you think of it as a mere summer place. If you are willing to go into this thing right, build an all-year house and put some people in it who will take care of it and the grounds. If it isn't that important, I shouldn't do it, at all, if I were you."

Then he began drawing some tentative plans for a house, part of it to serve the caretakers; two-thirds of it for the master, a couple of guest bedrooms, and—most important of all—a large living-room with a grand view. As the design unfolded, my interest increased. I need a place of this sort. I have stuck too close to my work.

"If you mean business," said Fred, "you would do well to have a good landscape man come out here and get some of your heavier plantings started. It takes a little time to do that."

"I would probably not live long enough to see trees of any size," I said.

"Not like the ones across the lake, certainly," agreed Fred, pointing to the beautiful panorama on the western shore. "The Fosters' grove of firs must be very old; big trees long before they built their place. Nick Merrick paid a pretty penny for his landscaping."

"You built that house; didn't you?"

"Yes. It's a great place; don't you think?"

"Gorgeous! But I wouldn't want it. Too big."

"Neither would I," agreed Fred. "I wonder if the old boy is happy in it."

"Ought to be," I said. "He has everything; all the modern conveniences; fancy livestock, flower gardens, fresh air, the lake."

"I don't think Nick makes much use of the lake," drawled Fred. "Young Bobby has a little fun, occasionally, in that big speed-boat. Have you seen him lately?"

I said I hadn't. Fred grinned enigmatically.

"Have you?" I asked, surmising that he wanted a little encouragement.

"Bobby's going to be a second edition of Cliff," muttered Fred. "A good deal brighter than Cliff—but a waster. They tell me he is doing a fairly good job at the University; finishes in February. But he goes at a pretty fast clip."

"Does your Arthur see anything of him, over there?" I inquired.

"No," snapped Fred. "I put my foot down on that. He's no fit company for any young fellow with an ounce of ambition. Art was considerably upset because I wouldn't let him go to Bobby's house party that's on now at Windymere."

"You must have your boy under good control," I observed, "or he would have gone, anyhow."

"Oh—he knows better than to pull a trick like that on his daddy. However—I must say for the boy that he generally votes the right ticket. We haven't had much trouble with him. I've explained to him that we're not well enough off to let him grow up to be a bum. He has got his living to make. Young Merrick will never have to work." After a little pause, he added, "I expect that bunch, over there to-day, is plastered to the eyebrows."

I made no reply for a long time; then I couldn't help saying, "My Joyce is there."

"Sorry," said Fred, a bit flustered. "I guess I spoke out of turn. However—I daresay your girl can take care of herself, all right."

"I hope so," I said. "It's hard to know just what to do when these youngsters insist on having their own way."

"Yeah—that's right, Doc," said Fred, soothingly. "Big problem." He scrambled to his feet. "Well—shall we call it a day—and go home?"

Our conversation had suddenly depressed me. We drove another mile north on the gravelled road, at Fred's suggestion, to see what the country looked like, further out. I

376

hadn't been that far, before. Half a mile from my place we found an unoccupied house, not in bad repair, and sauntered around it, peering in through cobwebbed windows.

"Somebody tried to live here," I said, "and gave it up."

"They probably hoped to make a living," said Fred. "Anyone who wants a house in this neighbourhood will have to make his living somewhere else."

We had some difficulty keeping our conversation alive, on the way home. It was still a bright day, but my own sky was overcast. I let Fred out at his house, and returned to the hospital to see if everything was all right. Or, perhaps my car proceeded over to Brightwood by force of habit. Or, perhaps I felt, subconsciously, that was the one stable fact left to reassure me. In any event, I went to the hospital, where things seemed unusually quiet. I did not talk to anyone.

I had my dinner at home alone. I suppose it was a good dinner, but I had no appetite. Afterward I began a letter to Helen, but found I had nothing in particular to say to her that I dared to say. So I tore it up. Then I decided to write a few pages in this journal, but you can see that I am in no mood for that either. Life is very flat to-night.

* * * * *

Nancy has succeeded in bringing Martha Ruggles and her irascible brother to Brightwood. Martha is proving to be the jewel that Nancy had thought her. Grim old Perry who, for all that he is Martha's twin, appears to be about ten years her senior, is going to be a problem. Can't work with anybody. Thinks he is being made fun of, and I daresay he is.

He regards everyone with suspicion. Nancy thinks he is jealous of Martha's responsible position and growing popularity with our Brightwood family.

My heart goes out to the old codger. I think it's the stiff knee that has made him so standoffish. If so, that means he is uncommonly sensitive. I have a notion he would respond to a little tactful attention.

Yesterday afternoon I waved a hand to him as he was hobbling across the grounds behind a big lawnmower. He paused, a moment, and regarded me with an impassive stare, but did not return my salute. An hour later one of the orderlies met me in a corridor and said, confidentially, "This here new feller, with the game leg, is out in the parkin' lot, a-tinkerin' with your motor. He's got the spark-plugs all out, a-fussin' with 'em.

"I know about that, Danny," I said, failing to add that I had just now found it out. "And perhaps you'd better get back to your own job before it outgrows you." I hate a tattler.

It annoyed me a little to have this report about Perry. I would have to tell him, too, to mind his own business. When I left the hospital, my car had more pep and snap than it had had for many a day. Perry had cleaned and readjusted the spark-plugs: probably had known they needed it when he heard the engine come into the lot.

I couldn't help chuckling over this droll affair. Perry is going to be worth cultivation, I think. Yesterday's episode is funny enough to make a dog laugh, but it has its pathos, too. Sour old Perry never gets an amiable word because he doesn't deserve it. I wave a hand to him, and he merely scowls at me. Then he ditches his lawnmower and goes out to do me a favour. I must see more of Perry, but I'll have to be very careful.

I think he has all the natural instincts of a squirrel. He could be trained to eat out of your hand, but it would be a mistake to pat him on the back.

BLACKSTONE HOTEL, CHICAGO
August twenty-eighth, 1919, 8.30 p.m.

I CAME here for a consultation with Russell. We had it this afternoon and I am going back to Detroit to-night. Russell really shouldn't have asked me over, for there was nothing to be done. A sixteen-year-old boy dived into a shallow pool. Anyone would know, from the character of the respiration, that the blow had fractured the odontoid process. You can't do anything about that.

Russell said, "I know—but the family wanted to do everything possible." And then he added that he wanted my confirmation of his own diagnosis. I told him I thought he could confirm that, in about three days, with an autopsy.

It was a great pity. They were very fine people, and the boy will be a sad loss to them. I can't get accustomed to these things. After the consultation, I had an hour's talk with the parents. They were bewildered; hungry for almost any kind of consolation. I am not sure that I gave them anything but my time and sympathy. I suggested that they have a talk with Dean Harcourt, after they have laid their boy away. They know he can't live more than a day or two. We gave them no false hopes. I do not think it is a kindness, in such cases, to offer any encouragement. And neither does Russell. The truth—taking it by and large—is more satisfactory than a lie, however kindly meant. You encourage a family to hope—when there isn't the ghost of a chance—and they keep themselves strung up almost to the breaking-point for a period of days; and then they have to take the blow when their nervous equipment is disabled.

I used, occasionally, to practice that sort of benign deceit, but stopped it when I realized—with a start—that it wasn't their own feelings I had been trying to protect so much as mine. I had thought I was being humane when I was only being cowardly. I didn't want to witness their grief. I wanted them to take their hard wallop when I wasn't present to see them writhe. You'll find, if you look into it, that your sympathies can play some queer tricks on you. There's a lot of fraudulent consolation offered by people who are merely trying to protect their own emotions against a distressing scene.

Somebody is in an awful mess, and you say, "There, there; don't fret. Maybe this is going to come out all right." And you damn-well know it isn't going to come out all right. It's already out—and it's all wrong! What you're really trying to do is to give them a little sniff of ether until you've had time to escape.

Of course, it is a mistake to argue with grief, but it's a bigger mistake to dismiss it with "Now, now; there, there."

Pyle had an interesting patient at Brightwood, a few weeks ago; a serene and friendly little woman, who had been hospitalized for some deep surgery. Pyle asked me to call on her, when she was convalescent. In the course of our talk, I inquired about her family. She had lost a boy, an only child, when he was twelve. I said, "That's too bad." She shook her head and smiled. "No," she said, quietly, "I've never felt that way about it. It was the great experience of my life—having him for twelve years. I live it over and over. Those memories are very precious. They comforted me so much when I was sick."

I repeated this conversation to the Brownings, this afternoon. I told them they couldn't hope that their Lawrence would recover, but they had a right to hope for an early arrival of the day when their possession of him—for sixteen years—would become an enduring blessing. Mrs. Browning murmured, "Larry has had such a short life." I told her they might extend it by investing something—in Larry's name. Her husband, eager to comfort her, said they would do that; a gift to the hospital, maybe.

"Or, better, an investment in a person," I suggested. "Stake some worthy young fellow to an education that will fit him for constructive service—and that will be Larry, carrying on; Larry as a doctor, perhaps; Larry as a teacher; Larry as a violinist. Find a chap that can be trained to make people well, or informed, or happy. Then Larry will live for a long time yet."

I never stepped out of a professional consultation before, to go into a lay consultation with the family. Perhaps I might not have done so to-day if I hadn't been out to the Cathedral this morning. I arrived here at nine, coming early on purpose to hear Harcourt. I have been under the spell of this, all day.

Harcourt is a straight and steady thinker. And everything he says sounds as if it was coming from Somewhere Else. Of course, the environment has a good deal to do with that. After you've been stilled by the impressive music and the ancient ritual, you drift into a sort of hypnosis which makes you peculiarly amenable to Harcourt's suggestions.

And yet he doesn't make the slightest effort to impose on your emotions. I can't quote the text he used. There is a Gideon Bible here on the chiffonier, but that doesn't do me any good; for I have forgotten where the text was: something about "The eye cannot see, nor the ear hear, the things God hath prepared for those who love Him; for He reveals them to us by His spirit."

For a little while, the Dean talked very beautifully about one's aesthetic response to the God we find in Nature. It was a prose poem. God in the sunrise; God in the sunset; offering two entirely different revelations of Himself; the eastern view at dawn inviting joy and work; the western view proposing a tranquil thought of rest. "That is what sunsets are made for," said the Dean, "to give you mental repose."

If you use your imagination a little on this, you will get the Dean's general idea of God's appeal to the human eye; in the silent, patient majesty of big trees; in the august austerity of high mountains; in the confident onrush of rivers cascading toward the sea, and never coming back until—chastened and humbled—they return in quiet showers falling on still pastures and in snowflakes on the hills. That sort of thing.

Then he talked about God's self-disclosures to the human ear; in music, of course; and in the eternity-message of the surf; and in the cadences of a voice beloved.

These were aesthetic appeals, said the Dean, and nobody was to minify their importance. "These messages," he went on, "are in the nature of spiritual oxygen. Without them, we cannot live as spiritual beings." Then he talked a little about the properties and phenomena of oxygen. We have to breathe to live, and it's the oxygen that we're after. We can't get on without it, and we recover it from the air by breathing. "When people become anaemic, spiritually, it may be for lack of oxygen. Perhaps there are no sunsets where they live. Perhaps they never see mountains or hear a waterfall. We get our spiritual oxygen through the eye and ear—and the other senses."

Then he talked about nitrogen. You can't live without it, but you must work for it. You can't breathe it. It is not free. It is in the soil, in the plants, in the wheat, in the meat; but not free.

Spiritual nitrogen, on which the soul feeds, must be captured. You must invest, you must be willing to wait with the patience of a farmer, you must not quit sowing because there was a drought. But if you strive, God will reveal to you, by His spirit, some self-disclosures which He cannot give you in a sunset, or by starlight, or by music. "Many people who can breathe," said the Dean, "are hungry."

Then he talked about what one may do to acquire this needful nitrogen; the investment of one's life in the upbuilding of other people, the steady alignment of oneself with the forces that lead up and on; costly adventures, sometimes; the more costly, the more rewarding.

The sermon was in the nature of a strong stimulant. I wish I had easier access to this man. I have not met him personally, and I shall not seek to do so. He is—from the distance in feet and inches that has been between him and me—the most engaging personality I have ever seen or heard; but I shall not risk a disillusionment by asking for an introduction to him: I do not want him to inquire how the weather is in Detroit, or tell me he is glad I came to his church. I don't want anything out of Harcourt when he isn't standing in his pulpit with his black gown on. Maybe I should find him just as helpful, in private talk; but I am not going to venture the experiment.

Back in the country, when I was a youngster, they always inquired whether the candidating preacher was a good mixer. Maybe that was the reason the people never kept one preacher very long. He was a mixer, and while he mixed, the people starved to death spiritually. At least, I surmise they did; for they were always in rows with one another, which couldn't very well have happened if they had been spiritually alive.

THE SHOREHAM, WASHINGTON
September seventeenth, 1919, 10 p.m.

I AM in good spirits to-night, after a month or more of anxiety. Joyce is again in Helen's custody, and everything is going to be all right.

Their school resumed work to-day. I came down with Joyce, explaining that I had an errand in Baltimore, which is true, though I purposely timed my appointment there to coincide with her journey. She was candidly suspicious of my motive, and inclined to be resentful when she learned we were travelling together.

"I hope you aren't afraid I might elope with some stranger," she said, ineffectually trying to be jocular.

"Not at all," I declared, "*but I have to go down, anyway, and I shall be very proud to be seen in your company. Of course," I added, pensively, "if you're ashamed to have your infirm parent along, I can go on a later train."

There wasn't much she could do, after that, but assure me of her great joy, so we planned the trip; and, on the surface, it was pleasant enough. But Joyce's surmise that, in my opinion, she needs a bit of supervision, isn't a bad guess. In fact she knows that I have been disturbed about her recent social activities. She has been playing around with a pretty gay set, seeing entirely too much of young Merrick and a chap named Masterson, who thinks he is going to be a story-writer.

I made an effort to learn something about the nature of these frequent engagements, some of which have kept her out late, but her accounts of their various diversions have been disquietingly sketchy, and her attitude on the subject decidedly cool. I have been less in Joyce's confidence, during the past couple of weeks, than ever before.

I think I once adverted, in this journal, to the very close relation between one's emotional states and certain types of heart trouble. I cannot too strongly insist that this is true. I have discovered, in my own case, that a few days of fretting will so intensify my heart disability that I am obliged to add that anxiety to the other worry.

My aneurism has bothered me so constantly, of late, that I decided to consult Ramsey at Johns Hopkins. I have an engagement to see him to-morrow afternoon. But I am feeling ever so much better, to-night; so very much better that I am half minded to call him up and cancel the appointment.

I know very well the reason for my sudden improvement. My girl is safe in Helen Brent's hands. I still have an aneurism—and it will unquestionably get me some day—but, to-night, I am fit as a fiddle.

Joyce gave herself the pleasure of teasing me, this morning, when I said I would go out to Chevy Chase with her.

"Why—how funny!" she shrilled. "I thought you detested getting yourself messed up with a lot of fond mammas and old maid professors. There must be something else out there, darling, that you want to look at. What could it be?"

I think she had repented a little, by the time we arrived; for she was prompt to find Helen, and when we met, her attitude was intended to put us at ease. I feel assured, now, that Joyce—however scatter-brained on occasions—has not abused my confidence by reporting to Helen the conversation we had about her.

By special dispensation, the girls were permitted to come down-town to dine with me. It was a delightful evening. How quickly Joyce reacted to the gracious presence of her charming friend. Instantly, she dropped her recent role of blasé and world-weary cynicism—a part she is quite too flighty to play convincingly—and became what she is, and ought to admit being, an impressionable school-girl, with a wide knowledge of the movie stars, a low opinion of Trigonometry, and an insatiable appetite for chocolate fudge. She is about as sophisticated as a pet rabbit. I have been so exasperated over her silly attempts to be a bored duchess that it was refreshing, indeed, to witness her return to a becoming simplicity.

Joyce never does things by halves. Having decided to set her clock back, she came very near recovering her perambulator, which had the effect of increasing the three years between herself and Helen to about ten, and lessening by that much the chasm between her lovely friend and me. I think Helen was a little bewildered, at first, over this manoeuvre, but soon adjusted herself to my child's metamorphosis.

While we were lingering over our coffee, Joyce—who hadn't wanted any—said she was anxious to get a note off in the mail and thought she would go and write it, if we'd excuse her.

"I am greatly relieved, my dear," I said, as Joyce moved off. "She is a different person when she's with you."

"I'm not conscious of doing anything to her," said Helen.

"That's just it!" I said. "You don't admonish or criticize. It's effortless. That's the charm of your influence. It's not because of anything you do. It's simply because you're you."

Her lips parted in a slow smile and her eyes lazily met mine.

"You always say nice things to me," she said. "They build me up." There was a little pause. "You like to build people up; don't you?"

"You don't need any building up, Helen," I said, sincerely.

"More than you'd think," she replied, soberly. "In my home no one goes to much bother about it." Then, impulsively candid, she added, "I think I'm at my best with you."

Perhaps she was hoping only to say something that would please me, but her tone was so obviously sincere that it stirred me deeply. I have been thinking seriously about it, since they left, a while ago.

Suppose it is true. Suppose that Helen really feels that way. I wonder if she might think that a constant companionship between us would give her a self-assurance valuable enough to compensate for the sacrifice she would have to make—of her youth.

Of course I would make a gallant effort to meet her age halfway. I think her comradeship might rub out a few of my years. She would unquestionably take on a quick maturity. But would it be fair?

I reason this all out, neatly, and almost persuade myself that the thing is possible, feasible, practical, commendable. And then the implacable figures—unadorned by any elaborate circumstantial extenuations—stand out like a problem in simple arithmetic. I am a fool for giving way to this desire. I shall not make a middle-aged matron of this radiant girl. It wouldn't be right. But—God!—how I need her!

* * * * *

And I am going over to Baltimore to-morrow to see Ramsey. The fact that my heart doesn't worry me to-night is of no lasting significance. I daresay the present apparent well-being of my heart is a simple psychological phenomenon, on the order of the bad toothache that suddenly lets up when one is on the way to the dentist.

I'll go to Baltimore in the morning. And I'll make an honest effort to put Helen out of my mind. The thing is impossible; and I may as well reconcile myself to that fact before I commit some serious blunder. As it stands, I can have her for a devoted friend. Perhaps I should be satisfied with that.

AT HOME
November twenty-seventh, 1919, 10.30 p.m.

TO-DAY was Thanksgiving. My chief grounds for gratitude were provided by a telegram from Joyce saying that Helen's attack of flu—of which I was informed, day before yesterday—is very light, and that she is already on the mend.

Helen is going home for a few days, to rest up, according to Joyce's wire; though I think she would be far better off where she is, in the hospital. I had a big notion to telegraph her to that effect, but decided it was none of my business.

Joyce thought it better to remain in Washington through the Thanksgiving recess and avoid the danger of picking up a flu germ on the train, which I felt showed uncommon wisdom. I wish now that I had urged them both to leave early and come here for the vacation. We could have put Helen into Brightwood, when she took sick.

This evening I had a little party at The Pontchartrain. I've had a private tip that this fine old hotel is presently going out of business. No announcement has been made yet, but it won't be long.

My guests were Natalie, Dorothy, Harry, young Minton— who has just come to Brightwood as assistant to Carter, and Nancy Ashford. My decision to invite Nancy was somewhat of a surprise to both of us. I never take her anywhere. Our business relations at the hospital require us to see so much of each other that I have thought it a safe policy to restrict our friendship to the contacts we have there. It would be so easy to set people chattering, if we went out together socially. I hate gossip.

Yesterday afternoon, in the course of a little conference with Nancy, she wanted to know whether I expected to be in town to-day. I told her I had no other plans, except for an informal dinner down-town with some young friends.

"Why don't you join us?" I asked.

"Sure you want me to?" countered Nancy, candidly.

"Of course!" I told her who would be there. "Do you good to get out of here for a few hours."

"Won't Doctor Minton think it's odd?" Nancy's eyes registered perplexity.

"Well—" I observed, loftily, "Doctor Minton's thoughts haven't become very important around here yet."

"Don't you like him?" asked Nancy.

"Sure!" I said, firmly. "Only he has no right to do any thinking about anything at Brightwood until he has been with us for ten years, at least."

"Very well," said Nancy. "Thanks. Shall I meet you down there—in Peacock Alley?"

"I'll come for you," I said. "About seven."

"Don't be silly," said Nancy, stringing out the last syllable derisively. "I'll go down in a taxi."

So—we left it that way. Damn it! If I'd had sense enough to ask Nancy Ashford to marry me, ten years ago, she might have done it; and we would have been immensely congenial. She would have taken Joyce in hand and made a normal, stable child of her. But Brightwood needed Nancy more than I did. If I were a little more wise than I am, I might propose this to Nancy—even now. But I doubt whether she would be the least bit interested. We have been associated in business too long to pitch our relations in any other key. We are very fond of each other—but—that's as far as it goes.

Nancy nearly took my breath away to-night. I haven't seen her in anything but hospital harness for a long time. She is certainly a stunningly beautiful woman, with that youthful face and white hair and trim lines. She was in black. It fitted as if she'd been melted and poured into it.

Naturally, she had the opposite side of the table. I admired the poise and assurance with which she accepted her hostess role. I was very proud of Nancy Ashford, to-night. Occasionally I caught her eye, and it came over me that she and I were very close friends; very dependent on each other; very much more intimately bound up together than I had thought. As a matter of fact, I haven't thought much about it—for a long time. We had our work to do. I wish I had a map of her mind.

Natalie, who sat on my right, showed me her engagement ring. It hadn't been bought at the ten-cent store. I suppose Harry will be paying for it over a considerable period. Natalie was starry-eyed. I think this match is perfect. Harry is thoroughly fine.

Dorothy, as usual, was very pretty, and self-contained. Dorothy doesn't say much, but her eyes are bright. Doctor Minton seemed to enjoy looking into them.

It was the traditional Thanksgiving dinner; turkey, mashed potatoes and gravy, baked squash, cranberry sauce, etc. I wonder what it is that a hotel does to a turkey that utterly relieves it of any taste, at all. Have you ever noticed that? It always looks fairly appetizing, and tastes like a lukewarm slice of linoleum.

I drove Nancy home, over her mild protest. We talked mostly about hospital affairs. When I let her out, she said, "It's none of my business, but if I were you I shouldn't throw young Minton and your Dorothy Wickes at each other."

"You think he's a trifler?" I asked.

"It wouldn't surprise me," said Nancy.

"I hope he hasn't been making passes at any of our girls, here at Brightwood," I growled.

"Oh no," said Nancy, quickly. "He is far too clever to do that. But—I think he feels pretty sure that women ought to find him practically irresistible."

"Do you think Dorothy was impressed?"

"Well—Doctor Minton is a handsome young fellow, witty, amiable. Doubtless she enjoyed his attentions which, I thought, were quite marked. Don't take this too seriously, please. Only—as I said—if I were you I shouldn't contrive occasions to further their acquaintance."

"Thanks for the tip," I said. "Your hunches are usually right."

* * * * *

I wrote a letter to Helen to-night, inviting her to spend the Christmas holidays with us. Perhaps I shouldn't have done it.

I have again and again explained to myself how imprudent it would be to pursue this hopeless friendship any farther. But, in the face of my sober judgment, I wrote the letter. I even pressed the invitation urgently. Heretofore, on similar occasions, I have merely added my hope to Joyce's that she would come for a visit. This time I told her that I was very anxious to have her come, adding that Joyce—of course—joined heartily in the invitation.

After I had written the letter I walked down to the corner and mailed it, which is certainly proof enough that I wanted to make sure my commonsense—possibly restored by daylight—will have no chance to deter me from committing this indiscretion.

AT HOME
December second, 1919, 9 p.m.

JOYCE arrived home unexpectedly this morning. I was at the hospital when she telephoned from the house. She was sullen, sore, and uncommunicative. As soon as I could get away I drove home and queried her.

The story was hard to extract. She has not yet confided the full details, and may not do so. The most I can make of this half-hysterical, disjointed, incoherent report is that she slipped away from the school, just before dinner, the day before yesterday, and went down-town in a taxi.

At the Raleigh she met, by appointment, two local girls who had been expelled from the school, last spring, for insubordination. They were her guests at dinner, and afterward they went to a night club with three young men friends of the Washington girls, and danced. She showed up in Chevy Chase shortly after two, which she thinks is not very late for a young woman of her age to be out, but the management seems to have thought otherwise.

So they suspended her for the remainder of the year; and here she is, at home, apparently much pleased over her recollection of the things she said to the Principal before she left. I surmise that these final impudences were of a flavour to insure my daughter's future status in the esteem of the institution. It is very unlikely that they will ever take her back.

I tried to be patient and sympathetic as Joyce shrieked and blubbered her story. According to her view of the scrape, she has been persecuted. She had done nothing deserving of censure; much less suspension. It was just a few hours of innocent fun. She had been in respectable company, and behaving discreetly. These unwanted old prissies, instead of being cattishly jealous because a girl had been invited out of their stuffy little reformatory for some fresh air and lively music, should have been glad that at least one of their charges still had enough pep left to exercise her human rights—and so forth—and so on.

I knew better than to come to the defence of the school management, at this stage of Joyce's dramatization of her woes, and when I said, "Too bad," she shouted, "How do you mean—'too bad!' I'll bet you don't mean it's too bad the way they've thrown me out! You mean I'm too bad, and it's too bad I am human, and too bad I like a little fun! That's what you mean!"

By two o'clock I felt that I had had about all of this that was good for me, and returned to the hospital. Before I left the house I heard Joyce telephoning to one of her girl friends whose acquaintance she made in the summer.

I came home early for dinner, this evening, hoping to find her in a less rebellious mood. She had left a note for me, saying she would be out for dinner. I suspect that I am now in for an indeterminate period of anxiety. I wish I knew what to do. I can't lock her up.

* * * * *

There is one comforting ray of hope. I had a letter from Helen to-day, in reply to my latest to her, saying she is almost well again and is planning to be with us through the Christmas holidays. Of course she had not yet learned of Joyce's misfortune. I hope this does not affect her decision to come, and I don't think it will; except possibly to make Helen more sure she should come—and see what may be done for our unhappy girl.

* * * * *

Nancy tells me to-day that our Perry Ruggles slapped old Danny Ulrick yesterday. She says there has been bad blood between Perry and Danny for some time. Yesterday Danny made some remark that annoyed Perry. There was no fight. Danny, having been soundly— and no doubt appropriately—slapped, immediately demobilized himself and went at full gallop to report his injury to the superintendent.

"I sent for Perry to come to my office at once," said Nancy.

"And what did he have to say for himself?" I asked, with much interest.

"He didn't come," said Nancy.

So—I suppose we will have to let Perry out of our organization. I shall try to see him to-morrow and find out whether there is anything we can do to save Martha. Nancy says Martha is much chagrined. But if old Perry goes, Martha insists that she will have to follow him.

I wouldn't have Nancy Ashford's job if it was the last bit of employment left in the world.

* * * * *

Carter told me this afternoon that he wanted me to be more circumspect with my digitalis. I had been feeling so well, for a few weeks, that I had let the dosage run down. I feel like an old man to-night.

AT HOME
December twenty-third, 1919, 4 p.m.

I HAVE not been well for the past three weeks. Until yesterday, I have been going to the hospital in the mornings and coming home early in the afternoon. Joyce does not realize that I have been ill. This is not her fault, for I have made light of the fact that I am not pursuing my usual schedule of work.

She sleeps all forenoon, and is gone for the remainder of the day. A few times I have waited up for her, but she resents it and is frank to say so.

Yesterday things came to a little crisis with me. I passed out cold in the operating-room. It was an intracranial tumour— a long, tiresome, exacting task. Fortunately I had Tim Watson with me.

I have no recollection of fainting. When I roused, I was propped up in bed, with Carter counting my wrist. I suddenly remembered that I had been operating, and tried to raise up; but I was too weak. Carter said, "You're all right. Take it easy. Watson's carrying on. You were all done but the sutures. He can manage."

"Queer," I mumbled. "Nothing like that ever happened to me before. Didn't have the slightest bit of warning."

"It needn't happen any more," said Carter, encouragingly. "It was a long job—and you're not quite up to par. You'll be fit, after you've rested a little."

"I think I'll get up now," I said.

"Not yet," advised Carter. "I want you to stay right where you are for a couple of hours. I'll be back presently."

I settled back on the pillows and noticed a hypodermic syringe on the table. The Bates girl was standing there. I said, "What was that?" She pretended she didn't know, which was of course the proper behaviour for her. I said, "Hand it to me." She did so, rather reluctantly. There was a minute particle of the solution adhering to the point of the needle. I touched it to the tip of my tongue. It was nitroglycerine. I hadn't fainted because of fatigue. It was a heart attack.

Carter drove me home about four, Minton following in Carter's car to pick him up. I didn't go to bed and Carter didn't insist on it; said I would be just as well off lounging on the davenport, not too flat. It sounded like good advice. Joyce did not come home for dinner.

I feel ever so much better, to-day, than for several days. I'm not fretting about myself. Carter said I should be quiet to-day, and he evidently reinforced his suggestion. I know the stuff he gave me has codeine in it. It accounts for my peace of mind.

* * * * *

Helen is coming to-morrow. I am not going to try to meet her. Joyce can tell her I had to be at the hospital. I hope I shall be well enough to entertain her properly. It would be too bad if her visit were spoiled. Perhaps I can keep her from finding out that I have had this little upset. If I am as much better to-morrow as I am to-day, maybe she will not notice. Joyce hasn't remarked about it. Gladys knows, but I told her not to say anything.

Joyce insists that she is very happy over Helen's coming for Christmas, but seems a bit embarrassed. Helen has been back at school and of course knows the story of Joyce's escapade. Perhaps they have had some correspondence about it: I don't know.

I am looking forward to to-morrow with mingled feelings.

AT HOME
Christmas Eve, 1919, Midnight

THIS is indeed a Merry Christmas! My heart is overflowing with joy!

I must try to record to-day's experiences in orderly fashion, but it will not be easy to do. Five minutes ago I parted with Helen at the foot of the stairs. I know that as long as I live the memory of that enchanted moment will quicken my pulse.

This morning I rose in better health than I have had for a month. I had a notion to accompany Joyce to the station. But I had told her that she was to meet Helen without me, and she had seemed pleased over the prospect. Perhaps she felt it was going to be easier for her if she had an hour alone with Helen, at the outset.

I drove to Brightwood. There had been a brain tumour operation scheduled for nine-thirty this morning but they had postponed it. I amazed my colleagues—and worried them, too, I fear—by announcing that I was going to do the operation. While we were scrubbing up for it, Tim said, "Are you sure you want to do this? We can put it off a few days, you know. Give you a little more time to get your strength back." I assured him I had never felt more fit. So—we went into it. My hand was never steadier. I think Tim and the nurses were relieved when I had finished. I know they thought I ought to be at home in bed.

It was after one before I could leave the hospital. For many years it has been my custom to give small Christmas presents to the nurses, orderlies, and all the help. Nancy always makes out these cheques in figures consistent with the nature of the employment and seniority in service. The cheques are enclosed in gay greeting cards and distributed during the morning of the day before Christmas.

It is difficult to account for the way some little traditions get themselves established. I suppose that the first time we issued these Christmas cheques, some employee—eager to show his gratitude—came to my office at once to extend the season's greetings. And then all the rest of them followed suit.

At all events, I can expect—on the day before Christmas— that before I leave the hospital our entire outfit will swarm in on me with assorted felicitations and expressions of thanks.

This morning I forgot about it. I daresay my absent-mindedness was to be accounted for by my eagerness to go home and welcome Helen. Shortly after eleven, I was on my way out of the building when I met Nancy.

"You can't go," she said, in a stage whisper. "Have you forgotten?"

It suddenly dawned on me what she meant.

"Sorry, Nancy," I said. "I'm afraid it slipped my mind."

"You feel all right; don't you?" she asked, anxiously. "You mustn't stay—if you don't."

I assured her that wasn't the reason. I had forgotten; that was all.

"Then you'd better wait," she advised. "They will be disappointed if you don't."

I hesitated a little.

"Think so?" I queried. "I was hoping I might get away early."

Nancy shook her head.

"If it isn't something positively urgent, you ought to wait." Nancy seemed to have something on her mind. "You see," she went on, slowly, "there's a rumour going around that you're not very well. Everybody knows what happened. I think it will be just as well if they all have a chance to see you to-day, and find out for themselves that you're all right."

I have always despised loose chatter and indiscriminate gossip. Nancy's report that there was a lot of buzz at Brightwood over my little collapse annoyed me.

"You saw to it that they all had their usual gifts?" I asked.

"Of course," said Nancy.

"And now I'm expected to sit in my office, for a couple of hours, just to prove to them that I haven't had a stroke of paralysis—or something. Well—I don't like the idea."

"But you'll do it," wheedled Nancy, "because I asked you."

I turned about, took off my hat and coat, and trailed along after her to my office. Presently they began streaming in, the word that I was ready to receive them having got about quickly by the mysterious grapevine process of communication. I tried to greet them all with the usual exuberance, but I'm afraid the affair wasn't quite satisfactory. Most of them came to my desk with anxious, questioning eyes, as if they were trying to make a quick diagnosis. Their attitude perplexed me; chilled me a little. Some of them seemed almost strangers. I tried my best to be natural, probably overdoing it; and a few of the brassier ones showed an enthusiastic cordiality that was too strident to be spontaneous.

When it appeared that my large family had all been in, and I was making ready to leave—with the disturbing sensation that if they had been apprehensive about me before, they would probably be even more so now—grim old Perry Ruggles hobbled through the doorway and confronted me with a heavy frown. I was pulling on my overcoat.

"I ain't a-takin' it," he growled, deep in his throat. He laid the cheque down on the desk, and pushed it toward me with a work-worn finger. "I ain't been nothin' but a lot o' trouble to yuh." It was plain to see that Perry had composed this speech with all the wormy abasement of the Prodigal Son. I could hardly keep my face straight. "Yuh've paid me more'n I earned," he rumbled. "Ef 't-waren't fer Martha, yuh wouldn't hev me around, 'n' I wouldn't blame yuh. I'm no good here."

I walked to the door and closed it, returned to my desk, and seated myself. "Sit down, won't you?" I said. "Let's have a little chat about it."

Perry gingerly lowered himself into the chair, and sat on the edge of it, scowling inquiringly.

"Perhaps you haven't been entirely happy here. Perry," I began, "but that's probably because the work you have been asked to do has not interested you very much. You have known you were employed here because we needed your sister. I understand your feeling, and I know I should feel the same way myself. I have been trying to think of something more pleasant for you to do."

Perry's lips were still pursed tightly, but his brow had smoothed a little.

"I don't like it—in town," he muttered. "Neither does Martha, fer that sake. Ef 't-waren't fer Miss Ashford, a-bein' so good t' her, she'd go back t' the country with me."

Suddenly I had an inspiration.

"Perry," I said, "I have a little place up on Lake Saginack where I am going to build a house in the spring; soon as the weather permits. I have had a lot of trees planted there, and shrubbery. How would you like the job of caretaker?"

Perry rubbed his jaw carefully, which I interpreted as a bargaining gesture. This, I felt, was enough progress for one session. And I was anxious to get away.

"What all would I hev t' do?" he asked.

"We can figure that out," I said, rising. "You stay here and try to content yourself for the present—and we'll talk about the other thing when we get around to it. And as for this little Christmas gift," I added, "I shall be more pleased if you take it. If you feel you do not deserve it, how about converting it into a present for someone else?"

Perry's upper lip lifted in amazement, and he blinked a few times. I suppose it was the first time that an idea of this nature ever collided with Perry. His expression was so amusing that I had to hold on tight to keep from ruining our delicate relationship.

"Didn't you ever do anything like that?" I asked. "It's great fun." Then—perhaps because I had already startled Perry with a strange suggestion, I thought I would see whether he could survive another harder jolt. "It's even more fun," I went on, "if you give the present to someone who isn't expecting anything, and will be surprised."

Perry drew a crooked grin and said he 'lowed almost anybody'd be surprised ef they got a present frum him. This struck us both as being very funny indeed and we laughed together. Perry's merriment was noisily uncouth, but short-lived. He quickly resumed his habitual frown, apparently repenting that he had let himself go in this unseemly manner.

"If you don't happen to know anyone to try this out on," I said, "I'd like to make a suggestion. Have you ever noticed this sharp-nosed little kid that comes every day with somebody's lunch?"

Perry eyed me suspiciously from under shaggy brows.

"Yeah," he replied, unpleasantly. "That's this here Ulrick feller's grandson."

"He's certainly a ragged little rascal," I remarked. "I suppose everything he wears has been passed along to him, after it has been worn out by his brothers."

"Yeah," agreed Perry sourly. "I guess so. Old man Ulrick has to feed a passel of 'em."

I picked up the cheque and handed it to Perry.

"There you are," I said. "You go and see how much fun you can have with it."

"Yuh mean—get some shoes, er sumpin, fer that kid?" Perry's tone was loaded with distaste. "By Gar! That's more'n old Ulrick'd ever do fer any o' my kin, I'll bet!"

"I think you're probably right," I said. "I imagine that Danny has missed a lot of fun in his life. I suppose he has had his nose on the grindstone so hard that he never had a chance to give himself a treat."

"Himself a treat?" echoed Perry, derisively. "Yuh mean— I'd be givin' myself a treat ef I got this kid some shoes?"

"Of course," I declared. "I must go now. Perry. Good luck with your experiment."

Perry blocked my way.

"Yeah—but see here," he muttered. "Ef I do that, old Ulrick will think I'm a-tryin' t' be friendly like, and we ain't spoke fer weeks."

"Oh, well, in that case," I remarked casually, "maybe you'd better not do anything about it. If it's more fun not to speak to old Danny than to get his grandson some shoes, let it go. I expect you're right. If you gave the shoes to the kid, old Danny would probably want to speak to you—and, of course, that would be annoying. Just forget about it. Perry. Bye-bye. Merry Christmas." I went out and left him standing there.

On the way out, I met Nancy again. I had a broad grin on my face, and Nancy said, "What have you been up to?" Perry was hobbling down the hall. She tipped her head slightly in his direction and asked, "Have you, by any chance, been entertaining yourself at that poor thing's expense?"

I nodded, and assumed the guilty look of a child caught in the jam-jar.

"Does—does he know it?" asked Nancy, anxiously.

"I think so," I said, soberly. "And I believe he was entertained a little, too. Did you ever hear Perry laugh?" I asked.

"Impossible!" she declared. "Want to tell me?"

"No," I said. "Not now. Merry Christmas, Nancy!"

* * * * *

Helen's greeting was very tender, giving me both hands, her smiling eyes full of sincere affection. I wanted to kiss her. Had my feelings toward her been simply that of a middle-aged parent, welcoming his child's best friend into his home, I might have done so. But I knew I could not pretend to exercise a doting father's privilege in greeting a young guest. If I kissed Helen, it wouldn't be a mere gesture of hospitality. So—I rejected the impulse, but retained her hands, and I am afraid that as I looked into her uplifted eyes she must have divined my wish; for she flushed a little, and seemed anxious to include Joyce quickly into our mutual expression of happiness.

They were dressed for the street, Joyce having secured tickets for a matinée. It was suggested that they might be able to find a seat for me, but I declined, thinking it much better to let them be alone together. I was very happy. The old relationship between the girls had been resumed, and it was easy to see that Joyce was finding much satisfaction in readjusting herself to match Helen's poise and manner. The strained, half-rebellious expression had vanished from my child's mobile face. Helen exercises some strange witchery that transforms Joyce into a person of beauty and charm.

I spent the afternoon alone with my thoughts. It was good to feel physically fit again. It was good to see Joyce doffing her brittle affectations. It was very healing to my spirit to have Helen near me again.

It was almost six when they returned, tarrying before the open fire, for the temperature had dropped, and they were chilled. At Joyce's suggestion, we dressed for dinner. I was glad she had not wanted to go out. We met in the library at seven. I was proud of my dinner companions. They were very lovely. Joyce was in blue and Helen in coral.

Our talk skipped about, with no central purpose; no serious intent. When the dessert came on, there was a little lull in our conversation, and I remarked—quite fervently—that it was a very happy occasion; that it was delightful to have Helen with us. I surprised myself by saying, "I don't see how we can ever let you go."

"Why need she ever go?" said Joyce, turning fond eyes toward Helen. "You're happier here than anywhere else; aren't you, darling?"

My heart skipped a beat. I hoped Helen would appraise the remark as one of Joyce's undeliberated disbursements, and make some rejoinder that would tag it as a spontaneous outburst of affection.

Helen did not reply, for a moment. A slow flush crept up her cheek, and she did not lift her eyes.

"See?" exclaimed Joyce, ecstatically. "It's true! Let's keep her, Daddy!"

It was a pretty tense moment. At least it was for me. And when Gladys popped in to tell Joyce that Mr. Masterson wanted her on the telephone I was pleased that something had intervened to remove her until we could tug the conversation back to firmer ground.

"Joyce," I said, when she was gone, "sometimes does her thinking afterward." I chuckled a little, as if I had thought the situation mildly amusing. Helen, still pink, smiled, but made no comment.

"Of course," I went on, drawing an aimless little design on my ice-cream, "I couldn't imagine anything more wonderful— than to have you with us—always."

Helen slowly reached out her hand and laid it on mine. I wrapped my fingers tightly about it, and searched her eyes. She gave a quick little intake of breath. I rose and drew her to her feet. She came into my arms, and I kissed her. Her response was all that a starved heart could wish.

After a long moment, I released her a little, and said, rather breathlessly, "My darling—I have wanted you—so very much!"

"I know," she whispered. "It's all right."

"Can you forget how many years there are between us?" I asked.

"I forgot that," she murmured, "a long time ago."

I held her close to me again.

"Joyce will be coming back," she said, softly.

"Shall we tell her—now?" I asked.

"Of course. She would know, anyhow. And we mustn't leave her out. That would spoil everything—for all three of us."

What a sensible creature she is! I suppose that's the first and biggest reason I have for loving her. She intuitively understands. She knows what to do, what to say, how to say it, when to say it. She has *savoir faire*. *Savoir faire* is not an achievement, but a talent. You have it, or you don't. No amount of cultivation will give it to you. Helen possesses it in its perfection.

We resumed our places at the table. Joyce rejoined us, and asked airily what we had been talking about in her absence.

"Well—for one thing"—I tried to keep my voice steady— "I repeated to Helen your wish that she remain with us— always."

Joyce's eyes widened and she stared at us with curiosity.

"It was all your fault," said Helen.

"You darlings!" exclaimed Joyce. She pushed back her chair, threw her arms around Helen's neck, and kissed her. Then she came to me, hugged me tight, kissed me—and cried like a little child; because she was excited, I think. I know she didn't cry because she was unhappy.

Arm in arm we went back to the library for coffee. Joyce, who had quite recovered her balance, said she didn't want any, and would be back after a while.

Helen said, "I hope Joyce is going to like this idea."

"After she gets accustomed to it," I said. "It's new to all of us."

"Not to me," murmured Helen.

"I mean—the idea that it has really come to pass," I said. "As for wishing it might happen, I haven't thought about anything else for a long time."

"Yes," she whispered. "I know."

My sense of well-being surged through me like a transfusion. I remembered an old text that I hadn't thought of for years, and repeated it, half to myself. "They shall mount up on wings as eagles. They shall run and not be weary. They shall walk—and not faint."

"Is that the way you feel?" asked Helen, softly, knowing the answer.

"Exactly."

"That wasn't said of people in love," she said, smiling, "but of those who trust in the Lord."

"Very well," I said, "I also trust in the Lord. He has been very kind—and I am on His side."

Joyce came down, at eleven, in a fluffy dressing-gown and asked us whether we were getting along all right without her chaperonage. I hope she isn't going to adopt this role permanently. It's bound to be an awkward situation if she poses us as lovers who need her mature counsel.

She left us, after a while, kissing us both and telling us not to sit up too late.

Helen and I practically discussed our future plans. I asked her if she could consent to an early marriage and she seemed entirely willing. I suggested a trip to Europe for the three of us, and she thought it a grand idea.

I put my arm about her and went with her to the stairway. I kissed her good night. She moved up on the next step, where she was on a level with me, and kissed me again.

I am very happy. Life has been very good to me.

AT HOME
December twenty-seventh, 1919, 11.30 p.m.

THE three of us spent the evening discussing travel plans. Joyce is entering whole-heartedly into our program, seeming to be in full approval of our early wedding; and, of course, bubbling with enthusiasm over the prospect of our trip to Europe.

Helen goes home to-morrow. She had expected to remain until after New Year's Day, but feels now that she should not delay her preparations for our marriage which, we have agreed, is to occur on the eleventh.

It is really at Helen's insistence that we are being married so soon. I was content to wait until she had graduated in June. But she thinks that if I need her at all I need her now. Naturally we have talked over Joyce's problem candidly. Helen thinks that if Joyce is permitted to run at large here, for another five or six months, it may be difficult to reclaim her. She thinks, also, that my own worry over Joyce should be relieved at the earliest possible moment.

I do not know exactly how much sacrifice it entails, on Helen's part, to give up school, this close to graduation. She assures me that she is glad to do it, and seems not to be fretting over it.

So we are arranging to be married in a fortnight. It will be a very simple wedding, with a half-dozen friends in attendance. And on the next Thursday afternoon we sail on the *Aquitania* for Cherbourg.

* * * * *

In spite of Nancy Ashford's tactful but urgent warning, the other day, that all Brightwood was chattering about my ill health, it had not occurred to me that this anxiety had become a subject of formal discussion by the staff.

I had no operations scheduled for to-day, and did not arrive at the hospital until half-past ten. After making a few visits on patients of mine, I put in a call to Ann Arbor and told Doctor Leighton I was going away presently on a two months' vacation. There are only three head cases here now, under observation, and waiting for surgery. Two of them Watson can handle alone. Leighton promised me he would look after the third, and any other cases which may show up, though I think Tim can give a good account of himself in all but a few problems. Leighton says he will be available whenever Watson wants him.

At noon, when I was preparing to leave, Nancy came in and said that Doctor Pyle wished to see me. I thought this odd, for I had encountered Pyle two or three times in the course of the morning and he had had every opportunity to talk. Apparently this was something private.

"Know what Pyle has on his mind?" I asked, casually.

"Yes," said Nancy—but she did not elaborate and I respected her prudence.

"I hope it isn't anything that will detain me very long," I said. "I have an engagement at home."

"Shall I see if I can find him?" suggested Nancy. "Perhaps he can come at once—and get it over with."

I said, "Very well," and Nancy slipped away. I confess I didn't like her employment of the phrase—"Get it over with"—a stock remark with us when counselling agitated patients to submit to surgery.

Pyle seemed quite a bit flustered when he came in. Ever since I have known the testy old chap—and that is a very long time—he has had a funny trick of tipping up his lower lip, when embarrassed or bewildered, and gnawing absurdly at the tip of his diminutive goatee. In order to accomplish this manoeuvre, he is obliged to spread his mouth almost from ear to ear, achieving a mirthless grin that startles persons who observe this phenomenon for the first time.

He was pursuing this little whisker with his upper incisors as he took the chair opposite me, and I knew that something had gone wrong. Pyle had come on a difficult errand.

I gave him a cigar, lighted it for him, and said, "What's the matter, beloved? You look as if you might have taken the wrong kidney out of somebody."

"We must have a little chat, Hudson," he began, ignoring my chaff. "About your health. It's getting breezed around that you're in bad shape. Also that you insist on keeping up with your usual schedule. Now, if that goes on much longer, it is going to hurt you—and it might hurt Brightwood. We think you should take a vacation."

"Who are 'we'?" I snapped.

"The staff," replied Pyle. "All of us. It's unanimous. We met, afternoon before Christmas, and talked it over. Felt like traitors, of course. Hated to do it in your absence. Everybody was agreed to that. Everybody was sympathetic—and on your side—and wanting to do the right thing. I hope you will understand that. Nobody thinks you're done for. But we all feel that you should get away—for six months, maybe. Rusticate. Travel. Play."

Without giving me an opening, the good old boy carried on with his suggestions. He had a large envelope, crammed with cruise advertisements. Apparently he had gone to no end of bother to set up a half-dozen tentative trips for me.

"Now, here you have—" said Pyle, spreading out a map of the world on my desk, and inching his chair closer, after the approved manner of a high-pressure salesman. "Now, here you have a delightful tour around the world. Go west, stop at Honolulu, smell the flowers, listen to the marimbas—"

"You mean the ukuleles," I put in. "Do I? Very well, then. The ukuleles! And then you go to Tahiti! Think of that, Hudson! Tahiti! Marvellous! I confess I've always wanted to do that, but I've been so damned healthy that nobody ever thought of shipping me away for a rest. This will be a great thing for you, Hudson. Take your daughter along. Stop in Europe on the way back. Spend some time in Germany with the brain tinkers. Now—you do that! This is very important!"

Of course I knew it would be up to me to tell Pyle—and all the rest of them—about my plans for the European tour, but I hadn't quite got myself nerved up to confide about the wedding. Perhaps this irresolution means nothing less than that I expected Pyle to be utterly disgusted when he learned of it. The fact that I was postponing the hour when this news must come to light disturbed me. I wasn't ready to tell him; not yet. I would organize a little speech, explaining it all, so he could understand how I happened to decide on matrimony. I couldn't tell Pyle that I had fallen in love with a girl young enough to be my daughter, but I could tell him she would be a steadying influence for my Joyce. And this would be true enough for all practical purposes. But I must have a little more time to consolidate my campaign of self-defence.

So—I heartily agreed with Pyle that I had been working too hard; told him I had plans made to build a cottage up on Saginack and go up there, for two or three days every week, soon as the nice weather came along.

Pyle gnawed his goatee, while I was elaborating on this, and it was easily to be seen that I wasn't making much of an impression. He interrupted me, presently, to inquire what was going to become of me—and all the rest of us—in the meantime.

I saw then that I might as well let him have it. I said, "Pyle, I hope this won't knock you cold. I'm going down to Philadelphia, week after next, to marry my daughter's school friend. Miss Helen Brent."

Pyle was stunned. If I had pulled a pistol out of my pocket and shot myself, I doubt if his strained expression of incredulity could have registered a bigger shock. I couldn't help grinning. I waited a moment for him to recover, and when it was obvious that the blow had struck his speech centre, I went on to give him some details; told him about our projected trip to Europe—and everything.

He gradually came up out of his semi-conscious condition, and I gave him a fresh cigar. He bit the end off mechanically, and drew back a little, defensively, when I approached with a lighted match. I know he thought I had lost my mind. I laughed. And he finally found his tongue.

"Er—well," he croaked feebly. "That's very—surprising. Many happy returns."

Then I began at the beginning and told him all about it, making no bones about the worry I had had with Joyce, Helen's remarkable hold on her, and the circumstances leading up to our recent decision. I don't know whether Pyle accepted any of it as reasonable, but when he left he was at least able to get away without assistance. At the door he wanted to know how much of this was a secret, and I told him it should be sufficient—for the present—to say that I was going abroad with my daughter. They could learn the rest of it when it happened.

Then, after some hesitation, he asked how much of the story he should tell to Mrs. Ashford. This distressed me a little. The fact is, I should have confided in Nancy at once. It isn't quite fair for me to have kept this a secret from her, seeing how close we have been, through all these years.

I daresay Pyle has had it in the back of his old head, for a long time, that Nancy and I would marry, some day. And I suppose it might strike him that such a match would be immeasurably more suitable.

"I'll tell her myself," I said. And Pyle went out, and closed the door.

* * * * *

I called up Fred Ferguson, this afternoon, and told him I was going away for a couple of months, and wondered whether he could get the plans for my house in the country ready for me to see by the end of next week. He thought he could. I hope they can get going on it, so I can have some use of it during the coming summer.

This has been an eventful day and I am very tired. I am feeling the reaction from the difficult interview I had with Pyle. I suppose I should have sent for Nancy, after he left. I mustn't let much more time slip by until I tell her.

There is really no reason why I should feel any embarrassment about this. The relations between Nancy and me certainly do not call for any apologies. I never gave her any reason to think that we belonged to each other, except in the bonds of an invaluable business friendship. Perhaps I'm making a mountain of a mole-hill. Maybe Nancy has no such thoughts in her head. I hope not. Still, I wish I didn't have this to look forward to. Damn it!—why should I feel so sensitive about letting my friends into this secret? It's nobody's business—is it—whom I marry? I don't owe anyone an explanation. Perhaps I should have said something to Tim.

AT HOME
January eighth, 1920, 11.30 p.m.

THIS is undoubtedly the last entry I shall make in my journal until after our return from abroad. The day has been confusingly crowded with last-minute duties. I hope I have not forgotten anything of importance. Joyce and I are leaving to-morrow for Philadelphia where the wedding occurs on the morning of the eleventh. The time is growing short.

I am very restless to-night, and in need of diversion. To be quite frank, I might not otherwise be writing this. I have no inclination to read, I am not sleepy; besides, I told Joyce I would wait up for her, hoping it might encourage her return at a reasonable hour. She has gone somewhere with young Masterson.

There is no need for anxiety about the successful management of affairs at Brightwood during my absence. The staff is harmonious, loyal, efficient; and Nancy is at the helm. Nancy has given her full approval of my plans. There has been no constraint. I am glad of that.

I find that for many years I have been assuming that Brightwood, without my constant oversight, might promptly disintegrate. Of course I haven't been vain enough to say that to myself in so many words, but the bare fact that I have never felt free to take an extended vacation is proof that I felt the hospital could not get along without me.

It occurred to me to-day, after interviewing several members of the staff, that it wouldn't matter much if I never came back to Brightwood at all. When I bade good-bye to Nancy I remarked to that effect. Naturally she comforted my vanity by saying they would be simply marking time and hoping to keep things running smoothly until I returned.

I told her I had discovered a sin that the prayer-book had not taken into account. I recited what I could remember of the litany used at Trinity Cathedral in Chicago. This quaint confession had invited the good Lord to deliver us from all evil and mischief; from the crafts and assaults of the devil; from envy, hatred, and malice; but, I observed, it should also have prayed that we be delivered from indispensability. And in all seriousness I believe it disrupts a man's honest dealings with himself when—perhaps unwittingly—he begins to think that his home and his business couldn't possibly carry on without him.

Among the many callers who came this afternoon to extend their good wishes was my excellent old friend Caleb Weatherby. I had not seen him for nearly a year. He is spending the worst of the winter here. Before our return from Europe, he will have gone back to his home on Lake Moosehead in Maine. He had read in the papers that I was going abroad and came to pay his respects.

I cannot remember having spoken of him in this journal. He insists that I saved his life, and this may not be far from the truth, though the rescue was effected in a manner that may strike you as amusing. And if you have any fondness for baked beans, the story may make you hungry.

Late last fall, a year ago, Doctor Grant, one of our local physicians, called up one day to ask if he might bring in for observation a patient who had attempted suicide and was so deep in melancholia that he would probably finish the job at the first opportunity. Grant said the case history indicated a healthy and stable mind, until quite recently, and he felt that only a pathological condition could account for a depression so stubborn and dangerous.

Weatherby was brought in, the next morning, by his son. I did not at once see the old gentleman but had an hour with the son, a personable and fairly prosperous business man of thirty-eight to forty, who seemed loyally concerned about his father's plight.

He gave me the facts briefly. Weatherby, senior, had spent his life in Maine. He had always been active and most of his time had been spent out of doors, cutting timber, running a mill, making maple products. A few months before his wife had died, Weatherby, junior, and his wife had proposed to the old gentleman that he come to Detroit and live with them, because he was lonely and without employment. It was his first experience in a large city. After a few days, he began to be moody, taciturn, and glum. They tried to interest him in their own affairs, took him to the movies, made an effort to include him in their social life; but to no avail.

I thought I had a pretty good picture of the old fellow's dilemma. The problem of an old man, who comes to live with his son and his daughter-in-law, is much more serious than for the old lady who finds herself in the same circumstances. There are plenty of little things she can do to entertain herself, and small services she can perform which preserve her self-respect as a useful member of the household. She can knit stockings, sew on buttons, feed the baby, help in the kitchen on the maid's day out. There is very little that an old man can do. In the case of Weatherby, the enforced idleness and sense of dependence had made him loathe himself. He would sit for days on end, refusing to speak, and now he had gone to the limit of desperation by attempting suicide.

That afternoon I went up to my new patient's room. For a man approaching seventy, he was as fine a specimen of physical fitness as I have ever seen; nor have I ever seen anyone more stolidly depressed. He was sitting by the window, with his big, shaggy head in his hands, and when I told him who I was he did not look up. I sat down near him and began asking him leading questions but could get nothing out of him but grunts and growls and shrugs.

After a while he grew exasperated and barked out shrilly that I could go to hell with my questions, that he was tired of living, that he had lived too long, that he was only a nuisance, that he wished he was dead, that he was sorry the poison hadn't got to work before they pumped him out, that he was going to do a better job, next time; that it was none of my damn business how he felt, and would I go away and leave him alone?

I then resorted to the familiar technique of agreeing with him, which occasionally has the effect of making a functional—but almost never a pathological—melancholic rouse to his own defence. Slipping to the edge of my chair and pocketing my notebook and consulting my watch, to sign that I had lost interest and was about to depart, I ostentatiously stifled a yawn, the old man regarding me with sour distaste but with a trace of grim curiosity.

"You're probably right, Mr. Weatherby," I drawled. "You are sixty-eight. A man at that age is, as you say, a nuisance and far better off dead. Any old duffer of your years is practically worthless, even if he has fairly good health; and I suppose you've been puny and sickly, most of your life."

That popped him! If I had touched off a cannon cracker under his chair he couldn't have responded any more promptly. It delighted me to see how mad he was!

As soon as he had yelled, "Puny! Sickly! Me!" I knew there wasn't anything the matter with that fine old head. "Puny?" he shouted. By Gemini, he'd bet he could take me outside and tie me into a hard knot! Then the glitter faded from his eyes and he suddenly subsided, with slumped shoulders, into his habitual gloom. But this did not discourage me. Apparently it had been a long time since he had blown the whistle, and the noise had startled him.

"Well," I remarked, with an infuriating grin, "we frequently find frail people making big threats. Now, tell me the truth, Mr. Weatherby, didn't you have quite a lot of lung trouble when you were a young man?"

This time he got down to business! "Lung trouble! Who? Me? Hell!" Then he proceeded to inform me that at the age of fifteen he was doing a man's work in the woods; came from sturdy stock; his father had been killed by a falling tree at the age of seventy-six, still able to swing an ax with the best of 'em. Then he melted back into his chair again and scowled at the window.

"How did that happen?" I inquired. He shook his head crossly and did not reply. I thought I would try another bait. "I saw your son," I said. "Sort of mean-looking fellow. Not much wonder you're tired of living with such a sour crab. I suppose his wife's a nagger. Probably that's what makes him abuse you. Two of 'em in cahoots to drive you out of their house."

At that, he turned on me venomously. He'd have me understand that his son was one of the finest men in the world, and his wife had done everything to make him comfortable. And anybody who said she was a nagger was a dirty liar. Nobody could be any sweeter than Florence. Then the old man's eyes gushed sudden tears, and I saw that we were really making some headway. His hands were shaky as he filled his pipe, and his noble old nose was a-drip. He was still mad at me, but I knew now that I could make him talk, and felt it was time to conciliate.

"Of course I don't think your boy is mean," I said, gently. "And I don't think his wife is a nagger. And I know they both love you. But—you wouldn't talk to me, and I had to do something about it."

He nodded, understandingly, and puffed in silence.

"And the fact is," I went on, "I never saw a healthier man than you are. You don't look as if you'd ever seen a sick day in your life. That probably comes from living in the woods. Must be a great experience to live up there in Maine. I wish you would tell me something about it."

That was exactly what he wanted to talk about, and for the next hour he gave me a treat. In the coldest weeks of the winter they felled the trees and dressed out the timber. Then, at the first thaw, they reopened their little mill. It ran by water-power, and operated only for a couple of months while the early spring freshets made the stream bank-full. In the mill, they sawed up lumber and ground meal and feed. There was a fine maple grove, hard by. They gathered the sap and boiled it down. In the mill there was a big brick chimney and a huge fireplace.

And it was at this point that we came to the beans, which played so important a part in Caleb Weatherby's reconditioning.

"We used to bake beans in that fireplace," rumbled the old man. "And they were beans, let me tell you! No beans like that any more. People have forgot how to make 'em."

"How?" I demanded. "I like baked beans. But it's hard to get them cooked right. Too dry, I think."

"There you are," agreed Weatherby. "Hard as buckshot, and dry enough to choke you to death. The way we fixed our beans: first we soaked 'em, of course, and then boiled 'em; put 'em in a stone pot, with plenty of salt pork, and salt and pepper and mustard, and an onion with a clove stuck in it—"

"And molasses," I assisted, when he paused to recollect.

"Yes—but not sorghum. We boiled down the maple syrup until it was thick as sorghum, and poured in plenty; and then we did the thing that made 'em different! Level teaspoonful of ginger. Ever hear of ginger in beans?"

I hadn't, but it sounded all right, for I was hungry. It occurred to me that we might now tap the old torpid cistern again and see if we could get into it and bounce out of it.

"Look here!" I said. "If you're really serious about committing suicide, how about coming over to my house, some day, before you do it, and make up a nice big pot of those beans for me?"

The old man pulled a twisted grin and relighted his pipe.

"By Gemini—that's a pretty cool way to talk," he growled, with a mirthless chuckle. "You want me to make you a pot o' them Maine beans—and then I can go and kill myself, if I want to."

"Well," I explained, brightly, "you said you were going to kill yourself, anyhow, and the beans do seem very good. I thought—"

"All right," declared Weatherby, nodding his head. "I'll just do that for you. When shall I come?"

* * * * *

Our Gladys has had the run of the house for so long that she lacks the discipline of a well-trained servant. She has had no illusions about her value to my establishment and talks back quite freely. Whenever our views have failed to coincide, I have promptly abandoned my position. Gladys is indeed a treasure; but, unfortunately, she has long since found that out. I confess it was with some diffidence that I informed her, in the morning at breakfast, that a fine old gentleman from Maine was going to spend the next day in her kitchen, making us a nice big pot of baked beans.

Gladys was a bit stunned at first, but presently recovered sufficiently to inquire what was the matter with her baked beans, and since when did we have to hire some old man to come all the way from Maine—

"Just a minute," I broke in, firmly, though I suspected it was going to take longer than that; "this gentleman is so lonely in Detroit that it has made him ill."

"In the head?" inquired Gladys, remembering my specialty.

"Well—he's not insane, if that's what you're wondering. He has nothing to do, and he's tired of sitting around idle. But he does know how to make marvellous baked beans. And I want you to let him do anything he wants to do in the kitchen—all day to-morrow."

Gladys sniffed and was about to deliver an oration. I had heard them before, and recognized the early symptoms. I held up my cup for more coffee and proceeded with my remarks. I told Gladys she had a chance to do something for this good man.

"Lots of people," I went on, "are going around half dead, and wishing they were wholly dead, because there's nobody to talk to about the only thing they're interested in. And one of the finest investments you can make, in restoring life to such wilted and discouraged people, is to make them see that this one thing they've got is important; worth doing; worth talking about. If you want to give yourself a happy day, Gladys, stand by this old man and make a big fuss over his ability to cook beans."

"And keep the kitchen in a muss all day," grumbled Gladys, quite truthfully, no doubt.

"Very well, then," I capitulated, with a beaten sigh. "If it's more important that you keep your kitchen nice and tidy, to-morrow, than to humour a lonesome old fellow who needs somebody to build him up and make him think more of himself, you just forget it."

I waited for Gladys to retire to her domain, but she stood there thoughtfully scowling. Gladys is not pretty when she meditates.

"Of course," I went on, mumbling through my toast, "I said to myself, 'Gladys will get the idea at once, and be glad to do it. Gladys will stand at the old boy's elbow and watch him mix up his mess, which she could probably do very much better—and she will oh and ah and be surprised—and pleased to learn; and that will make the old fellow so proud of himself that he'll be glad he's alive; swell up until he'll pop a button off his waistcoat.'"

Gladys kept on standing there, after I paused, so I thought I might as well finish her off.

"But—that's all right, Gladys. I know how necessary it is to keep things neat and clean, and not be bothered by strangers that we don't know. After all, it's none of our business whether this old man's lonely or not. He has got some folks here in town. They can look after him."

I pushed back my chair and left the room, but was in no great rush to leave the house. I knew that Gladys needed a little time to digest the dose I had given her. Sometimes I have wished I could administer an idea hypodermically. She was waiting at the foot of the stairs, when I came down.

"You can bring him," she said. "I'll treat him decent."

"Thanks," I said. "I rather thought you might, when you had considered it a little more." Then I added, confidentially, "Now—you can either let this be a tiresome burden to you, or you can have a grand day. Don't try to pity this old fellow. He has probably had too much of that now. You just pretend to let him teach you how to make baked beans—and it will be the best day's work you've ever done—and the happiest, too, I'll bet."

Gladys said she'd try, and grinned a little over our conspiracy. I reflected, on the way to the hospital, that Gladys would have a chance to build herself up a little, too—an interesting by-product of my adventure.

* * * * *

I had told the nurse to send Mr. Weatherby over in a taxi next morning, and he arrived at eight. Gladys had been instructed to soak the beans in cold water overnight. She was waiting for my patient when he came, and seemed pleased when he consented to have a cup of coffee with me in the breakfast room. Now that she had gone into this thing, she was going to do it right: I could see that.

"You'll probably have some time on your hands, Mr. Weatherby," I said, "and you are quite welcome to sit in my library and smoke your pipe and read anything that attracts you."

He nodded, dignifiedly, and thanked me. Before I left the house I found an illustrated copy of Wallace Nutting's *Maine Beautiful*, and laid it in a conspicuous place beside the tobacco jar.

* * * * *

They were, as Mr. Weatherby had declared, great beans. I had not suggested that he remain for dinner. It had been a long, exciting day for him, and I didn't care to risk an anticlimax. I had him sent back to the hospital where, I learned later, he had eaten a good dinner and tumbled off to sleep without grousing about anything.

But Weatherby's melancholia had cut in pretty deep, and I knew he would skid back into the same old mudhole if we didn't stay with him until he was safe on firm ground. Many worried people tinker with the idea of suicide, as a possible escape from their frets, and come through that phase of depression without serious harm; but if a man ever gets to the point where he actually tries it, you want to look out!

One pleasant day of bright endeavour wouldn't be enough to insure old Weatherby's life. I told him I should be greatly obliged if he would come again to my house, on Saturday, and bake a big pot of beans for a party I was giving to a few friends. I hoped the anticipation of this engagement would entertain him in the meantime.

Gladys had made no complaint about turning her kitchen over to the old gentleman, and I believed I could safely risk a repetition of my request. So, at dinner that night I gingerly ventured upon the subject, after informing her that nobody but herself knew how to cook creamed sweetbreads.

"I hope I am not imposing on you, Gladys," I said, "but I should consider it a great favour if you would consent to have Mr. Weatherby come on Saturday and bake another pot of beans. I think this will be the last time."

"Sure!" said Gladys, pleasantly.

"Was he very much in your way?"

"No—I liked having him here. He told me all about cutting down trees, and what they did in the mill."

"That must have been interesting."

"Not at first, it wasn't," said Gladys. "But I listened, like you said, and made believe I was interested, and pretty soon was."

"That's what makes people interesting, Gladys," I said. "You let them see that you're interested—and presently they begin to be interesting. Nobody can be very interesting," I added, "if he thinks the other fellow is bored by what he says."

"It's funny, that way," agreed Gladys. "I had a real good time with Mr. Weatherby. And I think it did him a lot of good to talk."

"You'll probably be wanting to try that on someone else, I suppose, now that you see how nicely it works."

"Well," admitted Gladys, confidentially, "it was like you said. I had a good time. And it made me feel good—like I'd done something for somebody."

"Gladys," I said, "you haven't told anyone about this—but me?"

"And Mert," she added.

"Of course—Mert. Now—don't tell anyone else. You have done a fine thing. You have helped that old man—perhaps more than you realize. And it has made you happy. Keep it a secret. Because—if you tell your friends what you did for Mr. Weatherby, and how pleased he was, and how pleased you are—you'll lose it."

"That's funny," said Gladys, doubtfully. "You mean—if I tell about it I won't feel good about it, any more?"

"That's what I mean, Gladys," I replied, soberly. "And it is funny. But it's so. And the next time you do something for someone, and are very happy about it, don't tell anybody! Not even Mert; nor me."

Gladys's eyes were wide with mystification. She slowly moved toward the swinging door leading to the pantry, and went through. Then she returned. Her eyes were now alight with discovery.

"That's what *you* do!" she said. "I know now—about a lot o' things I've wondered at! For instance—"

I put up a hand, and shook my head.

"No, no, Gladys—if you please," I said, firmly. "You keep your nice secrets—and I'll keep mine. Then we'll both be glad."

The Weatherby beans were getting to be very important.

* * * * *

The next experimental pot of beans was ready for me at six o'clock on Saturday. I sent Mr. Weatherby back to his son's home, that night, to spend Sunday. I had kept in contact with his son, advising him to make the old man talk about his youthful experiences, and send him back to Brightwood on Monday.

I had Gladys wrap up the pot of beans in a small blanket and we put it in a big wooden bucket. I had asked Pyle to join me at The Pontchartrain for dinner, and went down a bit early with my strange luggage.

It is barely possible that you may remember Louis, the famed *maître d'hôtel* at The Pontchartrain. Louis is beyond all question the best cook in town, a product of the Cordon Bleu, insufferably snobbish, and quite forthright with his cold contempt of patrons who think of food as something to sustain life. I have known Louis for a long time and he has done me the honour of his friendship.

He was standing stiffly at the door, in his evening dress, when I appeared at the Gold Room, carrying my bucket. I drew him aside and guardedly muttered into his ear.

"I have a hot pot of Weatherby baked beans in this bucket, Louis," I confided. "Perhaps you know about them; made according to an old Maine logging- camp formula; Weatherby's. I got wind that the old man was in town visiting his son; happened to do a little favour for him, and he paid me off by baking these beans. I want them for dinner. Doctor Pyle will join me here presently."

"Oui," said Louis, bowing. He signed to one of the bus boys and the beans made off toward the kitchen.

"And Louis," I continued, "if you have a minute, taste those beans. You know, it occurred to me, to-day—this grand old fellow is retired now, and hasn't much to do—if you could say, on your luncheon menu, about twice a week maybe, and on Saturday nights, that you were serving the famous Weatherby beans, made by Weatherby himself, in your kitchen, after an old formula concocted in the logging-camps of Maine, where maple syrup was easier to get than sorghum—"

"Merci," said Louis, bowing. I could see that the thing had bit him.

* * * * *

Monday afternoon I drove Mr. Weatherby down to The Pontchartrain for an interview with Louis, and he held forth there on Tuesdays, Thursdays, and Saturdays—as beanster-extraordinary—until the warm weather came along. Then he went back to Maine and opened up a little roadside place where he served nothing but Weatherby's Baked Beans—with brown bread and other suitable accessories. I had insisted that he stick to the bean *motif*; and, seeing that the beans had saved his life, he seemed glad enough to do so.

"And print on your menu," I advised, "that you may be found, during the winter season, baking beans at The Pontchartrain. That ought to fetch 'em."

* * * * *

He is spending the roughest part of the winter in his son's home where, he told me to-day, he is entirely contented. The novelty of Weatherby's beans has worn off, at The Pontchartrain, and the old gentleman is not working there now; but he is glad enough for a little rest, he says.

"Had a mighty busy summer," he reported. "I am fixing up the place a little, this season, and taking on a couple more girls to help. Ain't as spry as I used to be."

And that, I noticed by his gait, is true. He ain't as spry as he used to be; but, at least he hasn't killed himself, and I don't believe he is going to. He inquired, warmly, about Gladys, and said he had had a Christmas card from her. His beans did more for Gladys than he realized. Her little investment in Weatherby has given her something new to think about.

The old man told me to-day that I had saved his life. He was not effusive, however, and made the statement calmly. I assured him I had been abundantly rewarded by his friendship.

Perhaps you may think that this narrative is too trivial to be worth recording, but I want you to know that I put a great deal more into old Weatherby's salvation than appears on the surface. To justify Louis's experiment, I talked Weatherby's Baked Beans to all my friends until they thought I was losing my mind.

Several times that winter, when I had occasion to get a few men together for a business luncheon, we met at The Pontchartrain and I insisted on their having beans. Tim Watson was in on a number of these affairs. One day he said to me, "I'm so damn tired of Weatherby's beans that if the old fellow doesn't commit suicide pretty soon I think I will."

It is two o'clock, and I am going to bed. I wish my girl had come home. I do not like these late parties. It will be a great comfort when I can put Joyce into Helen's keeping.

BRIGHTWOOD HOSPITAL
August sixth, 1921, 11 a.m.

DOUBTLESS it has often occurred to you, while deciphering this journal, that the book was not only a private repository for certain experiences and impressions which I did not care to share with any of my contemporaries, but was in the nature of a little sanctuary where I might solace my loneliness.

For many years, this journal has served as my most confidential friend, and many a long evening has been made endurable by the somewhat laborious game of burying these observations in the code.

You will not think it strange, therefore, that since my marriage I have had no inclination to resume this eccentric pastime. Helen's sweet companionship has completely filled my life. I have had no temptation to slip away by myself, in the late evening, to document the events of the day; though there have been plenty of occasions when the events were even more worthy of record here than some of the items you have read.

I have not given this journal a thought for a long time. And I might not be writing these words, to-day, but for the fact that I want you to have access to a few of the thoughts expressed yesterday in Chicago at the funeral of my valued friend, Doctor Clark Russell.

Before I attempt to recover these significant words, let me sketch briefly the present state of my various interests. I pursue much the same program of work as formerly, except that I have been assigning to Watson most of the post-operative care. The personnel at Brightwood is practically unchanged. Doctor Minton is not here. The Ruggles twins are taking care of my place in the country. Pyle is on a vacation cruise in the South Seas.

Helen has gone to Philadelphia, suddenly summoned by a not very explicit telegram from her cousin Monty who appears to have got himself into some scrape which he prefers to discuss with her in person. She did not want to go, but she would have fretted about it; so I told her she had better set her mind at ease. She left on Thursday night, and will not be back until Monday or Tuesday.

As it turns out, my advice was not very good, and Helen will probably be sorry she went; for Joyce, who had decided to decline an invitation to spend the week-end at Windymere, impetuously changed her mind, and is out there now. Young Merrick has just arrived home from France and is having a party. I tried to persuade Joyce not to go. Perhaps it will turn out all right, but I dislike the prospect of Joyce's getting interested again in the fast set that Bobby Merrick gathers about him.

I fear that, little by little, Joyce is exerting her independence of Helen's quiet and affectionate supervision. Perhaps we should all have foreseen that Helen, in the role of stepmother, could hardly retain the influence she had as a comradely schoolmate.

I am lonesome and restless to-day. In a few minutes I am going to drive out to Flintridge and spend the week-end. It is very peaceful out there.

Russell's death was very sudden. I had seen him, only a couple of weeks ago, and he was in his usual health. It is hard to think of him gone.

Dean Harcourt conducted the funeral service in Trinity Cathedral. I think it was the most impressive affair I ever attended.

Of course my emotions were easily accessible, for the loss of Clark Russell is a serious grief to me. Moreover, I have a great admiration for Harcourt, and whatever he says carries much weight.

There is something about the Cathedral, too, that inspires me. I have had several uplifting experiences there. In my regard, it is indeed a holy place.

It was very quiet, when we took our seats. It was after four o'clock, and the declining sun was flooding the rose window in the apse. The candles on the altar glowed.

The Dean was led into the chancel by his curates. He sat down in a tall Gothic chair, his face impassive, serene, saintly. I think Harcourt has suffered much pain. He has probably paid a pretty high price for his nobility of soul.

The casket stood at the head of the broad, stone-flagged, central aisle, covered with a pall. There were no flowers on it. People who come to the Cathedral for the last time are not expected to bring their floral displays along. You needn't fret because your cheap little bouquet won't make much of a showing. Trinity Cathedral, like God, is no respecter of persons.

The organ played "Lead, Kindly Light."

Dean Harcourt read the ritual.

I understand that it is not customary for any additional remarks to be made in an Episcopal Church on such occasions. But, when the Dean had concluded the formal reading of the funeral service, he talked quietly, for a few minutes, about the eternal life.

This was—as I have said—the most impressive thing I ever heard, and the memory of these simple words is haunting me. I have not come out from under their spell.

"If we are immortal, at all," said the Dean, "we are immortal now. If we are to survive, the future life will be a continuation of our life now. It will be different only in respect to its larger freedom, and the chief attribute of that freedom will be our escape from the dread of death and transition.

"We all have our ambitions," said the Dean, "and many of them lack fulfilment. Our houses burn up, our ships go down, our bubbles burst. All our ends are uncertain but this. Whatever we may or may not come to, this is inevitable. It is the shadow that clouds our sky. Our friend has emerged from that shadow."

The Dean did not specify any of Clark Russell's scientific contributions to medicine and surgery or his other well-known philanthropies. Perhaps he knew that every one of the five or six hundred people present was fully aware of Russell's invaluable career. But, by implication, he recognized this exceptional service.

"It is given to some men," he said, "to achieve immortality in two worlds. They go hence—but they linger here. This is very fortunate for them. They have earned a right to live on—Here and Elsewhere. We shall not weep for them. They do not need our tears."

Of course I realize that my written impressions of this inspiring event cannot convey the full flavour of Dean Harcourt's quiet words; but, to me, they were august!

I seem still to be in this other-worldly mood. I can't shake it off. The Dean's sonorous sentences were punctuated by impressive silences. Two or three times I thought he had finished, and I was sorry. I hope this doesn't sound like cant—but what this man said was nourishment to my soul. I could feel it building me up! It was majestic! How it would have stirred Russell!

It seems that at five o'clock, every afternoon, no matter what is going on in Trinity Cathedral, the chimes in the tower play the "theme-song" of this great institution—the tune to the ancient hymn, "O God Our Help in Ages Past, Our Hope for Years to Come."

The Dean closed the service while the big bells were booming this soul-stirring confession of faith. The air was vibrant with these tones while he recited Browning's imperishable lines, "So—if I stoop into a dark, tremendous sea of cloud, it is but for a time. I press God's lamp close to my breast: its splendour, soon or late, will pierce the gloom. I shall—emerge—one day!"

And the great bells in the high tower carried on, "Our Shelter From the Stormy Blast—and Our Eternal Home."

* * * * *

Printed in Great Britain
by Amazon